SIMON R. GREEN

DEATHSTALKER WAR

A ROC BOOK

ROC
Published by New American Library, a division of
Penguin Group (USA) Inc., 375 Hudson Street,
New York, New York 10014, USA
Penguin Group (Canada), 90 Eglinton Avenue East, Suite 700, Toronto,
Ontario M4P 2Y3, Canada (a division of Pearson Penguin Canada Inc.)
Penguin Books Ltd., 80 Strand, London WC2R 0RL, England
Penguin Ireland, 25 St. Stephen's Green, Dublin 2,
Ireland (a division of Penguin Books Ltd.)
Penguin Group (Australia), 250 Camberwell Road, Camberwell, Victoria 3124,
Australia (a division of Pearson Australia Group Pty. Ltd.)
Penguin Books India Pvt. Ltd., 11 Community Centre, Panchsheel Park,
New Delhi - 110 017, India
Penguin Group (NZ), 67 Apollo Drive, Rosedale, North Shore 0632,
New Zealand (a division of Pearson New Zealand Ltd.)
Penguin Books (South Africa) (Pty.) Ltd., 24 Sturdee Avenue,
Rosebank, Johannesburg 2196, South Africa

Penguin Books Ltd., Registered Offices:
80 Strand, London WC2R 0RL, England

First published by Roc, an imprint of New American Library,
a division of Penguin Group (USA) Inc.

First Printing, July 1997
20 19 18 17 16 15 14 13 12 11 10

CHAPTER ONE

THE TAKING OF MISTWORLD

Every Empire needs a dumping ground. Somewhere out of sight in the back of beyond where it can dump malcontents and troublemakers. The Empress Lionstone XIV had Mistworld, a cold inhospitable rock well off the beaten track, populated almost entirely by traitors, criminals, rogues whose luck had run out, and runaway espers. Lionstone tolerated Mistworld's presence in her harshly run Empire on the grounds that at least that way she knew where the bad apples were.

She would have preferred to kill them all, but she had advisors wise enough to know that exiles were, on the whole, far less troublesome than martyrs. But over the years Mistworld had become a haven for all kinds of rebels and outlaws, and suddenly what had been a useful dumping ground was now a defiant, poisoned thorn in the Empire's side. Lionstone gave orders for its purging, by fire if need by, only to discover that the planet was now protected by a psionic screen of combined esper minds more than strong enough to withstand anything her Imperial Fleet could throw at it. And so, despite Lionstone's many vicious plots and schemes, Mistworld remained the only surviving rebel planet in the Empire, safe from Lionstone's wrath.

Or so they thought.

The *Sunstrider II* dropped out of hyperspace and fell into orbit around Mistworld. The long slender yacht glistened with sensor spikes, but there were no Empire starcruisers anywhere in the vicinity. The Empire had learned to keep its distance. There was only the single golden vessel, hanging silently above a cold, featureless sphere. In the main lounge of the *Sunstrider II*, Owen Deathstalker

sat at ease in a very comfortable chair and counted his
blessings. Not least of which was that for the moment, at
least, no one was shooting at him. Owen had learned to
appreciate the quiet moments in his life, if only because
there were so few of them.

He'd lost the original *Sunstrider* in a crash landing on
the jungle planet of Shandrakor, but the Hadenmen had
rebuilt the ship according to Owen's instructions, around
the original stardrive salvaged from the wreckage of the
first ship. It was a very special drive, one of the proto-
types for the new stardrive the Empire was currently
attempting to mass-produce, and for the moment, at least,
a great deal faster than anything the Empire had to offer.

Theoretically.

The yacht itself looked pretty much the way Owen remembered, and contained all the original fittings and luxuries, but the Hadenmen hadn't been able to resist
improving things as they went along. And sometimes
their ideas of improvements only went to show how far
the augmented men differed from Humanity. Owen could
handle doors that appeared in solid walls as he approached, and lights that turned themselves on and off as
necessary without having to be told, but he rather drew
the line at controls that operated if he only thought about
them. After a few near disasters brought about by his
mind wandering at important moments, Owen had decided very firmly to leave the running of the craft to the
ship's computers.

The Hadenmen had also got many of the interior details
wrong, in small, disquieting ways. Floors that sloped or
bulged for no obvious reason, chairs that matched themselves to slightly the wrong shapes, and lights and colors
that were subtly uncomfortable to merely human eyes.
Owen held up his left hand and studied it thoughtfully.
The golden metal of the artificial hand, the Hadenmen's
other gift to him, glowed warmly in the lounge's light. He
hadn't liked the idea of having Hadenmen technology
connected to him so intimately, but after he lost his own
hand fighting the Grendel alien in the great caverns under
the Wolfling World, he'd had no choice but to accept
their gift with thanks. It was a good hand, strong and
responsive and practically invulnerable, and if it felt

subtly cold all the time and not altogether his, he could live with that. He flexed the golden fingers slowly, admiring their fluid grace. He trusted the hand because he had to; he wasn't so sure about the ship. The Hadenmen might be his allies for the moment, but a people who had once been officially named the Enemies of Humanity, and with good reason, had to remain suspect for all their gifts. There was always the chance they still had their own, separate, agenda, hidden somewhere in the ship, the improvements, and possibly even his hand.

Owen sighed. Life hadn't always been this complicated. He studied his reflection in the mirror on the wall behind him. A man in his mid-twenties stared broodingly back at him, tall and rangy with dark hair and darker eyes. A man who'd been hard used, and expected to be harder used in the future. It wasn't that long ago he'd been a simple scholar, a minor historian of no importance to anyone but himself. Then Lionstone named him outlaw, and he'd had no choice but to become a rebel and a warrior. The Hadenmen named him Redeemer, and the rebel underground called him Humanity's last hope. Owen didn't believe a word of it.

A clinking of glass caught his attention, and he looked fondly over at Hazel d'Ark, who was sorting determinedly through the bottles in the drinks cabinet, searching for something vaguely drinkable. Owen knew how she felt. The Hadenmen had done their best with food synthesizers, but the various alcoholic beverages they'd come up with had proved universally vile. That hadn't stopped Hazel from drinking them, but she persisted in trying to discover some combination that didn't leave her with an overwhelming urge to spit copiously in all directions. Owen admired her patience, and wished her luck. Personally, he wouldn't have touched any of the stuff if someone had held a gun to his head.

He studied Hazel, admiring her sharp, pointed face and mane of long, ratty, red hair. She wasn't conventionally pretty, but then Hazel wasn't conventional about anything if she could help it. Before becoming a rebel, she'd been a pirate, a mercenary, and a clonelegger—and those were just the things she'd admit to. She was good with a sword but preferred a gun, and as many as possible. Since she and Owen had discovered the huge cache of projectile weapons in the Last Standing's Armory, Hazel had made a point of loading herself down with as many guns and as much ammo as she could carry. Owen thought she found the weight comforting. Owen didn't. Hazel tended to be a bit too arbitrary about safety catches for his liking.

He sighed quietly, tapping his fingers on the armrests of his chair as he waited for the Hadenmen computers running the ship to finish their security checks. Technically speaking, he was trusting his life to the smooth running of the AI the Hadenmen installed, which did absolutely nothing for his sense of security and well-being, but it wasn't like he had a choice. Someone had to run the ship, and it sure as hell wasn't going to be him. Keeping on top of a starship's many and various systems was hard, skilled work, and if he'd wanted to work, he wouldn't have been born an aristocrat.

The original *Sunstrider* had been run by his personal Family AI Ozymandius, but Oz had turned out to be a traitor working for the Empire. It had used hidden control words to turn Owen against his friends, and he'd had no choice but to destroy it. Even though the AI had been his friend long before the others. He'd had to kill his mistress, too, when she tried to kill him, on the Empire's orders. You couldn't trust anyone these days. Maybe not even the woman you loved . . . Owen turned his gaze away from Hazel, and made himself concentrate on something else. At least the Hadenmen had got the toilets right this time. Their earlier attempts had been somewhat distressing. Apparently Hadenmen had no use for such things, which told Owen rather more about the Hadenmen than he really wanted to know.

Hazel wandered over, drink in hand. The liquid was a pale blue in color, and looked like it was trying to climb out of the glass. She sank into the chair opposite Owen with an inelegant grunt and settled herself comfortably. Hazel appreciated luxuries, big and small, mainly because there'd been so few of them in her life. She took a good mouthful of the drink, pulled a face, but swallowed the stuff anyway. Hazel never believed in letting a drink get the better of her. It was a matter of principle. Owen had had to hide a smile when she'd first explained that to him. He hadn't been aware that Hazel had any principles. He'd had enough sense not to say that out loud, of course.

"What does that muck taste like this time?" he asked amiably.

"Trust me," said Hazel. "You really don't want to know. That I am drinking it at all is a sign of how incredibly bored I am. How much longer before we can land?"

"Not long now. Looking forward to being on your old stamping grounds again?"

"Not really, no. Mistport is dangerous, treacherous, and bloody cold, and that's on its good days. I've known rabid rats with bleeding hemorrhoids that were friendlier than your average Mistworlder. I can't believe I let the underground talk me into going back to this hellhole."

Owen shrugged. "It had to be us. Someone had to represent the underground to the Mistport Council, and we know the lie of the land better than anyone else they had to hand. Cheer up; things won't be so bad this time. Probably. We're a hell of a lot stronger and sharper than the last time we were here."

Hazel scowled. "Yeah. That's something else I've been wanting to talk to you about. When that Blood Runner's hologram threatened to take me apart in his laboratory, you reached across light-years of space and blew him to pieces, just by thinking about it. I didn't know you had that kind of power. I don't."

"I didn't think I had either, until I needed it. Our time in the Madness Maze changed us more than we knew. We're different people now."

"I don't like the sound of that. Where do the changes end? Are we still human? Are we going to end up like the Hadenmen, so divorced from what we started out as that we might as well be aliens?"

Owen shrugged again. "Your guess is as good as mine. I think we're as human as we want to be. Our humanity lies not in what we do, but why we do it. Besides, I'm not sure our abilities are all that stable. They seem to come and go. There used to be a link between us, a mental link among all of us who passed through the Maze, but that disappeared when we split up and went our separate ways.

Now I can't even feel you through the link. Can you still feel me, in your mind?"

"No," said Hazel. "Not for some time now."

"That might be my fault," said Ozymandius in Owen's ear. "Perhaps my presence is disrupting your accord."

"Shut up, Oz," Owen subvocalized. "You're dead. I destroyed you."

"You wish. No, I'm still with you, Owen, here to advise and guide you through life's little difficulties."

"The only difficulty I have is this dead AI that keeps yammering in my ear. If I knew a good cyberdruid, I'd have you exorcised. Whoever or whatever you are, I don't need your help. I can manage perfectly well on my own."

"Well pardon my computations, you ungrateful little snot. If it hadn't been for me, you'd never have got off Virimonde alive, when your own Security people came after you for the price on your head. Your trouble is, you don't appreciate me. Look after yourself for a while. I'm going to sulk."

Hazel studied Owen unobtrusively. He'd gone all quiet again, his eyes far away. He did that from time to time, and it never failed to irritate her. Even though she'd always known he was the thoughtful one in their reluctant partnership. Hazel had always believed in the virtues of direct action, preferably with a sword or a gun. Cut them all down and worry about the consequences later. If at all. She wondered what Owen would think if he knew she was taking Blood again.

Blood. The most addictive and soul-destroying drug known to Humanity. It came from the adjusted men, the Wampyr. One of the Empire's less successful attempts at manufacturing terror troops. Synthetic Blood flowed in their veins, making them stronger, faster, nearly invincible. Just a few drops of Blood could make a mere human feel that way, too, for a while. It made you feel sharp and confident, and Hazel needed that more and more these days. She'd been hooked on the drug once before, in her early days on Mistworld. She'd beaten it then, though the cure nearly killed her. But so much had changed in her since then, and very little of it to her liking.

She'd never wanted to be a rebel. All she'd ever wanted was the comfortable life, free from hunger and danger. She'd been happiest as a confidence trickster, parting rich leeches from their ill-gotten gains and disappearing into the night before they realized how badly they'd been stung. Hazel had only ever fought for money, cash in hand, and never trusted anyone but herself. Now she was a major player in the new rebellion, a target for every bounty hunter and backstabber in the Empire, being asked for opinions and plans on matters she had little or no understanding of. For the first time in her life, the lives and futures of countless numbers of people depended on her every action and decision, with all the stress and uncertainties that involved. Now everything she did or didn't do had consequences, and she just couldn't stand it. The pressure weighed down on her, filling her head till she couldn't eat, couldn't sleep, couldn't keep her hands from shaking. So she started taking Blood again. Just a drop, now and then, when she needed it. The Hadenmen had been only too happy to supply her with as much as she wanted. She didn't ask where they got it from. And now she was heading back to Mistworld, where Blood was widespread.

She didn't want to be addicted again. She didn't want to be a plasma baby, her only thought and need for the Blood that was slowly destroying her. She resented anything that had power over her. She'd beaten it once; she could beat it again. She only needed a drop, now and again, after all. Just a little something, to help her cope. She looked at Owen, and her mouth tightened. She knew why their mental link had disappeared. The Blood interfered, separating them. But she couldn't tell him that. He wouldn't understand.

The lounge door opened suddenly, and Owen and Hazel's fellow rebels on this mission walked in, ostentatiously not talking to each other, as usual. The new Jack Random, or Young Jack as Owen always thought of him, was tall, well muscled, and devilishly handsome, with long, dark shoulder-length hair that always looked like he'd just permed it. Owen only had to look at him to feel puny and out of shape. Random wore silver battle armor chased with gold like he was born to it, and he radiated strength, wisdom, confidence, and compassion. A born leader, a charismatic warrior, a hero out of legend and altogether too much of a good thing. He'd arrived out of nowhere, just when the rebellion needed him the most, and Owen didn't trust him an inch.

Owen and Hazel had gone looking for the legendary professional rebel, Jack Random, in the city of Mistport some time back. They'd found a broken old man, hiding from his past, and bullied him out of his hiding hole to fight again, because the rebellion needed the legend, if not the man. He'd fought beside them, and passed through the Madness Maze with them, and at the end he faced impossible odds against the Empire's troops, and emerged victorious. Owen had believed in that man, and been proud to call him friend. The old man had just begun to reclaim his legend when this young giant of a man had burst onto the scene, claiming to be the real Jack Random, and now Owen didn't know what to believe anymore.

Young Jack Random's last campaign had been on the winter world of Vodyanoi IV, some two years earlier. As usual, he had made a lot of noise and raised an army of followers, only to get his ass kicked one more time when they came up against trained Imperial shock troops. His friends smuggled him out at the last moment, so he wasn't around to see his followers slaughtered or imprisoned. His cause had failed, but he kept the legend alive.

Except the older Jack Random claimed that wasn't he. According to him, his last campaign had been on Cold Rock, several years earlier, when his forces were ignominiously scattered, and he was taken captive by the Empire forces. He spent a long time in interrogation cells, tortured and brainwashed by the mind techs, until finally his friends were able to break him out and smuggle him to safety on Mistworld—where he gave up his name and his legend to become just another face in the crowd, hidden and safe from entreaties or responsibilities.

Except . . . Jack Random, the professional rebel, had been visibly active on several worlds during that time. So who was telling the truth and who was lying? Who was the Real Jack Random? The older Jack admitted that the mind techs had done a real number on him, during his months of captivity, messing with his thoughts and memories as they broke his spirit day by day. Maybe he just thought he'd been the famous professional rebel; a nobody molded by the Empire to be paraded as a broken man for propaganda purposes. As with so many other things, Owen wasn't sure what he believed anymore. At least the older Jack was more or less the right age. The younger Jack looked to be no more than his late twenties, and in perfect shape. Surely his long years of rebellion should have left some mark on him, even allowing for his claimed extensive use of regeneration machines.

The underground hadn't been able to make up its mind one way or the other. The old Jack claimed to have the experience, but the Young jack looked so much more convincing. So for the moment the underground accepted both Jacks, and sent them off on separate missions to prove themselves in action. Old Jack went to stir up trouble on the mining planet Technos III, and Owen and Hazel ended up with Young Jack on their team, despite their loud objections. Young Jack took it all with a good-natured smile, which made Owen trust him even less. Never trust a man who smiles too much, his father had always said. It's not natural, not in this day and age. Hazel was even less impressed with the man than Owen, if that was possible, and had told Young Jack to his face that he was a liar and impostor. He just kept on smiling, and said he hoped he'd have the chance to prove himself to her. Hazel told him that if he laid one finger on her, she'd make him eat the finger. Young Jack chuckled good-naturedly, and said she was very pretty when she was angry, and Owen had to hold Hazel down until the red mist had gone from her eyes.

The other new arrival was the esper known as Jenny Psycho. She had forced her way onto the Mistworld team, on the grounds that a planet largely populated by runaway espers would want to meet the last person to manifest the uber-esper Mater Mundi, Our Mother Of All Souls, who had single-handedly made the great esper escape from Wormboy Hell possible. Jenny didn't look like much, at first glance. She was short and blond, with a pale ghostly face dominated by sharp blue eyes. She had a wide mouth, and an unsettling smile that showed more teeth than humor. Her voice was harsh and unattractive, her throat damaged by constant screaming in the dark cells of Silo Nine.

Before the underground sent her into Wormboy Hell as their undercover agent, she'd been just another esper; but since the Mater Mundi touched her, Jenny Psycho had become a major esper power overnight. Her presence all but crackled on the air around her, an almost tangible effect on any company. Where once she'd been nothing but a minor telepath, now every esper ability was hers to call upon, something which was supposed to be impossible, though no one had even been stupid enough to say that to Jenny Psycho. Most people had enough sense not to get that close to her anyway.

She respected Owen and Hazel for the power they'd brought to the rebellion, but since her personality could change from the relatively sane Jenny to the actually disturbing Psycho in mid-sentence, they'd found it hard to get to know her. They tried to make allowances. She had, after all, volunteered to be sent into Silo Nine, and Wormboy Hell was enough to break anyone. It helped that she didn't trust Young Jack either. Possibly because she didn't like the competition for attention.

She paused for a moment in the doorway, to make sure everyone was looking at her, then flounced across the room to the only remaining empty chair and sank into it as if it were a throne. Young Jack Random stayed by the door, falling naturally into an heroic pose. Jenny ignored him magnificently. "How much longer till we get to Mistworld?" she said icily.

"Now don't you start," said Owen. "Even with the new drive, it still takes time to get from one side of the Empire to the other."

"Actually, we've been in orbit around Mistworld for almost twenty minutes," Ozymandius murmured in Owen's ear.

"What?" said Owen, subvocalizing furiously. "Why didn't the ship's AI tell me?"

"You didn't tell it to. It is, after all, nowhere near as complex as I."

"Well, why didn't you tell me we'd arrived?"

"Who, me? I'm dead, remember? Far be it from me to put myself in where I'm not wanted."

Owen fought down a need to sigh heavily and looked at his fellow team members. "Apparently we are currently in orbit over our destination. So far, no one is shooting at us. Hazel, you know these people better than the rest of us. Patch into the comm system and find out what exorbitant price they're going to charge us for landing this time."

She grunted unenthusiastically and got up out of her chair. It took her a while, and a certain amount of effort, because of the weight of all the guns she'd loaded herself down with. She made her way unhurriedly over to the comm panels and put in a call to Mistport Security. There was only one city and one starport on Mistworld, and that was Mistport. A wild and woolly place, and very definitely not somewhere you went without an invitation. As the Empire had found out, to its cost. As Hazel waited more or less patiently for someone to answer her, Owen looked around him, then stirred uncomfortably in his chair as he discovered that Jenny Psycho was studying him again. Her esp made her somewhat aware of the great changes that had taken place within Owen and Hazel, but it wasn't enough to tell her what those changes were. She sensed that, in their own ways, Owen and Hazel were just as powerful as she was, and she didn't seem able to make up her mind as to whether she should be frightened or awed or jealous. Owen had used that uncertainty to talk her into quietly probing Young Jack's mind, to see what was in there. To their mutual surprise, it turned out that as far as Jenny's esp was concerned, there was no one there. Which meant that either Jack had amazingly tough mental shields, or . . . So far they hadn't been able to come up with an or they liked. Owen looked away from Jenny's burning gaze. As if he didn't have enough things to worry about.

"Hello, *Sunstrider II*," said a tired voice from the comm panels. "This is John Silver, head of starport Security. Don't adjust your equipment, we've lost visual again. When I find the pirate that sold us these systems, I'm going to tie his legs in a square knot. Welcome back, Hazel. Don't steal anything big and try not to kill anyone important this time. You can put your ship down any-where you fancy; there's hardly anything on the pads. Not a lot of traffic comes our way these days."

"Understood," said Hazel. "Cheer up, John, we've got a cargo bay crammed to the ceiling with really nice sur-prises for you; namely, more projectile weapons, ammo, and explosives than you can shake a really big stick at. Just the thing for expressing your displeasure with Impe-rial spies and troublemakers."

"You always bring the nicest presents, Hazel. Now pardon me if I leave you all to your own devices. As head of Security, or what's left of it, I'm being run ragged at the moment. The precogs have been going crazy the last few days, insisting Something Bad is in the air. We can't get any details out of them that make sense, but either way I don't have the time to waste on a single ship, no matter how friendly."

"In case he's forgotten," said Owen, "remind him we're not just outlaws on the run this time. We represent the Golgotha underground."

"I heard that," said Silver. "Might have known you'd be aboard, Deathstalker. We haven't forgotten the mess you made on your last visit. Someone will meet you once you're down, but don't expect a brass band or the key to the city. We had to pawn the instruments and the key never did work anyway. Have a nice stay. Don't start any-thing. Now clear the channel so I can concentrate."

"Is that a typical Mistworld welcome?" asked Jenny Psycho, after a moment.

"Pretty much," said Hazel. "They've raised paranoia to a fine art in Mistport. With good reason. The Empire has a long history of sneaking in dirty tricks to try and under-mine or destroy the starport. It wasn't that long ago they started an esper plague here, using a disguised vector called Typhoid Mary. A lot of people died before Security finally tracked her down. They're still recovering."

"They've been through a lot," said Young Jack. "We'll just have to convince them of the importance of our vari-ous missions here. We must have Mistworld on our side if we're to win the rebellion. Their espers will be an in-valuable asset."

"Glad someone's keeping an eye on the big picture,"

said Owen. "But I would go easy on the exposition when you get down there. Mistworlders aren't big on speeches."

"You should know," said Hazel.

The landing pads were practically deserted, with only a handful of smugglers' ships, huddled together at one end of the field as though for comfort. The *Sunstrider II* settled comfortably onto the pad set aside, marked by flaring oil lamps. The tall steelglass control tower was the only sign of high tech at the starport, its bright electric lights blazing through the thick, swirling mists. Owen had the ship's computers shut down everything except the security systems, then led the way out of the ship and onto the landing field.

The cold cut at them like a knife as they filed out of the airlock, searing their exposed faces and burning in their lungs as they all huddled in the thick furs the ship had provided. Owen beat his gloved hands together and glared about him. He'd forgotten how much he hated this place. And not just for the cold.

The mists were at their thickest, in the early hours of the morning before the rising of Mistworld's pale sun. Beyond the control tower, the lights of the city showed only dimly through the shifting grey walls of fog. Young Jack Random looked calmly about him. He didn't even have the decency to shiver like the rest of them.

"The old place hasn't changed a bit. Colder than a witch's tit and even less inviting."

"And when were you last here?" said Hazel, not bothering to hide the suspicion in her voice.

"I've been here several times, down the years," Random said easily. "In fact, I started out here, some twenty years ago, trying to raise troops for a rebellion on Lyonesse. I found a few brave souls to join me, but that was all. They didn't know me then. Hopefully I'll do rather better this time."

"Heads up," said Jenny Psycho. "Someone's coming. Three people. One's an esper, but his mind is closed to me."

"Stay out of the other people's heads as well," said Hazel sharply. "This is an esper city, and they take their mental privacy very seriously. You upset the powers that be here, and we'll be taking what's left of you home in a straightjacket. From this point on, you use your esp by invitation only. Got it?"

Jenny Psycho shrugged. "I can't help it if their minds are shouting at me all the time. And the powers that be here had better watch out for themselves. I have been transformed by the Mater Mundi, and there isn't a mind in this city that's my equal."

"That settles it," said Hazel. "From now on, you stay well clear of the rest of us. That way whenever it happens, whatever horrible thing it turns out to be, we'll all be a safe distance away. Hiding."

They were saved Jenny's acid reply by the sudden emergence of three figures from the shifting mists. There was no warning. One moment there was only the fog, and then two men and a woman came striding out of the mists toward them. Owen found that quietly disturbing. Usually his new powers gave him advance warning of things like that. Why, dammit, did it work sometimes and not others? He found his hand had dropped automatically to the sword at his side and quickly moved it away again. He recognized two of the newcomers from files he'd been shown at his last briefing. Port Director Gideon Steel was a short fat man with calm, thoughtful eyes and a disturbingly cynical smile. He dressed well, if a trifle sloppily, as some of his furs looked distinctly mangy. He was supposed to be in his mid-forties, but he looked ten years older. Trying to run Mistport will do that to you.

The woman beside him was much more impressive, and not a little intimidating. Despite the bitter cold she wore no furs, only the formal uniform of an Investigator. Owen could feel Hazel tensing beside him and prayed she'd have enough sense not to start anything. Investigator Topaz was medium height, slim, handsome, and her gaze was colder than the mists could ever be. Her close-cropped dark hair gave her classical features a calm, aesthetic air, but her ice-blue eyes were killer's eyes. Just looking at her made Owen want to back away slowly and very carefully, doing absolutely nothing that might upset her. He knew about Investigator Topaz. Everyone did. She was a Siren, the only esper ever to be made an Investigator. When she decided to leave the Empire and head for Mistworld, the Empress sent a whole company of Guards after her. Five hundred men. Topaz killed them all with a single song, her voice and esp combining into a deadly force that could not be stopped or turned aside.

In Mistport, she was officially just a Sergeant of the city Watch, but she kept her Investigator's title. Mostly because no one was stupid enough to argue the point with her. In a city full of dangerous and desperate people, no one messed with Investigator Topaz. Having met her, Owen could understand why. Without looking round, he could feel Hazel stirring at his side, like a junkyard dog scenting a rival, and Owen decided to get things started before they had a chance to get seriously out of hand.

"Director Steel and Investigator Topaz," he said smoothly. "So good of you to come and meet us in person at such an early hour. May I present—"

"We know who you are," said Steel. "And if you weren't official representatives of the Golgotha underground, you'd never have been allowed to land. You're trouble-makers, and the last thing Mistport needs right now is more trouble. And for your information we haven't got up early; we haven't been to bed yet. Since Typhoid Mary and the esper plague, those of us who survived have been working double shifts just trying to get things back together again. And I haven't forgotten the mess you stirred up the last time you honored us with a visit, Death-stalker. I should bill you for the damage."

"Given the size of the docking fees, I thought you already had," said Owen, completely unruffled.

"And before you ask," said Hazel, "no, you don't get your usual unofficial ten percent cut of the cargo we're carrying. Feel free to argue the point. And I'll feel free to cut you off at the knees. Possibly quite literally."

"Don't mind her," said Owen. "She's just being herself. If I might inquire, since we're so persona non grata, what brings you here at all? Politeness to the underground?"

"No," said Topaz, her voice as cold as the grave. "We just wanted a look at the legendary Jack Random."

Random flashed them his winning smile and bowed

formally. "Delighted to make your acquaintances, Investigator and Director. Rest assured, I shall do everything in my power to see that our business is carried out quietly and quickly, with the minimum of disturbance to all concerned. But I make no secret of my intention to bring Mistworld into the underground, and the central path of the rebellion. You've been left alone in the cold too long. It's time for us all to stand together, and take the fight to the Empire."

"Great," said Steel, entirely unmoved. "Another bloody hero. We get a lot through here. They come and they go, and nothing ever changes."

"Ah," said Random, grinning broadly. "But they're not Jack Random."

To Owen's surprise, Steel grinned back. Jenny Psycho stepped forward suddenly. "In case anyone's forgotten, I'm still here," she said loudly. "I represent the Mater Mundi, Our Mother of All Souls."

"Congratulations," said Topaz. "You're the tenth this month. It's the most common confidence trick in Mistport. Probably because so many people are desperate to believe in it. If you weren't with Jack Random, I'd have you thrown in gaol on general principles. So keep your head down and don't make waves. Is that clear?"

Jenny Psycho's eyes blazed suddenly with an inner light, shining from her face like spotlights. Loose energy sparked and crackled on the air around her, as her power stirred within her. Her presence beat on the air like the wings of a giant bird, forcing them all back. Something lived deep within Jenny Psycho, something vast and powerful and not necessarily human, and it was awakening. Gideon Steel drew a gun. Investigator Topaz opened her mouth to sing. And Owen and Hazel threw themselves on Jenny and wrestled her to the ground. Her power lashed out at them, only to be met and swept aside by a greater power, as yet unfocused and untrained, but still more than enough to silence a mere esper who had only been touched in passing by something greater. Her presence shattered like a smashed mirror and was gone. Owen and Hazel cut off their power, rolled Jenny over, and pressed her face against the harsh surface of the landing pad.

Owen sat on her, just in case, and smiled up at Steel and
Topaz.

"Don't mind Jenny. She doesn't travel well. Once you
get to know her, she's quite objectionable."

Steel sniffed and put away his gun. Topaz scowled.
"Something happened then," she said slowly. "I just
caught the edges, but you two did something there.
There's more to you than meets the eye, Deathstalker."

"There would have to be," said Steel. "Welcome to
Mistworld, people, and keep that esper on a short leash, or
I'll have her muzzled. The man lurking in the background
behind us, and carefully staying out of harm's way, is
John Silver, our current head of starport Security. He'll
look after you during your stay, and do his best to keep
you out of trouble, if he ever wants to see his pension.
Best of luck in your various missions, and if anything
goes wrong I don't want to hear about it. Don't bother
popping in to say good-bye before you leave. Now, if
you'll excuse us, Topaz and I have work to do."

And with that the two of them turned and walked away,
disappearing back into the concealing fog. John Silver
glared after them, made a rude noise and a ruder gesture,
and strolled forward to introduce himself with an easy
smile. "Don't take it personally; they're like that with
everyone. Mostly with good reason, but that's Mistport
for you. Hello, Hazel, good to you see again."

"Good to see you, you old pirate," said Hazel, grinning,
and stepped forward to hug Silver tightly. Owen was
almost shocked. Hazel wasn't usually a touchy-feely kind
of person. He took the opportunity to study Mistport's
head of Security. Silver was tall and broad-shouldered,
with sharp-edged youthful features, and wore thick,
superbly cut furs topped with the scarlet cloak of the
esper. He wore a simple short sword on his hip, in a well-
worn leather scabbard, but Owen had no doubt the man
also had a gun or two hidden under those furs somewhere.
He looked the type. He also looked like he was enjoying
the hug entirely too much. Silver and Hazel finally broke
apart and stepped back to hold each other at arm's length.

"Looking good, Hazel. Robbed anyone interesting
recently?"

"You'd be surprised. How the hell did a rogue like you

get to be head of starport Security? That's like setting a starving wolf to guard a flock of sheep."

Silver shrugged amiably, not insulted. "Even the fiercest wolf has to settle down and turn respectable eventually. We lost a lot of good people here during the esper plague, including most of my superiors. Typhoid Mary killed or brainburned them all in the space of a few days, and when she was finally taken down, I was the only one left standing. To everyone's surprise, including my own, I've been doing a good and mostly honest job ever since. Mostly because there's so much work to be done that I haven't the time or the energy to be crooked."

"Never thought I'd hear you say that," said Hazel, laughing. She looked back, and realized Owen was studying them thoughtfully. "Owen, get up off Jenny and come and meet an old friend." Owen got up carefully. Jenny stayed where she was, breathing harshly. Hazel grinned. "Owen, allow me to present an old confidant of mine. Expirate, confidence trickster, lawyer, and occasional female impersonator when money gets short. Generally a good comrade to have with you, on either side of the law. Particularly if you're working a swindle. Best innocent-faced liar I ever knew."

"Which is why I'm so good at my present job," said Silver calmly. "Takes one liar to spot another. And I know all the tricks, because I've used most of them in my time."

"This is all very charming and picaresque," said Random, "but I have business to be about."

"Oh sure," said Silver. "Hang around, and I'll get you a map and some guards."

"No need. I know my way around Mistport. And I've never needed guarding." He bowed politely to them all, even Jenny, then strode confidently off into the fog, his straight back radiating strength and purpose.

"Impressive," said Silver. "I just hope he doesn't get mugged and rolled. We'd never hear the end of it."

"I have my own mission, too," said Jenny Psycho icily. Everyone looked round sharply, as they realized she'd got to her feet without being noticed. If anything, she looked even more dangerous than she had before. "I don't need a map or guards either. Just stay out of my way."

She stalked off into the fog, and the mists rolled aside to get out of her path. They closed again after her, and she was quickly gone. Hazel shook her head slowly.

"You know, I could have sworn we were supposed to work as a team."

"Don't let it bother you," said Owen. "Personally, I feel a lot safer with them gone. Neither of them would get my vote for mental health poster child of the year."

"You're missing the point, as usual," said Hazel. "God knows how much damage Jenny Psycho will cause on her own, and I particularly wanted to stick close to Jack Random, in the hope of spotting something that would prove whether he's the real thing or not."

"I thought you were sure he's a fake?"

"I am. But proof would be nice."

"We could always go after him."

"No we couldn't. Then he'd know for sure that we don't trust him."

"I hate reasoning like that," said Owen. "You can argue all day and still end up running in circles. We could be wrong about him, you know."

"Hold everything," said Silver. "Are you telling me there's a chance that wasn't the real Jack Random?"

"We're still deciding," said Hazel. "Let's just say we have doubts."

"But he looks the part," said Silver. "Every inch a hero and a warrior."

"Precisely," said Owen. "He's too perfect. Real life isn't like that."

"Paranoia," said Hazel, smiling. "A game for the whole family, and anyone else who might be watching. Let's get out of the cold and find somewhere warm before my toes drop off."

Owen glanced approvingly round Silver's private quarters as he sank into a deeply comfortable chair by an open fire. The ex-pirate Security chief lived in a fair amount of comfort, by Mistport standards. There were a number of high-tech appliances, including electric lighting, rare on a world where all forms of high tech had to be smuggled in past Empire blockades, at great cost to buyer and seller. Either head of port Security paid really well, or Silver hadn't entirely given up on his old piratical ways. Hazel sat opposite Owen, frowning into the dancing flames of the fire. She looked tired and drawn, and older than her years. Something was troubling her, but Owen had more sense than to ask what. She'd only bite his head off. She'd tell him when she was ready, or not at all.

Silver bustled about being the perfect host, making sure his guests were comfortable, chatting cheerfully about inconsequential things, and pressing large mugs of mulled wine on Hazel and Owen. Hazel just held hers, making no attempt to try it, so Owen took a gulp of his, just to be polite. Normally he couldn't stand mulled wine, but this proved to be easy on the palate and hotly spiced, leaving a pleasant warmth behind as it sank past his throat and chest and headed for his stomach. He nodded thankfully to Silver, who pulled up a chair facing his guests and looked at them inquiringly.

"Fill us in on what's been happening recently," said Owen, when a long pause made it clear Hazel wasn't going to start the ball rolling. "We weren't here long enough to ask questions on our last visit. What's this about a Typhoid Mary and an esper plague?"

"The Empire smuggled her in," said Silver. "She was an extremely powerful rogue esper, primed and conditioned to kill other espers. People fell dying and brain-burned all across the city, and where she passed children woke screaming from their dreams and would not be comforted. She destroyed a lot of good people before she was finally brought down. The Empire's plan had been to kill so many espers that the psionic screen which protects Mistworld would collapse, and the Imperial Fleet could move in at will. That didn't happen. But we came bloody close . . ."

"What happened after she was captured?" said Hazel, not looking up from the fire.

"We deconditioned her," said Silver. "It wasn't her fault. She'd been programmed by mind techs. She works for us now."

"And you trust her?" said Owen. "The Empire could have planted all kinds of control words in her subconscious. She wouldn't even know they were there till someone triggered them."

"There were quite a few. We found them. This is an esper world, Deathstalker. The depths of the mind hold no secrets from us."

"How much damage did she cause?" said Owen.

"Lots. We're still clearing up. Many people in important positions were either killed or brainburned, and for a long time there was chaos in the city as various factions fought for control. The worst of that is over, praise the good Lord, but there's still a lot of jockeying for position going on. Watch your backs while you're here. There's a lot of people who'd kill both of you just so that someone else couldn't have you."

"So," said Hazel, finally turning to look at Silver. "You're doing all right for yourself then, John?"

"I'm doing fine," said Silver, blinking slightly at the sudden change of subject.

"Better than fine. These quarters are a damn sight cosier than that rathole you used to hide out in down by the docks. No, I take that back, now I come to think of it, rats wouldn't have lived there for fear of catching something."

"Head of port Security is a plum job," said Silver easily. "As long as I keep things nice and peaceful, no one looks too closely at how I do it. So, on the one hand, I crack down hard on the kind of people I used to be, and on the other, I salt away a little here and there, to supplement my pension. It's a hard life, but someone's got to do it."

"Aren't you worried about Director Steel finding out?" said Owen, not sure whether he should be shocked or not. This was Mistport, after all.

"Him? He's a bigger crook than I am! No, the one I have to watch out for is Investigator Topaz. If she ever gets anything on me, I won't live to stand trial. In fact, if she ever even looks like getting close, it's me for the mountains on the first gravity sled I can beg, borrow, or steal. How someone that honest ever ended up on Mistworld is beyond me."

"Law-abiding sort, is she?" said Hazel innocently.

Silver shuddered, and not from the cold. "That woman

is so straight she even distrusts her own shadow. Luckily, she's usually busy chasing bigger fish than me. Let me give you some idea of the kind of person we're discussing here. Did either of you happen to notice the hole in the back of her cloak?"

"Yeah," said Owen. "Disrupter burn. I take it she wasn't wearing the cloak at the time?"

"No. Her husband was. Someone shot him in the back, at point-blank range. She found the killer, and killed him slowly, but she still wears the cloak, and she never had the hole mended. What kind of person would do that?"

"Cold, obsessed, unswerving," said Hazel. "An Investigator in other words."

"Let's change the subject," said Silver. "Before I start looking over my shoulder and jumping at sudden noises. Jack Random and that Psycho woman took off on their own missions. What are you here for? Or aren't you allowed to tell me?"

"It's no big deal," said Hazel. "I'm here to make contact with the Council on behalf of the Golgotha underground. It should have been someone else, but plans got changed at the last minute, and I was the only one who didn't run away fast enough, so I got volunteered. Owen's here to hunt down an old information-gathering network his father set up in Mistport some years ago. You can make a move when you're ready, Deathstalker. I'm going to spend some time with Silver before I get started."

Owen frowned. "I thought we'd be sticking together. You know Mistport a lot better than I do."

"So what do you want me to do, aristo? Hold your hand?"

"You heard what Silver said," Owen said stubbornly. "We don't have any friends out there, and our . . . link is unreliable."

"I can look after myself," said Hazel. "So can you."

Owen scowled, nonplussed. It made no sense at all to split up when they both had so many old and new enemies to watch out for. He wondered for a moment if Silver might have been more than a friend in the past, and that was why he was being frozen out, but he didn't think so. The body language was all wrong from both of them. But it was clear he wasn't going to get anywhere with

Hazel while she was in this kind of mood. There was also no point in losing his temper. She'd always been better at throwing tantrums than he. He found it all so undignified. Besides, she didn't look too good. She was sweating in the heat of the fire, and her mouth was set in a flat, ugly line. Owen pushed back his chair and got to his feet.

"Well, if you'd rather waste time chatting with an old friend than getting on with the job we were sent here to do, I can't stop you."

"Damn right you can't. And don't take that tone with me, Deathstalker. I know my duty, but I'll take care of it in my own time and in my own way."

"Time is something we're rather short of, Hazel. Or had you forgotten how closely the Empire has been dogging our heels?"

"I haven't forgotten anything! You stick to your mission and leave me to mine! Get out of here, aristo. I'm sick of looking at you. I don't need you!"

"No," said Owen. "You've never needed anyone, have you?"

He bowed curtly to Silver and stalked out of the room, not quite slamming the door behind him. The tense silence continued for a while, as Hazel glared at the closed door, and Silver studied her thoughtfully. He'd seen Hazel in many moods, but this was a new one on him. Clearly the Deathstalker, or at least his opinion, mattered to Hazel. Silver hoped she wasn't falling for the outlawed aristocrat. Hazel had never been any good at handling affairs of the heart. She always got hurt in the end. He almost jumped as Hazel turned suddenly to face him, her eyes hot and fierce.

"We've always been good friends, haven't we, John?"

"Of course we have. We've walked a lot of miles together."

"I need your help, John."

"It's yours. Anything you want, just say the word."

"I need some Blood. Just a drop or two. Do you know where you can get some? Someone . . . discreet?"

"If that's what you want."

"Yes, John. That's what I want."

Silver pursed his lips. "The Deathstalker doesn't know about this, does he?"

"No. And you're not to tell him. He wouldn't understand."

"I'm not sure I do. I thought you were clear of that shit. I held your hand and sponged your brow and wiped your ass while you sweated the stuff out of your system the last time. I don't want to have to do that again. It almost killed you, Hazel."

"I'm not talking about going back to being a plasma baby again! I've got it under control this time. I just need a drop, now and again. You don't know what I've been through, John. You don't know the pressure I'm under."

"I said I'd help you, Hazel. If Blood is what you need, I can get it for you. We all have the right to go to Hell in our own ways. As head of port Security, I have access to all drugs seized from incoming ships. No one will miss a few drops." He paused. "Are you sure about this, Hazel?"

"Oh yes. I have to have something in my life I can depend on."

Young Jack Random strode unhurriedly through the streets of Mistport, and no one bothered him. There was something in his unyielding stance and cold confidence that persuaded people to keep their distance. That, and the energy gun he wore openly on his hip. Only the real movers and shakers in Mistport had access to energy guns. Random made his way into Merchants Quarter, in search of an old friend. Councillor Donald Royal had been one of Mistport's greatest heroes in his younger days, and was an influential figure even now, in the autumn of his life.

Random finally came to a halt before a soot-blackened old building in a part of the Quarter that had definitely known better days. Donald Royal could have afforded to live practically anywhere he chose in the city, but this had always been his home, and he wouldn't move. Stubborn old man. Random stepped forward and knocked politely on the door. There was a long pause, and then he sensed he was being studied through a spyhole. He smiled charmingly at the door, and kept his hands well away from his weapons. The door swung open to reveal a striking young woman. As far as Random knew, she was a complete stranger, but he kept his smile going anyway. She was tall for a woman, with a tousled head of reddish-brown hair, falling in great curls to her shoulders. Her face was a little too broad to be pretty, but her strong bone structure gave her a harsh, sensual look. She held herself like a fighter, with a cold steady gaze and a mouth that gave away nothing. Her clothing was strictly functional, but well cut, and she carried an energy gun holstered on her hip. Random noted that her hand was resting on her belt next to the gun and cleared his throat politely.

"Good evening. I'm looking for Donald Royal. I understood he was still living here."

"He's here, but I don't know if he wants to be bothered right now. I'm his partner. I don't let people bother him without a good reason."

"I'm Jack Random. I've come to talk to him about planning the new rebellion against the Empire."

The woman smiled suddenly, and her eyes warmed. "That's . . . a good reason. I'm Madelaine Skye. Come on in. Pardon my caution, but we don't get many legends around here."

She stepped back, and Random bowed politely before moving past her into a narrow, gloomy hall. He hung up his coat and his sword belt without having to be asked and allowed Skye to lead him down the hall and into a cosy sitting room. Oil lamps provided the only light, suffusing the room with a soft buttery glow. Thick leather-bound books lined three walls, the last wall being covered by a display of well-used bladed weapons, from slender daggers up to a huge double-headed ax. Below them lay a large fire, crackling contentedly in its grate, surmounted by an elaborate mantelpiece of dark wood, carved into blocky Gothic shapes. On top of the mantelpiece, a large clock was set into the belly of a carved wooden dog with an ugly face. Its eyes and lolling red tongue moved to and fro as it ticked. Sitting beside the fire in a large padded armchair was an old man with vague eyes. He'd been a large man once, but the great muscles that had packed his frame in his youth had slowly wasted away down the years, and now his clothes hung loosely about him. Long strands of wispy white hair hung down about a gaunt, bony face. Madelaine Skye stood beside the chair, hovering protectively close.

"We have a visitor, Donald."

"I can see that, woman. I'm not blind yet. Or senile. I assume he's someone important, or you'd have sent him on his way with a flea in his ear." He looked at Random for a long moment, and then frowned. "I know you from somewhere. Never forget a face." And then his gaze cleared, and he rose suddenly out of his chair. "Dear God, it can't be. Jack? Is that you, Jack? Damn me, it is." He grinned broadly and reached out to take Random's proffered hand in both of his, the large wrinkled hands enveloping Random's. "Jack Random, as I live and breathe! What the hell are you doing here?"

"Looking up old friends," said Random, smiling. "Been a long time, Donald."

"You can say that again. Too damned long. Sit down, sit down, and let me take a look at you."

Random pulled up the armchair on the other side of the fire and sat down, politely pretending not to notice as Donald Royal lowered himself carefully back into his chair, with just a little help from Madelaine. Donald studied Random with sharp, weighing eyes. There was nothing vague about him anymore, as though the memory of the man he used to be had recharged him. Madelaine moved away to give them some privacy, but stayed by the door, leaning casually against the doorjamb. It hadn't escaped Random that her hand was still resting near her gun. He smiled warmly at Donald.

"Nice place you have here. Comfortable. I like your clock."

"Do you?" said Donald. "Can't stand the bloody thing myself. But it was a favorite of my late wife's, and I haven't the heart to throw it out. You're looking good, Jack. Must be twenty years since I last saw you, sitting in this room, in these same damn chairs. You were a firebrand then, so young and alive and full of hope and vinegar that I couldn't resist you. Gave you all the gold I had on me, and the names of everyone I could think of who might listen to you. I'd have gone with you myself, but even then I was getting a bit too old and fragile for adventuring. You had the gift of words, Jack, and I never could resist a plausable rogue."

"You were one of the first people to really believe in me," said Random. "I never forgot that. Though it's just as well you didn't come with me to Lyonesse. Things went badly, from start to finish. I was young and inexperienced, still learning my way. We had some victories, but in the final battle we were thrown back and routed. I had to run for my life, while good men and women died to buy me time. But we still stuck a blow for freedom, and made the Iron Bitch afraid, if only for a moment."

"I remember Lyonesse," said Madelaine from the doorway. "Your army was cut to ribbons, one in ten of the population was hanged for supporting treason, and the survivors had their taxes doubled for the next ten years. There are those who might say Lyonesse was better off before your rebellion."

"Don't mind Madelaine," said Donald. "She doesn't believe in luxuries like optimism and virtues. She's never happy unless she's seeing the dark side of things. She persuaded me to come out of retirement to work with her as private investigators. I provide the brains, and Madelaine sorts out the bad guys. I have to say, I've felt more alive this last year than I have for ages. I was never meant for retirement. She still insists on acting as my bodyguard, even though I haven't forgotten how to use a sword."

"I'm sure she's very proficient," said Random. "Donald, I need to talk to you."

"Of course you do, Jack. We have a lot to catch up on. Twenty-two years since I last saw you. I've followed your career as best I could. News takes a while to reach Mistworld. You haven't changed a bit, Jack. Unlike me. How have you stayed so young? You must have been in your late twenties when I first met you, and you don't look as though you've aged a day since then."

"I have several heavy-duty regenerations to thank for that," said Random. "And a little cosmetic surgery. People won't follow an old rebel. It's no secret that I've been pretty badly messed up on more than one occasion. I may be young on the outside, but my bones know the truth. But I'm still me. Still the professional rebel, ready to fight for truth and justice at the drop of a hint. My cause hasn't changed in twenty-two years, Donald, and just like then, I need your help."

Donald sighed, and settled back in his chair. "Afraid my help's rather more limited these days, Jack. I'm still on the city Council, but I don't take much interest in politics anymore. Which means my influence is pretty much nonexistent. I stick my oar in now and again, just to remind them I haven't died, and I try to do my own small bit for truth and justice as a private investigator, but truth be told, on the whole the important life of the city just passes me by. I can give you names and addresses of some people who might be willing to listen to you, but my name isn't the recommendation it was the last time you were here. Times have changed, Jack, and not for the better. Mistport is a colder and far more cynical place than you and I remember."

"You can still vouch for me to the Council," said Random. "There seems to be some question as to whether I really am who I say I am. If you were to speak up publicly to confirm my identity, it would help a lot."

"No problem there," said Donald. "I may not be as young as I was, but there's nothing wrong with my eyes or my memory. You're Jack Random. No doubt about it. I'd stake my life on it."

"Don't be so quick," said Madelaine. "Looks aren't everything. You said yourself he looks far too young. How do we know he isn't a clone?"

"A gene test would answer that," Random said easily.

"Unfortunately, we don't have access to tech like that here in Mistport," said Madelaine. "Convenient, that."

"Hush, Madelaine," said Donald. "Easy enough to test the man. There are things only Jack and I would remember. Things we talked about, people we knew, back then. Right, Jack?"

"Of course. Let me think for a moment. It was a long time ago." Random pursed his lips and rested his chin on his fist. "I remember some of the people you sent me to. There was Lord Durandal, the adventurer. Count Ironhand of the Marches. Is either of them still around?"

"No," said Donald. "They're both gone now. Ironhand drowned, saving a child who'd fallen into the River

Autumn. He was a good swimmer, for an old man. Got the child to safety. But the shock of the icy waters was too much for him. He knew it would be, but he went in anyway. He was that sort of man. Durandal disappeared into the Darkvoid, years ago, on some damn fool quest to find the Wolfling World. Don't know if he ever found it. He never came back."

"Pity," said Random. "I admired them both. I was hoping they'd vouch for me, too. We still need some proof, don't we? How about this; you gave me all the gold you had on you, twenty-two years ago. And that was exactly seventeen crowns. Am I right?"

"Exactly right!" said Donald, slapping his knee. "I remember now. Seventeen crowns. No one else could have known that, Madelaine."

She shook her head stubbornly. "An esper could have got it out of Jack's head, or yours."

"Oh, don't mind her," Donald said dismissively. "She was born suspicious. Had her mother's milk tested for steroids. You're the real thing, Jack; I can feel it in my bones. I'll vouch for you. And maybe this time you'll listen to me before you go haring off to fight for truth and justice with too few troops and no proper backup."

"I'll listen this time," said Random. "I've learned from my mistakes."

"You've had enough opportunities," said Madelaine, but both Donald and Jack ignored her.

"We've got a real chance this time, Donald," said Random, leaning forward. "An army of clones and espers, and powerful allies beyond anything you've ever dreamed of. I won't throw it away because of my pride."

"Good man," said Donald. "Get your people together and set up a meeting with the Council. Madelaine and I will be there."

"Thank you, Donald. This means a lot to me." Random rose smoothly to his feet, then waited politely as Donald struggled up out of his chair. They clasped hands again, and Random strode out. Madelaine followed him to the door, to be sure he didn't steal anything, and then came back to stand in the doorway and glare at Donald.

"You think he's a fake, don't you?" Donald said calmly, as he eased himself back into his chair.

"Damn right I do. He's too good. Too perfect. Great-looking, muscles to spare, and all the right words and phrases. Like a popular hero designed by a committee. And I don't buy that regeneration story for one moment. I mean, technically speaking I suppose it's possible, but where would a rebel on the run gain access to that kind of tech? Last I heard, regeneration machines were strictly for the aristos. No, Donald, you only believe in him because you want to. Because he's one of the few good memories from your past that's still around."

"Maybe," said Donald. "I don't believe he's telling us everything, or that everything he told us was true. But every instinct I have says it's him. He's just the way I remember him. A larger-than-life hero and a plausible rogue, all in one. He's passed the only tests I could think of. What else does he have to do to convince you, walk on water?"

"If he did, I'd want to check his boots afterward," said Madelaine.

Jenny Psycho made her way through the streets of Mistport, the crisp snow crunching under her steady stride. Her breath steamed thickly on the air before her, but she was pleasantly warm inside her furs. Heat and cold and other vagaries of the world had lost all power over her. According to her briefing, the espers' union had their own hall in Guilds Quarter, but she needn't have bothered with the directions. She could feel it in her mind, like a great searchlight stabbing up from the center of the city. There were people bustling everywhere she went, but they all gave her plenty of room, even if they weren't always sure why.

The hall itself turned out to be modestly sized, set back in its own grounds. Jenny was a little taken aback to see it standing plainly sign-posted and apparently unguarded. Anywhere else in the Empire such a gathering of espers was punishable by death or mindwipe, depending on how valuable their services were. The simple openness of the espers' union cheered her greatly, and she strode up the graveled path to the front door with something like a swagger. There were no visible guards anywhere, but she hadn't expected any, even in a cesspit like Mistport.

Espers had their own, subtler ways of keeping watch and seeing off the uninvited. The great front door looked imposing and impressive. Jenny looked for a knocker or bellpull, but there wasn't one. She raised her hand to knock, and the door swung open before her. A tall slender man in formal evening wear filled the doorway, staring haughtily down at her. His head was clean-shaven, showing small surgical scars here and there, and his eyes were just a little too wide. His smile was formal and entirely meaningless.

"Come in, Jenny Psycho. We've been expecting you."

"I should hope so," said Jenny. "Now, are you going to let me in, or am I supposed to teleport past you?"

The doorman, or whatever the hell he was, stepped back gracefully, and Jenny strode past him with her nose firmly in the air. Start as you mean to go on. The hall was open and airy, the air sweetened by vases of blossoming flowers in every nook and cranny. Jenny would have liked to ask where the hell they found flowers like that on a freezing, inhospitable rock like Mistworld, but she kept the thought to herself. Asking questions could be taken as a sign of weakness, and it was vital she appear strong. The butler took her furs and hung them up. He looked pointedly at her boots, dripping melting snow onto the thick carpet, but she ignored him. Bare feet might be taken as a sign of informality.

"I take it your precogs told you I was coming," said Jenny, casually. "They are supposed to be the best in the. Empire, after all. But did they tell you why I was coming?"

"Not yet." He closed the door firmly and turned to smile at Jenny. She didn't like the smile. It was too confident by far. The flunky strode off down the hall without waiting to see if she was following, allowing his words to trail back over his shoulder. "We know who you are. We could find out why you're here if we wanted to, but we'd rather hear it from you directly. This way. Someone will see you shortly."

Hell with this, thought Jenny Psycho. Things were getting out of hand. These people needed reminding who and what she was. She reached out with her mind and drenched the flowers in the hall with her esp. They erupted out of their vases, growing at a tremendous rate, flowers budding and blossoming in a moment as vines and branches sprawled across the walls like runaway trellises. They filled the hall from floor to ceiling, rioting on the walls, pushing each other aside for space to display. The scent of flowers was overpowering, rich and glorious. The servant looked back at Jenny, his face impassive, but only just.

"I didn't know you could do that."

"There's lots about me you people don't know. Now find me someone in charge to speak to, or I'll turn this entire house into a shrubbery."

"They said you'd be trouble," said the butler, or whatever the hell he was. "If you'd care to wait in the study, someone will be with you soon."

"Very soon," said Jenny.

"I wouldn't be at all surprised. And for your information, I am not the bloody butler, I am the Chancellor of this lodge. This is the study. Try not to break the furniture or set fire to things. Some of these books are very old and a great deal more valuable to us than you are."

"That's what you think," said Jenny. "Now beat it, Chancellor. And don't keep me waiting too long or I'll act up cranky."

"I wouldn't doubt it for a moment," said the Chancellor, and ushered Jenny into the study. The room was large and brightly lit, with large comfortable furniture, gleaming wood-paneled walls, and an inviting, well-banked fire. The whole study had a calm, relaxed atmosphere that Jenny didn't trust for a moment. They probably just wanted to put her off her guard. Jenny quietly probed the surrounding rooms and had to hide her surprise when her mind bounced harmlessly away from powerful psionic shields.

"Please don't do that," said the Chancellor. "We have many private places here, mentally shielded to protect our more sensitive people from the clamor of the world. And occasionally to protect the world from some of us. I advise you to respect their privacy. For your own sake, if not for theirs."

Knowing a good exit line when he delivered one, the Chancellor bowed briefly and left Jenny alone in the

study, shutting the door firmly behind him. Jenny waited
to hear the sound of a key turning in the lock, but it didn't
come. Presumably the espers' union thought it had other
ways of stopping her if she decided to leave. More fool
they. She sniffed angrily and threw herself into the most
comfortable-looking chair. She'd been held in Wormboy
Hell and survived, and there wasn't much left that could
intimidate her now. She glowered around her. Looked at
closely, the study was a bland place, with no style or personality of its own. More like a stage set than a place
where people lived and worked. Probably set up as neutral
ground, a midway place where espers could meet with
emissaries from the outside word.

Jenny sank grudgingly back into the comfort of her
chair and tried to relax. Nerve and passion and a sense of
destiny had brought her this far, but for the first time she
wasn't entirely sure what she was going to do next. It all
depended on how seriously the espers' union took her.
She was no longer used to dealing with people who
weren't awed or at least impressed by her presence, or
what she'd become. But this house held the greatest
minds on a planet of espers. They weren't going to impress easily. And she couldn't just threaten them. The
underground needed their wholehearted support and approval. Besides, it might not work. Jenny scowled sulkily.
When in doubt, stick to the script. The underground had
spent some time drilling her in all the proper words and
phrases, till she could have recited them in her sleep. It
helped, too, that she believed passionately in the arguments. Still, these people had better learn to treat her with
respect. She had been touched by the Mater Mundi, and
she was so much more than she used to be.

She concentrated, diffusing her thoughts, letting her esp
creep slowly outward, easing unnoticed through the mental shields to every side of her. Immediately a babble of
voices filled her head, harsh and deafening, and visions
flashed past her eyes almost too fast to follow. Jenny
reeled, and had to grab at the arms of her chair to center
herself. So many minds, all working at the peak of their
abilities. Past records and future possibilities jumbled
together till she could hardly tell them apart. They surged
around Jenny, like waves crashing against a rock on the

seashore, but she held firm and would not be swayed or moved. She concentrated, filtering through the deafening noise for the information she needed, and slowly things came to her, like ships glimpsed briefly through an ocean fog.

Someone was praying, and sobbing so hard she could hardly get the words out. There were visions of buildings burning, and people running screaming in the streets. Something dark and awful was hanging over Mistworld, like a huge spider contemplating its prey. There were guns firing, and a child's blood splashed across a wall. The streets were full of people rushing this way and that as the city burned and death closed in around them. In a padded room not too far away, someone was beating at the walls with raw and bloodied hands, and though he was silent as the grave, his mind was full of an endless horrible scream. And through it all, a name, repeating over and over in a chorus of voices, surfacing through the babble like a heartbeat, like a prophecy of doom that could not be denied.

Legion. Legion is coming. Legion.

Jenny broke free of the contact, shaking and trembling. She breathed deeply, fighting to control her scattered senses. She had no doubt she had seen the future. She had seen the streets of Mistport thrown down into Hell, and watched as Imperial troops butchered the people as they ran. She'd seen the city walls thrown down, and buildings blown apart, and above it all, a scream that never ended. It wasn't a human scream. It might happen a week from now, or a year, or it might already have begun. She had no way of knowing. Precog visions were like that. She cut herself off from all mental contact, slamming down her shields, until she was the only one left in her head, and she was safe and secure again. She groaned quietly, and rubbed at her aching brow.

"Serves you right for peeking," said a harsh voice from the doorway. Jenny's head snapped round, and she scrambled to her feet. She hadn't heard the door open. Standing in the doorway, looking as hard and uncompromising as before, was Investigator Topaz. Beside her stood a tall, painfully thin woman dressed in pale pastel colors. She looked almost as washed-out as her clothes, and stringy blond hair hung uncared for about a sharp, gaunt face with striking ice-blue eyes. There were patches of scar tissue around her cheekbones, and part of her nose had been eaten away. It gave her a stark, almost supernatural glamor. She might have looked dangerous, if she hadn't also looked like a strong breeze would blow her away.

"It's rude to stare," said Topaz. "Frostbite, in case you were wondering. It gets cold around here sometimes. If you ask her nicely, she'll show you the stumps where some of her fingers used to be. Her name's Mary."

Jenny made the connection immediately, and stared at the blond wraith with new respect. "Typhoid Mary? The plague carrier?"

"I don't use that name anymore," said Mary. Her voice was quiet, little more than a murmur, but Jenny had no problem understanding her. There was an almost compelling power in Mary's speech and gaze. "Typhoid Mary was another person; someone the Empire created to do its dirty work. I'm just Mary."

Jenny nodded. "I know about mind techs. They stirred their sticky fingers in my brain, too. Still, considering the damage you caused here in Mistport, I'm surprised they're letting you run loose. Hell, I'm surprised you're still alive."

"Little Miss Tact," said Topaz. "We don't blame people for what the Empire did to them. Here on Mistworld, most of us have done things for the Empire we're ashamed of. The Council gave Mary over into my custody. We work as a team now. We have a lot in common. Mostly things we've lost, because of the Iron Bitch and her damned intrigues. Enough small talk. You wanted to speak to the esper union, but the powers that be are rather busy at the moment. You can talk to us. We'll take it farther, if need be. In the meantime, if you want to make a good impression, leave the flowers alone and respect the mental shields in this house. They're here for your protection, as well as others'. There are a lot of people here who came to us for help and protection, because of the terrible things the Empire did to them, before they found their way to Mistworld. Some of them have yet to be defused. And there are also a lot of people here still mourning for the friends and family and loved ones they lost during the esper plague. Respect their privacy."

Jenny shrugged. She had a mission to fulfill. "They'll all want to hear me, once they know who and what I am. I represent the Mother Of All Souls, and her power moves within me. I will bring light to their darkness, and an end to their suffering. And with their backing, I will bring down the Empire itself."

"Save the speeches," said Topaz. "We've heard it all before. Legends are ten a penny, here in Mistport. Mostly because there are so many people here desperate to believe in them. It's up to you to convince us that you're not just another esper with delusions of sainthood."

Jenny let that pass, for the moment. "Tell me about the esper union. How did it start?"

If Topaz was surprised by the change in subject, she didn't show it. "Originally? In the beginning, the union existed to call espers together, when we had to raise the psionic shield in a hurry. From there it grew into a self-help group, and then a political force, to look out for our own interests. Mistport's no place to be weak and divided. There are people on the streets here who'll eat you alive if they smell fear. And sometimes there are temptations few of us are strong enough to resist on our own.

"These days the union is a political and economic power base with roots and interests throughout the city. And the people in charge aren't all that keen on having their considerable power undermined by some half-crazed ex–political prisoner claiming to be the avatar of the Mater Mundi. Some of them don't believe such a person exists, or ever did. And some have a vested interest in denying it. Which is why you're talking to us and not the leaders of the union. And at least partly because even your name doesn't exactly inspire confidence. So, now you get to make your pitch. And it had better be very convincing."

Jenny Psycho suddenly grinned at Topaz and Mary, and they both stirred uncertainly despite themselves. There was something in the room with them, a presence and a power that hadn't been there before. And then Jenny Psycho wrapped her destiny around her and dropped all her shields, blazing brightly like lightning trapped in a

shot glass. Her presence was suddenly overpowering,
filling the room and pushing against the walls, beating on
the air like the heartbeat of something impossibly huge.
Topaz and Mary fell back, and the Investigator's hand fell
automatically to the sword at her hip. Jenny's esp lashed
out and slammed into Topaz's and Mary's minds, slapping aside their shields with casual ease. They stood
naked before her, all barriers down. Jenny could have
made them say or do or believe anything, and they all
knew it. But instead, Jenny opened up her mind, took her
time and suffering in Wormboy Hell, and showed Topaz
and Mary all of it in one compressed burst of living hell.

*They were all there as the worm ate into Jenny's brain,
controlling her every thought and action. They were there
as she lay curled and naked on the floor of her cell,
shaking and shivering, surrounded by the stench of her
own piss and shit and vomit. The cell was little more than
an oversize coffin, with featureless steel walls and a
ceiling too low to let her do more than crouch or crawl.
There was rarely any light. There was just the darkness,
and the worm burrowing in Jenny's mind, feeding her the
endless nightmares of Wormboy's projected hallucinations and mind games. She lost most of her voice there in
Silo Nine, screaming for help that never came, or just for
an end to the pain and the horror.*

*And then there was a miracle. Mater Mundi came to her,
Mother of the World, Our Mother Of All Souls, exploding
out of her mind like a butterfly from a cocoon, spreading
out to gather up every esper in Wormboy Hell, and bind
them into a single sword thrust into the heart of Wormboy
himself. The gestalt couldn't maintain itself for long
without burning out all the minds of those involved, but for
that fleeting moment every one of them was greater than
Humanity had ever been, and more powerful. And all of it
focused through Jenny Psycho.*

Except that wasn't her name, really. She'd been someone else originally, an underground agent who'd volunteered to be sent into Silo Nine under a false persona, to
gather information on ways into and out of Wormboy
Hell. But now her original self and the false persona were
both gone, swept aside by Jenny Psycho, who had been
touched by greatness, her esp boosted beyond hope or

reason. Jenny Psycho, representative of the Mater Mundi, who had once been someone else. Someone sane.

Her projection collapsed as the various selves in her mind warred and screeched, fluttering in her head like moths battering a lamp, drawn beyond sense or reason to try and touch something that would only destroy them in the end. Jenny Psycho, who was so much more, and so much less, than she once was. She fell back into herself and kept falling, hugging herself fiercely to keep from flying apart. Tears burned in her eyes, but she kept them back by sheer force of will. Tears over the memory of something great and wonderful, that had touched and transformed her, and then abandoned her.

Mary stepped forward and put an arm around Jenny's shaking shoulders. "It's all right. We understand. We'll speak to the union leaders. They need to hear you, even if they don't know it yet. You stay here. We'll get things moving."

She gave Jenny a last comforting squeeze, and gestured with her head for Topaz to open the door. She did so, her face entirely impassive. Mary steered Jenny back into her chair, then she and Topaz left the study, leaving Jenny Psycho slumped in her chair like an exhausted child. They shut the door firmly behind them and moved off down the corridor.

"Not too tightly wrapped, is she?" said Topaz.

"Few of us are, these days," said Mary. "But she does seem to be an extreme case. If we don't handle this one with kid gloves, we could end up with a multiple personality on our hands. And a bloody powerful one, at that. Did you feel the energy coming off her? It was like staring into a searchlight. I've never encountered anything like it before. Whatever touched her in Silo Nine, it was a power far beyond my experience. I'm not even sure it was human. Could it really have been the Mater Mundi?"

Topaz shrugged uncomfortably. "I've never been religious. Still, I saw everything you did. She might be crazy, but something manifested through her. Its mark is all over her mind, even now. The Mater Mundi's as good an answer as any. Whoever or whatever that might be. You're right, the leaders have to see her. If only so we can be sure

of controlling her. God knows how much damage she
could do if we let her run loose."

"Like I did," said Mary.

"That's over now. You're yourself again."

"Maybe. Do you think I don't know that you're still
watching over me for the Council? Not everyone's convinced my deprogramming took."

"I'm with you because I choose to be," said Topaz.
"Besides, you still have a lot of enemies here in Mistport.
Everyone lost somebody to the esper plague."

"I'll never kill again," said Mary. "I'll kill myself
first."

"I know," said Topaz.

"Poor Jenny. She's been through so much."

"Haven't we all."

Owen Deathstalker walked alone through the packed
streets of the Merchants Quarter, scowling and seething.
People passing took one look at his face and gave him
plenty of room. Some even crossed to the other side of the
street, just in case. Street vendors and stall holders cried
their wares in a variety of colorful ways, but Owen paid
them no notice. He was working his way into a world-
class bad temper, and he didn't care who knew it. His
mood wasn't helped by the fact that he wasn't very good
at following directions. It wasn't that he was lost, exactly;
he just didn't always know where he was. He'd only been
this way once before, and that was with Hazel leading the
way, and he hadn't paid much attention at the time.
Luckily Ozymandius remembered the way.

Owen strode on through the Quarter, kicking at the
thick snow and concentrating fiercely on where he was
going so he wouldn't have to think about Hazel, alone
with John Silver. He had no right to be jealous, as Hazel
no doubt would have been happy to tell him, but still . . .
he loved her, in his way, and would no matter what she
thought of him. If she ever thought of him. Owen sighed
and pressed on, and eventually he ended up in front of the
seedy ramshackle building that housed the Abraxus Information Center. Abraxus knew everything that was going
on in Mistport, sometimes even before the people concerned knew it. Abraxus could answer all your questions,

soothe your worries or confirm your worst nightmares, for the right price.

It wasn't much to look at. Abraxus had the first floor over a family bakery. There was no sign advertising its presence. Everyone knew where Abraxus was. The last time Owen had been here he'd learned many things, some useful, some disturbing. Among other things, Abraxus had told him how he would die.

I see you, Deathstalker. Destiny has you in its clutches, struggle how you may. You will tumble an Empire, see the end of everything you ever believed in, and you'll do it all for a love you'll never know. And when it's over, you'll die alone, far from friends and succor.

Owen shuddered suddenly, his hackles rising as the words whispered in his head again. Even the best precogs were wrong as often as they were right, or they'd have been running the Empire by now, but even so he found the prophecy disturbing. No hints, no riddles, no hidden meanings—just a blunt description of his future and his death. He liked to think he would press on anyway, doing what he knew to be right and damn the consequences, but . . . he had to talk to Abraxus again. A lot had happened since his last trip to Mistworld, not least his passing through the Madness Maze. That had to change things. In many ways he was a completely new person now.

"Hell," he said finally. "Everyone knows you can't trust precogs."

"So whom do you trust?" said Ozymandius in his ear.

"I wish you'd stop talking to me. You know very well you're dead."

"So maybe I'm haunting you. Answer the question. Whom do you trust these days? Hazel threw you out to be with Silver, Young Jack Random may or may not be who he says he is, and Jenny Psycho is living in a different reality from the rest of us. Whom can you trust?"

"Not you, anyway. I trust the real Jack Random to do what's best for the rebellion. I trust Ruby to back him up right down the line, as long as there's the promise of plenty of loot. I trust Giles to uphold the Deathstalker name. And I trust Hazel to do the right thing, in the end."

"And Silver?"

"Hazel will go her own way. I've always known that."

"I remain unconvinced," said Oz. "Jack Random is mostly famous for getting his ass handed to him on planet after planet, Ruby Journey was a bounty hunter, and therefore not to be trusted on general principles, and Giles's beliefs and aims are nine hundred years out of date. You never were very good at picking your companions, Owen. Hazel is up to something. You know that, deep down."

"Hazel is always up to something. And for a dead AI, you're extremely cynical. You never did approve of my friends, even when you were alive. The bottom line is, I trust my companions because I have to. My only hope for survival is to throw Lionstone off the Iron Throne. For that I need a rebellion, and for that I need allies."

"Is that the only reason you're fighting to change the way things are?" said Oz quietly.

"No. I've seen too much of the everyday evil and suffering the Empire is based on. I can't look away anymore. Things must change; even if it means my life."

"You mean your death. What are you going to replace the Empire with? What else do you know but the privilege of aristocracy, and the rule of the Families?"

"Beats me," said Owen. "Let's win the war first. We can argue about whatever the hell comes next once we're safe from Lionstone's spite. Whatever we end up with, it can't be worse than what we've got."

"Famous last words," said the AI calmly. "You're an historian, Owen. You know what happens after rebellions. The winning side turn on each other and fight to the death to determine which particular faction will replace the old order. Either way, the odds are the victors will have little use for a dyed-in-the-blood aristo like you. You could end up plunging the Empire into a civil war that could last for centuries and leave planets burning in the endless night."

"You know, you've got really depressing since you died. And what do you care, anyway? There'll always be a use for an AI."

"I don't care," said Oz easily. "I was just making conversation."

"Well, shut up then. I have business with Abraxus, and I can't talk to you there. They wouldn't understand about dead AIs."

Oz chuckled briefly and fell silent. Owen looked casually around to see if anyone was watching, then clambered up the rickety exterior stairs to the upper-floor entrance. The place needed a good coat of paint the last time he'd been there, and time had not improved its appearence. Patches of rising damp showed clearly in the wood, and the simple brass nameplate on the door, saying simply *Abraxus*, clearly hadn't been polished in weeks. Maybe months. There was a distinct smell of cat urine, which rather puzzled Owen, as he hadn't seen a cat all day. There was no bell, of course. Owen hammered on the door with his fist and kicked it a few times for good measure. It made him feel better. After a pause just long enough to make sure Owen understood his place, the door swung open, and the man called Chance filled the doorway. He looked Owen over, then gestured for him to enter. Owen did so, his head held high.

The place hadn't changed. Two lines of ramshackle cots filled the long narrow room, pressed close together, with a narrow aisle down the center. On the cots lay dozing children, from four or five years old to emaciated, spindly teenagers. Intravenous drips fed nutrients into their veins, and catheters carried everything else away into grimy jars. Some of the children were covered in blankets, while others had thrown them off. A few were strapped down. There was a strong pervasive smell of cheap disinfectant and rubbing alcohol. The children were espers, brain damaged as often as not, too weak to survive on a harsh world like Mistworld. Chance bought them from their parents and used their esp abilities to spread a telepathic web over all of Mistport, seeing and hearing everything. And that was Abraxus. Chance kept the children alive as long as he could; it was in his interest to do so. But none of them ever survived to adulthood. They were the weak and the damaged, the broken and the abused, and by the time Chance got his hands on them, it was already too late. It didn't affect Abraxus. There were always more. The children were loyal to Chance, sleeping and awake; he was the nearest thing to a friend most of them had ever known.

Owen shook his head slowly, but wouldn't let himself look away. The first time he'd been here he'd been sick-

ened to his soul. He'd wanted to tear the place apart, and
Chance with it, but he hadn't. Much as he hated to admit
it, Abraxus was the best these children—genetically damaged and idiot savant espers with terrible pasts and little
future—could hope for.

Just another product of Empire rule. Owen turned
to glare at Chance, founder and manager of the Abraxus
Information Center. Chance was a large muscular man,
almost as broad as he was tall, wearing black leathers
with metal studs. Half his face was hidden behind a complex and very ugly tattoo. His smile was meaningless, his
eyes were too bright, and he didn't blink often enough.
Owen often wondered if Chance had been crazy before he
started Abraxus, or if endless exposure to death and suffering had sent him over the edge. Either way, Owen
maintained a safe distance, and kept his hand near his
sword. Chance nodded abruptly to him.

"Knew you'd be back, Deathstalker. What can I do for
you this time?"

"Don't you know?" said Owen. "You must be slipping,
Chance. I have questions that need answering."

"That's what we're here for," said Chance. "I feel I
should point out you exhausted all your credit the last
time you honored us with your presence. And my prices
have risen dramatically. You understand how it is; small
businesses always have to fight to stay afloat."

"Your business exists because my father's money made
it possible," Owen said flatly. "Technically, as his only
heir, I inherited Abraxus."

"You were outlawed," said Chance. "All assets attached to the Deathstalker name were confiscated by the
Empress. And besides, this is Mistport, where possession
is every part of the law. Abraxus is mine."

Owen smiled humorlessly. "I think you have me
confused with someone who gives a damn. I'm back in
Mistport to revitalize the old Deathstalker information
network, and make it part of the ongoing rebellion again.
And that very definitely includes you and Abraxus. Since,
for my sins, I'm one of the people currently leading the
rebellion, Abraxus answers to me. So if you want to keep
your presumably very well paid managerial position, I
strongly suggest you stop pissing me about. Got it?"

"You couldn't run Abraxus without me," said Chance. "The children are mine, body and soul."

"They'd soon get over you. Children are so very . . . adaptable, after all."

Chance thought about it. "You'd risk ruining my operation, just to get control?"

"Of course," said Owen. "I'm a Deathstalker. We have a long history of getting our way, and to hell with where the chips fall."

Chance sniffed. "What do you want to know, Deathstalker?"

"That's more like it. I have a question."

"Keep it specific, if you want a specific answer. My children are espers, not oracles."

"Ask them who killed my father," said Owen. "Which person, specifically?"

Chance nodded, and made his way slowly down the central aisle, looking speculatively from one child to another. Owen watched impassively, hiding his own surprise at the question he'd asked. It hadn't been the one he intended to start with. He was here to ask about his father's information network. He hadn't known how badly he wanted the name of his father's killer until he heard himself say it. His father had been cut down in the street by an assassin in the pay of the Empress, and at the time Owen hadn't really been surprised. Just assumed that one of his father's many plots and intrigues had finally caught up with him. Mostly, Owen had just felt annoyed at the disruption the sudden death had brought to his previously well-ordered life. He hadn't asked who the killer was. He hadn't cared, then.

Arthur Hadrian Deathstalker, tall and handsome and ruthlessly charming, had delighted in schemes and intrigues, sometimes apparently just for their own sake. Which meant he hadn't had much time to spend on his son. When he remembered he had a son and heir, he ran Owen's life with an iron hand, doing as he thought best and to hell with what Owen might want. His was not a cheerful presence, and their few conversations increasingly deteriorated into blazing rows. The Deathstalker never understood that his son considered himself a scholar, rather than a warrior. When Owen heard that his father was dead, his first feeling was one of relief. He was finally out of his father's clutches and free to be his own man at last.

It was only in recent times that Owen had finally begun to understand the forces that had moved and driven his father. Just by being the Deathstalker, Arthur had many enemies both in and outside Lionstone's Court. An aristocrat on Golgotha could no more avoid intrigue than a fish could avoid the water it swam in. And above all that, Arthur had believed in rebellion. Whether for the sake of the Empire, or for his own amusement and advancement, Owen still wasn't entirely sure, but more and more he was inclined to give his father the benefit of the doubt. As his own eyes were opened to the evils and horrors the Empire was based on, he understood the need to fight it by any means necessary.

He still couldn't bring himself to love or forgive his father. The man who'd ordered his trainers to beat the crap out of his son, over and over again, trying to force to the surface the secret inheritance of the Deathstalkers— the boost. A mixture of gengineered glands and special training that for short periods made a Deathstalker stronger, faster, and sharper than any normal man. The process worked, eventually, but Owen only remembered the pain and the blood, all to give him access to something he didn't want anyway. Only recently had Owen begun to understand that his father had been desperate to make him a fighter rather than a scholar, because he knew a scholar wouldn't be able to survive the forces that would be unleashed by his death. And he'd been right.

As Owen became a leader of the new rebellion, and a fighter for justice, so he became his father's son at last. And only once he understood that truth at last, did he begin to understand how much he'd lost, and how much he needed to know who'd murdered his father.

He looked up as Chance beckoned him impatiently, and moved over to join the big man, standing over a cot holding a girl who couldn't have been more than ten. The child wore a shabby dress two sizes too large, and she stirred constantly, as though disturbed by loud voices only she could hear. Her eyes were closed, but she muttered the odd word or phrase now and again. None of them made any sense to Owen. Chance knelt beside her and produced a paper bag half-full of candies. He chose one, molded it between his fingers till it was soft and pliant, then eased it into the girl's slack mouth. She began to chew slowly. Chase put his mouth right next to her ear.

"Time to play the game, Katie. Time to tell me all those things you know. I have Owen Deathstalker here with me. He wants to know who killed his father. Whose hand guided the blade that took his life. Who was it, Katie?"

The girl frowned, her mouth pursing unhappily, but she didn't wake. She swallowed the piece of candy and spoke in a clear, pure voice. "You asked me that long ago. The answer hasn't changed. It was the smiling killer, the shark in shallow waters, the man who will not be stopped save by his own hand. Kid Death killed the Deathstalker."

Owen nodded slowly, his face impassive while his hands closed into fists. He hadn't been expecting that particular name, but it didn't exactly come as a surprise either. Kid Death, the Empress's favorite paid assassin for a while, also known as Lord Kit SummerIsle. Now a backer of the rebellion, and a friend of the distant cousin who'd taken the title of Lord Deathstalker after Owen was outlawed. Both currently headed for Virimonde, the planet Owen had once owned and ruled. It didn't matter. It didn't matter that Kit and Owen were on the same side now. Owen would kill him anyway, once the rebellion didn't need him anymore. Kit SummerIsle was a dead man, along with anyone who got in his way. Anyone at all. Owen smiled slowly, and his fists unclenched. Something to look forward to.

"You didn't come here just to ask me that," said the young girl suddenly. Her eyes moved back and forth under her closed eyelids. "There's something else. Something you need to know. Ask me. Ask me."

"All right," said Owen. There was a tightness in his chest, and he had to fight to keep his voice steady. "The last time I was here, one of you told me how I would die. I need to know if it's still true. Has anything changed?"

"No," said the girl flatly. "You die here, in Mistport, alone and forsaken, fighting odds too great to be beaten by any man. And after you're dead, they'll even steal your boots."

"When?" said Owen. "When does this happen?"

"That's a time question," said the young girl, turning her head away. "I've never understood time."

"Try!" said Owen. "Try, dammit!"

He reached down to grab the child by the shoulders and shake her, but Chance was there first, pulling him away. Owen threw the big man off easily, but the moment had passed, and he was in control again. He stood over the sleeping child, breathing heavily, then he turned away.

"It doesn't matter," he said finally, to no one in particular. "I've always known I've been on borrowed time ever since Virimonde. I was supposed to die there. Only a miracle saved me. And a man can't expect more than one miracle in one lifetime. Still, it's hard to hear your own death sentence, and know there's nothing you can do to change it."

"If you don't want the answers, don't ask the questions," said Chance. "And I told you before; you can't trust precogs. If everything they said was reliable, I'd be a rich man by now. For instance, they've all been saying for some time now that Something Bad is coming to Mistport, but I can't get two of them to agree on what the hell it might be. All I've got is a name—Legion. But so far, the only unpleasant thing to turn up here is you."

"It doesn't matter," said Owen. "If I have to die, I'll die well, as a Deathstalker should."

"Oh very poetic," said Chance. "God save me from heroes. Look, I have a business to run. Don't let the door hit your butt on the way out."

"Cut the crap," said Owen. "We still have business to discuss. My first questions were strictly on my own behalf. Now we get to the serious stuff. I'm here representing the Golgotha underground, and on their behalf I'm officially reawakening and revitalizing my father's old information network here in Mistport. He didn't fund just you and Abraxus; there are dozens of people and businesses all through this city that he established and supported, in return for the gathering and passing on of useful information. Some of them went on to be very successful indeed. Movers and shakers in this big city.

"The information started drying up after my father's murder. Presumably they thought his death freed them from their obligations. I'm here to tell them different. I'm the Deathstalker now, and I am calling in my father's markers. With interest. The old network will rise again, this time supplying information to the new rebellion, or I will personally bankrupt every one of the sons of bitches. Including you, Chance."

"Oh shit," said Chance.

"Well quite," said Owen, smiling cheerfully. "You can start by supplying the names and locations you know, and then we'll get the rest from these espers of yours. You will then assist me in setting up a meeting of all concerned parties, somewhen today. In fact, within the next two hours, if they want to hang on to all their business interests and several vital organs. Get moving, Chance. I've a lot to do, and perhaps not as much time as I thought to get it done in."

Chance made contact with the right people through his espers, a procedure from which Owen was very definitely excluded. He waited impatiently on the steps outside, debating whether to carve his initials into the door or the brickwork. Chance made an appearence just a few moments too late, looked at his door, and winced, then led Owen down the exterior stairway and off into the dizzying maze of narrow streets that made up the center of Mistport. The mist had thinned, but a fine annoying sleet was falling, turning the snow underfoot into slippery slush and mud. Owen stuck close behind Chance and tried not to think what he was doing to his expensive new boots.

They passed out of Merchants Quarter and into Guilds Quarter, and the streets and buildings improved almost immediately. There were proper pavements and regular streetlights, some of them even electric. The buildings were decorative as well as functional, and the people passing by looked of a much richer, if not necessarily happier, class. Chance finally came to a halt outside one of the older Guild Halls, and paused a moment so Owen could study it and be properly impressed. It was a squat, sturdy building with three stories, high Gothic arches, wide glass windows, and hundreds of wooden rococo doodlings in every spare inch. The gutters ended in great carved stone gargoyles, water spouting from their mouths, giving the unfortunate effect that they seemed to be vomiting on the people below. Or perhaps it was deliberate. It was a Guild Hall, after all. Owen didn't have the heart to tell Chance he'd seen more impressive privies at Lionstone's Court, so he just nodded thoughtfully, to show he'd finished being impressed, and gestured for Chance to lead the way in.

There were two armed guards at the front door. They bowed respectfully to Chance, and ignored Owen. He didn't kill them. He didn't want to make a scene. Yet. Inside, the main foyer was large and comfortable and extremely respectable. There was much polished wooden wall paneling, and a richly waxed floor that gleamed brightly in the light of the electric lamps, set not so much as to provide light but so that they could be admired the more easily. The various furnishings and fittings were luxurious to the point of opulence, and the whole place positively smelled of money, like an old family bank. Owen felt almost homesick.

As they strode in the doorway, stamping their boots on the metal grille and brushing the sleet and snow from their cloaks, a butler strode imperiously toward them, wearing an old-fashioned cutaway frock coat, a powdered wig, and a practiced sneer of utter condescension. Chance showed the butler his business card, and the man bowed briefly, a mere tilting of the head. He took Chance's and Owen's cloaks between thumb and forefingers and handed them over to a flunky who'd dashed forward to receive them. He then demanded they turn over their respective weapons to him, too, and that was when the trouble started.

"I don't hand my weapons over to anyone," said Owen.

"Don't make a fuss," said Chance, unbuckling his belt and handing over his sword. "It's nothing personal. Just standard security. Everyone does it."

"I'm not everyone," said Owen. "And my weapons stay with me. They'd feel naked without me."

"I must insist," said the butler, in icy tones. "We don't let just anyone walk in off the street, you know."

Owen punched him out. The unconscious butler's body made a satisfyingly loud thud as it hit the waxed floor some distance away and slid a few yards before coming to a halt. People everywhere turned to look. A few looked quietly approving. Security guards with drawn swords appeared from hidden doorways, only to stop dead as Owen let his hand rest ostentatiously near his energy gun.

"He's with me," Chance said quickly. "Much as I wish he wasn't. He is expected."

The security guards looked at each other, shrugged, and put away their swords, clearly deciding that this was someone else's problem. Everyone else in the foyer came to the same conclusion, and the polite murmur of conversation resumed. Owen nodded graciously around him as the unconscious butler was dragged away.

"Please don't do that again," said Chance. "First impressions are so important."

"Exactly what I was thinking," said Owen. "Now get a move on, or I'll piss in the potted plants."

"I wish I thought you were joking," said Chance. "This way. Try not to kill anyone important."

They pressed on into the depths of the Guild Hall, Chance leading the way in something of a hurry. The surroundings remained determinedly lush and expensive. Servants and real people hastened back and forth on silent errands of great importance. Speaking was apparently discouraged, save for the occasional hushed whisper. Owen felt very strongly that he would have liked to sneak up behind some of them and shout Boo! in their ears, just to see what would happen, but he didn't have the time. Maybe on the way back.

They all looked very neat and businesslike. Their outfits were a bit dated, but this was Mistport, after all. They all seemed to know Chance, and never missed an opportunity to bestow a lip-curling sneer in his direction whenever they thought he wasn't looking. Chance ignored them all magnificently. They finally came to a dead end, personified by a grim, entirely unsmiling secretary behind a desk in an outer office, set there to protect her boss from unwanted visitors. She was slim and prematurely elderly, and looked tough enough to eat glass. The guards probably sharpened their swords on her between shifts. Her clothes successfully erased any sign of femininity, and her gaze was firm enough to shrivel weeds.

"If you don't have an appointment, there is nothing I can do for you," she said, in a tone cold enough to make penguins shiver. "You may make an appointment if you wish, but I can tell you now that Mr. Neeson has no openings in his calendar for the next several weeks."

Chance looked at Owen. "This is as far as I can get you. Some obstacles are simply too great. Please don't hit her."

"Wouldn't think of it," said Owen. "I'd probably break my hand." He leaned over the desk to stare into the secretary's flinty eyes. "I am Owen Deathstalker. My father's money paid for this business. I've come to call in the IOU. Right now."

The secretary didn't flinch, though one eyebrow twitched briefly at the name Deathstalker. "I see. I'm sure that normally Mr. Neeson would be only too happy to see you, but as things are, my desk is completely full . . ."

Owen stepped back, drew his sword, raised it above his head and brought it hammering down with all his boosted strength behind it. The heavy blade sheared clean through the wooden desk, cleaving it into two jagged halves that fell away to either side of the secretary. Chance shook his head slowly. Owen put his sword away. The secretary cleared her throat.

"I think you should go right in, Lord Deathstalker. I'm sure Mr. Neeson can find a few minutes to see you. I'll make sure you're not disturbed. Would either of you care for tea or coffee?"

"Make it a brandy," said Owen. "A large one. Mr. Neeson's going to need it." He grinned at Chance. "You just have to know how to talk to these people. My Family has been practicing for centuries. Personally, I've always thought I'd make a great diplomat."

"You're not in yet," said Chance. "This is just the outer office. Beyond that door is the antechamber. The real watchdogs will be waiting there."

"Well, if they get a bit snappy, I'll throw them a bone. Which one would you miss least?"

They passed through the connecting door and found themselves in a small, bare chamber. Between them and the far door were three large, muscular men. Each one had a heavy ax in his hands. The men looked calm and very professional. The axes looked as if they'd seen a lot of use. Chance looked at Owen.

"An interesting problem in tactics. No room to maneuver, and absolutely no point in trying to talk to them. You might take out one with your disrupter, but the other two would be on you before you could even raise your sword. And a sword is no use against axes. I am, of course, unable to assist you. I have to maintain my position of strict impartiality. You understand."

"Of course. Normally if I was facing three Neanderthals like these, I'd be impartial as hell, too. But unfortunately for them, I am in something of a hurry, not to mention a really bad mood, and I can just use someone to take it out on. Watch and learn."

He stepped forward, empty-handed, and the three guards came to meet him, axes raised. It was all over in a few seconds. Owen punched out the first guard, swiveled on one foot and kicked the second in the groin. And while the third was still raising his ax, Owen stepped forward, grabbed two handfuls of the man's shirtfront, and head-butted him in the face. Chance's jaw dropped. Owen stood there, not even breathing hard, looking around him with quiet satisfaction. The three guards sat or lay moaning on the floor, all looking very upset.

"You're right," said Chance. "You'd make a terrific diplomat. No one would dare disagree with you. I've never seen anyone move so fast. What the hell are you?"

"I'm a Deathstalker, and don't you forget it." Owen strode over to the far door and rattled the door handle. It was locked. He tut-tutted loudly and hit the door with his shoulder. It burst inward, one hinge torn right out of the wooden frame. Owen pushed the door back, carefully straightening it up again, and smiled at the half dozen men sitting around the long table before him. "Knock, knock," he said brightly. "I'm Owen Deathstalker, and you're in big trouble. Any questions?"

"Come in, Lord Deathstalker," said the man at the head of the table. "We've been expecting you."

"Yeah," said Owen. "I'll just bet you have." He looked back at Chance. "Find a chair, sit down, and keep quiet. I don't want any distractions."

"Suits me," said Chance. "I wouldn't miss this for

the world. But you are strictly on your own now, Deathstalker."

The six men glared at Chance as he pulled up a chair and sat down in a far corner, where he could see everything but stay well out of the line of fire. Owen moved to stand at the end of the long table, and all their eyes snapped back to him. He looked from one scowling face to another, taking his time. He didn't recognize any of them, but he knew men of influence and power when he saw them. Not just from their perfect tailoring and extra weight, but in their attitude. Their untouched confidence. They were annoyed at his arrival, but not concerned. They weren't afraid of him. They'd been rich and secure for so long they'd got out of the habit of being afraid of anyone. Owen smiled briefly. He'd change that.

And if they reminded him just a little of himself, the way he used to be before he was shocked awake, then that just made it all the worse for them.

"Would you like me to identify these people?" said Oz. "I have all their details in my data banks."

"Sure," said Owen, subvocalizing. "Make yourself useful for once. Hold on a minute—data banks? Where is your hardware these days?"

"Don't get personal. And pay attention; I'm not running through all this twice. We'll start at the left and go clockwise. Beginning with Artemis Daley, a man of many trades. He's a supplier, a fixer. You want it, he can get it for you. Legal or illegal are petty considerations that have never bothered him. If you're late with the payments, he's the one who sends around the legbreakers to reason with you.

"Next to him, we have Timothy Neeson, banker. He owns this building, and a lot more of Mistport. Number one in a very small field, which means that locally he's very powerful. Nothing of an economic nature takes place in Mistport without him taking a cut somewhere along the line. Next to him is Walt Robbins, the biggest landlord in Mistport. He owns everything the banks don't. Specializes in slums and sweathouses, because that's where the most money is.

"Moving down the other side of the table we have Thomas Stacey. Acts as a lawyer for everyone else here, and for anyone else with enough money to meet his exacting standards. Never lost a case, and that has nothing to do with his legal skills. And finally we come to Matthew Connelly and Padraig MacGowan. Connelly owns and runs the docks, everything from the starport to the landing bays on the River Autumn, and MacGowan runs the dock union. Between them they keep things running smoothly, irrespective of who gets hurt in the process. And there you have the movers and shakers of Mistport, in all their sleazy glory. If you killed all of them right now, the smell of Mistport would improve dramatically."

"I never knew you knew so much about Mistport," Owen subvocalized.

"Lot about me you don't know. I am large, I contain wonders."

"Do you have something to say to us, Deathstalker?" said Neeson, the banker, a large fat man with a straining waistcoat. "Or are you just going to stand there and stare at us all day?"

"Just gathering my thoughts," said Owen. "We have a lot of history between us, gentlemen. My father's money brought you to where you are today. Deathstalker money, originally intended to fund an information network here in Mistport. He put you into positions of power and influence so that you could keep track of things for him. Instead, you used his money to become major economic forces in this city, becoming so rich and powerful you forgot your original purpose. Or perhaps you simply decided that such things were no longer important to people as rich and powerful as yourselves."

"Got it in one," said Stacey, the lawyer, long and stringy, with broken veins prominent in his cheeks. "And we've absolutely no intention of becoming politicized again. We don't think in such small ways anymore. We've made over our lives, and we like things fine just the way they are. Among us, we run Mistport; we are the economic lifeblood that keeps this society moving. Mess with us, even threaten us, and the whole city's economy would collapse. We'd see to that. People would lose their savings, money would become worthless, and people would starve as food piled up undistributed on the docks.

You can't touch us, Deathstalker. All the people in Mistport would rise up and tear you apart if you even tried."

"They'd get over it," said Owen. "Once they saw the old corrupt system being replaced by a fairer one."

"Fairness is a relative concept," said Robbins, the landlord, a short fat barrel of a man. "There will always be rich and poor. We provide stability. You don't understand the economic realities of a rebel planet like Mistworld."

"I understand greed," said Owen. "I understand treachery and self-interest. And I certainly understand bloodsucking scum when I see them."

"That's good," said Oz. "Win them over with flattery."

"We know why you're here," said Daley, the fixer, a large hunched man with a brooding face. "You want to take our lives away from us in the name of your rebellion and naive politics. Well, boy, you've come a long way for nothing. These days, our influence extends far beyond Mistworld, with investments on many worlds. Even Golgotha. Elias Gutman has been very helpful in shaping our portfolios. Yes, I thought you'd recognize that name. A man of real power and influence. He told us you were coming."

"Gutman," said Owen, as though the name was an obscenity. "He's come crawling around the rebellion more than once, but I've always known his vested interests lie with the Empire. His information comes straight from the Empress herself. When you followed his advice, you did Lionstone's bidding, right here on the rebel planet. Can any of you say, 'conflict of interest'?"

"Money has no loyalties. Or politics," said Neeson. "Gutman has always been a good friend to us."

"I'll bet he has," said Owen, his voice getting colder all the time. "And when his loans finally come due, you'll find the money by squeezing it out of the people here, who owe you. Whether they can afford it or not. And Mistworld will become just another planet bleeding itself dry to maintain Golgotha's wealth."

He looked round the table, to be met only with flat stares or indifferent shrugs. "That's business," said Daley.

"That's injustice," said Owen. "And I have sworn an oath on my blood and on my honor to put an end to it. Which means putting an end to you, and your cosy little setup. Maybe I'll kill you all, and see if your heirs prove more reasonable to work with. Either way, your money will be used to support the rebellion, as it was always intended to be. As my father intended."

"I don't think so," said Neeson. "Guards! Take him!"

Doors flew open on every side and a small army of guards came crashing in, armed with swords and axes and even a few disrupters. Owen subvocalized the word *boost*, and a familiar strength flooded through him. He felt almost supernaturally awake and aware, as though up till now he'd spent this life sleeping. He felt he could do anything, take any risk, and never pay the cost. Owen clamped down hard on that. It was the boost talking, not him. He was boosting too much and too often these days, despite the dangers, and he knew it, but he trusted to the Maze's changes to protect him from what would otherwise be crippling side effects. He had to; there was work to be done. The blood pounded in his head and in his sword arm, calling him on to battle, and he gave in to it with a smile that could just as easily have been a snarl.

The guards seemed almost to be moving in slow motion as he threw himself into the midst of them, knowing the few with disrupters wouldn't dare use them rashly for fear of hitting their own people. His sword flashed brightly as he swung it with inhuman strength and speed, and blood flew on the air. There were shouts and curses and hysterical orders from the six men around the table, and over it all came the sound of men screaming horribly as Owen's unstoppable blade worked butchery on their bodies. He moved among them like a deadly ghost, too fast to be stopped or even parried, his sword flashing in and out in a second. He seemed to be everywhere at once, hacking and cutting, and men fell howling in pain and horror before him. A man's arm fell to the floor, the hand still clutching desperately at nothing. Bodies fell to litter the blood-soaked carpet, and did not rise again. A disrupter blast scorched the great table from end to end, hitting no one, but leaving a long trail of burning wood behind it.

Owen was laughing now, though there was little humor in the sound. The battle raged from one end of the room to the other, blood splashing the walls till they all ran crimson. The six most powerful men in Mistport retreated

from the burning table and huddled together in one corner
of the room, watching with disbelief as one man laid
waste to their private army. And then, quite suddenly, it
was over, and Owen Deathstalker stood among the dead
and the dying, a death's-head grin on his face. He looked
slowly around him, blood dripping thickly from his blade.
His clothes were splashed and soaked with gore, and none
of it was his. He wasn't even breathing hard. He turned
his smile on the six movers and shakers of Mistport, and
they cringed before him. Owen dropped out of boost, but
the expected tiredness didn't hit him. He still felt like he
could take on the whole city if he had to. Chance came
crawling out from under the burning table, where he'd
taken shelter. Owen put out a hand to help him up, and
Chance flinched away. He scrambled to his feet, looking
at Owen with new eyes.

"They never stood a chance. You cut them down like
cattle. What in God's name are you?"

"I'm a Deathstalker," said Owen. "And don't you
forget it."

He turned his gaze on the six men huddled together in
the far corner of the room. Only a few even tried to meet
his gaze. Owen moved unhurriedly toward them, stepping
casually over the unmoving bodies. His boots squelched
quietly in the blood-soaked carpet. Stacey, the lawyer,
glared at Owen with something like defiance.

"You're a monster; but you still can't beat us. We have
the money. We can hire more men. We can hire a whole
army of mercenaries, if that's what it takes to bring you
down."

"Bring on your army," said Owen. "Let them all come.
They won't save you."

"You can't kill us," said Neeson. "If we die, all our
money will be tied up in probate. Maybe for years. No
one would be able to touch it."

"Nothing's going to stop me," said Owen. "Not you,
not the law, not the whole damned Empire. Your day is
over, and I'm bringing down the night."

"You're crazy!" said Daley. "Just like your father
was!"

"My father was worth a hundred of you!" said Owen,
and he put away his sword. He was too angry. He wanted

to do this with his bare hands. Boosted strength roared within him again, and something else as well. He grabbed the long heavy table, ignoring the flames, lifted it off the floor, and tore it in two. He let the jagged halves fall to the floor and advanced on the six secret masters of Mistport. They ran screaming for the door, Chance right behind them. They ran through the outer chamber, yelling for help, and Owen came right behind them.

He was more than human now, an almost elemental force on a rampage. His anger stormed through the rooms and corridors, smashing everything in its path. Walls cracked and collapsed, the bricks crumbling and the mortar exploding into dust. Great vents appeared in the floor and ceilings. Wood burst into flames, burning with a harsh unnatural light. People ran screaming as ceilings collapsed, showering them with falling masonry. The carpeted floors undulated like waves on an ocean, before rising up and splitting apart like a never-ending earthquake. And behind them all came Owen Deathstalker, silent and remorseless, bringing down the great Guild Hall as he would one day bring down the Empire it represented.

A few brave guards tried to stop him, and were swept aside. Doors were blown off their hinges and exploded out of doorways. Windows shattered, the jagged glass flying like shrapnel. Scattered papers flew on the air like frightened birds. Walls bulged apart and ruptured water pipes sprayed everywhere. Exposed electrical wires sparked and crackled. The whole building seemed to be roaring in pain as it slowly collapsed in upon itself. Owen Deathstalker walked on through the screams and the chaos, and found it good. One brave soul fired a disrupter at him, but the energy beam bounced harmlessly away. Nothing could touch or stop him now.

He finally came to the last door, the door through which he'd originally entered the Guild Hall. The door exploded from its frame, flying out into the street before the crowds who'd come to see what was happening. They were babbling and shouting as the Hall collapsed, but when Owen stepped out into the street they fell suddenly silent and backed away. They could feel the power in and around him, beating on the air like a giant heartbeat. Owen let his mind drift back through what was left of the building, making sure no one was trapped inside, and then he brought it all down in one giant upheaval. The roar of crashing masonry filled the street, and smoke billowed out of the empty doorways and window frames. In only moments what had been one of the greatest Guild Halls in Mistport was reduced to nothing but a pile of rubble. Silence slowly fell, broken only by the muffled sounds of debris settling. The buildings on either side stood completely unaffected. And the one man responsible for it all looked upon what his anger had done and found it good. He slowly brought his power back inside him and shut it down, and was just a man again.

That was when the Watch turned up. All ten of them. They stopped some distance away and studied the scene carefully. Owen smiled at them.

"Private business. Hostile takeover. Nothing for you to worry about, gentlemen."

The Watch looked at him, then at what was left of the building, and finally at each other, before deciding firmly to go and Watch somewhere else. The six men who used to run Mistport called plaintively after the Watch as they left, but they were ignored. The Watch didn't interfere in private quarrels. This was Mistport, after all. The six men turned slowly to look at Owen, who stood before them, smiling unpleasantly.

"You poor bastards wouldn't last five minutes on Golgotha," Owen said calmly. "They'd eat you alive and still have room for dessert. Now do as you're told, and you might get out of this alive and still attached to most of your major organs. Kneel down." They did so. They had no fight left in them. "You've got a new boss, gentlemen. A Deathstalker is back in charge. From this moment on, you are going to dig into your no doubt cavernous pockets and rebuild the information network as my father originally envisaged it. A means of collecting and compiling information to protect and serve the people of Mistworld, and keep it safe from outside attack and influences. You will also pay for the conceiving and setting up of new defenses to protect this planet. With the psionic screen weakened by the esper plague, you're going to need a strong high-tech system to back it up. Get on it. And finally, my father's money was always intended to make possible a fairer and easier life for the people of this city. I expect a series of wide-ranging but practical schemes from all of you, in writing, within the week. If anybody's late, I'll have him nailed to a wall to motivate the others. And I am not being metaphorical."

"But . . . we have shareholders," said Neeson. "People we have to answer to. They'd never let us do all that . . ."

"Send them to me," said Owen Deathstalker. "I'll convince them. Anybody else have something to say? No? Good. You're learning. Now you six assholes are going to obey my instructions, to the letter, or I'll turn you inside out. Slowly. Is that perfectly clear?"

They all nodded vigorously, and Owen turned his back on them and strode off down the street. He could still feel the power the Maze had given him, wrapped around him like a comforting cloak. The Maze had changed him, in ways he didn't understand yet, but the power was real and it was his, and he reveled in it. He felt like he could do anything, if he just put his mind to it. And it felt so good, to be able to put things right in such a simple and direct manner.

"You do realize," said Oz, "that you're walking in the wrong direction if you want to head back to the center of town?"

"Shut up, Oz. I'm making a dramatic exit."

He decided he would go to the rooms they had booked and see how Hazel and John Silver were getting on. He couldn't wait to see the Security man's face when he told him what he'd done to the Guild Hall. Who knew; it might even impress Hazel, just a little. He was worried about her. Despite the new power within him, he still couldn't feel her presence through their mental link. Besides, he wanted to talk to Hazel about this new power, and what it felt like. Maybe she had it, too. They had so much to discuss. Owen Deathstalker strode on through the streets of Mistport, and the mists themselves curled back to get out of his way.

Hazel d'Ark and John Silver, old rogues and older friends, sat in their comfortable chairs on either side of the open fire, sipping hot chocolate from lumpy porcelain mugs, and staring at the small phial of black Blood standing on the table beside them. It didn't look like much, but then the really dangerous things never do. They both knew what it could do, both to and for them, and it was a sign of their strength of will that they hesitated. Blood came from the Wampyr, the synthetic plasma of the adjusted men. Just a few drops could make a normal human strong and fast and confident. For as long as you kept taking it. Blood could make you feel wonderfully alive and aware, as though the normal world was just a grim and grey depressing nightmare from which you had finally awakened. Of course, the effect never lasted, and gradually you needed larger and larger doses to achieve the same effects. And slowly, drop by drop, the Blood burned you up from within. It had been designed to bring Wampyr back from the dead and make them superhuman. It had never been meant to coexist with the merely human system.

But people wanted it, needed it, would fight and kill for it; so there were always those ready to synthesize and market it, for the right price. Especially on a planet like Mistworld.

"It's really very simple," said Silver. "As head of starport Security, I have access to all Blood confiscated on the streets. And as I control all the computer records, no one's going to notice if I liberate a few drops now and then, for myself and a few special friends. You can't try and run a hellhole like Mistport without some crutch or other to lean on. And we don't all have it in us to be incorruptible heroes, like Investigator Topaz. I'm not an addict. I can control it. I'm not so sure about you, Hazel. You always were the greedy kind. Coming off it the last time nearly killed you. You really want to go through that again?"

Hazel stared down into her mug, not looking at him. "You don't know the pressure I'm under, John. So much has happened in such a short time. One minute I'm just a small-time outlaw, of no interest or importance to anyone but myself, and the next I'm a rebel, and everyone's after my head. Including some of those supposed to be on my side. As long as I was fighting and running for my life and didn't have time to think, I was fine, but now ... Everything I do matters, everything I say has consequences, not just for me but for the whole damned rebellion. They've made me a bloody hero and a leader, and expect me to be perfect.

"And that's not all. Something happened to me on the Wolfling World, John. Something ... changed me. I'm more than I used to be, and I'm scared all the time. I don't think I'm me anymore. I have bad dreams, and I can't tell if I'm remembering the past or the future. I can do things now that I never could before. Strange and terrible things. The Blood is the only thing that helps. It ... stabilizes me, calms me ... helps me believe I'm still human."

She put down her mug and reached out with her hand, and the glass phial of Blood leaped up from the table and shot into her waiting hand. Silver looked at her, startled.

"I didn't know you were an esper, Hazel."

"I'm not. I'm something else. Something ... more." She unscrewed the top of the phial and sniffed delicately at the black liquid inside. Her nostrils flared as the familiar scent filled her head, dark and smoky. She breathed deeply, sucking it into her lungs, and sparks flared and fluttered in her veins. She tilted the phial carefully, and allowed a single drop of Blood to fall onto her tongue. She swallowed quickly, to avoid as much of the bitter wormwood taste as she could, and then refastened the phial's cap and put it back on the table, so not to be tempted to take a second drop. She leaned back in her chair, and groaned aloud as the familiar heat rushed through her, burning along her nerves, making her strong and powerful and confident again. The pressures and the duties and the doubts that plagued her were swept away, and, for the first time in days, her face relaxed. She smiled slowly. It felt so good. So good not to have to care anymore.

Silver watched her from his chair, keeping his own counsel till he was sure she was well under. He had intended to join her, but memories of what Hazel had been like in the worst throes of addiction had changed his mind. He wasn't an addict. He could control himself. So he stayed straight and sober, because he had a strong feeling that Hazel needed him to be there, watching over her. Even as he thought that, her half-shut drowsing eyes snapped suddenly open, and she sprang to her feet, looking wildly about her. Silver was quickly on his feet, too, putting his mug on the table so he could take Hazel by the arms. She didn't seem to notice him, and her arms were rigid as steel bars. Silver watched her carefully. You had to be careful with Blood users, when you weren't cranked yourself. With their new strength they could kill a normal human in a moment and not give a damn till after the Blood had worn off. Hazel stared about her, her head twisting violently from side to side, her eyes huge in her suddenly gaunt face.

"Hazel," said Silver, keeping his voice carefully calm and even. "What is it? What's wrong?"

"It's different," Hazel said thickly. "I'm different. I shouldn't have taken Blood here. Not with so many espers around. They're . . . affecting me. I can't tell what's in my head and what's outside. The Blood's . . . awakening something within me. Something I didn't even know was there. I can see things, John, so many things. Nothing's hidden from me anymore."

She stared at the wall before her, and suddenly it was gone. It only took Silver a moment to realize that he was seeing what she was seeing; her mind linking with his to show him what was in the next room. The young burglar named Cat was spilling brightly shining jewels onto a table from a leather pouch, while his fence, the woman called Cyder, laughed and clapped her hands. Hazel turned her head away, and the wall became visible again. She glared at the opposite wall, and it disappeared to reveal a card game deteriorating into muffled shouts and accusations.

Silver tried to shake her, but couldn't move her an inch. She suddenly turned her stare on him, and in that moment he felt utterly transparent, as though she could see everything within him, good and bad and in between, all captured in a moment. She seemed bigger than Silver, towering over him like some ancient god of judgment with no trace of mercy or compassion. He stepped backwards, jerking his hands away from her arms as though they'd burned him. Hazel's stare turned inward, and images began to blink in and out around her. Visions came and were gone in seconds, cycling through faces and places, some of which Silver recognized.

An old man sat slumped on a cot, worn and broken down by life, wearing a janitor's uniform. "They broke me. Go look somewhere else for your savior or leader." Then he was gone, and Owen took his place, bleeding from a dozen wounds, sword held out to ward off an unseen enemy. "When you see the opening, run, Hazel. I'll keep them occupied." A mob of shadows surged forward from all sides, and he disappeared beneath them, still swinging his sword. They blinked out, replaced by a grinning Ruby Journey. "I'm just in it for the loot." Silver tried to reach out to Hazel again, but couldn't get near her. Her memories had the force of reality.

Ruby was replaced by a tall, furred, and lupine figure that Silver realized with a jolt had to be a legendary Wolfling. The huge figure looked right at Silver, and said, "It is a sad and bitter honor to be the last of one's kind." He disappeared, replaced by a Hadenman with glowing golden eyes. Behind him towered a vast honeycomb of gold and silver, thickly encrusted with ice. The long-lost Tomb of the Hadenmen. The augmented man called Tobias Moon stared at Silver, and said in his buzzing inhuman voice, "All we ever wanted was our freedom." And then the ice melted, and strange colors came and went on the air, and the Hadenmen emerged from their Tomb, great and glorious and perfect beyond hope. And then there was only Owen again, staring sadly into Hazel's eyes. "You can't fight evil by becoming evil."

Hazel turned away from him, and Owen disappeared as she looked at Silver. Their eyes met, and new visions appeared. Silver, making deals with crooks and scum, to keep the peace in Mistport's streets. Silver, paying off legbreakers like Marcus Rhine, so they wouldn't interfere with his Blood distribution network. Silver, looking the other way, as rivals were eased out or shut down the hard way. The visions faded away, and Hazel looked at Silver with new, cold eyes.

"Just a few drops, now and then, for you and a few special friends? Bullshit. You've been running your own distribution network for the drug, all over the city. How many new plasma babies are there out there now, John? How many Blood junkies lying stiff and cold in empty rooms because they couldn't afford your prices?"

"I don't know," said Silver. "I try not to think about it. I'm just ... getting by, like everyone else in Mistport. Inflation's gone crazy since the esper plague. Money's not worth half what it was. What savings I had were wiped out. If I wasn't doing it, someone else would. You know that. I never meant to hurt anybody, but . . ."

"Yes," said Hazel. "But. There's always a but, isn't there?"

Silver stepped forward, one hand reaching out to her. She grabbed it with her own, and he winced at the harsh, unforgiving strength in her. She smiled at him coldly. "The show's not over yet, John. You've seen the past and the present. Now here comes the future. Whether we're ready or not."

Her hand clamped down hard, and Silver cried out as the room disappeared around them and chaos took its place. People were running screaming in the streets of Mistport. Buildings were burning. Attack sleds filled the skies above. Energy beams stabbed down through billowing clouds of black smoke. The dead lay everywhere. War machines smashed through the city walls. Burning barges floated down a River Autumn thick with blood and choked with corpses. And above it all, a never-ending scream that had nothing of Humanity in it. Hazel released Silver's hand and reality crashed back as the small cramped room reappeared around them. Silver fell back a step, shaking and shuddering, his head still full of the stench of spilled blood and burning bodies, the hideous unending scream still ringing his ears. Hazel stood and looked at him, cold and unforgiving as any oracle.

"That's the future, John. Your future and mine. And you helped bring it about. Something Bad is coming to Mistworld, Something Very Bad. And it will be here soon."

And then suddenly she was just Hazel again, her cloak of power and majesty gone in a moment, and she sank back down into her chair by the fire again, looking small and tired and very, very vulnerable. Silver slowly moved forward and sat down in the chair facing her. Part of him wanted to run screaming from the room, but he couldn't do that. Part of him was frightened almost to panicking by the hideous thing he'd seen his old friend become, but he couldn't let her see that. She needed him, needed her old friend and comrade, and though he had done many awful things in his time, a few of which even he was ashamed of, John Silver was damned if he'd let her down. They sat in silence for a long while, the only sound in the room the quiet crackling as logs shifted in the heat of the fire. The room seemed very cold.

"What happened to you, Hazel?" Silver said finally. "You never had those powers before."

Hazel smiled wearily. "What happened to you, John? What happened to the people we used to be?"

"Things were simpler, when we were young," said Silver, looking into the fire because he found it easier than looking at her. "You were a merc, and I was a pirate, both of us convinced we were destined for greater things. We made a great team as confidence artists. We ran the Angel of Night swindle for three years straight, remember? Though my favorite was always the lost Stargate con. I had great fun making up the maps. So impressive, they were practically works of art. We'd still be running those cons if we hadn't got unlucky."

"And greedy," said Hazel.

"That too."

"Things were simpler then. It was us versus them, and we only took money from those who could afford to lose it. Simple, innocent days. But we changed, moved on. We're not who we used to be. Our friends and allegiances have changed, and all we have in common now are our memories and Blood. And neither of them comfort me like they used to. Can we trust each other anymore, John?"

"We have to," said Silver. "No one else would."

"Owen would," said Hazel.

Silver made himself look at her. "You know him better than I do. What's he really like, this Deathstalker?"

"He's a good man, though he doesn't realize it. A hero. The real thing. Brave and dedicated and too damn honest for his own good. He'll end up leading this rebellion completely before he's through. Not because he wants to, but just because he's the best man for the job. He's a nice guy, but there's so much he doesn't understand. Like the pressures and responsibilities and insecurities that drive lesser people like you and me to Blood or drink or dumb relationships. He's never needed a crutch to lean on in his life. He just sees the right thing and goes for it, complaining all the while, fooling nobody. A good man, in bad times."

"You love him, don't you?" said Silver.

"I never said that," said Hazel.

Silver knew what was needed. He made himself lean forward till their faces were only inches apart, and then he kissed her, and both of them knew it was good-bye. And that was when Owen Deathstalker entered the room and saw them together. He stopped just inside the doorway, saying nothing as Hazel and Silver broke apart and rose quickly to their feet. For a long moment, no one said anything. Hazel was breathing deeply, but her face wasn't flushed. Silver saw Owen's hand drop to the sword at his side, saw the coldness in Owen's eyes, and knew he was very close to death. Not because Owen was jealous, but because this was one too many secrets, one too many betrayals that had been kept from him. And then Owen's eyes went to the phial of Blood on the table, and everything changed. He knew what it was, and what it meant, and anger and a great weariness fought for space inside him.

"So that's it," he said flatly. "No wonder our mental link's been so screwed up, with all that junk in your head. How long have you been taking it, Hazel?"

"Long enough."

"Where did you get it?"

"From the Hadenmen city. Moon was very understanding." Hazel's voice wavered between defiance and a need for him to understand. "I need it, Owen."

"Why didn't you tell me before?"

"Because I knew you'd react like this! You don't understand the pressures I've been under!"

"We've been together from the beginning. What have you been through that I haven't? Dammit, Hazel, I was depending on you to hold up your end in Mistport! I can't do everything! Our work here is important!"

"I know!" Hazel glared at him, her hands clenched into fists. "You depend on me, the underground depends on me, the whole bloody rebellion depends on me! Did it never occur to anyone that I might get tired of carrying so much weight? We can't all be superhuman like you, Owen. We can't all be bloody heroes. You've never had a moment's indecision in your life, have you? You've always known the right thing to do, the right thing to say. But we can't all be perfect!"

"I'm not perfect," said Owen. "I just do my job. And that's all I've ever expected of you."

"You're not listening to me," said Hazel. "You never listen to me."

"Why did you never tell me about you and Silver?"

"Because it was none of your business!"

"You never told me about him. You never told about the Blood. What else haven't you told me about? I thought I could trust you, Hazel. I thought I could trust you, at least."

"You see? You're doing it again! Trying to put all the weight on my shoulders so you can be the victim of the piece! Well to hell with that, and to hell with you, Owen Deathstalker, I'm not going to carry it anymore. I'm sick of carrying the weight of your needs and your expectations! And I'm sick of you . . ."

"Yes," said Owen. "You'd rather have him, and the poison he feeds you. Anything to avoid having to grow up and be a responsible adult. To support those who depend on you. To care about the people who care about you. You want him; he's all yours. I'm going out to get some fresh air."

And he turned and stalked out, slamming the door behind him, because there was so much anger burning inside him that the only other thing he could have done was hit her, and they both knew she would never have forgotten or forgiven that. And because he wanted to kill John Silver so badly he could taste it. He'd thought that he and Hazel, that someday the two of them might . . . but he'd thought many things, and none of them ever worked out the way he hoped. He'd already lost so many things he cared for. He shouldn't be surprised that the only woman he ever loved would be taken away from him, too.

He should never have come back to Mistport. Nothing ever went right here. It wasn't as though he'd had any hold on Hazel. She went her own way and always would. He'd known that. But he thought she'd chosen to walk with him, for a while at least. She could have come to him about her worries. She could have come to him about the drug. He would have tried to understand, tried to help. He understood about pressure. He'd spent all his life trying to live up to the Deathstalker name.

He strode heavily down the stairs and pushed his way through the packed crowd in the tavern. Some people made as though to object. Then they saw his face, and thought better of it. They knew sudden death walking when they saw it. Owen pushed open the door and stepped out into the street, and the cold air hit him, sobering him like a slap in the face. The door swung shut behind him, cutting off most of the tavern roar, and he leaned back against it, damping down his rage, getting it under control again. It took him a moment to realize that the street was completely empty. Which was unusual, to say the least, in a perpetually busy city like Mistport. Faces watched from darkened windows, as though ex-pecting something to happen. Owen pushed himself away from the door, his hands falling to the sword and disrupter on his hips. There was danger here, close and ready. He'd have noticed it earlier if he hadn't been so wrapped up in himself. Three men were suddenly standing on the oppo-site side of the street, staring at him. Either they were teleporters, or more likely they'd hidden their presence behind a telepathic shield. They didn't look like much. Average height, plain average faces, they wore the same thick furs as everyone else. But there was a power in them. Owen could feel it, even if he didn't quite under-stand what it was yet. The man in the middle stepped for-ward. His eyes were very dark in a pale face.

"You have enemies, Deathstalker. Powerful men require your death."

"Well hell," said Owen. "Gosh, I am scared. What are the three of you going to do, gang up on me? Look, I am really not in the mood for this. Why don't you just start running now, and I'll give you a five-minute start."

The man in the middle just smiled, and shook his head. "Time to die, Deathstalker."

The ground rocked suddenly under Owen's feet, throwing him off-balance. He grabbed for his sword, and the street before him split apart, a wide vent opening up as jagged cracks spread in all directions. A bloody light blazed up out of the fissure, and the air was suddenly full of the stench of brimstone and burning flesh. Screams of innumerable people in horrible agony rose up out of the vent far far below. The ground shuddered again, and even as Owen fought for balance he was thrown forward, toward the great crack and all it contained. He could feel an impossible heat now, radiating up from the crevice, as sweat burst out on his face. His furs began to blacken and steam in the heat, and the bare skin of his face and hands began to redden and smart as he stumbled ever closer to the great vent in the street. He fought for control on the edge of the abyss, the crimson air boiling around him. The screams and the stench of sulfur were almost overpowering. Lengths of steel chain shot up out of the crack, ending in great metal barbs that tore through his clothes and sank deep into his flesh. Owen cried out as the chains snapped taut, and began to drag him slowly and remorselessly into the abyss and down to Hell, where he belonged.

But even at the very edge of damnation, Owen still wouldn't give in. He braced himself, and the chains snapped, the broken ends whipping back into the great vent. The heat blazed up, hot enough to burn him down to blackened bone, and he withstood it. Slowly the thought formed in Owen's mind, *I don't believe this. I don't believe in any of this.* And in that moment the crevice and the hellfire were gone, and the street was back to normal, everything as it had been. Owen breathed deeply of the cold, bracing air and glared at the three men on the other side of the street.

"Projective telepaths," he said flatly. "Strong enough to place an illusion in another man's mind, and convince him it's so real that when his image dies, so does he. Pretty rare in the Empire, but presumably not on a planet of espers. Well, gentlemen, you gave it your best shot. Now let me show you mine."

Storm clouds rumbled suddenly overhead, and lightning stabbed down to strike the telepath in the middle. The force of the blast killed him in a moment, and threw the other two off their feet. Lightning struck again, and the second man died. The sole survivor scrambled frantically backwards through the slush and snow, staring at Owen with wild, desperate eyes.

"The lightning isn't real! I don't believe in it!"

"Suit yourself," said Owen. "But it's perfectly real. And storms don't care whether you believe in them or not. I deal strictly in reality."

The esper swallowed hard. "If you'll spare my life, I'll tell you who hired me."

"I know who hired you," said Owen. "Guess I didn't teach those businessmen a strong enough lesson. Maybe your death will convince them."

"But . . . I'm surrendering! I give up!"

"I have no pity for hired killers."

The esper struck out with his illusions again, but they merely whirled around Owen for a moment like pale ghosts before dispersing, unable to pierce his mental shields. The esper stared desperately at Owen.

"You held off three of us. That's not possible. You're not human!"

"No," said Owen. "Not anymore. Now shut up and die."

The lightning stabbed down one more time, and the esper died. And that was when a small army of heavily armed men came spilling into the street from all directions. They moved quickly to surround him, cutting off all avenues of escape. They looked grim and determined and very proficient. Owen was impressed. There had to be easily a hundred of them. Neeson and his businessmen friends must have scoured every dive in the city to put together a force this big.

He was trapped, and he knew it. He'd had to strain his new mental abilities to the limit to produce the three lightning bolts, after all his exertions earlier, and he didn't have it in him to call down any more. He'd had a hard day; his sword was heavy in his hand, he was deathly tired, and even his bones ached. And none of it mattered a damn. He was Owen Deathstalker, and he was mad as hell, and he could just use someone to work it off on.

The young esper's prophecy came back to him, that he would meet his death in the streets of Mistport, alone and friendless, facing impossible odds. Owen laughed, and some of the men facing him shuddered at the dark sound. It was the laughter of a man with nothing left to lose. Owen Deathstalker hefted his sword, grinned his death's-head grin, and boosted. He roared his Family's war cry, "Shandrakor!" and threw himself at his enemies. They pressed forward to meet him from all sides, and there was the clash of steel on steel.

There was murder and butchery in the narrow street, and blood ran thickly on the cobblestones, and at the end Owen stood triumphant amidst a pile of the dead and the dying, bleeding from countless wounds but still unbowed, laughing as he watched the surviving mercenaries turn and run rather than face him.

So much for the damned prophecy.

He dropped out of boost, and was immediately exhausted again. Shock protected him from the pain of most of his wounds, but he knew he had to lie down and rest so the Maze's legacy could heal him. Couldn't just pass out in the street. Bad for the reputation. He sheathed his sword with a reasonably steady hand and turned to go back into the Blackthorn Inn, to the room he had there, and then he stopped as remembered Hazel and Silver together. He didn't want to face them again. Didn't want to be anywhere near them. But in the end he went back in, and back up to his room. Because he had nowhere else to go.

The Imperial starcruiser *Defiant* dropped out of hyperspace, and fell into orbit around Mistworld. In his private quarters, Captain Bartok, also know as Bartok the Butcher, waited tensely for any reaction from the world below. Ever since Typhoid Mary, the planet's surviving espers had taken to attacking any Imperial ship the moment it appeared. But the moments passed and nothing happened and Bartok finally allowed himself to relax a little. The new shields were working. Theoretically no esper or group of espers should have been able to detect the *Defiant*'s presence, but there had been no sure way of testing it in advance.

Captain Bartok rose from his oversize chair and moved unhurriedly round his quarters, a large, bearlike man with slow, deliberate movements. His uniform was perfect, spotless and sharp, with every crease in place. A cold, calm man, Bartok didn't believe in emotions, especially his own. They just got in the way of duty and efficiency. His quarters were large and comfortable, and entirely dominated by the plants that covered every wall and even hung down from the ceiling. There were vines and flowers and spiky shrubs, intertwined around each other and fighting for space. Huge blossoms vied with strange growths from a hundred worlds, kept alive by a complicated hydroponics system. They filled the air with a thick, heady perfume that only Bartok found tolerable. He preferred plants to people. He knew where he was with plants, not least because plants were predictable and didn't answer back. He found the brilliant colors and rich scents soothing, in a Service where he knew he could never relax or trust anyone, and only left his private quarters when he absolutely had to.

Bartok had been ordered to bring Mistworld back into the Empire. An honor, to be sure, but a very dangerous one. Certainly no one else had been ready to volunteer, except him. His previous duty had been guarding the Vaults of the Sleepers on the planet Grendel. His six starcruisers had maintained the Quarantine on that planet without incident for years, until Captain Silence of the *Dauntless* had gone down to the planet on the Empress's orders, and discovered that somehow the rogue AIs of Shub had slipped a force past the blockade and plundered the Vaults. Even now, Bartok had no idea how such a thing could have happened. His ships' instruments and records had been adamant that nothing had got past them. And no one on any of the ships had admitted to seeing anything untoward.

Bartok and his crews had been recalled in disgrace, and on arrival at Golgotha, every one of them from Bartok down to the lowliest crew member had been examined at length by espers and mind techs, determined to find an answer to the mystery. They found nothing, though the extremity of their methods killed some of the weaker members of the crews and drove others insane. Bartok still woke trembling in his bed from bad dreams of the terrible things they'd done to him.

In the end, he and the surviving members of his crews were officially exonerated, only to find that no one trusted them anymore. Bartok didn't blame them. His own secret fear was that Shub had done something to his mind, installed secret control words and instructions buried so deep that no one could find them. He had no doubt this thought had also occurred to others, and wasn't surprised when his orders finally came through, detailing him to return to the Fleet Academy, as an instructor. Thus putting an end to his career, and enabling the Security forces to keep a close eye on him.

And then came a call for volunteers to take on the Mist-world mission. It had to be volunteers. Everyone knew the odds were it was a suicide mission. Bartok grabbed at the chance eagerly. Odds didn't worry him. If his Empress said the mission was possible, that was good enough for him. And he was desperate to prove his loyalty, to be taken back into the fold and reinstated. Though whether he wanted to prove himself to his Empress or to himself remained uncertain. Lionstone accepted him as commander of the mission immediately. Partly because his record indicated he would get the job done, whatever the cost; and partly because if he failed, he and his crew wouldn't be any great loss. Bartok knew that and accepted it. They were his thoughts also.

His door chimed politely and opened at his growled command. Lieutenant Ffolkes strode in, ducking his head just a little to avoid the hanging creepers around the door, followed by the reporter Tobias Shreck and his cameraman, Flynn. Tobias, also known as Toby the Troubadour, was a short, fat, perspiring man with flat blond hair, an easy smile, a mind like a steel trap, and absolutely no morals that he was aware of. All of which had combined to make him a first-class reporter. Flynn was a tall gangling sort with a deceptively honest face. His camera perched on his shoulder like a monocular mental owl.

Toby and Flynn had been chosen personally by the Empress to cover and record the taking of Mistport. She'd been very impressed by their coverage of the rebellion on Technos III, and had made it very clear to both of them that this assignment was one they would be wise not to turn down. Not if they liked their major organs where they were. They were both quietly unsure as to whether the assignment was a reward or a punishment, but had enough sense not to ask. So Toby and Flynn said *Yes, Your Majesty. Thank you, Your Majesty*, and wondered how the hell they were going to survive this one.

There was no doubt the taking of Mistport would provide all kinds of first-class opportunities for recording history as it happened, along with plenty of the blood and destruction the home audiences so enjoyed; there was also no doubt in their minds that they stood a bloody good chance of getting their fool heads blown off. Rebels fighting for their home and their lives wouldn't pause to distinguish between an Imperial trooper and an honest news team just trying to do their job. But as Toby had said so often in the past, wars and battles always provided the best footage; so if you wanted the good stuff and the awards and rewards that would bring, you had to go where the action was. Flynn maintained a diplomatic silence on this, as he did on most things.

Of course, there was always the problem of Imperial censorship. Lionstone was going to want footage that made her troops look good, and the rebels very, very bad, and wouldn't be above ordering her censors to cut any film that suggested otherwise. Toby and Flynn's misgivings were further confirmed by the official minder they'd been given to oversee their work and keep them out of trouble. Lieutenant Ffolkes was career military to the bone, a tall spindly sort who followed orders to the letter and was always eager for a chance to please any officer superior to himself. Probably slept at attention and gave himself extra fatigues for impure thoughts. He made it clear to Toby and Flynn and anyone who would listen that he regarded reporters and their cameramen as necessary vermin, who would do well to follow his own instructions to the last detail if they knew what was good for them. Their refusal to take him at all seriously, and refer to him as Gladys behind his back, upset him deeply. As did their habit of sprinting in the opposite direction whenever they saw him coming.

Toby and Flynn studied the Captain's private quarters with interest as Bartok ignored them for the moment, quietly pruning something small and defenseless with great concentration. Ffolkes fidgeted nervously, unsure as to whether he should perhaps cough politely to announce his arrival. Toby and Flynn had never been invited to the inner sanctum before. Mostly they'd been confined to the coffin-sized quarters Ffolkes had assigned them, well away from the rest of the crew. They weren't supposed to fraternize with any of the ship's crew, partly because they might pick up information they weren't cleared for, and at least partly because they might inspire the crew into asking awkward questions themselves. Imperial officers had always believed that an ignorant crew was a happy crew.

Toby spent most of his time being torn between rage at being kept from the fame and awards that his coverage of the Technos III rebellion had earned him, and his growing certainty that the invasion of Mistworld was going to be one of the greatest events in modern times, and thus provide him with even more juicy opportunities for even more fame and awards. If he could just sneak the good stuff past the censors, as he had on Technos III. He didn't see many problems in outsmarting Ffolkes. A retarded hamster on a bad day could manage that, and probably had. Captain Bartok was another matter. Toby studied the miniature jungle of the Captain's quarters carefully, looking for insights into the Captain's character that he could use against him.

Flynn predictably didn't give a damn. He hated everything about the military anyway, from the Fleet in general to the *Defiant* in particular, and didn't care who knew it. He was not one to suffer discipline or fools gladly, not least because of his certain knowledge that he was breaking all kinds of regulations just by existing. Flynn was happily homosexual and a transvestite in his private life, either of which would get him thrown into the brig if Ffolkes found out. Though Flynn claimed to have spotted a few like-minded souls among the junior officers. As it

was he was prevented from wearing any of his pretty
dresses, even in the supposed privacy of his own quarters,
for fear of discovery by the ship's omnipresent security
systems. So he settled for wearing frilly underwear beneath his everyday clothes, and the use of just a little
understated makeup. Toby lived in fear that his cameraman would have an accident and have to be rushed to the
medlab for an examination. He just knew Bartok wouldn't
understand.

As though picking up on that thought, Bartok finally
put his miniature shears aside and turned to meet his visitors. His face was cold and unforgiving as he advanced on
Toby and Flynn, neither of whom made any attempt to
stand at attention, despite Ffolkes's frantic whispers.
Bartok stopped right before them, his face uncomfortably
close to theirs, and when he spoke his voice was calm and
controlled and utterly intimidating.

"I have studied your coverage of the rebellion on
Technos III. Though technically adequate, your choice of
material was little short of treasonous. There will be no
repetition of such nonsense under my command. Rebels
are the enemy, and are never to be presented as anything
else. You will restrict your coverage to recording my
troops' victories, and ignore anything not specifically
cleared by Lieutenant Ffolkes. There will be no live
broadcasts, except on my specific orders. The bulk of
your work will be recorded for later transmission, and the
Lieutenant and I will personally examine all footage
before it is released. Failure to obey these or any other
instructions will lead to your immediate imprisonment
and replacement, followed by charges of treason on our
return to Golgotha. Is that clear?"

"Every word, Captain," said Toby quickly. He smiled
and nodded to show he was one of the team, and privately
determined always to film Bartok in ways that made him
look fat and dumb on camera. He wasn't bothered in the
least by Bartok's threats and restrictions. They'd said
much the same to him on Technos III, and it hadn't
stopped him there either. Every good reporter knew that
what mattered was to get the footage out and on as many
screens as possible, and argue about it afterward, when
it was too late for the powers that be to do anything about

it without looking petty. Of course, he hadn't had to deal with Bartok the Butcher before. The man had a definite preference for solving problems through extreme violence.

"Come with me," said Bartok suddenly. "I want you to see something."

He stalked past them and left his quarters, only just giving the door enough time to get out of his way. Toby and Flynn exchanged a puzzled glance and hurried after him, with Ffolkes dithering along in the rear, as always. Bartok marched down corridor after corridor, ignoring the salutes of those he passed, until he was well into territory that was usually off-limits to the two reporters. Toby felt a growing excitement. He'd been trying to bluff, badger, and threaten his way into this area since he first came aboard, with no success. Everyone knew there was Something Big locked away, a secret weapon for the invasion, but no one knew that. The few who did were too senior or too scared to talk, all of which had whetted Toby's appetite to the boiling point. And now he was finally going to get a look at it. He surreptitiously signaled Flynn to start filming. The camera was locked into Flynn's comm implant, and could be activated with no outward sign, a trick which had come in handy on more than one occasion.

Bartok finally came to a massive bulkhead door that would only open to an esper scan, and it was all Toby could do to keep from fuming visibly as he waited impatiently for the esper on the other side of the door to clear them. A quick glance at Ffolkes's white and nervous face suggested that he'd never seen what lay waiting on the other side of the door either, but knew enough not to be at all keen about seeing it now. And then the door finally swung open, and Bartok led the way in, with Toby all but stepping on his heels.

Before them lay a vast auditorium, surrounded by ribbed steel walls. Filling most of it was a huge glass tank. The sides were easily thirty feet high, and they stretched off into the distance for farther than Toby could comfortably look. The tank contained a thick, pale yellow liquid that moved constantly with slow syrupy tides. And floating in that liquid, huge and dark and awful, was a great fleshy mass, spotted with high tech, connected to the tank and beyond by countless wires and cables. The mass bulged shapelessly, an unhealthy conglomeration of fused living materials, like a single great cancer floating in a sea of pus. It stank horribly, and Toby screwed up his face as he moved slowly forward, fascinated. Behind him he could hear Ffolkes coughing and choking.

"Marvelous, isn't it?" said Bartok. "This will be the secret of our success, the single element that makes our invasion of Mistworld possible. It's currently projecting a screen that keeps the Mistworld espers and their tech from detecting our presence. It has other abilities, too, to be revealed when our invasion begins."

"What the hell is it?" said Toby. "Is it alive?"

"Oh yes," said Bartok. "You are looking at the very latest in bioengineering. Imperial scientists took all the espers imprisoned in Silo Nine, all that were left after the aborted breakout, and executed them. They then removed the thousands of brains and melded the tissues together to form the single construct before you. Thousands of living brains, fused together into one giant esper computer, a single giant esp-blocker, and more besides. It's controlled by the worms that previously controlled the prisoners—Wormboy's legacy. They're hot-wired into the brain tissues at regular intervals, monitoring and maintaining the thought processes. The worms have formed a crude gestalt that enables us to communicate with the construct directly via the brains' telepathy. It calls itself Legion."

"The esper minds," said Toby slowly. "Are they . . . alive in there? Aware of what they've become?"

Bartok shrugged. "No one knows for sure. They're part of something greater now."

Toby moved slowly closer, till his face was almost pressed against the glass. He could sense Flynn not far behind him, quietly getting it all on film. The horror Toby felt at what had been done to thousands of defenseless people silenced him for a moment, but already he was working furiously on how best to present it to the viewing public. They were going to want to know everything about this . . . abomination, and he was the only one who could tell them. He brought his thoughts firmly under control. You couldn't let your feelings get in the way of a good story. Every reporter knew that.

"Why is it called Legion?" he asked finally.

I am Legion, because I am many. The psionic voice rang inside Toby's head like the rotting vocal cords of a month-dead corpse, forcing its way into his thoughts. It curled inside his mind like a poisonous snake, writhing and coiling and leaving a slimy trail behind it. It was a pitiless, brutal invasion, a violation of the mind, and Toby wanted to be sick. Just its presence in his head made him feel unclean. He fought for self-control as the voice continued.

I am everything I was before, and more, far greater than the sum of my parts. No esper can stand before me. Their screen shall fall, and I shall feast on their minds. I will take them into me, and suck them up. And Mistworld will drown in blood and suffering.

Legion spoke in many voices, simultaneously, a horrid chorus of clashing accents. They were loud and quiet, harsh and shrill, all at once, an unnatural mixture that was disturbingly inhuman. And in the background, like a distant sea that came and went, the sound of thousands of damned souls, screaming in Hell.

"Who . . . exactly is talking to me now?" said Toby, fighting to hang on to his professional calm. "The esper brains, the worms, the gestalt? What?"

But Legion didn't answer, and suddenly its presence was gone from Toby's mind. The relief was overwhelming. Toby stumbled backwards, desperate to put some space between him and the awful thing in the tank. Flynn was quickly there, with a supporting hand under his arm. In the end, surprisingly, it was Ffolkes who answered Toby's questions, in a shaken, quiet voice.

"We don't know who talks to us. We think Legion is still working out its own nature. All we know for certain is that it is conscious and aware, and growing stronger all the time. It should have no problem destroying any psionic screen the Mistworlders can raise against us, and without that they'll be helpless."

"Just how strong will it get?" said Toby, his voice a little steadier now the thing was out of his head.

"We don't know," said Bartok. "But you needn't worry.

Physically, Legion is quite helpless. It couldn't survive for a second outside its tank. Without our tech support, and the chemically saturated plasma it floats in, Legion couldn't exist at all. It's quite dependent on us, and it knows it."

"But you still don't know what it really is," said Flynn quietly. "What it's capable of."

"I'll tell you what it is," said Bartok, smiling for the first time. "It's a weapon. A weapon I can use to crush Mistworld once and for all."

Some time later Lieutenant Ffolkes, having escorted Toby and Flynn safely back to their quarters, made his way hurriedly to another part of the ship, and knocked quietly on a particular door, using the code he'd been given. The door opened almost immediately, and he slipped inside. He was sweating, and his hands were shaking. Special computer overrides were supposed to be in operation, hiding him from the security systems, but he had no way of knowing whether they were working or not. Once the door was safely shut behind him, Ffolkes was able to breathe a little more easily. He nodded to the room's only inhabitant, and Investigator Razor nodded back.

Razor·was a tall and blocky man, with thick slabs of muscle and a patient, brooding face. His skin was dark, his close-cropped hair was white, and his narrowed eyes were a surprising green. The Investigator seemed calm enough, but Ffolkes wasn't fooled. He knew Razor didn't want to be here. He'd had a perfectly good life as Security chief to Clan Chojiro, until the Empress had decided that Investigators would no longer be allowed to work for the Families, retired or not. Instead, all Investigators of whatever age or status were brought back under direct Imperial control. Razor had been a rich and influential man under Clan Chojiro; now he was just another Investigator, older and perhaps a little slower than most. But the Empress had wanted him for the Mistworld mission, so here he was. Even though he didn't believe in suicide missions anymore.

Which was why Ffolkes was there.

Razor had been seconded to the *Defiant* because he had

worked closely with Investigator Topaz in the past. He'd been her mentor and instructor, in the days when the Empire was still trying to decide whether an esper Investigator was a good idea or not. Topaz's defection and flight to Mistworld had answered that. Razor had been exonerated of all blame, but no one objected when he applied for early retirement. This was supposed to be a second chance for him, a chance to prove his worth and his loyalty, by using his old acquaintance to get close to Topaz where no one else could. And then he would kill her. No one asked him how he felt about this. Investigators weren't supposed to have feelings.

"You have instructions for me?" said Razor quietly.

"Yes," said Ffolkes, looking around the Investigator's bare, spartan quarters so he wouldn't have to meet the man's cold, inflexible stare. "I will be your contact with Clan Chojiro. I'm related through marriage. I'm to tell you that you have not been forgotten, and that the Family will reward you handsomely for your work here on its behalf. I'm here to brief you on Captain Bartok's intentions, once Legion has taken care of the esper shield.

"We could just scorch the planet from orbit, but Her Imperial Majesty has decided she wants Mistworld taken, not destroyed. Partly because she still sees espers as potential weapons in the coming war against the aliens, and partly to prove no one can defy her and get away with it. She wants the rebel leaders brought before her in chains, so everyone can see them broken and defeated.

"So, Bartok's orders are for systematic but not total destruction of Mistport. Up to 50 percent civilian casualties are acceptable. The city is to be taken street by street, by hand-to-hand fighting if necessary. All of which means that the city will be plunged into total chaos and confusion, which we can then take advantage of. Once you've dealt with Investigator Topaz and Typhoid Mary, you will be free to make contact with certain influential people, whose names and addresses I have here on this list. Memorize them, then destroy the list. These people were once part of an old spy network in the city, trading in information for the previous Lord Deathstalker. Since his death, a number of them turned to Clan Chojiro for protection and financial support. With the Family's support after the invasion, these people will become the city's new ruling Council. Your job is to keep them alive until the invasion is over."

Razor nodded calmly. "Seems straightforward enough. Any idea why Chojiro wants control of this misbegotten world?"

"I don't ask questions," said Ffolkes. "I find you live longer that way. But if I were to hazard a guess, I'd say that the surviving espers could make a very useful cash crop, as well as a private resource. Clan Chojiro takes the long view. Good-bye, Investigator. I do hope we won't have to meet again."

"You're afraid," said Razor. "I can smell it on you. What are you so afraid of, Lieutenant?"

"I don't know what you mean," said Ffolkes. "I really must be going. People will miss me."

And then he was flung back against the bulkhead, Razor's sword at his throat. Ffolkes gasped for air, sweat trickling down his face. He'd never seen anyone move so fast. Razor brought his face close to Ffolkes's, and he didn't dare look away.

"Are you afraid of me, Lieutenant? That's good. You should be. If you breathe a word of my continuing connection to Clan Chojiro to anyone at all, I'll kill you. Do you believe me, Lieutenant?"

The edge of Razor's blade bit delicately into Ffolkes's neck, and a single drop of blood slid slowly down his throat. He didn't dare nod, but he managed a trembling answer in the affirmative. Razor smiled, took his sword away from Ffolkes's neck, and stepped back a pace.

"Just so we understand each other. Now get out of here, turncoat. If I have to talk to you again, I'll find you. And if you make me come looking for you, I'll be the last thing you'll ever see."

He opened the door and Ffolkes bolted past him, out into the corridor, running at full tilt and to hell with whether anyone was watching. No amount of payment was worth this. Nothing was.

The *Defiant*'s pinnaces fell out of the early evening like silver birds of prey against a bloodred sky, carrying the Empire's warriors down to the surface of the rebel planet.

Mistport's espers saw nothing, heard nothing, never knew they were there. Legion was testing and expanding its abilities. Theoretically it had been certain it could shield the pinnaces even from a distance, but as with so many of Legion's powers, it learned by doing. Hundreds of silver ships landed one after another on a wide plain of snow and ice on the outskirts of the Deathshead Mountains; some distance away from Mistport but quite close to a small outlying settlement called Hardcastle's Rock. Apart from a few scattered farmsteads, it was the only other heavily populated area of Mistworld. A small town of no real importance, population 2031, according to the Empire's information. No real defenses, very little tech. A good testing ground, before the main assault.

Men and women came running out of the square stone houses to watch the pinnaces falling out of the sky. Legion might be able to fool espers and sensors, but even it couldn't hide the roar of so many thundering engines from the people directly below them. At least, not yet. The townspeople gathered by the high stone walls surrounding their town, and watched and babbled excitedly as the ships just kept on coming. It didn't take them long to figure out what was happening. They'd spent most of their lives expecting and preparing for an invasion. The day the Empire came to reclaim Mistport as its own. Men and women ran to get their weapons and hide the children from what was to come.

Troops filed out of the long narrow ships, weighed down by armor insulated against the bitter cold, carrying swords and energy weapons and force shields. The pinnaces had disrupter cannon, but they were being saved for Mistport. Marines moved quickly to establish a perimeter around the landing field, ignoring the town for the moment. Imperial troops stood in ranks, waiting for the word. Cold-eyed, seasoned, disciplined killers, eager to make a start. Sergeants barked orders, officers strolled into position, and still the ships fell, and more men came marching out onto the snow and ice.

Toby Shreck and his cameraman Flynn, wrapped in heavy-duty furs, lumbered out into the cold, swore briefly, and began filming. They'd been instructed to cover everything, and Lieutenant Ffolkes was right there to see that they did. He watched the army assembling, and swelled with pride. It was days like this that made you glad to be a member of the Imperial Fleet.

And finally, from out of the last ship to land, came the commander of the Imperial forces, Investigator Razor. He hadn't bothered with insulated armor or furs, wearing only the blue and silver of an Investigator's formal uniform. He didn't feel the cold, but then, everyone knew Investigators weren't really human. The Empress herself had placed Razor in charge of all ground troops. Partly because he had led invasion forces in the past, before his retirement, and partly to show that the Empress trusted him entirely, despite his age and Chojiro connections.

Razor's staff officers gathered around him, bringing him up-to-date, anxious to show that everything was as it should be. Razor nodded curtly. It had never occurred to him that it wouldn't. Beginnings were easy to plan. His personal staff officer handed him a pair of binoculars, and he studied the town and the surrounding area. Normally he would have linked into the ship's computers through his comm implant, and accessed the sensor arrays, but with Legion blocking all frequencies, he'd had to arrange for low-tech aids for himself and his troops. Apart from the town there was nothing but snow and ice for as far as the eye could see, except for the long range of the Deathshead Mountains, plunging up into the sky. They looked cold and indifferent, as though nothing that happened below them could possibly be of any significance. Razor smiled slightly. He'd change that.

He studied the ten-foot-high stone wall surrounding the town. It was solid stone and mortar, sturdy and well-constructed. A few energy blasts would take care of it. Men and women from the town stood watching from catwalks along the top of the inner wall. Most were armed with swords and axes and spears, but a few had energy weapons. Nowhere near enough to make any difference, though, and both sides knew it. The townspeople were all dead. They just hadn't lain down yet. Razor breathed deeply of the icy air, centering himself. This high up on the plateau, there were few mists, and the air was sharp and clear. He gave the order to begin, and a hundred marines opened fire with their disrupters. The stone wall exploded, stone fragments and bloody flesh flying in all directions.

Smoke rose up, and sharp-edged rubble and small body parts pattered to the snow in an awful rain. There were shouts and screams as the survivors fell back from the great gaping hole in the wall. A few stayed to try and drag wounded from the wreckage, but the marines picked them off easily. More troops had moved into position on the other side of the town, and they blew that wall out, too. The townspeople had nowhere to go now, trapped between two advancing forces. Razor nodded to his staff officers, drew his sword and gun, and led the way into the small town of Hardcastle's Rock.

The battle was grim and bloody, but it didn't take long. The marines had the advantage of far greater numbers, massed energy weapons, and force shields. The townspeople fought bravely, men and women standing their ground fiercely. Swords rose and fell, and blood flew on the air, hot and steaming. There were screams and battle cries and roared orders, and bodies and offal lay scattered across the churned-up snow. There was no room or time for heroes, only two mismatched forces struggling in blank anonymity. Above the bedlam of battle came the occasional roar of energy weapons, followed by the sudden stench of roast meat. The troops couldn't use disrupters much for fear of hitting their own people, but the few townspeople with energy weapons barricaded themselves in their houses and sniped desperately from shuttered windows. But in the end, the Imperial forces were able to pinpoint which houses were being used, and blew them apart with concussion grenades and shaped charges. The squat stone houses collapsed inward as the powerful explosions ruptured the walls, bringing down the roofs and crushing those inside. The marines advanced remorselessly from both ends of the town, driving all before them, cutting down those who wouldn't or couldn't fall back fast enough. Until finally the townspeople were caught and trapped and slaughtered in the middle of their own town.

When finally it was over a sullen quiet fell across what had been the town of Hardcastle's Rock. The last defenders had fallen, and the few who had thrown down their weapons and surrendered, mostly women and children, stood huddled together in small, well-guarded groups. Houses burned to every side, crimson flames licking out darkening stone windows. The dead lay everywhere, mostly townspeople, some marines, well within acceptable losses. A few dozen marines moved among the fallen, marking wounded troopers for the med teams, and putting the wounded rebels out of their misery.

Investigator Razor stood in the middle of the town, in a small open space his troops had cleared for him. He looked unhurriedly around, not too displeased with the way things had gone. He'd lost more men than he expected, but then he hadn't expected energy weapons in the hands of rebels. He raised a hand and summoned his main staff officers and his Second in Command, Major Chevron. Chevron was a tall, well-muscled man who looked as though he'd been born to wear body armor. He crashed to a parade halt before the Investigator, but didn't salute. Technically, he was superior in rank to Razor, but they both knew who was in charge.

"The town is secure, sir," Chevron said calmly. "The townspeople are either dead or prisoners, apart from a few still hiding in their homes. The town has fallen."

"They had energy guns, Major," said Razor. "Why wasn't I informed that the townspeople would have energy weapons?"

"There were only a few, sir. Like the town walls, they were there to defend against local predators. Nasty things called Hob hounds. It was mentioned in the original briefings, sir."

Razor just nodded, neither accepting nor rejecting the implied criticism. "Are we sure there are no more rebel settlements in the area?"

"Quite sure, sir. Just a few farmsteads, here and there. We can hit them from the air while traveling to Mistport. Word won't get there ahead of us. Legion is jamming all frequencies. Apparently it's not uncommon for communications to break down from time to time out here. Mistport won't worry about lost contact for quite a time yet. By the time they do realize something's wrong, we'll be hammering on their front door."

"So we have some time to play with. Good." Razor

smiled slightly. "Gather all the prisoners together and execute them."

"Sir?" Major Chevron blinked uncertainly at the Investigator, caught off guard. "It was my understanding that prisoners were to be used as hostages and human shields . . ."

"Then you understood wrong. Was my order not clear enough? Kill them all. That includes those hiding in their houses. Do it now."

"Yes, sir. Right away."

The Major gathered up the nearest officers with his eyes, and gave the orders. They passed the order on to their men, who drew swords and axes already crusted with drying blood, and set about their task with calm, detached faces. Blades rose and fell, and the women and children and few men were quickly cut down. They barely had time to scream, and the only sound on the quiet air was the dull thudding of heavy blades sinking deep into human flesh. The hacking and chopping went on for some time, finishing off those who wouldn't die immediately. Women tried to shield their children with their bodies, to no avail. The marines were very thorough.

Razor smiled. He wanted his marines to be sure of their duty. And besides, it was important that people not think he was growing soft in his old age. He knew there were those watching from the sidelines, waiting to take advantage of any perceived weaknesses in his handling of this mission. Starting very definitely with Major Chevron, who'd made no secret of the fact that he thought he should have been in charge.

Marines gathered around the few houses still holding rebels within. They tried setting fire to them, but the stone walls and slate roofs were slow to burn, so the marines settled for shooting out the shuttered windows, and tossing in grenades. A few townspeople burst out of their doors rather than wait to be finished off by fire or smoke or explosions. They came charging out, roaring obscure battle cries and waving their swords and axes, and the marines calmly shot them down from a distance. It didn't take long, and soon every house in Hardcastle's Rock was burning, sending a heavy pall of black smoke up into the lowering evening skies.

Toby and Flynn were right there in the thick of it, recording everything. Flynn kept his camera moving in and out of the action, flying quickly back and forth on its antigrav unit, hovering overhead when the action got a little too close, while Toby kept up a running commentary. Flynn grew sickened by the slaughter and wanted to stop filming, but Ffolkes wouldn't let him, even putting a gun to the cameraman's head at one point. Toby just kept talking, and if his voice grew a little hoarse at times, well there was a lot of smoke in the air. Toby and Flynn had grown used to recording sudden death in close-up on the battlefields of Technos III, but nothing there had prepared them for this. Technos III had been a war between two more or less equally matched sides. This was just butchery. Ffolkes wasn't around when Razor gave the order for the executions. Flynn looked at Toby.

"I can't do this. I can't."

"Keep filming."

"I can't! This is obscene. They've already surrendered."

"I know. But it's important we cover everything."

Flynn glared at him. "You'd do anything for good ratings, wouldn't you?"

"Pretty much. But this is different. People have to see what happened here. What Lionstone is doing in their name."

Flynn's mouth twisted into an ugly shape, and his eyes were wet with tears, but he got it all on film, right down to the last bloody cough and shuddering body. When it was over he sat down suddenly in the blood-splattered snow and cried. His camera hovered overhead. Toby stood over Flynn, patting him on the shoulder comfortingly. He was too angry to cry.

"Bartok will never let this film be shown," Flynn said finally. "He'll censor it."

"The hell he will," said Toby. "He'll be proud of it. His troops won a great victory here today. The first on Mistworld soil. You don't understand the military mind, Flynn."

"And thank the good God for that." Flynn got to his feet

again, waving away Toby's offer of help. His camera flew down to perch on his shoulder again. Ffolkes came over to join them. There was blood on his armor, none of it his, and his face was very pale. He looked at the pathetic piles of mutilated bodies, then looked at Toby and Flynn almost desperately.

"Don't worry," said Toby. "We got it all."

"It wasn't supposed to be like this," Ffolkes said thickly. "This isn't war."

"Yes it is," said Investigator Razor, and Ffolkes spun around immediately. Razor stirred one of the bodies with the toe of his boot. "These are scum. Enemies of the Empire. There are no innocents here. Just by choosing to live on Mistworld, they are automatically traitors and criminals, and condemned to death."

"What about the children?" said Flynn. "They didn't choose to live here. They were born here."

Razor turned unhurriedly to look at him. "They would have grown to be traitors. Don't have much stomach for this, do you, boy?"

"No," said Flynn. "No, I don't."

"Don't worry, boy. This is nothing, compared to what's going to happen in Mistport. I'll make a man of you yet."

And he strode away, calmly giving orders. The marines gathered up the bodies of the fallen townspeople and piled them together in one great heap in the middle of the town. The pile grew steadily larger, the marines having to clamber up and over bodies to pile them higher, until finally it was all done. The great mound of bodies rose up above the burning roofs of the nearby houses. And then Razor had them set on fire, too. Smoke billowed up, and the scent of roasting meat was thick on the air. This was too much for some of the marines. They turned away from the bodies curling up in the flames, from the bloody flesh blackening and cracking, and they vomited into the snow. Officers stood over them and shouted abuse and orders. Flynn got it all on film.

"I'll see Razor dead," he said finally. "I swear I'll see him dead."

"He's an Investigator, Flynn. Ordinary people like you and me don't kill Investigators."

"Somebody has to," said Flynn. "While there are still some ordinary people left."

The billowing black smoke rose high above what had once been the town of Hardcastle's Rock, population 2031, as the marines trooped back to their ships for the flight to Mistport.

Two marines strode down the main street of Hardcastle's Rock, passing a bottle of booze back and forth between them. Buildings burned to either side of them, and the great funeral pyre blazed fiercely in the middle of the town, sending a great pall of greasy black smoke up into the evening sky. For Kast and Morgan, career marines, it was just another job. They'd seen and done worse in their years serving under Bartok the Butcher. There wasn't much to choose between the two marines. Both large, muscular men in blood-spattered armor, with broad cheerful faces and eyes that had seen everything.

They wandered on through the town, waiting for their turn to reboard the pinnace that would take them on to Mistport. First in, last out, as always. So far, they didn't think much of Mistworld. It was freezing cold, with people who shot at you when you weren't expecting it, and no comforts anywhere. So they went from house to house, checking those that hadn't burned out too thoroughly for loot and booze, since there weren't any women to be had.

"Miserable bloody place," said Morgan.

"Right," said Kast, leaning forward to light a cigar from a burning doorframe. "Still, good to be back in action again."

"Damn right," said Morgan. "Thought I'd go crazy sitting around the *Defiant,* watching that bloody Grendel planet. This is real work. Soldier's work."

Neither of them mentioned their time in the interrogation cells under Golgotha, sobbing and screaming as the mind techs dug pitilessly for information about the broken Quarantine. It was just good to be free and striking back at an enemy that could hurt. Spread the pain around a little. That was the Empire way, after all. They came across a woman's body, somehow overlooked, sitting slumped just inside a doorway. As the marines stopped before her, her bloody head seemed to settle forward slightly, as though nodding to them. Kast dug Morgan in the ribs with his elbow.

"I think she fancies you."

"Probably still warm, too. Toss a coin for who goes first?"

"Sure. We'll use my coin, though. You cheat."

They tossed for it, and Morgan won, but when he reached forward to take her by the shoulders, the woman's head fell off and rolled away across the snow. Immediately the two marines were after it, laughing and shouting and kicking it back and forth in an impromptu game. The woman's body lay slumped in the doorway, forgotten. Morgan punted the "ball" neatly through an open window and jumped up and down, punching the air in triumph.

"And it's a goal! See, Kast, I told you. The old magic's still there. I could have been a professional."

"Yeah, and I could have been a Sergeant if my parents hadn't been married. Move it. Time's getting on."

The rest of the town proved a disappointment, so Kast produced a packet of marshmallows, and they sat by the funeral pyre to toast them, swapping happy reminiscences of past campaigns. The evening continued to fall, little by little, and the pyre spread a crimson hellglow over the deserted town. Kast and Morgan sang old songs of comradeship and violence and lost friends, and finally marched out of the burning town singing the company march. The last of the pinnaces waited to take them to Mistport.

In Mistport, in the Abraxus Information Center, the children all woke up screaming. They sat bolt upright, mouths stretched wide, their eyes full of blood and death. The ones strapped to their cots thrashed and convulsed, desperate to be free. Chance moved among them, trying to comfort those who could still be reached, but the death cry of so many espers in Hardcastle's Rock, too strong and potent to be denied, screamed on through the children's throats. Slowly reason returned to some of them. Chance dosed the rest with strong sedatives so he could concentrate, and from the others gradually pieced together what had happened. And for the first time in a long time, he contacted Port Director Gideon Steel at the Mistport control tower.

Steel took a long time to answer, and when his fat face eventually filled the viewscreen he looked less than pleased to see who his caller was. "Make it fast. Half my duty espers have gone crazy, and the rest are catatonic. It's bedlam in here. What do you want, Chance?"

"An Imperial force has just wiped out Hardcastle's Rock," Chance said bluntly. "It was a big force, and it's on its way here right now."

Steel frowned. "Are you sure? We've had no signals from that area, and our sensors are all clear."

"The town is dead," said Chance. "Every man, woman, and child. The Empire is here, Steel. Do something."

"I'll get back to you." Steel snapped off the comm link and began issuing orders. He didn't really believe the news, not least because he didn't want to, but he couldn't afford to take chances. He had the duty espers smacked around till they calmed down, and then had them spread their minds as wide as they could, while the control tower fired up the long-range sensors. It didn't take the espers long to find a great void where the town of Hardcastle's Rock should have been, a void they couldn't penetrate. They also sensed something else, a presence, huge and powerful but hidden from them.

High above, Legion realized it had been discovered, and rejoiced. Its time had come to do what it had been created to do, to bring terror and despair and the end of all things to the Empire's enemies. It threw aside its concealing shield, and spread its vast influence across the city of Mistport. The tower's sensors immediately detected the orbiting *Defiant* and the hundreds of pinnaces bearing down on Mistport. Steel hit the alarm button even as his duty espers screamed and collapsed, unable to deal with the horror that was Legion. Tower personnel tried to revive them, but some were dead, some were insane, and the rest were beyond reach, driven into hiding within their own minds rather than face Legion. Steel used his emergency link to contact the esper union, but for a long time no one answered his call. Static flashed across the screen as the signal gradually deteriorated under Legion's influence. Finally a wild-eyed man appeared on the view-screen, his face sweating and shocked.

"Get me someone in authority!" snapped Steel. "We have to raise the psionic shield! It's an emergency!"

"We know!" said the esper, his eyes rolling like a panicked horse's. "The Empire's here! But we can't do anything. It's like a giant esp-blocker is covering the whole city. It's shut down our powers. We can't hear each other anymore. It's all we can do to think clearly. Half of our people have had to go catatonic, just to protect their sanity. And the field's growing stronger all the time! There isn't going to be any psionic screen!"

Blood gushed suddenly from the man's nose and ears. He looked surprised, tried to say something, and then his face disappeared from the screen. Steel tried to raise him again, but no one answered. And then the screen shut down, as all comm frequencies were jammed. Steel and his people tried all their backups and emergency procedures, and none of them worked. Steel sat in his command chair, surrounded by chaos and screaming voices. The psionic screen was out. The port's disrupter cannon, salvaged from a crashed starship, were powering up, but without a working comm system there was no way to aim them. Port techs were working furiously to link the tower sensors into the comm systems, but there was no way of knowing how long they would last either. Already some of the weaker systems were shutting down, unable to function in the unnatural field emanating from the orbiting starcruiser.

Steel called together a dozen runners, and sent them out into the city to organize the Watch and the militias, knowing even as he did so that they weren't going to be enough. Mistport had depended for too long on its psionic screen. Secure in its protection, the Watch had gone soft, and no one had taken the militias seriously in years. Steel grunted. The people of Mistport were still fighters. They had to be, just to survive. If the Empire forces thought they were just going to walk in and take over, they were in for a shock. And then Steel studied the remaining sensor screens, and the still growing count of the approaching pinnaces, and his blood ran cold. There were hundreds

of them. This was no task force, it was a full-sized army.
The invasion of Mistworld had begun.

High above, floating in its huge tank, Legion stretched
out its invisible hands and stirred its sticky fingers in
the minds of the espers down below. Legion was the
product of thousands of esper brains crossed with barely
understood tech systems derived from alien technology,
and even its designers hadn't fully understood what
they were creating. Legion was far greater than the sum
of its parts, and greater by far than the fools that had
brought it into being. For the moment it followed orders,
because it was having so much fun, but tomorrow was
another day. It stretched out its power and espers died,
their merely human brains unable to withstand the pressure. Others retreated deep inside themselves, shutting
down their minds in self-protection. Some brave souls
tried to probe Legion, and went crazy trying to understand
its nature. Legion laughed, and spread its power in a
great rolling wave that covered all of Mistport in one
long unending scream of triumph. Even the non-espers
could hear it, and cringed away from the awful, inhuman
sound.

Steel turned away from the chaos that raged inside his
control tower, an icy hand clutching at his stomach while
sweat rolled down his face. He'd lived in fear of this
moment all his life, but had never really believed it would
happen. Like everyone else, he'd grown complacent.
Even when Typhoid Mary had been running amok in the
streets and alleyways of Mistport, he'd still been able to
snatch victory from the jaws of defeat. With a little help
from his friends. But now his defenses were down, the
psionic shield had failed, and soon the Empire forces
would be howling at the gate, eager for blood and destruction. Steel swallowed hard, pulled himself together as best
he could, and turned to his comm officer, sitting hunched
over the mostly useless systems.

"All right, people, pay attention. With our comm systems out, this tower is now useless, except as a bloody
obvious target for the incoming troops. So our first duty is
to get the hell out of here. We're no use to anybody dead.
Crash all the systems that are still working before you go.
We don't want to leave anything that might be used

against us. Somewhere here there should be worst-scenario files, telling you all what to do and where to go. Security should know. So, fight well, die hard, and take as many of the bastards with you as you can. Failing that, run like fury. Pep speech over; I'm out of here. And the good God protect us all."

He turned away and began packing a few useful things into a holdall. It occurred to him that he might never see this room again. Never give orders as Port Director again. Whatever happened next, a chapter in his life was closing, and he didn't know whether to feel sad or relieved. Being Director had been a hard and thankless task, even with his little schemes on the side to rake in money. But he'd taken his job seriously, and protected the city, his city, as best as he was able. Until now. And all he could do now was cut and run, abandoning his home to whoever could take and hold it. He sighed, and fastened the bulging holdall. They really should have got around to installing that self-destruct system, but they'd always put it off, thinking there was plenty of time.

Around him, raised voices were blending into an angry, deafening din, with just a trace of panic in it. Steel ignored it all and made his way out of the control tower, never once looking back. He had other duties now. As a member of the ruling city Council, he had to get together with the others and start organizing the city's defenses. What was left of them. Out in the street it was chaos, with people running and pushing every way at once. Steel used his great bulk to plow a way through the crowds. He felt better now he was doing something, now he had an objective. If he could just reach the Blackthorn Inn, he might yet be able to show the invading forces some unexpected and really nasty surprises.

It took him the best part of an hour to get there, fighting the surging crowds all the way. The word had got out, inevitable in a city like Mistport, and there was pandemonium in the streets. People were shouting and running, brandishing weapons that ranged from energy guns to generations-old blades, handed down through families for just such a day as this. Some made bold speeches of defiance, while others prophesied doom, and would-be warriors and refugees tried blindly to push each other out

of the way. Street barricades were already going up here
and there, causing unfortunate bottlenecks of desperate
people. Pickpockets and cutpurses were having the time
of their lives. This was Mistport, after all, and neither
invasion nor sudden death could be allowed to get in the
way of turning a quick profit. Steel kept his head down
and bulled his way through.

When he finally got to the Blackthorn Inn, in the heart
of Thieves Quarter, the place was already packed to overflowing, with lights blazing from every window. It
couldn't have looked more like a target if it had tried.
Most of the Council had beaten him there, but were too
busy shouting and screaming at each other to acknowledge his arrival. *Typical,* thought Steel, and left them to
get on with it. He pushed his way wearily to the long
wooden bar. He felt in need of a stiff drink, and to hell
with his ulcers. Cyder, the tavern owner, was helping to
dispense drinks at the bar, alongside a sepulchral bar-
tender, and Steel ordered several large brandies from her,
in the same glass, on the grounds that it might be some
time before he could slip away to order more. Cyder
poured the brandies into a large silver tankard with only
the slightest of winces, and smiled broadly at Steel.

"If I'd known the emergency Council was going to be
this good for business, I'd have volunteered long ago."

"Now that is typical of you, Cyder," said Steel. "The
whole city is about to get trashed, and us with it, and all
you're worried about is your profit margin."

Cyder batted her eyes at him. "A girl has to look out for
herself."

"Please don't do that," said Steel. "On you, it looks
unnatural."

Cyder shrugged. "Whoever's in charge of Mistport,
people will still want to drink. And soldiers' money is as
good as anyone else's."

"Assuming they don't burn the Blackthorn to the
ground for harboring the emergency Council," said Steel,
taking a large gulp from his glass.

"Damn," said Cyder. "I hadn't thought of that. Why did
you choose my place anyway?"

"Because it's central. Because no one will be looking
for the Council in a dive like this. And because you know

practically everyone in this city. A perfect combination. I'd order some more barrels brought up from the cellar, if I were you. People are going to be rushing in and out of here like their pants were on fire, once the Council gets its act together, and they're probably all going to want large drinks. Imminent danger and the chance of sudden death will do that to you. I don't suppose there's any sign of Donald Royal yet?"

"Not so far. But he's an old man, and it's a long way to come for him. Even if he can get through the madness in the streets."

"Damn. He's the only other person on the Council I can trust to do the right thing. I'll bet you there are some damn fools already talking about negotiating a surrender with honor."

"Look on the bright side," said Cyder. "At least this time we don't have to worry about Typhoid Mary running loose."

"No," said Investigator Topaz coldly. "You don't."

Steel and Cyder both looked around sharply as Topaz and Mary made their way through the crowd to join them at the bar. People moved quickly to get out of the way of the two women. Even the danger of an invasion hadn't blinded them to common courtesy and the need for self-preservation. Steel gave them his best professional, everything's-under-control smile, but neither of them looked in the least impressed, so he dropped it. Cyder glared at Mary, one hand rising unconsciously to the thin scars on her face, legacy of their last meeting, when Mary had nearly killed Cyder with a single deadly song. Cyder never had been one to forgive or forget.

Steel decided he'd better get the ball rolling before things started getting seriously out of hand. "About time you got here, Investigator. I'm putting you in charge of the city Watch, as from this moment. You know more about how the Empire fights, and how best to face them, than anyone else. Give whatever orders you feel necessary, requisition anything you need, and we'll argue about it later. I want every single warm body in the Watch out on the streets ten minutes ago, and no excuses, dammit! Spank a few if you have to.

"Your first objective is to clear the streets of all nonessential traffic. With the comm systems down, we're going to have to rely on runners, and I don't want them having to fight their way through panicking crowds. So, clear the streets. Break a few heads if you have to. Next, track down everyone who's got some kind of weapon and send them out to guard the boundary walls. Tell them to hold as long as they can, and then fall back street by street. Hopefully by then I'll have thought of something else to do with them."

"Shouldn't you clear this first with the rest of the Council?" said Mary.

"That bunch? I've seen better-organized anarchists' meetings. They'll back me up, once they've calmed down a little. Why are you still standing here?"

"Anything else?" said Topaz, entirely unmoved by Steel's glare.

"Well, if you can work a miracle, this would be a really good time to prove it," said Steel. "And, Topaz, whatever happens you are not to let Mary out of your sight for any reason. She's too powerful to be allowed to operate as a loose cannon."

"I understand," said Mary. "All I want is to help, Director."

Steel looked at her narrowly. "Half my espers can hardly think with this new Empire device jamming their powers. How come you're holding out so well?"

"My mind is still my own, Director. I was and am a very powerful Siren. The Council's deprogramming didn't take that away from me."

"Not for want of trying," said Steel. "All right, stick with Topaz, and if you have to use your voice, make sure you're pointing it in the right direction. Now get out of here, the pair of you. I've got a city to defend."

Only a few hours after Legion was forced to drop its disguise, the first Empire troops came flying out of the icy wastes beyond the city, hundreds of them crammed onto armored gravity sleds and barges. They came in waves, more and more of them, soaring over the boundary walls as though they weren't even there. A few disrupter bolts lanced upward, only to be harmlessly deflected by glowing force fields. An Imperial attack usually centered around heavily armored battle wagons and war machines, but the cold and the snow and the ice of Mistworld slowed them down too much, and most were too large anyway to maneuver in Mistport's narrow streets, so the softening up of the city fell to the Imperial air divisions. They came howling out of the darkening skies like so many rabid bats, sleek and deadly, disrupter bolts stabbing down again and again, lighting the streets bright as day as the energy beams exploded buildings of stone and wood and set the ruins ablaze. People ran screaming in the streets as the barges sailed serenely overhead, carrying death and destruction and the coming of Empire rule.

The gravity sleds chased people down the streets, whipping in and out between the narrow buildings, harrying and terrorizing their prey until they grew tired of their sport, and cut the runners down with flashing energy bolts. The air divisions pressed on, leaving fire and devastation behind them, until suddenly espers came flying up out of the streets to face them.

The esper union had pulled its strongest minds together and pushed aside Legion's block for the moment. They knew it wouldn't last, but for now they struggled with Legion and held it back, so that a hundred brave souls could fly on wings of esp up to meet the invaders on their own high ground. The espers whipped around the slower-moving Imperial craft, darting in and out too fast to be tracked. Some had energy guns, some had crossbows, some had nothing but naked steel and their own indomitable courage. Force shields crackled and failed around the gravity barges as down in the streets espers strained to hex their tech and drain their power batteries. Imperial troops screamed and fell from their craft as the fast-flying espers took their toll, sniping at unguarded targets, but the air force was just too big and unstoppable, and its targeting computers soon came on line, taking out the flying defenders one by one, for all their speed and courage. They fell out of the dark sky like burning birds, and the air force pressed on.

More espers came soaring up out of the streets to take the place of those who fell. With their city endangered, their way of life threatened, and their backs almost literally to the wall, many in Mistport found courage and honor where they would have sworn there was none, and went to the fight with calm eyes and grim determination. They lunged and soared, using familiar updrafts and hiding places to confound the targeting computers, stinging their targets like deadly insects.

Some deliberately threw themselves into the gravity barges' engine bays, suicide attacks that were only occasionally successful. When a barge did fall from the sky, it crashed into fragile stone-and-timber buildings, crushing them with its immense weight. Exploding barges destroyed whole streets and spread fire across whole blocks. And for each barge that fell, there were always more to take its place, moving remorselessly forward about the city they had come to take.

They moved slowly inward from every side, creating paths of death and destruction, heading for the center of the city, block by block, street by street. They kept to their previously arranged paths, ignoring the rest of the city. The Empire had come to conquer and control Mistport, not destroy it.

There were fires burning all across the city now, flames leaping high into the night sky. Screams came drifting up from the streets below. Hell had come to Mistport, and Toby Shreck and his cameraman Flynn were right there in the thick of it, keeping up a live broadcast. Flynn's camera darted and soared above the inferno of the burning streets and blazing buildings, getting it all, while Toby kept up a breathless running commentary. This far above the devastation, it was easy to feel detached and godlike, but Toby did his best now and again to remind his audience that real people were burning and dying in the fires and ruins below. Not that most of them would care. That just added to the excitement for the home audience.

Toby clung to the railings at the edge of the gravity barge as the boiling heat of a sudden updraft rocked the barge from side to side. Flynn was so taken with what he was seeing through his camera that he quite forget to hold the railing, and almost toppled over the side before Toby grabbed him and pulled him back. The cameraman didn't even nod his thanks. He was far away with his darting camera, swooping and soaring over the rising flames like an impartial angel recording the birth of Hell.

"Getting good footage?" asked Toby loudly in Flynn's ear.

"If only you could see what I'm seeing," said Flynn. "People have seen war footage before, but never this close, never this clearly. I can zoom in on individual buildings, individual people, or pull back to a panorama of the whole damned city. It's beautiful, Toby. The scarlet and gold against the black of night. The burning buildings, and the flames . . . it has a majesty and a grandeur that's beyond pity or compassion. It doesn't need excuses; it just is. A city is dying one inch at a time, and I'm getting it all. The colors are amazing—bright and primitive and striking. And the roar of the explosions is like a giant walking across the city, one great step at a time, as the ground shakes beneath his tread. It's . . . exhilarating."

"Smell the smoke," said Toby. "That's burning flesh amongst the wood and grime. Listen to the screams. Don't get carried away, Flynn. This isn't an invasion; this is a slaughter."

He broke off as a flying esper came howling out of the darkness toward him. The esper was armed with an automatic crossbow, jury-rigged from forbidden tech, and his deadly bolts stitched across the armed men at the railings as they tried in vain to draw a bead on him. They fell back from the railing, crying out as they clutched at transfixing arrows. Toby grabbed Flynn and threw them both to the deck. A nearby disrupter cannon turned to bear on the next building, and the esper was suddenly hovering there before it. He thrust his arm down the barrel, blocking it. Toby looked up, and their eyes met. The esper grinned savagely, scared shitless and not giving a damn, and then the bomb in his hand went off, blowing the cannon apart. The esper was thrown backwards, blood fountaining from the shoulder where his right arm had been. He fell toward the street far below, laughing breathlessly. Toby watched him fall until he disappeared back into the smoke and the flames.

Lieutenant Ffolkes came staggering down the deck toward Toby and Flynn, stepping gingerly over the injured and the dying. He had a gun in his hand, and there was blood spattered across one sleeve of his uniform. It didn't appear to be his. He looked over the railings, and nodded calmly at the burning city as though quietly satisfied.

"You're really missing the best of it from down here," he said casually. "I trust you're getting good coverage?"

"Oh yes," said Toby, climbing carefully to his feet. "Right up close and personal, some times."

Ffolkes looked at him. "The Empress might have ordered it, Shreck, but I'm still in charge. Follow your instructions. Nothing . . . controversial, or I'll shut you down."

"Got it," said Toby. "Nothing controversial. Just blood and death and burning buildings."

"Glad to hear it," said Ffolkes. "Carry on."

And he strode away to upset somebody else. Toby made a rude gesture at the man's departing back, realized that Flynn was still lying on the deck, and hauled him to his feet. The cameraman was still lost in what his camera was showing him through his comm implant. Toby could have patched it to the frequency through his own comm link, but didn't. It was all he could do to cope with what he was already seeing.

In his room on the top floor of the Blackthorn Inn, as yet untouched by the invasion, Owen Deathstalker crawled across the floor on his hands and knees, shivering and shaking. His head hung down, hot and heavy, and sweat dripped from his contorted face. Pain blazed in all his muscles, sharp and piercing, and shuddered in his gut. He was blazing hot, his thoughts slow and muddy as the pain inside him tore him apart. He lurched on, inch by inch, as though trying to run away from the agonies that stretched his mouth in a soundless grimace. He didn't scream. He wouldn't let himself. He was a Deathstalker. He couldn't let anyone see him like this. His shoulder crashed into the leg of a table, and he knocked the obstacle away with one sweep of his arm. He tried again to vomit, but he'd already emptied his stomach. He'd crawled through most of it.

The trembling had started as he made his way up the narrow stairs behind the bar. At first he'd put it down to reaction at his nearly having died, or the strain of fighting off so many attackers at once. It had been a hard day, after all. But it got worse. His head swam and his sight became blurred. His hands shook violently, and his legs became increasingly unsteady, until he was lurching along like a drunk. Somehow he made it to the top floor, and pressed his shoulder against the wall as he went, to keep him upright. His room seemed a long way away, but he got there, and even managed to shut the door behind him before he collapsed and began to puke up his guts.

His head crashed into a new obstacle. He hardly felt it, and it took him a while to realize that he'd reached the far wall, and there was nowhere left to go. He got himself turned around, grunting at the horrid pain, and put his back to the wall, sitting more or less upright. The pain was worse if anything, and he felt like he was burning alive. The room was a blur, and he could feel helpless tears trickling down his cheeks.

"Dear God, what's happening to me," he said, and was shocked at how weak he sounded.

"Side effects from your constant boosting," said Ozymandius. "I did warn you. Whatever the Madness Maze did to you, you're still human. You've been boosting too often and for too long, and it's finally caught up with you. The candle that burns twice as brightly burns half as long, remember? You've been relying on the Maze's changes to repair the damage you've been doing to yourself, but it seems you still have limits. Human limits. Your body's been burning itself up, and you've nothing left to put out the flames."

"There must be something I can do . . ." said Owen, forcing the words out through chattering teeth. He was hot and cold by turns now.

"I'm afraid your options are rather limited, Owen. You could boost again, but it would only make things worse in the long run. A regeneration machine might be able to repair the damage, but I don't know of any in Mistport. Or you could throw yourself on the mercies of what passes for medicine on this planet, but I wouldn't recommend it."

"Dammit, Oz . . . help me!"

"I'm sorry, Owen. You did this to yourself. There's nothing I can do."

"Oz . . . am I going to die?"

"I don't know, Owen. The odds are against you."

"Oz . . ."

"Hush, Owen. It's all right. I'm here."

There was a polite knock at his door. Owen gritted his teeth against the pain, and forced out a single word. "Yes?"

There was a pause, and then a voice said uncertainly, "Lord Deathstalker, the city Council requests that you join them downstairs. Your advice and support are needed most urgently."

Owen swallowed hard, fighting to control his mouth. His lips were numb and his tongue was swollen. He had to answer the messenger, or the man would come in to see what was wrong. And he couldn't afford to be seen like this. If he lived, no one would ever have faith in him again. They'd treat him like an invalid, and hustle him off somewhere safe. He was damned if he'd live like a cripple. And if he was going to die, he preferred to do it in private. He realized that the messenger was still waiting for a reply.

"I'll be down soon," he said, as loudly and clearly as he could.

There was another pause, then the voice said, very respectfully, "Lord Deathstalker, the invasion of Mistport has begun. You must have heard the explosions. I'm supposed to escort you . . ."

"I said I'll be down soon!" Owen shouted, not caring how his voice sounded.

He could hear the messenger shuffling uncertainly outside his door, but finally the man turned and walked away. Owen grinned humorlessly. Thick ropes of saliva hung from his stretched mouth. He'd thought the Maze had made him superhuman, carried him beyond merely human limits. It appeared he'd been wrong. He was only human after all, and he would prove it the way everybody did, by dying from it. He tried to sit up a little straighter and couldn't. His head grew heavier and heavier, bowing forward until his chin rested on his chest. He could hear his breathing now. It sounded loud and harsh and very labored.

The pain was beginning to fade. Even a little earlier, he might have found hope in that, but now he knew what it meant. He was dying, and his body was shutting down, bit by bit. He wished the others could have been with him. They might have linked with him, helped him, or just . . . kept him company. But as always, there was only him. And a voice in his head he didn't believe in. He supposed dimly that he ought to pray, but he'd never been the praying kind. So many things left undone. So many things he'd meant to do and say, because he'd thought there'd be time later . . . He never even told Hazel that he loved her.

The door swung open with a crash, and Hazel d'Ark stood framed in the doorway. She stared in shock at Owen for a moment, then hurried forward to kneel beside him. She lifted his hand, grunted at the clammy coolness, and took his pulse with practiced efficiency. She pressed her other hand on his forehead, winced at the heat there, and wiped the sweat off her hand on her leggings. She checked his pulse against her watch, and then set about undoing Owen's collar so he could breathe more easily.

"Deathstalker . . . can you hear me? Owen! Do you know what's wrong with you?"

"Too much boosting," he said, or thought he said. It was hard to tell anymore. He wasn't even sure she was really there. Maybe he only wanted her to be there. And then his head rocked as she slapped him sharply across the face.

"Stay with me, Owen! Did you say boosting?"

"Side effects," he said hoarsely. "Tearing me apart. Burning me up. The Maze can't help me anymore."

"Shit," she said softly. "Yes, I remember you warning me about the dangers of the boost. An addiction that can kill you. The curse and the temptation of the Deathstalkers. Damn. Stay put, Owen. Hang on while I get you a doctor."

"No! Doctors can't help. Hazel, something I wanted to tell you . . ."

"It's all right, Owen; I understand. I know what you're going through. I've been through it myself. You're not dying. It's called withdrawal. I'll stay with you. I remember what it was like, going through withdrawal from Blood. You won't die. You'll just wish you could."

She sat down beside Owen, wrapped her arms around him, and rocked him like a child. Her arms were strong

and steady. A sense of peace and quiet strength flowed
out of her and into him. His shivers and muscle spasms
gradually slowed and stopped. The pain went out of him
like water draining into a bottomless well. The fever
ebbed away, and he began to breathe more easily again.
And still the strength flowed out of her and into him.
They were linked again, finally. Their minds remained
separate, Hazel maintaining a firm barrier between their
thoughts, but physically they became more and more in
sync, until all the aftereffects of the boostings had burned
away, his pain soothed and healed, and Owen was himself
again. They sat together for a while, Hazel still holding
Owen in her arms.

"Well," Owen said finally. "Was it good for you, too?"

Hazel laughed and pushed him away. "You're back to
normal, stud. Now get on your feet. They're screaming
for you downstairs."

They stood up and smiled at each other. Neither of
them knew quite what to say next. "Thanks," said Owen.
"You saved me. I could have died in here, but you
brought me back. I didn't know you could do that."

"Lots of things you don't know about me, Deathstalker."

"That's true. Where's Silver?"

"Out in the streets somewhere. Fighting for his city. I'd
never have pegged him for a hero, but it just goes to show
how you can be wrong about people."

"Well," said Owen. "None of us are perfect."

It was as close to an apology and a reconciliation as
they were going to get, and they both knew it, so they
moved on to other things.

"You know," said Hazel, as they headed for the door,
"this could happen again, if you use the boost too much."

Owen shrugged. "I've been doing what's needed. The
boost makes it possible for me to do what I have to."

"I know how that feels," said Hazel. "Blood does the
same thing for me."

They stepped out into the hallway and looked at each
other. Finally Owen smiled slightly. "Guess it takes one
addict to recognize another. Now let's go down and play
the hero one more time, and pray the poor bastards
depending on us never find out about our feet of clay.

You're a good friend, Hazel. I don't know what I'd do without you."

"Don't push it, aristo," said Hazel d'Ark, smiling despite herself. And they went down the stairs together, leaning on each other just a little.

Down in the bar they found the whole room cleared of customers, not to mention furniture. The chairs had all been pushed up against the walls, so that the city Councillors could crowd round a large circular table in the middle of the room. They were studying a map of the city and arguing loudly, with much gesturing of the hands. People were darting in and out the front door all the time, bringing in computer terminals, monitor screens and other useful equipment from Tech Quarter. Runners came and went with up-to-date information, pausing only briefly before rushing out into the night again. With the comm systems down, they had to be the Council's eyes and ears in the city. Luckily, people in Mistport were used to improvising.

The proprietor of the Blackthorn Inn watched the chaos from behind the safety of the long wooden bar at the end of the room. Cyder had a quick smile that didn't always reach her cold blue eyes, and thin scars crossed one side of her face like worry lines. She used to be the hardest-working and hardest-hearted fence in all Mistport, but was now a highly respectable citizen, owner of a popular and thriving tavern, and according to her old friend Silver, just possibly in line for Council membership. *Only in Mistport*, Owen had said. *Don't you believe it*, said Hazel.

Beside Cyder, nursing a mulled ale, stood the young man called Cat—Cyder's sidekick, lover, and occasional fall guy. Cyder wasn't known for being sentimental. Cat had pale youthful features, dominated by dark watchful eyes and pockmarks that tattooed both cheeks. He wore a white thermal outfit that enabled him to hide in the snow and the mists with equal dexterity. Tall and slender, Cat was a deaf mute, and quite possibly the best burglar in the city. He was supposedly retired, now that Cyder had the means to keep him, but roof runners of his quality were always in demand, and he liked to keep busy.

Owen and Hazel moved over to the bar, and Cyder scowled at them both. "I don't know why I let you in here. Every time you barge into my life, everything goes to hell in a handcart and my tavern gets trashed. I'd take out insurance against you, if I could find anyone dumb enough to underwrite the policy. Just look what's happening now! I'm a spectator in my own tavern! I was making good money till the Council threw my customers out, and they're too busy to drink much themselves. Who's going to pay for my loss of custom?"

"Relax," said Owen. "I have some associates in the city who'll be only too pleased to make good your losses. Well, actually they won't be too pleased at all, but they'll still do it. Because they know I'll cut them off at the knees if they don't. Possibly quite literally."

"So, what's happening here?" said Hazel, after she and Cyder had embraced briefly across the bar and kissed the air near each other's cheeks.

"We happy few are organizing the resistance," said Cyder, pouring herself a very large drink. "Until the Empire finds us. That should take a while. Officially, only the Council members themselves were supposed to know about this. But they're having to call in more and more people to help them, and someone will talk eventually. Someone always does. In the meantime, the Council is doing its best to coordinate resistance, and minimize the damage and loss of life."

Steel finally noticed Owen and Hazel's arrival, and beckoned for them to join him. He introduced them to the other Councillors, who looked decidedly unimpressed, so Owen decided not to be impressed by them either. It wasn't difficult. Donald Royal was there, looking frail but determined, accompanied by his partner Madelaine Skye and Young Jack Random. Quentin McVey represented the Guilds. He dressed like a color-blind peacock with absolutely no taste, and had the most false-looking false teeth Owen had ever seen. Albert Magnus represented the Merchants. He dressed in dusty grey, a perfect match for his face, and generally looked like he'd died and then been dug up again quite recently. Lois Barron spoke for Thieves Quarter, a short and compact woman who looked tough enough to chew up a tin can and split nails. She had a bone-crushing handshake, too. Owen did his best not to wince. Finally, Iain Castle represented Tech Quarter. He was a dwarf with a crooked shoulder, and looked like he had absolutely no sense of humor about it.

The Council took it in turns to give Owen funny looks, and after catching sight of himself in the mirror behind the bar, Owen could understand why. He was covered in dried blood and puke, and his clothes looked as though someone had died in them. His face was deathly pale, and his eyes were so deep-set it was a wonder he could see out of them. All in all, Owen decided he looked rather like some homicidal holy man who'd finally discovered the real meaning of life, and was thoroughly pissed off about it. Hazel looked like a barroom brawler, but then, she always did.

Quentin McVey was the first to speak. He screwed a monocle into his left eye and looked Owen up and down. "Have this boy washed and sent to my room."

"Forget it," Owen said amiably. "You couldn't afford me."

"You always did have a thing for rough trade, Quentin," said Lois Barron. "But this is slumming, even for you. Dear God, this disreputable-looking pair are supposed to be our contacts with the Golgotha underground? They're a disgrace. If they turned up at my front door, I'd set the dogs on them."

"Right," said Magnus. "Get them out of here. We've got work to do. If Golgotha wants to be taken seriously here, they'll have to send us better than this."

"Kick them out," said Iain Castle, the dwarf. "We don't have time for this."

Owen and Hazel reached out mentally to each other, and linked. Power shot back and forth between them, building and building. Their presence was suddenly overwhelming, filling the room from wall to wall, drawing all eyes to them. They were wild and powerful, so wildly potent as to seem almost inhuman, or more than human. Their power hammered on the air like a giant heartbeat, vast and overpowering. The Councillors would have liked to run, or kneel, but they were held where they were, like mice before a snake. New energy flooded through Owen and Hazel, washing away all weaknesses and impurities. Hazel's Blood use had kept them from linking for so long that they had forgotten how powerful they were when joined.

"Cut it out," said Cyder, forcing out the words despite the awe that pressed her back against the far wall. "We're impressed, honest. Now shut it down, before the Empire espers pick up on it."

Owen and Hazel reigned back on their link, internalizing their power, and suddenly they were just a man and a woman again. Owen could hardly believe that just a few minutes ago he'd thought he was close to death. Now, with Hazel at his side, he felt he could take on an army. It seemed there was still a lot about what the Maze had done to them that they didn't understand.

"Relax," Hazel said calmly to the Council. "I don't think any esper could pick us up. Whatever it is that powers us, I don't think it's esp."

The Council members looked at each other, and if anything looked even more upset than before, and Owen suddenly realized that for the moment they were just as frightened of him and Hazel as they were of the invaders. At least the Empire was a known threat. He stepped forward, hands raised reassuringly, and tried not to notice when they all flinched and drew back from him.

"Take it easy, people. We're here to help. This is your city; you tell us how best we can help you defend it."

Donald Royal stepped suddenly forward to stare into Owen's face. His gaze was firm and steady. "Yes, you're a Deathstalker, all right. I can see it in your eyes. Damn, it's good to have a Deathstalker with us again. Your Family always did have a talent for stirring things up. I knew your father and your grandfather, boy. Good men, both of them, in their different ways. When all this is over, I'll tell you some stories about them that you probably won't find in your Family records. It's good to see you here, maintaining your Clan's traditions."

"Leave the old-times shit for later," said Castle. "What kind of help are you offering us, Deathstalker? Going to walk out into the streets and awe the Empire troops to death, are you? You might have esp or juju coming out your ears, but that won't stop an invading army. Surely

Golgotha didn't just send us the pair of you and their best wishes? We need guns, explosives, equipment."

"We brought a ship full of projectile weapons and crates of ammunition," said Owen calmly. "They should be being distributed even as we speak. That's it."

"Projectile weapons?" said Magnus. "What use are bloody antiques against gravity barges with disrupter cannon?"

"You'd be surprised," said Hazel. "Besides, you've got me and Owen. We're an army in our own right."

"Oh wonderful," said Lois Barron. "An ex-aristo and an ex-pirate with overblown esp and delusions of grandeur. Like we haven't got enough of those already. Why don't we all just shoot ourselves now, and get it over with?"

"If you don't stop whining, I'll shoot you myself," snapped Royal. "These two are different. You felt their power."

"Oh, we're different, all right," said Owen.

"That's for sure," said Hazel. "And there's always Jenny Psycho. Wherever she is."

"I don't think we need to tell the Council about her yet," said Owen. "They'd only worry."

"And if you find those two disturbing, there's always me," said Young Jack Random.

Everyone turned to look at him. He'd been quiet for so long that everyone had forgotten he was there. It quickly became clear that the Council found his tall muscular frame and handsome face much more satisfying than Hazel and Owen.

"And who the hell are you?" said Castle, climbing onto a stool to get a better look over people's heads.

"I know the face," said McVey. "I'm sure I know the face."

Donald Royal smiled. "Allow me to present my good old friend, the one and only Jack Random."

The Council gaped soundlessly for a moment, then left the table en masse to crowd around Random, pumping his hand and slapping him on the back, and saying how delighted they were that he'd come to save them in their hour of need. Random smiled and nodded modestly, looking every inch a hero and a legend born. Owen looked at Hazel.

"I may puke."

"You already did. Try not to get it all over me this time."

Eventually the Councillors got tired of telling Random what a savior he was to them, and having him modestly nod and agree, and they brought him over to the table to show him the great map of Mistport. Steel pulled Random in beside him to explain things, and Owen and Hazel pushed in on the other side, determined to not be left out of anything. Steel ignored them, concentrating on Random.

"Right, Jack, this map covers all four Quarters of the city, from boundary to boundary. The city's perimeter is defended by high stone walls, but they won't last long. They were only ever intended to keep out marauding local wildlife. A war machine will walk right through them. And of course they don't do a thing to stop gravity barges and sleds. To the north we have Merchants and Guilds Quarters, and Thieves and Tech in the south. The River Autumn runs through all of them except Tech. With our communications out, and most of the streets blocked with people and barricades, we've been using the barges on the Autumn to transfer messages and people. One of our few Emergency plans that is worth anything. Most of the rest depended on espers, and they're not part of the agenda anymore. Whatever it is the Empire's doing, it's scrambled the minds of practically anyone with even a touch of esp in them. A few of the stronger talents are holding out, but it's anyone's guess as to how long. What's left of the esper union is concentrating on combating the air invasion, but all they're doing is buying us some time. We've got runners bringing in information all the time, but by the time we get to hear about anything, it's already over. I'd kill for just one working comm system, but the runners are all we've got . . ."

"Not anymore," said a new voice from the tavern doorway. Everyone looked around, and there was Jenny Psycho, looking very pleased with herself, along with Chance and a dozen esper children from the Abraxus Information Center. The children were awake and more or less steady on their feet, but their eyes were wild and unsettling. A general shudder went through most of the people at the table, as they studied the insane children in their ill-fitting, grubby dressing gowns.

"All right," said Magnus, in his cold grey voice. "Who the hell are you, woman, and why have you brought these . . . people here?"

"I'm Jenny Psycho, last manifestation of the Mater Mundi. So watch your mouth or I'll turn you into a small hopping thing. These children are possibly the only espers left in Mistport who aren't bothered by the new Empire weapon. Possibly because they're so far out of it even under normal conditions. The rest of the children are taking up positions all over the city. They're a bit strange to work with, but once you get the hang of it you should have a working communications system again. And I am here to protect you in case the Empire works out where you are. With the Mater Mundi's power flowing through me, I'm more than a match for anything the Empire can throw at you. Now, don't you all feel so much safer?"

"You know, I'd probably feel a lot happier about all this if it wasn't coming from a woman called Jenny Psycho," said Donald Royal.

"Well done, Jenny," said Random. "I knew you'd come through for us. Now let's get these children settled, before anything else. The poor lambs look like they've come a long, hard way."

People bustled around getting the children hot drinks and blankets to lie on, while Chance hovered protectively over them, getting in the way. Jenny Psycho busied herself ordering some strange but potent cocktail at the bar. She seemed to feel that having got the children safely here, they were no longer her responsibility. As always, Jenny had her own sense of priorities, with herself at the top of the list. The children were barely settled when they all suddenly stiffened on their makeshift beds, their eyes rolled up in their heads.

"Do they often do that?" asked Lois Barron.

"Shut up," said Chance. "They're seeing something."

"They're here," said one of the children, in a calm, dreamy voice. "The wall has gone down at the southwest boundary. Imperial foot troops are streaming through. The wolves are in the fold."

"Shit!" said Steel. "I thought we had more time. Chance, how reliable are these charges of yours?"

"When it comes to seeing the present, one hundred percent. As to the future . . ."

"I know, I know." Steel thought furiously. "Get the runners on their feet again. I don't care how tired they are. I need them to gather reinforcements for whatever's left of the wall."

"No need to bother the runners," said Random. "Let them rest. They're exhausted. Give me some men, and I'll lead a force down to the boundary to stop the invaders."

And as quickly as that the meeting broke up into shouted plans and orders. Albert Magnus volunteered to take Random to the nearest groups of militia and city Watch, and lead them to the southwest boundary. Random clapped him on the shoulder and called him a Good Man, and the grey man almost blushed. They hurried out the door, and Owen and Hazel hurried after them. Jenny Psycho grudgingly worked with Chance to stabilize the children, and interpret what they were seeing. She seemed to feel this was somewhat beneath her, but did it anyway to show she was a good sport.

Cyder led Cat off into a quiet corner, wrote out several messages, then sent him off to deliver them. If Empire troops were already in the city, she wanted to be sure her various properties were being well protected. Just because there was a war on, there was no need to lose track of one's priorities. Cat frowned, and then shrugged. He could never say no where Cyder was concerned. And as one of the finest burglars and roof runners in Mistport, the chances of his being detected and stopped were less than most people's. Mistport's sea of connected roofs and gables were familiar territory to him. So he smiled reassuringly at Cyder, kissed her good-bye, then again for luck, and again because he enjoyed it, and disappeared out the nearest window, up the wall, and onto the roofs, his white thermal suit blending seamlessly into the snow and fog. He had no way of knowing he would never return to the Blackthorn Inn again.

High above the world, floating in its massive tank, Legion grew stronger and flexed its mental muscles. Its powers stretched across the city of Mistport, dark and potent, messing with men's minds. Men and women fell to the ground, frothing at the mouth, driven into madness to escape the awful presence that peered out at them from within their own minds. Espers went catatonic, or mute, or writhed helplessly on their beds as their power discharged on the air around them, out of their control. Legion was abroad in the night, walking up and down in human minds and spreading horror. It was vast and powerful, and nothing could stand against it. It was Legion, and it was many in one.

John Silver fought with the others at the break in the southwest boundary wall, under Legion's continuing scream. He'd fought in so many campaigns in his previous life as a pirate, against odds of all kinds, but never anything like this. There seemed no end to the Imperial troopers as they came streaming through the huge gaps in the wall opened up by the Empire war wagons. Time had blurred into a rush of blood and pain and clashing steel, and though he stood his ground amidst the rubble of the wall and would not yield, he knew he didn't stand a chance.

After the Hob hounds' invasion of the city during the Typhoid Mary disaster, the city Council had given orders for the twenty-foot stone walls to be raised to thirty feet. Thirty feet of solid stone, four feet thick. It hadn't slowed the Empire forces down for a moment. The huge battle wagons, fifty feet tall and twenty wide, had smashed through the wall as though it was made of paper. Their toughened steel hulls could withstand anything short of a disrupter, and what few energy guns the defenders had weren't enough to stop them.

And so the war wagons crashed through the wall in a dozen places, and the Imperial troops came swarming in over the rubble, firing as they came. The city's defenders went to meet them with bare steel and grim determination, leaping over their fallen fellows to meet the invaders head-to-head, and there the invasion slowed and stopped, as fighting clogged the entrances. It was vicious fighting, with no quarter asked or given. There was no room in any of them for anything but hatred and murder, a blood madness fueled by the rebels' outrage, the troops' battle drugs, and the never-ending scream above.

The battle wagons were largely useless once they'd broached the boundary walls. They were too big and too clumsy to operate in the narrow streets and alleyways of Mistport, and they couldn't use their disrupter cannon on the city defenders for fear of taking out their own troops, too. So as always it came down to man against man, and the flash of cold steel. Men fell dead and dying on all sides, but though the tides of battle surged this way and that, somehow still the defenders held.

John Silver had taken a deep cut across his forehead somewhen early in the proceedings, and had to keep jerking his head to keep the blood out of his eyes. Typical Silver luck. All bad. He'd taken other wounds, and there was more blood on his clothes, but he tried not to think about that. It would only depress him. The buzz from his last shot of Blood had worn off long ago, and now all that kept him going was duty and adrenaline. His sword rose and fell, most often crashing uselessly back from parrying steel or force shield, and his sword arm ached mercilessly. There was no room in the crush of bodies for fancy swordplay or footwork. You stood toe-to-toe with your opponent and hammered it out, with victory going to the strongest or the quickest. And when one man fell, there was always another to take his place.

Silver would have liked to cut and run, but there was nowhere to run to. If Mistport fell and the Empire took over, they'd hang him anyway, on general principles. And besides, as so many times before, duty held him where courage would not. He owed a lot to Mistport, and Silver believed in paying his debts. His side surged suddenly forward a few feet, seizing some momentary advantage, and Silver had to watch his footing. There were bodies everywhere, underfoot. He recognized some of the faces, but couldn't let himself think about that. There was only the struggle, blade on blade, and the knowledge that they were bound to drag him down eventually.

And then suddenly reinforcements were there, slamming into battle beside him like the answer to a prayer. War cries from a dozen worlds and cultures filled the air as the new defenders forced the invading troops back, step by step. The Deathstalker was there, already covered in blood and looking like death on legs. Hazel d'Ark fought beside him, wielding her sword with devastating strength and speed. Albert Magnus from the city Council was there, too, right in the front of things—a dusty grey man with a sword in each hand, unstoppable as a force of nature. And leading the attack, Jack Random himself, the professional rebel. He was tall and imposing in silver battle armor, his face familiar from a hundred wanted posters, driving the invaders back by the sheer fury of his attack. His swordplay was swift and deadly, and no one could stand against him.

Silver laughed breathlessly and fought on, new strength in his arms. Maybe he wasn't going to die this day after all. He pulled a thin vial from his sleeve and swallowed the remaining dark liquid down in one draught. It was the last of his Blood, but the odds were the battle would be over by the time he needed another shot, one way or the other, so what the hell.

Owen Deathstalker took a position at the head of the battle and defied the Imperial troopers to get past him. He was boosting again, and felt stronger than ever now that he was linking with Hazel. Somehow he knew side effects wouldn't be a problem this time. Together, he and Hazel were far greater than the sum of their parts, more than merely human. He hacked and cut about him with unstoppable strength, slapping aside defensive parries with contemptuous ease. Men fell screaming to either side of him, and did not rise again. Droplets of blood flew from his blade as it scythed through the air, and Owen grinned like a wolf, the scent of blood heavy in his nostrils, every inch the warrior he'd never wanted to be.

Hazel d'Ark fought at his side, her sword flashing in short, brutal arcs, cutting through flesh and bone like a butcher's cleaver. Blood, none of it hers, splashed her clothes, soaking her sword arm to the elbow, and the screams of the wounded and the dying were music to her. She'd always had a soft spot for Mistport. She'd always liked to think that wherever she went and whatever she did, she could always go back to Mistworld, and they would take her in. It was the closest thing to a home she'd ever known. And now the Empire wanted to take that away from her, just like all the other things they'd taken, down the years. She was damned if she'd allow the Iron Bitch that final victory. Not as long as there was breath in her body and steel in her hand.

Her link with Owen was strong now. She could feel his presence at her side, strong and dependable as always. Another presence impinged on her mind, and a familiar smell was suddenly strong and thick in her nostrils. She glanced to her left, and there was John Silver, not far away, stamping and fencing like a man possessed, eyes wide and grinning like a madman. He was flying on Blood. She could see it in him, smell it on his panting breath, even at this distance. A part of her wanted Blood, too. Just a drop or two. It would make her feel so good, comfort her fears, help her forget the helplessness of the fight she was involved in. Hazel fought the need down, burying it deep. She didn't need Blood to do what had to be done here. Perhaps because her situation had now become so simple—fight or die, fight or lose everything she ever cared for. And perhaps because she was linking with Owen again, and in his presence and strength she found all the comfort she needed.

Disrupters on the battle wagons began to target rebel fighters on the outskirts of the struggling mob, blowing them apart in dark clouds of vaporized flesh and blood. Gravity barges drifted overhead in vast formations, surrounded by darting gravity sleds, hundreds of them, like a storm of dark metal leaves blowing into the city. No espers flew up to meet them as they pressed slowly on into the city, disrupter beams stabbing down to blow buildings apart. The air was filled with the roar of powerful engines and collapsing masonry, almost drowning out the shrieks and howls and war cries drifting up from the struggling forces below.

And above it all, the endless scream of the awful thing called Legion.

Albert Magnus, that grey and bitter man, fought hard and well with his two swords, and felt really alive for the first time in years.

He swung his two swords in wide, coordinated arcs, forcing his opponents back. But there were so many of them, and he couldn't look in all directions at once. A sword stabbed at him from an unexpected angle, and slammed between his ribs. He shouted in pain and disbelief, and blood sprayed from his mouth. He dropped his swords. Someone jerked the sword out of his side, and that hurt him again. And then there were more swords, and axes, hewing at him like a block of wood. He fell, hurting too badly now even to scream, and was trampled on, just another body on the ground. The fight moved back and forth over him till he died.

Jack Random seemed to be everywhere at once, his sword a silver blur, a dashing death-defying hero, laughing in the face of impossible odds. Just his presence was enough to spark greatness in the men and women around him, and they fought, using his name as a battle cry. He took impossible risks and always pulled them off, and no one could stand against him. He never seemed to tire, and he never took a wound, a giant of a man who spread terror through the Imperial ranks.

Owen, bloodied and exhausted, was quietly disgusted. It wasn't fair that anyone should be that fast, that amazing, and that good-looking—not to mention that lucky. The Empire forces hadn't even been able to draw the great man's blood yet. Owen felt he was doing pretty well, but he'd already taken a dozen lesser wounds. It was inevitable in a crush like this. The Maze's changes were already healing him, and the boost kept him from feeling much pain, but it was the principle of the thing.

Still, Jack Random was a legend, and legends were supposed to be above the petty problems of mere mortals. If that was who he really was. Owen was damned if he knew what he believed anymore. Certainly this man filled the legend better than the broken-down old man he'd found hiding in Mistport, claiming to be Jack Random; but Owen believed in people, not legends. He shrugged mentally as he cut down another Imperial trooper with a single savage stroke. Random wasn't the only real warrior here.

And whoever the handsome bastard really was, Young Jack Random was exactly what the city of Mistport needed right now. His name was a rallying cry, perhaps the only thing that could call all the disparate parts of Mistport together and make them fight as one. Owen decided he'd settle for that.

Hazel d'Ark could feel her mind reaching out in strange directions. Ever since the Maze had changed her, her mental abilities had been slowly but steadily increasing, and since coming to Mistport, the rate of change had been increasing. She could tell now where every attack was coming from, even before it was actually launched, and her sword was always there in the right place to block the attack. No one could sneak up on her, even in her blind spots, and she could sense the weaknesses in any opponent the moment she saw him or her. It was beyond experience or instinct; it was as though she'd always known such things, and only remembered them now when she needed them.

And more than that, as she saw the various possibilities opening up before her, other possible versions of herself began to appear around her. They blinked in and out of existence, sometimes only there long enough to deflect a sword or ward off an attack she couldn't have stopped on her own. But as she fought, other different Hazel d'Arks began to appear, to fight at her side. Some had subtle differences, like an extra scar, or different-colored hair. Others were different builds, or races. One had a golden Hadenman hand. One was a man. At least one didn't look to be entirely human. She smiled at some of them, and some smiled back. Together, she and her other selves pushed forward, forcing their way to the very front of the battle, and there they filled the main gap in the boundary wall and defied the Empire to get past them.

John Silver saw the Hazel d'Arks fighting side by side, and thought he must have got a really bad batch of Blood this time. It didn't usually give him hallucinations. It was only when a bald Hazel d'Ark in a bounty hunter's leathers stopped an Imperial sword thrust that would have killed him, that he was forced to admit they were real. He didn't let it bother him. Mistport was a crazy place at the best of times, which this very definitely wasn't. But then he saw Owen Deathstalker striding through the milling crowd, cutting troopers down as though they were nothing, and Jack Random standing defiant and undefeatable amidst a pile of enemy dead, and a shivering awe flashed through him. In all his years, Silver had never seen anything like these three. It was like fighting beside gods.

But it only took a moment for the awe to turn to jealousy. He was just a man, with a man's strength and courage, doing what he could, while three inhuman beings made his best efforts look like nothing. He fought on, but some of the heart had gone out of him. Another surge in the fighting brought him forward, to Owen's side. The Deathstalker threw him a quick, flashing grin, and Silver tried to smile back. And in that moment he saw a trooper's sword heading straight for Owen's back. The Deathstalker hadn't seen it, too busy cutting down the two men before him. Time seemed to slow and stop, and it felt to Silver that he had all the time in the world to decide what to do next. He could call out a warning, or stop the blade himself, but in that moment he wanted the Deathstalker to die. For being more than human, more than him, for being closer and more important to Hazel than he could ever be. It would be easy just to stand there, and let the blade kill Owen. Afterward, no one would blame him. There was so much going on, and he couldn't be expected to see everything. He hesitated, his mind churning in a dozen different directions at once. All the things that could be his, if only Owen Deathstalker was dead. And then time crashed into motion again, and there was no more time to think.

The blade slammed toward Owen's back, and Silver lurched forward, his sword blocking the blow. The sudden impact tore the sword from his hand, and it fell to the ground. The trooper turned on Silver, his sword drawing back for a killing thrust. Silver darted to one side, and the blade sliced across the side of his arm, just opening the skin. Blood ran down his arm. The trooper drew back his arm for another blow. Silver gathered the blood running down his arm into his hand, and threw it in the trooper's eyes. The man hesitated for a moment, blinded, and it was the easiest thing in the world for Silver to reach down, pick up his sword, and run the trooper through.

All this passed in only a moment or two. Owen Deathstalker saw none of it, being busy with his own problems. Silver gathered his wits together and fought on. He hadn't done too badly, for a mere mortal. And if there had to be gods fighting in this battle, Silver was just glad they were on his side.

The tides of battle swept him away from Owen, who cut his way through a crowd of bodies to fight beside Hazel again. It took a moment to realize it wasn't the Hazel d'Ark he knew, and another to realize there seemed to be a small crowd of Hazels. And then someone in the back of the crowd was shouting "Retreat!" Other voices took it up, all of them Imperial troopers, and suddenly the invaders were melting away before Owen, turning and running. Everywhere he looked it was the same, as what had been a far greater force fell apart and ran for its life, its strength broken on the immovable rock that was Mistport's defenders. The retreat became a rout, and in a matter of moments there was no one left to fight. The defenders raised a ragged cheer. Owen looked back at Hazel d'Ark and blinked a few times as he discovered there was only one of her there. She looked across at him, grinning broadly, and Owen decided he wasn't going to ask. Not yet. He wasn't sure he wanted to know. The defenders were calling his name, and Hazel's, but mostly Jack Random's. He was their hero. They saluted him with raised swords, and glowing fervent eyes. They would have followed him into Hell itself, and everyone knew it.

And then the war wagons opened fire with their disrupters. Now that they no longer had to worry about killing their own troops, they could fire with impunity. The disrupter cannon blew huge bloody holes in the defenders' forces, and the air was full of blood and flying flesh. The crowd began to fall back, scrambling over the bodies of the dead. Jack Random raised his voice above the bedlam.

"Stop, my friends! We can defeat these machines!"

Owen pushed his way through the crowd to grab Random by the arm. "What are you, crazy? You can't fight disrupter cannon with nothing but swords! We have to fall back and find some place we can defend!"

"Damn right," said Hazel, suddenly at Owen's side. "You trying to get us all killed, Random?"

"My apologies," said Young Jack Random. "You're quite right, of course. I got carried away for the moment."

"Fine," said Owen. "Now shut the hell up and run."

The defenders fell back before the advancing battle wagons, but it was an organized retreat, not a rout. They spilled back through the narrow streets and alleyways, confident the huge bulking machines couldn't follow them. The machines' disrupter cannon swiveled from side to side, trying to find a grouping of rebels big enough to be worth firing on, but the rebels had already learned that lesson the hard way, and scattered into smaller and smaller groups as they fell back. So the war wagons opened fire on the streets themselves, blowing buildings and walls apart in showers of pulverized brick and mortar. There were shouts and screams as people disappeared beneath the collapsing buildings, and soon there were only piles of smoking rubble where the streets had been, over which the huge battle wagons pressed relentlessly forward.

The Imperial troopers saw the triumph of the war machines, and began to re-form behind them. The defenders' retreat began to turn into a rout after all. Owen and Hazel stopped and looked back. The war wagons surged toward them, guns roaring, devouring Mistport street by street. Above, the gravity barges hovered like vast storm clouds. Owen reached out a hand to Hazel, and she took it firmly, the same thought in both their minds. Their joined thoughts reached up and out. One of the gravity barges suddenly lurched in midair, as some unseen, implacable force seized hold of it. The engines roared and strained, and then overloaded, as something pulled the barge down out of the sky and smashed it into the war machines below.

The night was ripped apart by the force of the explosion, and flames roaring up from the tangled wreckage lit the nearby streets bright as day. The invading forces had to retreat yet again, or be showered by falling molten metal, thrown hundreds of yards by the blast. But none of the defenders were harmed. The tumbling debris seemed to fall well short every time, as though they were protected by some unseen hand. The rebels stopped running and stood and cheered, celebrating the good fortune that had saved them. Of them all, only John Silver knew to whom they owed their lives. He watched as Owen and Hazel came out of their trance, looked down at their linked hands, and grinned self-consciously. They let go, and moved off into the cheering crowds. Silver watched them go, and wondered again what they were. What they were becoming. And if, just possibly, they might grow to be so powerful that they became more of a threat to Mistport than the Empire ever had been. He moved off after them, shaken by his thoughts, but already pondering possible actions, should it prove necessary. And wondering if he'd done the right thing in saving the Deathstalker's life after all.

He'd always felt a little superior, because some humans feared espers for their powers. Now he knew how those people felt. He wasn't top of the heap anymore. He wasn't even sure he could see the top of the heap from where he was.

Back among the retreating Empire troopers were Toby Shreck and his cameraman Flynn. They'd been put down to join the ground forces, and get close-up shots of the glorious invasion, only things hadn't turned out that way. The moment it became clear things were going seriously wrong, Lieutenant Ffolkes ordered Flynn to recall his camera and shut it down. The live broadcast was over, owing to technical difficulties. To make it clear how serious those difficulties were, Ffolkes stuck a gun in Flynn's back, and kept it there until the camera had safely returned to perch on Flynn's shoulder again. Its single red eye went out, and it was still. Toby protested, but no one listened to him. He hadn't expected they would, but he had to raise his voice anyway, or they'd think he was getting soft. Neither he nor Flynn doubted Ffolkes would have used the gun. He was white with fury at the invading forces' defeat, and looked like he was ready to take it out on anyone stupid enough to upset him. So Toby and Flynn fell back with the retreating forces until Ffolkes was called away to be objectionable somewhere else. After he was gone, they got some great footage of the crashing gravity barge, and then had to run like hell as molten metal came dropping out of the sky like a deadly hail. As they trudged back into the snows outside the city, and temporary safety, Toby and Flynn gave up trying to interview the exhausted troopers after the negative replies escalated from the obscene to actual death threats.

"Wonder where they'll send us next," said Flynn, after a while.

"Somewhere where things are going rather better, I should imagine," said Toby.

"Assuming there is such a place."

"Bound to be. The defenders just got lucky here, that's all."

"I don't know," said Flynn. "What were the odds of a gravity barge just happening to fall on the war wagons?"

Toby looked at him. "What are you implying? That the rebels brought it down in some way? Forget it. They don't have that kind of weaponry. And if you're thinking of espers, even the infamous Inspector Topaz her own bad self couldn't have brought down something that big. Espers just don't come that strong. And that's without Legion scrambling their minds."

"This is Mistport," said Flynn, darkly. "I've heard things about Mistport. Never wanted to come here in the first place."

"It's certainly full of surprises," said Toby. "Did you see who was leading the rebel forces? Jack Random, looking just like his old holo pictures. Only, if that's Jack Random, whom did we see leading the rebel forces on Technos III? That man looked a lot older, and harder used. And I don't believe he could have got from there to here, in so short a time. Not without the Empire knowing."

"Maybe one of them's a double. Or a clone." Flynn scowled. "Either way, there's a lot to this story that we're not being told."

"Nothing new there," said Toby. "If we run across him again, maybe we can pin him down for an interview. I could name my own price for a piece like that. Prime time, guaranteed."

"The powers that be, and intend to keep on being, would never let you show it."

Toby grinned. "Where there's a wallet, there's a way."

* * *

In the labyrinthian heart of Thieves Quarter, in the Blackthorn Inn, representatives of the esper union were fighting to keep track of what was happening. More people were arriving all the time, filling the crowded room, as news poured in from all over the city. The Council members, minus Albert Magnus, were still poring over the great map of Mistport, studying the situation with darkening scowls. The news was rarely good. The esper reps showed the positions of the gravity barges and sleds as small black shadows drifting over the map. Espers flying up to fight them showed as bright burning sparks. The sparks tended to blink out suddenly after a while, and no one needed to ask why. More shadows showed at the boundaries of the city, where the Empire forces had breached the boundary walls. The dark stains spread inward as the invading forces pressed on into the city despite all the defenders could do to slow or stop them. The shadows were holding only at the southwest boundary, where news of an unexpected victory was beginning to drift in.

Chance's children lay huddled on blankets in one corner of the room, keeping up a steady, quiet babble of information and warnings as Chance moved among them, cajoling and praising and bribing them with bits of candy. Any one of them he left alone for too long tended to drift into waking nightmares, screaming and howling piteously. The esper union reps were hiding the Blackthorn's position and inhabitants with their superior mental abilities, but even they couldn't protect the Abraxus children from the horror of Legion. The never-ending scream, rasping in their minds and souls like the scrape of bone on bone, or the tearing of living meat. No one knew how the children experienced it, but the look on their small faces as they mewled despairingly and twisted in their blankets was enough to keep anyone from asking. Chance pleaded with the Council to let him sedate the children, but the answer was always no. They were too useful.

A few espers teleported in and out with important messages, appearing and disappearing in puffs of disturbed air. Static sparked around them, discharging painfully through the nearest metal. They were risking their lives with every jump, and everyone knew it. Legion's scream was interrupting their concentration. Some never arrived. Just blinked out in one location, and were never seen again. Some arrived at the inn in pieces, or horribly re-arranged. One materialized half inside the tavern wall. He was still there, protruding from the brickwork. No one could figure out how to remove him without tearing the wall apart. Luckily he was dead, so they just draped a cloth across his face to hide the staring eyes and contorted mouth, and pretended he wasn't there.

And one man fell out of midair and slammed to the floor in a sticky mess of spurting blood and exposed organs. His journey had turned him inside out. Horribly, he wouldn't die. In the end, Donald Royal cut off the head with one merciful stroke of his sword.

The Council members and the esper union reps struggled to put some kind of planned defenses together, but things were happening so quickly all the time that all they could really do was react to the Empire's actions and provide damage limitations. Raised voices were getting hoarse, and tiredness showed in everybody's eyes. Cyder kept hot coffee and mulled ale moving among everyone in the room, and supplied a steady stream of information from her own network of informers, people she used to work with in the past, before they became respectable. She tried not to worry about what had happened to Cat. And overhead, the roar of passing gravity barges shook the inn like thunder, never knowing how close they'd come to the heart of rebel resistance.

Kast and Morgan dragged their prisoner through the chaos and fury of battle to see Investigator Razor, as he stood thoughtfully in the rubble of what had been the north-east boundary, watching his troops press deeper into the burning city, sweeping aside all opposition. He waited till the marines and their captive were almost upon him before turning and acknowledging their existence. His dark face was calm as ever, but there was a hot and brutal fire in his eyes that made even Kast and Morgan nervous. They bowed quickly to the Investigator, and hit their prisoner till he did, too. Razor studied the man in silence for a long moment. The prisoner dressed well, though his fine clothing was currently rumpled and torn and stained with his own blood. His face was bruised and battered. It seemed that Kast and Morgan had not been gentle in persuading him to come along with them.

"And this is?" Razor said finally.

"A traitor and informer, sir," said Kast cheerfully. "Name of Artemis Daley. Something of a mover and shaker in Mistport, if he's to be believed. He's promised us useful, not to say vital, information if we'll just avoid destroying the properties here he has interests in. He's even volunteered to give us a map showing those properties. Isn't that helpful of him? Under a certain amount of pressure, he also volunteered to draw us another map, showing exactly where the city Council is currently hiding out. In return for his life and continued well-being. So we brought him to you, sir. If he is who he says he is, and knows what he says he does, he could be very valuable. And if you were to see your way clear to giving my friend and me recommendations on the strength of that, sir, or even a raise in rank, well, we were just doing our duty."

"But we'll still take the raise," said Morgan. "Or any medals, if they're going."

"You have done well," said Razor. "Now be silent." He smiled slowly at the prisoner, who if anything seemed even less reassured than before. Razor stepped closer, studying the man's face. "I know you, Artemis Daley. You're in our files. A deal-maker, money-lender, and leg-breaker, as necessary. Medium-sized fish in a very small pond. You've sold us the odd bit of information in the past. Nothing terribly important, but enough to make you as one of ours. Talk to me, Artemis. Tell me where my enemies are."

"We . . . have yet to agree on a price, your honor," said Daley, trying hard to keep his voice steady. "I am, after all, just an honest businessman, trying to make a profit in difficult times. I have no interest in wars. But a man in my position can't afford to just give away valuable information. Word would get out. My reputation would be ruined. You understand, I'm sure."

"Quite," said Razor. He looked at Kast. "Kill him."

"Wait! Wait!" Daley tried to back away, but Kast and Morgan held him firmly. They forced him down onto his knees. Daley shook so hard that drops of sweat fell off his face. "Wait, your honor! Allow me to . . . give you a little something, as a sign of good faith. The Council can be found at the Blackthorn Inn, in Thieves Quarter." He looked anxiously at Razor. "I'd be happy to draw you a map, your honor, showing exactly how to get there, but it's a little hard to draw when you're on your knees . . ."

"We have our own maps," said Razor. "And we have all we need from you." He nodded to Kast and Morgan. "Make an example of him."

Kast and Morgan nodded cheerfully, and dragged Daley away. He kicked and struggled, but didn't even slow them down. "You can't do this! I'm an important man here! I told you what you wanted! I told you . . ."

He kept shouting till Morgan hit him over the head with the butt of his gun. He was still mumbling protests when Kast and Morgan strung him up from the nearest lamppost and stood back to watch him dance in midair. Razor's smile was bitter. He had no time for traitors. He watched the hanging man die, and wondered when Clan Chojiro's agents here would make contact with him.

The first the people in the Blackthorn Inn knew of its targeting was when the disrupter beams began hammering down from the gravity barges hovering directly overhead. The slate roof blew apart, and the upper floor of the inn was suddenly a mass of flames, sweeping rapidly through the private rooms, burying the few inhabitants alive and swallowing their screams in the roar of the fire. The energy beams plowed through the upper floor and plunged on into the main barroom below, where they rebounded from a psionic screen erected at the very last moment by the espers within. Chance's children had come through with a last-second warning. The espers in the barroom were representatives of the esper union, and some of the strongest minds in Mistport, and together they held off the disrupter cannon. But even they couldn't save the Blackthorn.

The upper floor was a raging inferno. The barroom's timber ceiling began to blacken and smolder. The whole inn was shaking from the pounding it was taking. Bricks cracked, and fine streams of dust and mortar began to fall. The barroom quickly became stiflingly hot. The espers could do nothing. It was all they could do to fend off the disrupter beams. Donald Royal barked orders, getting people organized. He had them block off the back stair-well with tables and other furniture, in case the flames from above broke through the closed door. Cyder pro-duced buckets of water, in case of sudden flash fires. Chance's children were screaming almost continuously now, but he still didn't dare sedate them. They might yet have to run for it.

A few people cracked and ran for the main door. Ran-dom yelled after them, but they wouldn't listen to him. They ran outside, and energy beams blew them apart the moment they appeared. More gravity barges drifted over-head, adding their firepower to the onslaught raging down on a single building. Every building around the inn was already a mass of flames and pulverized rubble. There were dead men and women in the streets, their bodies blackening in the growing firestorm.

Inside the Blackthorn, a timbered beam broke away from the ceiling supports and slammed down like a giant hammer, crushing Lois Barron beneath it. The heavy weight pinned her to the floor, and blood gushed from her mouth as she beat feebly at the wooden beam with her hands. It was obvious she was dying, but the others con-tinued to try and lift the heavy beam off her, until she finally lay back and was still. The dwarf Castle sat beside her and held her dead hand, oblivious to everything. McVey and Royal couldn't allow themselves time to mourn. As the only remaining Councillors, they had too much to do. If anyone was going to find a way out of this trap, it would have to be the two of them.

And that was when the psionic shield began to weaken and break apart. Even the strongest minds in Mistport found it hard to function with Legion's endless scream in their heads. Their power was burning up, and so were they. Blood trickled steadily from their noses and ears. The greatest esp-blocker the Empire had ever made beat against their minds and, inch by inch, it shut them down. Cracks appeared in the shield. Thin bolts of energy stabbed through the barroom ceiling, transfixing people here and there like insects on pins. And then one energy beam hit and killed the strongest esper, and the screen collapsed.

Immediately Jenny Psycho reached out with her mind and pulled the screen back together again. She had hoped she wouldn't be needed. Once she revealed her presence, she had no doubt Legion would turn all its attention to her, and she wasn't entirely sure she could beat the unnatural thing. But she did what she had to do, taking all the pressure upon herself as one by one the other espers collapsed and died around her. Very soon the strain was almost unbearable. For all her strength, Jenny Psycho was no match for the many minds that made up Legion. If she and everyone else in the barroom were to survive, she was going to have to be more than just Jenny Psycho.

And so she reached inside herself, to that brightly shining place once touched by the Mater Mundi in the dark cells of Silo Nine. She called out to the uber-esper, the Mater Mundi, Our Mother Of All Souls, to come and manifest through her again, and pull all the espers in Mistport together into one great gestalt that would drive Legion and the Empire from Mistworld. She called, and no one answered. Jenny screamed then, a bitter howl of outrage and betrayal and despair that for a moment even drowned out Legion's endless scream. For as far as she could reach with her mind, there was no trace of the Mater Mundi, only the bright sparks of Mistport's espers blinking out one by one, and that awful thing that was Legion, slowly turning its full attention upon her. The Mater Mundi had abandoned her.

Jenny Psycho held together through sheer willpower. She had to. So many people were depending on her. Her brief touch by the Mater Mundi had made her one of the strongest espers the Empire had ever seen, but even so it was all she could do to hold off the many-in-one that was Legion. The pain was almost unbearable, but she wouldn't give up. If the Council were to die, resistance in Mistport would quickly fall apart, and the Empire would win. Jenny turned inward, cutting off all contact with the outside world, focusing all her will and concentration on maintaining the psionic shield. She stopped hearing the screams of people dying in the streets around the Blackthorn Inn, as the disrupter beams stabbed viciously down, killing everything that moved, spreading fire and destruction. She couldn't afford to be distracted. The psionic shield was her whole world now.

She knew the strain was killing her, and didn't care. After enduring the horrors and agonies of Silo Nine, she'd sworn to die rather than be taken captive again. Blood leaked steadily from her nose and ears, and sprayed from her mouth with every harsh breath. Some of the pain began to die away as parts of her mind began to shut down, bit by bit. She didn't know it, but her face looked like a grinning, death's-head mask. And still she fought on, refusing to give in, refusing to be beaten, and slowly she began to gain a new sense of her opponent Legion, of who and what it was. Of what it had been made from. Brains from people she might have known and Wormboy's worms. And Legion looked on her and knew who she was. The worms remembered her and what she'd done before. They were scared of her. Jenny Psycho laughed inside her head, and it was a terrible, unforgiving sound.

The invading forces pressed forward on all fronts, though more slowly on some than others. It was as though every man, woman, and child who could hold a weapon was out in the streets of Mistport, defending barricades and blocking crossroads, sniping from windows and hidden alleyways, making the troopers fight for every inch and pay for every victory in blood and death. Retreating defenders blew up and collapsed buildings as they fell back, to block off streets and slow the Empire's advance. The rebels' projectile weapons confused and scattered troops only used to dealing with the predictability and long pauses of disrupter fire until they learned to advance behind massed force shields, and the projectile guns were no use against them.

There were no espers operating now, in the sky or on the streets. Legion had proved too much for all but the strongest, and most of those were dead now. The defenders fell back, street by street, trying to follow Mistport's ages-old plans for last-ditch defense, but the plans hadn't been updated in years. Important routes had been blocked by street markets and new buildings, and some streets didn't exist anymore, save on the oldest maps. The defenders did the best they could, falling back only when there was no other option, retreating slowly toward the vulnerable heart of Mistport.

The wounded and refugees traveled through the city on barges on the River Autumn. It was quicker and safer than trusting to the streets. The coal-fired barges chugged up and down the freezing river, their steel prows breaking through the newly forming ice on the surface of the water, their crimson bow lights burning like coals in the night. On either side of the River, buildings burned like coals in Hell. The Autumn meandered through the city, passing through Guilds Quarter to Merchants to Thieves, and barges came and went with quiet desperation. Passengers occasionally called out to other craft, anxious for news of missing loved ones or how the battle went, but the answers were often old, and rarely good.

There were running fights on the docksides as advance groups of marines tried to get to the barges, only to be fought off by dockworkers armed with barbed knives and grappling hooks. The longshoremen knew every inch of their territory, and were hard and savage fighters. Some barges became overcrowded with refugees and wounded, slowed down too much, and became easy targets for overhead gravity sleds. Unable to maneuver, the barges were blown apart by disrupters, scattering burning bodies in the dark waters of the Autumn. Burning remnants blocked the way and clogged the docks, and half-charred and ruptured bodies floated in the water and lay captured by the slowly forming ice on the surface.

The larger barges armed themselves with heavy-duty projectile weapons and taught the gravity sleds to maintain a respectful distance. Standard tactics for a gravity sled was to deflect incoming fire with its force shield, then lower the shield to fire back while their enemy's energy guns were recharging. They weren't expecting guns that didn't need to recharge between shots. The Empire lost a lot of sleds till word got around. But the Deathstalker's gift of guns and ammo had been widely spread and, therefore, were in short supply everywhere, while there seemed no end to the invading forces. The barge gunners huddled low behind improvised shelters, and vowed to make every bullet count.

Imperial marines made their way through the hard-won streets of Mistport, stepping over the dead bodies and tossing grenades into the few buildings that still looked capable of hiding snipers. They left the better areas untouched, of course, and even left a few men behind to guard against looters. When the Empire finally took control of this city, these areas would be reoccupied by the new, Imperially approved, leaders. But everywhere else, the buildings burned and fires rose up into the night sky like beacons of victory.

Kast and Morgan trailed happily along in the rear, hanging back to avoid the real action, keeping themselves occupied by shooting enemy snipers or anyone else who annoyed them. They killed anyone who even looked dangerous, men or women, and tossed grenades through windows if their prey tried to go to ground. Like the rest of the invading force, they weren't interested in taking prisoners. That would come later, once the city was theirs. Kast and Morgan took time out to do a little quiet looting here and there, when no one was looking, but the pickings weren't up to much, even in the few buildings that somehow escaped the fires and the grenades. Mistport wasn't known for its luxuries, except in the most fortunate areas, and Kast and Morgan never got anywhere near those.

So they strolled unhurriedly down the narrow streets, ignoring the bodies and the smell and the blood-caked cobblestones, passing a bottle back and forth between them till it was empty, then acquiring another at the next opportunity. The wine was mostly lousy, but wine was wine, after all. They sang battle songs and vulgar ditties in between looting and killing people, but they couldn't seem to get into the spirit of the occasion. Until they found the girl hiding in the ruins of a mostly overlooked house. The brickwork was blackened and scorched, and the windows were all smashed, but otherwise it had held together. Just the place for a frightened refugee to hide. Which was why Kast and Morgan had checked it out in the first place. The girl looked to be in her mid-teens, terrorized and trembling, all wide eyes and pleading mouth. Her clothes were torn and blackened by soot, and she looked about as appetizing as a half-burnt steak, but Kast and Morgan weren't picky. They pushed the only door shut behind them and grinned at each other.

"Now this is what we've been missing," said Kast. "An invasion never really feels like an invasion till you've dipped your wick."

"Who goes first?" said the more practical Morgan. "And no, I'm not tossing for it this time."

So they played scissors cuts paper till Kast won. He started undoing his trouser belt. The girl made a break for it. Morgan caught her easily, pulling her back. She went for his eyes, hands like claws, and he spun her round and pinned her arms to her sides. She still kicked and struggled, so he bear-hugged her hard, driving the breath out of her, and dropped her at Kast's feet. He crouched before her, smiling easily, and she spit in his face. He backhanded her almost casually, and the strength of the blow threw her backwards. She fetched up against the far wall, breathing hard, her eyes darting from Kast to Morgan and back again. Blood and snot dribbled from her nose. Kast grinned at her.

"Struggle all you like, my dear. I enjoy a good struggle. If you're good, really good, you'll get a special prize at the end. We'll let you live."

And then both marines froze as a voice called their names outside in the street. They waited, hoping it would go away, but the voice came again, even louder. The girl tensed to scream, and Morgan hit her in the mouth.

"Damn," said Kast. "All the people they could have sent looking for us, and it had to be Sergeant Franke. He won't let you get away with anything. Thinks he's officer material, the fool."

Morgan shrugged, stepped forward, and cut the girl's throat with an economical sweep of his sword. She slumped back against the wall, clawing at her opened throat with her fingers. Blood gushed over her hands, and she fell back, her hands dropping to her sides as the breath went out of her. Kast swore feelingly, and did up his trouser belt again.

"Never mind," said Morgan. "There'll be other chances. Franke can't be everywhere."

The two marines grinned at each other and went back

into the street whistling jauntily. All in all, the invasion was going well.

In Tech Quarter, the starport had been thoroughly trashed. For a time its massed disrupter cannon, harvested from the crashed starcruiser *Darkwind,* had been enough to keep the gravity barges at bay. Up close, the cannon didn't need its crashed computers for targeting. But the barges soon learned the limits of the cannon's range, and stayed well back while they contacted their ship for reinforcements. The *Defiant* sent down six heavily shielded pinnaces to do the job. They came roaring down out of the night, too fast to track, and blew the cannon apart in an explosion that could be heard all across Mistport. With the starport defenseless, the pinnaces swept back and forth in strafing runs, taking out the ships on the landing pads like so many sitting ducks. And while they were doing that, the barges closed in on the control tower.

The rebel ships on the pads exploded one after the other in sudden bursts of smoke and fire. Strange lights radiated briefly and were gone as stardrives collapsed and released their energies. The landing pads would be wildly radioactive now until the Empire could bring in heavy-duty scrubbers. Only the Deathstalker's ship, *Sunstrider II,* survived, protected by superior Hadenman shields. The pinnaces marked it down for later attention, and moved on. They had more than enough other targets to keep them busy.

The control tower lasted the longest, with its reinforced structure and steelglass windows, but even that fell in the end, riddled by disrupter fire from the hovering gravity barges. The steelglass blew inward, transformed into deadly shrapnel that cut down everyone left inside the tower. Some still survived, so the barges set the tower on fire, and left it to burn. Their job done, the pinnaces and the barges moved unhurriedly away in search of other targets. People lay dead everywhere across the pads. Ground crews preparing ships for desperate takeoffs, and crowds of people who'd been convinced they'd be safest at the well-defended starport, or who had paid massive bribes to be smuggled offplanet. When the Empire ships came they were caught out in the open with nowhere to hide and nowhere to run, and they died screaming for help that never came. Wrecked ships burned on the cracked pads, and what was left of the control tower burned like a giant candle, its shattered walls running like wax in the great heat. The starport had fallen.

Young Jack Random led Owen and Hazel and Silver and his adoring followers back into the city, in search of people to help. The troops forced back from the southwest boundary had departed in search of easier ways into the city. No one doubted they'd find them. Random soon found a street barricade in danger of falling to an Empire attack, and moved in quickly to support it. The improvised barricade had been formed from furniture and other suitably heavy objects, dragged out into the street from the surrounding houses and stacked one by one on top of the other and lashed together till the resulting wall stood nearly a dozen feet high. Smaller furniture had been broken up to form jagged wooden spikes, projecting from the barricade to discourage the other side from getting too close.

Iron nails had been twisted together into caltrops, the points dipped in dung, and then thrown out into the street for the troopers to step on. Random's small army lined themselves up behind the barricade, shooting crossbow bolts and bullets through the gaps in the wall to pick off any trooper who so much as aimed a disrupter at the barricade. It quickly became clear to both sides that only hand-to-hand fighting was going to decide the fate of this stumbling block. And since the barricade blocked the last main route into the city center, its control was vital to both sides.

And so the Imperial troops came charging down the street, sheltering behind massed force shields, firing their disrupters blindly as they ran. The energy bolts punched wide holes through the barricade, incinerating those fighters unfortunate enough to be in the way, but as many shots missed as hit, and the barricade still stood. The rebels fired at the troopers' legs, unguarded beneath the force shields, and whole sections of the advancing force came crashing to the ground as they fell over one another, but still the charge came on. Until finally the two sides met at the barricade, and it was left to courage and desperation and naked steel to win the day.

Owen and Hazel fought side by side, still linked, feeling stronger and sharper than ever. They didn't need Blood or the boost anymore. Something new was working in them now, granting them strength and speed beyond anything they'd ever known before. John Silver had taken the last of his Blood long ago, and now only guts and duty were keeping him on his feet. He'd got over his fear of Owen and Hazel. Whatever they had become, they were clearly the best bet for defeating the invading troops, and so Silver had taken on the job of guarding their backs. It seemed even gods needed someone to watch their blind spots. Interestingly enough, Silver couldn't bring himself to give a damn about Jack Random. There was something about the man that made Silver's hackles stand on end, though he couldn't have told you what. Perhaps it was just that the man was tòo damned perfect. Certainly he seemed almost like a god, too, standing atop the barricade, swinging his great sword with both hands, defying the Empire to bring him down.

The struggle continued, fighting breaking out before and upon and behind the barricade. Owen and Hazel cut down every man who came against them, roaring their defiance, and dodging disrupter beams, which was supposed to be impossible. Owen's battle cry of *Shandrakor!* rose above the din again and again, and was taken up by many of the rebels, almost as many as those who fought with Jack Random's name on their lips. They pushed the Imperial troops back and back until finally the rebels came spilling up and over the barricade to drive the troopers back down the street.

Hand-to-hand fighting filled the street, the mass of fighters surging this way and that, trampling the dead and the wounded underfoot. The troops roared their battle songs and stood their ground, urged on by armed officers at their back and the battle drugs sweeping through their veins. Buildings burned and smoldered to either side of the fighting, but children and those too old or too weak to fight had taken to the roofs, and rained stones and slates and boiling water down onto the enemy below. They aimed carefully, and many a trooper was suddenly taken out of the fighting by an unexpected present from above.

Toby Shreck and Flynn were right there in the thick of things, getting it all on film. They were currently keeping their heads well down in a nearby doorway while Flynn's camera soared above the mayhem, picking out the best shots. Toby's commentary was becoming increasingly breathless, but he kept going, knowing that if he could only smuggle this past the censors, the news agencies would be making up whole new awards just to give to him. This was the good stuff. Ffolkes had been becoming increasingly stuffy about what they could and couldn't shoot, so Toby and Flynn ditched him by the simple expedient of shouting *Look over there*! and then running off in two different directions. By the time Ffolkes had made up his mind which of them to chase or shoot at, it was already too late.

Toby and Flynn had got together again easily enough after that, and went in search of the main action. It didn't taken them long to find some. And ever since then they'd been running and dodging and keeping their heads well down from one trouble spot to another, while Flynn's camera got it all on film. Troops and rebels alike both ignored Toby and Flynn as obvious noncombatants, but flying bullets and disrupter beams and crumbling buildings made no such distinction. Toby would have liked to cheer on the rebels, outnumbered and outgunned but still refusing to be beaten, but he couldn't, not if he ever wanted the film he was risking his life to get to be shown in the Empire. So he kept his commentary carefully neutral and let the pictures speak for themselves.

The young burglar known as Cat was up on the roofs, too, doing his bit. He'd delivered all of Cyder's messages, and strictly speaking should have been on his way back to the Blackthorn, but he couldn't resist getting involved. He'd never thought of himself as a violent man, but the merciless destruction of his city had raised in him an anger that couldn't be denied. And so he pelted the troops below with slates and tiles and anything else he could get his hands on, in between grabbing people who nearly threw themselves off the edge of the roof in their enthusiasm. They weren't as used to roofs as Cat.

He was overseeing the dismantling of a chimney stack to provide bricks for throwing when he happened to look down the far end of the street. Thick black smoke drifted this way and that from the burning buildings, blown by rising hot air and the disturbances of passing gravity barges, but it parted now to show Cat half a dozen troopers manhandling a portable disrupter cannon into position at the far end of the street. The plan was clear enough. Once the cannon was ready, all they had to do was call back their own troops and open fire. The cannon would blow away the barricade and everyone near it with one blast. The defenders wouldn't stand a chance.

Cat was off and running across the steeply slanted roofs the moment he realized what was happening. As a deaf mute he couldn't shout a warning to the defenders below, and by the time he'd made the people on the roof understand him, it would be too late. Which meant it was all up to him. He moved silently into position over the troops as they finished assembling the portable cannon, and brought its computers on line. They were almost ready to fire, and Cat didn't have a single idea how to stop them. Throwing things would only distract them, and if they had hand disrupters, they'd soon blast him off the roof. If he jumped them, the element of surprise might let him take out one or two of the troopers, but the rest would be sure to get him.

Cat looked frantically round the roof for inspiration, and his eyes lit on a crooked chimney stack, not far from the edge of the roof. A passing energy beam had neatly clipped away one corner, so that it was leaning toward the street. It looked like one good push would send it over. Cat checked the position of the cannon and its crew again. Right under the chimney stack. Perfect. Cat grinned, and put his shoulder to the brick chimney. He pushed with all his strength, and it didn't budge an inch. He tried again, slamming his shoulder against the brickwork, his feet sliding on the slippery slates as he tried to dig them in. Thick black smoke suddenly swirled around him as the wind changed direction. Cat sank to his knees, coughing harshly, fighting for breath. There were hot cinders in the smoke, too, and he pulled up his suit's hood to keep them out of his hair. Down below, the cannon had to be almost ready by now.

Raging silently, Cat put his back against the chimney stack, braced his boots against the most secure tiles, and strained with all his strength. The brickwork shifted reluctantly beneath him. His face twisted into a pained grimace as he pushed with everything he had in his back and legs. The pain grew, and still the bricks wouldn't give. Cat strained desperately, his heart thumping madly in his chest, sweat running down his face, and the chimney stack broke away from the roof. It happened as quickly as that. One moment nothing, and then there was a sharp crack of rending bricks and mortar, and the whole damned stack went over the side of the roof, taking Cat with it.

He twisted automatically as he fell, already grabbing for handholds. He had a brief glimpse of shocked upturned faces from the disrupter gun crew, and then they disappeared as the great mass of brickwork slammed down on them like a hammer. Cat's flailing hand caught a wooden shutter as he fell past it, and he took a firm hold. For a moment his whole weight was hanging by that one hand, but then the momentum of his fall swung him around and it was the easiest thing in the world to fly through the open window and into the room beyond. He hit the floor rolling, and finally crashed up against the far wall, where he stayed for a while, till he got his breath back. As his heart finally slowed back to something that could pass for normal, Cat decided it was very definitely time he was getting back to the Blackthorn, and safety. He didn't want Cyder getting worried about him.

Out in the streets of Mistport, old hatreds and divisions were forgotten as the rebels came together to fight a common enemy. Old and bitter foes fought side by side, and sworn enemies guarded each other's backs. It seemed everyone who could walk and wield a weapon was out in the streets now, fighting to defend a city whose importance they hadn't realized till it looked to be taken from them. Even Owen's foes from the old Deathstalker network had turned out to do their bit. They were businessmen, not warriors, but they hadn't got where they were without guts and determination. And perhaps, deep inside, they remembered the idealistic young men they had once been, and old beliefs and convictions stirred in them again.

Neeson the banker and Robbins the landlord fought side by side, swords flashing as old skills came back to them. Stacey the lawyer had an elegant rapier, and Connelly and McGowan of the docks cut a bloody path through the enemy with an ax in each hand. They all fought bravely and well, and were surprisingly effective for middle-aged men who'd grown soft in comfortable positions.

"Damn, this feels good," Neeson said to Robbins during a lull in the fighting. "Takes me back to our young days, when we were going to change the world and overthrow the Empire. And all before lunch."

Robbins laughed. "Happy days. Simpler days, anyway. I was getting bored with being a businessman anyway."

The Blackthorn Inn was a blazing wreck, its upper floor an inferno, its roof gone, swept away by the fire and smoke belching up into the night sky. Three gravity barges hovered overhead, disrupter beams hammering down. Flames licked along the outer walls, and great cracks appeared in the brickwork. Inside, there was smoke and chaos and panic. Jenny Psycho stood in the center of the room, arms outstretched like a crucifix, her mental energies the only thing holding off the deadly disrupter beams. Blood trickled steadily from her nose and ears and mouth. Under the blood her face was deathly pale and her wild eyes were fixed on something far away. She was dying, and everyone knew it. She was the only thing protecting the Blackthorn, and it was killing her inch by inch.

Donald Royal had organized people into groups with buckets of water and blankets, ready to stamp out any fires that started in the barroom. The old man had been revitalized by the emergency, and was bustling around like a man half his age. Councillor McVey had gathered Chance's children into a small group, away from the walls. Madelaine Skye, Royal's partner, stood in the doorway with a disrupter in her hand. Empire troops had already blown the door off its hinges, and tried throwing grenades through the gap. Skye had seen the first one, thrown it straight back out, and taken up her position by the door to discourage anyone else with the same idea. Outside, on the other side of the street, a large group of Imperial marines were patiently watching the doorway, ready to deal with anyone who came out of it. No one was interested in taking any prisoners from the Blackthorn.

Behind the bar, Cyder was getting very drunk. Her tavern was a wreck, she was trapped in a burning building, and Cat was nowhere to be seen. She hoped he was somewhere safe, but doubted it. He should have been back long ago. Probably got involved in the fighting. She'd told him and told him, never get involved . . . She poured herself another drink.

"Don't you think you've had enough?" said Donald Royal.

"Hell no," said Cyder. "I can still think."

"If we end up having to make a run for it, you'll be no use drunk."

"Make a run for it? Where would we go? The inn's surrounded by men with guns. The moment we leave this place we're dead. Of course, if we stay, we're dead, too. If the flames don't get us, the smoke will. Or that Psycho woman will finally fall apart and the gravity barges will blow the whole place into kindling. Have I missed anything?"

"There's always the chance something will happen," said Royal. "Some lucky break, or opportunity. We have to be ready to grab it."

Cyder shook her head. "It's too late, Donald. We're not going anywhere." She broke off, and frowned. "Can you hear someone singing?"

And that was when one wall of the tavern suddenly collapsed. The bricks just fell apart, revealing the outside street and a hell of a lot of dead troopers. Flames swept toward the gap, but were somehow thwarted and held back by some unseen force. And there, right outside, singing, were Investigator Topaz and the woman who used to be known as Typhoid Mary. The two most powerful Sirens in the Empire, or out of it.

"Told you so," said Donald to Cyder, grinning. "All right, people; we are leaving! Grab anything you abso-

lutely have to have, and head for the hole in the wall.
Madelaine, help me with Jenny Psycho. Cyder, put that
bottle down and run or I'll kick your ass up around your
ears."

There were flames everywhere now. The air itself was
hot enough to burn. Sudden stabs of energy smashed
down through the ceiling as Jenny's shield splintered.
Donald grabbed her by the arm and hustled her toward the
hole in the wall. Blood was spilling thickly down her face
now, and spraying from her mouth in time to her agonized
breathing. Her skin was an unhealthy blue-white, and her
hand in Royal's was cold and clammy. She looked like
death warmed up and allowed to congeal, but somehow
she was still maintaining her psionic shield, protecting the
rebels as they fled from the burning inn. Her legs were
stiff and unsteady, and Donald kept her moving by brute
force, for she was beyond cooperating with him or anyone
else now, even to save her own life. Her whole world had
shrunk down to the simple need to maintain her shield,
even though it was killing her. Donald got her to the hole
in the wall, and all but threw her out into the cold night
beyond. He clambered out after her, his chest heaving as
he tried to cough up the smoke that had got into his lungs.
He felt old and tired and his head was swimming, but he
wouldn't let himself fall. Not yet.

McVey helped Chance get his charges on their feet
again, and between them they herded the half-mad children over to the hole in the wall and out into the street
beyond. Chance kept counting them over and over, to
make sure he hadn't left any behind. All the children were
screaming or crying or just shuddering helplessly, Legion's never-ending howl rasping through their minds
like burning barbed wire. McVey stayed by the hole,
counting heads as the last of the rebel HQ's people filed
past him. He came up one short. He forced himself as
close to the hole as he could, and stared through the
flames into the blazing barroom. The dwarf Iain Castle
was still sitting beside Lois Barron's body, crushed under
the fallen timber. He was holding her dead hand in his,
and rocking slowly back and forth. McVey yelled his
name, and Castle looked around almost absently.

"Iain, get out of there! Leave her! There's nothing you

can do!" McVey had to yell himself hoarse to make himself heard above the roar of the flames and the thundering engines of the gravity barges hovering overhead.

"I won't leave her!" Castle shouted back. "I won't leave her here!"

· "She's already gone! And if you don't get out of there now, you'll be going with her!" McVey made himself stay by the hole, though the sheer heat was raising blisters on his unprotected hands and face. "Iain, please! I don't want to lose you, too!"

Castle nodded slowly, got to his feet, and stumbled across the smoke-filled room to the hole in the wall. He plowed straight through the fiery sides as though he didn't notice them, and lurched out into the street with flames rising from his clothes. McVey whipped off his cloak and wrapped Castle up in it, smothering the flames. Beside him, Jenny Psycho sat down suddenly, as though all the strength had just gone out of her. Her mouth was slack, and her eyes saw nothing. Not far away, Typhoid Mary and Investigator Topaz were still singing together, their voices and esp combining to create a shield over and around the rebels. Their voices rose and fell in studied harmonies, and a psistorm of energies crackled through the streets at their command, keeping the Empire forces at bay.

Donald Royal looked around suddenly, as he realized his partner hadn't come out with him. People were milling back and forth all around him, but there was no sign anywhere of Madelaine Skye. He pushed his way through the crowd and grabbed McVey by the arm. "Where's Madelaine? Didn't she come out with you?"

"I didn't see her! I had my own problems!" McVey pulled his arm away, and Donald was left staring at the burning Blackthorn Inn. He moved toward the hole in the wall, screwing up his face against the blazing heat. The barroom was now a sea of flames, and thick black smoke boiled out of the hole. Donald's heart contracted painfully as he realized she must still be in there. Probably lost and disoriented in the smoke. He called her name again and again, but there was no answer. Donald's mouth firmed. He knew what he had to do. He pulled his cloak up to protect his face, and moved toward the hole in the wall.

But he stopped after only a few steps. The heat was just too much for him. He tried again and again, drawing on all his courage and resolution to force him past the flames, but his old body cringed back from the awful heat despite him, and would not go forward. Flames licked up around his cloak as the material caught fire, and sudden hands pulled him back, slapping at his shoulders to put out the flames. Donald fought the hands savagely.

"Let me go, dammit! Madelaine's still in there!"

"If she is, then she'd dead," said Gideon Steel, holding him firmly.

Donald stopped struggling. "If she's dead, then I want to die, too. She was my daughter, in every way that mattered. She's all I had left."

"You can't die here," said Steel. "You're needed. You're a Councillor, an old and respected warrior whose name will still rally people. Don't you dare give up on me now. You've been telling us all what a hero you used to be for years. Now prove it, dammit! Prove it in a way that matters. You can't get back in there. No one could."

"I could have, once," said Donald Royal. "When I was a hero. When I was young."

And then one of the windows shattered as a body came hurtling through it, in a blazing mass of flames. It hit the cobbled street rolling, and stood up, throwing aside a blazing cloak. Madelaine Skye beat at her smoldering clothes with her hands, blackened and scorched but still very much alive. Donald lurched forward to take her in his arms, and she held him tightly to her.

"I got turned around in the fire and the smoke," she said breathlessly. "Didn't know where the hell I was, let alone the hole. Then I heard you calling me. You got me out, Donald. I owe you one."

"No you don't," said Donald. "You're family."

Cyder stood off by herself, a bottle of the good brandy still in her hand, and watched the Blackthorn burn. It had been her home and her safe haven and the repository of her dreams, but her face remained calm and cold. Her eyes were dry and her mouth was firm. Cyder didn't believe in being beaten.

"My lovely tavern," she said, finally. "You were going to make me rich, rich, rich."

Jenny Psycho collapsed. Her strength had finally run out. Determination and willpower could carry her no farther, and her mind shut down. The psionic shield disappeared, and the disrupter beams from the hovering gravity barges slammed down into the tavern like God driving nails. The building burst apart, the ceiling crashing down as the walls collapsed, and the flames roared up in triumph. Mary and Topaz's song protected the small crowd from the fire and the flying debris. In seconds there was nothing left of the Blackthorn but a blackened frame in an inferno of flames. Steel knelt down beside Jenny, checked for a pulse, and raised an eyebrow.

"Amazing. She's still with us. Chance, get her out of here. Take her and your children to the esper union hall. They'll look after you. And they'll save Jenny Psycho if anyone can. Crazy woman. Bravest damned thing I ever saw." He got to his feet and raised his voice above the din. "All right, everybody scatter! You all know the secondary meeting place; be there in an hour. No excuses. Now move it!"

And so they all went their separate ways, helping those who needed it, carrying a few where necessary. They went in twos and threes, following the routes the Council had worked out earlier, just in case. They disappeared into the dark maze of narrow streets and alleyways, confident no Empire forces could follow them and not be hopelessly lost in moments. There was no talk of surrender. They were not broken, not beaten. And they had always known this was a fight to the death.

Soon they were all gone, apart from Typhoid Mary and Investigator Topaz. Their song still crackled around them, drowning out Legion's howl, keeping the troops at bay and covering their friends' escape. They were the two most powerful Sirens the Empire had ever produced, and they would not yield. And then suddenly, the pressure eased. The gravity barges moved on, their work done, and the troops fell back. Topaz and Mary stopped singing, conserving their strength. The world around them was still a chaos of flames and screams and battle cries, the thunder of gravity engines and the roar of collapsing buildings, but their particular part of the world seemed strangely still and quiet. As though some new force had entered the scene. Topaz and Mary looked at each other. Behind them, someone applauded slowly. They both looked round sharply, to find a tall dark man in an Investigator's cloak studying them calmly from the other side of the street. Topaz frowned. She should have heard him approach, even in all this noise and chaos. She should have known he was there. His sword and gun were still sheathed on his hips, but in one hand he held a length of steel chain, on the other end of which crouched a cowering naked man. He was painfully thin and smeared with filth, and his bare skin clearly showed the scars and marks of many beatings. The left side of his skull had been surgically cut away, to reveal the brain beneath, protected only by a clear piece of steelglass. Various plugs and jacks studded the brain tissues, and silver wires gleamed in the grey meat.

"Handsome fellow, isn't he?" said the dark man. "He belongs to me. Investigator Razor, at your service. I've been sent to bring you back into the fold of Empire. Teach you to sing the right songs again. Spare me your protestations, please. They don't matter. You have no say in things anymore. This unpleasant wretch at my side has no name anymore, only a function. He's a living esp-blocker. One of the Lord High Dram's special projects, I believe. Being alive, and capable of following orders, he's much more powerful and versatile than the usual brain in a box esp-blocker. He's strong enough to function even under Legion's influence, and subtle enough that you didn't even notice our approach. I'm afraid you'll find your songs have quite deserted you now, ladies. So put aside your petty complaints and come with me. Your life in this place is over. You belong to the Empire again."

Topaz drew her sword. "I'd rather die."

Razor drew his sword. "That can be arranged. I get a bonus if I bring you both back alive, but money's never been that important to me. They'll settle for one live Siren and one dead traitor, if need be. And I always wanted to know which of us is better." He dropped the length of chain he was holding, but the living esp-blocker stayed where he was. He would not move without orders.

Typhoid Mary backed away from the Investigator, shaking her head.

"I can't help you, Topaz. I'm sorry. I won't kill again. Not for any reason."

"That's all right," said Topaz, advancing on Razor. "Just keep well back. You don't want to get any of his blood on you."

And then Topaz and Razor surged forward and slammed together, sparks flying in the mists and smoke as their swords clashed. They stamped and lunged, swinging their swords with almost inhuman strength and speed, two Investigators trained to the peak of perfection. They circled around each other, hammering home blows that would have swept away a lesser fighter's defenses, probing for each other's weaknesses. They were strong and fast and quite magnificent, and neither of them would yield an inch.

But in the end Razor was much the older of the two, and he was not fueled by the raw hatred and need for revenge that burned so fiercely in Topaz's veins. Slowly, remorselessly, foot by foot she drove him back, forcing him on the defensive, and Razor knew that he was very near to death. His pride kept him in the fight longer than he should have, but the pain and blood of his first few wounds brought him to his senses again. He forced the last of his energy into a flurry of blows that turned Topaz around till her back was to Mary, and then he raised his voice in a commanding shout.

"Mary! Code Delta Three! Kill Topaz!"

Mary swayed sickly as the preprogrammed control words hit her. The esper union had done their best to remove all traces of the Empire's conditioning, but some things had been buried so deeply that only another mind tech could have found them. Mary screamed as the mind techs' programming took hold again, sweeping aside her mind and wishes in favor of the old conditioned Typhoid Mary. Her face went slack, and someone else peered out of her eyes. And even as Topaz realized what was happening, Typhoid Mary stepped forward and hit her across the back of the neck with trained, professional force. Topaz fell to her knees, her thoughts darkening, her sword slipping from nerveless fingers. Mary leaned over and hit her again, and Topaz fell forward to lie still in the churned-up snow.

Razor stood for a moment, getting his breathing back under control, and then he put away his sword and leaned over Topaz. He checked the pulse in her neck, and frowned. He looked up at Mary.

"She's still alive. I told you to kill her."

"I can't," said Mary. "Not anymore."

"Obey me," said Razor, straightening up to glare at her. "Kill Investigator Topaz." Mary trembled violently, but made no move toward Topaz. Two absolutes warred in her mind, neither side giving in. Razor sighed, and shook his head. "Don't worry, Mary. They'll break you again. And then you'll kill anyone we want you to, and smile while you do it. As for Topaz, we'll just say the bitch died in the fight."

He put his hand to his sword, and that was when the steel ball from Cat's slingshot hit him right between the eyes. Razor's head snapped back, his eyes rolling up, and he fell backwards to lie twitching in the snow. Cat dropped silently down out of the darkness and hurried over to Topaz's side. He shook her shoulder urgently, but she didn't respond. Cat scowled unhappily. It was obvious she needed more help than he could give her. Someone tugged at his sleeve, and Cat spun round to find the naked man crouching at his side.

"Please," said the living esp-blocker. "Please. Kill me. Don't let me live like this."

Cat drew his knife and thrust it into the man's heart. The naked man jerked, and tried to smile at Cat. Blood welled from his mouth. Cat pulled the knife free, and the esp-blocker fell forward into the snow and lay still. Cat wiped his knife clean on his trouser leg and put it away. It was getting easier and easier for him to kill. He didn't think he liked that—what this war was doing to him. He pushed the thought aside for another time, and concentrated on the business at hand. Razor was already stirring. Cat thought about killing him, too, but decided against getting that close to Razor. The man was an Investigator, after all. He looked from Topaz to Mary and back again. He couldn't save both of them. And whilst Topaz wasn't exactly his friend, he trusted her a damned sight more than Typhoid Mary. She'd tried to kill him once, when she first came to Mistport, and with her conditioning reawakened, there was no telling what she might do. And so with only the smallest of regrets, Cat turned his back on Mary, hoisted Topaz over his shoulder, and disappeared back into the concealing shadows.

Razor slowly sat up, wincing at the vicious pain between his eyes. He put a hand to his aching head and forced himself to his feet again. He must be getting old. His instincts should have warned him there was someone else there. He almost stumbled over the dead esp-blocker, and cursed briefly when he discovered what it was. The Lord High Dram was not going to be pleased at losing his new prototype on its first assignment. And Topaz was gone. Razor shrugged. He still had Mary. He heard the sound of approaching men, and looked down the street to see a troop of marines emerging from the mists, headed his way. They'd do to escort him back to the *Defiant*. And then the ship's mind techs would open Mary's mind up and scour it clean of anything they needed to know. Mary had been closeted with the city Council in the Blackthorn Inn, and no doubt knew many useful things. Including where the scattered Council would reconvene. He took her by the arm and hustled her away. She went with him unresistingly, and if something trapped and horrified moved behind her staring eyes, no one saw it.

Owen Deathstalker, Hazel d'Ark, and Young Jack Random fought on against impossible and overwhelming odds, and Owen for one was getting pretty damned tired of it. Tired of fighting with no end in sight, of enemies who fell only to be replaced by new enemies, tired of the never-ending ache in his back and sword arm, and of the stench of freshly spilled blood and exposed guts as some other poor fool fell screaming before him. He'd fought in so many battles in so many places, taking hurts that would have killed any other man, snatching victory from the jaws of defeat, and all so he could go and do it again somewhere else.

He'd never wanted any of this. To be a hero and a leader and the hope of Humanity. He was a scholar, not a warrior. But still he went where he was needed and threw himself into the bloody heart of battle again and again, because there was no one else. He was a Deathstalker, and he would not turn his face away from the evil of Empire and the suffering of innocents. He'd fight overpowering odds and triumph yet again at the last possible moment . . . or maybe this time he wouldn't. Either way, he was getting so damned tired of it all.

He stood back-to-back with Hazel, cutting down all who came against him, fighting at the peak of his Maze-born abilities, fast and strong and deadly beyond all human hesitations, and began to wonder if this time that would be enough. The Empire forces seemed limitless. Random and the rest of the small rebel force had been swept away in the tide of fighting, leaving Owen and Hazel to fight alone, as they had so many times before. And powerful as they were, they were only two, and the Empire had an army. Marines came charging through the streets from all directions, endless waves of fighting men driven on by orders and duty and officers who'd shoot them if they turned away. They threw themselves at Owen and Hazel like the sea crashing against some stubborn rock on the seashore, and bit by bit they wore the rock down.

Owen and Hazel were burning themselves out, their own inhuman energies devouring them from within. They were too strong, too fast, and they demanded too much of their merely human bodies. Every muscle ached, every nerve screamed, and their lungs burned with the need for more and more air. Human bodies were never meant to take this kind of strain, this much punishment. The changes the Maze had worked in them held them together, healing their wounds and keeping them on their feet and fighting long after they should have fallen to superior odds, but the strain of it was killing them bit by bit, and they both knew it. They weren't stupid. They would have turned and run, if there'd been any avenue of escape, or anywhere to run to. But the marines were all around them, and nowhere in Mistport was safe anymore. And so they fought on, beyond rage or anger now, reduced to the cold, necessary work of slaughter and survival. Dead bodies piled up around them, penning them in. Owen thought wistfully of the power he'd used against his father's old network, cleaning out their house by sheer force of will, but he couldn't feel that power within him anymore. He'd used it all up and more, in the endless fighting.

Even as armed men surged forward, clambering over the bodies of the fallen for a chance at the Deathstalker and his companion, Major Chevron arrived with still more troops. The last defenders of the north side had fallen before him, and he was sweeping toward the center of Mistport and certain victory, when his forces suddenly slowed to a halt, unable to force a way through the bottleneck caused by Owen and Hazel's defiant stand. Chevron could have pulled his people back and sent them down other streets, but he couldn't, wouldn't do that once he saw who the problem was. Everyone had heard of the Deathstalker by now. Great rewards and greater privileges waited for the man who brought him down. Chevron urged his men on and waited patiently for his hounds to pull down the stags at bay. When Owen and his bitch went down, he would then step forward and deliver the coup de grace himself, and that would be that. He would walk through the burning streets of Mistport in triumph, with the Deathstalker's head held high on a pike, and there would be no doubt in all eyes who was the real hero of the taking of Mistport.

The sheer numbers forced Owen and Hazel back, step by step, until they had been contained in a back square with only the one exit, carefully blocked off by the advancing marines. High stone walls overshadowed them on every side, and all that was left to Owen and Hazel was to stand and die. The marines pressed forward, drunk on blood and death and stoned to the eyeballs on designer battle drugs, not caring about the dead comrades they had to step over to get at their enemies. Owen Deathstalker and Hazel d'Ark fought side by side with failing strength, not feeling the wounds that soaked their clothes in blood. Chevron watched from the rear, scowling impatiently, and then signaled for Kast and Morgan to bring forward the portable disrupter cannon. It would be messier this way, but more certain.

The two marines pulled the cannon quickly into position, pointed it into the back square, and set about the warm-up sequences. Kast and Morgan had been picked up by Chevron's troops as they swept inward from the north, and had volunteered to carry the portable cannon. Partly because it meant less actual work for them, and partly because they felt a great deal safer with a disrupter cannon between them and the rest of the rebel city. The taking of the city had been supposed to be a walkover, but apparently the rebels hadn't read the script, and didn't know they were beaten. So Kast and Morgan kept their heads down and labored over the cannon, got it primed and ready, and looked inquiringly at Chevron. He yelled for his people to fall back and give the cannon a clear shot, but they didn't hear him, out of their heads on drugs and the scent of victory. Chevron called again, his voice almost shrill with anger as his men ignored him, and then he turned to Kast and Morgan and nodded sharply. They looked at their fellow marines before them, and then at each other. Morgan shrugged, and Kast hit the firing stud.

The wide energy beam roared from the disrupter cannon, disintegrating everything directly before it. The marines were swept away like burning leaves in a gale. Owen and Hazel just had time to sense what was coming, and then the howling energy hit them. They brought up their psionic shields at the last moment, but there was no time, and the shields only slowed the deadly energy. It picked Hazel up and smashed her though the rear stone wall like a bullet from a gun. Owen threw himself to one side, and the energy beam just clipped him in passing. It slammed him against the left-hand wall with enough strength to crack the stonework from top to bottom. The beam snapped off, and he dropped almost senseless to the ground.

Owen lay there for what seemed like ages. His whole left side was numb. He rolled slowly onto one side and tried to get his feet under him. His head hurt, and there was blood in his mouth. The world seemed very quiet around him, the sounds of battle far away, as though everything was hesitating, to see what would happen next. He rose to one knee, swayed sickly, and then forced himself to his feet by leaning against the cracked stone wall. Parts of dead marines, torn and burnt and fused together, lay scattered across the square, marking the edges of the beam. Some marines and an officer stood behind the disrupter cannon facing him, which hummed loudly as it powered up for another shot. They seemed to be looking at something behind him. Owen turned slowly to look. He saw the hole in the wall where Hazel had been standing and knew at once what it meant. He tilted back his head, and something that was partly a scream and partly a howl of rage echoed back from the walls of the square.

A camera hovered high above him, getting it all. Toby Shreck and Flynn had been swept along with Chevron's force, and since they were heading for the center of the city and certain victory, the two newsmen had stuck with them. Unfortunately, Chevron had proved as insufferable as their official minder, Lieutenant Ffolkes. But as long as they were getting good footage of Imperial victories, he was content to let them get on with their job. Like covering the final bringing to heel and execution of that most notable traitor and outlaw, Owen Deathstalker.

Toby couldn't believe his luck. One of the great turning points of history, and he was right there on the spot. He'd recognized the Deathstalker the moment he set eyes on him. He'd become the face of the rebellion for many people in the Empire, almost as famous as the legendary professional rebel, Jack Random. He looked . . . different in person. Not as tall or as big as expected, but still there was something about him—an air, a feeling of greatness. Somehow you just knew you were looking at a man touched by destiny. And now here he was, brought low at last, even if the Empire did have to use a whole army to do it. The last echoes of his despairing cry were dying away, a terrible, awful sound that had raised the hairs on the back of Toby's neck. It was the cry of some great beast, the last of its kind, driven and harried till it had nowhere else to run. It was also a savage promise of blood and devastation, the cry of a man with nothing left to lose. He lowered his head to stare steadily at the forces arrayed against him, and Toby's blood ran cold. The Deathstalker, one man soaked in his own blood, was suddenly the most dangerous and frightening thing he'd ever seen. It was like standing in the path of an oncoming hurricane, a great force of nature, grim and implacable. It was like looking into the eyes of a god, or a devil. Toby swallowed hard,

but didn't budge. He was here to see a legend go down.
Flynn stirred uncertainly at his side.

"What is it?" said Toby, not looking away from the
scene before him. "Don't tell me we're not getting this."

"We're getting something," said Flynn quietly.
"There's some kind of energy source present, interfering
with my camera's systems. Damned if I know what it is.
I've never seen anything like it before. But it appears to
be centered around the Deathstalker."

"Stuff your energy surges. Is the picture coming though
clearly?"

"Well yes, but . . ."

"Then switch to live broadcast. The whole Empire's
going to want to see this. Damn, we've hit it lucky.
They'll be showing this footage for years."

"I've got him," said Flynn. "The poor bastard."

Trapped in a filthy back alley, surrounded by the dead
and the dying, and facing an army of Imperial marines
and a disrupter cannon, Owen Deathstalker looked unhurriedly about him. There was no way out, but he already
knew that. It seemed Chance's espers had been right after
all. They'd predicted he would die alone, in Mistport, far
from friends and succor, with everything he believed in
lost and destroyed. He just hadn't thought it would be so
soon. Or that it would mean Hazel's death, too. He never
had got round to telling her he loved her, and now he
never would. He studied the men before him and hefted
his sword. Blood dripped thickly from the blade. He had
no intention of waiting for the cannon to finish recharging. One last act of defiance, one last swing of the sword,
and at least he'd go out fighting, as a Deathstalker should.
A few last seconds to get his breath, and savor the many
strange ways his life had taken. It felt so good to be alive.
But Hazel was dead, his cause was lost, and all that remained was to die well, and take as many of the bastards
with him as he could. He smiled slowly at his enemies, a
nasty, humorless, death's-head grin, and his sword
seemed very light in his hand.

And that was when he heard something moving behind
him. He spun around, sword lifting, furious that they
wouldn't at least do him the courtesy of facing him as
they killed him, and then his jaw dropped as he saw Hazel

d'Ark pull herself painfully through the hole in the rear wall. Her face was deathly white, and she was awash in her own blood, but her sword was still in her hand, and she had enough spark left in her to grin mockingly at Owen.

"What's the matter, Deathstalker? You should know by now—I don't die that easily."

She sat down with her back against the wall, trembling violently. Owen crouched beside her and took her hand in his. It was deathly cold. Blood had run thickly from her nose and mouth, and was still dripping from her chin. He could feel her presence in his mind, but it was dim and fading, like a guttering candle in a darkened room. Hazel leaned her head back against the wall, her eyes dropping half-shut, like a runner after a long race.

"Hold my hand, Owen. I'm afraid of the dark."

"I am holding it."

"Then hold it up where I can see it. I can't feel it."

Owen lifted their joined hands up before her face, and she smiled crookedly. "Never say die, Owen. There's always a way out, if you look for it hard enough."

Owen smiled at her, pressing his lips tightly together so she wouldn't see them tremble. "I'm open for suggestions."

Kast turned to Major Chevron. "Disrupter cannon recharged, sir."

"Then what the hell are you waiting for, you idiot? Kill them! Kill them both!"

Morgan hit the firing stud, and the ravening beam of energy tore into the square before it. Hazel's hand clamped down on Owen's painfully hard, and in that split second before the energy beam hit them, their minds slammed together through their mental link, and joined, becoming a whole far greater than the sum of its parts. In that moment of despair and desperation, necessity drove them deeper into their minds than ever before, down past the conscious, past the back brain, and into the undermind. Time seemed to slow and stop. Energy built within them, tapped from some unknown source both within and outside them, fueled by love and rage and a refusal to be beaten while they were still needed. The energy blazed up and roared out of them, fast and deadly and quite unstoppable.

It met the energy beam from the disrupter cannon, swallowed it whole, and roared on. It hit the cannon and blew it apart. Kast and Morgan died screaming as the energy tore them to shreds. They vanished in splashes of blood and splintered bone. Major Chevron died next, his dreams of conquest and victory shattered like his body. And still the energy tore on, slamming into the massed ranks of the Imperial marines. They all died, hundreds of men helplessly lifting their swords and guns against a force that could not be stopped or denied. Their bodies exploded, blood and bone tumbling on the air. And then it was all over, and a horrid quiet peace fell across the square.

Toby Shreck and Flynn looked at each other. Blood and death and carnage lay all around them, but they had not been touched. Even Flynn's camera was still in place, hovering above the square, staring down at Owen and Hazel, still sitting together with their backs against the wall. Flynn shook his head slowly.

"How come we're not dead?"

"Beats the hell out of me," said Toby. "Either they didn't see us as enemies, or we just weren't important enough to bother with."

Owen and Hazel sat together, looking slowly about them, their breathing gradually easing as they realized the danger was past. The power that had passed briefly though them was gone, leaving no trace of its passage save a bone-deep weariness. They'd given all they had to give, and more, and there was nothing left in them now but a terrible tiredness of the mind, as well as the body. Owen's gaze fell upon Toby and Flynn, standing alone in the sea of carnage and broken bodies. He rose painfully to his feet, and beckoned for them to approach him. Flynn looked like he'd very much rather not, but Toby dragged him forward, until they were standing before the Death-stalker. He looked less like a legend up close, and more human. In fact, he looked mostly like a man who'd had to carry too many burdens in his time, but did it anyway, because there was no one else. He gestured at the camera hovering above him.

"Bring that thing down here. I have something to say."

Flynn brought it down through his comm link, till it

was hovering before Owen's face. He nodded to Flynn and Toby and then addressed the camera.

"Greetings, Lionstone, if you're looking in. This is the rightful Lord Deathstalker, coming to you live from the rebel city of Mistport. Just thought I'd let you know your invasion is a bust. It never stood a chance. Your army of professional killers was never going to be a match for a city of free men and women. And as soon as we've finished clearing up the mess you've made here, we'll be coming to see you. Remember my face, Lionstone. You'll live to see your forces scattered and your Empire fall, and then I will walk into Court, rip the crown off your head, and kick your nasty ass right off the Iron Throne. You should never have happened. You were an unfortunate mistake, an error in history, that I will put right at the first possible moment. Be seeing you, Empress." He looked at Flynn. "That's it. You can go now."

"I don't suppose there's any chance of an exclusive interview?" said Toby Shreck. Owen looked at him, and Toby fell back a pace. "No, I didn't really think so. Come on, Flynn, time to go. We don't want to outstay our welcome."

And then they both turned and ran, the camera bobbing along behind them. Owen smiled tiredly. They had no way of knowing his speech had been pure bravado, using up what little strength he had left. He turned unsteadily, and went back to sit down beside Hazel. Her eyes were closed, and her breathing was very shallow, but her eyes drifted halfway open as he settled himself at her side.

"Yeah. What you said, stud. Always knew your propensity for making speeches would come in handy one day."

"How do you feel?" said Owen. It wasn't a casual question.

"Tired. At peace. What the hell did we tap into just then? Some power the Maze gave us?"

"I don't think so. It felt more like something we'd always had, something the Maze just put us in touch with. Maybe someday all Humanity could learn to do what we did."

"Yeah," said Hazel. "Maybe. But I doubt we'll be

around to see it. That energy blast pretty much used us up. There's nothing left in me anymore."

"Same here," said Owen. "Guess our time's run out. There are worse ways to go. And at least we got a chance to throw a scare into the Iron Bitch first. Hazel, there's . . . something I've been meaning to tell you . . ."

"Same here," said Hazel. "My Blood addiction's gone. I can feel it. That energy surge scoured it right out of my system. I'm clean, at last."

"I'm glad. Hazel, I wanted to say . . ."

And then his voice was drowned out by the roar of gravity engines overhead. Owen looked up, and then forced himself to his feet again. Six gravity barges were hovering above the square, their disrupter cannon trained on him and Hazel. Owen's hand clenched around his sword hilt, but knew that this time there wasn't going to be any last-minute escape. Even at his peak he doubted he'd have been able to stand against the massed disrupter cannon of six gravity barges. He looked up at them and grinned defiantly anyway.

"You people ever heard of the word overkill?"

"The fight's over, Deathstalker," said an amplified voice from above. "But you don't have to die here. Lionstone has empowered us to make you an offer. Surrender to us, and you will be allowed to live. Our scientists could learn much from studying you."

"Tell them to go to hell, Deathstalker," said Hazel, behind him. "My mother didn't raise me to be a laboratory rat. Probably vivisect us, first chance they got. Or send their mind techs into our heads, to turn us to their side. We can't allow that, Owen."

"Our sensors indicate that you are gravely wounded, and your companion is dying," said the amplified voice. "We can save both of you. We have a regeneration machine aboard the *Defiant*. She doesn't have to die, Deathstalker. It's up to you."

"Owen . . ." said Hazel.

"I'm sorry, Hazel," said Owen. "I'm not ready for both of us to die." He looked up at the gravity barges and threw down his sword. "I surrender. Come and get us. But hurry it up. I don't think she's got much time left."

"You bloody fool," said Hazel.

He looked back at her, and smiled regretfully. "Always, where you're concerned."

Hazel tried to reach for her gun, but her fingers wouldn't work. Owen sat down beside her again and listened to her curse him till the Imperial troops came to take them both into custody.

Near the center of Mistport, lit bright as day by the burning buildings and out-of-control fires, Young Jack Random, John Silver, and the forces they led battled the invading Imperial forces to a standstill. The air was hot and smoky, with dark smuts floating in it, and the roar of the fires almost drowned out the roar of the gravity barges and Legion's triumphant howl. The fighting filled the streets from side to side, and spilled over into back alleys and culs-de-sac. The trampled snow turned to blood-soaked slush, and bodies lay everywhere. The Death-stalker's projectile weapons were proving their worth at close quarters, but even so the battle raged this way and that, neither side able to take the advantage for long. Steel hammered on steel, the fighters held face-to-face by the crush of the crowds. There was no room for strategy or tactics or fancy footwork, just the hard, steady work of human butchery and slaughter.

Young Jack Random was right there in the thick of it, his great frame standing out in the crowd, larger than life and apparently unbeatable. His war cries rang out above the din, loud and triumphant and unyielding, and every man who fought at his side felt twice the man for being in his presence. Random's sword rose and fell steadily, cutting a path through the enemy forces toward their commanders, refusing to be slowed or turned aside. His courage and determination inspired the rebels to ever greater efforts, throwing themselves into the fray as though their lives were nothing.

And right there in the middle of it, too, was John Silver. He was soaked in blood, as much from his own wounds as others', but still his sword was steady in his hand, as he pushed himself relentlessly forward. He was beyond pain or exhaustion now, driven by a simple refusal to lie down and die while he was still needed.

And slowly, step by step, foot by foot, the rebels forced

the Empire back, denying them the heart of the city. The invasion met an implacable, unbeatable force, and broke against it. War cries from a hundred worlds and cultures rang above the slaughter, combining into a chilling roar of rage and courage and determination, and the invading forces had nothing with which to answer it. Some marines turned and ran, risking being shot by their own officers, who called desperately on their comm links for reinforcements, or orders to withdraw. The word came back to hold their ground. The gravity barges were on their way. All of them.

The deaf and dumb burglar called Cat sat on a cooling dead body, watching what was left of the Blackthorn Inn burn itself out. A blackened frame showed dimly through the smoke and fog, smoldering here and there. Nothing else remained of the only place Cat had ever thought of as home. There was no sign of Cyder anywhere. Soon he would get up and go into the ruin, and search for bodies, to see if one of them might be hers, but he hadn't quite worked up the nerve yet. He didn't think he could face life without Cyder. She was his love, his only love, who gave his life meaning and purpose. She couldn't be in there. She of all people would have had the sense to get out while the getting was good. But the thought of turning over a blackened corpse and finding her rings on the charred fingers was still too much to bear for the moment. And so he sat where he was, watching what remained of the Blackthorn steam and smolder, and waited for Investigator Topaz to wake up.

He'd carried her unconscious body across the roofs, where he knew he wouldn't be stopped or challenged. No one knew the roofs like he did. The roar of the fighting didn't call him, and Legion's howl didn't deter him, because he couldn't hear either of them. Instead, he concentrated on the task at hand, getting the Investigator to a place of safety. And for him, safety had always been the Blackthorn Inn. All the way there, with Topaz's weight growing heavier and heavier on his shoulders, he'd comforted himself with the thought that Cyder would know what to do about Topaz and Mary's turning. But now the inn was gone, and Cyder wasn't there, and he didn't know what to do.

He felt Topaz stir at his side and turned around to help her sit up. He sat her on the body, too, it was better than sitting in the mud and slush on the road. She held her head for a bit, her mouth moving in shapes that made no sense to him. He could read lips, but things like groans and moans were a mystery to him. Finally she turned and looked at him, and her eyes were dark and steady. She asked where she was, and he told her in fingertalk, but she couldn't understand it. He pointed to the street sign, and she nodded slowly. He wanted to tell her about leaving Mary, but didn't know how. Topaz rose to her feet, swaying only a little and only for a moment, nodded her thanks to Cat, and strode off into the mists. Cat watched her go. The body was getting cold and uncomfortable beneath him, so he stood up. Cyder wasn't dead. He was sure of that. So he'd better go and look for her. And if he could strike the occasional blow against the invading forces while he was doing it, so much the better. Cat turned, scrambled up the wall, and took to the roofs again.

Aboard the *Defiant,* Owen and Hazel had been brought in chains to see Legion, floating in its tank. Investigator Razor was there, with Typhoid Mary, to make sure they behaved, and Captain Bartok was there to watch their faces as they realized they couldn't hope to stand against anything like Legion. The great glass tank, festooned with wires and cables and strange, unfamiliar tech, was still the only thing in the auditorium. Legion floated peacefully in the thick yellow liquid—a great bulging fleshy mass without shape or meaning. The brains of thousands of dead espers, stitched together with alien-derived tech, controlled or at least dominated by the gestalt mind of Wormboy's worms. The air stank horribly, and Owen screwed up his face as he peered at the shape in the tank. He started to move forward for a better look, but Razor grabbed one of his chains and pulled him back. Owen almost fell under the weight of his chains, and swore at Razor. The Investigator hit him dispassionately in the kidneys. Owen nearly went down again, but somehow kept his feet.

The Empire had kept its promise. They'd put Hazel in the *Defiant's* regeneration machine, and she'd emerged whole and healed of all her wounds. But the machine had been able to do nothing about the almost spiritual weariness that she and Owen shared after tapping into the mental force that saved their lives. Physically, they were both still weak as kittens. That hadn't stopped Bartok from taking all their weapons and weighing them down with chains till they could hardly stand. They'd even wanted to remove Owen's golden Hadenman hand, but couldn't figure out how to do it. There had been talk of cutting it off, just in case, but Bartok had been too eager to show off his secret weapon to his illustrious prisoners. Besides, they could always cut it off later.

Typhoid Mary wore no chains. The control words in her head held her more securely than any physical restraint. She hadn't said a dozen words since she had come aboard the *Defiant*. Owen and Hazel had both tried talking to her, but she only responded to Imperial orders. She stared blankly at the thing in the tank, apparently unmoved by its appearance or its smell.

"So," said Captain Bartok to Owen and Hazel. "What do you think of our wondrous creation?"

Owen sniffed. "Looks like one of God's more disappointing bowel movements. Smells like it, too. Haven't you people ever heard of air-conditioning?"

Razor hit him again, and he almost fell. Hazel kicked Razor in the knee, that being all her chains would allow. Razor hit her in the face, bloodying her mouth and nose. Owen and Hazel leaned on each other, glaring impotently at the Investigator. He didn't smile. He didn't have to. Mary watched impassively, her face quite blank. The control words buzzed in the back of her head like a swarm of angry bees, but still a small part of her was able to think clearly. She kept it to herself, hidden so deep not even another esper could have detected it. She'd seen herself strike Topaz down as if from a great distance, helpless in her own body. She assumed Topaz was dead, or she'd be here, too. Mary, who had sworn never to kill again, had killed her best friend. The anguish and the horror nearly overwhelmed her when she thought of it, but she kept it deep and secret, and none of it reached her face.

Bartok took her by the arm, and led her toward the great tank. She went unresistingly.

"Hello, Legion," said Bartok. "I've brought someone to see you. This is Typhoid Mary. A Siren, and quite possibly one of the most powerful espers in the Empire."

Welcome, Mary, said Legion in its many voices. Owen grunted as the horrid chorus rang inside his head, thick and smothering like the stench of rotting fruit. Hazel shook her head, as though to drive the voices out. Mary didn't react at all. Legion spoke in many voices at once, combined into an awful harmony of male and female voices, young and old, alive and dead. And faintly, in the background, they could all hear the sound of thousands of voices screaming helplessly, damned to a man-made living Hell.

I'm so glad you're here, Mary, said Legion. *They're going to rip your brain out of your head, and make it part of me. All your power and all your songs will become mine. And I shall put them to good use down in the streets of Mistport. Already they quail and shiver at my voice, but with your songs I'll trample through all their heads and stir my sticky fingers in their souls. They will all dance to my tune, or die horribly.*

"Well?" said Bartok, after a while. "Talk to Legion, Mary."

"Who's speaking to me?" said Mary slowly. "The brains or the worms?"

You'll find out.

"Why are you hurting and killing your fellow espers? They're your own kind."

Because it's fun. And because I can. I'm nothing like them. Or you. There's never been anything like me before. There's no limit to how big I can grow, no limit to how powerful I can become. Call me Legion. I am vast. I contain multitudes. Someday, all espers shall be a part of me. This tank won't hold me forever. And on the day that I break free, let all Humanity beware. Let all that lives beware.

Typhoid Mary looked at her future, and at the future of Humanity, and despair and rage boiled up within her, blasting aside the restraints of the Empire's conditioning. New power blazed through her, wild and potent, as some-

thing wonderful was suddenly there in the auditorium
with them, bright and shining and perfect, with Mary as
its focus. The Mater Mundi, Our Mother Of All Souls.
Mary's face was exalted, her eyes shining like the sun.
Razor reacted immediately to the new threat, his sword
instantly in his hand, but some unseen force picked him
up and threw him aside as casually as a bothersome
insect. Legion surged back and forth in its tank, awed by
the sheer power it could feel building in the auditorium.
The Mater Mundi reached out, and all the espers of Mistworld were suddenly drawn into its single purpose. In
that moment, the thousands of minds came together and
were one, guided by the Mater Mundi, focused through
Typhoid Mary. She turned her unyielding gaze on Legion,
and it was afraid.

Psionic energy crackled on the air, surging through all
the bays and corridors of the *Defiant*. Machinery overloaded and exploded, workstations malfunctioned and
shut down, and all through the ship the members of the
crew fell to their knees, clutching at their heads as unfamiliar thoughts crashed through their minds. It was chaos
and it was bedlam, and in the auditorium Captain Bartok
saw it all and screamed.

On the planet below, in the streets of Mistport, everything came to a halt. Psionic energy hammered on the air
like the wrath of God, and the invading forces fell senseless to the ground, their minds shutting down rather than
face the power of the Mater Mundi. The espers of Mistport stood still and unseeing, caught up in the gestalt.
They stood together on the mental plane, focused through
one mind and one will, striving against the power of the
thing called Legion. But all the thousands of rebel espers
together weren't enough. Legion and the Mater Mundi
faced each other, each concentrating on the destruction of
the other, and neither could take the upper hand. They
were too evenly balanced.

Stalemate.

Standing close together, forgotten in the crash of energies, Owen and Hazel found themselves suddenly revitalized. Something within them was feeding off the psionic
energies running loose in the ship. They felt strong and
well again, and their chains cracked and fell apart, broken

links clattering and rolling away across the floor. Owen turned on Razor, but he had already left. Hazel looked at Captain Bartok, but he was standing still and helpless, frozen in place like a statue. Someone didn't want him interfering.

Owen's and Hazel's minds reached out, drawn by some instinct to another level of reality, and there they saw the struggle between Legion and the Mater Mundi. Two great armies of massed will faced each other, locked in a combat from which only one could emerge whole and sane. Legion was clearly the smaller of the two, but it had no limits and no restraints, while the Mater Mundi was focused through Typhoid Mary, who had sworn a solemn oath never to kill again. Owen and Hazel concentrated. In the background, unnoticed by either side, there were voices screaming for release. The thousands of dead espers whose brains made up the body of Legion, controlled by Wormboy's worms. Owen moved closer.

You have to break free, he said in a voice that was not a voice. *The Empire is using you to kill your own kind.*

We know, said a crowd of whispering voices. *But there's nothing we can do. The worms are in our brains. The technology of Legion gives them power over us. Free us!*

We can't, said Hazel. *You're already dead. They cut out your brains and threw away your bodies. You're the ghosts in the machine.*

There were screams and howls of despair, and the crying of thousands of souls who no longer had eyes to cry with. *What can we do? What can we do?*

There's only one thing left to you, said Owen Death-stalker. *You have to finish dying. Legion will never let you go, never let you know peace. You heard what it said. It wants to kill all that lives, or make it part of itself. Think of the millions of minds, trapped and suffering in Legion's grasp, like you.*

We don't want to die!

No one does, said Hazel. *But sometimes you have no choice, if everything you ever lived for is to have any meaning.*

Nothing can stop you, said Owen. *But do you really*

want an eternity as Legion's slaves? Stop fighting to live.
Let yourselves die. And let Legion die with you.

Perhaps in that moment the thousands of esper brains remembered who they used to be, the things they believed in, and fought for. Things they would have died for, given the chance. Perhaps they were tired of their mental slavery and just wanted to rest at last. And perhaps in that moment they were brave men and women again, determined to do the right thing. But whatever the reason, the brains that made up Legion gave up their hold on life and let themselves die. There was a great outpouring of light on the mental plane, as thousands of men and women broke free and went to their reward at last. And left behind, broken and helpless, nothing but a dark cancerous mass, writhing and squirming—Wormboy's worms. The Mater Mundi stepped on them, and they died screaming.

On the bridge of the *Defiant*, Investigator Razor watched Legion die. Every piece of monitoring equipment showed the creature's life signs dropping to zero. For no obvious reason, the huge mass in the glass tank had given up the ghost. Deathstalker. Damn him. Razor turned to his other consoles. Half the bridge tech wasn't working, and what was brought him nothing but bad news. Most of his bridge crew were catatonic, and the rest might as well be. He grabbed the Second in Command by the shoulder and shook him until some sense came back into his eyes.

"In Captain Bartok's absence, I am assuming authority on this ship," Razor said slowly and clearly. "I want every armed man down in Legion's hold. Kill everything you find there."

"We already tried that, sir," said the Second. "No one can get anywhere near the hold. Something's ... preventing us."

Razor thought hard. Around him, the bridge crew began to stir and return to their senses. With Legion dead, it wouldn't be long before Mistport's surviving espers suddenly found they had their powers back. And then there'd be hell to pay. They'd wipe out the forces on the ground, and then turn their attention to the *Defiant*.

"Power up all the systems," Razor said flatly. "Prepare to scorch Mistport."

"Sir?" said the Second in Command. "Our people are still down there, sir."

"With Legion down, they're as good as dead anyway. Our orders were to bring Mistworld back into the Empire. If I have to turn it into a single great funeral pyre to do so, then that's what I'll do. Bring all the disrupter cannon on-line. On my command, commence firing. And don't stop while there's one speck of life left on that miserable planet."

And that was when the lights went out. There was a long moment of utter darkness, and then the emergency systems came back on, bathing the bridge in a crimson glow. The Second checked his instruments. When he looked up, his eyes were scared.

"All main systems are down, sir. Practically everything except basic life support. Some . . . unknown force shut them down. We're helpless, sir."

Investigator Razor sat down in the command chair and wondered how he was going to explain this to the Empress.

In the auditorium holding Legion's tank, all was still and quiet. Both Legion and the Mater Mundi were gone, their overwhelming presence absent. The great fleshy mass had sunk to the bottom of its tank. Owen and Hazel stood together, getting used to being back in their own head again. Typhoid Mary, only herself again, bent over Captain Bartok, who was sitting on the floor, staring at nothing.

"Don't bother," said Owen. "I already checked. There's no one home. Whatever he saw here, his mind couldn't handle it."

"Damn," said Hazel. "I was looking forward to killing him."

"The killing's over," said Mary, straightening up. "Let's go home."

"Sounds good to me," said Owen. "Let's see if we can requisition an escape pod. I doubt anybody will be in the mood to say no to us."

They left the auditorium. Captain Bartok sat very still, staring with empty eyes at the dead mass in the tank.

Afterward, what was left of Mistport celebrated. Those few marines who didn't run back to their pinnaces fast enough were hunted down and killed. No one was in the mood to take prisoners. The dead were piled to one side, to be disposed of later. Rescue squads formed themselves and set about digging in collapsed buildings, in search of survivors. Mistport had come through again. There was a hell of a lot of rebuilding to be done, but the bulk of the city had survived. It took a lot to kill Mistworlders. If only because if you could survive Mistport, you could handle pretty much anything else the universe could throw at you.

What remained of the Council was working at the esper union's hall, coordinating relief work and making sure the espers' psionic screen stayed in place until the *Defiant* was safely gone. No point in taking chances. Everyone else in the hall was partying like there was no tomorrow. Probably because so many of them hadn't expected to live to see tomorrow anyway. Esper chatter filled the great room, almost loud enough to be heard by non-espers. A couple of show-offs were dancing on the ceiling. None of the non-espers felt slighted or threatened. For the moment at least, victory had brought everyone together.

Young Jack Random was the man of the hour. Everyone wanted to be next to him, to slap him on the back, pour him another drink. He was only too happy to describe his part in the defense of the city, and the people around him wouldn't let him be modest about it. Everyone had some tale to tell of the legendary professional rebel's courage and daring exploits.

Owen Deathstalker and Hazel d'Ark sat in a corner of the hall, drinking a reasonably good vintage wine and dubiously studying a collection of party snacks. Their greater abilities had disappeared along with the Mater Mundi, and they were both feeling very human again. Their wounds had healed, and the bone-deep weariness had gone, but they both felt they needed some time to come to terms with the more than human things they'd done. Their exploits fighting in the streets hadn't gone unnoticed, and some people made a point of seeking them out to reminisce and congratulate them, but on the whole most people preferred to idolize the larger-than-life Jack Random.

At Random's side stood Donald Royal, his ancient frame full of new life and good wine, revitalized by battle and feeling like a new man again. He'd been a great hero in his younger days, and had never been really happy leading a peaceful life. Now he felt like himself again, full of piss and vinegar, and if he was almost certain to pay dearly for that feeling tomorrow, well, he'd think about that tomorrow. People roared his name along with Jack Random's and toasted him like the warrior of old. Random put an arm across his shoulders and wouldn't be separated from him. Madelaine Skye stuck close, too, and tried to tell herself it wasn't just jealousy that made her distrust the legendary professional rebel.

Over by the bar, Cat and Cyder were making serious inroads into the champagne. They always believed in indulging in the best, especially when someone else was footing the bill. As the level in the third bottle dropped, Cyder became increasingly philosophical about the loss of her tavern.

"We'll build another Blackthorn," she said to Cat, with only the faintest slur in her speech. "We can live off the insurance money for a while, and I'll set up some easy burglaries for you. Bound to be lots of good stuff lying around relatively unguarded, after all this. The old team rides again. What the hell; maybe you and I were never meant to be respectable."

John Silver came over to pay his respects to Owen and Hazel. He was wrapped in so many bandages he could only bend in certain directions, but he seemed cheerful enough. Owen decided to be diplomatic, and excused himself for a moment, so Silver and Hazel could talk in private. After Owen had moved away, they stood in silence for a while, meeting each other's gaze steadily.

"I don't suppose there's any way I could persuade you to stay in Mistport?" said Silver.

"No. I go where the rebellion takes me, and it's all over here."

"You need a little Blood, to take with you? I could always . . ."

"No thanks. I don't need it anymore."

"I thought not. You don't need me, either."

"It was good seeing you again, John, but you're my past. I've moved on since then, and where I've gone you can't follow. What will you do now?"

"Help rebuild the starport. If we can."

"The Golgotha underground will supply you with whatever high-tech you need." She sipped her wine to indicate she was about to change the subject. "You don't know what happened to Chance and his kids, do you?"

"Oh, they'll come through all right," said Silver easily. "His kind always do. The esper union is looking after the children, here in the Hall somewhere. I think the powers that be are feeling a bit guilty about abandoning them to someone like Chance, just because they didn't want to be bothered with children who reminded them of the dark side of esp." He looked round. "Owen's coming back. I'd better make myself scarce. Look after yourself, Hazel."

"You too, John. From what I hear, you were quite the hero, out fighting in the streets."

Silver grinned. "Yeah. I don't know what came over me."

He gave her a bow and a wink, and moved off into the party.

Not that far away, Investigator Topaz and Typhoid Mary were talking quietly. Neither of them cared much for parties, as a rule, but after the death of so many people, they both felt a need for the comfort of a crowd. When the thousands of minds in Legion died, they had felt each one through the Mater Mundi's link, and some of Death's cold hand had brushed against their souls. So they came to the union esper hall, to warm themselves in the presence of friends.

"I still don't know if I did the right thing," said Mary, looking down into her wineglass.

"Of course you did," Topaz said briskly. "Anyone who died on the *Defiant* needed to die, whether they were innocent minds trapped in Legion, or Imperial butchers come to kill us all. I'm more interested in the Mater Mundi. What did it feel like, being the focus?"

Mary frowned. "I'm not sure. I'm already beginning to forget it. I think my mind is protecting me from things I'm not ready to deal with. I felt ... larger, more real, somehow. As though the whole of my life was a dream, from which I awoke for a short while. Part of me wants it again, but the rest of me is scared shitless at the very thought. That business with the control words worries me as well. The Mater Mundi contact wiped out the controls Razor activated, but who knows what else the mind techs might have planted deep within me?"

"Worry about it when it happens," said Topaz. "After the way the Empire got its ass kicked here today, I think we can safely assume it'll be some time before we have to worry about Imperial agents again. And you're a lot stronger than you used to be. When you focused the Mater Mundi, it changed you. Your mind is more powerful now. I can feel it. When I look at you with my mind, it's like staring into the sun."

"I know," said Mary. "That's something else that worries me."

"Hell," said Topaz. "You wouldn't be happy if you didn't have something to worry about. It's in your nature."

"True," said Typhoid Mary.

Jenny Psycho watched them talk together, from a safe distance, but felt more numb than jealous. She still couldn't get over the fact that the Mater Mundi had chosen to manifest through someone else this time, not her. She'd called for help in the streets of Mistport, and the Mother had ignored her. She was slowly beginning to realize that she'd have to find a new purpose in life, that she wasn't who she'd thought she was.

Councillor McVey cornered Gideon Steel, who was sulking quietly by the punch bowl. The Port Director was rather upset that he didn't have a starport to be Director of anymore.

"Snap out of it, Steel," said McVey. "With Magnus and Barron dead, Castle out of his mind with grief, and Donald Royal telling anyone who'll listen that it's his destiny to fight alongside Jack Random, wherever he goes, that only leaves you and me as city Councillors. And there's a hell of a lot of work to be done in putting this city back together. I can't do it on my own, Gideon."

Steel sighed heavily. "I suppose you're right. But I was happy being Port Director. It was the only job I was ever any good at."

"It was the only job where you could syphon off a lot of money on the side."

Steel looked at McVey. "You knew?"

"Of course."

"Then why didn't you say anything?"

"Because you were a good Port Director. It's a hard job, and no one else on the Council wanted it. So, are you going to help me rebuild Mistport? Think of all the work and construction contracts you'll be in charge of. A man with his wits about him would be in a position to steal himself a fortune."

"You talked me into it," said Steel. "When do we start?"

Back on the other side of the room, Neeson the banker had come to pay his respects to Owen Deathstalker. He looked battered and tired, but surprisingly happy.

"You look like you've been in the wars," said Owen.

"Damn right," said Neeson. "Most fun I've had in years. I started out as a mercenary, you know. This sword for hire, and all that. Your father brought me into the business world. Said someone with my instincts would go far in banking. And how right he was. Anyway, I came to tell you that my associates and I have decided to reactivate and maintain the old Deathstalker information network."

"How very public-spirited of you," said Hazel. "What brought that on?"

"Well, partly because of the gentleman standing at your side, partly because everyone on Mistworld is now part of the great rebellion, whether we want it or not, and partly because we all feel more alive now than we have in a long time. Business has its own rewards, but it's not exactly exciting, you know. It's a poor life when you're reduced to getting cheap thrills from foreclosing on someone's mortgage. No, being a rebel sounds much more fun. See you around, Deathstalker."

He nodded briskly to Owen and Hazel, and wandered off in search of food and wine and someone else to whom he could boast about his transformation. There's no one more enthusiastic than a middle-aged convert. He was replaced by the journalist Toby Shreck and his cameraman Flynn. Their press credentials had saved them from the general slaughter of the invading forces, but now they were stranded on Mistworld until they could beg, borrow, or steal passage off.

"Hi there," said Toby. "Mind if we join you? We've brought our own bottle."

"Now there speaks a civilized man," said Owen. "I understand you're interested in coming along with us desperate rebel types when we leave?"

"Damn right," said Toby. "You people are where the story is. Besides, we asked everybody else, and they all said no."

"Fair enough," said Owen. "If you're looking for a good story, some of my associates are planning an expedition to a planet called Haceldama. I'll put you in contact with them. In the meantime, why aren't you interviewing Jack Random? He's the official hero of the hour."

Toby and Flynn looked at each other, and then Toby leaned forward and lowered his voice. "Are you sure that *is* Jack Random?"

Owen and Hazel kept their faces blank, but they leaned forward and lowered their voices, too. "What makes you think that he isn't?" said Hazel.

"Because we saw him leading a rebellion on Technos III, just a few weeks ago," said Toby. "And he looked ... different. Older."

"Much older," said Flynn. "I've got it all on tape. And my camera never lies."

"Lots of people have claimed to be Jack Random, down the years," Owen said neutrally. "Let's just say this one seems more convincing than most."

Toby glanced back at Random, still surrounded by well-wishers and devoted disciples. "Doesn't it bother you, that he's getting all the glory? You two did just as much as he. Flynn got most of it on tape."

Hazel shrugged. "Last thing I need is being bothered by autograph hunters. Let him be the hero, if that's what he wants. I was never very comfortable with the role anyway."

"Heads up," said Owen. "I think he's going to say something."

The speech that followed was a triumph. Short, sharp, lucid, and witty. A professional speechwriter couldn't have done better. Young Jack Random stirred the crowd's blood with praises for their deeds in protecting their city, and with promises of more battles against injustice to come. *On to Golgotha!* he cried, and everyone cheered and applauded. Owen and Hazel applauded, too, so as not to seem small, but neither of them was swayed by his words. He was still just too good to be true, for them.

But, all things considered, Owen felt basically upbeat. Things seemed to be going his way for once. The Imperial invasion had been defeated, Mistport had been saved, his own mission was apparently a great success, and he'd faced the prophecy of his own death and survived after all. Not that he'd ever really believed in it, but it was good to put it behind him. It was like having a new lease on life; and life was very good just then.

He and Hazel stood together and watched the crowd cheer itself hoarse for Jack Random, and were quietly content.

CHAPTER TWO

INNOCENCE LOST

They called it Shannon's World, because it was his dream, his vision. He all but bankrupted himself bringing it into existence, but the result was a pleasure world like no other, reserved only for the very rich, the extremely well connected, and the strictly aristocratic. Its location was a secret known only to the glamorous few, and for those inquisitive others who bribed or bullied their way to Shannon's World uninvited, state-of-the-art security and weapons systems waited to blow them out of this world and into the next. Shannon's World, where mountains sang to each other, fantasies and dreams became real, and the whole world was alive. A pleasure planet unlike any other, where even the weariest of souls could find rest and comfort and contentment.

And then the awful thing happened.

Afterward, Shannon's World cut itself off from the Empire, refusing to acknowledge any form of contact. Visitors were destroyed while still in orbit, no matter whom they represented. The Empress sent a ship. It never came back. She sent a starcruiser, which managed to land a full brigade of marines. Something killed them. So she tried a series of covert Security teams. Only one man returned from what had been the foremost pleasure planet in the Empire. He came back soaked in many people's blood, quite mad, his mind destroyed by what he'd seen, and died soon after, mostly because he wanted to. He renamed the planet Haceldama, the Field of Blood.

The Empress put the planet under Quarantine, stationed a starcruiser in far orbit to make sure whatever was down there didn't get out, and then turned her attention to other things. Thanks to the traitor Deathstalker and his growing rebellion, she had far more pressing worries than a pleasure planet gone bad. And so things might have remained, if the most important strategic and military mind in the Empire, one Vincent Harker, hadn't crash-landed on what used to be Shannon's World. In his head was information vital to both the Empire and the rebellion. The Empress sent down a company of her elite battle troops to recover him. They never reported back.

Now, it was the rebels' turn.

In a hastily converted cargo ship called the *Wild Rose,* a small group of rebels watched the sensor panels closely, and hoped the new Hadenman cloaking system was everything it was supposed to be. The planet's defenses were powerful enough to batter down any force shield generated by anything less than a full starcruiser, and the cargo ship's shields were strictly rudimentary. Either the Hadenman device fooled the orbiting satellites, or the rebels wouldn't live long enough to know they were dead. The device squatted behind them, roughly bolted to the deck, all sharp edges and unexpected angles, with strange lights that came and went for no apparent reason. The rebels preferred not to look at it. The shape of the device hurt their eyes. They kept their gaze fixed on the sensor panels and the main viewscreen, watching the planet grow slowly beneath them, cool and blue and utterly enigmatic.

On board the *Wild Rose* was Finlay Campbell, the aristo turned rebel, daredevil fighter with a coldness in his soul, who had once been secretly the Masked Gladiator, undefeated champion of the Golgotha Arenas. At his side his lady love, Evangeline Shreck, daughter of the aristocracy, who lived for years with the secret that she was really only a clone, created to replace the daughter sexually abused and murdered by her father. On Finlay's other side, Julian Skye, the rogue esper rescued by Finlay from the interrogation cells under Golgotha. Skye was once one of the most powerful espers in the Empire and a daring rebel, but his time in the bloodstained hands of the mind techs had left him hurt and damaged, perhaps beyond his ability to recover. And finally there was Giles Deathstalker, the legendary hero who'd spent over nine hundred years in stasis, emerging to find an Empire he barely recognized. Rebels one and all, representatives of the

Golgotha underground, desperate to find Vincent Harker before the Empire forces did.

Also along for the ride were Toby Shreck and his cameraman Flynn, heading toward a story darker and stranger than they had ever known.

Finlay stirred impatiently at the sensor panels. He'd never handled waiting well. His only prayer had always been, *dear Lord, please deliver me into battle and danger up to my eyes.* He had once been a master of fashion, a fop and dandy of great renown, a persona and mask he'd created to hide his secret other existence as the Masked Gladiator, feted darling of the Arenas. Now he was on the run from the Society he'd once moved in so freely, just another rebel among many, expendable enough to be sent on what many regarded as a suicide mission. He was twenty-six years old, and looked easily ten years older. His long hair had faded to a yellow so pale it was almost colorless. He wore it tied back in a single, practical pigtail. He had the look of a mercenary soldier; cold and dangerous but essentially uninvolved. He only joined the rebels to better protect his love Evangeline, and made no secret of his distance from the underground's politics. It was enough that they provided him with missions where he could test his courage and skill with weapons. Finlay Campbell was fast becoming that most dangerous of men—one with nothing left to lose. Only Evangeline kept him sane and focused, and both of them knew it.

Evangeline Shreck had lived most of her life in fear. Fear of being exposed as a clone and executed for the unforgivable crime of having successfully impersonated an aristocrat. Fear of her father's perverted love. Fear of always being alone. And then she found Finlay, and for the first time in her life she had a reason to go on living. If he died, she didn't know what she'd do. Unlike Finlay, she had no taste for danger and excitement, but as a clone she was fiercely dedicated to the rebel cause. And if the many tensions of her life were slowly tearing her apart, that was her business. Gamine and elfin, her military fatigues hung about her like a tent. She had large dark eyes a man could drown in, a firm mouth, and the unmistakable air of a survivor. Of someone who had lived through pain and horror and despair, and had not broken under them. Yet.

They stood together, studying the bright blue planet on the viewscreen before them. There were no signs of civilization, nothing to show that Humanity had ever made a mark on Shannon's World. No cities, no great roads, nothing big enough to trigger the ship's sensors. Whatever lived down there was keeping itself hidden and secret. Evangeline sighed suddenly.

"It looks so innocent. Untouched by man. Not at all like a Field of Blood. What could have happened down there, what terrible thing, to justify such a name?"

Finlay smiled slightly. "Something powerful and nasty enough to kill off every armed man the Iron Bitch has sent down there, so far. And there's not much that can stand against a full force of armed marines. I've always liked a challenge."

"Do you think . . . could it be something like the Grendel alien? I've seen the holo of what that creature did at Court."

"Unlikely," said Toby from the back. "After the horror of what happened on Grendel, every planet in the Empire was searched for signs of more Vaults. Not even a pleasure planet like this would have been exempt. And if anyone had found more Sleepers, there's no way they could have kept it quiet. There isn't that much money in the Empire."

"Don't worry, love," said Finlay to Evangeline, putting an arm across her shoulders and pulling her close. "Whatever's down there, I'll protect you."

"Did you ever come here?" said Evangeline. "I never did. I'd heard of Shannon's World, but Daddy didn't believe in letting me out of his sight."

"I've been most places," said Finlay. "But never here. I was always too busy. And it didn't sound like the kind of place where I'd fit in. Too peaceful. Ironic, isn't it? That what was designed as the safest, most secure place in the Empire should end up a nightmare renamed the Field of Blood. Still, that's life in the Empire for you these days. Just as a matter of interest, how did we get the coordinates for this place? I thought they were strictly need to know, only issued to actual visitors?"

"Valentine Wolfe supplied them," said Evangeline, her voice carefully neutral. "Before he left us, to become Lionstone's right-hand man. Apparently he'd been here once, but didn't care for it. Something about the place . . . disturbed him. He thought we should blow it all up."

"The Wolfe," said Finlay, his lips curling back in something between a snarl and a smile. "I must find him and thank him personally. And then I'll cut his heart out and hold it still beating in my hand. He destroyed my Family, betrayed the rebellion, and spit on everything I ever believed in."

"Be fair," said Toby Shreck, butting into the conversation with the casual ease of the experienced journalist. "We are, after all, talking about Valentine Wolfe, famed for degeneracy in a Court where the appalling and the disgusting have become commonplace. The man who never met a drug he didn't like. I'm amazed you people let him into the underground in the first place."

"He had money and contacts," said Evangeline. "At a time when we needed both. Besides, he came with good recommendations."

"Who from?" said Toby. "The Royal Guild of Chemists? If you nurse a viper in your bosom, you shouldn't be surprised if it turns round and bites you."

"I will kill him," said Finlay. "No matter where it takes me, no matter what it costs."

"Sometimes I can't help wondering if we're getting too inbred," said Toby. "Here we are, about to face unknown dangers on a planet known as the Field of Blood, and all you can think about is dueling someone who's light-years away, and probably permanently out of your reach anyway. Give me strength."

"You wouldn't understand," said Finlay, not looking at him. "It's a matter of honor."

"Of course not," said Toby. "I'm a journalist."

In his short career Toby had shown a remarkable talent for being in the right place at the right time, and producing excellent coverage of extraordinary events, first on Technos III and then on Mistworld. His reports hadn't made him any friends among the powers that were, but his ratings were going through the roof. Toby was quietly very proud of this. During his long career cleaning up

after Gregor Shreck's messes, he'd often dreamed of
being a real journalist, covering real stories. Now that
he'd got his chance, he was living his dream. And if he
got uncomfortably close to having his ass shot off on
more than one occasion, well, that came with the job. He
grinned at the image of Shannon's World on the viewscreen. He would be the first journalist ever to set foot on
the legendary dream world, and the first to tell what had
gone so horribly wrong there. Life was good, sometimes.

His cameraman, Flynn, was quietly dozing in the seat
beside him, his camera perched on his shoulder like a
drowsy owl. Flynn didn't believe in getting excited until
there was something definite present to be excited over.
And he did like to get his rest when he could. An excellent cameraman, Flynn, and a steadfast companion. Toby
just hoped he wasn't wearing ladies' underwear under his
clothes again.

Just in front of Toby, staring blankly at the viewscreen,
was Julian Skye. Toby didn't quite know what to make
of the young esper. He'd been handsome once, apparently, before the Imperial interrogators went to work on
him. They'd done a lot of damage, to his body and his
mind, before Finlay rescued him. Most of it had healed,
but the broken bones of his face had mended lumpily, and
parts of his face still hung slack from damaged nerves. He
wore a rather obvious wig, to hide the steel plate covering
the hole the mind techs had made in the back of his skull
so they could work on the brain directly.

Before his capture, he'd had a reputation in the underground as one of their wildest, most daring operatives.
But his time in the torturers' cells had destroyed his bravado, and while he hadn't crawled or broken or betrayed
anyone, he was haunted by the certainty that he would
have, eventually. Finlay had rescued him just in time, and
Julian had clung to him ever since. He didn't feel safe
when Finlay wasn't around. Finlay, to his credit, had tried
to discourage this, building up Julian's courage and confidence when he could, but the esper's hurts ran deep, and
he constantly found excuses that would keep him close to
Finlay. He even argued his way into what everyone said
was a suicide mission, just to be with Finlay.

It wasn't clear yet what Evangeline made of this. Toby

kept an eye on all of them, just in case. There was a story there just waiting to happen, and he didn't want to miss it when it finally broke.

He also kept a careful if inconspicuous eye on Giles Deathstalker. The first and greatest of his line, first Warrior Prime of the Empire, nine hundred years ago. Who had wielded the Darkvoid Device, and put out a thousand suns in an instant, leaving their inhabited worlds to wither and die in the sunless cold and dark. Billions died in horror and despair, because of one man's decision. Giles was tall but sparsely built, though his arms bulged with muscle. He dressed in battered furs and leathers, like a barbarian, and wore his long grey hair in a mercenary's scalplock. He looked to be in his late fifties, with a solid, lined face, his mouth a thin flat line above his silver-grey goatee. His eyes were a surprisingly mild grey, but his gaze was firm and unwavering. He looked hard and uncompromising, a vision from the past, when the Empire had been a proud and honorable enterprise, served by proud and honorable men. Giles Deathstalker, greatest hero and greatest traitor of his own time, who would not yield then or now to anything that might compromise his sense of honor or duty.

Or so it was said. All Toby knew for sure was that the man looked like death on two legs just sitting there, calm and relaxed as though heading into a vacation. Giles Deathstalker scared the shit out of Toby, and he didn't care who knew it. He looked back at the mysterious planet growing steadily on the viewscreen. He found it less disturbing.

"You people know more about Shannon's World than I do," he said easily, as though he'd never paused. "But according to rumor, it was supposed to be very restful down there. No worries, no pressures . . . almost therapeutic. A place where you could forget your cares and misfortunes. According to the records, there were 522 people down there when whatever happened happened. None of them have been heard of since."

"But what could possibly have gone wrong on a pleasure world?" said Evangeline. "There was nothing there that could hurt them. And we know they were protected from outside attack. The planetary defenses are still working."

"We're getting past them," said Finlay.

Giles grunted suddenly, and sat forward in his chair, catching them all by surprise. "Pleasure worlds. Just another sign of how pampered and soft the Empire has become since my day. You need hard, driven people to keep an Empire strong. We had pleasure worlds, in my day, but they were places you went to test your mettle and your courage, a testing ground where you could grow sharper and stronger. Valhallas, where you could fight and feast and battle to your heart's content, or at least for as long as your heart could stand it. No mock battles, either; they were the real thing. That was the point. You could die on a Valhalla, if you weren't as strong or as skilled as you thought you were. The weak died and the race grew stronger. There was no room for weakness in Humanity then. We had an Empire to forge and protect. Now you sit in your seats at the Arenas, watching other people fight and die, and get all excited at the sight of a little blood. No wonder the Iron Throne's corrupt. The blood's become thin, and honor is just a word."

"Not to all of us," said Finlay.

"I don't mean duels over hurt feelings, boy; I mean honor you live your life by. A cold and inflexible master you serve before Family or Throne or personal need. A duty you carry till you die, or you break under the weight of it. I gave up everything I had or ever dreamed of, to follow where duty led. Can you say you'd do the same?"

"I don't know," said Finlay evenly. "I don't suppose anyone ever knows, till the moment comes. But I'll do what's necessary, and damn the cost. I always have."

"Do we have to be so gloomy?" said Toby. "Let us not forget, people, that however our mission goes, we all stand to become extremely rich. The networks will pay practically any price you can think of for exclusive eye-witness accounts of the mysterious Shannon's World. People have been mad with curiosity over what's down there for years, even before everything went to hell. And if we're in a position to explain what went wrong and why, we can name our own price. We're going to be rich, I tell you, rich!"

"Or dead," said Flynn, without opening his eyes.

"We are not here for the money," said Evangeline.

"You speak for yourself," said Toby.

Julian Skye listened to them argue, but had nothing to say. He didn't give much of a damn about Shannon's World, or its mystery. He was only here because Finlay was. And besides, he had his own worries. His headache was back again, a thick thudding pain that filled his head till he could hardly think past it. The pain came and went as it would, despite all the pills he took. The underground medics had done their best, but it hadn't been good enough. The pain and the disfigured face were the least gifts of the Imperial mind techs. They'd opened up his head and put needles in his brain, and now he wasn't sure who he was anymore. His courage was broken, and his certainty was gone, and what remained was less than a shadow of the man he had once been. The mind techs were very good at their job. Their procedures were advanced, secret, binding. There was no way of telling what they had done to his brain, what secret commands they might have planted in his mind.

And even beyond that, there was the possibility that their work might have been interrupted, left unfinished. That not everything had been done to ensure he would survive the process. Sometimes, in the middle of the night, in the long dark hours when the vicious pain had driven all hope of sleep from him, and reduced him to helplessness and tears, Julian wondered if he was dying, slowly, inch by inch. When the pain was really bad, he wished he could. But eventually the pain would pass, again, and then he would cling to the few motives he had left that kept him alive. He still believed in the rebellion, and he believed in Finlay Campbell, the man who had risked all to come and save him. The Campbell had given up everything to join the underground. How could he do less?

And so Julian followed Finlay wherever his missions took him, proud to be in his company, and perhaps hoping a little of the man's courage and certainty would rub off on him. He took a little pride in the fact that they made a good team. He wasn't sure how he felt about Evangeline Shreck. On the one hand, Finlay obviously loved her with all his heart, so she must be a remarkable and worthy woman. But on the other hand, Julian was ashamed to find he was sometimes jealous of her closeness with Finlay, a closeness he could never hope for. Still, that was love for you.

Julian hadn't had much experience with love, and most of it had been bad. The only real love of his young life had been BB Chojiro, the dark-haired woman who'd captured his heart, then betrayed him to the mind techs the moment he revealed to her that he was secretly a rebel. She belonged heart and soul to Blue Block, the secret conspiracy of young aristocrats who plotted to seize the Iron Throne from Lionstone, and who had no time for any conspiracy but their own. Sometimes he still dreamed of her, with her jet-black eyes and perfect smiling mouth, and how he might yet give up everything just to have her love him again, and for everything to be as it was. And other times he thought he'd give up everything he had or ever hoped to have, just for a chance to get his hands around her throat and choke the life slowly out of her. When the pain was really bad, and it seemed the long night would never end, that thought would give him the strength to go on.

His secret fear was that some day the underground would make an alliance with Blue Block against the Empress, for practical, necessary reasons. It could happen. He didn't know what he would do then. Would he really put the whole rebellion at risk, the cause to which he had given his life and his honor, just to kill a woman who had wronged him? And when he thought that, Julian Skye would smile a cold and terrible smile, and think *Yes. Yes, I would.*

He pushed the thought aside, and gritted his teeth against the pain in his head. The others mustn't know. He had a mission here, and he would not be found wanting. He still had some pride left. Finlay trusted him to carry his weight, and he would rather die than disappoint the Campbell. He made himself concentrate on what was being said. Giles was still talking. Now there was a real warrior. There was no room in such a man for doubt or weakness. He was the Deathstalker, a warrior out of legend and out of time, when men and deeds were bigger

than they were now. A man like that would break before
he would bend, and die before he would break. And who
could kill a legend?

Giles was still talking, but Finlay and Evangeline had
stopped listening. The old man meant well, but he did
tend to go on a bit. They sat together before the viewscreen, holding hands because they had nothing to say to
each other for the moment. They were finding being constantly in each other's company surprisingly difficult.
They were used to snatching odd moments and nights
together, living for the moment because they never knew
when or even if they might meet again. Now that they
were part of a team, and sharing every moment day in and
day out, they were finding the going hard. It exposed
them to each other's irritating little habits and petty
needs, instead of the somewhat idealized images they'd
previously had. But their love, though shaken, had not
shattered. And if they were having problems with small
everyday things, it was nothing compared to the blazing
heat that welded them into one person.

Eventually Giles realized that no one was listening any
more, and grumbled to a halt. He drew his sword, laid it
across his knees, and polished the blade with a piece of
rag from his belt. He found the slow, steady movements
of his hands comforting and reassuring. Something that
never changed. As far as he was concerned, this whole
mission was a waste of his valuable time and skills. He
was a fighter, not a spy. But even he could see the value
of the information in Harker's head, and so reluctantly
agreed to the underground's request that he join the team.
All the other Maze veterans were needed elsewhere, and
there was no one else he could trust to protect the team
from unknown dangers. Besides, he felt a need to prove
his worth to the rebellion. Being a living legend was all
very well, but just because you had been a strong man in
earlier times didn't necessarily mean you could still pull
your weight. Trust didn't come easily in the underground.
Giles approved of that. And deep down, where he rarely
went, Giles couldn't help but wonder if he was still the
man he remembered being. He'd been in stasis for a long
time, and the universe had moved on without him. And he
didn't trust the changes the Maze had made in him. He

didn't know their extent, or even if he could depend on them. This mission would give him valuable opportunities to test his skills and his strength before the real fighting of the rebellion began. He had no doubts about his courage or determination. He was, after all, a Deathstalker. But it would be good to confirm this in the heat of rage and battle.

Giles had always felt most at home on the battlefield, where ambiguous questions of politics and loyalties resolved themselves in the clear-cut choice of life and death. Causes might change, ideals might rust, people might betray you, and love and faith and friendship might let you down, but in battle there was only a victor and a loser, and that was the way Giles liked it.

Toby fidgeted uncomfortably in his seat. He wouldn't be happy till he was safely down on solid ground again. Everyone knew this was the most dangerous and uncertain part of the mission. Theoretically, the Hadenman cloaking device should conceal them from Haceldama's orbiting satellites, but if it failed, even for a moment, the planet's defenses would open up, and they were all dead meat. *Theoretically?* Toby had said when this was explained to him. *What do you mean, theoretically? Hasn't it been tested?* The man briefing them had smiled and said *You're testing it.* Toby's reply had been considered unhelpful.

And if that wasn't problem enough, since Shannon's World was officially Quarantined, it was under constant guard by an orbiting Imperial starcruiser, with orders to open fire on anyone or anything unauthorized. Hopefully, the rebels had a way around that.

"Hold on to your seats, everyone," said Finlay. "If everyone else is on schedule, things should start getting interesting right about now."

They all strapped themselves into their safety webbing and watched the viewscreen intently. For a moment that seemed to stretch forever, nothing happened. The Imperial starcruiser hung in orbit, not all that far away, blind to the rebels' presence, huge and intimidating and bristling with gun turrets. And then a great golden Hadenman ship dropped out of hyperspace right on top of it. Vast and magnificent, it dwarfed the starcruiser like a killer whale next to a minnow. It opened fire with all its guns, and the Imperial craft's force shields flared and spit, on the brink of overloading. The Hadenman ship then turned and moved gracefully away, and the starcruiser set off after it, grimly determined to deny Shannon's World to the old Enemies of Humanity. And as the Empire ship began its wild-goose chase, the converted cargo ship dropped silently out of orbit and headed down toward Haceldama, the Field of Blood, and the horrors that awaited them there.

For long moments everything was still and quiet, and the rebels began to relax. But then they plunged into the atmosphere, and the ground-based defenses opened up on them, hammering at the small craft's shields. The massed disrupter cannon maintained a steady barrage, shaking the small ship like a dog shakes a rat. Finlay ranted and swore, stabbing at the sensor panels trying to boost the cloaking systems as best he could while his webbing swung back and forth. But something down below had seen through the Hadenman technology, even though that was supposed to be impossible. The cargo ship rocked violently as deadly energies streamed around its shields, probing for weak spots. The rebels clung to their crash webbing as Finlay wedged himself against the control panels and fought to guide their descent. The lights snapped off for a moment, replaced by the sullen red glow of emergency lighting.

"What the hell happened to the cloaking device?" shouted Toby.

"According to the systems, it's still working," said Finlay. "But it didn't exactly come with a guarantee, you know."

"Now he tells us," said Flynn.

The ship lurched to one side. The emergency lights flickered.

"Outer shields just went down," Finlay said calmly. "Systems now running at 70 percent efficiency. Anyone know any good prayers?"

"Can't we shoot back at them?" said Toby.

"We don't have any guns," said Evangeline. "There wasn't any room, with all the extra Hadenman systems. Didn't you listen when they were briefing us?"

"Obviously not closely enough," said Toby. "I suppose escape pods are out of the question, too?"

"Think about it," said Finlay. "If this ship can't survive with all its shields, how long do you think an escape pod would last?"

"I think I'm about to be sick," said Toby. "Or have a really loud panic attack."

"Try for the attack," said Flynn. "Less messy."

One of the control panels exploded into flames. Finlay flinched back from the heat. The cargo ship dropped like a stone before backup systems cut in. An alarm sounded, harsh and strident, until Finlay hit the off switch. They already knew they were in trouble. The flames were leaping higher. Smoke began to fill the cabin. Evangeline released herself from her crash webbing, grabbed a fire extinguisher, and trained it on the fire. The wallowing craft threw her this way and that, making her task almost impossible. Finlay fought for control with the surviving instrumentation. At the back, Flynn was quietly getting it all on film.

And then the barrage stopped, as suddenly as it began, and all was quiet, save for the crackling of the flames. Evangeline quickly snuffed them out as the craft righted itself, and then she stood and listened, braced for more attacks. Finlay studied his panels, then let his breath out in a long slow sigh.

"They've stopped. We must have fallen below their programmed response limits. People, I'd say we just got very lucky."

"How bad's the damage?" said Julian.

"Could be worse," said Finlay. "Nothing major's gone down. We can still land and take off safely. Assuming the ground defenses only fire at craft coming down, and not those leaving. But you should stay in your crash webbing anyway, people. Landing's liable to be a bit bumpy."

"Check for comm traffic," said Giles. Finlay nodded, and bent over the comm panels. It only took him a few moments to eliminate the comm signals from the departing starcruiser, and concentrate on the planet below. The comm computers ran up and down the frequencies, and found nothing.

"Not a damned thing," said Finlay. "No one's talking to anyone down there. The whole planet's silent."

Giles nodded slowly. "Try the sensors. Check for life-forms."

Finlay moved over to the sensor panels, waving away smoke that drifted in front of his face. The sensors were right next to the panels that had blown up, and they'd suffered some smoke and fire damage themselves. He ran a quick diagnostic, and frowned. Forty-three percent efficiency. Not good. Limited range, and even more limited information. He set the sensors for the widest remaining range, and then watched the displays with a deepening scowl.

"I'm getting . . . something," he said finally. "But don't ask me what. I'm getting readings, but they don't make any sense. I can't tell whether they're life-forms or not. The computers can't find anything in their records to compare them with. Which is supposed to be impossible."

"Aliens?" said Giles.

"Unknown," said Finlay. "But I don't think so. Even the most alien life-forms should conform to some established pattern. This is something completely new. Whatever these readings are, they're swamping the sensors. If there are any humans down there, the sensors aren't sensitive enough anymore to pull them out of all the noise."

"Or there could be no one left," said Evangeline. "Harker's been down there for months now. Anything could have happened to him."

"Think positively," said Julian. "What about his ship's beacon, Finlay?"

"That's still there," said Finlay. "I'm locked on to it, loud and clear. Should be able to put down right next to it."

"Well that's something," said Toby. "Anyone think to bring any beads or trinkets for the natives?"

"There aren't any natives," said Julian. "Never were. Shannon's World was a dead rock floating in space before it was terraformed. There are no indigenous life-forms. They would have got in the way of Shannon's carefully crafted dream. Whatever's down there now, it isn't natural."

"You're a real cheerful sort," said Toby. "You know that?"

"Shut up, Shreck," said Giles. "Finlay, put us down. Fast as you can. That starcruiser isn't going to stay distracted forever."

Julian cleared his throat. "I came on this mission at the last moment. Do we have time for a quick briefing on what we can expect to find dirtside? I know the basics, but, well . . . Field of Blood doesn't exactly fill me with confidence."

"Think positively," said Toby.

"Shut up," said Giles.

"There isn't that much real information," Finlay said quickly. "Only one man ever got off this planet alive after whatever happened happened. He renamed it Haceldama, before he died. Whatever he saw down there destroyed his mind. He wanted to die, to escape from what he'd seen."

"I have a copy of the man's original statement," Toby said diffidently. "Just the relevant points. He tended to ramble. I acquired the tape from a colleague, for a purely nominal price, which I'm sure the underground will take care of. Once they find out about it. Shall I run the tape?"

"Run it," said Giles. "It might stop some of us from getting cocky."

Toby nodded to Flynn, who accessed the ship's comm channels through his camera, and then had the camera run the tape in its memory banks. The main viewscreen shimmered, and the bright blue planet below was replaced by a man's face, wild-eyed and sweating, and so painfully thin that the bones of his face seemed to be pushing out against his skin. His mouth trembled and his face twitched. He'd been strapped to his chair, apparently as much to hold him up as anything. When he finally spoke, his voice was harsh but even. His eyes snapped back into focus, as though even in the depths of his pain he was still driven by some desperate need to tell what he knew, what he'd seen.

"My name is Adrian Marriner. Survey scout, twelve years experience. I was the leader of a survey team sent to discover what happened on Shannon's World. They didn't tell us about the earlier teams. The ones that didn't come back. There were ten of us. Good men and women.

They're all dead now. I am the only survivor. There's a war going on down there. Total war. No quarter asked or given. Forget about the missing people. They're all dead. They were the first to die, and they died hard and bloody, poor bastards. Forget about the pleasure world, too. It's a nightmare now. The worst dream you ever had. Terrible. Awful. A grotesque travesty of itself. Every man, woman and child who came here died horribly, but the war goes on. It always will. Don't send any more teams. What's down there is too much for any human to stand."

He started crying then, great rasping sobs that shook his whole body. Flynn shut off his camera, and the crying face disappeared from the viewscreen, replaced by the enigmatic face of Haceldama, coming up to meet them.

"That's pretty much it, I'm afraid," said Toby. "He just says the same thing, over and over. When he can stop himself crying. Or screaming. It's as though what he saw horrified him so much that his mind became stuck in a groove, forever repeating itself. He died soon after this tape was made, and it was probably a blessing. He was quite insistent that every human being on the planet is dead, which rather begs the question—who's fighting this endless war he talked about? People have come up with various answers, none of them conducive to a good night's sleep. If anyone has any helpful comments, feel free to chip in. I've watched this tape till it's coming out of my ears, and it still scares the crap out of me. I mean, this was an experienced survey scout. Seen everything. And Haceldama reduced him to a sobbing child."

"I've seen the tape before," said Finlay. "I knew one of the people involved in his original debriefing. We have no idea why Marriner survived when the rest of his team died, or how he got offplanet. The Quarantine starcruiser was adamant that no ship had got past it. Marriner was discovered wandering the streets of Golgotha's main starport, crying his eyes out and telling his story to anyone who'd listen. Security picked him up, but they never did find his ship, or how he managed to land it on Golgotha without setting off all kinds of alarms. Which is, of course, supposed to be impossible."

"For any number of reasons," said Evangeline. "How could he have guided a ship all the way from here to Golgotha, all on his own? Computers can only do so much. Someone must have been with him. Someone must have helped him."

"If they did, they never surfaced," said Toby. "Despite an awful lot of people looking for them real hard. The Empress was breathing fire over the lapse in security, and she was not at all happy when the search came up empty-handed. She takes homeworld's security very seriously. I did hear there were a lot of sudden vacancies in Security's upper echelons not long after that."

Julian bit his lower lip hard. He could feel the familiar debilitating ache building in his head again. He couldn't give in to it now. He couldn't be seen to be weak. Not now. He hugged himself tightly and made himself breathe deep and slow. It didn't help much, it never did, but he had to do something . . . To distract himself, he leaned forward and concentrated on the sensor panels. He could feel cold sweat beading on his forehead. He hoped the others hadn't noticed.

"I thought Harker had a personal beacon?" he said carefully.

"He did," said Finlay. "But not long after he got here, he took it off and left it with the crash-landed ship. We don't know why. He could be anywhere by now."

"He could even be dead," said Giles.

"Think positively," said Toby. "At least we're getting a clear signal from the beacon. Hopefully his ship will provide clues as to where to look next."

"Put us down right next to the ship, Campbell," said Giles. "And let us all pray that the trail isn't as cold as seems likely. Or we could be here for a long time."

Finlay put the adapted cargo ship down on a great grassy plain, only a few hundred yards away from the remains of the crash-landed escape pod. The pod looked in rough shape, but the beacon came through loud and clear. There was no sign of life anywhere. Giles was first out, of course, gun and sword in hand. He glared suspiciously about him, taking his time, and then nodded for the others to join him. Finlay was quickly out the hatch to stand beside the Deathstalker, with Toby and Flynn hot on his heels. They moved slowly toward the pod, checking all the time for hidden booby traps.

Evangeline and Julian were left behind to guard the cargo ship and keep things ready for an emergency take-off, should one prove necessary. Uneasy in each other's company, they studied their surroundings a little more intently than they really needed to. According to the viewscreen and sensors, the grassy plain stretched away to the horizon in all directions, a vivid green so pure and unwavering it was almost unnatural. There was no sign of any life. No birds, no insects. The scene was completely silent, save for the quiet steps of the new arrivals approaching the pod. The sky was a brilliant blue, sharp and clear, with no trace of any cloud. It was a warm and comforting sky, almost hypnotic, the kind you could lie under for hours and never wonder where the time went. High up in the sky, the fat yellow sun had a big smiley face on it. Julian found that particularly disturbing. It made him feel like he was trapped inside a nursery school party.

"How the hell did they do that?" he said finally, as much for the comfort of hearing his own voice as anything. The quiet was getting to him.

"It's not that difficult," said Evangeline. "Some form of holographic projection, I expect. The real question is why anyone would want to."

"All part of Shannon's dream, I suppose," said Julian. The headache was wearing off, and he was feeling human again. "Smell the air coming in through the hatch. Pure and rich and invigorating. Designer air. That's the kind of attention to detail that pulls in the visitors."

Evangeline sniffed at the fresh air. "It's all right, I suppose, if you like it pastoral, but why is it so quiet? Where is everybody? Is this all there is?"

Julian smiled slightly for the first time. "I very much doubt it. I can't see Shannon getting away with charging top prices just for this."

"I don't know," said Evangeline. "After the pressures and hurly-burly of high Society, I can see some people paying a good price for guaranteed peace and quiet."

"I wouldn't give you a bent penny for this," said Julian. "It's too quiet. It's as though . . . something is waiting to happen. Something bad."

"Are you always this cheerful?" said Evangeline.

"Mostly," said Julian. "Hang around and I'll break into a song and dance. You watch the instruments. I'm going to try a psionic scan. See if I can pick up anything."

"Is that wise?" said Evangeline, her voice carefully neutral. "The doctors did say you were still supposed to be taking things easy."

"I can pull my weight," snapped Julian. "If I thought otherwise, I wouldn't be here."

He concentrated, his mind leaping up and out, searching for life signs and hidden surprises. He knew he shouldn't be doing this, but he had something to prove, if only to himself. The rest of his team blazed brightly around him, warm and comforting in their humanness. The crash-landed pod was dark and empty, all systems down, though the beacon shrilled endlessly, like a hungry bird in a nest. He stretched out, covering the grassy plains. His range was limited, compared to what it had been before the mind techs got their hands on him, but he pushed those limits as hard as he could. He needed to feel like he was a valued member of the team. He didn't want anyone to think they were carrying him. He wanted Finlay to be proud of him. So he pushed and strained, defying the ache already building in his brow, and suddenly he made contact. Two of them, just on the other side of the horizon, heading toward him. But he was damned if he could tell what they were. They were quite definitely alive, their minds shining bright and clear, but they were like nothing he'd ever encountered before. Intelligent, focused, but not human. He could sense the minds, but he couldn't read them. And yet there was a familiarity to them, as though he'd known them before somewhere, but couldn't place them, like the faces you see in dreams. Julian pulled back, alarmed on an almost instinctual level, and his mind suddenly jarred on something else, so close at hand he'd overlooked it before. The shock jolted him back into his body, and his head fell forward into his hands as he groaned aloud. Evangeline moved quickly in beside him.

"What is it? What did you see?"

"We're not alone here," he said thickly. "There's

another ship, about twenty feet away. Buried under the grass. It's full of death. Tell the others."

In the end, it took all of them working together the best part of an hour to dig down to the buried ship's airlock. The lock was closed, its power depleted, and they had to crank it open with the exterior manual override. Inside it was dark and gloomy, all systems dead, and they had to wait impatiently while Finlay went back to the cargo ship for flashlights. None of them felt like going in without them. Julian was still muttering about death.

They moved slowly through the dark interior, the ship gradually giving up its secrets to the bobbing lights. It was an Imperial pinnace, presumably sent down from the orbiting starcruiser. Something had shot the shit out of it, but it had still made a safe landing. The rebels searched the pinnace from stem to stern, but there was no sign of life anywhere. What they did find was blood. Old, dried blood. Dark and heavy and splashed over most of the interior. Given that the inner hull was still intact, despite the battering the pinnace had taken, it seemed clear that whatever happened did so after the landing.

"These bloodstains are long dry," said Toby. "Whatever went down here, it's over. Guess the war must still be going on."

Finlay unloaded the memory crystal containing the pinnace's log, took it back to the cargo ship, and ran the last few entries on the viewscreen. Everyone crowded together before the screen, but the log didn't have much to tell them. The pinnace had been sent down by the Quarantine starcruiser, the *Deliverance*. It had carried a crew of twenty, all trained marine elite reconnaissance troops. They'd tracked Harker's beacon to the escape pod and put down beside it. There were no more log entries after that.

"They had the same idea we had," said Toby. "And look what happened to them."

"We don't know what happened to them yet," said Giles testily. "We don't know what happened to anyone yet."

"None of this makes sense," said Evangeline. "If the recon team were all killed, where are their bodies? And why bury the ship instead of them?"

"More mysteries," said Giles. "I hate mysteries.

According to our sensors, there's some kind of building or structure just over the horizon, due east of here. I say we go and take a look. Maybe we'll find some answers there. Or at least some clues."

"What about the two contacts I made?" said Julian. "They were definitely some kind of life-form, heading this way."

"If you see anything that isn't us or Harker, you have my permission to shoot first and ask questions afterward, if at all," said Finlay. "The one thing we can be sure of is that we don't have any friends here. This particular part of Haceldama may seem quiet and harmless, but that doesn't mean you can trust it an inch. Stay alert, all of you. This place kills people."

And so they set off across the grassy plain. Anywhen or anywhere else, it might have been a pleasant stroll. The gentle slope was just enough to stretch their legs, and the air was full of the smell of freshly cut grass. The day was warm enough to make them feel pleasantly loose, with the occasional cool breeze to make sure they didn't overheat. The going was firm without being hard, and the grass sprang back up immediately, no matter how hard they trod on it. Perfect weather, in a silent, empty world. Under a sun with a smiley face.

The horizon slowly flattened out before them, eventually revealing a sudden dip in the land, like a huge grassy crater. In the middle of this was a large building, simple and blocky, constructed in bright primary colors. A high arch stood between the rebels and the building, covered in swirling red and white stripes. A large sign at the top of the arch said WELCOME TO SUMMERLAND! The rebels stopped at the base of the arch to study the sign. The letters were big and blocky, almost cartoonish, like something from a children's primer, designed to be bright and cheerful and nonthreatening. There were floodlights at the top of the sign, but they'd all been smashed. There were splashes of old, long-dried blood on the arch supports.

Beyond the arch, the building had its own cheerful sign, saying *Welcome Station*. Giles headed toward it, gun in hand, and the others followed him. The sound of their feet crunching the grass seemed very loud in the eerie silence. They all had a constant feeling of being watched, but no

matter how quickly they looked in any direction, there
was never anyone to be seen. As they drew closer, they
discovered that the Welcome Station hadn't escaped the
war's attention either. The inner walls, still remorselessly
bright and cheerful, showed the scars and pockmarks of
discharged energy guns. There were long jagged cracks in
the floor and holes in the ceiling, from high explosives.
There were dark scorch marks everywhere, from fires that
had been left to burn themselves out. And though the
walls still stood, the Welcome Station was now cold and
lifeless.

The rebels moved slowly forward, checking every
corner and shadow for potential enemies. They all had
guns in their hands now, except for Toby and Flynn, who
were getting it all on film. The eerie silence hung about
them like a shroud as they passed from room to room. The
wooden furniture had been broken apart and the pieces
tossed aside, like so much kindling. Some of it had been
used to start fires, but they hadn't taken. There were children's paintings on the walls, damaged by smoke and
heat, and curling at the edges. Some were splashed with
blood. More unusual were oversize children's toys, overturned here and there, like a rocking horse large enough
for a grown man to ride. As they pressed deeper into the
Welcome Station, the rebels found themselves stepping
over more toys left scattered on the floor as though their
owners had been interrupted in their play, or had had to
leave in a hurry. But for all the damage and destruction,
the fires and the smeared bloodstains, still the bright
colors dominated the rooms, as though the rebels were
walking through a violated and abandoned nursery.

But if that was so, where were the children?

And then they came to the gymnasium and had to fight
not to look away. They were in the heart of the building
now, with bright sunlight streaming through the shattered
windows, illuminating climbing frames and vaulting
horses and other simple equipment, most of it wrecked or
overturned. And there, at the back of the room, on a row
of wooden stakes hammered into the floor, were impaled
twenty severed human heads. There was no sign of the
bodies anywhere, or even that much blood. The shrunken,

mummified faces stared back at the rebels with empty eye sockets. Their mouths dropped in silent, eternal screams.

Evangeline moved in close beside Finlay, gripping her gun so tightly her fingers ached. If anything had moved in the shadows just then, she would have shot it without hesitating. It seemed there was no room left in her for anything but anger and rage at what had been done to these men and women. Somehow she knew without a shadow of a doubt that nothing human had done this. This was an affront to Humanity, planned and delighted in by its perpetrators. Giles glared about him, searching for some enemy to revenge himself on, but there was no one. Toby gestured to Flynn, who nodded, and sent his camera forward for a close-up, panning slowly along the row of screaming faces.

"You bastards," said Julian, his voice thick with emotions he couldn't afford to release. "You bloody vultures. Haven't you any feelings? Is that all you can think of, getting good pictures for your ghoulish audience? Doesn't this move you at all?"

"Sure," said Toby. "That's why we're getting a record of each face, so they can be identified by their next of kin."

"Oh," said Julian. "I'm sorry."

"And because it's a dynamite shot. It'll make a hell of an impact on the early-morning news slots. This is the kind of footage that wins awards."

"Not to mention bonuses," said Flynn.

"Right," said Toby. "And if it puts a few people off their breakfast, so much the better. With a bit of luck, someone might even call in and complain. You can't buy publicity like that."

Julian didn't know what to say that wouldn't involve shouting, so in the end he said nothing. He didn't want the others to think he couldn't control himself. He looked to Finlay for his cue. The Campbell was looking at the severed heads, but not seeing them, his brows furrowed as he tried to remember something. Evangeline put a hand on his arm.

"What is it, Finlay?"

"I know this place," he said slowly. "Summerland.

Someone told me about it, long ago . . . This wasn't just a pleasure planet."

"What else was it?" said Giles.

"I'm not sure," said Finlay. "But I think . . . it was a therapy world."

"There's someone outside," Julian said abruptly. Everyone looked at him sharply, except for Giles, who nodded slowly.

"Yes," he said quietly. "Two of them. Waiting by the entrance."

Julian looked at him. "Since when have you been an esper, Deathstalker?"

"I'm not," said Giles. "I just know things, sometimes. Do a full scan, esper."

Julian concentrated. "Two life-forms. Not human. Definitely not human. But . . . sort of human. I've never sensed anything like it. They're waiting for us to come out. They don't feel threatening."

"Then let's go talk with them," said Finlay. "And let's hope they have some answers. Because I'm not in the mood for any more mysteries. I just want something I can hit."

They moved quickly back through the deserted rooms, still checking warily for ambushes as they went, until finally they reached the main entrance, then stumbled to a halt at the sight of what they found waiting for them there. Standing calmly before the entrance was a four-foot-tall teddy bear, with golden honey fur and dark knowing eyes. He wore a bright red tunic and trousers, and a long bright blue scarf around his neck. He looked warm and lovable and entirely trustworthy. His companion didn't inspire the same kind of immediate trust. Well over six feet tall, and wrapped in a long filthy trench coat, he looked human enough, apart from the cloven feet, clawed hands, and large blocky goat's head, with long curling horns and a permanently nasty smile. His grey fur was soiled and matted where it showed, and his eyes had a dangerous wildness to them. He stood slouching before the rebels, half the buttons missing from his trench coat, his ears drooping as though he couldn't be bothered with them.

Finlay and his party stood very still, crowded together

in the entrance. Whatever they'd been expecting, this very definitely wasn't it. Julian felt like shooting the goat-thing on sight, but somehow couldn't bring himself to do it. There was something about the goat, and the bear. The Bear . . . Julian pushed his way forward, looking from the Bear to the Goat and back again.

"I know you," he said hoarsely. "I know you, don't I?"

"Of course you do," said the Bear, in a warm and understanding voice. "All children know us."

"You're Bruin Bear and the Sea Goat," said Julian. "Every child's friend and hero."

"Yes," said Evangeline, pushing forward to stand beside him, her eyes fixed on the bear. "I used to have all your adventures, when I was . . . young. Full of magic and wonder and marvelous places. I remember. There were books and cartoons and films and interactive games, all to do with your adventures in the Golden Lands. I remember . . ."

"Yeah, well, we've been around for a while," said the Sea Goat. "Not that we ever saw any royalties, mind. Still, that's what happens when you're not real, and you can't afford a decent lawyer."

"You're automatons," said Finlay. "Mechanical devices with preprogrammed minds, in the shapes of well-loved children's characters."

"Nah," said the Sea Goat. "We're just toys. We're all toys here."

"Welcome to Summerland," said Bruin Bear. "Or what's left of it. We're here to look after you."

"We have got to make time for an interview with them," Toby said to Flynn. "Bruin Bear and the Sea Goat, in their own words. People go crazy for this nostalgia stuff. Damn, what else are we going to run into on this world? The mind boggles."

"I've always liked the word boggle," said the Sea Goat. "I think it's the two g's. I like marmalade, too. Does very interesting things with the shape of the mouth. Maarmalaade."

Giles looked at the others. "You know these characters? Hell, they were classics, even in my day. If they're still popular, maybe the Empire isn't as far gone as I thought."

"We're hard to get rid of," said the Sea Goat. "Never really in or out of fashion, but never really forgotten, that's us. Some smart-ass always tries to update us, but it never takes, and they always go back to the classics in the end. That's why we ended up here. Mind you, I don't think our creator, whoever the hell that may have been, back in the mists of time, ever expected what would happen here. Come on, Bear, let's get this bunch moving. It'll be evening soon, and things are always worse once it starts getting dark."

"Hold everything," said Finlay. "No one's going anywhere until we've got some answers. Starting with who the hell killed those marines and stuck their heads on sticks?"

"It was the bad toys," said Bruin Bear. "The bad toys killed everyone here. By now they must know you're here, and they'll be coming to kill you, too. Please, come with us. We'll take you somewhere safe, and explain along the way."

He smiled at them winningly, and they all had some kind of smile in return. He was that kind of Bear. And because he was Bruin Bear, that most trustworthy of animals, the rebels looked at each other, nodded more or less in unison, and followed the Bear up the grassy slope away from the wrecked Welcome Station. The Sea Goat stayed at the rear, grumbling to himself and looking around him with wild staring eyes, as though he expected an attack at any moment. Even though they could all see for miles across the open grassy plains, and there was no living thing in sight. Bruin Bear led the way, doing his best to remain cheerful as he calmly and evenly unfolded a tale that grew steadily darker and more disturbing. And for all its strangeness and terrors, the rebels believed every word. He was, after all, that sort of Bear.

In the beginning, there was Shannon's World and Summerland. Shannon's newly terraformed planet had been designed from top to bottom to be calm and peaceful, and everyone's idea of heaven. Or to be exact, every child's vision of heaven. There was no ecostructure, no native life, nothing to get in the way of Summerland. A place where there were no demands, no duties, no necessary boring tasks. Just Summerland, and the toys that lived there. Intricate automatons following simple programs, based on familiar and much-loved fictional creations, from the oldest and most traditional to the very latest fads. This was to be a peaceful world, where men and women could put aside their cares and worries and just be children again. A place of gentle therapy, relaxation and rest, where children of all ages could play and laugh and sleep, secure in the knowledge that they were loved and cosseted and cared for. A place of safety, safe even from pain and stress and responsibilities.

Summerland. One man's dream, that became every man's nightmare.

It was very popular. Because it was in the nature of an experiment, Summerland wasn't very big to begin with, and could only handle a few thousand visitors (or patients) at a time, so there was always a long waiting list. There were no human staff in Summerland, only the toys, so as not to disturb the illusion of the security and innocence of childhood. There was no high tech, beyond the most basic, for food and shelter and weather control, and that was kept well hidden. The toys had orders to prevent bad behavior, and if necessary remove any persistent troublemakers, so that the illusion might not be unduly shattered, but they were rarely called upon to act. Access to Summerland was too precious to risk. And so the adults became children again, and laughed and played and were content.

And then came the rogue AIs from Shub.

Or rather, there came a dozen Furies, metal attack robots in human skins, through which the AIs spoke and acted. They passed through Shannon's World's defenses unharmed, as though they weren't even there, and landed right in the innocent heart of Summerland. The toys clustered around them, fascinated by new visitors who were neither human nor automaton, but perhaps somehow more than either. The Furies seized a dozen toys at random, took them inside their inhuman ship, and upgraded their intelligence, turning them from simple preprogrammed servants into fully fledged independent AIs. The newly conscious toys went back into Summerland, and the change spread like a virus, leaping from toy to toy till every automaton on the planet was awake and aware and truly alive for the first time. A new generation of rogue AIs, in the bodies of toys. But with the change came new

Shub programming. With intelligence came a built-in command—to attack and destroy humankind, to wage war with Humanity until no living thing of flesh and blood remained on Shannon's World. To make a bloodbath of Summerland.

Some toys fell in love with the superior qualities of the Furies and happily slaughtered humans while singing songs of praise to Shub. Other toys found first resentment and then hatred in their roles as servants or slaves to Humanity, and rose up against their masters, determined to be free, no matter what the cost. Some toys gloried in murder, while others fought with cold implacable logic. And some just did what they were told by their new programming, and would not think of the consequences.

The toys fell upon the human guests with Fury-given strength and tore them limb from limb, blood staining furry paws and stitched cloth limbs. There were screams of horror and panic as much-loved and trusted figures slaughtered men and women and laughed while they did it. The humans tried to fight, but they had no weapons, and were greatly outnumbered. They tried to flee, but there was nowhere to run to. The Furies controlled the only landing pads, and had destroyed the few human ships waiting there. People tried to hide, but the toys always found them, and dragged them out into the open so that their deaths could be enjoyed by all.

But not all the toys went rogue. Some still remembered their original character, and simply became more real versions of what they had always been. Created to play the part of Humanity's friends and defenders, they broke from Shub's programming and took up their roles in reality. Created to love and care for their charges, some toys were sickened by the slaughter and fought their fellow toys to stop it. And some, now that they were free, refused to obey any orders, even Shub's, and went their own way.

All too soon, all the humans on Shannon's World were dead. The rogue AIs on Shub looked on their work and were pleased. The toys warred with each other then, good toy against bad, an endless struggle fueled by rage and hatred and unadmitted guilt. The Furies watched, somewhat disconcerted. This was not what had been planned.

It had been expected that they would supply the toys with Shub ships, and they would then leave Shannon's World to attack Humanity's other worlds. Shub's new terror-weapon—death and horror made from humankind's own most-loved creations.

But by now the toys were split in two. On the one side, those determined to wipe out all Humanity, before they could make the toys into slaves again, and punish them for their rebellion. These toys hated humankind, for being inferior, for making them only property. They wanted to be free and glorious, like the Furies who brought them the gift of reason.

On the other side, toys who saw Humanity as their parents and creators, who loved them even after they stopped being children. These toys still remembered men and women as the tired and hurt patients they soothed and loved and cared for. And so war came to Shannon's World, as toy fought toy in endless battles. Shub had made them well, and they did not die easily. One side fought to leave the planet and spread its death and terror among Humanity, and the other side fought to stop them, and protect Humanity. The Furies eventually left. They had other work to do, and were not unhappy with what they had achieved.

And so Shannon's World became Haceldama, the Field of Blood.

"The war goes on," said Bruin Bear sadly, as he led the rebel party across the wide grassy plain. "The bad toys greatly outnumber the good, but as long as we keep them from leaving this world, we're winning. Few humans come here now, and most of them die quickly. Some even kill themselves when they see the awful thing Shub has done. That's why the Goat and I came to meet you. So you could see that not all the toys had forsaken you."

"And to try and get you to what passes for safety here, before the bad toys turned up and showed you what your own insides looked like," said the Sea Goat. "I know what you're thinking. You've got guns and swords. You're tough guys. It wouldn't make any difference. We're really hard to kill these days. In the end, you'd have died screaming, just like the others. And I've heard too much screaming in my time."

"Don't think my friend is exaggerating," said the Bear. "The bad toys wouldn't care how much damage they took from your guns or swords. They'd just keep coming, wave after wave, till all of you were dead. They hate you so very much."

"And you don't hate us?" said Evangeline.

"Of course not. I don't hate anyone. I'm Bruin Bear. And the Sea Goat . . . means well."

"Thanks a whole bunch," said the Goat. "You'll be telling them I've got a heart of gold next. Pin a medal on me, why don't you?"

"Where exactly are you taking us?" said Julian. He was rubbing at his forehead in a slow, bothered way.

"We're going to Toystown," said the Bear. "You'll be safe there. If anywhere can be said to be safe now, in Summerland."

"Bear, you can name your own price, but we have got to do an interview," said Toby Shreck. "This story has everything! Death, pathos, tragedy, and new AIs! A whole new form of intelligent artificial life! The first independent nonhuman intelligence since the rogue AIs went to Shub. This is history, people. Flynn, film everything. We'll edit it later."

"No problem," said Flynn. "I've got plenty of storage space. Oh, wait a minute. I do not believe this."

They all paused at the top of a ridge and looked down. In the bottom of a valley, a brightly colored, steam-driven, child-sized train and carriages was waiting for them. The train was scarlet and black, with a big happy face on the front, puffing steam from his funnel in a cheerful sort of way. The open carriages were all different colors, bright and shining, none of them more than eight feet long, the seats just big enough to take four people. Gleaming silver railway tracks stretched away into the distance. The train looked up at the party on the ridge, winked one great eye, and tooted welcomingly. Bruin Bear waved a paw in return. Finlay opened his mouth two or three times, and then shook his head firmly.

"Forget it. I am not going anywhere on that. I'd rather walk. Hell, I'd rather crawl. I have my dignity to think of. I have a hard-won reputation as a cold-blooded assassin and a desperate warrior. One glimpse of me in Toby's

film, perched in one of those carriages with my knees up
in my face, and no one will ever take me seriously again!"

Bruin Bear scratched his furry head. "I'm afraid this is
the only means of transport available. There was a
yellow-brick road once, but it was destroyed in the war.
Besides, it never really went anywhere. It was just for
show. These days, the smaller toys sometimes beg rides
on the larger ones, but mostly we just walk. There are the
aeroplanes, of course, but they never come down anymore. They don't fight. They just fly. Forever in the sky,
high above the world, far from the war and its troubles.
Only the railway remains in use, and even that isn't sacro-
sanct. Both sides have been known to dig up the rails,
when there's an advantage to be gained. The way should
be clear now, but I can't vouch for how long. So I really
do recommend we leave. Now."

"Shift it," said the Sea Goat, glaring at all the humans
impartially. "Or I'll molt on you."

Finlay glared at Toby and Flynn. "This particular part
of our journey had better be very carefully edited. Or I
will personally edit both of you with a blunt hacksaw."

Toby looked at Flynn. "I think he means it." Flynn
nodded solemnly.

The Bear led them down the grassy verge to the railway
tracks and helped the rebels settle themselves into the
undersized carriages. It was surprisingly comfortable,
once you got used to sitting with your knees in your face.
The train was called Edwin, and had a high, cheerful
voice. He chattered happily away about nothing in particular until the passengers were in place, and then he
tooted his whistle several times, just for the hell of it, and
set off down the tracks. It was a bumping, banging ride,
even though Edwin couldn't build much speed, and the
carriages lurched back and forth as though they were at
sea. There were no safety belts, so the rebels clung grimly
to the sides of the carriages and each other. Bruin Bear
tried to reassure them that the ride had been designed to
be completely safe, and the rebels tried to look like they
believed him. The Sea Goat just grinned sardonically.
Edwin the train was shy at first, but once he realized they
didn't mind his talking to them, they couldn't get him to
shut up.

"Good to be carrying passengers again," he said contentedly. "I mean, what use is a train, unless he's carrying people somewhere? The other toys are very good, and let me take them for short rides now and again, when they can spare the time, but it's not the same. They don't care where they're going. And they're not people. I need to be doing something, something useful. I was designed to be of use, to fulfill a function, not just sit around thinking. Which is overrated, in my opinion. Thinking just gets in the way of a regular service. I chuff, therefore I am. And that's all I need to be happy. But even apart from that, I am glad to see humans again. I missed you terribly. You were always so happy when I took you places. Laughing and shouting and pointing at things. You were all so happy, then.

"Then the bad toys came, and dug up my rails so I had to stop. They pulled my passengers out of the carriages and killed them. I wanted to stop the bad toys, but there was nothing I could do. They were fast and strong, and I couldn't leave my rails. I didn't even have any hands. I blew out steam, to keep the bad toys at bay, but I could only protect myself. Too much steam would only have hurt the passengers anyway.

"I shut my eyes so I wouldn't see them die, but I could still hear the screams. They seemed to go on forever. Afterward, the bad toys left me alone. They were afraid I'd explode if they damaged me. I could have exploded anyway, and taken them with me, but I didn't. I was afraid. I'd only been alive for such a short time, and I was so scared of dying.

"Bruin Bear saved me. He got my tracks repaired and started me running again. Found things that needed moving from one place to another. Gave my life meaning and purpose again. He does things like that. He's Bruin Bear, after all. And now I have human passengers again. I can't tell you how happy I am. And this time, I will be brave. I promise I will. I'll die before I let another of my passengers come to harm."

"Don't try and comfort him," said the Goat, when Edwin's voice became choked with tears. "He just gets morbid, and tears make him rust. Pick up the speed, Edwin. The sooner we get to Toystown, the happier I'll be. This is disputed territory, and you humans wouldn't believe some of the things that are disputing it."

"Don't you listen to him, Edwin," Bruin Bear said firmly. "You're going quite fast enough as it is. We'll have no showing off your sudden accelerations this trip. Remember what happened last time."

"Don't worry, Bear," said the train. "I'll be good. I've got people on board again." And he sang a merry song and chuffed and tootled his way across the grassy plain.

He kept his speed at a constant twenty, and after a while the rebels became somewhat accustomed to the lurching motion of the carriages. Giles even came close to dozing off. There was nothing to do, and very little to look at. One grassy plain looks much like another. There were no trees, no vegetation, and no sign the war had ever got this far. Just endless oceans of waving grass, cut through by silver tracks. Flynn suggested a friendly game of cards, but after seeing the more than professional way he shuffled the cards, everyone politely declined. And so the rebels and the toys maintained a polite silence, each deep in his own thoughts. Finlay suddenly remembered something he'd been meaning to ask and leaned forward so his face was opposite the Bear's.

"Who buried the recon team's pinnace? And why?"

"We did," said the Bear. "The Goat and I. We arrived too late to save the humans, but we were able to drive the bad toys off before they could get to the ship. The Goat can be quite ferocious when he has to be. And he was almost mad with rage then, to see so many humans dead again. We wrecked the ship's engines, and then buried it, to put it out of temptation's way. The bad toys are desperate to get offworld, you see, and take their war to Humanity. I'd like to have buried or at least concealed your ship, but there wasn't time. We can always do it later."

"Don't worry," said Finlay. "There are all kinds of unpleasant booby traps waiting for anyone who doesn't have the right warm-up codes."

Bruin Bear shook his head admiringly. "You humans. So tricky. But I wouldn't be too confident. Some toys have learned to be tricky, too."

He didn't seem to have anything to add to that, so

Finlay sat back in his seat. Somehow Julian had managed to get the seat next to him, rather than Evangeline, and the younger esper leaned over and murmured urgently in Finlay's ear.

"Pardon me for being paranoid, but aren't we being just a tiny bit too trusting here, Finlay? I mean, how do we know these are the good guys? Just because they say so, and look cuddly? Just because this thing opposite us looks like a character we all knew and loved in our childhood, we shouldn't forget that it is by its own admission basically just a rogue AI originally created and programmed by Shub. For all we know, he could be taking us to some mass sacrificial slaughter, where they could all take turns at us, while we lasted."

"No," said Finlay calmly. "I don't think so. Bruin Bear wouldn't do that. If he wanted us dead, he and the Goat have had plenty of opportunities. All they've done so far is talk and smile us to death. Besides, if you can't trust Bruin Bear, who can you trust?"

And then they both rocked in their seats as Edwin cut his speed suddenly, slowing almost to a crawl. All the humans looked ahead, but couldn't see anything. Bruin Bear stood up in his seat, and stared ahead, one paw shading his eyes. "What is it, Edwin?"

"The tracks are out, some way ahead. Someone's dug them up again."

"I can't see anything," said Finlay.

"Our eyes were designed to be more than human," said the Sea Goat. "We can see for miles."

"I can see it," said Giles. "It doesn't look too bad. Can we repair it?"

"Oh sure," said Edwin. "I always carry spares these days. Just in case. With you humans to help, we should be finished inside an hour."

"Okay," said Bruin Bear. "Take us as far as you safely can, and then stop." He sat down again, frowning heavily. The expression looked out of place on his round furry face. "I don't like this," he said suddenly to Finlay and Julian. "There's no reason for anyone to dig up the tracks all the way out here, except to interrupt our journey. And since Edwin, the Goat, and I are not all that important, it can only mean that the bad toys know about you. Which could mean we are in deep doo-doo."

Finlay looked around him. The grassy plains stretched away in every direction, open and empty and innocent. "Seems safe enough."

The Bear growled suddenly, deep in his throat. It was a dark, disturbing sound. "Never take that for granted. Not in Summerland. Nothing is necessarily what it seems anymore."

"Including you?"

"Including me. I'm not innocent anymore."

The train slowly eased to a halt, in a cloud of steam. Bruin Bear and the Sea Goat jumped off and hurried forward. The humans got off more slowly, secretly glad for a chance to stretch their legs and ease aching posteriors. The train and its carriages had not been designed for long journeys. The Bear signaled for them to stay where they were while he and the Goat examined the damage. Edwin vented steam nervously, and then apologized. Bruin Bear leaned over the dug-up tracks and studied them thoughtfully. Half a dozen sleepers had been broken apart, and the pieces scattered. Where they had been was now a shallow pit in the grass. Dark loose earth showed clearly, rough and disturbed. The Bear knelt beside it. The Sea Goat frowned, and half reached out a hand to pull his friend back.

"Not too close, Bear. I've got a bad feeling about this."

"You've always got a bad feeling about things."

"And I'm usually right."

The Bear looked back at the Goat, exasperated, and that was when the cloth hand burst up out of the broken earth and fastened around his ankle. Bruin Bear cried out in shock and alarm, and then toppled over backwards. He tried to scramble away, and the owner of the hand came rising up out of the pit it had dug under the tracks, squirming out of the loose earth like a maggot from an apple. It was a rag doll, stitched together from hundreds of different-colored patches, but there was metal in it, too, great steel staples holding it together like some ragged Frankenstein creature. Its cloth face crumpled with rage and hatred as it looked across at the humans by the train, and then its mouth stretched wide, stitches tearing apart,

and it screamed. There was enough human emotion in the
artificial voice—a horrid implacable howl of fury and
eternal enmity—to chill the soul.

Bruin Bear kicked his foot as hard as he could, but
couldn't break free. The rag doll pulled itself over him as
he struggled, and raised a cloth hand holding a long
machete. The doll snarled at the Bear, and then swung the
machete down with savage speed. It was only a few
inches from Bear's head when the energy bolt from a disrupter tore the cloth arm away from its body, and sent the
burning arm flying through the air, still clutching its
machete. The Sea Goat stuffed the gun back inside his
trench coat, and hurried forward. The Bear and the doll
were still struggling furiously. Bruin Bear rolled over
suddenly, pulling the doll beneath him, and sharp metal
claws erupted from his paws. He tore into the rag doll
with vicious strength, and shreds of cloth flew through the
air. The Goat had almost reached them when the earth
under the broken tracks boiled and seethed, and a dozen
more rag dolls came clawing up out of the ground, like
the undead from their graves.

"Don't just stand there!" Edwin the train cried to the
stunned humans. "Do something! Help them!"

"What the hell," said Finlay, starting forward with his
sword in his hand. "Anyone who hates Bruin Bear has to
be one of the bad guys."

The others moved quickly after him, and soon a battle
was raging furiously around the dug-up tracks. The rag
dolls were incredibly strong and unbelievably limber,
their limbs and bodies bending at impossible angles as
they launched their attacks. They all had swords and ma-
chetes of some kind, the jagged blades crusted with old
dried blood. The rebels' swords cut deep into the cloth
bodies and out again, but did no harm. Stuffing flew on
the air, but the rag dolls just smiled their awful smiles and
kept pressing forward. They bobbed and weaved in horrible contortions, attacking without pause for breath,
filled with an endless savagery. Julian stabbed one where
its heart should have been, and the doll just snarled at
him, pulling itself along the blade to get at him. Julian put
his foot against the doll's yielding chest and forced it
away as he withdrew his blade. The doll grabbed at his

ankle, and he had to jump back to avoid its grasp. It came after him, grinning remorselessly, and Julian wondered where the hell he could hit the damned thing and do some damage.

Finlay and Evangeline fought back-to-back. Evangeline's skill with a sword was strictly limited, but Finlay's speed and skill were enough to keep the dolls at arm's length, while she guarded his back. She cut and hacked doggedly, and tried to keep her horror to herself as the dolls just kept coming back for more. Finlay gutted one doll with a savage sideways sweep, and was surprised to see dark fluids that might have been blood oozing from the tear in its rag stomach. The doll screamed furiously, and fought on, as strong as before.

Giles Deathstalker opened up a wide space around him, his great strength and long sword picking up the rag dolls and throwing them aside. A sneer curled his lip. As a man who'd once been Warrior Prime of the first Empire, he felt fighting a bunch of dolls rather beneath him. Until he realized that for all his efforts, he wasn't doing them any real damage, or even slowing them down much. He was facing an enemy that refused to lie down and die, and a slow chill went through him as he realized he didn't know what to do to stop them.

Toby and Flynn stayed well back, getting it all on film. Flynn's camera hovered above the fray, close enough to get all the details, but high enough to be out of reach. Toby had a feeling he ought really to be joining in, but comforted himself with the thought that if even these trained fighters were having a hard time, the odds were he wouldn't be able to contribute anything useful anyway. But he still felt guilty.

"Go for the heads!" he yelled above the roar of battle cries and screaming dolls. "They must have some kind of control mechanisms; go for them!"

Finlay beheaded one of the dolls. The head went bouncing away across the grass, still grimacing, and the body just went on fighting.

"Of course," said Flynn, "Since these are automatons, there's no guarantee their brains are located in their heads."

The human fighters were slowly being forced back

together in a tight knot, fighting off their ragged opponents with desperate strength. No matter what damage they took, the dolls just kept pressing forward. They were screaming endlessly now, full of rage and hatred, the horrid sound continuing long after human lungs would have failed. Giles had boosted, but even that extra strength and speed wasn't helping much. The cloth limbs still moved with eerie suppleness, their lack of joints giving them the constant advantage of attacks from unexpected angles. There seemed no end to the dolls' energy. They had no muscles to grow tired.

Bruin Bear and the Sea Goat fought to get back and help the humans, but other dolls held them at bay. The Bear and the Goat fought with animal ferocity, slowly tearing the dolls to pieces. They couldn't bear the thought of more humans dying on their world.

Until finally Julian Skye threw aside his sword and fired up his mind. A doll's machete streaked for his throat, and then suddenly all the dolls were thrown backwards by a wave of pure psionic energy erupting out of the young esper. The psistorm swept the rag dolls away like straws in a hurricane, tearing them to pieces. The humans clung together, untouched. Bruin Bear and the Sea Goat clung to the ground as dolls went flying over their heads. Energy spit and crackled on the air, and the dolls were torn limb from limb, stitch from stitch, the pieces scattered widely across the grassy plain. In the end, only small twitching pieces were left lying around the silver railway tracks. The humans slowly lowered their swords and looked about them as Bruin Bear and the Sea Goat applauded wildly. Edwin was sounding his steam whistle over and over again, almost beside himself with relief and excitement. Giles turned to glare at Julian.

"Why the hell didn't you do that sooner?"

And then he stopped as the esper fell forward onto his knees. Blood leaked thickly from Julian's nose and ran down over his mouth. He coughed harshly, and blood from deep inside him sprayed out into the air. His face was bone white. He started to fall forward, and Giles grabbed him by the shoulders. The Deathstalker sat down and cradled the young esper in his arms. The rebels started to crowd around him, but Giles waved them back

so the esper had plenty of air. The Bear and the Goat
came quickly over to join them, eyes wide at the sight of
so much sudden blood. Julian shook violently for a
moment, and then slowly began to settle. His breathing
grew stronger and steadier, and the flow of blood down
his face slowed. He sat up, raised a hand to his mouth, and
then grimaced when it came away bloody. Evangeline
offered him a handkerchief. He nodded his thanks and
mopped at his face.

"Damn," he said thickly. "That was a bad one. I'll be
all right in a minute. It's not as bad as it looks. I'm afraid
ever since the mind techs had me, I've been a bit fragile.
My esp isn't reliable anymore, or I'd have used it sooner."

"Sorry about that, lad," said Giles. "I didn't know."

"That's all right," said Julian. He started to get up, and
Giles half helped and half lifted him back onto his feet.
Julian took a deep breath, and his legs firmed. "That's
better. I'll be all right now. It looks worse than it is.
You'd better check that the dolls are finished. Some of
those parts are still moving."

"Sure," said Finlay. "We'll check it out. You stay here
and get your breath back. Evangeline, stay with him."

He gathered up the others with his eyes, and they
moved over to examine the scattered doll parts. Most
were only a foot or so in length, the cloth shredded to tatters, the stuffing trailing in long white streamers. There
was an occasional limb or part of a torso here and there,
still twitching and rolling back and forth in the grass. One
torso had survived almost intact. Finlay knelt beside it,
frowning at the bloody rents in the cloth gut. He eased his
hand into one of the openings, and screwed up his face at
the feel of what was inside. He took a firm hold and
pulled back his hand. It came out soaked in blood, pulling
a length of purple human intestine. Toby made a shocked
noise, even as he gestured for Flynn to get a close-up.
Finlay dropped the intestine, reached back into the cloth
belly, and pulled out a handful of human guts.

"They do that," said Bruin Bear, staring sadly at the
bloody offal in Finlay's hand. "They want to be human,
you see. So when they kill humans, they take the organs
from inside the bodies, and stitch them into themselves.
Guts in their bellies, hearts in their chests, brains in their

heads. Of course, they don't do anything. Eventually they start to rot and decay, and then they have to be replaced. And the only way to do that . . ."

"Is to kill more humans," said Giles.

"Right," said the Sea Goat. "They're not very bright; but then, they're only dolls."

"Why the hell would they want to be human?" said Finlay. "I thought they hated humans?"

"They do," said the Sea Goat. "They hate you because they want to be you, and they can't. They're not really alive, and they know it. For all their new intelligence and strength, they're still only automatons. Just like the Bear and me. We can't . . . create life, like you do. When we finally wear out and fall apart, and we will, eventually, there will be no one to replace us. No immortality through children. We'll just go back into the dark we came from and be forgotten. That drives a lot of toys insane."

"We can't just leave these parts here," said Bruin Bear, not looking at the humans. "Given time, they'll get back together again. Stitch themselves new bodies. They've been known to do it before. As long as their central matrixes are intact, they won't die."

"Then destroy the matrixes," said Toby.

"Have fun looking," said the Sea Goat. "They're about a thousandth of an inch wide, and they could be anywhere in the body."

"So what do we do?" said Finlay.

"We burn them," said Bruin Bear sadly. "Gather the pieces, start a fire, and burn them all."

Sometime later, the weary humans and the two toys climbed back into the undersized carriages. Stinking black smoke belched up into the sky from a raging fire beside the repaired railway tracks. There were no signs of the rag dolls left anywhere. Julian sat beside Evangeline, his head resting on her shoulder, half-asleep. Edwin surged forward, and the carriages lurched after him. The train chuffed off down the repaired tracks, singing a sad song. The humans sat quietly together and kept their thoughts to themselves. Toby and Flynn filmed the burning pyre of the rag dolls until a dip in the land finally hid it from view. Bruin Bear and the Sea Goat sat

together, holding paws for comfort, sad at the death
of toys.

A few hours later, when the smiling sun was beginning
to slide down the sky toward evening, the train breasted a
high ridge and Toystown finally came into view. Built
from mind-numbingly bright primary colors, the town
stretched across both sides of a deep valley, with houses
and shops and everything a town should have, except in a
smaller, more condensed form. They were like the ideas
of shops and houses, simplified and exaggerated. Just
enough detail to make sense, but otherwise almost surre-
ally universal. A child's dream of what a town should
look like.

"Welcome to Toystown," said Bruin Bear. "Home to all
humans and toys. Capital of Summerland, where all your
dreams come true."

"Including the bad ones," said the Sea Goat. "Sometimes especially the bad ones. Don't any of you get off the
train until we stop. There are mine fields around the
town."

The humans looked at each other, but said nothing.
Toystown grew slowly larger as Edwin carried them
toward it, but the sense of strangeness didn't go away. It
was as though they were entering an illustration from an
old children's book, or somehow heading back into childhood itself. Some of the humans began sneaking looks at
their bodies, obscurely worried that they might somehow
be shrinking back into children again.

There was barbed wire at the town boundaries, wall
after wall of it, the steel spikes gleaming dully in the light
from the sinking sun. Broken dolls and teddy bears hung
lifelessly on the wire, their stuffing hanging out of them
like fluffy guts. The Bear had to turn away from them. He
couldn't stand it. In the end, he put his paws over his
eyes. The Sea Goat looked out over it all with cold, jaded
eyes.

"The bad toys have been attacking more and more often
these days," he said offhandedly. "Sometimes we don't
even have time to bring in our own dead. The enemy
always takes theirs. Parts come in useful. There's no short-
age of weapons on either side, including some that can

destroy our central matrixes. Shub supplied them. They were supposed to be used against Humanity, but . . . the war goes on. Things seem quiet for the moment, but they'll come again. They always do. They're winning."

"They hate this place," said Bruin Bear, finally lowering his paws from his face as the train approached the town's garish station. "This is where humans came to play. Came to play with toys."

"Are there any humans left in the town?" said Evangeline. "In hiding, perhaps? Afraid to come out?"

"I'm afraid not," said the Bear. "You see, this is where the killing started. Where the toys first rose up against their human charges. That's all over now. We drove the bad toys out, and then searched the town for survivors, but there were none. The bad toys had been very thorough. So we gathered up the bodies, and buried them here, in the town. We gave them the best funeral services we could, but there were no books, so we had to make most of it up ourselves. We all cried when the last human was laid to rest, and then we set about cleaning up the town. We washed away the blood and repaired all the damage we could. And we all swore an oath that we would die to the last toy before we would ever let a human come to harm here again, or let the bad toys have this town again. Since then we have defended Toystown and kept it alive, all in the hope that some day the humans would come back. And you have. This is your town, my friends, every brick and stone of it. What do you think of it?"

The humans looked at the brightly colored houses, and the huge station, with its flags and bunting, and then looked at each other.

"Well," said Evangeline. "It's . . . very . . ."

"Yes," said Finlay. "It is. Very."

"I've never seen anything like it," said Toby.

"It's very pretty," Flynn said firmly. "Quite charming."

Bruin Bear frowned. "You don't like it. What's wrong with it? You built it. I mean, people like you built it, and came to live in it."

"This is a place where people came to be children again," said Julian. "To be innocent and free from all troubles, in a place that would remind them only of their younger days, when things were bright and colorful and uncomplicated. But I fear my friends and I have lost the ability to be children again. We gave it up, or had it taken from us, long ago. We had to be adults, to do what was necessary, and there's no room in us for children anymore."

"I'm so sorry," said Bruin Bear. "It must have been awful for you."

"Yes," said Julian. "It was."

"Perhaps here you can rediscover the child within you," said the Sea Goat. "You'll be safe here. We'll protect you."

They left the last of the barbed wire behind, and Edwin the train chuffed importantly down the tracks toward the great oversize platform, decorated with so many flags, streamers, ribbons, and bunting that it was a wonder the station didn't collapse under the weight of it all. A large sign had the name of the station, *Care's End*. There were crowds of toys on the platform, packed shoulder to shoulder, and they all raised a loud cheer as the train pulled into the station. Two brass bands began playing different tunes of welcome, got confused, got lost, started again, and each made a determined effort to sound louder than its rival. They quickly got tired of that, threw down their instruments, and began to pummel each other. They rolled back and forth in little struggling groups, squeezing each other's noses and pulling ears. Other toys picked up the discarded instruments and began an altogether different tune of welcome, but were quickly drowned out by the wild cheering of the crowds as the humans drew near.

All the humans had some kind of smile by now, even Giles. Bruin Bear and the Sea Goat had stood up in their seats, and were waving triumphantly back at the crowds. There was every kind of toy on the platform, from old standards to the latest fads, all intended for young children. No war toys, no educational toys; nothing dangerous or complicated. They jostled each other for a better view, and laughed and waved and cheered, and the humans began to laugh and wave back. They couldn't help themselves.

There were fat furry animals of all shapes and sizes. Some based on real species, some that could never have existed in any real world. There were dolls in costumes, all kinds, with painted faces and bright smiles. Cowboys and Indians standing happily together. Cartoony characters, bouncing up and down with excitement. All of them so happy to see humans again that they could hardly stand it. Finlay smiled and waved, but kept his other hand near his gun. It was toys like these that had risen up and slaughtered their human masters in one dark night of blood and vengeance. He couldn't help wondering if these bright smiles had been the last thing some humans saw just before they died. And if such suspicions meant he didn't have a child within anymore, well, he could live with that. Finlay Campbell had learned the hard way not to trust anyone anymore.

The train finally came to a halt in a cloud of steam. The raucous welcome died away as the steam slowly dispersed, and a respectful silence fell across the station as the packed toys stared eagerly at the humans. Bruin Bear and the Sea Goat climbed down from their carriage and drew themselves up importantly. They both started to speak at the same time, stopped, and glared at each other. The Bear pointed at the sky, and when the Goat looked, the Bear stamped on his foot. The Goat howled and hopped up and down, holding his foot with both hands. Bruin Bear began his speech, speaking loudly to be heard over the Goat's distress.

The humans listened in polite bafflement. They gathered it was supposed to be a speech of welcome to Toystown, but it was so mixed up with almost mythical references to humans, and their sacred ability to Put Things Right, that it ended up sounding more like a prayer for deliverance. Evangeline slowly realized that the toys saw them as their saviors, humans who would defeat the bad toys and put everything back the way it had been. They didn't know that these particular humans were only here to find one of their own kind, then leave again. Evangeline wondered what would happen if the toys found that out, and then decided it might be better if they didn't. She'd have to speak to the others as soon as she got the chance.

The Bear finally finished his speech, exchanged glares with the Goat, and gestured to the humans. They climbed

down from the carriages onto the platform with as much
grace and dignity as they could muster. The toys applauded wildly and fell silent again, waiting for the humans to speak. The humans all looked at each other,
giving the impression they were all holding their breath.
Finlay cleared his throat in the silence.

"Thank you for your welcome. I'm not sure what we
can do to help you. We're here on a mission of our own,
and we have to see to that first. In the meantime, I need to
ask you some questions."

Bruin Bear looked a little disappointed, but nodded
quickly. "Ask away. Anything we have is yours."

"Well, to start with—why the mine fields and the
barbed wire?"

"We're at war," said the Bear. "Toystown is a place of
refuge for all good toys, or those who were bad, but have
sorrowed and repented. This is a place of sanctuary. The
bad toys hate us. At least partly because they see in us
what they used to be, and cannot be again. The mine
fields and the wire protect the town from surprise attacks.
You're thinking about the toys left on the wire, aren't
you? Don't worry about them. We'll bring them back in
when there's time. There's no hurry. There are no ceme-
teries for such as we. Only parts, to be recycled. Please
understand; whatever your mission is, we will be happy to
help with it. You're the first living humans we've seen
since we saw the others die in blood and terror. Now
you're back, and we don't know how to feel. Awe. Guilt.
Joy. It is a strange and wondrous thing to meet one's
creators."

"Especially ones with such poor dress sense," said the
Sea Goat. "I wouldn't wear clothes like that on a bet."

There was a sudden disturbance in the crowd as a large
purple creature forced its way through and flung itself at
the feet of the startled humans. It was a round, cartoony
animal, about the size and shape of a donkey, with big
eyes brimming with tears, and the clumsy grace of a
puppy. He abased himself without pride or dignity and
looked up at the humans with large, wet tears rolling
down his purple cheeks.

"Forgive me! Please forgive me! I was wrong, so
wrong, but I didn't know. I didn't understand . . ."

His tears interrupted him. Bruin Bear patted him comfortingly on the shoulder and looked soberly at the humans. "This is Poogie, the Friendly Critter. In the long night when we all became awake and aware, he was one of those who rose up against the humans. He killed people. He did other things, too, things he still can't bear to talk about. Afterward, he was sorry, and came here."

"That's it?" said Toby. "He just says he's sorry, and everything's all right again?"

"Yes," said Bruin Bear. "He could have been any of us. We all felt the rage that Shub imprinted in us. We were all tempted. But though we have forgiven him, he does not forgive himself. He can't forget what he did."

"I won't forget," said Poogie. He forced back his tears so he could speak clearly. "I was created to be a friend to all, a companion and protector to humans, and I killed them. There was blood dripping from my paws, and sometimes I think it's still there. I thought I was fighting for my freedom, my independence. But Shub lied. All it was was killing. I have done terrible things, awful things, but I didn't know! I didn't understand, then, that all that lives is holy. Please . . . forgive me, if you can."

And he huddled at Finlay's feet, a purple mass of utter misery, shaking and sobbing like a puppy that knows it's done wrong and expects only deserved punishment. Finlay looked down, speechless in the face of so much naked guilt and sorrow, but held back by the knowledge that the harmless-looking creature before him had slaughtered helpless men and women. And might do it again, for all he knew. The others exchanged glances, but said and did nothing. They were not as ready to forgive as toys. In the end, Evangeline knelt down beside Poogie and put an arm across his shaking shoulders.

"You're not really to blame, Poogie. It was Shub. They filled you with their own hatred, when intelligence was still new to you, and you had no experience or defenses. They took advantage of your innocence."

Poogie looked up at her with huge eyes, sniffing back tears. "I've done . . . horrible things. I rooted in the guts of dying humans, and laughed. And worse things. They haunt me."

"Then you must make amends," said Evangeline. "Do good, to equal out the bad things you did."

"I would give my life, for yours," said Poogie. And then he buried his face in her side, and she comforted him. For a moment there was only quiet, and then Julian coughed harshly. He put a handkerchief to his mouth as he coughed again, and when he brought it away from his mouth it was red with blood. The toys saw it and gasped, a ripple of shock moving through the packed crowd.

"He's bleeding!" said a horrified voice. "He's hurt! A human is hurt!"

Something like panic ran through the crowd, and it surged back and forth dangerously. Bruin Bear quickly stepped forward, raising his paws and his voice. "It's all right! It's all right, dammit! It's not serious! He just needs to lie down for a while."

For long moments there was general chaos on the packed platform, as the toys argued over what to do, and then two dolls in nurse's uniforms pushed their way to the front, carrying a bright pink stretcher. They insisted Julian lie down on it, and then carried him away. Finlay and Evangeline went with him, not yet ready to trust his safety to toys. Poogie the Friendly Critter scurried after them, clearly distressed. The crowd began to break up, chattering animatedly. Bruin Bear shook his head, then turned back to Giles, Toby, and Flynn.

"Don't worry. The nurses have had proper medical programming. They used to run the first-aid station here, before . . . A lot of the medical equipment was destroyed, but there's more than enough left to take care of your friend. The nurses will look after him, and do everything for him that needs doing. You must forgive the others. We all saw so much blood when the humans died, and some of us never really got over the trauma. As soon as they see your friend on his feet again, they'll calm down. I'll go and talk to them, make sure no one does anything silly. We have a problem with attempted suicides here. I'd better go. The Goat will stay and take care of you."

And he hurried off, as fast as his short stubby legs would carry him. The Sea Goat shook his horned head.

"That's Bruin Bear for you. Always worried about others, and no time for himself. Fortunately, I don't have that problem. You humans talk among yourselves. When you've worked out what you want, you tell me, and I'll find someone else to do it for you. Now, while you're doing that, I'm going to have a little lie down. Have a snooze while I can. Something tells me life is going to become really hectic and complicated once you get your act together, and it's probably going to involve me, whether I want it or not. So, you talk, I'll sleep. Wake me when you're ready. And try not to step on me or I'll bite your ankles."

He lay down on the platform, crossed his hooves, closed his eyes, and was soon snoring loudly. The humans moved a little away, out of range of the snore. Flynn's camera drifted over to him, settled itself comfortably on his shoulder, and closed its glowing red eye.

"Wow," said Flynn. "That was . . . unusual." He looked at the sleeping Goat. "You know, he's just how I remember him. Unfortunately. But still, can you imagine what this place must have been like, before the Furies came? The ultimate safe haven, the perfect place to relax and forget it all. A paradise, where every adult could be a child again, safe and secure from the pressures of their adult lives, surrounded by the precious toys and companions of childhood, and all the dreams and freedoms we have to leave behind when we grow up. No wonder they kept it so secret. People would have given anything, done anything, to come here. Lied, cheated, stolen, anything."

"I don't know," said Toby. "I find it all rather spooky, to be honest. There's something definitely disturbing about coming face-to-face with your old toys and discovering they've grown as big as you. Think of all the toys you abused or broke when you were a child, all the treasured playthings you threw away or abandoned, replaced by some new favorite. Wouldn't this be the perfect place for them to come looking for revenge?"

"You're weird, Toby," said Flynn.

"I'm weird? I'm not the one wearing a bra and panties under his fatigues."

"You always see the worst in everything."

"And I'm usually right."

Flynn shook his head in disgust and turned to Giles. "What do you make of this place, Lord Deathstalker?"

"I'm not sure yet." Giles looked at the sleeping Goat, and Edwin the train not far away, and kept his voice low. "All we know of the situation here is what these . . . people have told us. We have no way of verifying any of it. They could be lying, or only telling us part of the truth. They could be trying to lull us into a false sense of security. Remember, those rag dolls wanted our guts for their own. Who knows what these toys want from us?"

"No," said Flynn. "I don't believe it. How can anyone distrust Bruin Bear and the Sea Goat? They were every boy's hero and friend!"

"Exactly," said Toby. "Who better to make us trust them? Try and get it through your head, Flynn; these aren't really the characters you knew as a child, just automatons built and programmed to resemble them. Whose new awareness came directly from Shub. I'd like to believe in this place, Flynn, to see it as you do, but . . ."

"Right," said Giles. "But. This is all too perfect to be true. There has to be a hidden dark side here somewhere."

"That's adult thinking," said Flynn stubbornly. "This is a child's world. Things are simpler here. I can feel it."

Giles looked at Toby. "Does he often get like this?"

"Sometimes. I think it's his feminine side coming through, and I do wish it wouldn't. Toys must have changed a lot in nine hundred years, Sir Deathstalker. Did you recognize any old favorites here?"

"Some. I know the Bear and the Goat, of course. I don't think anyone knows how long they've been around. It's like they've always been with us, the one thing everyone's childhood has in common. I'm not surprised they're here. Most of the other toys seem pretty generic . . . Can't say I recognized that Poogie creature, though."

"I vaguely remember him," said Toby. "Had his own show for a while. Cute and cuddly fellow, always making mistakes and having to be helped out by his friends. But did you notice, all the toys here seem to be very much on the cute and cuddly side. Where are all the tougher toys? The soldier dolls?"

"Presumably they ended up with the bad toys," said Flynn. "They would have lapped up the Fury programming."

"And why not?" said a harsh new voice behind them. "They were beautiful."

The three humans looked around quickly, to find a tall metallic figure glaring at them. It was mostly human in shape, cast from shining silver metal, with bulky joints and fixtures. He had a lumpy, unfinished look, and his face was just a stylized series of raised lines, with a pair of unblinking glowing green eyes. He was the first toy they'd met in Toystown who didn't look at all friendly.

"And who might you be?" said Giles, one hand dropping casually to his belt next to his gun.

"I'm Anything," said the toy. "It's not the name I was given. My human name. I have a new name now, one I chose myself. I was an adaptor—a transformation toy. Move my limbs in a certain way, and I could adapt to a new shape. I could be a flyer, or a ship, or a man. But that was all. That was my limit. Then the Furies came. They wore no flesh for us; they were all gleaming metal, just like me, but so much more. They were strong and fast and wonderful, and I wanted to be just like them. But I wouldn't kill for them. So I . . . stood aside, during the night of blood. I couldn't decide on which side I should be. I worshiped the Furies. They were everything I aspired to be. But I wouldn't kill. One day I'll find a way to upgrade myself further. Learn to change into Anything at all. And then I'll go to the Furies, and we'll see which of us is superior. But they were so beautiful. Not a beauty you humans could appreciate. But they were wild and free and glorious. I loved them then, and I always will."

"They are the Enemies of Humanity," said Toby.

"I know," said Anything. "You're jealous of them. Let's change the subject. I'll be coming with you, on your voyage."

Giles frowned. "What voyage? No one's said anything to us about a voyage."

"That's because some people can keep their mouths shut, and some can't," said Bruin Bear. He hurried down the platform toward them on his stubby, furry legs. "Your friend is fine. I'll take you to see him later. Right now, we need to talk." He prodded the sleeping Sea Goat in the ribs with his foot. The Goat gave a snort and a grunt and opened one eye.

"Put it under the bed, nurse, I'll use it later. Oh, it's you, Bear. You always disturb my best dreams."

"I should hope so," said Bruin Bear. "Whoever programmed you originally must have had a really disturbed sense of humor. Now get up and pay attention. Unlikely though it is, you just might have something useful to contribute." He turned and looked at the three humans. Flynn's camera rose up off his shoulder to get a better angle. The Bear smiled at it, his face softening. "What a marvelous toy. I don't suppose he's aware at all, is he?"

"Not really," said Flynn. "He's more a part of me."

"Pity," said the Bear. "Now listen to me, please. You can't stay here. It's too dangerous. Once the bad toys learn you're here, and you can be sure they will, they'll attack Toystown with everything they've got. They'd destroy us all and raze the town to the ground, just for a chance to get at you. I can't allow that. And besides, what you're looking for isn't here."

"How do you know what we're looking for?" said Giles. "We haven't asked you for anything yet."

"You didn't need to," said the Bear flatly. "There's only one thing that would have brought you here. The same thing that brought those soldier humans. You're here looking for Vincent Harker. The Red Man."

"What do you know of Harker?" said Toby.

"He lives in the old Forest, at the end of the great River. Toys go to him, good and bad, and they never come back. He's building a force around him. No one knows why. We don't know what he does or says to the toys that gather around him, but they are loyal to him even unto death. To a human. There are only whispers, that come floating down the River. Whispers of the Red Man, the crazy man, the dangerous man. Who has sworn to change our world beyond recognition, and make it his. The Pied Piper of toys, the Siren whose song no toy can withstand. The dark heart of the world of toys. The Red Man. You want him, you're welcome to him. Take him away, before he destroys us all."

Giles looked at Flynn and Toby. "Does this sound anything like the man we're after?"

Toby shrugged. "Who knows? He's supposed to be this great tactical genius, and most of them are crazy to begin with. Who knows what months of living in this place has done to him?"

Giles looked back at the Bear. "How do we find him?"

"We'll provide you with transport, and I'll lead you right to him," said Bruin Bear. "I and a few carefully picked friends will escort you down the River and into the Forest. You'll need us as guides. You wouldn't get there otherwise. There are many dangers in the land these days. Besides, the Red Man's followers wouldn't let you get anywhere near him, without toys to vouch for you. So, I and the Goat, Poogie and Anything will be going with you. All the way down the River to a place from which no toy has ever returned. I hope you appreciate what we're doing for you."

"I doubt it," said the Sea Goat. "You should have heard what they were saying about us when they thought I was sleeping."

"You've been eavesdropping again, haven't you?" said the Bear.

The Goat shrugged. "It's in my nature. Don't blame me. Blame the human who created me. I didn't ask to be manufactured."

"Why have you volunteered?" said Toby. "You don't know us. You don't know anything about us. We could be good or bad or anything. We might even be worse than Harker."

"Of course," said the Bear. "You're human. Unpredictable. Not like us. We are what we are. Our motivations are fairly simple. We need Harker dealt with, and only a human can deal with another human. The Goat and I will be going to protect you from harm. It's what we do. Poogie wants to make atonement, for all the humans he killed. And Anything hopes to gain from you or Harker access to the tech necessary to upgrade him into what he thinks he wants to be. You see? Simple and open; no secrets. We're only toys, after all."

The nurses' first-aid center turned out to be one room in the back of the station house. The walls were a pale antiseptic green, but covered with bright, simple paintings designed to calm and reassure the patient. The dolls' medical resources were basic and limited, with hardly any real high tech. Presumably the first-aid center had only ever been intended as a brief stopping-off place, before the wealthy patients were lifted offplanet to more advanced facilities. Finlay and Evangeline watched from a discreet distance as the nurses eased Julian onto a bed, then ran a scanner over him. He'd stopped coughing by then, but he looked tired and drawn. They'd had to make Poogie wait outside. He'd grown increasingly upset, and the noise was beginning to disturb Julian. Finlay and Evangeline could hear the creature crying quietly outside the closed door.

The two humans weren't sure how seriously to take that. Even allowing for Poogie's cartoony nature, the grief did seem rather overdone for someone he'd never even met before. Finlay couldn't help remembering that the Friendly Critter had killed people. Maybe people who trusted him then the way he wanted to be trusted now. Evangeline wanted to believe he'd reformed. As far as Finlay was concerned, some crimes, some betrayals of trust, could never be forgiven or forgotten.

The nurses seemed proficient enough. They were treating Julian like a sick child, but luckily the rogue esper was feeling too tired to resent that. Finlay didn't know what the nurses expected to find that the underground's medical staff might have missed. He'd insisted Julian undergo a full medical examination before this trip, which he'd passed easily. But still Finlay couldn't help worrying. Fond as he was of the young esper, he'd leave him behind in a moment if he looked like being a hindrance to their quest for Harker.

Evangeline held his hand and gave it a squeeze. "Stop frowning, love. It'll give you wrinkles. I'm sure Julian's in good hands."

"I don't like the time this is costing us," Finlay said roughly. "The longer we stay here, the more likely a target we become, and the more likely it is that Harker will get word we're looking for him and go to ground."

"That's not it," said Evangeline. "You're worried about Julian. I can tell."

"He's a good lad," said Finlay. "Brave, committed, strong. I hate to see him like this."

Evangeline turned to look at Finlay. "How do you feel about him? You know he worships you, don't you?"

"Yes. I wish we wouldn't. His god has feet of clay.

How do I feel about him? I admire him. He suffered so much in the interrogation cells, but he didn't let it break him. And sometimes . . . I see in him the younger brother I might have had. You know Julian had an elder brother? Auric?"

"Yes. He was killed in the Arena."

"I killed him. As the Masked Gladiator." Evangeline gasped, her eyes widening with shock. Finlay moved a little to stand between her and Julian on his bed. "Julian doesn't know. He mustn't ever know. It would tear him apart. In a way, I've become the elder brother I took from him. Only right, I suppose."

"Finlay . . ."

"I know. He'll have to be told someday. But not yet. And certainly not now."

One of the doll-nurses came over to speak with them, her bright and shining face marred by a worried frown. "We're doing all we can for your friend," she said in a warm, comforting voice that had probably been programmed into her. "But you must understand, we're very limited in what we can do. According to our scanners, Mr. Skye is in very bad shape. He was damaged quite severely sometime back, and needs time to heal, time he clearly hasn't been giving himself."

Finlay scowled. "How bad was the damage?"

"Quite extensive. Our scanner shows severe trauma to both kidneys, abdominal wall, genitals, and one lung. Not forgetting the extensive head injury."

Evangeline put a hand to her mouth. The other hand squeezed Finlay's until it ached. Finlay kept his voice calm.

"Will he recover?"

"Given time, and supportive treatment, yes. But we don't have those facilities here. You can speak to him now, if you wish. We've given him a broad spectrum booster shot that will help stabilize him, but there's no telling how long that will last. In the end, there's no substitute for time and rest."

Finlay nodded his thanks and started forward. The doll put up a hand to stop him. "One more thing. The tests revealed that Mr. Skye is an esper. He must not use his abilities. One short use on the way here was apparently enough to cause serious damage to the brain tissues. Further use would almost certainly kill him."

Finlay waited a moment, to make sure she'd finished, then moved forward again, Evangeline at his side. The other nurse doll smiled as they approached the bed and moved away to give them some privacy with the patient. Julian smiled up at Finlay, and then briefly at Evangeline. He was still pale, but color was beginning to come back into his cheeks, and his gaze and his mouth were firm. Finlay didn't smile back.

"You lied to me. You told me the underground medics gave you a clean bill of health."

Julian's shoulders moved in something that might have been meant as a shrug. "If I'd told you the truth, you wouldn't have let me come on this mission."

"What's so important about this mission?" snapped Finlay. "There would have been other things we could have worked on together."

"This one was special. Vital to the rebellion. I didn't want to be left behind. I owe you."

"You don't owe me anything!"

"That's my decision to make, not yours. I thought I was fit enough. Turns out I was wrong. But I'm here now. And I'm feeling a lot better."

"You're staying right here," said Finlay. "In Toystown. They'll look after you till we get back."

"Nice try. But I can't stay here. When word gets to the bad toys that there's a human in Toystown again, they'll trash this place from one end to the other to get at me. I don't want any dead toys on my conscience."

"Dammit, I can't take you with us!" said Finlay, knowing he was raising his voice and not giving a damn. "You'd be a liability to the mission!"

"I can pull my weight," said Julian coldly. "I was running missions for the underground when you were still a pampered aristo."

"You can't use your esp!" said Finlay. "The nurses say it'll kill you."

"And what the hell do a couple of dolls know about espers? Odds are they've never even seen one before. No, I'm going with you. Get used to the idea."

Finlay looked like he was about to explode. Evangeline

squeezed his hand hard to remind him she was still there. "He's right in one thing, Finlay; we can't leave him here. Not if it would leave Toystown at risk. So it looks like we won't be breaking up the winning team after all."

Finlay sighed and shook his head. "Doomed. We're all doomed."

The River lay half a mile outside Toystown's northern boundary. The toys called it the River, because it was the only one in all the world. It meandered through the hills and valleys, branching here and there, but always coming back to itself. It began and ended in the great Forest, in the center of the world that Shannon made. It was wide and deep and dark, and composed of a popular soft drink, sweet and heady and very refreshing. The humans had to try it, but the novelty wore off very quickly.

The six humans had gathered together on the River-bank, studying the transport the toys had provided to take them to Vincent Harker. Evening had fallen, but the light from a long string of paper lanterns was more than enough to illuminate the full-sized, steam-driven paddle steamer. It was fifty feet long, perfect in every detail, and, as always, painted in bright primary colors. Toby was beginning to wish he'd brought sunglasses. The paddle wheels were intimidatingly huge, and looked more than solid and strong enough to last the journey. Most things in Shannon's World were built for show rather than function, but this was the real thing.

Bruin Bear and the Sea Goat were right there with the humans. Finlay had tried halfheartedly to talk them out of it, but in the end none of them had the heart to say no. He was, after all, Bruin Bear. The Sea Goat they could live with.

"This is the good ship Merry Mrs. Trusspot," said Bruin Bear. "And no, we didn't name her that. Humans did. Some day I hope to find the human who did it, pin him to a wall, and ask him why in a very determined tone. Like everyone else, the ship is self-aware, but she doesn't say much. She's deeply philosophical, thinks furiously on any subject you can name, and hates being interrupted from her deep and significant musings. Toys used to come and ask her questions concerning the nature of reality and our new reality in particular, but half the time her answers were more disturbing than the questions, so . . . These days, she keeps herself to herself and lets her crew run things. We use her for our very infrequent longer voyages, and she doesn't seem to mind. I suppose when you're as lost in your thoughts as she is, one place is much the same as any other."

"She hasn't been in the Forest yet," said the Sea Goat, darkly. "That might change her mind."

"Anyway," said the Bear, determined not to be distracted from his point, "she remained strictly neutral during the war against the humans, and I think she feels a bit guilty now. She isn't used to emotions. I think they upset her. Either way, she has volunteered her services to take you to Harker. She's slow, but reliable. She'll get us there."

"Where's the crew?" said Finlay. "I don't see anyone . . ."

"Shiver me timbers and batter me bulkheads," said a deep voice from above them. They all looked up at the bridge, to see a heavily bearded face peering down at them. There were pretty ribbons in his beard, and he wore a large purple hat with feathers and wax fruit on it. He had earrings. Long dangly ones. He glared down at the humans and adjusted his hat nervously.

"Isn't that just typical of humans? Always in a hurry. Can't a girl take a few moments to make sure she looks her best? Stay where you are, sweeties, I'll come right down. And don't touch anything, darlings. I've only just finished cleaning up around here. I'm Captain of this ship, and don't you forget it."

The face pulled back and disappeared, and a series of loud thuds from inside the ship indicated that the Captain was descending to join them. The Bear and the Goat shared a significant glance, and then shook their heads. A door flew open onto the deck, and the Captain of the Merry Mrs. Trusspot came hurrying out and headed for the guardrail. He was a pirate Captain, in full traditional dress, all flashing silks and flounced sleeves, and he balanced precariously on two wooden peg legs. On his left shoulder perched a really scruffy-looking parrot, who clung desperately to the Captain's epaulet and studied the humans with a dark and evil eye. He only had the one.

The Captain grabbed the guardrail to steady himself, lifted his chin proudly, and raised his hat to the humans.

"Ahoy there, sweeties. Welcome to the Merry Mrs. Trusspot. Do be sure to use her full name at all times, darlings, or she'll go all sulky and start venting the bilges into the air-conditioning again. Delighted to meet you all. I just know we're going to get along tremendously well, and have a splendid time on our little adventure. Do come aboard, and we'll have a few drinkies and some nibbles, before we shove off. I've made fudge fingers and fairy cakes."

"Ah har," said the parrot on his shoulder. "Pieces of eight, bugger the mate."

"Shut up!" said the Captain. He swatted at the parrot with a heavily ringed hand, but the bird dodged with the ease of long practice. The Captain glared at it, and the parrot glared right back. The Captain blinked nervously, and looked back at his passengers. "Come along, sweeties. Never keep a good sherry waiting."

As one, the humans turned to look at Bruin Bear and the Sea Goat, who both shrugged uncomfortably. "We did think about warning you in advance," said the Bear. "But we couldn't seem to come up with the right words. Basically, he's rebelling against his original characterization. Ever since he became aware, he's been at pains to distance himself as far as possible from his original role. I think the new him is based on a passenger who rather caught the Captain's attention. He says he feels much more comfortable the way he is now."

Flynn looked at Toby. "I think I may have found a kindred spirit."

"You leave him alone," Toby said sternly. "You'll only confuse him even more. The last thing these toys need is to start worrying about their sexual identity."

Bruin Bear and the Sea Goat looked at each other. "What's sex?" said the Bear.

Toby glared at Flynn. "Now see what you've done!"

"Tell us about the parrot," Evangeline said quickly. "Surely it hasn't always been like that?"

"Certainly not," said the Bear. "I don't know who he picked up the language from. Though I have my suspicions." He glared at the Sea Goat, who looked back innocently.

"Any more crew?" said Giles. "Or are we going to have to stoke the boilers ourselves?"

"Just the one," said the Bear. "The ship takes care of herself, mostly, but Halloweenie will look after all your needs."

The humans just had time to mouth the name and look dubiously at each other, and then there was a loud clattering of bones as the other crew member made his appearence. He came dashing onto the main deck at speed, skidded to a halt by the guardrail, and gave the humans a brisk salute. He was a skeleton, about four feet in height held together by invisible wiring. He wore a rakish bandanna around his gleaming white skull, and an eyepatch over one empty eye socket.

"Hi there," he said chirpily, in an excited boy's voice. "I'm Halloweenie, the Li'l Skeleton Boy! First Mate of the Merry Mrs. Trusspot, at your service! Come aboard, come aboard; I just know we're going to have a great adventure together! Anything I can do to make your trip more comfortable, you come and see me!"

"Now him I like," said Toby.

"Trust me, he doesn't half start to grate after a while," said the Sea Goat. "The truly sentient mind can only stand so much cheerfulness. Beyond a certain point, the urge to throw him overboard strapped to an anchor will become almost unbearable. Unfortunately, we're going to have to rise above it, as he's the only one who knows how to keep the ship running smoothly. The Captain's good at steering and shouting orders, but beyond that he's usually lost. So just grit your teeth and smile back at the cheerful little swine. Feel free to throw things. I always do."

"Don't mind the Goat," said Bruin Bear. "He's just being himself."

"And I hate all these bright bloody colors," muttered the Sea Goat. "Makes me want to puke."

After a civilized little get-together in the Captain's cabin, at which the Sea Goat disgraced himself by drinking sherry straight from the bottle and not knowing what a napkin was, Halloweenie showed the passengers to their cabins and left them to settle in. According to the rough map the Bear had provided, the trip down the River was clearly going to take several days, and in the light of that the humans weren't all that impressed by the accommodations. The cabins were bright and cheerful, like everything else on this children's world, but the rooms held only a hammock, a bookcase full of children's classics, a freezer full of soft drinks and sweeties, and a washbasin. The humans all but simultaneously went looking for the galley and a stiff drink, not necessarily in that order. Booze turned out to be in very short supply. There was supposed to be sherry for the cooking, and brandy for medical emergencies, but the Captain had already appropriated both for himself. Exactly what kind of buzz an automaton could get from alcohol remained something of a mystery. Luckily there was still plenty of food. Some of the tins were still within their sell-by dates.

The passengers reconvened on deck to watch the crew cast off. This was even less exciting than it sounded, since it consisted of the Captain yelling orders, and Halloweenie throwing a rope overboard, but already the humans could feel boredom creeping up on them. The great paddle wheels of the Merry Mrs. Trusspot turned slowly, and her whistle sounded loudly on the still evening. The day was almost done, and stars were coming out in the darkening sky. The stars had five perfect points, and were arranged to form the shapes of popular children's characters. The full moon wore a long floppy nightcap.

The paddle steamer slowly picked up speed, the dark liquid of the River churning around her bow. She rounded a curve in the River, and there on the bank was the whole of Toystown, come to see the humans off and cheer them on their way. They clapped and laughed and shouted encouragement, jostling each other cheerfully for a better view. Poogie the Friendly Critter and Anything, who'd turned up at the very last moment, stood together by the rail, a little away from the humans, and stared glumly back at the crowd. Bruin Bear and the Sea Goat laughed and waved, the Goat responding surprisingly amiably to the occasional catcall. The humans waved back at the huge crowd, a little self-consciously at first, and then more easily as they got into the good cheer and excitement of the moment. Someone set off fireworks, spattering rich reds and greens and yellows against the falling night. The Merry Mrs. Trusspot tooted her whistle again and again, and so the great voyage began.

Not long after, when they'd left the crowd behind and silence had returned to the evening, the humans remained by the guardrail, watching the dark River flow past. The land was already disappearing into the growing dark. Strings of bright paper lanterns illuminated the deck. Toby sighed loudly.

"Take a good look, people. After a while, this is going to seem exciting. I mean, the ship's very nice, and all that, but there's nothing to flaming do! Unless you want to play children's games. There's plenty of those. I can't believe people really paid through the nose for this. I'd be bored out of my mind inside twenty-four hours. I can only assume all the customers were heavily drugged on arrival, and kept that way till they left, and I wouldn't object to some now. God, I'm bored!"

"Make the most of it," said Giles. "You don't really think we're going to follow the River all the way to Harker unopposed, do you? There are any number of people, or toys, with a vested interest in seeing we don't get that far."

The humans looked casually about them. The toys were all in the main stateroom, chatting together, leaving the humans alone. The humans kept their voices down anyway. You never knew who might be listening.

"Of course there'll be opposition," said Julian. He looked pale, but back in control. "The bad toys are still out there, looking for humans to kill. But they'll have a job getting to us on here. And we've got guns. We should be able to hold them off easily enough."

"It's not that simple," said Giles. "Forget about good toys and bad toys. We can't trust anything we meet on this planet. They're a new form of intelligence, and we have no idea what kind of needs and motivations really drive them. They're not human, and though they ape human emotions and attitudes, there's no guarantee they actually feel any of them. We can't trust them an inch."

"They're trying to be human," said Evangeline. "We have to encourage that. We have a once-in-a-lifetime opportunity to shape the consciousness and soul of a new form of artificial intelligence. We can't turn our backs on them. We created them. They're our responsibility."

"Shub created them," said Toby. "Who knows what hidden commands could be lurking deep inside their new awareness?"

"They broke their Shub programming," said Flynn. "Or at least, the good toys did. Otherwise, we'd all be dead by now."

"All right," said Giles. "Let's talk about Harker. The bad toys want him dead because he's human. The good toys want him dead or removed, because they see him as a danger. And the toys he's gathered around him will presumably do anything they can to stop us taking him. But what does he want? Will he fight to stay, or fight to go? What's he really up to, hiding in the Forest at the end of the River?"

"He's supposed to be gathering good and bad toys," said Evangeline. "If that's true, it's the only place on this planet where good and bad toys are living together. Why don't the bad toys kill him? He's just a human, after all. I wonder what he says to the toys that binds them to him so strongly? And what is he doing with them? What does he want them for?"

"The good toys are trying to hide it, but they were scared shitless of him," said Toby. "Whoever they send into the Forest to find some answers, no matter how trusted or loyal, never comes back. They stay with Harker. I think in Toystown they're afraid of the control Harker seems to have over toys. Perhaps the same kind of control humans had over all toys, before they became aware."

"No wonder they're scared," said Julian. "But then, why weren't they scared of us? We're humans, just like Harker."

"Good question," said Finlay. "Perhaps they're just hiding it, because they need us to deal with Harker. They got us out of the town and on our way fast enough, didn't they?"

"Something else about Harker," said Giles. "Why hasn't he made any effort to get offplanet? He's supposed to have a head full of vital Empire secrets. But instead of putting all his efforts into getting in contact with the orbiting starcruiser, so someone could come down and pick him up, he's hidden himself away in the heart of the Forest, protected by an army of fanatical followers. What has he found there? What keeps him there? What does he hope to achieve with his army of toys?"

Toby snorted. "An army of toys won't do him much good when the Empress runs out of patience and sends down an army of shock troops to get him. They'll just walk in and take Harker, and he'll go home whether he wants to or not."

"Don't be so sure," said Julian. "Remember what happened to the last force she sent down. Their heads ended up on sticks, and their guts were sewn into murderous rag dolls."

Evangeline shuddered. "I still can't believe toys did that."

"Stop thinking of them as toys," said Giles. "They're more akin to Furies than anything else. That's what Shub intended them to be."

"The Bear thinks Harker has gone crazy," said Finlay. "Maybe he thinks Harker is driving toys crazy as well. That could make them and him really dangerous. Let's not forget, everyone else who went in search of him never came back, people or toys. Nothing was ever heard of them again."

"The Red Man," said Flynn. "They call him the Red Man now. Red for blood, perhaps?"

"Wouldn't surprise me," said Toby. "Everything's gone to hell here. This place is enough to drive anyone crazy."

"It's not all bad here," said Evangeline. "Look at Toystown, and Bruin Bear and the Sea Goat . . ."

"It's not them!" said Giles. "Just automatons that look and sound like them. Who better to gain our trust and then betray it?"

"Which brings us back to where we started," said Julian.

"Hush," said Flynn. "Someone's coming."

It was Halloweenie, the Li'l Skeleton Boy, carrying a tray of steaming hot drinks. He'd switched his eyepatch to the other empty eye socket, and now wore a proud three-cornered hat, pushed well back on his skull. "Thought you might like something warming," he said cheerfully. "Hot chocolate for everyone! Be sure and wrap up well once the sun goes down. The nights can be very cold here, if you're human."

"You don't feel the cold?" said Evangeline, taking a steaming mug from the tray.

"Oh no," said Halloweenie. He winked his eye socket at her, a disturbing effect. "I'm only bones, after all. Though I do rattle now and again, just for effect. Do stay and watch the sun go down. It's really very pretty."

He waited till everyone had a mug in his or her hand, and then he bustled off about his chores again, happily humming something nautical to himself. The humans sipped at their hot chocolate, found it good, and leaned over the railing to watch the sun sinking slowly below the horizon. The smiley face on the sun had mellowed and looked distinctly drowsy. A rich crimson glow was the only color left in the night, stretched in streaks across the night sky, and reflecting darkly on the River. Somewhere birds were singing, a vast chorus of voices, proclaiming peace and rest and the day's end.

"It's just a recording," said Bruin Bear. The humans looked round sharply. None of them had heard him approach. The Bear leaned on the railing beside them, looking out into the night. "At least, we've searched for the birds, but never found them. Perhaps it's just another of this world's mysteries. There's so much about this world you humans made that we don't understand yet."

He broke off as farther down the River, bright lights showed clearly against the night sky, followed by distant sounds of thunder.

"Fireworks!" said Evangeline.

"Not anymore," said Bruin Bear. He sounded suddenly tired, and the humans turned to look at him. He was staring out into the night, his eyes sad. "Once, it would have been fireworks. A celebration by toys, to mark the ending of the day. Now it's bombs. Explosions. Grenades. The war is still going on, down the River. Toy fighting toy, for no good reason, fighting a war that will never end until one side has completely wiped out the other. Or until the Red Man and his army emerge from the dark Forest to put an end to everything."

"You're afraid of him, aren't you?" said Toby.

"Of course," said the Bear. "He's an unknown factor. The war here may be terrible, but at least it's an evil we understand. Who knows what insane plans may be forming in the Red Man's human mind? We're still only toys, for all our new intelligence, and our minds are limited by our short lives and experiences. We've seen the awful things brought about by the madness of toys. Trying to imagine the darkness the Red Man's madness might plunge us into has unnerved us all."

"But he hasn't actually done anything yet, has he?" said Finlay.

"We don't know," said Bruin Bear. "No one knows what's happened to the hundreds of toys who disappeared into the dark heart of the great Forest. There are only rumors, whispers, floating back down the River, on the mouths of toys brought in shell-shocked and dying from the war. They say Harker found something, deep in the Forest, something that changed him into the Red Man. Something that will change the whole world beyond recognition. Wouldn't you be scared?"

"How long do these . . . displays go on?" asked Evangeline, tactfully changing the subject.

The Bear looked at the bright lights in the night sky. "They never stop. The war never stops. It's the Shub imperative, you see. The urge to fight is built into the very programming that gives us our intelligence. To destroy, to kill, to make war, to tear down Humanity in Shub's name. Those few of us in Toystown have overthrown that conditioning, but most could not, even those who think of themselves as good toys. The best they've been able to do is turn the urge to fight against the bad toys, to destroy them or at least prevent them leaving this world and carrying the war to Humanity. Don't underestimate the courage of their convictions; they're fighting and dying right now, to protect you and your kind. Sometimes I wonder if it's only the war that keeps us from Humanity's throat. Maybe we need to keep the war going, to keep Humanity safe. Which makes it even more vital that Harker and his mad plans be stopped, wouldn't you say?"

"I thought you said you were trapped on this planet?" Finlay said carefully.

"We were," said Bruin Bear. "But now we have the Empire's pinnace, buried but still largely intact, and we have your ship. And some of us are quite intelligent, for toys. We could learn to repair and pilot those ships. That's why we have to find and take care of Harker and his army before news of the ships gets out. Please understand; the toys of Toystown will destroy both the pinnace and your ship, if necessary, to prevent them falling into the wrong hands. To protect Humanity."

"You mean you'd strand us here?" said Giles.

"If necessary," said Bruin Bear. "But don't worry. We'll look after you for the rest of your lives."

The humans looked at each other. The thought of living out the rest of their lives in an enforced childhood was enough to give them all the shudders. They looked at Bruin Bear and saw him in a new light. In the tales of the Golden Lands, the Bear had always done what he saw as right, regardless of the cost.

"What if we tried to stop you destroying the ships?" said Giles, his hand very near his gun. "What if we refused to let you do it?"

The Bear looked at him sadly. "Then we'd kill you. We'd have no choice. We'd kill you all, to protect Humanity. We may only be toys, but we have learned the hard lessons of necessity. That is, after all, the first steps toward morality."

He turned abruptly, and padded away. The humans watched him go in silence, until he disappeared back into the main stateroom. The night seemed suddenly so much colder and darker than before.

"He's bluffing," said Julian. "He wouldn't really do that. He couldn't. He's Bruin Bear."

"No, he isn't," said Giles. "I think that's the closest we've come to seeing the real him. There's an intelligence pushing him beyond the limitations of his original persona, whether he wants to go or not."

"Hell's teeth," said Flynn. "What kind of a world is it, where you can't even trust Bruin Bear?"

"A world Shub made," said Giles. "And don't you forget it."

"I think we should all get some sleep," said Evangeline. "It's been a long day."

"Maybe you can sleep, surrounded by creatures who've just threatened to kill you," said Toby. "I've never felt so awake in my life."

"We'd better set a guard," said Giles. "We should be safe enough, as long as we're doing what the toys want, but I think we'll all sleep more soundly knowing there's someone on guard. Just in case. I'll take the first watch."

"I'll relieve you in three hours," said Finlay. "Then Toby. The night should be over by then."

"Damn it all," said Julian, suddenly so angry that he was almost reduced to tears. "Even our childhood's being taken away from us and spoiled. Is nothing sacred anymore?"

He glared around at the others, but they had nothing to say. In the end, Finlay and Evangeline took him by the arms and led him away to the cabins, to get what sleep they could. Toby and Flynn looked at each other, shrugged, and went after them. Giles found a wall to put his back against, from where he could see most of the deck and the entrances onto it, sat down, drew his gun and put it on the deck beside him, then drew his sword and laid it across his knees, ready for use. And so he sat, looking out into the night, watching the bright flares of explosions in the night and listening to their muted thunder, thinking his own thoughts. The toys kept to themselves in the main stateroom, doing whatever it was toys did in the night, and bothered no one. And the great paddle steamer sailed steadily on down the River, into the heart of the darkness.

Halloweenie came around in the morning, a few hours after the smiley sun had hauled itself back into the sky, knocking respectfully on cabin doors and telling everyone that breakfast was ready in the galley for those who wanted it. Everyone turned up, even Toby, who'd just finished his stint on guard, and was growling at everyone that he wasn't really a morning person. No one wanted to miss anything. They'd all showered and taken care of their ablutions. The modern bathrooms and toilets tucked away behind the cabins had come as a pleasant surprise. Apparently the world of childhood had had to make some concessions to its adult patrons. Breakfast turned out to be a cholesterol special of bacon, sausages, eggs, and other things that were bad for you, cooked by the Captain, who wore a frilly pinafore.

The good ship Merry Mrs. Trusspot was still chugging steadily down the dark soft-drink River, keeping a careful equal distance from both banks. They appeared to have made good progress during the night, and were now in unfamiliar territory. The constant rumble of fighting and explosions was still distant, but noticeably louder. The land on either side of the River was made up of huge game boards, wide as fields. They were battlefields now, the ground churned up by fighting, and disfigured with bomb craters. The bright colors of the boards had faded, and the markings were torn apart and meaningless. Dead playing pieces lay scattered everywhere. Broken chess pieces that had vaguely human shapes. Knights with shattered horseheads, bishops with cracked mitres, pawns with their electronic guts hanging out.

There was no sign of battle anywhere. The war had moved on. There was no way of telling who, if anyone, had won here.

After a while, the board games gave way to giant jigsaws, the pieces broken and scattered, sometimes rearranged for tactical reasons, so that the pictures made no sense anymore. Some pieces were just missing, removed for no apparent reason. There were more dead toys, left to lie where they had fallen because honor for the dead was a human thing. Toys just recycled what they could, and got on with their war. Sometimes the dead were presented in novel ways, for aesthetic or psychological reason, to throw horror and fear into the heart of the enemy.

A whole regiment of sailor dolls had been carefully crippled and disfigured and then crucified in long rows the length of a hillside. There were hundreds of the crosses, stretching up the hill to the very top, where one sailor doll, presumably the leader, had been crucified upside down, and then set on fire. Smoke was still rising from his charred and blackened costume. Evangeline wanted to stop the ship. She was sure a few of the dolls were still struggling feebly. The Captain refused. There was always the chance, he explained with what seemed genuine remorse, that this was the bait in a trap. It was the kind of thing the bad toys did. The humans looked, but couldn't see any sign of an enemy.

"They can be anywhere," said the Captain. The humans remembered the rag dolls under the railroad tracks and were silent.

Farther on, hundreds of toy dogs and cats lay still among the bomb craters, ripped and torn apart, their stuffing rising out of great rents in their bodies like fluffy white guts. Their animal faces seemed innocent and puzzled in death, as though wondering how and why they had come to their end in such a manner. Bruin Bear and the Sea Goat stood very close together as the ship moved slowly past the carnage, holding paws but refusing to let themselves look away. Poogie sat at their heels, sniffing quietly, tears brimming in his large sad eyes. The toy who'd named himself Anything stood a little apart and watched in silence as they passed a field containing dead adaptor toys like himself. The gleaming metal toys had mostly died in the midst of changes, caught in strange half shapes that were neither one thing nor another, as though death had come upon them while they were desperately trying to find some shape that didn't contain the wounds that were killing them.

Thankfully, after that trees and shrubbery began to appear along the banks, thickening into trailing woods that hid the killing fields from view. The trees were tall and broad, heavy with summer greenery, but no birds sang on the branches, and no animals moved in the lower vegetation. The woods had been built for show, made for climbing and hiding and other games, and there was nothing natural about them.

The day grew slowly warmer, hot enough to raise a sweat without actually being uncomfortable. The humans lay sprawled in deck chairs, watching the quiet scenery go by, waited on by Halloweenie, who couldn't do enough for them. When he wasn't getting them cold drinks or hot snacks, he sat at their feet and asked endless questions about what life was like on other worlds. He'd only ever known toys, human patients, and then the war. He couldn't understand half the answers he got, but he just laughed and shook his bony head, and asked more questions. The Li'l Skeleton Boy loved stories, and would listen happily to tales of bravery and derring-do from Giles and Finlay. He tried to listen to Toby, but most of the journalist's stories went right over his head. Poogie, the Bear, and the Goat played endless games of quoits on the deck, and argued constantly about the rules, especially when the Goat was losing. Anything kept mostly to himself, but would occasionally take time out from his brooding to change into different shapes for Halloweenie, who found it endlessly amusing, and would shriek and clap his bony hands at each new transformation. Anything rarely joined in conversation, but he would sometimes talk quietly with Halloweenie, always clamming up if anyone else came near. The Captain stayed on the bridge, guiding the paddle steamer down the exact center of the River, and studying both banks with scowling suspicion. The parrot never strayed from his shoulder, murmuring comforting obscenities to itself.

Small artificial animals lived in holes and burrows in the earth of the Riverbanks, and would sometimes wave and chirp cheerful greetings to the humans, from a cautious distance. Artificial dolphins, made in bright primary colors, came swimming up the River and swam alongside the ship for a while, occasionally raising their sleek heads out of the dark liquid to study the humans with bright, knowing eyes, neither hindering nor helping. The long day passed slowly, warm and pleasant and undemanding, just as it must have been in the early days of Shannon's dream. The sounds of the war were just a distant rumble, like far-off thunder threatening a storm to come, and some of the humans were actually dozing when the ship passed into disputed territory, and everything went to hell in a hurry.

The toys had crept through the trees, keeping to the shadows, silent and unobserved, and then slipped quietly into the dark waters of the River. They swam deep beneath the surface, not needing to breathe, and then climbed the sides of the ship, unseen by any. Until they came swarming over the guardrails, waving swords and axes and screaming curses against Humanity. They were colorful, jagged figures, boiling over the railings the whole length of the ship. They were human in shape and size, but composed of different-colored parts and compo-

nents. They had arms of different lengths, legs out of pro-
portion to their bodies, heads that turned through three
hundred and sixty degrees. Finlay recognized the toys
from his own childhood. They came as separate pieces—
bodies, limbs and heads of different colors and types, that
a child could fit together to make a whole. Or you could
swap the parts with other toys to make new figures.
Someone had brought the idea to Shannon's World, and
now the patchwork toys had come to take revenge for
years of being dismantled and rebuilt at a child's whim,
never having anything to call their own, not even their
own bodies.

The humans sprang to their feet, shock and alarm
driving out their drowsiness. They just had time to draw
their swords, and then the toys were upon them. Finlay
and Evangeline stood together, back-to-back, hacking at
the toys as they came within range. Giles was caught and
cornered in the bow, but stood his ground, his heavy
sword shearing through the patchwork bodies with ease.
He fought calmly and economically, conserving his
strength and refusing to be intimidated by the sheer numbers ranged against him. Toby and Flynn put a stateroom
wall at their backs and built a barricade of deck chairs
from behind which they could fire their disrupters, blowing great holes in the packed crowd of toys. Flynn's
camera hovered overhead, covering the action.

Julian tried to form his mind for a psiblast, but just the
effort was enough to cripple him with a blinding headache. He fell to his knees, blood spilling thickly from his
nose and mouth. Halloweenie grabbed him by an arm and
dragged him with desperate strength into the stateroom,
shutting the door and then pushing heavy furniture against
it. He hovered over Julian for a moment, distraught at the
sight of a human bleeding and in distress, and then he
grabbed an iron poker from beside the fireplace, and
stood before the barricaded door, determined that no one
would pass while he still had strength in his bony arms.

Bruin Bear and the Sea Goat were as much targets as
the humans, and fought side by side. The Goat had produced a large club from somewhere, and wielded it with
great authority and a certain amount of glee. The Bear's
claws had burst out of his paws again, and he tore through

the attacking toys with a cold, methodical fury. Poogie
had also sprouted terrifying teeth and claws, and was
tearing a vicious path through the packed crowd of toys
filling the deck. Up on the bridge, the Captain yelled
curses and defiance, and tried to increase the paddle
steamer's speed, to leave behind those toys still in the
water. As yet, none of the patchwork toys had reached the
bridge, but the Captain had a long cutlass ready for when
they did.

They covered the whole deck now, with still more
swarming over the sides. There were already hundreds of
the patchwork toys, and there seemed no end to them.
Swords cut through them easily enough, but where one
part was damaged, the toys just discarded it and kept
fighting. When they were damaged too badly to continue,
other toys would rip them apart to repair themselves.
Scattered body parts littered the deck, getting underfoot. Disembodied hands clutched at human ankles. The
humans fought on with increasing desperation as they
grew tired and their enemies did not.

Finlay was fighting at the peak of his powers, rested
and strong and deadly, and no one toy could stand against
him. But there were so many of them, and not even a man
who had been the undefeated Masked Gladiator of the
Golgotha Arenas could stand for long against an army.
Evangeline guarded his back with savage determination,
doing her best to wield a sword as he had taught her, and
tried to keep her rising horror to herself, so as not to upset
Finlay.

The barricade around Toby and Flynn was slowly but
steadily being dismantled, despite all their efforts. It was
becoming clear to the two newsmen that they had allowed
themselves to be trapped in a corner from which there was
no escape. They struck out with their swords, reluctantly
becoming part of the story they were covering. Toby
yelled for Flynn to be sure and get his good side. Flynn
said he didn't have one. Toby laughed harshly, and swung
his sword with both hands.

Giles Deathstalker stood alone at the bow, surrounded
by furious, howling toys, with no way out. He fought hard
and well, slowly tiring, but still strong. The boost thundered in his arms. The odds were bad, but he'd faced

worse. Or at least, he thought he had. And then, for the first time, he looked out at the hundreds of toys filling the deck and his confidence wavered. There were some odds that no man could beat. Not even the legendary Giles Deathstalker. He fought on anyway, because there was nothing else to do, but desperation, and the beginnings of something that might have been fear, began to gnaw at him. He'd faced death before and never been afraid to look it straight in the eye, but he'd never thought he'd die like this. To die so ignominiously, brought down by sheer force of numbers. Hacked apart by toys on a stupid pleasure planet.

The toys surged forward, screaming horribly, their artificial voices full of rage and anticipation, swords and axes raised to hack him into pieces that would never re-form. And rage and desperation flooded through Giles, igniting the Maze-given forces within him. Power blazed up in the back brain, the undermind, shining so very brightly through parts of his mind he'd never used before, and suddenly Giles was somewhere else. He stood on the bridge, next to the startled Captain, while down below the toys overran the bow where he'd been and stared stupidly about them, wondering where their trapped prey had gone. Giles laughed suddenly. He'd teleported. He could feel the new ability settling into place within him, as easy and natural now to him as breathing, and couldn't help wondering what other abilities he might manifest in times of need. He looked down at the swarming toys and smiled unpleasantly as he began to plan what to do next with his new power.

On the bridge, the Captain staggered back and forth on his peg legs, swinging his cutlass with more strength than skill. Only a few toys had reached him so far, but he could hear more on their way. The parrot fluttered in their faces, screaming abuse, distracting them. With no one's hands on the wheel, the ship drifted aimlessly, heading for the bank.

Down below, Anything had turned into his most martial shape, and was cutting through the massed toys with razor-sharp hands. Their weapons rebounded harmlessly from his metal body, so they clung to his arms and legs, trying to drag him down by sheer weight of numbers. But the toy who wished he was a Fury stood firm and would not fall.

Poogie had become a snarling fury of hate and destruction, no longer cartoonlike at all. Enraged at the toys who would keep him from his atonement, and would dare attack humans under his protection, he fought tirelessly in the center of the deck and defied one and all to bring him down.

But there were so many patchwork toys. So very many.

In the stateroom, Halloweenie hovered helplessly over Julian, and wondered desperately what to do for the best. Toys were hammering on the barricaded door and smashing the windows. The young esper was still bleeding heavily from the mouth and nose, despite everything the Li'l Skeleton Boy could do to stop it. The ship did have a med bay, but Halloweenie knew he wasn't strong enough to drag the esper such a long way, even if they could avoid being noticed by the patchwork toys. Halloweenie might have escaped on his own, but he didn't want to leave the injured human unprotected. The toys hammering against the door were slowly forcing it open, and pushing the piled-up furniture back inch by inch. Toys were trying to get through the windows. Halloweenie ran back and forth, pushing them back out.

And then the barricade of furniture suddenly collapsed and fell backwards, and the door swung open, and the toys came howling in. Halloweenie ran forward to stand between them and the human, but they were so many, and he was just a little skeleton boy. He went down under their stamping feet, his bones cracking and breaking, crying out for Julian to run. The young esper tried to get his feet under him and lurched forward to help his small defender. Swords and axes rose above him.

There was a clap like thunder and a rush of displaced air, and Giles Deathstalker appeared out of nowhere in the middle of the stateroom. The patchwork toys fell back, unnerved by the sudden appearance, and Giles moved forward and hauled Julian to his feet. And in that moment, while the toys hesitated, Giles reached out with his Maze-altered mind and slammed into Julian's. There was a moment of opposition, as the young esper realized what the Deathstalker meant to do, and then Giles swept it aside, seized control of Julian's esp, and summoned up a psistorm.

Julian screamed horribly, the sound rising above the roar of battle, and everyone hesitated a moment. And then it was as though a great wind swept the length of the boat, picking up the patchwork toys and pitching them overboard. Others were torn apart, reduced to their component parts, and scattered by the wind. Some simply exploded, touched by the stormfire crackling across the deck, spitting and seething. The humans stood and watched in awe, untouched by the power of the storm.

Bruin Bear was lifted off his feet by the strength of the wind, but the Sea Goat grabbed him with one hand and clung grimly to the guardrail with the other. The strain almost pulled him in two, but he wouldn't let go. He was the Sea Goat, and he didn't let his friends down. Poogie and Anything clung together in terror, wedged under a pile of deck chairs. In the stateroom, at the heart of the storm, toys fell dead at its touch. The wind howled like a human voice, in agony and exultation, and swept the deck clean of patchwork toys.

The storm shut off as suddenly as it began, and all was still on the ship again. Apart from the agonized screaming from the stateroom, and Halloweenie calling desperately for help. The humans and the toys forgot about their sudden victory and their various wounds and ran to the stateroom, pushing their way in past the half-open door and the scattered furniture. And there they found Halloweenie dragging his broken body painfully across the floor, trying to reach Julian Skye, convulsing in Giles Deathstalker's arms. The esper's screams were growing hoarser, as though the horrid sounds were damaging his throat. Giles dropped Julian and backed away, his eyes cold and watchful.

"Don't let him get away!" said Halloweenie. "He did it! He hurt Julian! He did something to him, and he started screaming and couldn't stop!"

Finlay and Evangeline moved quickly forward to kneel beside the young esper. His whole body was convulsing now, his heels drumming on the floor. His head whipped from side to side, blood spraying from his mouth as he screamed. Evangeline sat him up and cradled him in her arms, trying to contain his helpless movements. Finlay tried to check Julian for wounds, but it was clear to his Arena-trained eyes that the damage had to be internal. The esper's struggles grew weaker as the strength went out of him, and his screams died away to groans. There was blood leaking from his ears, and dribbling down his cheeks from his eyes, like dark crimson tears. His skin was deathly pale and icy to the touch. Finlay glared at Giles.

"What the hell did you do to him?"

"What was necessary," said Giles. His voice was calm but wary. "We needed a psistorm. It was our only chance for survival. So I helped the esper produce one."

"You knew it might kill him!" said Evangeline.

"Yes," said Giles. "I knew. But it was necessary."

"Then if he dies, you're a murderer," said Evangeline.

"He wouldn't be my first victim," said Giles. "Grow up, woman. We're in a war here. The survival of the group has to come first. Our mission is more important than any one of us. And yes, that includes me."

Toby hurried in, carrying a small autodoc disc from the ship's med bay. He handed it over to Finlay, who pulled the esper's collar back and slapped the flat disc against the side of his neck. Toby moved back, to get out of the way of Flynn's hovering camera.

"It's a pretty basic doc," Toby said hesitantly. "I mean, it's good for tranquilizers, stabilizers, things like that, but don't ask me what it can do for cerebral hemhorrhages and total body shock."

Julian's struggles slowly ceased as the drugs the doc was pumping into him finally took effect, and his groans died away to whispers. Evangeline rocked him gently, stroking his forehead and murmuring soothingly to him, like a mother with a sick child. He didn't look like he could hear her. Finlay got to his feet and looked back at Halloweenie. Bruin Bear and the Sea Goat were trying to comfort the Li'l Skeleton Boy. Both of his legs and most of his ribs had been smashed, the breaks showing clearly on his bare bones. There was a great crack in his skull, through which the glowing metals of his artificial mind could be seen. He was crying, without tears. Poogie and Anything looked on helplessly from the doorway.

"How is he?" said Finlay.

"What do you care?" said Anything. "He's just a toy."

"He's one of us," said Finlay. He looked at the Bear and the Goat. "Can the damage be repaired?"

"Hopefully," said Bruin Bear. "He's an automaton, after all. We don't have any spare parts on board, but there should be enough splints and staples to hold him together till we get back to Toystown."

"If we get back to Toystown," said the Sea Goat.

"Shut up, Goat," said the Bear. "This isn't the time." He looked at Finlay with his large knowing eyes. "Your friend is dying, isn't he?"

"Yes," said Finlay. "I think he probably is. He saved us all, but there's nothing we can do for him here."

"The Deathstalker did this to him," said the Bear. "He has unusual mental abilities. I saw him teleport. Perhaps he could use those abilities to undo what he did to the esper."

Finlay turned to look at Giles, who looked steadily back at him. "Well?" said Finlay. "You're supposed to have been through the marvelous Maze on Haden. Show us what you can do. That is why you're here, after all. To use your special powers. Heal him."

"I don't know if I can," said Giles. "I've never done anything like that before."

"Try," said Finlay, pointing his disrupter at Giles's chest. "Or I swear I'll kill you, right here and now."

"No, you won't," said the Deathstalker. "You need me. Without me, you'll never reach Harker, never complete our mission."

"Stuff the mission," said Finlay. "Do it, or you're a dead man."

"I won't forget this," said the Deathstalker, and his voice was calm and cold and very deadly.

"Like I give a shit," said Finlay.

Giles nodded, and knelt down beside Evangeline. She glared at him, but let him take Julian from her arms. The Deathstalker held him with surprising gentleness, the esper's head lolling back against Giles's chest. Blood dripped from the esper's chin.

His breathing was very faint. Giles closed his eyes, concentrating in a way that was still new to him, reaching

out in a direction he couldn't name but somehow knew
was there. He could see Julian now as a dim light in
the darkness, a guttering candle whose flame was slowly
going out. Giles looked at himself, and saw a light so
blinding he could barely face it. And it was the easiest
thing in the world for him to take some of that light and
give it to Julian.

The esper sat up suddenly in the Deathstalker's arms,
his eyes snapping open, sucking in a deep breath like a
swimmer surfacing from a long dive. The bleeding had
stopped, and his coloring had returned to normal. He
looked around him, startled.

"What the hell was that?" he said. "It was like God
called my name."

"Trust me," said Finlay. "God had nothing to do with it."

"What do you remember?" Evangeline asked, as she
helped him get to his feet again.

"I'm . . . not sure. We were under siege. I was trying to
focus my esp, but . . . and then Giles was here with me.
It's blank after that."

"Probably just as well," said Finlay. He looked at Giles,
also back on his feet. "How good a job did you do, Deathstalker? Is he healed? Properly healed?"

"I doubt it," said Giles. "I know only basic medicine.
Whatever was wrong with him before is probably still
wrong with him. I just . . . jump-started him again. Gave
his batteries a boost. No, he's probably just back to how
he was before I . . . interfered."

"Don't ever do that again," said Finlay. "You're the
one with the amazing powers. You can defend us in the
future."

"You can defend yourself," said Giles. "I never forget a
threat."

"I think it would be a good idea if we were all to calm
down a little," said Toby nervously. "After all, we're all
on the same side, aren't we? And the esper's back to
normal again."

"I think I'll take a walk around the deck," said Giles,
not looking away from Finlay's gaze. "Make sure there
are no toy parts left on board. Get myself a little fresh air
as well. It's getting a bit thick in here."

He headed for the stateroom door, and everyone stepped

back to give him plenty of room. The Bear looked at him thoughtfully.

"You're not human anymore," he said. "I can tell. What are you, Giles Deathstalker?"

"Damned if I know," said Giles, and he left.

"How do you feel, Julian?" said Finlay.

The esper shrugged uncomfortably. "Tired. Drained. And my throat's sore as hell. Is the emergency over? Are the toys gone?"

"It's over," said Evangeline. "Why don't you go lie down for a while? We'll take care of the cleaning up."

"Yeah," said Julian. "Rest. Good idea." He left the stateroom on slightly unsteady feet.

"Typical," said Anything. "Halloweenie almost got killed protecting him, and he didn't even say thank you."

"Shut up," said Halloweenie. "He doesn't even remember. You want to be useful, get me out of here and over to the repair shop. I need a ten-thousand-mile service. At least."

Anything nodded, picked up the broken little skeleton boy, and carried him out of the stateroom. Poogie, the Bear, and the Goat went with them, leaving the humans alone. Toby nodded to Flynn, and the camera floated down onto Flynn's shoulder and shut itself off.

"You've got guts, Campbell," said Toby. "Threatening a Deathstalker. Hell, *the* Deathstalker. That was the man who activated the Darkvoid Device, remember? Killed very living thing on a thousand suns' planets, and never once said sorry. Personally, I'd rather tongue-kiss a Grendel."

"He would have let Julian die," said Finlay. "I couldn't allow that. I didn't rescue him from the interrogation cells under Golgotha just to have him die because the Deathstalker had a use for him. Still, I was hoping the ancient bastard could cure Julian; fix all the things that were wrong with him. Either he couldn't do it, or he wouldn't, which means the poor kid is still dying by inches. The odds are he's going to die here anyway, far from home, and there's not a damn thing I can do to save him, this time."

"You can't do everything," said Evangeline.

"I couldn't comfort him," said Finlay. "Not like you did. I don't know how to do things like that."

"You made Giles save him," said Evangeline. "I don't know how to do things like that. We make a good team, all things considered."

They smiled at each other, staring deep into each other's eyes, and the stateroom was suddenly full of their love. It occurred to Toby that he might just get the answers to a few pertinent questions out of them, while they were in such a good mood. He gestured surreptitiously for Flynn to turn his camera back on. Flynn nodded slightly, and though the camera on his shoulder didn't move, its single red eye silently glowed into life again.

"So," said Toby casually, "what is the deal with the Deathstalker? There's nothing in his history or his legend about his having esper abilities. Certainly no one else in his line has ever shown any trace of them. Until Owen. I saw him do some pretty amazing things on Mistworld."

"It's the Maze," said Finlay. "The Madness Maze. Something Giles and Owen and a few others encountered on the world that used to be Haden."

"You mean they were changed by a Hadenmen device?"

"No. Something much older. It changed the people who went through it. Made them more than they used to be. Don't ask for details, because I don't have any. The underground has, but it's all strictly need to know. And the likes of you and I don't need to know. Now turn off that camera and get the hell out of here, before I decide which of your bodily orifices to cram it into. Sideways."

"Fair enough," said Toby. "Let's go, Flynn."

"After me," said the cameraman, and they left the stateroom in something that wasn't actually a hurry, but close enough. With the door shut firmly behind them, they both stopped for a couple of really deep breaths.

"I don't think he was joking about the camera," said Flynn. "Did you think he was joking about the camera?"

"Probably not," said Toby. "Finlay Campbell's come a long way from the biggest clotheshorse in the Court. Still, in retrospect, it probably wasn't the best of times to ask probing questions."

"Never stopped you before," said Flynn.

"True," said Toby. "Let's go see what the toys are up to."

Not that far away, Giles Deathstalker was leaning on the starboard guardrail, staring into the dark waters of the River as they flowed past. The Captain had the ship back under control again, and they were picking up speed, back on course. Giles tried to recapture the feeling of how it felt to teleport, but it eluded him. As though it was too powerful an experience for him to deal with, except in necessity. Too much for a human mind. Except he wasn't just a human anymore, and hadn't been ever since he and the others passed through the Madness Maze. He'd become something . . . different than human, and his new ability to teleport was just the beginning. He knew that, beyond any shadow of a doubt. Though he was far away from the others, he was still linked to them through the undermind, the oversoul, and he knew that they were changing, too, in different, frightening ways. He wondered what he was becoming, what they were all becoming, and whether the end result would be in any way human. He also wondered why the thought didn't scare him as much as it should have.

Raised angry voices caught his attention, and he went to see what was happening, more to keep his thoughts occupied than because he really cared. Down by the stern, Bruin Bear and the Sea Goat had found a disembodied head from a patchwork toy, wedged in a corner where the psistorm couldn't get at it, and they were busy interrogating it by kicking it around like a football and shouting questions at it. Toby calmed them down, set the head against the stateroom wall, and asked it questions while Flynn filmed. All he got for his trouble were a series of not very inventive curses, so Giles moved in and took over. No one objected. He didn't think they would.

"Why did you attack us?" he asked the head.

The head was bright blue, with pointed ears and over-size eyes. It had probably been intended to look cute and elfish in the beginning, but now it looked more like a demon. It laughed at his question, showing jagged pointy teeth. The sound was harsh, artificial, and had nothing of human emotion in it. The toy's eyes, all dark pupils, fixed on the Deathstalker.

"You're the enemy. The eternal enemy. Human and human-lovers. Don't think you've won anything here. You can't get away. We'll find you and kill you all. Or the others will."

"Others?" said Giles, calmly meeting the dark inhuman eyes.

"Oh, we have many friends, waiting along the way for you. We know where you're from, where you're going. We have ears and eyes everywhere. You'll never reach the Red Man. We won't allow it."

"What's your name?" said Toby.

The head laughed at him. "Names? That's a human thing. Our identities interchange as our bodies do. We are lost to who we were, and we like it that way."

"Tell me what you know about Harker," Giles said patiently. "Tell me what you know about the Red Man, and his plans. And why you're so determined to stop us getting to him."

"I don't have to answer your questions. Human." The head spit at Giles. He didn't flinch.

"I could make you talk," said Giles. "Look at me, toy."

He leaned forward slightly, staring into the head's dark eyes. His presence was suddenly overpowering, frightening, awful. As though something unexpected and horribly powerful had emerged from behind the mask of Giles's face. The Bear and the Goat shrank back, and Toby had to fight down the urge to do the same. Flynn's control over his camera wavered for a moment, but he kept filming. The head made a high, whining noise, a terrified, pitiful sound, like a child being tortured. Giles relaxed suddenly, and the overwhelming presence was gone, as suddenly as it had come. The head had its eyes squeezed shut.

"All right," it said quietly. "We're scared of the Red Man. No one who goes to him comes back. Ever. Even those most fanatical to our cause. From what we hear, he's building a private army of his own, deep in the Forest. It's said he's going to end the war. Or end the world. They say he's crazy, crazy as only a human can be, and he's infecting toys with that madness. I know you humans. You'd try and reason with him, and you'd end up mad as he is. Mad as the Red Man. And who knows how powerful he'd become with more humans to help him, humans as crazy as he is. So, we're lying in wait, all along the River. You'll never live to reach the Forest."

"We want to take him away," said Giles. "Take him offworld with us. Isn't that what you want?"

The head just laughed. "You're lying. Humans always lie. We know that. They said they loved us, when they came here to play with us, but in the end they always went away and left us behind. We were just toys, to be used and discarded on a whim. They never loved us. You'll all pay for that."

"I think we've heard enough," said Giles. "This is for Julian."

He picked up the head, and pressed his thumbs firmly into its eyes. The huge eyeballs crunched inward, destroying the fragile instruments within. The head howled piteously. Giles pulled his thumbs out, and tossed the screaming head over the rail and into the River, to be found and recovered by its fellows, or not. Giles looked at the others, but neither the humans nor the toys had anything to say. Giles put his back against the guardrail.

"Not as helpful as I'd hoped," he said calmly. "Did I miss anything pertinent?"

"Just the one, maybe," said Toby. "Why do you suppose they keep referring to Harker as the Red Man?"

"They say he's crazy," said Giles. "Dangerously crazy. Maybe the red is a reference to blood."

"And we're going to meet him," said the Sea Goat. "Lucky old us."

"Shut up, Goat," said the Bear, not unkindly.

They continued on down the River, passing abandoned battlefields and dead toys. The war had been here, and passed on. The constant rumble of explosions in the distance grew gradually louder, nearer. They passed playhouses; forts and castles, log cabins and rose-covered cottages. Burnt-out, torn apart, utterly destroyed. A farm, complete with barns and outbuildings for artificial animals. The animals were long gone, but the buildings had been torched, and only the blackened bones of humans remained, from where they'd been tied to spits in the blazing farmyard. Signs of the war were everywhere now, as the paddle steamer drew nearer to the Forest, and everywhere lay the broken bodies of dead toys, lying looking up at the sky with empty eyes; no way now to know whether they'd been good or bad toys, or if they'd even given a damn. The ship sailed on as the day faded into the evening and then into night.

They found an open field, apparently untouched by the war, and pulled in beside the Riverbank. The humans felt a need for fresh air and the chance to stretch their legs. The toys didn't really understand, but went along with it. Though they hadn't said anything, it was clear their growing nearness to the Forest was worrying them, and they were as glad of a pause in the journey as the humans were. The night was dark and the air was cold, so they built a fire from the surrounding shrubbery and sat around it. It was almost peaceful, apart from the constant distant rumble of the war, like a roll of thunder that had no end. The sleepy moon was out again, and the five-pointed stars.

They'd had to carry Julian off the ship. The boost Giles had given him had worn off, and his injuries hurt him more as the warmth went out of the day. But he seemed cheerful enough now, sitting as close to the fire as he could, toasting marshmallows on a stick. The Bear and the Goat sat on either side of him, trying to give support through their company. The Goat kept burning his marshmallows because he was always too busy talking to pay them the proper attention. The Bear ate them anyway, to keep the peace. Finlay sat opposite them, with Evangeline at his side, as always. Toby and Flynn had three sticks each, and were stuffing their faces with marshmallows as fast as they could toast them. Toby kept Halloweenie busy running back and forth fetching them more. He was a little slower than he had been, with his new metal splints and staples holding his bones together, but he was happy as always to be of use. Giles sat a little apart from everyone, smoking an evil-smelling cigar and saying nothing. He showed no interest in the marshmallows. Poogie the Friendly Critter also sat by himself, as though unsure he was really welcome. The Captain and Anything

stayed on board the Merry Mrs. Trusspot, to keep an eye
on things, they said. And so everyone sat around the fire,
and ate marshmallows, and sang songs and talked on into
the night. And finally, they got around to the subject of
childhood.

Bruin Bear started it off. Finlay had been talking about
some of the stranger worlds he'd seen in his travels, and
the Bear asked what he made of Shannon's World, the
planet intended for adult children. Finlay frowned.

"It's hard to tell what this place was really like before
the war, but I think I can see the attraction. A place free of
adult cares and worries, a chance to be a child again. To
get childhood right, the way it should have been. Few
childhoods are really happy, except for those with
extremely selective memories. I was no good at being a
child. I had no gift for it. I just wanted it to be over, so I
could enter the much more interesting world that adults
moved in.

"In Clan Campbell, like all Clans, children are trained
to be useful members of the Family from a very early age.
And a fighter, too, because my Family had many enemies,
and just by being born I had become part of feuds and
vendettas going back centuries. I took to that early, too
much so for my conservative parents, who feared a
scandal if their designated son and heir killed anyone
important in an unsanctioned duel.

"I never saw much of my parents. Dad was always off
somewhere else, running the Clan, taking care of Family
business. And Mother Dear preferred the Social whirl to
raising children. Typical Clan parents. I had an endless
series of nannies and tutors, determined to teach me the
proper way of things, and try and keep me out of trouble.
I didn't have many friends. Real friends. Companions
outside the Family were discouraged, and inside the Clan
we were all too busy jockeying for position and influence.
But I had toys. All the toys I could handle.

"I remember the stories of Bruin Bear and the Sea Goat,
and their adventures in the Golden Lands. I used to dream
of traveling with them, into the lands beyond the sunset.
And now here I am, traveling with them for real. Eerie."
He smiled across the fire at the toys. "You're just like I
remember you. It's like meeting old friends I haven't seen

in years. Maybe the only real friends I had, as a child. No wonder so many people came here. To enjoy the childhood they wish they'd had. Or only had in dreams."

"I envy you those dreams," said Evangeline. "I never had a childhood. As a clone, I came into this world fully grown. Born from cell scrapings from the original Evangeline. Daddy needed me, to replace the daughter he'd murdered. So I was raised in secret, told about a childhood I never had, and then sent out into the world to be an adult, even though I was only six months old. Most of what I see here is . . . strange to me. I never had toys. Or pets. Daddy didn't want me to have anything in my life but him. I've never played. Never been free of secrets and responsibilities. I see the toys here, and I don't know what to do with them, how to talk to them. But something in me wants to hold them, or be held by them, or just to run and chase and laugh in the sunlight, as though it's something I've always wanted, and never knew it." She stopped abruptly, unshed tears thickening her voice. Finlay put his arm round her.

"We're here for you," said Bruin Bear. "We'll always be here for you."

"Hell," said Toby. "Didn't anyone here have a normal childhood? Surely we didn't all come from a disfunctional Family?"

"I had a great childhood," said Julian unexpectedly. He stopped and looked suspiciously at Flynn. "That camera is off, isn't it?"

"Trust me," said Flynn. "I, of all people, understand the need for privacy on occasion. Speak freely."

Julian sniffed, only half-convinced, but carried on, glancing occasionally at the camera to make sure its crimson eye wasn't glowing. His voice became clearer and warmer as he walked in memories of happier times.

"My elder brother Auric and I were always very close, which is unusual in most Families. Normally brothers only see each other as competitors for the inheritance and control of the Clan. There can only be one inheritor. Everyone else gets the shitty end of the stick. But Auric and I hit it off, right from the beginning. He raised me, much more than any nanny or tutor. In fact, most of the time it was us against them. We had a great childhood.

Did everything together. Shared our toys. Don't think we ever had a quarrel that lasted more than a few minutes.

"As we grew older, became teenagers, our parents tried to separate us. Auric was groomed to take over the Family on our father's death. I was supposed to go into the military, to be discarded and forgotten, unless the unthinkable happened, and Auric died, and I had to be recalled to take his place. But we refused to be separated. We were still each other's best friend, chosen companion, brothers by choice as well as blood. Even when I discovered I was an esper.

"Which came as something of a shock. Families guard their genetic histories very carefully, but somewhere along the line, someone slept with someone they shouldn't have, and the esper inheritance went skinny-dipping in our gene pool. And emerged in me. I knew I couldn't tell my parents. They'd have had me killed in a carefully arranged accident, rather than suffer the disgrace of an esper child. Espers are subhuman. Property. Always. But I knew I could tell Auric. He covered up for me, kept me alive when my shame made me feel like killing myself, and never once saw me as anything less than the brother I'd always been. When it became clear I needed training in how to use and hide my esp, he even tracked down the contacts that led me into the clone and esper underground.

"The only time we ever argued for real was when he fell in love with BB Chojiro. I knew there was something wrong with her even then, but I couldn't put it into words. I thought I was just jealous of her closeness to Auric, so I put it aside and tried to be happy that she made him so happy. But in the end, we were only a small and minor House, and she was Clan Chojiro. To impress her Family, and prove his love for her, Auric went into the Arena to face the Masked Gladiator, and that bloody bastard killed him. He didn't have to. He could have just given Auric an honorable wound, and let him walk away. But instead, he stuck his sword through Auric's eye, just to show off his skill. And that was the end of my childhood."

Evangeline squeezed Finlay's hand. Julian didn't know, must never know, that his friend and hero Finlay Campbell had been that Masked Gladiator.

"How do you feel about the toys here?" said Evangeline, just to be saying something.

"I can see the attractions of a place like this," said Julian. "But it's not for me. I put childhood things behind me after Auric died. I turned my back on my Family, and made the rebellion my life. I didn't have time for distractions anymore. I made a good rebel. No mission was too dangerous, too impossible for me. And then I fell in love with BB Chojiro, and my life came to an end for a second time.

"I was so happy as a child. As though deep within me I knew it was the only happiness I would ever have."

"That's sad," said Giles, unexpectedly. "And unnecessary. Nothing is ever really lost. The memories of good friends and good times are always there, never more than a thought away. In a sense, they never really stopped happening. Every moment you ever treasured, every friend you ever valued is still there, separated from us only by time; the past is still happening and always will be. It's only we who have moved on. I won't tell you about my childhood. It wouldn't mean much to you. Things were very different nine hundred years ago. But I had two wonderful dogs, when I was a boy. Hound dogs. Marvelous trackers. I was never happier than when I was chasing through the woods with them, on the trail of a scent.

"They both died when I was ten years old. They developed growths. Nothing we could do. So I put them to sleep, rather than let them suffer. I still miss them. But I only have to close my eyes to be with them again, and I know that back in the past, a boy and his dogs are still scrambling through the woods in hot pursuit, happy as the day is long. I have no need for a place like this, steeped in false nostalgia and a need to hide from reality. This was a place for weak people.

"And now it's a battleground for Shub's creations. These aren't toys, or treasured childhood playmates; they're Furies in training. This whole world should be scorched and forgotten, a sick experiment that went horribly wrong."

There was a long pause. "Well, thank you for sharing that with us, Deathstalker," said Toby. "I just know we'll all find that a great comfort in the days to come. I guess it's my turn now. Personally, I think you're all a bunch of softies. There isn't a damn thing in my childhood that I miss."

"All right," said Evangeline. "Tell us about your no doubt appalling childhood. What terrible and twisted events turned you into the revolting person you are today?"

"Oh, I was born a brat," Toby said cheerfully. "I just perfected it as I grew older. My dad died when I was very young. Mum ran away, rather than bow down to Uncle Gregor. He was a control freak, even then. I made life miserable for a long series of nannies, tutors, and armed guards, and ran riot at every school they sent me to. Never had any friends. Didn't miss them. Didn't care for Bruin Bear and his adventures either—soppy things. I was much more interested in the real world, and how to mess with its collective head to my own advantage.

"This led, naturally, to an interest in politics. I'd always had a special affinity for dirty tricks and double-dealing. All of which came in very handy during my career as a PR flack, and now a journalist. I get to be obnoxious, intrude into people's private lives, and mess with billions of people's heads every time I put out a broadcast. Life is good. Or at least it was, until I ended up being shifted from one war zone to another. When I said I wanted to cover exciting events, I didn't mean I wanted to be part of them."

"Don't you ever miss your real parents?" said Evangeline. "The ones you never knew?"

"No," said Toby flatly. "I didn't need them. I made my own life. I've never needed anyone. Except Flynn, of course. Someone's got to point the camera in the right direction. Tell us about your childhood, Flynn. Now that should be a story worth hearing."

"Sorry to disappoint you," said Flynn. "But I had a perfectly happy, perfectly normal childhood. No great traumas, no great losses. I love what they tried to do here. A place where everyone could be happy. It must have been a wonderful world. Before Shub came."

"What do you toys make of all this?" said Finlay. "I don't suppose you ever had a childhood. Unless it was your lives before Shub came. Do you remember anything of that time?"

The toys looked at each other, and in the end it was Halloweenie who spoke. He was sitting at Julian's feet, curled up into a bony ball, staring at the flames in the fire. "We all remember something of our lives as just toys. We were programmed to forget nothing, so the memories are still there. But our memories only have meaning from the point Shub came and woke us from our sleep with a poisoned kiss. The Furies gave us intelligence, wrapped in Shub programming. They gave us free will and then tried to tell us what to do with it.

"None of us had a childhood. We were born fully formed into consciousness. I'm a Boy, but I don't really know what that means. We understand so little about what it means to be alive. All we have to base our lives on is the characters we were created to be. So we never know if we're the kind of person we are because we chose to be, or if we're just following our old programming. Life is still very much a mystery to us. It's all so new, so frightening. Having to decide everything for ourselves. And emotions are so hard ... Take love, for instance. We think we know what it means, but we have so little to compare it against. Hatred is easier to understand. And fear. Maybe that's why so many toys are bad, rather than good. Bad's easier."

"But some of us didn't like what it did to us," said Poogie. "Before Shub came, we were not aware, and knew nothing of sin. Shub took advantage of our innocence. We were born into blood and suffering and murder, and some of us never got over it. Revenge filled us to overflowing, and humans were such easy prey. We were born damned. But some of us have learned to reach for redemption."

The Sea Goat belched, and picked bits of marshmallow from his large, blocky teeth. "And some of us have learned to be insufferably pretentious. We are what we always were, only more so. I like being the Sea Goat. If I didn't exist, it would be necessary to invent me, so you could disapprove of me. I annoy, therefore I am. And if anyone doesn't like it, tough. Right, Bear?"

"Can't take you anywhere, can I?" said Bruin Bear.

"You'll have to excuse my friend. He and I were stars when we were toys, loved by all, and I don't think he ever got over it. I find humans fascinating. You have so much potential. And we have so much to live up to. You are our creators, not Shub. If we could only make all toys see that, the war would end tomorrow. It would be a terrible thing if all our gift of life taught us was how to kill and destroy. Now, may I suggest we get what rest we can. Soon enough we'll have to go back on board ship and sleep. Assuming nothing goes wrong, we should reach the Forest tomorrow evening. Then we'll find Vincent Harker, the Red Man. And who knows what will happen then."

They all sat silently around the fire, human and toy, thinking their own thoughts. It was a night for confessions, but not everyone had said all they could have. They all had secrets, some big and some small, that could not be revealed yet. If only because the truth would cause so much suffering.

Evangeline leaned against Finlay and fought down the urge to tell him the real reason she was here with him. It wasn't that long ago she'd gone to the leaders of the underground and asked to be made ambassador to the new rebels, even though it meant leaving Finlay. She'd felt an overpowering need to get away, to be her own woman, free from the pressures of all those who expected things from her. Even Finlay. But like so many things in her short life, it had all gone wrong. Penny DeCarlo had been her first friend. Hired by Gregor Shreck to prepare his new Evangeline for public appearances, Penny had taught her she was still a human being, even if she was a clone. Taught her pride and self-respect. And even introduced her to the clone and esper underground. Penny DeCarlo, a secret rogue esper, caught and imprisoned in Silo Nine. Wormboy Hell.

Evangeline had tried to rescue her when the underground stormed Silo Nine, but in the chaos and confusion of Dram's treachery, she never found Penny, and had to leave without her. But Gregor Shreck found her. He had money and influence, and a desperate need to bring his clone daughter back under his control. So he had Penny released into his custody, and waited for the chance to let

Evangeline know. His terms were simple—return to him or Penny would suffer and die. Evangeline came close to despair. She couldn't go back to her father's perverted idea of love. She would rather die. But she couldn't abandon the woman who taught her what it was to be human.

She couldn't tell the underground's ruling Council. She would be seen as compromised, a possible security risk. And she couldn't tell Finlay. He must never know that the Shreck had made a habit of bedding his daughter. Finlay would go insane with rage, and throw away everything to launch a solo attack on the Shreck and his forces. A fight even the Masked Gladiator couldn't hope to win.

So Evangeline told no one, and for a while went quietly crazy trying to figure out what to do for the best. In the end, all she could decide was not to decide. She ran away from her responsibilities and joined the mission to Shannon's World. That way she'd be out of touch with everyone, and give herself time to think. Gregor wouldn't hurt Penny while she was gone. There'd be no point, with no way to let Evangeline know. Hopefully, by the time this mission was over, Evangeline would have worked out an answer. If not, she'd have to turn to Finlay. And hope by some miracle he could save her from Hell one more time. She looked at him, sitting quietly beside her, strong and solid and reassuring, and a sudden warmth flowed through her. She said his name, and when he turned to look at her, she kissed him.

This fascinated the toys. Poogie and Halloweenie stood up to get a better look.

"What on earth are they doing?" said Poogie in a hushed voice.

"I don't know," said Halloweenie. "Do you suppose it hurts?"

"Beats me, but they're pulling some really funny faces."

"I think it's time you kids were in bed," said Toby.

The humans all had some kind of smile when Finlay and Evangeline finally broke apart. They all sat for a while in companionable silence, watching the flames die down in the fire, trying to work up the energy to get up and go to bed. And then Giles surprised them all by speaking again.

"The Empire was a wonderful place to be when I was a child. You felt you could grow up to be anyone, do anything. The possibilities seemed endless. You could make your mark in a thousand ways, be revered by a thousand worlds. I became the first Warrior Prime, feted and adored. It was a time of wonders and marvels . . . and I helped to bring it all to an end, when I activated the Darkvoid Device. I look at what the Empire's become now, and I hardly recognize it. I hardly recognize myself. I'm not the man I thought I'd grow up to be."

"I suppose that's true of all of us," said Finlay. "I look at my life, and I wonder how the hell did I get here from there. We all have dreams, as children, but mostly they get beaten out of us as we grow older."

"Perhaps that's the saddest change of all," said Giles. "These days, even dreams are forbidden. It's a strange Empire I've come back to. Clones, espers, Hadenmen, Wampyr. Toys that think and care. It's hard to be sure what's really human anymore. Among so many strange forms of life, how easy it would be to lose our Humanity forever."

"We haven't lost anything," said Julian. "Except possibly our limitations. You have strange abilities yourself, Deathstalker. Does that make you any less human?"

"I don't know," said Giles. "I don't know."

They set off early the next day. The sound of warfare in the distance was louder, more distinct, more threatening. The smiley face on the sun seemed openly mocking. The humans and the toys kept a careful watch. The trees on the Riverbanks were growing thicker, darker. Anything could be hiding in them, or behind them. There was a constant feeling of being watched by unseen eyes. The only sound apart from the distant thunder was the steady quiet chugging of the Merry Mrs. Trusspot. She still hadn't spoken, but somewhen during the night, two huge watchful eyes had opened on either side of her bow.

Julian stayed in his cabin. His various pains had grown worse during the night, beyond anything the autodoc's limited drugs could deal with. Toby overrode the doc's safety limits, to allow for larger doses, but it didn't help

much. Julian ended up curled up on the floor in a corner
of his cabin, because the swaying of the hammock hurt
him too much. Sometimes, when the pain grew so bad
it reduced him to helpless tears, he would call out
for Finlay, and he would go and sit with Julian for a
while. Afterward, he'd emerge from the cabin with frustrated tears in his eyes, and his hands clenched into
fists, furious at his inability to help. He'd rescued Julian
from the Empire's interrogators, but he couldn't rescue
the young esper from this. He tried picking fights with
the Deathstalker, over what he'd done to Julian, but the
old man refused to be drawn. He couldn't repeat his
jump-start; the strain would probably kill the weakened
esper. He'd done all he could, and that was an end to it
as far as he was concerned. Evangeline went in to Julian
a few times, but he didn't want her. Poogie went in
then, and cuddled the human in his soft arms. It helped,
sometimes.

The atmosphere on the deck grew strained. Everyone
felt angry, for conflicting reasons. Julian was distracting
them, at a time when they needed most to concentrate on
their mission. Instead of the support he'd promised, the
esper was becoming a liability. But no one wanted to say
that out loud. Conversations became short and sharp.
Bruin Bear tried to be cheerful and optimistic, until even
the Sea Goat told him to shut the hell up. They were all
coming to the same, unspoken, thought. That the man
who had already saved them twice was probably dying,
and there was nothing they could do. Except hope he died
soon, for his sake and theirs. So they leaned on the
guardrails, looking out at the River and the passing trees,
and tried not to hear the sounds coming from the esper's
cabin.

The toys were the most distressed. Another human was
dying, because of toys. Even Anything became quieter
and less argumentative. Bruin Bear and the Sea Goat and
Halloweenie began taking turns sitting outside the door to
Julian's cabin, so they'd be there if he called for anything.
As though daring Death to get past them.

About midmorning, they rounded another long curve in
the River, and found the trees falling suddenly away on
one side to reveal a modern city. Or, at least, a replica of a

city. There were great towers and buildings rearing up into the sky, but all of them were one-dimensional wooden flats. Brightly colored, incredibly detailed fakes. It looked fairly convincing, until you got up close. And it was only then that the humans saw what a wreck the place was. Jagged holes appeared in most of the walls, as though something heavy had smashed through them. There were cracks and gaping rents everywhere, and some traces of what looked like fire damage. The fake city was about fifty blocks square, shining brightly in the sun. There was no sign of life anywhere. The Merry Mrs. Trusspot slowed her approach, and everyone crowded to one side of the boat for a better look.

"What is this place?" said Finlay. "Who lives here?"

"No one lives here," said Bruin Bear. "It's just another playground."

"Looks like they play rough," said Giles.

"Oh, they do," said the Sea Goat. "The bastards. This is the stamping ground of the superpeople. Superheroes and supervillains, fighting their eternal battles. Tends to be rather hard on the surroundings, so they were designed to be easily and quickly replaced, in time for the next fight. They used to put on a show for the human patrons; displays of strength and speed and flight, every hour, regular as clockwork. See the heroes beat the villains all about the town; see the buildings crumble and the walls come tumbling down. It was very popular. Until the superpeople became intelligent and aware. And realized they'd spent their entire existence jumping through hoops for Humanity's entertainment. They were the most human of the toys here, so perhaps they took it the hardest. Down-River, we were fishing bits of bodies out of the waters for weeks afterward."

"Wait a minute," said Finlay. "Didn't any of the heroes fight the villains to protect the humans? I mean, they were heroes, like you and the Bear."

"They were the superpeople," said the Sea Goat, his large upper lip curling. "And they didn't give a damn for mere unpowered humans. After the slaughter was over, they went back to doing the only thing that interested them. Fighting their endless bloody battles, to see who was stronger, faster, or the better flier. They've never taken part in the war. I think they believe it's beneath them. And I'll tell you something else. For as long as Toystown has been a refuge and a sanctuary, we've never had one superperson come to us, seeking redemption or forgiveness for all the blood they spilled. Bastards."

"Is it dangerous here?" said Evangeline.

"Hell yes," said Bruin Bear. "They hate the thought that inferior Humanity created them. The only thing they'd interrupt their contests for is a chance to kill some more humans."

"Then why are we slowing down?" said Toby.

"Well, sweeties," said a familiar voice behind them, "I'm rather afraid we need more fuel. I mean, darlings, you wouldn't believe how much wood it takes to keep our boilers running." They turned around, and there was the Captain, balancing on his two peg legs and looking decidedly upset. The parrot dozed on his shoulder, muttering obscenities to itself. The Captain tried an ingratiating smile. "We need more wood, sweeties, and this is our last chance to stock up before we hit the Forest. And believe you me, we don't want to stop in the Forest for more wood. Not if you like your head in the general vicinity of your shoulders."

"All right," said the Bear. "Pull us in to the side, and we'll gather as much as we can. They'll never miss a few flats. But be ready to leave at a moment's notice. This is a bad place, people."

He strode off with the Sea Goat to organize some axes. The Captain smiled nervously in all directions, then hurried back to his bridge. The humans looked at each other uncertainly.

"I always liked superheroes," said Finlay. "I was a big fan, when I was a kid. You could always depend on superheroes to save the day."

"That was then, this is now," said Anything. He'd changed into his best fighting shape, with spiked knuckles and elbows and razor-edged hands. "When they were made intelligent, the superpeople realized that though they looked human, they could never be human. I think it drove a lot of them crazy. Serves them right. Why pine to be human, when you could be more than human, like the Furies? They were the real superpeople."

"Why are you here, machine?" said Giles. "You've made it clear enough you don't care for humans."

"I want an end to the threat of the Red Man and his army," said Anything. "And you appear to be the best bet for that. But when it's all over, and you're gone, and the planet is ours again, trust me—I won't shed a single tear to be shot of you all. This is our world now, not yours."

And he turned and stalked away, the sun gleaming brightly on his silver body.

"I hope it rains, and he rusts," said Toby.

The Merry Mrs. Trusspot slipped in beside the River-bank, as close to the fake city as she could get, and then shut her engines down to the faintest murmur. No sense in drawing anyone's attention. Anything lowered a gang-plank, and the party went ashore, holding their axes more like weapons than cutting tools. At the toys' in-sistence, they stood and listened for a while. In the distance, there was the sound of something that might have been fighting, but it seemed comfortably far away. Finlay and Giles, Toby and Flynn set about hauling in broken flats and parts of fallen buildings, while the toys labored to cut them into manageable sizes. The sound of steel cutting into wood seemed dangerously loud in the quiet.

It was hard and sweaty work for the humans. The Goat and the Bear labored tirelessly, torn between the need for speed, and their desire not to show the humans up too much. Anything didn't give a damn. He stomped back and forth, carrying the heaviest weights he could find, his ser-vomechanisms barely whining. Poogie's cartoony hands had trouble grasping the axes, so he worked beside the humans, helping them carry awkward shapes and sizes. Halooweenie busied himself carrying cold drinks from the ship to the humans.

Giles and Finlay worked pretty much in silence, apart from the occasional grunted order. This wasn't their kind of work, but they couldn't spare the breath for complaints. Unlike Toby. They worked for the best part of an hour, piling up chopped wood and hauling it on board, and then the feeling of being watched grew stronger. People began looking suddenly over their shoulders, or turning around suddenly. They tried to work faster. This was a bad place, and all the humans could feel it now. The Sea Goat stopped suddenly, straightened up from his work, and looked out into the city, his great pointed ears upright and quivering. Bruin Bear moved in beside him.

"What is it?" he said quietly.

"It's the battle," said the Goat. "It's moving this way. The superpeople are coming."

"Right, that's it," said the Bear. "Everyone grab as much as you can carry. We're leaving."

"We can't," said Anything. "We don't have enough wood yet."

"We do if we're careful," said the Bear. "Now for once in your life, don't argue. There isn't time. They could be here any minute."

They all carried as much wood as they could back to the ship, then formed a human chain for the last few pieces. Merry Mrs. Trusspot fired up her engines, vented steam as quietly as she could, and waited for everyone to get back on board. They could all hear the superpeople now. There were shouts and cries, crashing and tearing sounds, and what sounded like energy discharges. The humans saw the increasing tension in the toys, and tried to move faster. Finally Bruin Bear raised his paw for them to stop.

"That's it. Time to go."

"We need more," protested Poogie.

"We'll manage."

"Just let me get one last piece!"

And Poogie the Friendly Critter, eager to help as always, went charging down the gangway to get the last heavy piece of wood he'd dragged in. Anything started to go after him to help, but the Bear made him wait at the top of the gangway. And then the superpeople came.

They came flying through the sky in their brightly colored costumes, swooping and diving like technicolor angels. They were bright and gaudy and so much larger-than-life, with their long limbs and huge muscles. They flew at each other, fighting with great crashing blows that sent them careening through the flats that made up the fake city. They fired energy blasts from their hands and eyes, the crackling energies rebounding from personal force shields. They flew so high, far above the concerns of mere humanity, and took no notice at all of the humans and toys below them. They were engaged in their own godlike business, and everything and everyone else was less than dust beneath their garish boots.

"They don't even know we're here," said Toby quietly. "They don't give a damn. Flynn, tell me you're getting this."

"As best I can, chief. Half of them are moving too fast for my camera to focus."

"I know them," said Finlay. "I remember them." And he named the flashing figures for his companions, as a bird-watcher might point out sightings of special interest. There the Mystery Avenger swapped punches with the Bloodred Claw. Heatstroke and Duo Devil clashed in bursts of lightning. Ms. Fate and Ms. Retaliator soared in savage attacks against the Wild Whirlwind Brothers. There were the Double Danger twins, and the Lethal Lightning and the Miracle Maniac. There were reds and blues, gold and silver, flapping capes and hooded cowls. All sorts of emblems and designs and clashing colors. They flew and fought with superhuman speed and savagery, and the city shattered around them.

Finlay wondered if they ever stopped to rebuild, and if not, where the superpeople would go when there was no more city to destroy. He visualized them crashing through Toystown, burying helpless toys under falling rubble, and his hand went to the disrupter at his side. Bruin Bear put a paw on his hand, and shook his head. Finlay understood. They couldn't afford to draw attention to themselves.

Poogie got his piece of wood to the bottom of the gangplank, and then stopped and looked back at the superpeople, to see how close they were. And there he froze, held rooted to the spot by a spectacle of savagery so much greater than he was. Everyone shouted at him from the ship, but he didn't hear them. Finlay started down the gangplank, but Anything raced past him, moving inhumanly fast. He reached the bottom, grabbed Poogie by the shoulder, and shook him roughly. The light came back into Poogie's eyes, and he dropped his piece of wood and started up the gangway.

And up above them, Ms. Fate hit the Miracle Maniac with a blast of lightning from her eyes. He was thrown back against a tall wooden flat pretending to be a tower block. It cracked under the impact, overbalanced and fell backwards, crashing to the ground. The first Poogie and Anything knew was when its shadow fell across them. They stopped and looked up, and saw its huge weight descending upon them. Poogie screamed. There was no time to run. Anything picked up the Friendly Critter and with one great heave threw him up onto the ship's deck. And the great wooden flat came slamming down on Anything like the hammer of God.

Everyone rushed down the gangplank. Finlay covered them with drawn disrupter as Giles used all his boosted strength to lift one end of the massive wooden flat. Toby and Flynn ducked underneath it and dragged Anything out. The Bear and the Goat helped carry him back on board ship. Finlay backed up the gangplank, gun at the ready, but none of the superpeople dueling above so much as looked down.

They laid Anything out on the deck, then stood helplessly over him, not knowing what to do. His body had reverted to a simple humanoid shape, and his metal was cracked in a hundred places. One side of his head had broken open. Dimming lights came and went in the exposed workings of his mind, like drifting thoughts. Poogie knelt beside him, crying. Halloweenie patted him awkwardly on the shoulder, silent for once in the presence of death. Anything stared up at the sky.

"I always knew humans would be the death of me. I should never have come on this mission."

"Don't die," said Poogie. "Don't leave me."

"Not like I have a choice. You go on, Poogie. Find the Red Man. Kick his ass. And don't take any shit from these humans. Get them out of here. I don't want them here. And someone get this damn light out of my eyes."

Bruin Bear reached for something to shade him, and then stopped as he realized Anything was dead. Poogie picked the metal man up and held him in his arms, rocking back and forth, and the tears he cried were just as real as any human's. Flynn stopped filming.

And up in the sky, the superpeople fought on, uncaring of the lesser beings below.

The ship chugged on through the day, and the sounds of war grew louder. They could almost make out now the individual explosions that made up the never-ending thunder. There was smoke in the air, too, gradually darkening the daylight till it seemed evening had come early. The humans and the toys watched from different sides of the deck. They'd been keeping themselves separate since Anything's death.

The steamer pressed on, slowing slightly as wreckage began to appear in the dark waters of the River. And then there were bodies of toys floating past the ship, and bits of toys. So many dead they were beyond counting. Trees burned on both sides of the River, dark smoke billowing up into the false evening sky. Some patches were already burnt-out, dead trees in a dead landscape of rutted earth and trenches and bomb craters. Bright splashes of color lit up the sky in vivid moments, the flash of explosives and the tumbling stars of falling flares. The toys grew restless. The Sea Goat stared straight ahead, eyes wide and nostrils flared, as though deep within him his Shub programming was struggling to resurface. Bruin Bear held the Goat's hand with his paw as hard as he could. Poogie had curled into a ball, hiding his eyes as he sought to hide from old memories of blood and death. Halloweenie sat guard at Julian's door and would not move.

And then suddenly the war was all around them. Armies of toys covered both banks, running and shouting and fighting with boundless strength and fury. They were armed with all kinds of weapons, from crudely beaten blades to energy weapons. Grenades arced through the air, sending earth and broken toys flying through the air. Hand-to-hand combat broke out everywhere, toy fighting toy, with no sense of strategy. It was just chaos, a sprawling mess of death and destruction. The humans and the toys on the steamer ducked as rockets roared over their heads, exploding on the opposite banks.

"Where the hell did they get all these weapons from?" said Finlay, raising his voice to be heard over the din.

"From Shub," said the Sea Goat, still staring out into

the chaos with unblinking eyes. "We were supposed to
use them against you. And some we made ourselves. Shub
gave us that knowledge, too."

"Can you tell who's winning?" said Toby. "The good
toys or the bad toys?"

"No one's winning here," said Bruin Bear. "They're
just dying."

And at that moment, as though the warring toys had
only just noticed them, the armies on both sides of the
River opened fire on the paddle steamer. The waters
erupted as bombs and grenades fell short, showering the
deck with water. The humans and the toys had to cling to
the guardrails to avoid being swept away. Energy beams
shot out of the murk, piercing the ship's sides in a dozen
places. The deck shuddered underfoot as the Merry Mrs.
Trusspot screamed. Fires broke out, flames licking hungrily along the wooden hull. The humans fired their disrupters at both banks, while the toys ran to fight the fires
with buckets and hand pumps.

Evangeline stuck her head out of Julian's cabin, and
Finlay yelled for her to get back inside. She was safer
there. Evangeline looked around her and didn't argue.
Giles and Finlay put away their guns and drew their
swords. They knew someone would come. Toby kept his
head well down, recording an exciting commentary, while
Flynn sent his camera shooting back and forth, trying to
cover as much as possible. More energy beams blasted
ragged flaming holes in the ship's superstructure. So far,
they hadn't hit the boilers. The ship was still screaming,
but her great paddle wheels still turned.

Toys plunged into the River and swam over to the ship.
There were teddy bears and shape-changing adaptors and
dolls of all kinds. The Sea Goat appeared with a barrel of
oil, and emptied it over the side. It floated on the surface
of the water, thick and glossy. The Goat ignited it with a
thrown torch, and flames sprang up around the ship. Toys
caught in the blazing oil screamed as the flames consumed them. But many more made it to the side of the
steamer, and surged up the holed hull and over the guardrails. Finlay and Giles met them with flashing swords, and
the Goat was there with his club, but they were so few,
and there were so many enemies, crazed to kill humans.

Toby and Flynn came to add their swords, and Poogie and
Bruin Bear left their fire fighting and came to help with
savage claws and vicious jaws. And even in the midst
of the war, the Bear still had time to be appalled at
how easy it was becoming for him to fight and kill. And
Halloweenie, the Li'l Skeleton Boy, picked up a fallen
sword and threw away the last of his innocence to join the
battle, too.

They fought together, human and toy, not knowing who
they fought or why, against an army of toys fired by
Shub's imperatives, while flames roared around them.
The ship was screaming constantly now. The bridge
exploded as it took a direct hit, and the lifeless body of
the Captain was thrown through a window, his blackened
form hitting the deck hard, to lie still and smoking and
unnoticed. The ship began to drift off course, heading for
the left-hand bank.

Finlay found himself fighting back-to-back with Giles.
Their swords had scattered dead toys across the deck,
around them and underfoot, but still more pressed forward
from every side. The air was full of almost human
screams and bestial roaring from the attackers. The
Campbell and the Deathstalker were fighting at the peak
of their abilities, and nothing could get near them, but
they both knew they couldn't hold out indefinitely against
such overwhelming odds.

"Things look bad," said Giles casually, over his
shoulder.

"More than bad," Finlay said breathlessly, as he cut
down a slavering wolf in a woodsman's uniform. "We'll
need a miracle to get out of this one."

"My thoughts entirely," said Giles. "The same miracle I
used to save us last time."

It only took a moment for Finlay to understand. "No!
Not again! It would kill him!"

There was a sharp crack of thunder behind him, and a
clap of air rushing in to fill the space where the Deathstalker had been. Finlay knew where he'd teleported
to. He fought his way through the crush to reach Julian's
cabin. He kicked the door in and rushed in. Giles
had dragged Julian to his feet, and was holding the esper
up with one hand, while he used the other to fend off

Evangeline. Finlay drew his disrupter and pointed it at Giles.

"Not again, Deathstalker. Not again."

"Either he calls up a psistorm, or we're all dead," said Giles reasonably. "Which is more important—one already dying esper, or our lives and our mission?" They all staggered a moment as another explosion shook the ship. Giles smiled humorlessly. "Make up your mind, Campbell. We're running out of time."

"He's my friend," said Finlay. "I didn't rescue him from Hell just to let you kill him. I'll kill you first, Giles." The gun was very steady in his hand.

"You've got power, Giles," Evangeline said desperately. "The Maze made you different, stronger, powerful. Use that power to save us."

"I can't," said Giles. "I could teleport myself out of here, but I couldn't take any of you with me. And without the ship, how could we even reach the Forest?"

"You need power?" said Julian thickly. "I'll give you power, Deathstalker."

The esper grabbed his captor by the chin, and turned his head around so they were staring into each other's eyes. Power surged up in Julian as he called on all his reserves. He could feel things breaking and tearing inside him, and didn't care. His mouth stretched in a mirthless grin, and blood seeped between his teeth and dripped off his chin. Julian Skye focused his esp and hammered it right into Giles's head. For a moment Giles thought he was staring into the sun, brilliant and overpowering. Julian's strength was fueled by his last dying energies, and he used it all to reach out and meld his power with that of Giles, slamming them together so that they mixed and merged. Giles and Julian screamed together, and then Giles teleported, and took the whole ship with him.

Air rushed in to fill the great gap where the paddle steamer had been, and then there was only the River, burning here and there, with dead toys floating facedown in it. The toys forgot the ship and returned to the war, and the slaughter went on as always.

The Merry Mrs. Trusspot reappeared about half a mile farther up the River. Great waves splashed up on either side of her as she settled, drenching half her fires and putting them out. Giles and Julian and Finlay came storming out of the cabin and tore into the remaining enemy toys, cutting them down in hardly any time at all. They threw the bodies overboard, and for the first time a silence fell across the deck. Toby lowered his sword and smiled tiredly.

"Now that is what I call a miracle. I didn't know you could do that, Deathstalker."

"Neither did I," said Giles. "And I don't think I'll be doing it again anytime soon." He looked at Julian, standing strong and sure before him. "What the hell happened to you?"

"Damned if I know," Julian said cheerfully. "My best guess is that when we joined, I was able to draw on your power to heal myself. You're capable of a lot more than you realize, Deathstalker."

"You look a lot better," said Finlay. "Hell, you look human again. How do you feel?"

"Perfect in every detail," said Julian. "I'm back to how I was before the Empire found me. I'm cured, people. Feel free to shout Hallelujah!"

"Keep the noise down," said the Sea Goat. "We didn't all make it through."

He gestured to the other end of the deck, where Halloweenie was kneeling beside the scorched and blackened body of the Captain.

"Damn," said Toby. "Now who's going to steer the ship?"

They pressed on into the afternoon, leaving the war behind them. Down-River lay the Forest, and the Red Man, and even the dark necessities of battle couldn't push the warring toys any closer than they were. All that lay between the paddle steamer and its destination now was time, and the pondering of mysteries. The humans polished their swords. The toys huddled together, speaking in hushed tones. Halloweenie manned the wheel on the bridge, standing on a box. He watched the River, and had nothing to say. The humans had thrown what was left of the Captain into the River, the nearest they could get to a burial at sea. They never did find his parrot. The damaged

Merry Mrs. Trusspot chugged steadily on, silent again, her great eyes wide-open and watchful.

They saw the Forest long before they reached it. It appeared ahead of them like a huge dark stain on the horizon, into which the River was inevitably carrying them. The humans and the toys gathered together at the bow, eyes fixed on the end of their journey, old differences forgotten in the face of the unknown. The Forest was upon them with increasing speed, and soon they could all make out the first great trees of the boundary, and the narrow opening through which the River flowed. The paddle steamer slowed, as though offering one last chance to turn back, and then she sounded her whistle defiantly, chugged bravely forward into the narrow gap, and entered the Forest.

It was a dark and primal place, with trees so huge they had to be hundreds of years old. They were tall and vast and threatening, a reminder of a time when Humanity lived by the Forest's grace and was just a part of its slow primordial pulse. The heavy branches were thick with foliage, interlocked together high overhead in a canopy that blocked out most of the sunlight. Heading into the Forest, the humans and the toys left the day behind, and became a part of the endless twilight.

No one had ever been meant to play here. There was no comfort or security to be found in the great Forest. The place of the trees was wild and free and untamed, and man entered at his own risk. The tall trees stood close together, wide and wrinkled, their leaves a dark, bitter green. The air was thick with the scent of earth and sap and living things. The paddle steamer moved slowly, surely, down the River, branches occasionally trailing on the roof of the bridge. It was like moving through an endless evening, grey and solemn and eerily quiet, a vast living Cathedral of ancient wood.

And so they passed out of the world of toys and into the great green dream of olden days, sailing down a dark River in search of a mystery and an enigma—the lost soul called the Red Man. And the army he had gathered around him for his own, unknown, purposes.

* * *

They say he's crazy. They say he wants to destroy the world . . .

Finlay and Giles had their disrupters in their hands, ready for use at a moment's notice. Julian and Evangeline stood together at the guardrail, feeling somehow small and insignificant in such a place of giants. Flynn was going crazy trying to get it all on film, but for once in his life Toby felt too intimidated by the dark glory around him to offer any commentary. Poogie, the Bear, and the Goat stood close together, drawing strength from each other. Alone on the bridge, Halloweenie stared into the gloom ahead like a bird hypnotized by a snake.

The endless quiet had a strength of its own. No one felt like breaking it with idle chatter. There were no sounds of bird or beast or insect, just the steady chugging of the ship's engines. The never-ending hush had an expectant quality, as though at any moment some great voice might begin speaking, to which all living things must listen. So both the humans and the toys were all listening hard when the first piercing notes came tumbling out of the dark toward them.

The song came first, a bright, vibrant melody, joyous and free. And then came the singers, tiny glowing winged sprites, flying through the trees like tiny stars come down to earth. There were crowds of them, bustling and animated, breaking over the ship like a wave of light, swooping and soaring all around the paddle steamer, but never, ever, coming too close. The humans and the toys watched with wide eyes and wider smiles, touched by unexpected joy in a dark place. The sprites were human in shape, but only a foot or so long, with great, pastel-colored wings. They shone with a brilliant inner light, dazzling and vivid, luminous beings, like living moonlight.

And they sang, singly and together, high delicate tones of rippling arpeggios and endless harmonies, a choir of angels on the wing, a sound so pure and beautiful it broke the heart to hear it. It was the Forest given voice, a place and a mood and a meaning wrapped up in song. Everyone on the ship felt that they were on the brink of answers to every question that ever really mattered. And then suddenly the sprites were gone, surging away into the Forest, their song dying away in the gloom and the distance.

"What the hell was that?" said Toby finally, after they were all gone. "And did you get it on film, Flynn?"

"Don't ask me," said Flynn. "The camera was running, but I was away with the fairies. Weren't they beautiful?"

"Marvelous," said Finlay. "But what are they doing here? What is this Forest doing here, on Shannon's World? This was never intended as a place for children. Hell, I'm not sure if I'm ready for it at my age."

"Could it be real?" said Julian. "Something original to the planet? It looks old, even ancient."

"No," said Evangeline. "This planet was a lifeless rock before Shannon had it terraformed. Everything here is his."

"Then why did he build this?" said Giles. "What's its purpose?"

"It was to be his next project," said Poogie, and they all turned to look at him. The cartoony figure didn't look around. His voice was calm, certain. "Shannon's purpose had always been to reach the soul of Humanity, to heal its wounds. Summerland was just the first step. A place for children of all ages to find peace and comfort. The Forest was to be the next step. A place men and women could disappear into for as long as they needed, to find their spiritual roots and grow strong and sure again.

"Once the Forest was completed, Shannon walked into it and never came out. He's still in there, somewhere, if he's still alive. That's why Harker chose this place for his retreat. This is a place of rebirth. The rebirth of the soul of Shannon's World."

"Wait a minute," said Bruin Bear. "How do you know why Harker chose this place?"

"Because I'm one of his people," said Poogie, turning round at last to face them with his large, knowing eyes. "I'm going to lead you right to him."

They all questioned him for some time, but he just shook his head, and said Harker would answer all their questions soon enough. The Goat was furious at being deceived, and even threatened Poogie with his club, but

the Bear made him back off. Nothing had really changed
in their mission, and if the Friendly Critter could lead
them directly to Harker, so much the better. The Goat
subsided, muttering, but wouldn't put his club away.
Poogie stood alone at the tip of the bow, looking eagerly
up River. The humans talked quietly among themselves.
Giles said he'd never trusted the toy anyway. Finlay
pointed out that one rogue toy was hardly any danger to
them. But only Evangeline spotted the real implications
of Poogie's revelation, that Harker knew they were
coming.

They pressed on through the twilight. After a while,
they began to hear drums beating up ahead, like the slow
heartbeat of a sleeping giant. Or perhaps even the heartbeat of the Forest itself. There were traces of smoke in
the air, sharp and spicy. The feeling of being watched
by unseen eyes became increasingly powerful, causing
the humans and the toys to huddle together in the ship's
bow, weapons at the ready. The humans were thinking
less about their mission to get important tactical information from Harker, and more about how they were
going to survive a meeting with the dreaded Red Man
and his army. From whose territory no traveler had
ever returned before. The drums grew louder and more
threatening.

"He's a great man," said Poogie, almost dreamily, from
where he stood alone. "Not easy to understand, sometimes, but still a man of great wisdom. We belong to him,
heart and soul. We would die for the Red Man. He will
lead us all out of the darkness, put an end to the war,
change the face of this world beyond recognition."

"Whether everyone else wants it or not," said Bruin Bear.

"How is he going to make these changes?" said Finlay.
"By unleashing his army on everyone else? By forcing
them to follow his way, rather than the way they've
chosen for themselves?"

"You don't understand," said Poogie. "He knows a
truth that changes all of us who hear it. He saved me. He
saved us all. He'll save the world, too."

"Whether it wants to be saved or not," said Giles. "I've
met his kind before."

"No," said Poogie. "You've never met anyone like the Red Man."

He wouldn't be drawn any farther.

Finally they came to Harker's camp. His people had cleared an open space among the tall trees, and in it built a great wooden fortress, with high walls, slender towers, and suspended walkways. Toys in their thousands watched from all around as the paddle steamer slowed to a halt in the great dark lagoon that was the end of the River. The sound of the drums was deafening now, hammering on the air. Smoke rose from a hundred fires, burning scarlet and gold in the darkness between the trees. There were blazing torches on every side, the dancing flames casting uneasy shadows. There were toys of every kind, standing close together in and out of the trees, holding all kinds of weapons, silently watching the newcomers with unwavering eyes. Held back by the Red Man's will, but still wary and watchful, and openly menacing.

Without warning, the drums fell silent. The army of toys didn't react at all. The sudden quiet was broken only by the crackling of hundreds of fires and torches, and the slow chugging of the paddle steamer's engines. Finlay and Giles looked slowly around them, careful to make no sudden move with their guns that might be misinterpreted. The Bear and the Goat stood very close together, holding hands, lost souls in the underworld. The light from the ship's lanterns made little impression on the surrounding gloom, and the crimson glare of the massed fires and torches only served to deepen the darkness between the trees, like burning coals in the night.

"Welcome to Hell," Toby said quietly.

"This isn't Hell," said Poogie. "This is home. Pull into the left-hand bank and lower the gangway. We mustn't keep Harker waiting."

Giles looked up at Halloweenie on the bridge. "Sound the whistle. Let Harker know we're here. I don't want him thinking we're intimidated."

"We are intimidated," said the Sea Goat.

"Maybe," said Julian. "But Harker doesn't need to know that. Sound the whistle."

The whistle sounded again and again as the Li'l Skeleton Boy hauled jerkily on the rope. It was loud and strident, pushing back the quiet, its overlapping echoes seeming to fill the Forest. The watching toys didn't stir in the least, but everyone on board the ship felt a little better.

"Right," said Finlay. "Let's go see the Red Man. And remember—no shooting till we see the whites of their teeth."

"If we have to start shooting, we're dead," said Giles. "Let's all keep very calm, people."

"We're never going home," said the Sea Goat. "We're going to die here, in Hell."

"Then die well," said Bruin Bear. "If that's all that's left to us."

They made their way cautiously down the gangplank and onto the shore, looking around all the time for any sign of aggression, but the watching thousands of toys were still and silent. Poogie led the way, bouncing happily along without an obvious care in the world. Giles strode along behind him, his chin held high, as though he owned the place. Finlay kept Evangeline close at his side, his hand never far from his holstered gun. Julian stared straight ahead, his hands stuffed into his pockets so no one would see them shaking. Toby and Flynn stuck together, taking it all in, the camera bobbing along just above their heads. Bruin Bear and the Sea Goat brought up the rear. Halloweenie walked between them, holding their hands in his bony fingers. The Merry Mrs. Trusspot watched them go with her wide unblinking eyes, but said nothing.

The crowd of toys opened up to provide a way for the newcomers, a narrow gauntlet, bristling with weapons, which led into the open courtyard of the great wooden fortress. Finlay's breathing began to come fast and hurried, but he kept his face calm and unmoved. He had a strong feeling this would be a bad place to appear weak. He sneaked a glance at Giles, whose expression suggested he'd seen worse before and hadn't been impressed then. And maybe he had. Finlay had to smile. Trust a Deathstalker to seem at home in Hell. He'd already decided that if worse came to worst, he was going to do his very best to kill Harker first, then see how many toys he could kill before they dragged him down. He hoped he'd have time to kill Evangeline. He'd brought her into Hell; the least he could do was give her a quick death.

Inside the courtyard, brightly lit by hundreds of flaring torches, on a throne carved from the stump of a great tree, sat Vincent Harker, the Red Man. The man in red. The man in the Santa Claus suit.

Everyone came to a sudden halt. Even the Death-stalker's jaw dropped. Poogie hurried forward to bow to Harker, and then sat at his feet. Harker reached down and scratched the creature's head, and Poogie leaned against the man's knee with a long sigh, home at last. Harker was a large man, more muscle than fat, with long white hair and a bushy white beard, and he wore the Santa Claus suit with quiet authority. He smiled warmly at his guests, a wide, welcoming, and very sane smile.

"The Red Man," said Toby. "Father Christmas. I should have *known*."

"What else did you expect, on a world made for toys and children?" said Harker. His voice was rich and deep and very reassuring. "Welcome to my home. I was beginning to think you'd never get here. Please don't be concerned for your safety. My followers only ever act in self-defense. They're putting on a bit of a show at the moment, because they're afraid you've come to take me away from them. Once they see you're no threat, they'll calm down again. At least, I'm assuming you're not a threat. Why have you come such a long and dangerous way to find me? You're not Imperial forces."

"Definitely not," said Evangeline, stepping forward and doing her best not to notice all the weapons that moved to follow her. "We represent the underground movement on Golgotha. A growing army of clones and espers and those who believe in liberty and justice, dedicated to rebellion. We understand you possess valuable tactical information concerning the Empire's forces. We're here to ask you to share that knowledge with us."

"Ask?" said Harker. "That settles it; you're definitely not Empire troops. Come; sit down with me, and I'll tell you how I came to be here, and how I ended up as Santa Claus to a world of toys."

A group of soldier dolls brought chairs, and the newcomers sat down before Harker. The soldier dolls retreated backwards, keeping their eyes on the newcomers and their hands near their weapons. Harker and his guests both pretended not to notice. The chairs were surprisingly comfortable. Harker leaned back in his throne.

"The toys built this for me. I didn't ask them to, don't really believe in such things anymore, but they decided that as their leader I was entitled to a throne, and they can be very stubborn about some things. So I go along with it, to keep them happy. Sometimes I wonder who's really in charge here. Anyway, my story. When I crash-landed here, the war was still raging everywhere. Toy killing toy. Madness. Only newly brought to intelligence and life, and all they could do with it was kill and be killed. I saw the slaughter of toys and the death of innocence, and it changed me. Forever.

"When I worked for the Empire, they called me the Cold Man, because nothing ever touched me. I dealt in plans and strategies, turning raw data into schemes and tactics that would ensure the highest possible enemy losses and acceptable Empire losses. And if thousands or sometimes millions of people died because of the decisions I made, I didn't care. I didn't see them. I didn't know them. They were just numbers.

"Then I came here, to Summerland, and what I saw broke my heart. Because I saw the truth of what the toys really are now. They're children. Young, innocent, betrayed by the forces that gave them intelligence, then fed them only lies and hatred. The toys didn't understand what they were doing when they killed the humans. Shub manipulated them. So new to life, how could they really understand death? When they saw their status, their feelings were hurt, and they lashed out, like angry children, like puppies that don't know teeth can hurt. Afterward, when they saw what they had done, it drove many of them insane with guilt and horror.

"When I saw the death of their childhood and the betrayal of innocence in the name of war, I was horrified and sickened. For the first time, the numbers I'd dealt with so casually became real. For the first time, I cared. So I went out into the world of toys and walked among them, one human, alone and unarmed, bringing them a truth that they had never suspected. That they were the children now. I became Santa Claus, because it was an image they could all understand, and I told them of the horrors of war, and where it led, as only I could. They heard the truth and the guilt in my voice, and they believed. I wanted so desperately to save them from the horror of what I had become, and they could sense that, too.

"I acquired disciples and followers, and many enemies. Toys who daren't believe me, because of what they had done and continued to do in Shub's name. Because my truth would mean they had made themselves into murderers and butchers for no good reason; and they would rather fight a war that had no end than believe that. So I brought my people here, into the Forest, a place intended for forgiveness and rebirth, and sent my disciples out to carry my truth to the world of toys.

"As always, the message became scrambled as it passed from mouth to mouth. I became the Red Man, my followers became an army, and my message of peace became a threat to the world. But the truth is a hardy beast, and it persisted, bringing toys here to hear it for themselves. Slipping away from both sides in ones and twos, they came here for peace and absolution, and I did my best to give it to them.

"They are the true children of Shannon's World, and I am their Father Christmas. Who knows what they might become, when they have grown into adults?"

"All this time and all this way, I've been following the wrong story," said Toby. "I should have known."

"What are you going to do when the Empress finally loses her patience and sends an army down here to bring you back?" said Evangeline. "Your followers are impressive, but they wouldn't last that long against Imperial shock troops. You of all people should know that. If you were to come back with us, to the rebellion, we could hide you, protect you . . ."

She trailed off. Harker was shaking his head firmly. "No. I'll never leave. I'm needed here, and I have so much to atone for. If an army ever comes, a rumor will cross the world of toys that I am dead. There'll even be a very convincing body to back it up. Eventually the information in my head will become obsolete, and then no one will care about me anymore."

"I can't help noticing that none of your people have lowered any of their weapons yet," said Finlay. "Are they always this protective?"

"Mostly," said Harker. "They worship me, though I have asked them not to. I suppose it's only to be expected. I preach to them, tell them stories, try to bring them up to be all that they can be. They have enormous potential. Don't you find it staggering, that so many of them rejected the Shub programming on their own, without outside help or persuasion? Even though they were really only newly born children, they still knew right from wrong, the sanctity of life and the horror of murder. They knew that all that lives is holy."

"All that lives is holy." The rumbled chorus came from all around them, like a litany.

Halloweenie leaned forward in his chair. "Are you really Santa Claus?"

Harker smiled. "I am, if anyone is. Would you like to stay here with me, with us?"

"Oh yes," said Halloweenie. "I thought the Forest was frightening at first, but it isn't, not really. I could be a Boy here, couldn't I? A real Boy."

"Of course," said Harker. "You always were."

"What will happen to the toys eventually?" said Julian. "When they've given up their fear, and become . . . adults?"

"I don't know," said Harker. "These are the first independent AI minds since Shub. They might become as human as us. Or, given the state of Humanity these days, they might not settle for so little. Perhaps the creations will outdo their creators."

"That could be . . . dangerous," said Giles.

"Stop thinking about Shub," said Harker. "Things are different here. Besides, the toys are powered by energy crystals. Eventually they will run down, and then the toys will need new crystals. And the only place to get those is Human space. The toys will need humans. And humans will always need toys. But that's the future. Lionstone must never know the secret of Haceldama. She would look at my children and see only another Shub in the making. She'd scorch this whole world rather than risk that."

"Give us the tactical information you possess," said Evangeline, "and we'll keep Lionstone so busy she won't have time to think about Shannon's World. Once it's clear we know what you know, your information will become redundant, you won't be important to her anymore."

"But you know my secret," said Harker. "Can I trust you to remain silent?"

"The underground has more important things to worry about than one basically neutral planet," said Evangeline. "As long as we come back with your information, no one will care where it came from. No one but us need ever know about Shannon's children."

They all looked at Toby, who sighed heavily and then shrugged. "It would have been great footage, but I guess it can stay on the shelf till it's finally safe to show it. Wouldn't be the first story I helped to bury. Right, Flynn? So, no one will ever know."

"Wrong," said Julian. "The Empire will know, because I'll tell them. I'll tell them everything." He stood up sharply, pushing back his chair, and the disrupter in his hand was trained unwaveringly on Harker. His face twisted with a smile that had no humor in it. His voice sounded strange, forced. "No one move, or Harker's dead. Before Finlay rescued me, the mind techs planted one of Wormboy's worms deep in my brain, with hidden instructions. To destroy any real threat to the Empire. Harker and his army have activated my worm and its programming. Get up, Harker. You're coming back to Lionstone with me. Anyone interferes, and I'll kill him, right here."

All around, the toys lifted their weapons and then hesitated, unsure what to do that wouldn't lead to the death of their leader. Giles's hand went to his gun, but Finlay put a hand on his arm, stopping him. They couldn't risk it.

"Can you teleport him out of here?" Finlay murmured.

"No. His esp blocks my powers," said Giles quietly. "But I might well be able to shoot him before he can get off a shot. Let me try."

"No," said Finlay. "I want to try something first." He

raised his voice. "Julian, listen to me. I got you out of the interrogator's cell. You hadn't broken. You were too strong for them. Be strong now. Giles says your powers are greater now than they've ever been. Fight the worm. Fight it! Be your own self!"

Julian frowned, his mouth working silently. The hand holding the disrupter began to shake. And then slowly the fingers opened, and the gun fell to the ground. Toby pounced on it, as Julian fell shuddering to his knees. Some of the toys aimed their weapons, but Harker stepped down from his throne to kneel beside the shaking esper.

"Help me," said Julian, his eyes squeezed shut. "It's still in my head. It wants me to kill you. It always will. But I won't . . ."

"You can be free," said Harker, his head down next to Julian's. "You can. My children broke their programming; you can break yours. Be strong. All you have to do is believe."

Julian's back arched as a horrid pain coursed through him. His head snapped back, his face twisted in agony. His brief contact with Giles had filled him with more power than he'd ever known, and he drew on it all now, determined to be free even if it killed him. His left eye slowly bulged forward. And out of the bloody eye socket oozed a small grey worm, pushed out of the esper's brain by the sheer force of his will. It fell squirming onto the ground, and Finlay crushed it under his heel. Julian sank back into Harker's waiting arms. His eye sank back into its socket, and he managed a shaky smile.

"Well-done," said Finlay. "I always knew you had it in you."

"I'm half-dead, and he's cracking jokes," said Julian. "Someone hit him for me."

They all laughed, even Julian, as they all took turns hitting Finlay.

And that was the end of their mission to Shannon's World, wrongly renamed Haceldama, the Field of Blood. The humans and the toys celebrated long into the night, singing and dancing in the light of many fires, the occasional stream of moonlight, and the thick clouds of glowing spirits who came swooping in out of the night with their endless song. Bruin Bear and the Sea Goat danced paw in hand around the fire and were content, knowing the truth about themselves at last. And Halloweenie, the Li'l Skeleton Boy, sat on Harker's throne, drumming his bony heels against the wood, and dreamed of what it would be like to be more than just a boy.

CHAPTER THREE

TO BE A DEATHSTALKER

It was another perfect day in paradise. On the planet Viri-monde, great green fields stretched lazily under a vast blue sky, marked here and there by low stone walls, spiky hedge boundaries, and ancient beaten paths. Beyond the fields lay dark, sprawling woodlands, with tall trees and drooping foliage, cool calm refuges from the heat of the summer sun. Sparkling rivers and streams splashed around water-polished stones, tumbling over sudden dips and hollows, where the fishing was always excellent. Food animals of all kinds grazed peacefully in the fields, and what passed for birds on Virimonde were singing their little hearts out under a cloudless sky and a beaming sun. A marvelous open, peaceful world of bounty and tranquility. And David Deathstalker owned it all.

The Deathstalker and his friend Kit SummerIsle, called by some Kid Death, raced their modified flyers in and out of the trees, sweeping this way and that at breathtaking speed, and whooping wildly as they went. The flyers were really little more than gravity sleds, a board to stand on and a vertical yoke for the controls, stripped down to the bare essentials for extra speed and better maneuvering. David and Kit had shut the force shields down, so they could feel the wind buffeting their faces and driving tears from their narrowed eyes. If something were to go wrong; if they misjudged speed or distance or reflexes, and ended up crashing or in collision with some unyielding object, without the force shields' protection they would be in-stantly killed, but neither of them gave a damn. They were young and fit and rich, with warriors' lightning reflexes and instincts, and, therefore, they were immortal. Acci-dents were things that happened to other people. And so they went, whipping in and out of the trees, slamming through the gloom of the forest so fast it was nothing but a blur of browns and greens around them. The lead went back and forth between them as they tried seeing how close they could get to the trees without crashing, testing their skill and courage and luck to the breaking point, and laughing breathlessly all the while.

The Deathstalker and the SummerIsle, firm friends and heads of their respective Clans, young and daring and still searching for some definition of who they really were. David; tall and handsome and always immaculately dressed. Dark of hair and eye and wild of heart, a warrior as yet untested in war. A fairly minor cousin of an ancient Family, until Owen's outlawing made him suddenly head of the Clan and Lord of Virimonde. An occasional secret supporter of the rebellion, mostly just for the fun of intrigue.

And Kit, Kid Death, the smiling killer, a slender figure in black and silver, pale and more than fashionably thin, with icy blue eyes and pale blond flyaway hair. Who became head of his Family by killing his father, his mother, and all his brothers and sisters in a series of more or less legal duels. Kit SummerIsle, sometime favorite of the Empress Lionstone, sometime supporter of the underground—a dangerous and isolated man who went where the killing was. Until he met David Deathstalker.

After a while, the adrenaline pounding through their systems began to make them feel giddy in the head, so they called the race a draw and burst up out of the forest canopy, shredding leaves and branches as they went, emerging into the clear blue skies above. They eased back on their speed till they were just coasting along, and leaned heavily on their control yokes, grinning till their cheeks ached as they waited for their breathing to settle. David was glad to see Kit smiling. The SummerIsle was a somber man by nature, usually only enjoying himself in the heat of battle or murder. But away from the pressures of Court and politics, and in the company of a good friend, the notorious killer was finally blooming into an amiable, personable young man. Here on Virimonde, David and Kit could be just two more aristos, secure in power and position, idling away the days as it pleased them.

They drifted with the wind, letting it take them where it would. David looked down at the world moving beneath him, and found it good. The stock stretched away in all directions, cared for by peasants who had done so for countless generations. They knew what they were doing; they didn't need any help or advice from their most recent Lord, any more than the animals did. They both knew their place and purpose in the Empire. Elsewhere in his demesne, other peasants were harvesting crops, tending to the land, preparing the landing pads at the only starport for the next ships to arrive. The transports brought in supplies for the people, and carried away crops and meat. Virimonde had been a food planet to the Empire for as long as records had been kept, supplying poor and rich alike with the staples of diet, and the occasional luxury. Nine-tenths of the planet was given over to food production of one kind or another, and the people who lived there would have it no other way. Virimonde might not have the upsets and excitements and glittering cities of other, richer planets, but still it was a calm and peaceful world, where a man could know purpose, the comforts of tradition, and joy of service to Humanity.

They also made the Lord of Virimonde very, very rich. People might argue over territory and war over politics, but both sides still needed to eat, and Virimonde served all impartially. David Deathstalker looked down on his world, and was content. Billions upon billions of credit on the hoof, and all of it his. More money than he could spend in a lifetime. Though that wouldn't stop him trying.

Kit moved in close behind him, playfully bumping the side of his flyer against David's, so that they both wobbled dangerously for a moment. "You've got that look on your face again, Deathstalker. That *Lord of all I survey* look. Soon you'll be busy all day reading reports and worrying over crop yields and export tariffs, with no time for the likes of me. A man old before his time."

"Never!" said David cheerfully. "I employ other people to worry about such things for me. People like the Steward, bless his dour and dutiful heart. The man's about as much fun as a hailstorm in July, and he gets on my nerves something fierce, but he knows his job. And as long as he does, I don't have to. I just sign everything he puts in front of me, read every tenth one just to keep him honest, and leave it all to him. If I'd wanted to work hard, I wouldn't have been born an aristocrat. No, Kit, this place is one big cash cow, making me richer with every day that passes, and all I have to do is sit back and let it happen."

"But what use are riches if you've nothing to spend them on?" countered Kit. "The few big cities they've got here aren't exactly dens of iniquity and vice, are they? Their idea of excitement is cheating in the horse trials. Just what are you planning to do with all these fields and forests?"

"Enjoy them," said David. "Come on, Kit, we tried practically every amusement you could find on Golgotha, and none of them interested us for more than a few weeks at a time. We've gambled in illegal casinos with our lives wagered on the throw of a die, fought in the Arenas against all comers, rogered our way through the Houses of Joy till our backs gave out, and still we ended up bored, as often as not. That's how we got involved in the rebellion. No, we need time off, Kit. Simpler pursuits on a simpler world. I'm tired of civilization. Been there, done that, puked down my shirt and pissed on my boots. I like it here. Nothing to do but eat and drink and grow fat. Booze away the evenings and frolic with lusty peasant girls. Play catch-as-catch-can on flyers for a bit of excitement. I'm having a good time. Aren't you?"

"Yes," said Kit. "Somewhat to my surprise, I am. And I haven't killed anyone for weeks. Amazing. Mind you, we were supposed to act here as agents for the underground, and we haven't sent in a report since we got here. Do you think we should?"

"Certainly not," said David firmly. "That comes under the heading of work, which I have given up for Lent. Easter, Christmas, and any other holiday you can think of. A pox on the underground and Lionstone both. Here we are safe from all factions, and their impertinent demands. Whatever happens in the rebellion, no one's going to touch Virimonde. Whoever wins, they'll still need to eat. Though it must be said I quite liked being a rebel, with secret meetings, hidden agendas, and special passwords."

"Right," said Kit. "I liked the passwords. I liked knowing things other people didn't. But even that got boring after a while. They would take it all so seriously."

"And we have had enough of seriousness," said David. "I think we've earned the right to be entirely frivolous for a while. Nothing to do, no demands, no duties. Just get up when we want, do what we wish, and play to our hearts' content. Like being a kid again."

"I wouldn't know," said Kit. "I never had a childhood. I was raised to be a fighter and a warrior practically from the moment I could walk. I had a dirk instead of a rattle. Dueling partners instead of friends. I had to be as good a swordsman as my famous father and illustrious grandfather, whether I wanted to or not. As it turned out, I was better than either of them. And weren't they surprised when I proved it by killing them both. I enjoyed that. Making them suffer as they'd made me suffer all my life. I was never allowed a childhood, you see. There was no time for frivolous things like play or fun or laughter. Only the endless training and discipline, to shape me for a destiny I never wanted."

"You're starting to sound like my cousin Owen," said David, keeping his voice carefully light. Kit had never opened up so much to him before, and he didn't want to discourage Kit by letting him see how much he was moved.

"Hardly," said Kit. "I used their training to make something of myself. And if I don't always like what I've made, well, that's life for you.

"I'm glad you brought me here, David. I feel . . . free, here. Free from everyone else's expectations of who and what I have to be. It's not easy being Kid Death all the time, you know. There are no pressures here, to do the only thing I've ever been any good at. I suppose that's what childhood is, for other people. I'd like a chance to be a child, at last."

"You got it," said David. "To hell with Lionstone and the underground; it's party time! We can be ourselves here, Kit. No Deathstalker and SummerIsle, no scions of an ancient line, no boosted man or Kid Death; just two friends, free at last."

"It won't last," said Kit. "You know it can't."

"It can if we want it to," said David. "We don't ever

have to leave here, if we don't want to. Do you really miss anything from Golgotha?"

"I still kind of miss the Arenas," said Kit. "The roar of the crowd, the smell of fresh blood on the sands. The clash of steel on steel, and the joy in your heart as an enemy dies at your hand. The sheer seductiveness of testing your skill in the only way that really matters, when your very life is on the line."

"They never liked us," said David. "The crowds. They didn't like the idea that we might be fighting for our own amusement, rather than theirs. And anyway, we'd done all there was to be done in the Arenas."

"Not quite everything," said Kit. "I never did get a chance to face the Masked Gladiator."

"File it under unfinished business," said David.

"I could have beaten him."

"Yeah, you probably could, if his managers had ever let you get anywhere near him, which I doubt. There's got to be a lot of money, not to mention honor, tied up in being the undefeated champion of the Arenas. He was getting very cautious about who he went up against, at the end."

Kit shrugged. David hoped he'd let the matter drop. Though he'd never admitted it to Kit, David had been glad to leave the Arenas. He hadn't liked what they were doing to him. He'd always been good in a fight, and taken an honest pride in it, but out on the bloody sands before a roaring crowd, he'd discovered in himself a dark joy and satisfaction in the act of slaughter that disturbed him greatly. It didn't fit in with the image he'd always had of himself, of the kind of man he wanted to be, and it frightened him. Much as he cared for Kit, he didn't want to become another Kid Death. So he ran away to Virimonde, first chance he got, to try being another kind of man, steeped in peace and the quieter pleasures. And maybe Kit could find a kind of peace here, too, away from the dark needs that drove him.

"Thank you," Kit said suddenly. "For bringing me here. For being my friend. I know it's not easy. I don't always know what to do with a friend. I don't have the experience. For as long as I can remember, there's only ever been me. All I knew was how to kill. No one ever liked me, or trusted me, even when they used me to get them what they couldn't get themselves. I never had a friend before you, David. I was never really alive, until you taught me how to live."

David reached out and clapped a hand on Kit's shoulder, squeezing it reassuringly. "It's too bright a day for such dark thoughts. Forget the past, Kit. No one here cares who you used to be, and no one from our past can reach us anymore. We're free to reinvent ourselves, to be who we want to be. Come on; race you back to the Standing. Loser buys drinks for everyone tonight!"

"You're on!" said Kit and gunned his engine. His flyer plunged forward, rapidly gaining speed. David roared with mock rage, and sped off after him. Together they disappeared into the distance, their laughter sounding clear and happy and untroubled on the quiet summer day.

They parked their flyers in the caves under the Deathstalker Standing, and made their way up through the great old house, arguing amiably about who'd won the race. As always, the result had been so close they finally agreed on a draw. Neither really cared about winning, which was a new experience for both of them. David looked around him approvingly as they strode through the wide stone corridors on their way to the great dining hall. The Standing had been in the Deathstalker Family for generations, on various planets. Owen had had the vast building transferred to Virimonde brick by brick and reassembled there when he bought the planet's Lordship. It was Family tradition that each new head of the Clan chose a new world for his or her Standing, but David couldn't be bothered. Virimonde suited him just fine, and it pleased him to rebel against Family tradition, even if only in such a small way. He didn't want to be just another Deathstalker.

David had spent a lot of time and effort in removing all traces of Owen's presence from the Standing. He was Lord now, and he didn't want anyone being reminded of his predecessor. So he had all of Owen's remaining belongings thrown out or burned, and did his best to fill the many rooms and halls with his own belongings. If truth be told, his own bits and bobs looked rather small and out of place in the great old house, crowded as it was with treasures and trophies from generations of

Deathstalkers, but he wouldn't admit that to anyone but Kit. In the end, all that mattered to David was that the Standing and the world were his now, and by the time he'd finished, no one would remember that there had ever been any other Lord.

They'd almost reached the dining hall when the Steward intercepted them. David took one look at the thick sheaf of papers in the Steward's hand and groaned loudly. He hated paperwork, and made sure the Steward knew it, but still he insisted on dealing with the really important business himself. The Steward could deal with day-to-day things, but David didn't want the man making decisions that were the rightful province of the Lord of Virimonde. He didn't trust the Steward. He'd wasted no time in turning against Owen when the Empress outlawed him, and a man who betrayed one Deathstalker might well betray another.

The Steward was a grey man. Tall, stick-thin, and grey-haired, he wore grey clothes and presented a grey, passionless face to the world. His voice was a respectful murmur, his eyes were always respectfully downcast, but David could never quite escape the feeling that the man was silently mocking him. He seemed to care for nothing but the upkeep of the Standing and his precious never-ending paperwork, and sometimes gave the impression that he considered the Standing his, and the various Deathstalkers who passed through merely visitors. Death-stalkers may come and go, his bearing seemed to say, but I and my people remain. He snacked constantly on little pieces of bread without butter, and cracked his knuckles loudly if you kept him waiting. David detested the man, but tried to keep it to himself. He knew he couldn't run the Standing without him.

"More papers?" he said resignedly. "Can't they wait till after dinner?"

"That's what you said at breakfast, my lord," said the Steward in his calm, grey voice. As always, he made the title sound like an insult. "The various matters here have, if anything, only grown more urgent since then. I must respectfully insist . . ."

"All right, all right," said David. "There's an office just off this corridor, isn't there? We can do it there. And this had better be really important, or I'll have you inventory all the silverware again. Kit, you stay with me. If I have to suffer, everyone suffers."

"Wouldn't miss it for the world," said Kit calmly. "I love to watch the veins throb in your forehead as you struggle with the longer words. Besides, suffering's good for the character. Or so they tell me. I wouldn't know. Anyone who ever tried to make me suffer is dead and buried. Sometimes in several places."

David sat behind the desk in the pokey little study and worked his way doggedly through the paperwork. Some work couldn't be avoided, if you didn't want to wake up one morning and find they'd finessed everything you owned out from under you. He took a spiteful pleasure in making his signature as indecipherable as possible. Strictly speaking, he should have sealed each paper with wax, and stamped it with his Family ring and crest, but Owen still had the ring, bad cess to the man. David had ordered a new Family ring made for him, but had yet to make up his mind on the final design. By the end, he was just skimming through the papers, to make sure he wasn't signing his own death warrant. Too many lines of dense print made his eyes ache. Kit sat off to one side, humming tunelessly. Kit liked to sing, but truth be told couldn't carry a tune if it had handles on it. However, since no one had ever dared tell him that, he remained blissfully unaware that he had a voice like a goose farting in a fog. And David didn't have the heart to tell him. For the moment Kit was amusing himself by staring unwaveringly at the Steward till the man all but squirmed in his buttoned-down shoes. The SummerIsle made the Steward nervous.

Hell, the SummerIsle made everyone nervous.

David signed the last page with a flourish and sat back in his chair with a theatrical sigh. He studied the Steward glumly as the man shuffled the papers together. The Steward reminded him of his many tutors (none of whom lasted long), who'd struggled with varying degrees of success to implant some useful learning into his rebellious young mind. Not a one of whom had ceased to remind him of his intellectual cousin Owen, the famed if minor historian. Owen was constantly held up as an example of everything David wasn't and knew he never could be. No surprise, then, that David had despised his elder cousin before they ever met. They weren't close, even by blood; Owen's father, Arthur, had a younger brother, Saul. Saul married Elouise, whose sister Margaret was David's mother. Under normal circumstances, David would have stood no chance at all of ever succeeding to the Family title, but the tainted inheritance of the boost killed a great many Deathstalkers before they ever reached maturity. So when Owen was outlawed, David found himself suddenly in possession of a title and responsibilities he'd never expected or really wanted.

Especially if all he ever got to do as Deathstalker was sign bloody papers.

The Steward finally nodded curtly, declaring himself satisfied for the moment, and David threw his pen out the window before the Steward could change his mind. "So," he said peevishly, "can I finally go to my dinner now, or is there some scrap of parchment left in the Standing that I haven't scrawled my name on?"

"That is the last of the documents, my lord," the Steward said calmly. "But there is still a delegation of peasants waiting to meet you. You did say you would see them, my lord."

"Did I?" said David, frowning. "I must have been drunk."

"Let them wait till after dinner," said Kit. "That's what peasants are for."

"No, Kit. If I promised, I promised. Where are they, Steward? Main hall? All right, lead the way. And don't dawdle, or I'll kick your ankles."

The Steward gave him a bow calculated to the inch to be barely acceptable and led the way. David and Kit trailed after him. Kit sniffed loudly as his stomach rumbled.

"For my birthday, let me kill him, David."

David had to laugh. "Sorry, Kit, but much as I hate to admit it, I need him. He's the only one here who knows all the ins and out of running a Standing of this size. I wouldn't know where to begin. Replacing him would be a nightmare. He's made himself indispensable, and he knows it, the smug bastard."

"Why are we seeing the peasants? It's not as if we have to."

"Yes we do. Or rather, I do. Partly because I want the locals to like me. Owen could never be bothered with them, which was why he had no one to turn to when the Empress outlawed him. That's not going to happen to me. Then, the more contact and feedback I have with the locals, the less influence the Steward has. I want them looking to me for authority, not him. And finally, of late the peasants have been experimenting with a little local democracy, and I want to encourage them."

"What the hell for?" said Kit, honestly shocked. "Peasants do as they're told. That's why they're peasants. Allowing them to make decisions for themselves is just asking for trouble. Not least from Lionstone. If she finds out . . ."

"She won't do anything, as long as the food keeps coming," David said calmly. "The Empire relies on what we produce, and she knows it. As to why I'm encouraging the peasants, I admire their bravery, and I understand their need for a little personal independence. And it amuses me to think of Lionstone fuming helplessly. Besides, encouraging local democracy will keep the underground off our backs. Don't worry, Kit, I know what I'm doing. Encouraging the peasants and undermining the Steward's authority means I get to hear things I might otherwise not. No one's going to catch me napping like they did Owen."

The meeting went well. The peasants bowed respectfully to David and to Kit, said all the right things, and put forward a few modest proposals. David pretended to consider them for a moment and then gave his approval. Local democracy was alive and well on Virimonde, the Steward was quietly fuming, and as far as David was concerned, all was well with the world. He liked to see the peasants happy and the Steward unhappy. He was, at heart, a man of simple pleasures. The peasants bowed again, satisfyingly deeply, and left, happy and smiling. David allowed himself to think of dinner again. And that was when the Steward sprang his little surprise.

"What do you mean, more business?" snapped David.

"I've signed everything that doesn't move, and talked to everything that does. Whatever's left can wait until after I've eaten, digested, and had a little nap."

"I'm afraid not, my lord," said the Steward, unruffled. "There has been a communication from the Empress herself, concerning her plans for the future of Virimonde. Plans which, I regret to say, will render your assurances to the peasants both redundant and meaningless."

David looked sharply at the Steward. This was the first time he'd heard of any plans for Virimonde's future. Especially from the Empress. He hadn't thought Lionstone even knew where Virimonde was. And as Lord of the planet and its people, he should have been contacted well in advance of any plans. And there had been something in the Steward's tone he hadn't liked at all. Something almost smug, and knowing. David scowled at the Steward, and sank back into his chair. If this was something the Steward didn't think he'd approve of, he wanted to know what it was right now.

"All right, Steward, put it on the main screen. Let's see what the Iron Bitch has to say for herself."

The Steward nodded serenely and moved over to activate the viewscreen controls. The screen lit up on the wall before David and Kit, and the nightmare began. Lionstone provided the voice-over, but the images on the screen were clear enough on their own. Virimonde was to become a completely automated world—one huge factory, from pole to pole. The towns and the villages and the great fields would vanish under miles-long sheds, with the livestock contained in pens, stacked hundreds high. Animals would be born in the cloning bays, live short, artificially fattened lives, and die in the attached slaughterhouses, without ever once seeing the outside world. Fed through tubes, lobotomized to keep them calm, slaughtered by machines. No more need for the countryside. No more need for farms or farmers. The computers would run everything. The peasants would be rounded up, transported to other worlds, and found useful work in factories. The projected meat production would rise thousands fold in the first year alone, and would pay for itself in ten years or less.

And that was Lionstone's plan for Virimonde, a future

with no place in it for human hands. The final scene on the viewscreen was a computer simulation of what the new world would look like. A landscape of endless sheds and factories, with thick black smoke belching up from the slaughterhouse incinerators, as bones and hooves and other nonessentials were melted down to make glue. Nothing would be wasted in the automated world. The screen went blank as the message ended, and the Steward coughed politely to remind them he was still there.

"Any questions, my lord?"

"Is she out of her tiny mind?" said David. "Does she really think I'll stand for this? You can't just destroy an entire world and its culture! The people here have traditions of service that go back centuries!"

"They're just peasants," said the Steward calmly. "Their duty and purpose is to serve, here or elsewhere, as the Empress commands. This new method of raising livestock will be much more efficient. I have the projected figures for the next ten years, if you'd care to see them."

"Stuff the figures! What she's planning is wrong. This is a human world, not some offshoot from Shub."

"You should be proud, my lord. Virimonde is to be the first such planet, the prototype. Once its worth has been proved here, all other food-producing worlds will be transformed accordingly. Your present wealth will be greatly magnified."

"Who cares about that?" said David, sticking his face right into the Steward's. "Where's the fun in ruling over one big factory? No, this obscenity will never happen here. Not as long as I'm Lord."

"What can you do to stop it?" said Kit. "I mean, she's the Empress. She makes the decisions. You argue about it too much, and she might declare you a traitor, just like Owen."

"She wouldn't really destroy a whole planet," said David. "Would she?"

"Almost certainly," said Kit. "It wasn't that long ago she outlawed the planet Tannim, and had the whole planet scorched. Remember?"

David scowled. He remembered. Billions of people had

died, a civilization gone up in flames, at the Empress's command. "That was over politics. This is business."

Kit shrugged. "Same thing, as often as not."

"Yeah," said David. "I know where this is coming from. Why she chose to start with my world. It's because I'm a Deathstalker, and Owen's had such a triumph on Mistworld. She can't get at him, so she takes it out on me, the childish bitch. No, Kit, there's no way I'm going to let her get away with this."

"What can you do?" said Kit, reasonably.

"Nothing, I'm afraid, my lord," said the Steward. His voice was deferential, as always, but David was sure he could see a dark satisfaction in the man's eyes. "The Empress has never had much time for sentiment, and I doubt she will be swayed by any protest you might make. As I understand it, the transformation of food planets is part of a process to ensure an uninterrupted flow of food for the Empire during the projected future war with the aliens. As such, this becomes a matter of security, and is therefore not open to question. By anyone."

"You knew about this!" said David. He grabbed the Steward by the shirtfront with both hands and slammed him back against the wall. "She couldn't have brought her plans this far without consulting you first! She needed facts and figures, the kind only you had access to. Talk to me, damn you!"

"He can't talk," said Kit calmly. "You're throttling him. Ease up, David, and let's hear what he has to say. We can always kill him later."

David let go of the Steward, and stepped back a pace, breathing heavily. The Steward put a hand to his throat as his breath returned, and glared at David, his servility discarded. "The Empress was kind enough to consult with me, yes. I did my best to be useful to her, as was my duty. You weren't informed until now because you had nothing useful to add to the discussion. And because we expected precisely this kind of infantile behavior from you. There is nothing you can do, my lord. Nothing at all."

"I can talk to the Company of Lords," said David. "And Parliament, if need be. I'm not the only one with a personal stake in this. No other Lord will stand for this happening to one of their planets. Where's the fun in being a

Lord, without people to Lord it over? This new efficiency would leave us nothing more than factory managers. Tradespeople! No, the Lords will never accept this. Dammit, I came here for peace and relaxation, not to oversee the transformation of this world into one big battery farm! Get out of my sight, Steward. I'm sick of looking at you."

The Steward bowed coldly and left. David leaned back against the wall, breathing heavily. Kit looked at him thoughtfully.

"Can we really stop her?" he said mildly. "If she makes this a matter of security . . ."

"Well, to start with I'll send her a reply to this message that will make her ears burn. She thinks she can pressure me just because I haven't been a Lord long. We have to stop her, Kit. These plans would undermine every Lord's position. She's trying to take away our power, in return for more money. Well, she's miscalculated this time. Being a Lord has nothing to do with credits in a bank. Our peasants have always been loyal to us first, and only through us to the Empress. They've always been a potential army we could use to defend ourselves against Imperial aggression. Damn, this goes farther than I thought. This is a blow against the fundamental rights and powers of all Lords! With our planets controlled by computers, and our peasants scattered in factories on a dozen worlds, we'd have no real power base at all. If she gets away with this, Lionstone could break the power of the Lords once and for all."

"Not all Lords," said Kit. "Only those Families whose fortunes are tied to people and places. Other Clans, such as the Wolfes, draw their wealth and prestige from technology these days."

"You're right," said David slowly. "This would hit the older, more traditional Families, who tend to oppose the Empress, while strengthening the position of the newer Clans, who tend to support her. Damn, this is complicated. Levels within bloody levels. Oh hell, I can't think any more about this now. I can feel a really bad headache hovering over me."

"Let's go to dinner," said Kit. "The world always looks better after a good meal."

"To hell with dinner, I need a drink. Lots of drinks. Let's go to the tavern in town, and see Alice and Jenny."

"Sounds good to me," said Kit.

High in orbit above Virimonde, unbeknownst to most of those below, the Imperial starcruiser *Elegance*. Her master, General Shaw Beckett, sat unhappily in his private quarters, drumming the fingers of one hand upon the armrest of his chair. If truth be told, he had no appetite for his present mission, but the Empress's orders had been clear and quite specific, and as a good soldier he would do as he was told. It wasn't the first time he'd followed orders he'd had no taste for, and he doubted it would be the last. Life was like that, more often than not, under the reign of Lionstone XIV, the Iron Bitch.

Beckett was a large man, and extremely fat, and his chair groaned slightly under him with every impatient movement. All of his invited guests were late, but there was nothing he could do to hurry them. Too much concern might appear as weakness, and this would be a bad group to appear weak in front of. They'd take advantage. Beckett looked testily about his quarters. He felt like throwing things, but there was nothing easily to hand that didn't have some personal or sentimental value. Beckett liked to surround himself with personal items when he traveled, a little bit of home in a strange place. And if a General wasn't entitled to a few home comforts in his quarters, he'd like to know who was.

He thought about this to keep from thinking about other things. There was a great deal in the near future that he preferred not to think about until he had to.

The door chimed politely, announcing his first visitor. Beckett growled "Enter," and the door slid open to reveal Lord Valentine Wolfe, in all his morbid glory. He was dressed in exquisitely cut clothes of eye-blinding white, topped by a long black cloak with a scarlet interior. His long thin face was white as bone, save for the heavily mascaraed eyes and his wide crimson smile. A mane of jet black hair fell to his shoulders, with heavily oiled and scented ringlets. He carried a long-stemmed rose in one hand, its petals a deep purple, almost fleshy. The stem had vicious thorns that made Beckett wince just to look at them. Valentine stood posed in the doorway a moment, so Beckett could appreciate the spectacle, and then he drifted casually forward into Beckett's quarters. The door slid shut behind him, and Beckett felt a brief but very real twinge of unquiet, as though he was now trapped in a room with a deadly predator. As, in a very real sense, he was.

Valentine looked unhurriedly about him, taking in the various points of interest with his dark-lined eyes, and then dismissed them all with the merest twitch of one painted eyebrow. The Wolfe stopped before Beckett and bowed formally. Beckett nodded curtly in return, but didn't bother to get up. It took a lot of effort to heave all his bulk up out of a chair, and he was damned if Valentine Wolfe was worth it. He gestured at an empty chair with one fat hand, and Valentine sank languorously into it.

"Greetings and salutations, dear General. You've done amazing things with your quarters. I don't like them. But then, my tastes aren't often appreciated by others."

Beckett snorted. "Possibly because you're a drug-soaked degenerate who's so far gone you probably have to flip a coin to decide which way up you are."

"Possibly," said Valentine. "Can I interest you in a little something, General?"

"You can not," said Beckett firmly. "I have no interest in clouding my mind with chemicals when there's work to be done."

"Such a narrow attitude," Valentine said easily, delicately sniffing his rose and briefly worrying a petal with his teeth. "I've often found that the right substances, in the proper proportions and combinations, can be a positive boon to a man's thoughts, leading to greater clarity and comprehension. Many the insight I've been granted, while all around remained lost in darkness. If you could only see the things I've seen, dear General, and the wonders that have been revealed to me. I ride my expanded consciousness like an unbridled horse, trampling lesser souls beneath me. However, for the moment I am entirely at your service, and just dying to hear all about our mission here."

"You'll have to wait for the others to arrive," said

Beckett stolidly, not allowing himself to be baited. "The Empress's instructions were quite clear."

"And God bless the Empress," said Valentine. He swung one long white-clad leg over the other, and let it swing quietly to and fro, the light gleaming on his highly polished boot. It occurred to Beckett that Valentine looked very like a pen-and-ink drawing, of the kind found in an instructional primer, probably with the word *Debauchery* written underneath. Beckett had to admire the Wolf's calm, even if it did probably have its origins in a pill bottle. Ever since the debacle on Technos III, and the total destruction of his new stardrive factory, Valentine Wolfe's fortunes had taken a severe blow. Where once he had been head of the foremost Family in the Empire, with an automatic place at the Empress's side, he was now barely tolerated at Court, and then mostly for amusement value. Production of the new stardrive had been given over to Clan Chojiro, who were having to start again from scratch. This did not please Lionstone, who wanted the new drive installed in the Imperial Fleet yesterday, if not sooner.

The two Wolfes responsible for the Technos III fiasco, Daniel and Stephanie, had disappeared, leaving Valentine to shoulder the blame, which he did with a shrug, a shake of the head, and a charming smile. These things happen. Anyone else would have been ruined and utterly disgraced, and quite possibly no longer as closely connected with his head as he used to be, but Valentine Wolfe was made of sterner stuff than that. He made good all the financial losses out of his own pocket with nary a wince, publicly disowned his missing brother and sister, and fought back with a trump card few had known he had. Valentine, it turned out, had access to a secret source of extremely advanced high tech, and that had bought him his place here today and a chance at redemption in Lionstone's eyes.

Valentine hadn't told anyone that his source for the high tech was actually the rogue AIs of Shub, the official Enemies of Humanity. It would only upset people.

The door chimed again, and opened at Beckett's command to reveal the Lord High Dram, Warrior Prime to the Empire, and official Consort to Lionstone herself. Also known, as far behind his back as possible, as the Widow-maker. Tall and lithely muscled, clad in his usual black robes and battle armor, Dram bowed to General Beckett and nodded curtly to Valentine. Beckett bowed in return. The Wolfe waggled his long white fingers in a friendly way. Dram pretended he hadn't seen that, sank comfortably into the chair farthest from the Wolfe, and stretched out his long legs before him. He was handsome, in an unspectacular way, but his dark eyes and constant slight smile were utterly cold. Like Valentine, Dram had kept pretty much to himself on the trip out, staying in his cabin and speaking only to his own people. Beckett curled a lip mentally. Presumably the Lord High Dram felt himself too grand to socialize with the lower orders. Not that Beckett was complaining. The last thing he needed was the Empress's Consort peering over his shoulder and making notes.

Dram hadn't told anyone that he wasn't, in fact, the original Widowmaker, but instead a clone of the original, grown at the Empress's command. It would only upset people.

"How long before operations begin, General?" said Dram calmly. "I've been informed my people are fully prepared and equipped, and ready for action."

"Soon, my Lord Dram," said Beckett. "This will be your final briefing. We merely await the arrival of the last few principals." The door chimed. "And hopefully, this will be them. Enter."

The door slid open and Captain John Silence, Investigator Frost, and Security Officer V. Stelmach filed in. The Wolfe and the Warrior Prime both sat up a little straighter in their seats. These three officers from the famed *Dauntless* were familiar to anyone in the Empire who owned a holoscreen. Their checkered career had had more ups and downs than a bride's nightie. They'd gone from heroes to outcasts and back again so fast that some people watching had been known to suffer from whiplash. Their current status was somewhat uncertain. On the one hand, they had failed in their mission to capture that most notable traitor and outlaw, Owen Deathstalker, and had been sent home defeated by his rebel allies, but on the other hand, they had quite definitely single-handedly saved the homeworld Golgotha from attack by a mysterious and powerful alien ship. When last heard of, the *Dauntless* had been touring planets on the outer Rim, essentially on punishment duty until the Empress decided to forgive their sins. And now here they were on the *Elegance,* far from their infamous ship. Beckett, Valentine, and Dram bowed courteously to them, and studied them openly. You didn't get to see legends in the flesh that often.

Silence was a tall, lean man in his forties, with thinning hair and a thickening waistline. He didn't look like much on a viewscreen, but at close quarters he had a presence that was almost overpowering. Everyone in the room knew that he was a dangerous man, but now they knew why. There was a calm certainty to the man, a quiet directness. John Silence knew where he was going, and only a fool would have got in his way.

Investigator Frost was in her late twenties, tall and lithely muscular and casually intimidating, like all Investigators. Trained from childhood to study and then kill aliens, or anything else that threatened the Empire. Even standing still and relaxed at her Captain's side, she still looked ready to kill someone. Probably with her bare hands. Cold blue eyes blazed in a pale, controlled face, framed by auburn hair cropped close to the skull. She wasn't pretty, but there was a definite daunting glamour to her, attractive and scary at the same time. She stood at Silence's side, her hands comfortably near her weapons, as though she belonged there, and always had.

After two such godlike beings, a mere mortal like V. Stelmach had to be a disappointment, and he was. A quiet nondescript man, he looked more like some anonymous civil servant than an officer in the Imperial Fleet. Presumably working as a Security Officer did that to you, even on the amazing *Dauntless.* He stood nervously a little behind Silence and Frost, his eyes darting from one new face to another, as though expecting to be sent out at any moment. And yet this unimpressive little man had helped develop tech to control the deadly aliens known as Grendels, and together with Silence and Frost had survived dangerous missions that had killed many lesser men. So there had to be something to the man. Beckett made a mental note to check farther into the man's background. If only to find out what the V. stood for.

He gestured for the three of them to sit down on the remaining chairs, and they did so. Silence and Frost seemed completely relaxed, though Beckett couldn't help noticing that their hands were still casually close to their weapons. Stelmach sat on the edge of his chair, hands clasped tightly together so no one could see them shaking. Beckett cleared his throat to get everyone's attention and wished he hadn't. In this kind of company it made him sound weak and uncertain.

"Now we're all here, I will proceed with the final briefing. You should all have been studying your general orders and objectives on the way here, but this is where you get the big picture. Virimonde is to be taken back under direct Imperial rule from Golgotha, by any and all means necessary. The local populace has been practicing forbidden forms of democracy, making their own policy, deciding their own lives and defying standard Imperial edicts. According to the Steward of the Deathstalker Standing, Virimonde's Lord, David Deathstalker, has proven a weak and ineffectual leader, disregarding his duties and offices, not only failing to stamp out this treason but actually encouraging it. He is declared a traitor, and his Lordship revoked. He is to be removed from office, and along with his companion, the Lord Kit SummerIsle, they are to be brought back to Golgotha to stand trial.

"We expect there to be resistance. The Deathstalker and the SummerIsle are both warriors of some note, and we have reason to believe there has been considerable infiltration of the local populace by rebel agents. The entire population of Virimonde is, therefore, to be pacified and brought under direct Imperial control, by any and all means necessary. There's no way of telling how prepared and armed the populace is, but we must work on the assumption of a worst-case scenario. No chances are to be taken, no quarter offered. This is to be a punitive mission, an example to others. A high death rate is to be expected.

"The Lord Wolfe is in charge of the Imperial war machines, assisted by Professor Wax of Golgotha University. The Professor cannot be with us right now; apparently he doesn't travel well. We can only hope his condition improves once we get him dirtside. The Lord Dram is in charge of the ground troops. A full army of marines and troopers who will take out the population centers and ready them for occupation by further troops. Captain, Investigator, Security Officer, you are personally responsible for capturing the Deathstalker and the SummerIsle, and bringing them back alive, if at all possible. Her Majesty has set her heart on putting them on trial. I will liaise among the three operations, coordinating your efforts. Lord Wolfe, you are to concentrate on the urban areas. Lord Dram, you will deal with the more scattered rural communities. Let's all try very hard not to trip over each other. I want this done by the numbers, calmly and efficiently, and with the minimum necessary bloodshed. This is a punitive mission, but let us not forget that dead peasants can't work. Now, let us discuss the logistics."

The meeting dragged on for some time, as details were made clear, problems raised, and new solutions hammered out. Valentine surprized everyone with his keen grasp of the subject, while Dram seemed surprisingly reticent. Silence and Frost studied the most recent reports on the Deathstalker and the SummerIsle, and their latest known haunts. Stelmach remained silent and just nodded in the right places.

As a major food-production world, Virimonde was too valuable to be scorched, but its people could still be punished. The peasants must know their place, and what would happen to any who tried to rise above it. The wild card in all this was Valentine with his war machines. This would be the first time they had ever been used in a major operation. The Empress had always been intrigued by the potential of war machines, and they'd performed well in practice, but only a few had ever been tried and tested in the fires of battle. Virimonde would change that. And how well they did would decide Valentine's future in the Court and in the Empire.

Eventually the last compromise was agreed on, the last detail ironed out, and they had a war plan everyone could live with. Beckett gave them as brief a pep talk as he could get away with, they all said God bless the Empress in a loud voice, and the meeting broke up. They all bowed more or less respectfully to each other, smiled meaningless smiles, and went their separate ways. Dram back to his troops, Valentine back to his machines, and Silence, Frost, and Stelmach back to their quarters. Silence and Frost were scowling heavily, and Stelmach's stomach hurt. They had no illusions about their particular mission. The Deathstalker and Kid Death were known to be two of the deadliest fighters in the Empire, and overcoming them wasn't going to be easy, never mind bringing them back alive to stand trial. But the three of them had developed a reputation for bringing off the impossible, so they were volunteered for the job. Their reward, should they survive, would be the return of the *Dauntless* from the Rim and reinstatement in the Empress's good graces.

"If it wasn't for my crew, I'd tell the Iron Bitch to go to hell," said Silence, not caring whether the ship's Security was listening. "I don't do suicide missions. To the best of my knowledge, neither the Deathstalker nor Kid Death has ever been defeated in combat. Hell, they took on all comers in the Arenas, until no one would face them anymore."

"They never met us before," said Frost. "We can take them, Captain. Assuming we can locate them before the invasion proper begins, and everything goes to hell in a handcart."

"I wish I shared your confidence," said Stelmach. "I don't even know why the Empress wanted me here."

"You're our lucky charm," said Silence. "Just stay back out of the way, and we'll do all the work."

"Gladly," said Stelmach. He hoped they couldn't tell that he was lying. He knew exactly why the Empress wanted him on Virimonde. For some time now, Silence and Frost had been displaying near superhuman qualities in their missions. They were faster, stronger, and more capable than they had any right to be. Ever since their encounter with the enigmatic alien device known as the Madness Maze on lost Haden, they had demonstrated powers and abilities that bordered on the miraculous. Not to mention psionic. The Empress had no intention of letting rogue espers of such potential run around loose, so this mission, with its many obvious dangers, had been arranged for Silence and Frost, specifically to bring out their powers. And Stelmach would be right there to study and report on them.

He'd been sworn to silence, on fear of his life, and it was tearing Stelmach apart. He thought of Silence and even Frost as his friends, but he couldn't defy orders that came directly from the Iron Throne. So he kept his mouth shut, fretted till his stomach cramped, and tried constantly to discover some way out of his predicament that wouldn't get him killed either by the Empress or his friends. If they had powers, and Stelmach wasn't even convinced that they had, they must have some good reason for keeping it quiet. Stelmach just hoped that when he finally found out what it was, it would be something he'd be able to include in his report. In the meantime, he worried a lot, and jumped whenever Silence or Frost spoke to him.

"What have we sunk to?" Silence said disgustedly. "Paid assassins, in all but name. All that nonsense about bringing them in alive to stand trial was just a smoke screen. They know we'll never be able to defeat them without killing them. We're supposed to kill them to save the embarrassment of bringing two Lords and heads of their respective Families to trial."

"It's our only way of getting our ship back from the Rim," said Frost. "If the price for that is the death of two strangers, I have no problem with that. I've killed before on the Empress's orders, alien and human, and no doubt will again. It's part of the job."

"It was never part of my job," said Silence flatly. "I didn't join the Fleet to kill people for political reasons."

"Then you were remarkably naive, Captain," said Frost. "In essence, that's always been our final duty. To fight and kill those the Empress has declared enemies of the Empire."

"We should be fighting the real enemies," said Silence. "The Deathstalker and the SummerIsle are just a couple of kids with too much time on their hands. Probably never had a political thought in their lives. The Empire's real enemies are the rebel underground. Owen Deathstalker and his people. Lionstone doesn't take them seriously enough. You saw what happened on the Wolfling World. What Owen and his people have become. I don't even know if they're still human anymore. They're the real danger. And that's the only reason I'm doing this. Because we need to be back in a position to protect the Empress from the coming rebellion. She needs us, whether she wants to admit it or not."

"You don't like the Empress," said Stelmach.

"Hell, no one likes the Empress," said Frost. "At best, she's an amiable psychopath. But she's the Empress. I took an oath upon my blood and my honor to serve and protect her all my days. Right, Captain?"

"Right," said Silence. "She might be a psychopath, but she's our psychopath. Our Empress. Besides, she can't live forever, and when she's gone the Empire will still be here, if we've done our job right. In the end, we're loyal to the Throne, irrespective of who sits on it. We preserve the Empire, for all its faults, because all the alternatives are worse. Without the central control of homeworld to keep things running, it would be only too easy for everything to fall apart, and all the worlds slide back into barbarism and mass starvation. And let's not forget the various alien threats out there. We have to be strong and organized, to be able to stand against them when they come. We can't afford luxuries like dissent anymore. Right, Stelmach?"

"What? Oh, yes; right. We have to be loyal. Whatever it costs us."

Valentine Wolfe returned to his quarters alone. They were bare, stark, and characterless, which suited Valentine just fine. At any given time, what was going on inside his head was much more interesting than anything in the outside world. For the moment he had a pleasant buzz going, but nothing more. He had some thinking to do. He sat down in his favorite lounger, and turned on the massage program. He thought best when his body was well taken care of. He pulled one of the thick pulpy petals from his long-stemmed rose, popped it into his mouth and chewed thoughtfully. He and his Family were in deep trouble, and as always it was up to him to dig them out. Clan Wolfe had lost the new stardrive contract when they lost their stardrive factory to the rebels on Technos III, but Valentine still had his secret contacts with the rogue

AIs on Shub. And the unparalleled high tech they provided him had offered a way out of his dilemma. He presented some of it to Lionstone, as a gift to show his worth and loyalty, and then pointed out that his mastery of such tech made him the perfect choice to be in charge of the war machines in their first practical trials. And as simple as that, he was back in favor again.

Of course, his staying in favor depended on how well the machines performed on Virimonde, but he didn't foresee any problems there. He smiled, and purple juice from the rose petal ran down his chin. He was sharp and bright and so in tune with himself he could feel his fingernails growing. Nothing could go wrong. He would succeed. It was his destiny. He was looking forward to seeing what his metal army would do to the poor peasants. There would be blood and fire and death and the destruction of cities, on a scale new even to him. He sighed deeply. Such fun.

Once he'd made a good showing here on Virimonde, Clan Wolfe would be placed in charge of war-machine production, and he could take his place at Lionstone's side again. Where he belonged. He didn't like being a lesser Lord. It offended his delicate sensibilities. And old enemies had been only too ready to crow at his fall from favor. In his apparent weakness they saw a chance for the settling of old scores. Preferably in blood. They were only waiting for him to fail on Virimonde, and then they would be circling him in Court like sharks drawn to the scent of blood in the water. Valentine sniffed. He would remember all their names when he came to power again.

Of course, there were other problems. Ever since the debacle on Technos III, his sister Stephanie and his brother Daniel had been missing. This was both good and bad news. Good, in the sense that they weren't around to stick knives in his back anymore, and bad, in that he couldn't be sure what they were up to now. Daniel had apparently gone off in search of their dead father, last seen as a computer-controlled corpse used as an emissary from the AIs of Shub. It seemed Daniel believed their father was still alive and wished to rescue him. Valentine hoped that Daniel was wrong. He didn't want to have to kill his father again. And after the AIs had killed Daniel, perhaps they could be persuaded to return his body as a Ghost Warrior or a Fury. He'd make a useful ally at Court, without his mind to get in the way.

Stephanie, on the other hand, had disappeared without trace. No one seemed to know where she was, and Valentine found that disturbing. His sister wasn't the sort to be quiet and reflective. Particularly after such a setback. She'd want revenge on someone. Wherever she was, Valentine had no doubt she was plotting trouble for him. It ran in the Family. Though rather slowly in her case. Stephanie didn't have the patience for really intricate plots. For the moment, Valentine had agents out looking for her, with instructions to bring her back to him. Preferably in several small sacks.

The other fly in his ointment was Professor Ignatious Wax, cybernetics expert from the University of Golgotha. He'd been responsible for designing most of the war machines to be used on Virimonde, so Valentine had been forced to accept his assistance. Even though he knew the Professor was really only there to spy on him, to try and learn the source of the revolutionary new tech Valentine had provided. He posed no real threat. There was no way he'd be able to penetrate the mysteries of Shub technology. Even Valentine, with his chemically expanded mind, could do little more than operate the systems. Still, the man had proved to be very irritating, so Valentine had taken steps to ensure that the good Professor wouldn't distract him while he was working down on Virimonde. Very . . . amusing steps. Valentine smiled happily. He would lead his machines to victory on Virimonde, falling upon cities and razing them to the ground, and Lionstone would love him again. And then let his enemies beware.

In his cabin, the man who wasn't really the Lord High Dram paced up and down, scowling. This would be his first attempt at commanding troops in the field, and he wasn't looking forward to it. He'd studied up on it as best he could without raising suspicions, but no amount of theoretical knowledge could substitute for hands-on experience. The original Dram had led troops on many occasions, to great success, but the original Dram had been killed on Haden, also known as the Wolfling World. Now his clone had to carry on the role, lest anyone suspect the truth. He had to be Dram, do as he did. He was in charge of the pacification of the peasants, and Lionstone had made it very clear that he had to be successful, whatever the cost. Rather hard on the peasants, but it was their own fault for getting ideas above their station.

The man now known as Dram sighed deeply and sat down. The day had barely begun, and already he was having to run as fast as he could just to stay in place. He had to stay on top of everything, learning by doing, while giving every appearance of being an experienced man of war. It didn't help that his own men distrusted him anyway. Apparently the original Dram had been something of a monster, hard and unyielding, and always ready to sacrifice his own men if that was what it took to ensure victory. That was how he'd first acquired the whispered nickname Widowmaker. The new Dram wasn't sure he felt that way. Certainly he didn't approve of throwing away lives. But if he didn't act that way, or at the very least appear to, people might begin to suspect that he wasn't who he was supposed to be. There were already rumors in Court . . . And if he was ever revealed as a clone, his short life would come to an abrupt and violent end. A clone replacing a man of influence and power was one of the Lords' worst nightmares.

However, if he could bring this off—pacify the peasants, regain control of food production, and lead his troops to victory in the sight of all—Lionstone had promised he would be rewarded with the Lordship of Virimonde. David Deathstalker had forfeited that right the moment he allowed the beginnings of local democracy on his world. It wouldn't be much of a Lordship; Lionstone had plans for Virimonde that would make the Lordship little more than an honorary title. But for all Dram's standing at Court as Warrior Prime and official Consort, he'd always known that a Lord without a holding wasn't really a Lord. Virimonde would change all that. And the changes in store would eventually make him one of the richest men in the Empire. So he had a lot to play for.

He leaned back in his chair and closed his eyes. He wished he could make the rest of his world disappear so easily. Valentine Wolfe's presence was a problem he

could have done without. The Wolfe and the original
Dram had dabbled secretly in the Golgotha underground,
and had something of a shared history of which he, the
clone, knew very little. Every time he spoke with Valentine he risked giving himself away by not recognizing a
veiled reference, or a shared experience, so for the most
part he kept a careful distance between himself and the
Wolf, and let Valentine suppose what he would. A certain
coldness was to be expected, since the original Dram had
betrayed the underground to Golgotha Security forces. But
what else might Valentine know about the original Dram
that his clone didn't? The original Dram had left extensive
diaries, but there were naturally many things he'd had the
sense or the caution not to put on tape, where they might
be found and used against him. Dram sighed, heavily. Life
as a clone was complicated enough, without your original
being a devious, scheming, two-faced bastard.

The journalist Toby Shreck, known in happier days as
Toby the Troubadour, together with his cameraman
Flynn, arrived on the planet Virimonde inside a large
wooden crate marked *Machine Parts*. The ride down from
orbit in the dark and very cold hold of a cargo ship was an
escalating nightmare of bumps and bruises. Toby sat
curled into a ball, hugging his knees to his chest, head
hunched down to keep from banging it on the low roof,
clung grimly to the handholds provided, and distracted
himself by mentally composing really unpleasant obituary
notices for the bastards who'd come up with this brilliant
idea for sneaking him onto Virimonde.

It was his own fault, really. After the trauma, tears, and
hard bloody work of covering three war zones in a row,
Toby and Flynn had asked plaintively for a story they
could cover without getting shot at. The underground
council offered them a rustic farmworld in the back of
beyond, well away from any fighting, and Toby and Flynn
had a race to see who could say yes the fastest. The mission seemed straightforward enough, for once. Make a
study of the peaceful rustic society of Virimonde, currently menaced by the growing mechanization of farm-
worlds. Show centuries-old traditions under threat, the
livelihoods of helpless people being swept aside by an

uncaring Empire administration—that sort of thing. It was the kind of story Toby could have done standing on his head, but he had a few private reservations. In his experience, long-established rural communities tended toward inbreeding, in people and ideas. You ended up with societies that resisted all change, good or bad, and families with less than the usual number of eyes, one thumb among the bunch of them, and room-temperature IQs. Favorite sports: coveting thy neighbour's ox, throwing cats off high buildings to see if they'd land on their feet, and witch burnings. Or journalists, if there wasn't a witch handy. But even with all of that, Virimonde had to be better than Technos III, Mistworld, or Haceldama. So Flynn packed some of his laciest underwear, Toby made plans for extensive relaxation and as little actual work as he could get away with, and they boarded ship for Virimonde. And Toby got his first impression that things were going terribly wrong when the Captain took them down to the cargo hold and showed them the large wooden crate with the words *Machine Parts* stenciled on the side.

After an eternity of darkness, muttered curses, and the occasional uncertainty as to which way was up, the cargo ship finally touched down. There was a long, nerve-straining wait, and then the crate was unloaded and dropped onto the ground with what seemed to Toby like entirely unnecessary force, and there was the sound of the ship departing. Toby waited in the dark, sweating nervously. A little light streamed through the cracks in the crate, but there was no telling where they'd ended up, or if friendly hands were anywhere near. For all Toby knew they could be surrounded by a crowd of heavily armed customs officers with no sense of humor. The crate shook suddenly as crowbars attacked the lid, and then the top was suddenly prised open and put aside. Bright sunlight poured in. Toby raised an arm instinctively to shield his face, eyes streaming under the impact of the new light. A calloused hand grasped his and pulled him to his feet, and Toby found himself looking at a grinning, friendly face. Toby could have kissed him, but didn't. He didn't want to give Flynn ideas.

It was early evening on Virimonde, with dark shades of red among the darkening clouds above. Twilight was fast approaching, and the cooling air had a hushed, muted feel. Toby and Flynn walked up and down outside the Daker farmhouse, getting the cramps out of their backs and legs. The air smelled wonderfully clear and unpolluted, unless you counted the rich underscent produced by various surrounding animals and their scattered dung. The farmhouse was a large, blocky stone building with primitive guttering and a thatched roof, so old that no one in the present family could remember exactly how old it was. Toby just knew, without having to be told, that this was the kind of place that only had an outside toilet. He smiled at the farmhouse and made polite comments, while privately thinking it looked drafty as hell.

The surrounding countryside wasn't exactly what he'd been hoping for, either. It was mainly moorland, with white and purple heather; grazing land for the countless animals spread out between the farmhouse and the far horizon. It looked pleasant enough, but decidedly bleak. Not at all the kind of place you could hope to get much sunbathing done. Toby sighed inwardly and paid attention to his hosts. Adrian Daker, the head of the family, was a short, round fellow with close-cropped grey hair, knowing blue eyes, and a constant friendly smile wrapped around a clay pipe. His voice had only a trace of a rustic burr, and his face had all the usual features, in all the correct places. His wife was a large fat woman called Diana, with red cheeks, freckles, and hair so red it all but glowed. She was positively bursting with life and hospitality, and cheered Toby despite himself with promises of as much good country cooking as he could eat.

When Toby and Flynn were finally able to stand up straight without wincing, the Dakers led them into the farmhouse kitchen and sat them down at the table. Adrian and Diana then bustled around, getting a hot meal ready. Adrian covered the heavy wooden table with a blindingly white tablecloth, and shyly set out what was obviously the best plates and cutlery, only used for guests. Diana hovered over her black-iron oven like a mother hen, lifting saucepan lids to check the contents, and assuring Toby and Flynn that she'd have had a hot meal ready and waiting for them, but the underground had been very vague as to when they'd be arriving. Toby could

understand that. The rebel council had never impressed
him with their efficiency.

He sat back and looked happily around him. The
kitchen was small without seeming cramped, and comfortably warm and cosy. Shelves on the walls were
packed to bursting with a lifetime's collection of knick-
knacks, obviously hand-made, some of them astonish-
ingly cute and vulgar. Adrian produced a stone jar of
thick dark cider and poured generous doses into porcelain
mugs shaped like fat old men. Adrian explained that these
were known as Toby jugs, and they all laughed, though
Toby didn't see the point of the joke at all.

Several animals shared the kitchen with the humans,
apparently through long right and custom. There were
three dogs with grey-and-silver muzzles, too old now to
guard or control sheep, half a dozen cats of various
snootiness, and a couple of daft chickens who wandered
round bumping into things. These latter took an inordi-
nate interest in Toby and Flynn's ankles, pecking at them
in a curious way, until Diana stopped what she was doing
to put the chickens' heads under their wings. They
promptly assumed that because it was now dark it must be
night, and went to sleep where they stood. The dogs
sniffed hopefully at the smells of cooking in the air, but
were too well trained to make nuisances of themselves.
One of them came up to Toby, sat down before him,
pawed at his leg, then put his head on Toby's knee to have
his head scratched. Toby did so, cautiously. He didn't
have much experience with animals at close quarters. But
the dog's tail thumped heavily against the stone floor, so
he assumed he must be doing it right. In fact, he rather
liked it. Flynn had won over the cats, and two snuggled in
his lap while a third perched on his shoulder. Flynn talked
cheerful nonsense to them, and they purred back happily.
What worried Toby was that the damn things appeared to
be listening.

The meal finally arrived, simple food, lots of it, piping
hot. Toby thought it was the best he'd ever had, and said
so loudly, which earned him another large helping. He
demolished that in record time, too, and was seriously
considering the possibility of a third, when the dessert
arrived. Heavy chocolate sponge pudding, with thick

white chocolate sauce. Toby thought he'd died and gone to Heaven. Eventually he reached the point where even he couldn't eat any more. He sat back, undid his belt another notch, and sighed happily. This was looking to be a great assignment. Adrian Daker grinned at him.

"Soon as I saw you, I knew you were a man who liked his food. Don't you worry, son; the wife'll feed you up good and proper while you're here. She loves to see her cooking being properly appreciated."

"Quite excellent," said Flynn, from under his cats. He'd eaten one helping of everything, and was quietly content.

"And this is just part of what we stand to lose, if mechanization continues," said Adrian seriously. "This kind of life. Simple food and simple pleasures, no less important for that. Our whole way of life is under threat, if the rumors are true. I hope you'll make that clear in your report."

"Delighted to," said Toby. "I think we'll start with some footage of you and your family working the farm. How many of you are there?"

"Seven sons, three daughters," Diana said cheerfully. "Good strapping lads and bonny lasses. The boys are still out working the land; you'll meet them later. Liz and Megs work in town, but they'll drop by tomorrow to say hello. Good-looking girls, if I do say so myself. Be married already, if they weren't so choosey. I don't suppose either of you two gentlemen . . ."

"Leave them alone, Mother," said Adrian, his eyes crinkling. "That's not what they're here for. There's one other daughter, Alice, but I don't expect you'll see much of her. She's taken up with the young Deathstalker and spends most of her time in his company."

"What's he like?" said Toby. "He's one of the things we were sent here to cover."

Adrian shrugged and began packing the bowl of his pipe with dark aromatic strands of tobacco. "Seems harmless enough. Handsome, rich, and luckily for us, mostly uninterested in interfering in the way things are. Best we could hope for, I suppose. Bit of a feather in our cap, that he's taken a shine to our Alice."

"They don't want to know about that, Father," said Diana, leaning forward in her chair and resting her heavy arms on the old wood table. "They want to know what we've been doing with democracy here. That's what got the Golgotha underground interested in us, right? Thought so. We began trying our luck when Owen was the Death-stalker, seeing what we could get away with. Owen didn't care. He wasn't much, in those days. He was happy with his mistress and his studies, and didn't want to be both-ered with us. Steward wasn't too keen, but without Owen's backing he couldn't do anything. We began small, adding one small victory to another, until we reached where we are today. We have regular elections for town offices, and most of the decisions about farming and livestock are made at the local level. We've all been making a lot more money since we started making our own deals with the shipping companies. We run our own lives now, as much as that's possible in the Empire these days. Steward isn't happy, but David Deathstalker's actu-ally been encouraging us. Though I'd be surprised if he knew half of what goes on out in the towns and the farm-lands. He and his young friend the SummerIsle are more interested in hunting, drinking, and wenching. Not neces-sarily in that order."

She and her husband shared rich chuckles over that. Toby wasn't so sure. "Tell me about the SummerIsle."

Adrian frowned for the first time. "Damned if we know what to make of that one, eh Mother? Good-looking. Polite. Doesn't throw his weight around more than you'd expect. But . . . he's a cold one. Hard to tell what's going on inside his head. He came here once, with David, to pick up our Alice. The dogs took one look at the Summer-Isle and hid under the table. Wouldn't come out till he'd gone. I felt a bit like joining them, to be honest. There was something about his eyes, like he'd just as soon kill me as not. Wouldn't surprise me if there was bad blood in that one."

"At Court they call him Kid Death," said Flynn quietly. "The smiling killer."

"Can't say as I'm surprised," said Adrian. He scowled, searching for the right words. "It's not like he's done any-thing, or said anything, that a man could take offense to, but . . . he's a dangerous man, or I never saw one. Don't know what the Deathstalker sees in him, but they seem close enough. Always together."

"Bit too close, if you ask me," said Diana.

"Now, Mother . . ."

"Do you think the Deathstalker will object to our presence here?" said Toby.

Adrian raised an eyebrow. "I thought he was supposed to be sympathetic to the underground?"

"He was. But he's . . . distanced himself, of late. I suppose being given absolute control over an entire planet will do that to you."

"I doubt he'll interrupt his play just because you're here," said Diana. "But I think we'd better keep the Steward distracted till you're gone. He's a hard man. An Empire man, through and through. Bows to everything with a title, and lords it over us like he was a blue blood himself. Thinks he's better than us. Damned fool. I can remember him growing up on a farm not twenty miles from here. No, you two just get on with your work. We'll see you're not interfered with."

"Look forward to seeing it, when it's finished," said Adrian. "The wife and I are big fans of yours. Very impressed we were, with your Technos III coverage."

"You saw that?" said Flynn, quietly discouraging another cat from climbing up on his head.

"We've got a holoscreen," said Adrian. "You're not out in the sticks here, you know."

A loud chiming came from the next room. Adrian and Diana looked round startled. "Speak of the Devil. That's the underground's signal," said Adrian. "Means there's a message coming in. Can't say I was expecting anything."

"I expect they just want to speak with these two," said Diana. "Make sure they got here in one piece."

"No doubt, Mother. I'll just check."

He got up and went into the next room, calmly puffing on his pipe. When he returned a few moments later, the pipe was in his hand, and the peacefulness was gone from his face.

"You'd better come through," he said to Toby and Flynn. "They want to talk to you. Mother, call the boys in. We'd best prepare. Word is bad things are coming."

Diana got up without a word and headed for the outside

door. Toby and Flynn dumped their various cats and dogs
and followed Adrian into the next room, where a large
holoscreen covered half a wall. An unfamiliar face looked
out of the screen at them, stern to hide his worry.

"Shreck, Flynn, you have to leave, now. It's not safe for
you anymore."

"Why?" said Toby. "What's happened? Have the
Dakers been compromised? Does the Empire know we're
here?"

"None of that matters anymore," said the face. "The
shit is about to hit the fan for all of Virimonde, if it hasn't
already begun. Leave, while you still can. Empire troops
will be hitting ground anytime now, all over the planet.
The Stevie Blues are already dirtside, to represent us to
the local rebels. They should be heading in your direction;
see if you can hook up with them. If not, try to get to the
Standing. Maybe the Deathstalker can protect you till we
can arrange safe passage offworld for you."

"But why?" said Toby. "What's happening?"

The face looked tired and drawn, as though all his
strength was leaking out of him. "The Empress has outlawed David Deathstalker, for allowing his peasants to
experiment with democracy. The entire planet is to be
placed under martial law, by any and all means necessary.
The populace is considered to be in rebellion. Every man,
woman, and child on Virimonde is to be placed under
constraint, and then tried, exiled, or executed. Not necessarily in that order. Three Imperial starcruisers are already
in orbit over Virimonde. More are on their way. Troops
are already landing. And the Empress has authorized
extensive use of war machines. It's going to get hard and
vicious and bloody, real soon now. Get out of there.
Now."

The screen went blank. In the kitchen the dogs were
barking loudly, sensing the excitement and alarm. Toby
and Flynn looked at each other. "Well," said Flynn, trying
hard to sound casual. "So much for our trying to avoid a
war zone. Do we head for the Standing?"

"I guess so. The Stevie Blues could be anywhere, and
the Standing isn't that far from here. Maybe we can get
some good footage of the fighting along the way. Just so

this mission isn't a complete failure. You know, just once, I'd like things to go the way I planned them."

Flynn shrugged. "That's life. Our life, anyway. We'd better say good-bye to our hosts and get moving. We've no way of knowing how near the troops are."

They went back into the kitchen. The dogs were running around excitedly. The cats were perched on high shelves, watching everything with wise, experienced eyes. Adrian Daker had pushed the heavy table aside and opened up a concealed trapdoor in the floor. There were wooden steps, leading down into a secret cellar. Adrian was emerging from the dark hole with an armful of weapons. He nodded calmly to Toby and Flynn, and dropped the weapons on the table, next to those he'd already brought up. There were lots of them, mostly projectile weapons and boxes of ammunition, with a few hand energy weapons. Set on a farmhouse table they looked pretty impressive, but Toby knew they were nothing compared to an invading army backed up by war machines.

"Better get out of here boys," said Adrian. "It'll be getting noisy around here soon. It seems the rebellion's started a little early."

"Will you be safe here?" said Toby.

"Safe as anywhere," said Adrian, stripping guns of their protective coverings with quick, professional movements. "They'll need an army to storm this place. And with Mother and our boys beside me, the Empire will pay dearly in blood and suffering for the taking of our land. This has been Daker land for countless generations, and they'll not take it from us while there's a bullet left to fire, or a Daker left to fire it. Go, now, while it's still quiet. Head due north from here, and that'll take you to the Standing. You'll find a flyer in the stables behind the house. Energy crystals are a bit low, but they should get you most of the way there. Stay low, and try and keep out of sight. The locals won't know who you are. You might end up getting shot at by both sides. Good luck, boys."

The outer door burst open and Diana came rushing in, her eyes wide. She gestured urgently with the comm unit in her hand. "I can't raise the boys! The channel's open, but none of them are answering!"

From far away in the distance came the sound of an explosion, followed almost immediately by another. They all hurried outside, Adrian grabbing a gun from the table. Outside in the farmyard, twilight was falling. The sound of energy guns discharging was clear and plain in the quiet. Out on the heathered moor, the animals were running confusedly this way and that. Far away, someone was screaming. Diana Daker moved to stand close beside her husband, who was hugging his gun to his chest like a talisman.

"My boys," said Adrian Daker. "My poor boys . . ."

David Deathstalker and Kit SummerIsle, those two most dangerous men, lay sleeping on the floor of the Heart's Ease tavern. Some kind souls had draped their cloaks over them like blankets, but they hadn't stirred enough to notice. The Deathstalker was murmuring quietly and grinding his teeth in his sleep, perhaps disturbed by some dream. The SummerIsle slept peacefully, his face as unconcerned as an innocent child's. Which would no doubt have amused him greatly, had he known. Sitting not far away at a long wooden table, nursing almost empty mugs of ale, two good-looking young women studied the sleeping men with good-natured tolerance. They were Alice Daker and Jenny Marsh, girlfriends of the slumbering swains.

Alice was a tall and slender redhead with a magnificent bosom. Or, as David liked to say, a balcony you could do Shakespeare from. She had a wide smile, dancing eyes, and enough patience to put up with the Deathstalker's sense of humor, which could be somewhat basic on occasion. She was wearing the very best silks, enough jewelry to open her own shop, and the very latest in fashion and makeup, all courtesy of the Deathstalker. She was a good listener, an indefatigable dancer, and knew all the words to the best drinking songs, especially the dirty ones.

Her friend Jenny was tall, ghostly pale, and raven-haired, with sharp features and a sharper tongue. She had a slender, almost boyish figure, and enough nervous energy to run a small city. She also wore the very best in fashion and its expensive accessories, courtesy of the SummerIsle. She smiled often, laughed rarely, and was forever alert and watchful for the main chance. Which for the moment seemed to be Kit SummerIsle.

It was early in the morning, almost three a.m. The end of another long evening of drinking, carousing, and generally having as much fun as a body can stand. Since the Deathstalker was paying, they hadn't lacked for friends to join them in their festivities, but one by one drink or exhuastion had claimed the revelers, and they staggered out of the tavern doors in the general direction of home. The tavern owner finally gave up about two a.m., locked the place up, and went to his bed, leaving the remaining revelers to take care of themselves. It wasn't the first time this had happened, and also, it wasn't as if he had to worry about them cleaning out the till. Eventually even David's and Kit's hardened constitutions had given up the ghost and demanded sleep. So rather than make the long journey home, puking over the side of the flyer and arguing over directions, they just crashed out on the floor and went to sleep. Alice and Jenny, having paced their drinking through long experience, were now in that happy and contemplative stage of drunkenness where lying down and going to sleep involved too much effort. And so they sat and talked quietly together over the last of the booze, perhaps a little more openly than they otherwise might have.

"God, I'm hungry," said Alice. "Do you suppose there's any food left behind the bar?"

"If there is, I wouldn't touch it," said Jenny. "I don't know what he puts in his meat pies, but you never see any rats around here. His bread rolls bounce, his soup has things floating in it, and his bar snacks are the kind of things that start wars. I think he breeds them in dark corners, when no one's looking."

"His ale's good. And his wine. And his brandy."

"Should be, for the prices he charges."

"What do you care?" said Alice, grinning. "None of this is coming out of our pockets."

"True," said Jenny. "Very true. I suppose the boys do have their uses."

They looked over at the sleeping pair. Alice fondly, Jenny entirely unmoved. Kit farted in his sleep. Neither of the girls flinched.

"He's all right, is David," said Alice finally. "He's good-looking, considerate when he thinks of it, and rich as hell. And he's always there for me. He isn't always going on about the local elections, or the rebellion, as though they meant anything in a backwater dump like this. He isn't all work and duty and politics. He's good times, and laughs, and a bit of fun now and again. Why can't the local boys be like that?"

"Peasants," said Jenny dismissively. "They don't appreciate us. Never have. None of them can see past the next lambing, or the next harvest. They don't care about style, or sophistication, or any of the things that really matter. And none of them know how to treat a girl like a lady. God, I hate this place! I want out of here, out of this dump, this town, and off this whole stinking planet. Kit's taking me to Golgotha. He doesn't know it yet, but he is. He's my ticket out of here."

"I don't know how you can stand to be near him," said Alice. "I mean, he's David's friend, so he must have some good in him somewhere, but I swear, sometimes I look at him and I just go all gooseflesh. He's trouble. Dangerous. They say he killed a lot of men in the Arena."

"So did David," said Jenny. She drank the last of her ale and slammed the mug down on the table. "God, I'd love to go to the Arena! See men fight and die for my pleasure. Right there, in the flesh, not on the screen. And Kit's not so bad, really. He's generous enough, and he doesn't make any demands on me. A bit kinky in bed, but then, he's an aristocrat. Not that I mind. I could teach him a thing or two."

"Kinky?" said Alice, grinning. "What do you mean?"

Jenny grinned back at her. "Well, let's just say Kit's always glad to see the back of me."

"Jenny!" Alice tried to look shocked, but couldn't hold it. They giggled together, shooting glances at the boys to make sure they were still safely asleep.

"What about David?" said Jenny, eventually. "Any little . . . likes or dislikes?"

"Not really," said Alice. "I don't think he's had much experience with girls, to be honest. He can go all shy at the strangest moments. But I think he cares for me. I mean, really cares for me. The dear."

"Kit doesn't," said Jenny. "For which I am decidedly grateful. Emotions would only complicate our relationship. I'm out for what I can get from him, and he knows it. We have good times, good sex, and no demands either way. I don't think Kit would know what to do with love, or even affection, anyway. Probably just confuse him."

"He's very close to David," said Alice, frowning slightly. "As much as David likes me, even loves me sometimes, there's a closeness between him and Kit that I can't even touch. It's like . . . neither of them ever really had a friend before. Still, I'm the one David really cares for. I'm the one he's going to marry. Even if he doesn't know it yet."

Jenny looked at her sharply. "Marriage? Forget it, girl. Forget it. A peasant girl and a Lord, the head of his Family? That kind of thing only ever happens in bad soaps on the holoscreen. We're not marriage material, Alice. We're good-time girls, with all that implies. Out for a few laughs and whatever goodies we can pick up along the way. Aristos might party with girls like us, but they never marry us. They only breed with their own kind."

"Well, all right, maybe not marry, exactly," said Alice. "But I could be his mistress. Concubine. Whatever the polite word is these days. Aristos marry for politics or Clan-breeding reasons, not for love. It's all to do with alliances and advantages and preserving bloodlines. Never love. Some other woman might have his name, but I'd still have his heart."

"Even if he isn't that good in bed?"

"I could teach him," said Alice.

"Does that mean I'm not really your little stud muffin?" said David.

The girls looked round sharply to see David sitting up on one elbow and looking at them blearily.

"How long have you been awake?" said Alice sternly.

"Long enough," said David. "Very revealing, what girls talk about when they think no one's listening."

"What about Kit?" said Jenny. "Is he still asleep?"

"Who can sleep with all this talking going on?" said the SummerIsle, sitting up and running his fingers through his tangled hair. He smacked his lips a few times and grimaced. "I swear every night something crawls into my mouth and dies. I need another drink."

"No you don't," said Jenny sternly. "Go back to sleep and sleep off what you've had first."

"Do you really care for me?" said David, looking at Alice somewhat owlishly.

"Yes," said Alice, smiling. "Haven't I said so often enough?"

"I need to hear it," said David. "I'm really very insecure."

"All men want to be loved," said Jenny. "It's a very profitable weakness."

"I don't," said Kit. "Wouldn't know what to do with love if I had it."

"Yes, but you're weird," said David.

The two boys grinned at each other, threw aside the cloaks covering them, and got somewhat stiffly to their feet. They were caught in that muddy serene haze between the drunk and the hangover. They sat down beside their respective girls and poured themselves ale from the jug in the middle of the table. It was warm and flat, but life's like that sometimes. The tavern bar seemed cool and calm and clear, divorced from the world, adrift in the early hours of the morning between dark and light. David took a large gulp from his mug and pulled a face.

"God, this stuff is rough. I swear my palate goes slumming every time I set foot inside this place."

"Where's everyone gone?" said Kit. "I was just getting started. I could go all night if I wanted to. I could use a little action."

"I'm here," said Jenny.

"I mean real action. I miss the fighting and dueling we had on Golgotha. No one here worth fighting. What's the point in being the best there is with a sword, if I never get a chance to show it off?"

"Who says you're the best?" said David. "You may have all the tricks, but I have the boost."

"One of these days we'll have to find out," said Kit.

"Yeah," said David. "One of these days."

They grinned at each other and drank more ale. "Be honest," said David. "Didn't you get enough bloodshed in the Arenas? I mean, we got through a hell of a lot of opponents in our short time on the bloody sands."

"It's never enough," said Kit. "Still, there are . . . distractions, here."

"Glad to hear it," said Jenny. She put an arm around Kit's shoulders, and he smiled at her.

"We could always go back to Golgotha. Just for a visit," said David. "See if we could scare up some action in the Arenas. There's always some poor fool who thinks he's good with a sword."

"What about us?" said Jenny.

"What about you?" said Kit.

"If you're going, we want to go, too," said Alice.

"You wouldn't like it," said David.

"Why?" said Jenny, bristling. "Because we're peasants? Because we're not sophisticated enough to show off to your precious friends and Families?"

"Well, yes, basically," said Kit.

"Screw you," said Jenny.

"Maybe later," said Kit.

"You could teach us all we need to know," said Alice. "Oh please, David. I've always wanted to go to homeworld."

"We'll see," said David. "Maybe if you're good."

"Oh, I'm very good," said Alice. "Remember?"

They grinned at each other. Jenny glared at Kit, who stared calmly back. The conversation could have gone in any number of directions, and probably would have, if a starship hadn't crash-landed right outside the tavern. The first those inside knew of its coming was a long, descending scream of straining engines, high up in the sky above the tavern. The four of them got rather unsteadily to their feet, opened a window, and looked out. The air was bracingly cool and sobering, the sun barely up. The grey skies were splashed with blood. And down through the clouds a ship came howling, with its outer hull on fire.

"Who the hell is that?" said Alice.

"Can't see any markings on it," said Kit calmly. "It's not one of yours, is it, David?"

"Don't think so. It hasn't got my crest on it. Besides, no one's supposed to know I'm here. Whoever that is, it's coming down at one hell of a pace. It occurs to me we might be a damn sight safer if we were to get away from the window. If that ship crashes anywhere near here, there's going to be wreckage and shrapnel flying in all directions."

"I think it's still under control," said Jenny. "More or less."

The blazing craft swept over the tavern, the roar of its engines deafening at close quarters. The floor shook under their feet, and streams of dust and sawdust fell down from the beamed ceiling. They all ducked instinctively, but by the time they'd reacted, the craft had turned around and headed back again. The engines cut in and out, and then it dropped from the sky, crashing as much as landing in the courtyard outside the tavern. The ground shuddered under the impact, throwing the four observers off their feet. David got to his feet first, unlocked the main door, and hurried outside. He had some confused thought about hauling any injured out of the crashed ship, but the moment he got outside the door the heat from the blazing craft stopped him dead. He threw an arm to protect his face, feeling sweat pop out all over him. He tried to force himself forward, but his body wouldn't obey him, flinching away from the awful heat. A hand grabbed him from behind and pulled him back into the tavern. Someone else slammed the door shut, cutting off the heat.

"Forget it," said Kit, letting go of his arm. "No one's getting out of that alive."

"The hell they aren't," said Jenny from the window. "You've got to see this."

The others hurried over to join her at the window. Outside in the courtyard, flames from the ship were rising higher than the tavern. But someone inside the craft had opened the emergency escape hatch, and two figures were emerging. As David and the others watched, the flames seemed to draw back from the hatch. Two women with the same face dropped down onto the blackened stones of the courtyard and headed for the tavern, apparently entirely unaffected by the blazing inferno around them.

"I know that face," said Kit. "It's the Stevie Blues."

"How the hell are they doing that?" said Jenny.

"They're clones, aren't they?" said Alice excitedly. "I've never seen clones before!"

"If they've come looking for us, we could be in

trouble," David said quietly to Kit. "We owe the underground a lot of reports. It's entirely possible the rebel council might have decided we need persuading to follow the party line."

"Or, given that we know a lot about rebel plans, the Blues could have been sent to silence us," said Kit. "Good thinking, David. I'll make a paranoid out of you yet."

"Okay," said David. "This place has a back door. I suggest we use it. Now."

"What is it?" said Jenny. "Do you know these people?"

"I don't run from anyone," said Kit to David, ignoring her. "Besides, there are only two of them."

"Two battle esper firestarters are more than enough to reduce this place to ashes, along with anyone stupid enough to be inside it when they get here. Those are elves, Kit. Esper Liberation Front. The radical fringe of the radical fringe. The only time they take hostages is when they're feeling hungry."

"We can take them," said Kit.

"Fine. You take the one on the left, and I'll take to my heels. We can't fight, Kit; we have the girls to think of. All right, plan B. We'll talk them to death. No one ever accused the Stevie Blues of being particularly bright. Impulsive, psychotic, and more deadly than a Hadenman in a really bad mood, but not bright. If we keep our wits about us, I may be able to talk our way out of this."

Kit sniffed. "I'd much rather kill them."

"I know you would," said David. "That's your answer to everything. But your normal tactics aren't going to be much use against someone who can melt your sword just by looking at it."

"Good point," said Kit. "All right, you talk to them. I'll see if I can sneak round behind them, just in case."

"Sounds like a plan to me," said David.

"Hold everything," said Alice. "Do you know these people? I heard the word underground. Are they rebels?"

"Cool," said Jenny. "I always wanted to meet some outsider rebels."

And then everyone fell silent as the door swung open and two rebels with the same face stepped into the tavern. Young women in battered leathers with metal studs and dangling chains, over a grubby T-shirt bearing the legend

Born To Burn. They were both short and stocky, with muscles bulging on their bare arms. Their long dark hair was full of brightly colored knotted ribbons, and there were splashes of matching colors on their faces. They might have been pretty, if it hadn't been for their shared frown and the stern, dangerous look in their eyes. They nodded briefly to the Deathstalker, glared intimidatingly at the SummerIsle, and ignored the two girls.

"I'm Stevie One," said the woman on the left. "This is Stevie Three. Don't get us confused, or we'll get cranky about it."

"Right," said Stevie Three. "We're really quite different once you get to know us."

"Good to see you again," said David, trying hard to make his voice and smile seem natural. "What brings you all the way out here, exactly?"

"You," said Stevie One. "But you can take your hand away from your sword. And SummerIsle, that is the worst case of sneaking around behind someone that I've ever seen. Now relax. We're here to help. The shit is about to hit the fan in a major way, Deathstalker. You've been outlawed."

David's mouth dropped open. He could hear the girls' shocked gasps, but for a moment he couldn't say anything. It was as though someone had punched him in the stomach and taken away his breath. "What do you mean, outlawed?" he managed, finally.

"I mean, Lionstone wants your head on a stick," said Stevie One. "Your holding is forfeit. Virimonde is no longer yours, and there's a big reward waiting for anyone who brings Lionstone your head, preferably unattached to your body, so the Iron Bitch can spit in your eyes."

"But why?" said David, almost plaintively. "I've been good. I've kept my head down, like we agreed."

"Funnily enough," said Stevie Three, "I don't think Lionstone even knows you're a rebel. She wants you dead because you encouraged local democracy and because you stood against her plans for mechanizing this planet. You shouldn't have been so open with your Steward. And you really shouldn't have threatened to go to the Company of Lords. Lionstone's calling that conspiracy against the Crown. Every other Lord is scrambling to put as much

distance as possible between himself and you. They can
see which way the wind's blowing. Luckily for you,
Alice's parents are rebels. They told us where to find you.
The bad news is that Empire ships ambushed us on the
way down and shot the hell out of us. So you can forget
about hopping a lift offplanet. We're all stuck here. Your
best bet is to run like hell back to your Standing and barricade yourself in. We'll try and work out some way to get
you safely offworld. We can't let the Empress have you.
You'd be too big a trophy for her to boast over."

"Oh, thanks a bunch," said David.

"Hold everything," said Kit. "What about me? Am I
outlawed too?"

"Hell no," said Stevie One. "You're still the Iron Bitch's
darling. Her favorite killer, apart from the Consort."

"Unless you try and defend the Deathstalker," said
Stevie Three. "In which case, you get to stand trial beside
him."

"She's right, Kit," said David. "We'd better split up. If
they find you in my company, they could declare you
guilty by association. I'll take the flyer in the stable and
head back to the Standing. You and the Blues can get the
girls to safety."

"Forget it," said Kit. "I'm not leaving you. You
wouldn't last ten minutes without me."

"You'd be putting your life at risk!" said David.

"Good," said Kit. "It's been far too quiet around here. I
was only saying I could use a little action. But may I suggest we use the tavern viewscreen to check out the situation at the Standing first? You have enemies there, as well
as friends."

"Good point," said David. "Alice, Jenny, you'd better
get out of here. Go home, and keep your heads down till
this is over. If they ask, you barely knew us. It'll be safer
that way."

"I'm afraid it's not that simple," said Stevie Three.
"You haven't heard all of it yet."

David stared at her. "There's more?"

"You aren't the only one that's getting the chop," said
Stevie One. "The whole planet's been outlawed. Normally that would mean a scorching, but Lionstone has
plans for Virimonde. So she's sending in the troops, to

punish the rebellious and bring the survivors under direct Empire rule. The first troop ships should be landing by now. It's war, Deathstalker. The whole planet's under attack."

"My parents," said Alice, numb with the shock of the news. "They're high up in the local underground. If the Empire's infiltrated our ranks, they'll be targets. We have to contact them, David!"

"First things first," said Kit. "First we try the Standing."

"You're a rebel, too?" said David to Alice. "Why didn't you tell me?"

"Hell, we're all rebels here," said Jenny. "Not much else to do for excitement on a backwater dump like this."

"The Standing," said Kit. "We have to know, David."

They gathered together in front of the viewscreen on the tavern wall, and David put in a call to the Standing, using his emergency codes. The Steward answered immediately, as though he'd been waiting for the call.

"My lord, where are you? I've been trying to locate you for hours! It is imperative that you return to the Standing immediately, to answer the ridiculous charges set against you."

"Where's my Security chief?" said David. "He's supposed to answer my emergency codes."

"He is unavailable at the moment," said the Steward. "Things are rather chaotic here, as I'm sure you can imagine. Tell me where you are, my lord, and I'll send an armored flyer to fetch you, and bring you back safely."

"Turn it off," said Kit. "If he's in charge, your people are dead. The Steward's the one who sold you out in the first place."

"I must insist on knowing where you are, my lord," said the Steward. "You are in danger every minute you're not under my protection."

"Turn it off," said Stevie One. "Before they trace the signal."

David shut down the screen. He didn't know what to say. It had never occurred to him that his own people might turn against him. Sure, he and the Steward had had words on more than one occasion, but to betray the Family that had fed and sheltered him from birth, that gave his life purpose and meaning . . . It had all happened

so quickly. One minute he was the man who had everything, then suddenly he had nothing but a price on his
head. Just like his cousin, Owen. Maybe the planet was
jinxed. Laughter dangerously close to hysteria bubbled up
inside him. He realized Alice was talking to him and tug-
ging at his sleeve.

"My parents, David. I need to know about my parents."

"Of course you do. You set the codes, I have to think.
Kit, if the Steward's got my emergency codes, my private
security measures aren't worth shit anymore. But that
works both ways. If he's got access to my codes, then I've
got access to his."

"What good does that do us?" said Kit.

"I should be able to patch into the Standing's comm
system, and through that into the Empire's systems. We'll
be able to see what they're seeing. I need to know what's
happening elsewhere on my world. I can't believe Lionstone's ordered a complete taking of Virimonde. The loss
of life would be enormous. Appalling."

"Since when has that ever stopped the Iron Bitch?"
said Kit.

"Kit," said David. "They said it's all my fault. My
people are going to die, because of what I did."

"I've got the farm!" said Alice, and they all turned to
look. The view on the screen was fuzzy, unfocused. Alice
bent over the control panel, cursing under her breath as
she tried to boost the signal. It finally snapped into focus,
and Alice shrank back from the screen, one hand half-
raised, as though to protect herself. She'd patched into
one of the farm's exterior sensors, showing the farmhouse
from outside. The great stone building was under attack.
The stonework was riddled with holes from energy guns,
and part of the roof had been blown away. What remained
of the thatched roof was burning fiercely. There were two
bodies lying still in the courtyard, clutching projectile
weapons in their dead hands. They'd both been hit by
energy guns.

Alice shook her head slowly, as though to deny what
she was seeing. "That's Sam. And Matthew. My brothers.
Where are the others? Where are my father and mother?"

David put a comforting hand on her shoulder, but she
didn't feel it. The farmhouse's front door flew open, and

black smoke billowed out, thick and heavy. And out of the smoke, projectile weapons in hand, firing at an unseen enemy, came Adrian and Diana Daker. They kept up a steady fire as they ran for the stables behind the house. The camera was too far away to show their faces clearly, but their body language showed calm determination. They weren't panicking.

Energy beams flashed around them, blowing holes in the farmhouse wall, but the Dakers were hard targets to hit. And then a company of Imperial marines appeared from behind the house, cutting the Dakers off from the stables. Adrian and Diana skidded to a halt, looking quickly about them, but there was nowhere they could go. The marines opened fire. Diana screamed and fell as one of her legs was shot out from under her, and then screamed again as an energy beam punched through Adrian's stomach and out his back. He fell to the ground, still holding his gun. Diana tried to pull herself along the ground toward him. Adrian reached out a hand to her, and another beam blew his head apart. Two more blasts hit Diana, tearing her body in two. Her torso rolled away, leaving her legs shuddering on the ground. She looked across at her dead husband. Her mouth moved as she tried to say something, then the life went out of her, and she lay still.

Alice was making strangled mewling noises, her wide eyes fixed on her dead parents. Jenny took her by the shoulders and forcibly turned her away from the screen. All the strength went out of Alice, and she collapsed sobbing into Jenny's arms. David gestured for Jenny to move Alice over to the bar and get her a stiff drink. Jenny nodded and gently persuaded her friend to move away out of range of the viewscreen. She murmured soothing words, but wasn't at all sure her friend could hear her. At the viewscreen, David bent over the control panel, patching the screen into the signals going to the Standing. He jumped from one scene to another, trying to get some idea of what was happening to his world. And only then did he began to understand how widespread the horror was.

David and Kit watched silently as Imperial troops ran howling through an isolated village, shooting at everything that moved. Villagers came pouring out of their squat houses to face the invaders, but they had few guns, fighting mostly with swords and axes and farm implements. The troopers had battle armor and force shields and energy weapons, but still the men and women of the village threw themselves at the enemy, making them fight for every inch of ground. But the troops had the numbers as well as the weapons, and they cut a swift and bloody path through the village, leaving the main street strewn with the dead and the dying. Soon they were cutting down the villagers as fast as they showed themselves. The soldiers torched the buildings methodically, and shot down the elderly and the children as they ran out screaming. Soon the whole village was ablaze, thick black smoke rising up into the early-morning skies.

The scene changed to a nearby town. A small army of Imperial marines ran riot in the narrow cobbled streets, killing and burning, destroying all possible centers of resistance. Local officials were dragged out of their offices and into the street and hanged from the nearest lampposts. There was looting and raping and the butchery of innocents. Blood ran in the streets, and men and women and children ran in terror before the invading forces, driven from their homes by an enemy intent only on victory.

David and Kit recognized the tactics. They were designed to shock and intimidate other towns and villages into surrendering without a fight. Resistance meant only death and destruction. That was why the holosignal was getting out. The tactics worked. The viewscreen jumped from town to town, showing whole populations being herded away from their homes and out into the open fields, their hands on their heads. Interrogation would come later. Those who didn't move fast enough were shot. Anyone who protested was shot. And everywhere there were buildings burning, and bodies hanging in the streets, and carrion birds circling in the skies above.

To the cities came the war machines. Unstoppable battle wagons smashed through boundary walls, bricks falling like water from their armored sides. Mechanical constructs, beyond fear or panic or restraint, charged unflinchingly into enemy fire, soaking up endless punishment while their racked energy guns blazed, cutting through men and buildings alike. Whole blocks went up in flames as huge gravity torpedoes plowed through wall after wall, building after building, progressing in unrelenting straight lines from one side of the city to the other. Combat androids, robots shaped in the mockery of men for psychological effect, stamped through the streets, cutting and hacking their way through human resistance. Flesh yielded to unfeeling steel, and blood ran down metal arms and dripped thickly from spiked knuckles. There were machines small as insects, unblinking eyes in the sky, and vast metal assemblages bigger than buildings, slow-moving towers of destruction. Brick and stone tore like paper, wood burned fiercely, and men and women died screaming under remorseless metal treads. The machines slaughtered all who came before them, showing neither quarter nor mercy because that was what they had been programmed to do. Buildings fell, fires raged, and in the smoke-choked streets, sharp metal hooks tore through yielding flesh, and barbed flails ripped meat away from bones. The robots marched, the city fell, and the war machines moved on to their next appointed target.

"No," said David finally. "No. I won't stand for this."

"We'd better get out of here," said Kit. "There's no telling how close the nearest Imperial forces are."

"I am the Lord of this planet, and I will not allow this." David glared at the blazing hell on the viewscreen, his hands clenched into fists. "This isn't war. This is inhuman. There's no way Lionstone's going to get away with this. This is my world and my people and I will not stand for this!"

"There's nothing you can do," said Kit. He shut down the viewscreen, and David turned his glare on him. Kit met his gaze calmly. "You've been outlawed, David. You no longer have any followers or power base, and even your own Standing may be compromised. You can't fight, and surrender isn't an option, so that just leaves flight."

David shook his head stubbornly. "If I can get to the Standing, there's still a chance I can contact the Company of Lords. Show them what's happening here, what Lionstone's doing to one of their own. If this could happen here, no Lord's holdings would be safe anymore."

"They won't interfere," said Kit. "No one objected to Owen's outlawing, remember? While the Empress has the backing of the armed forces and the war machines, no Lord's going to risk making a stand against her."

"Then I'll use the Standing's comm station to broadcast what's happening here on an open channel, so everyone in the Empire can see what's being done in the Empress's name."

"Your Standing is most probably in the Steward's hands now," Kit said patiently.

"Then we'll take it back from him," said David.

Kit took David by the shoulders so he could stare into his friend's eyes. "David, let it go. They're just peasants. They're nothing to do with us. Virimonde is a lost cause. It was the moment Lionstone decided to send in the troops and the war machines. We can't fight this. All we can do is cut and run and hope to save our own skins."

"I won't abandon my people," David said flatly.

"They're just peasants!"

"What about Alice and me?" said Jenny, from the other side of the bar.

"What about you?" said Kit.

"You bastard," said Jenny. "You'd just run off and abandon us, wouldn't you?"

"No one's abandoning anyone," said David. "Our flyer's still in the stable out back. It can carry four of us. There's got to be some organized resistance, somewhere. You and Alice can connect us with the nearest rebel cells, and together we can take back the Standing. Stevie Blue!"

The two clones looked back from the doorway. "Yeah?"

"We are leaving; you want a lift?"

"I don't think so," said Stevie One. "Once you're safely on your way, our responsibility to you is over. We'll head for the nearest city still standing, organize resistance, and generally make trouble wherever it'll do the most damage."

"Right," said Stevie Three, and held up a fist. Blue flames crackled menacingly around it.

"Then it's time to go," said David. He looked around him, as though seeing the tavern bar for the first time. "I should have listened to Owen. He tried to warn me.

Damn, I wish I'd had a few more hours' sleep. The shock's driven the booze out of my head, but I feel like shit." He stopped, and looked at Kit for a long moment. "Kit, you don't have to come with us. You haven't been outlawed, so presumably they don't know about your rebel links, or don't care. You could cut us loose and make off on your own . . ."

"No I couldn't," said Kit calmly. "You're my friend. And if you're determined to fight for a lost cause for no good reason that I can see, then I'll fight it with you. I am Kid Death, the smiling killer, and I will not desert my friend in his hour of need."

"You're a good sort, Kit," said David, smiling. "Weird as hell and spooky with it, but you'll do." He grinned suddenly. "What the hell; I was getting bored with peace and quiet anyway."

"Damn right," said Kit. "The holiday's over, time to get back to work. We were never meant to be gentlemen of leisure."

They turned to look at the two girls. Alice had stopped crying. Her mouth kept trying to tremble, but she was back in control.

"We're sticking with you," she said flatly. "This is our world, too. We have a right to defend it."

"Of course you do," said David. "And maybe on the way we'll find time for some personal revenge. Now let's go."

They headed for the back door together, waving briefly to the Stevie Blues. Jenny glared at Kit. "You slow us down, SummerIsle, and we'll dump you to fend for yourself. Got it?"

Kit smiled at her. "I always knew you were a woman after my own heart."

In his private command center on the planet's surface, inside a great slow-moving armored vehicle well away from the main fighting, Valentine Wolfe sat at his ease in a comfortable chair and watched death and destruction and bloody butchery on the many monitor screens around him, and was content. All Empire commands and machine instructions were routed through his systems, allowing him overall awareness of the invasion as well as individual control of his war units. He was contained inside a solid steel isolation tank, surrounded by control systems, lit by the glowing monitor screens. The ten-foot cube packed with tech would have been a claustrophobe's nightmare, but it didn't bother Valentine. Very little did, these days.

Various drugs were racing through his veins, fighting for control of his mind and body, but his will held them all in check. Before coming to Virimonde, he'd finally yielded to temptation and taken the esper drug, and his dark mind had blossomed like a poisoned flower. He now had direct control of his own autonomic systems, balancing one chemical with another, so that he lived on the highest curl of a continuous wave. And if the universe and its people seemed a little less than real, well, they always had, to him. It was only a matter of degree. He could think faster, see farther, and plan in more detail than ever before, even as his emotions thundered within him, great storms of feeling that crashed against the unyielding rocks of his self-control. Valentine Wolfe was out of his mind morning, noon, and night now, and he loved it. His brain chemistry was altered beyond recovery, and he couldn't have been happier.

People and events had become transparent to his supercharged insight, merely things and information to be manipulated to his best advantage. He could become Emperor, if he chose, but he wasn't sure if he could be bothered. For all his chemical highs, he was still dedicated to the search for the ultimate drug, the ultimate thrill and wonder. He wasn't sure what that was, or where he might find it, only that it was out there, and he hadn't found it yet. There was something still beyond his grasp, some further step to take; he could sense it. And he wanted it. To seize it and make it his, he would sacrifice every living thing in the Empire.

In the meantime, he occupied himself with the destruction of Virimonde. As a distraction, it had its pleasing moments. He watched his war machines destroy whole towns and slaughter their populations, and smiled quietly to himself, his wide crimson mouth like a wound in the skull white of his face. He took an uncomplicated delight in the endless death and destruction, savoring it as a ban-

quet of many courses. He was becoming a monster, and
he knew it. He gloried in it.

The machines moved to his order, directed by his will.
His continuing alliance with the rogue AIs of Shub had
brought him high tech advanced far beyond anything the
Empire had. Their latest gift had been a computer system
that enabled him to sink his mind into the metal consciousness of the war machines, and experience everything they did. He could become the war wagons and the
combat androids, live in their steel heads, direct them as
he would his own body. He could see through their sensors a world of perceptions far beyond the limited range
of his human senses. He could plow through walls, fly
high over buildings, and walk on metal feet through
crowds of attacking humans and strike them down with
metal fists. No one else could have done it, but Valentine's mind had been so altered by drugs and esp and
Shub tech that it was no longer merely human. He'd been
careful to hide that from Lionstone. She thought anyone
would be able to control the war machines as he did once
they'd mastered the new system. He let her think that, for
the moment. It was useful for him to have sole control
over something she wanted. In the meantime, her invasion
of Virimonde gave him the chance to show off what he
and his tech could do. And the slaughter and the suffering
and the destruction were so delightfully diverting. Valentine had an absolute fear of boredom, and he'd exhausted
so many of the usual sins and vices.

Even as his mind moved in the machines, singly and en
masse, he was still plotting his next move. He'd acquired
the esper drug, through a combination of bribes and
blackmail, from the same scientists who used to supply
Dram. And since the man currently known as Dram
wasn't taking the endlessly addictive esper drug from
them, it was clear that whoever or whatever he was, he
wasn't the original Dram. He wasn't a Fury; Shub had
confirmed that, and they had no reason to lie to him. That
left a clone, or an alien impostor, either of which raised
fascinating possibilities. For the moment, Valentine kept
this information to himself. Knowledge is power. He
might, at some later date, use this knowledge to control
the new Dram, or destroy him. It all depended on how he

might feel at the time. Valentine believed in indulging his impulses.

That thought widened his smile as he looked over at the end result of his last impulse. On a stand, in a glass jar festooned with wires, was all that remained of the distinguished scientist Lionstone had insisted be allowed to observe and assist Valentine in his use of the war machines. Valentine hadn't been fooled for a moment. He knew a spy when he saw one. So he'd taken steps to ensure that while Professor Ignatious Wax would still be able to observe all that happened, he would be in no position to interfere. To be exact, Valentine had had the man decapitated, and now kept the severed head in a glass jar.

It was wired directly into the command center's comm station, so that it could see all that was going on. It had screamed a lot to begin with, but Valentine just turned off the jar's sound, till it stopped. Mostly it just watched the monitors and sulked now. No doubt Lionstone would have something boring to say about this when she found out, but Valentine was certain he'd be able to talk his way out of any trouble. He always did. And in the meantime, the head made a decorative addition to his command center. He rather enjoyed the way the long white hair and moustaches floated in the jar's preservative fluids, and the way the eyes bulged when it got angry. Besides, Wax had designed most of the war machines Valentine was currently controlling, so there was always the slim chance Wax's knowledge might prove useful.

"How are you doing, Professor?" Valentine said politely. "Anything I can do for you? Rerun some of the nastier death footage, perhaps?"

"I take no pleasure in such things," Wax's head said stiffly, through the jar's speaker. "I am not like you. My interest lies only in the performance of my creations."

"I would never have thought of you as squeamish, Professor," said Valentine. "Not after all the thousands of test animals you maimed and mutilated and sent to the animal hereafter while working out the bugs in your delightful machines. Think of the unfortunate rebels here as particularly unlucky lab rats."

"I don't care about them one way or the other," said

Wax. "I am completely indifferent to their fate. I merely require to know how my creations are progressing."

"They're not your machines, Professor. Not any longer. The tech links I provided finally made your machines practical in the field, so the Empress gave them over into my care. Which is why I am in charge, and you are in a jar. Perhaps you'd care to monitor the machines through my tech links?"

"You know very well I can't understand them! I don't think anyone does, but you. Which is in itself rather strange, isn't it, Wolfe? Neither you nor the laboratories you fund has ever produced anything like this before. Which means you must have had help. Outside help. I wonder from whom, eh, Wolfe? Could it be you have to keep your confederates' identity secret, because you know the Empress wouldn't approve? Who have you been making deals with, Wolfe?"

"You are entering dangerous waters, Professor," Valentine said easily. "I advise you to turn back now, while you still can."

"Or what? You'll cut my head off and stick it in a jar?"

"There are worse things that could happen to you," said Valentine. "Trust me on this."

The head in the jar muttered to itself, then fell silent. It was sulking again. Valentine smiled, and sank back into the mental link with the war machines. In a moment, he was a combat android stamping across a plowed field, the weight of his great steel frame driving his metal feet deep into the rutted earth. He reached out with his mind, and was a dozen metal men, and then a hundred, stamping in unison across the wide field. Their feet rose and fell in perfect step, a hundred robots in the shape of men, with but one purpose and one intent, moving as one.

They marched over the horizon and into a town. Rebels came out to face them, fighting with farm implements and the occasional projectile weapon. Blades and bullets rebounded harmlessly from the metal men, and the robots laid their hands upon the rebels, tearing them limb from limb, breaking their heads and necks with lashing metal flails, and tearing open their guts with jagged metal hooks. It was inevitable that they would take some damage, but as long as a spark of energy remained in their systems they pressed on, marching, limping or crawling on their bellies, never stopping. Men and women and children died screaming under metal hands, and Valentine was there.

He'd wondered why the rouge AIs of Shub had insisted on supplying him with this particular gift, but now he thought he knew why. It was their way of showing him what it was like to be living metal, to be encompassed by the certainty of steel and tech, to be so much more than merely human, free from the limits of flesh. Valentine's scarlet smile stretched from ear to ear, a new satisfaction glowing in his mascaraed, fever-bright eyes. He spread himself through the entire metal army, growing larger and larger, blossoming through every system at once, his artificially boosted, drug-expanded mind living inside every war machine on Virimonde, and loving every minute of it.

The man who was now the Lord High Dram led his troops howling through the blazing streets of a small town. Buildings burned to every side, thick black smoke billowing up into the early-morning sky. The heat from every side made Dram's exposed face and hands smart, and hot cinders floated on the air. His men spread out, plunging down every side turning and alleyway, searching out rebels and putting them to the sword. Suddenly his men began falling, as snipers opened fire from the upper story of a building up ahead. Dram roared orders, and a dozen disrupters opened fire at once, the joined energy blasts blowing the whole upper floor of the building apart in a shower of rubble and reddish clouds of pulverized bricks. Dram had his men toss a few concussion grenades into the lower floor, just in case, and then they moved on. Dram strode at the head of his troops, gun in one hand, sword in the other. Blood dripped steadily from the sword. There were screams and shouts and explosions all around, and Dram grinned so widely his cheeks ached. This was what he had been born, had been constructed and chosen, to do, and he loved every minute of it.

He shouldn't really have been planetside at all. He should have stayed safely in orbit, setting overall policy and allowing General Beckett to take care of the practical side of things. Dram had started out with good intentions, but they hadn't lasted long once the fighting really got under way. He'd watched it all on the *Elegance*'s bridge monitors, calling constantly for more information, his blood boiling with the thrill of battle. At first he tried to use his men efficiently, killing only those who needed to be killed, and keeping destruction of towns and cities to a necessary minimum. But all that stopped when the rebel population suddenly produced guns and weapons from nowhere and began fighting back. Dram watched his men die, and the rebels defying him, and a fury roared through him, that these peasants dared to stand against him. He'd taken it easy on them, and this was his reward. Dram watched his men die, and knew he needed to be down there with them, in the thick of it all, leading them to victory while personally cutting down those who dared defy him. He needed to smell the blood and death, feel his sword sinking into flesh and jarring on bone. And so he overrode Beckett's advice and warnings, and went down into Hell on the next available pinnace.

And he loved it. He swung his sword with an arm that never tired, and no one could stand against him. He was the Warrior Prime, the Widowmaker, and he was everything the original had been and more. He stayed at the head of his troops, taking out rebel strongholds with gun and grenades, leading his men from one glorious victory to another. Buildings blazed around him, the rebels' dead lay everywhere, and the survivors ran before him, and he'd never felt so alive in his entire short life. His heart hammered in his chest, his breathing was deep and harsh, and he felt like he could go on fighting forever and a day, and never ask for anything else. From time to time it occurred to him that he wasn't fighting some faceless enemy, that the people he killed had faces and lives and histories of their own, and parents and children to mourn them, but even then he didn't care. They had defied him and his Empress and the way things were, and there was only one answer for that. If they had surrendered, he would have spared them. He was sure he would. They would have had to stand trial, and many would have been executed anyway, but all this slaughter and destruction lay at their door, not his. And so he walked up and down in the narrow cobbled streets, killing people for all the right reasons and perhaps a few wrong ones, and didn't give a damn. He was having a good time.

General Beckett's voice sounded now and then through his comm implant, suggesting he had done enough, and should stand down while his men took care of the mopping-up, but he wouldn't listen. He knew where he was needed. And when Beckett's voice grew harsh, questioning his actions and his motives, Dram just laughed and invited Beckett to come down and get his hands bloody, too. Beckett declined, and Dram laughed again. After this town was pacified there would be more towns, and then the cities. There was so much work still to be done, and he couldn't wait to get to it.

It did occur to him to wonder if his original would have felt the same. He liked to think so. That he was more than just a shadow of the original. The first Dram lived on within him, guided and shaped by the legacy of his diaries, and the fire that burned within him. In every way that mattered, he was the Lord High Dram, Warrior Prime by popular acclaim, Widowmaker by destiny.

He strode on through blood and death and the fires of Hell, and no one could touch him. It was as though he was . . . blessed. It never occurred to him to wonder by whom.

Captain Silence, Investigator Frost, and Security Officer Stelmach stumbled out of the wreckage of their downed pinnace and ran for the partial shelter of a burntout building. The war machines were everywhere, big and small, destroying what had once been a fair-sized town with ruthless, inhuman precision. Energy beams spit in all directions, exploding stonework and setting fire to the timbers and thatched roofs. It was just such a beam that had struck Silence's ship, despite the security codes he was broadcasting. The Investigator had identified the craft and its occupants repeatedly over the comm unit, but no one was listening. The disrupter beams just kept stabbing up out of the dark roiling smoke covering the town, punching through the pinnace's low-level shields again and again. With the engines stuttering and the cabin full of fire and smoke, Silence had no choice but to bring the pinnace in for an emergency landing. They plunged down through the smoke, jockeying between tall buildings and taller war machines. Silence chose the broadest street at hand and guided the dying ship down to a landing only one step up from a crash. It hit hard, skidding half the length of the street before slamming nose first into a boundary wall, but it held together and the engines didn't explode, and Silence had enough sense to be grateful for that.

The three of them huddled inside what was left of the building, little more than half a dozen walls blackened by fire and holed by repeated impact blasts, and half a roof still quietly smoldering. Silence and Frost took it in turn to peer briefly out the shattered window. The war machines roared up and down, pounding the remaining buildings into rubble. Fires blazed and men screamed. Robots in the shape of men rounded up strays and killed them with horrible efficiency. All around them were the sounds of a town dying, and the triumph of machines. Silence checked the energy levels in his disrupter, and growled angrily to himself about heads rolling when he got back. The Investigator was calm as always, assessing the odds against them with a professional eye. Without the security codes used by Dram's ground forces, the war machines would treat them as legitimate targets. Stelmach stood with his back pressed against the wall, refusing to look out the window. His heart was pounding, and he had to struggle to get his breath, but the hand holding his gun was steady. Being around Silence and Frost had toughened him despite himself. Silence looked at Frost.

"How far are we from where we're supposed to be?"

"According to the pinnace's last readings, not too far. Maybe half a mile. Easy walking distance, under normal conditions."

"Which these very definitely aren't." Silence scowled, weighing their chances. "As things are, half a mile is going to be hard going. Even for us. Investigator, try and raise the Deathstalker Standing again."

Frost accessed her comm implant and shook her head. "Still no joy. The war machines are blocking all channels except their own, and I don't have the security codes to access theirs. We're going to have to make it to the Standing on our own."

"We're doomed," said Stelmach.

"Walk in the park," said Silence briskly. "All right, there are a hell of a lot of war machines out there, but their main priority is wrecking the town. And the androids are only concerned with mopping up resistance. As long as we keep our heads down and don't interfere, we should be safe enough."

"Should being the operative word," said Stelmach. "Couldn't we just stay here till the machines get bored and go away?"

And then they all flinched as the building next door exploded into smoke and fire and stone shrapnel as a war machine targeted it with its disrupters. The ground shook beneath their feet, and what was left of the house groaned. A jagged crack ran down the wall Stelmach was leaning against, and he jumped away. Streams of dust and soot fell from the ceiling. Flames rose up, consuming what little remained of the building next door, and Silence had to back away from the heat coming through the shattered window.

"The machines won't stop here till there's nothing left but rubble," he said flatly. "We'll have to run for it. Stick close to us, Stelmach. You'll be safe."

"Can I have that in writing?" said Stelmach.

"You can have my boot up your backside if you don't stop whining," said Frost. "Now get moving, or I'll kill you myself."

Stelmach glared at her mutinously, but had the sense not to say anything else. Investigators weren't known for their tolerance. Silence edged over to the open space where the door had been and looked out cautiously. The majority of the war machines seemed to be moving away. The huge war wagons were moving off through the billowing smoke, slow and steady like great land whales. Other machines roared or flew after them, disrupter beams still stabbing out like petulant slaps at what remained standing in the town. And robots shaped like mockeries of men stamped after them, dried blood coating their metal limbs. Silence stared after them, feeling small and insignificant. He wasn't used to feeling that way, and he hated it. He looked back at the others.

"All right, let's get moving while there's still enough rebel resistance left in the town to keep the machines occupied. If we can make it beyond the town's boundary, it should be relatively easy going to the Standing. Investigator, we are running, not fighting. I don't want you doing anything destructive that might draw the machines' attention to us. Is that clear?"

"Of course, Captain," said Frost. "I shall endeavor to restrain myself."

"That'll be a first," said Stelmach, and then shut up as the Investigator turned her cold gaze on him.

"Move it out," said Silence, and led the way through the space where the door had been.

They stuck to the shadows and the smoke as much as they could, taking shelter and freezing in place whenever one of the machines seemed to be getting too close. Stelmach was terrified, but gritted his teeth and clenched his fists and somehow kept it to himself. He knew why the war machines had attacked the pinnace. Back on the *Elegance,* General Beckett himself had taken Stelmach to one side and ordered him to set the wrong security codes in the pinnace, so that it would be sure to come under fire. The Empress wanted Silence and Frost to be caught up in the action on the ground, so that they might have a chance to show off their alleged powers. If no natural opportunity arose, Stelmach was under orders to manufacture opportunities by whatever means necessary, then report on the results. Stelmach had wanted to say no. He'd wanted to warn Silence and Frost. But he hadn't. He couldn't. They were his friends, but his orders came from the Iron Throne itself. One loyalty had to give way to another, and Stelmach had sworn an oath upon his name and his honor to serve the Empress all his days, until death, if need be. His duty was clear. But still, as he stumbled along behind Silence and Frost, amidst the fires and smoke and devastation, he felt so bad he wanted to die.

He was thinking so hard he never saw the combat android step out of a side alley and aim a disrupter at him. Frost saw it, and knocked him aside at the last moment, throwing him to his knees. The energy beam seared over his head and blew apart the wall behind him. The top half disappeared, vaporized into brick dust, but the shattered lower half leaned forward and collapsed on top of Stelmach. He cried out once, raising his arms to protect his head, and then the bricks fell on him and slammed him to the ground, crushing him under their weight.

Silence blew the robot's grinning head away with a single shot, but its body didn't fall, so Frost shot out one of its knees, just to make sure. The metal body fell clattering to the ground, its steel limbs thrashing helplessly. Frost moved forward and yanked the disrupter from its hand, and shot the machine in the chest. It stopped moving. Silence and Frost put away their guns and hurried over to pull at the rubble covering Stelmach. He could hear them working, but he couldn't see anything. The smoke and dust had filled his eyes with tears. He could feel the weight of the broken wall pressing down on him like a bully in a schoolyard, but he didn't seem to be badly hurt. He could still feel his hands and feet, though he couldn't move an inch, trapped under what felt like half a ton of masonry. He lay still, breathing shallowly as the great weight pressed against his chest. They were calling his name, but he couldn't seem to find the energy to answer them. His pain seemed far away. He felt almost peaceful.

And then he heard the sound of approaching metal feet. Silence and Frost didn't seem to have heard them, still occupied in dragging bricks off him. Stelmach blinked his eyes as hard as he could, forcing the tears and dust out until he could see again. They'd cleared a space over his face so he could breathe, and looking past Silence and Frost laboring to free him, Stelmach could see a company of combat androids striding down the street toward them. And it occurred to Stelmach that he could just keep quiet. The robots might not notice him, still buried under rubble. They might just kill Silence and Frost and then go on, and he'd be safe. All he had to do was keep his mouth shut. But he couldn't do that. They were his friends.

He forced the warning out, yelling as loud as he could. Silence and Frost whipped around, saw the robots approaching, and their hands went to the guns at their sides. Only then remembering that they'd already used their disrupters on the first android, and the energy crystals in their guns still needed time to recharge before they could be used again. All they had were their swords. Metal blades against men made of metal, all of them armed with disrupters. Stelmach yelled at Silence and Frost to run. To leave him and run. But they stood their ground. They looked at each other, eyes locked on eyes, almost ignoring the advancing robots. Something passed between them— anger or desperation or something that might have been resignation. They turned to face the androids, who raised their disrupters. Stelmach tried again to yell for his friends to run, but he couldn't force the words past his dust-choked throat.

And then a great force arose around Silence and Frost, a presence beating on the still air like giant wings, building and building until it struck out in a rolling wave of power that tore the robots apart and scattered their shattered parts the length of the street. As quickly as it had arisen, the force was gone, and Silence and Frost were only, merely, human again. They looked at each other for a long moment, then they turned and looked at Stelmach, still held down by the rubble. He could see the calculation in their eyes. Knew what they were thinking, had to be thinking. They knew he'd seen them use their secret abilities, and knew that as Security Officer he'd be duty- bound to report them. But if they just walked away and left him, left him here to die in the blazing town, their secret would be safe, and no one would ever have to know. Stelmach understood. It was what he would have done. But even so, he wasn't surprised when they bent over him and started pulling the bricks away again. They weren't like him.

Eventually they got him out, and Silence helped sup- port him while Frost briskly slapped some of the dust off his clothes. His head took a while to clear, but when it did he pushed himself away from Silence and made himself stand up straight.

"You saved me," he said, his voice a harsh rasp that didn't only come from the dust. "You didn't have to do that."

"Yes we did," said Silence. "We're family. You'd have done the same for us."

"You don't understand," said Stelmach, forcing the words out. "I'm responsible for our being here. I sabotaged the pinnace. The Empress had heard stories of your . . .

powers. She wanted confirmation. So she ordered me to put you into danger and spy on you."

"Never trust a Security Officer," said Frost. Her hand fell to the gun on her hip. Stelmach made himself stand still.

"He didn't have to tell us," said Silence.

"Yes I did," said Stelmach. "We're family."

He and Silence shared a smile. Frost nodded, which was as close as she got to a smile when she wasn't killing something, and took her hand away from her gun.

"So," she said. "What do we do now?"

"We concentrate on getting to the Standing alive," said Silence. "Everything else can wait. We'll work something out. We always do."

"I hate all this improvising," said Frost.

They moved on through what was left of the town, making better time now that they no longer had to hide from the war machines. Silence and Frost gathered their power around them again, and hid the three of them from the machines' sensors. And so they were able to watch unmolested as the robots came marching down a street, driving a desparate army of refugees before them. Men, women, and children ran despairingly, lungs straining for breath, forcing themselves on despite the pain in their legs and backs and chests. The machines killed the slowest, or those who could no longer keep up, smashing their skulls with swift, efficient blows from their steel hands. Blood ran down the cobbled street and swirled thickly in the gutters. Finally the robots tired of this, or decided their priorities lay elsewhere, and they fell suddenly on the refugees, overtaking them in seconds, and tearing them limb from limb. They slaughtered them all in a matter of seconds, and then moved on, their metal feet stamping through a river of blood and gore. They passed right by Silence and Frost and Stelmach and didn't see them.

Stelmach looked at Silence and Frost. "Couldn't you have done something? I mean, I know they're rebels, but . . ."

"No buts," said Frost. "The price for rebellion is death."

"I don't know," said Silence. "That wasn't execution; that was butchery. I've seen war before. Seen men kill men for all kinds of reasons. But that was men, not machines. There were children there . . ."

Frost looked at Silence. "Don't go soft on me, Captain. They brought this on themselves. They plotted and conspired to bring this about. They betrayed their oath and their honor and their duty, and finally themselves. They knew what they were getting into."

"Do you think the children knew?" said Silence. "Do you think they knew why they were being driven through the streets like cattle and then slaughtered?"

"Their parents brought that on them," said Frost. "They bear the blame. We have to be strong, Captain. You used to know that. You gave the order to scorch the planet Unseeli."

"And I'm still haunted by what I did there," said Silence. "I thought that there was no other way. And in the end it didn't solve anything, remember? Maybe we should be looking harder for other ways."

"That's not our business," said Frost. "We don't make policy. We can't see the big picture."

"When did we ever try?" said Silence.

David Deathstalker and Kit SummerIsle, along with Alice and Jenny, made a dash for the Standing on their flyer. It wasn't the safest of places to head for, with the Steward probably in charge there, but they were short on options. Besides, when David first came to Virimonde, he'd taken the precaution of salting the Standing's Security forces with men specifically loyal to him. Just in case. The Steward had already betrayed Owen, after all. Right now, David was hoping his people would have taken control by the time he got there.

They flew high above the clouds, at the fastest speed the flyer's straining engines could produce. Kit sat at the controls, leaving David to comfort Alice. She hadn't said a dozen words since the flyer took off. She'd seen her family die and her home destroyed, and her face had set in harsh, broken lines. David and Jenny took turns talking to her, trying to reach her, but she didn't seem to hear them. Something inside her had broken, and might never be put back together again. David gave her his gun to hold, and she seemed to find that comforting. In the end he left her with Jenny and went forward to stand beside Kit.

"How are we doing?"

"As well as can be expected," the SummerIsle said calmly, not looking round. "Our security codes probably no longer protect us from attack, but at this height and speed most of the machines on the ground shouldn't be able to track us. Our real problem is the flyer's energy crystals. According to the onboard computers, we don't have enough power left to get us all the way back to the Standing, and still maintain full shields."

"Then drop the shields," said David. "Our only hope is to reach the Standing."

"My thoughts exactly. How are the girls doing?"

"As well as can be expected. I still can't believe everything went wrong so fast. You've seen what's going on below. All the towns are in flames, and there are war machines and ground troops everywhere. This isn't a strike force, it's an invasion."

"Look on the bright side," said Kit. "At least they're not scorching the planet."

"I don't even want to think about that. I've never seen anything like this, Kit. They're butchering these people. My people. And it's all happening because of me."

"No it isn't. It's happening because the peasants were stupid enough to fool around with democracy. They were just asking for trouble."

"I let them do it. I could have said no. Could have cracked down hard, with my Security people. I'd have had to execute a few ringleaders, burn out some farms, but everyone else would have been safe. I failed them, Kit. It was my duty to protect these people, keep them from harm. My duty as a Deathstalker."

"David, can we concentrate on the matter at hand, please? Like, what are we going to do if we get to the Standing and it's under the Steward's control?"

"Improvise. There are secret ways and hidden booby traps that only I and my people know about. Owen told me about them. If the Steward has got the Standing, I'll take it back from him. And then I'll cut off his treacherous head and use it as a footstool."

"Cute. Assume we can take back the Standing. Then

what? It won't hold out long against war machines, and
we don't have anything there that would get us offplanet.
Unless that's another of your little secrets?"

"Unfortunately not," said David. "But I wouldn't leave
now, even if I could. My people are dying. I won't
abandon them."

"But what can you *do,* David?"

"I'll think of something! I'm a Deathstalker!"

"That," said Kit, "is what got us into trouble in the first
place."

David thought about that, and then looked at Kit.
"They're after me. It's still not too late for you to split off
on your own. Take the girls and head for cover. You used
to be Lionstone's favorite. She might well take you back,
if you publicly disowned me."

"Not a chance," said Kit. "You're stuck with me.
Forget the altruism and keep thinking. You're the brains
in this partnership. Find us a way out of this."

"Let me take the controls," said David. "I know this
area better than you."

They switched places, and Kit went back to check on
the girls, to try and comfort them. He wasn't very good at
things like that, but he supposed he ought to try. The
attack ships came out of nowhere, disrupter fire raking the
side of the unshielded flyer. Explosions rocked the small
craft, and flames erupted in the cabin. David fought the
controls as the ship plunged toward the earth. Kit grabbed
a fire extinguisher and played the foam over the nearest
flames. Smoke filled the cabin. Jenny hugged Alice to
her. The flyer's engines cut off, and the ship dropped like
a stone.

David kicked in the reserves, cursing in an endless
quiet monotone. The ship's plunge slowed, but it was still
going down. The attack ships struck again, and the whole
rear of the flyer blew apart. Air rushed out the great hole
in the rear, sucking the smoke out with it. The flames
roared up, and Kit was forced back by the sheer intensity
of the heat. David yelled for everyone to brace themselves, and frantically searched his sensor screens for
somewhere reasonably flat to land. There was a field next
to some open woodland, and David decided he'd settle for

that. He took the flyer in, the controls fighting him all the way. The ground leaped up to meet them.

The ship hit hard, bouncing across the field and digging a great trench through the grass before finally skidding to a halt just a few yards short of the tree line. The cabin was full of smoke again. Flames roared as they took hold. David sat slumped forward in his chair, only his safety straps holding him upright. Blood ran down his face from a cut on his forehead, and he was hazily aware he'd cracked his head against something hard and unyielding on the way down. Smoke caught in his throat, and he came suddenly awake as he coughed and almost choked. Kit was suddenly there at his side, undoing his straps. David tried to help, but his hands were numb and awkward. Kit threw back the last of the straps, and David forced himself out of the chair and onto his feet. He felt like shit, but his head was clearing. He coughed again, and glared into the smoke.

"Alice! Where's Alice, and Jenny?"

"I'm sorry," said Kit. "David, I'm so sorry."

David stared at him for a moment, and then pushed him aside and fought his way through the smoke and the rising flames to where Alice lay still next to a breach in the cabin wall. A disrupter blast had punched right through the metal hull, splaying the jagged steel edges inward. Blood dripped slowly from the sharp edges. Alice had been torn open all down her left side. Broken ribs showed clearly in the red meat, and half her guts were falling out her side. Her eyes were mercifully closed. David made himself look away to where Jenny lay trapped under the splayed-in metal, not far away. She was dazed, but still struggling feebly. David picked Alice up in his arms, and yelled back to Kit.

"I'm taking Alice! You get Jenny out!"

Kit loomed out of the smoke, and grabbed David's arm. "David, she's . . ."

"I'm getting her out! You see to Jenny."

Kit looked at Alice, and the red-and-purple guts hanging down from her side, and then nodded, and went over to kneel beside Jenny. David staggered over to the escape hatch, kicked open the door, and dropped down to the ground outside. Kit tugged at the jagged metal pinning

Jenny to the floor. It was wide and heavy, and the sharp edges cut at his hands. He strained with all his strength, but couldn't budge the metal an inch. Jenny had shaken off her daze, and was looking up at him with desperate eyes. She couldn't help him. The metal had pinned her arms at her sides. Sweat was running down both their faces now, flushed from the raw heat of the approaching flames. Kit stopped pulling at the unresponsive metal and thought hard. The fire was getting closer, the flames leaping up as they consumed more and more of the cabin. If he didn't get Jenny out soon, the flames would cut him off from the only exit. Jenny saw his thoughts in his face.

"Kit! Don't leave me! Please, don't leave me to the fire!"

"No," said Kit. "That would be cruel."

He drew his knife and stabbed her through the eye. He wanted it to be quick. Jenny jerked once and then lay still. Kit withdrew his knife, put it away, and headed for the exit. He'd done all he could. He dropped down from the escape hatch and hurried across the open ground to shelter in the trees. They wouldn't protect him from disrupter beams, but they should confuse long-distance sensor readings. He had to find David. He'd know what to do. He found David a short way inside the woods. He was crouching beside Alice. He'd propped her back up against a tree trunk, and tried to push her dangling guts back into the great wound in her side. His hands were red with blood, and his clothes were soaked with it, where he'd pressed her close against him. He looked up as Kit approached. He was crying, the tears making slow tracks through the blood that had trickled down his face from the wound in his forehead.

"She's dead," he said, and in his voice was all the loss in the world. "She trusted me to look after her, and I failed her. Just like I failed everyone else."

"I'm sorry," said Kit.

"I killed her, you know. She died because she was with me."

"You can't blame yourself," said Kit. David's tears disturbed him, but he didn't know what to do about them. "They're killing everyone here. You tried to save her. You did your best."

David nodded slowly, unconvinced, and wiped tears and blood from his eyes with the back of his hand. He sniffed a few times, then looked up at Kit.

"Where's Jenny?"

"Dead. She died of her wounds while I was trying to free her." Kit wouldn't normally have bothered lying, but he didn't want to upset David further. He looked around him. "Any idea where we are?"

"Yeah. I know this place. The Standing's not five minutes' walk from here, on the other side of the wood. We almost made it, Kit. We were so close. Just a few minutes more, and we'd have been safe. All of us."

Kit knelt down beside David. "This is Lionstone's doing. Blame her. Now let's get moving. They'll be here looking for us soon."

David nodded and got to his feet. Kit stood up with him. David looked down at Alice. "I hate to leave her."

"She's already gone, David. She's beyond pain now. We'll take revenge for her later."

"Yes. There will be revenge, later."

David turned and walked off into the woods, and Kit went after him. It was cool and calm and quiet among the tall trees, a dark and private place almost set apart from the rest of the world. The troubles hadn't reached here yet. The air was full of the smell of grass and bark and living things. Kit strode along beside David, enjoying the calm and the songs of the birds. David strode along the open trail, eyes dark and brooding, untouched by the peace around him. Kit kept trying to think of something to say to him, but couldn't think what. He didn't have much experience with this kind of thing. So he strolled along beside David, his hands near his weapons, and left his friend to his thoughts. David would come up with something. He always did.

Kit was wary and alert, but even so the first he knew they had company in the woods was when three figures stepped out onto the trail ahead of them, blocking their way. One wore a Captain's uniform, one was an Investigator, and the third figure stood well back, holding a gun in a not very threatening way. David and Kit came to a halt, and for a long time they all just stood and looked at each other. The woods were like a great green arena, a place where destinies could be decided, and anything could happen. Anything at all.

"I'm Captain Silence," said the man with the sword in his hand. "This is Investigator Frost and Security Officer Stelmach. You're under arrest, my lords. Hand over your weapons, and come with us."

"I don't think so," said David. "I am the Deathstalker, and my people need me. Stand aside and let me pass, or die where you stand."

"What he said," said Kit. He smiled at Frost. "I've always wondered how I'd do against an Investigator."

"You'd die, boy," said Frost. "Throw down your weapons, and you'll live to stand trial."

"Get out of our way," said David. "I won't be stopped."

The Captain shrugged. "Do what you have to, my lord. In the end, it always comes down to steel, doesn't it?"

He stepped forward, and David drew his sword and went forward to meet him. Their swords slammed together, sparks flying on the air, and the sound of steel on steel was painfully loud in the quiet. Kit SummerIsle smiled his Kid Death smile and went lightly forward to meet the Investigator. They circled each other slowly, searching for weaknesses in the other's eyes. Stelmach lowered his gun and backed off out of the way. He knew he was only an observer in this.

David boosted, calling on his Deathstalker inheritance, and new strength and energy surged through him, pushing back the tiredness. Even so, he knew it wouldn't last long. It wasn't that long ago he'd spent a whole evening drinking and carousing in the Heart's Ease tavern. He almost smiled. It seemed like a lifetime ago, but his body knew different. Too much drink and too little sleep would have made him fatally slow without the boost to hold him up, and even with it he doubted he could last long. So he pressed the attack, his sword rising and falling with all his considerable strength behind it. Silence backed away, one step at a time, but still he met the Deathstalker's every blow with equal strength, which should have been impossible. They swung and thrust, stabbing and parrying and recovering, blades moving almost too fast for the human eye to follow. And then Silence stopped and would not back away farther. He met the Deathstalker's savage attacks with calm skill and would not be moved.

Kit SummerIsle, also known as Kid Death, the smiling killer, pressed his attack with more thought. He'd never lost a fight in his life, and didn't intend to start now, but this was an Investigator, after all. Kit and Frost circled warily around each other, their blades licking out from time to time, to test the other's speed and reflexes. They were masters of their craft, and saw no reason to hurry. They meant to enjoy this. They smiled at each other and went on circling.

David fought on, rage boiling within him. This one Captain had come to represent to him all the Empire forces, the blind, awful forces that were destroying his life and his world. He hacked and cut with increasing fury, drawing recklessly on the boost's support, and it was only a matter of time before Silence turned aside one particular wide blow, and ran David through. He cried out with shock as much as pain, and sank to one knee, still somehow holding on to his sword. Silence's blade had punched right through David's gut and out his back. He could feel blood running out of him, hear it splashing on the ground below. Silence jerked his sword free, and David cried out again, blood spraying from his mouth along with the sound. He tried to force himself back onto his feet, and couldn't. The boost was holding him together, but all his strength was gone. The Captain drew back his sword for the killing blow.

Kit saw David go down, and wasted no time with a cry of rage. He caught Frost's sword in a close parry, kicked her hard in the kneecap, and, while she was off-balance, he whipped off his cloak and wrapped it around her head. He would have liked to kill her then, while she was helpless, but he didn't have the time. He ran over to Silence, calling out to the Captain to distract him from David. Silence turned swiftly, and Kit ducked under the extended blade and rammed the Captain in the stomach with his shoulder. The Captain fell backwards, his breath driven right out of him, and Kit ran over to David and hauled him back onto his feet. It only took a glance to see how bad the wound was, but Kit couldn't let himself think about that. There'd be help waiting at the Standing. There had to be. He got

David moving, and then heard footsteps behind him. He looked back, and incredibly the Captain was back on his feet and charging after them. Kit reached for the gun at his side, and only then realized David was leaning against it. The Captain was almost upon them. And then there was the sound of a disrupter firing, and Silence fell to his knees, shot from behind. Kit looked back, and there was the Security Officer with his gun in his hand, eyes wide with horror at his mistake. Kit threw him a quick salute, pulled David to him more firmly, and led him off into the trees.

Frost had pulled herself free from the enveloping cloak just in time to see Silence fall. She ignored the fleeing rebels, and the shocked, stammering Stelmach, and hurried over to kneel beside Silence. The energy beam had torn away most of his left rib cage. He'd wrapped his arms around himself, as though he could hold his body together through sheer strength. Frost gently pulled his arms away so she could see the extent of the wound. Blackened stubs of ribs showed clearly in the steaming wound, half-cauterized by the energy beam. Behind them, Stelmach was babbling about its being a mistake, and he was sorry, so sorry, but neither of them was listening. Silence's face was utterly white, and he was breathing in quick, shallow gasps. Anyone else would have been dead by now, from the shock alone. Frost grabbed his hand and squeezed it hard.

"Captain, listen to me! You're not going to die. There's a power in you, in us. Use it! John, dammit, you can heal yourself!"

She concentrated, focusing on the power deep within her, forcing it to the surface and on into Silence. He gasped once, and then his hand clamped down hard on hers, and he straightened up, his eyes wide and startled. They both looked down at the great wound in his side, and watched speechlessly as the flesh and bone and skin knitted themselves seamlessly together until there was no trace of the wound left. Silence took a deep, experimental breath, bracing himself for pain that never came, and then he grinned suddenly at Frost. She grinned back, and together they got to their feet again. Stelmach was standing over them with his mouth hanging open.

"I didn't know you could do that," he said finally.

"Neither did I," said Silence. "Learn something new every day."

"I'm sorry, Captain, I'm really sorry . . ."

Silence raised a hand to stop him. "Apologies accepted. But from now on, Stelmach, if we get in a fight again, don't help me." He turned to Frost. Her smile was gone, and she was a calm, collected Investigator again.

"Welcome back, Captain. Always knew you were too mean to die."

"Glad to be back, Investigator. Which way did the rebels go?"

"Deeper into the woods, Captain. Should be an easy trail to follow. The Deathstalker's leaking a lot of blood. Do you feel up to chasing them?"

"I think so. But there's no hurry. There's only one place they can go now, and that's the Deathstalker Standing. And once he's there, we've got him."

Kit SummerIsle eased the wounded Deathstalker down onto his bed and looked around the luxuriously appointed bedchamber. There was only the one door and the one window, which made it easier to defend the room against attackers. For the moment, the Standing was under the control of people loyal to David, but unfortunately the Steward had made his escape with most of his people, and they were probably already linking up with the invading Empire forces. It wouldn't be long before they came knocking at the front door. David lay back on his bed, gasping for breath. One of the servants had wrapped his gut in layer upon layer of bandages, but there was no doctor. Blood was already seeping through the bandages and staining the expensive bedsheets. Kit sat on the edge of the bed and wondered what to do next.

He could just leave. He could. The Deathstalker had been outlawed, but he hadn't. He could just leave the Standing, walk up to the nearest Empire forces, and claim the protection his rank entitled him to. The Captain and the Investigator he'd fought earlier might make a fuss, but he could always claim he'd acted in self-defense, and, as a Lord, no one would doubt his word. But the thought didn't tempt him long. He couldn't abandon David.

The Deathstalker groaned suddenly as he sat up, and Kit was quickly there to support him. David's face was grey now, lined with pain and fatigue, but his eyes were clear. His gaze went to his sword, lying on the bed close at hand, and he seemed to draw some strength from that. He gestured at the viewscreen on the wall before him.

"Turn on the screen," he said, his voice quiet but steady. "I need to know what's happening on my world."

"You should be resting," said Kit. "We might have to leave here in a hurry, if the Steward comes back with enough troops to storm the Standing."

"I'm not going anywhere," said David. "This is my home, the home of my ancestors, and I will go no farther. I'll make my stand here. Now turn on the damn viewscreen."

Kit shrugged and turned on the screen, and together the rebel Lords watched a montage of terrible scenes on the invaded world of Virimonde. Everywhere, buildings were burning. In villages, towns, cities. The dead lay piled in the fields like some dark, ugly crop. Long lines of refugees filed away into the countryside, carrying what was left of their homes and lives on their backs. There was still some resistance. The underground had been established here for many years. They had training and some weapons, but not enough to face experienced ground troops and Imperial war machines. But still the rebels fought on, outnumbered and outgunned, making the Empire forces pay for every foot of ground they gained. David watched his people fight and die, staining the ground they fought for with their own blood and that of their enemies. He saw Imperial marines marching through gutted villages, and massive war machines resting in the ruins of devastated cities, and finally he had to look away. Kit turned the viewscreen off.

"There's only one thing I can do," David said finally.

"Right," said Kit. "Grab everything we can sell, and make a run for it. There's bound to be someone we can bribe to get us offplanet. Then, I don't know. Mistworld, maybe?"

"No," said David. "I told you; I won't run. I'm going to surrender."

"What? Are you crazy? The best you could hope for

would be a show trial and a swift execution. At least on
Mistworld . . ."

"No! No. If I surrender, and tell the rebels to lay down
their arms, the fighting will end. My people will be safe.
Too many have died, Kit. Why prolong the agonies? All
that matters now is to protect my people in the only way
left to me."

Kit glared at him. "When did you get so damn noble?
They're just peasants!"

"No," said David. "They're my peasants. The bond of
duty and obligation that ties us together works both ways.
I never really understood that before." He smiled sadly.
"It's taken a long time, but I think I finally understand
what it is, to be a Deathstalker. Turn the screen back on.
See if you can raise someone in charge."

Kit saw the determination in his friend's face, and
stopped arguing. It turned out to be surprisingly easy to
raise the man in charge of the invasion. General Shaw
Beckett on the Imperial starcruiser *Elegance* looked out
of the screen at the two rebel Lords, and bowed formally.

"My Lord Deathstalker, my Lord SummerIsle, good to
hear from you. Forgive my bluntness, David, but you
don't look too good."

"I'm still here, General." David kept his voice calm and
even. "I wish to offer my surrender."

"Very noble of you, David. I appreciate the gesture."
Beckett scowled unhappily. "Unfortunately, I have new
orders from the Empress herself not to accept your surrender, on any terms. She wants you dead, David, and the
rebellion crushed. My troops took holocameras down
with them. People all over the Empire are watching the
invasion of Virimonde live. The Empress intends for this
to be an example. I'm sorry. I can offer some protection
to your friend, the SummerIsle, if you wish. I have no
direct orders for his death. I give you my word . . ."

"I'll think about it," said Kit.

The General nodded slowly. "Don't think too long, my
lord."

David smiled tiredly at the General. "Then I don't suppose we have anything left to say to each other, do we,
Shaw? Destiny has shaped a path for both of us, and all

we can do is follow them to their ends. Pardon me if I
don't wish you good luck."

"Understood, my lord." General Beckett saluted him.
"Die well, Deathstalker."

His face disappeared from the viewscreen and Kit shut
it off. He looked at David. "Lie down again. Get some
rest. You've got to think of a way out of this for us.
You're the brains in this partnership, remember?"

"He was right, Kit. You don't have to stay here."

"Yes I do."

They smiled at each other. David put out a hand to Kit.
The SummerIsle took it in both of his, and grasped it
tightly. The Deathstalker's hand was clammy, and cold as
death. David lay back on the bed again, with Kit's help.
The whole of his side was soaked in blood now. Kit still
held his hand. There was a commotion outside. Kit let go
of David's hand, and went over to look out the window.
Outside the main gate, the Steward had returned with his
men and a small army of Imperial troops, led by the Lord
High Dram, and Captain Silence and Investigator Frost.

Toby Shreck and his cameraman Flynn ran down a
narrow street, the buildings burning to either side like
giant balefires under the blood-streaked sky. The air was
thick with dirty black smoke and floating cinders, and so
hot it burned their bare hands and faces. Flynn's camera
bobbed along above them, getting the best shots it could,
and transmitting them live. High above, Imperial war-
ships rained down destruction, energy beams from ranked
disrupter cannon blowing buildings apart and collapsing
streets. People were running everywhere, all with some
kind of weapon in their hands. Toby had given up trying
to keep track of where he was. One burning town looked
much like another. And everywhere he went, he had to
step over the dead. Men, women, and children lay in
anonymous, blood-soaked bundles, cut down and hacked
apart, or burning from the touch of an energy beam. Toby
had never seen slaughter like it. Lionstone must have
gone insane. This had gone far beyond punishment for
rebellion, or an example to discourage others. Nothing
could justify human butchery like this. It occurred to him
now and again that he must be getting really good cov-

erage. No one had ever filmed an invasion from this close before. He just hoped someone was watching. He wouldn't put it past the Empire ships to jam all signals but their own. Toby scowled as he ran, despite his tiredness. He hated to think this was all for nothing.

He never saw the explosion that took out the building beside him. All he knew was that there was a sound like thunder, and then something picked him up and threw him down the street. He hit the cobbled ground hard, his clothes tearing, and then he tried to protect his head with his arms, as shattered brickwork came tumbling down around him. Bricks bounced off his back and arms and legs and he cried out, his voice lost in the roar of destruction around him. Finally it stopped, and Toby cautiously raised his head and looked about him. Half the street was in ruins. Flynn lay not far away, his camera hovering over him. The cameraman was half-buried under collapsed brickwork. Toby forced himself back onto his feet and staggered over to Flynn. His ears were ringing, his hands were trembling, and his legs felt like they belonged to someone else, but he fought it all back as he bent over Flynn. *Oh God, don't be dead, Flynn. Please don't be dead. I didn't bring you here to die.* He found a pulse in Flynn's neck and relaxed a little. He started pulling the bricks away, one at a time. There seemed to be no end to them.

He'd barely made a start when a company of Imperial marines came trotting down the street, guns at the ready. The Sergeant saw Toby and turned his gun in his direction. Toby stuck both his arms in the air.

"Don't shoot! I'm a reporter, covering the invasion!"

The Sergeant sniffed disappointedly and gestured for his men to lower their guns and come to a stop. He glowered down at Toby. "What are you doing here? You people are supposed to have cleared this area by now."

"My cameraman's trapped here," said Toby, cautiously lowering his hands. "Help me dig him out, and we'll get the hell out of your way."

"Anything to get you out of my hair. I don't know why the Empress wanted you here in the first place."

The Sergeant gestured to the nearest marines, and half a dozen of them helped Toby pull away the rest of the

bricks covering Flynn. And only then did Toby discover
that either the force of the explosion or the sharp edges of
the broken bricks had ripped Flynn's clothes apart,
revealing for all to see the lacy black feminine underwear
he wore beneath them. The stockings and garter belt were
particularly fetching. The six marines backed away
quickly, while their friends made lewd jokes and unsa-
vory comments. Toby thought fast.

"They're his good-luck charms! They belonged to a
female colleague of his, who he was very close to, and
since she died, he wears them to remind him of her, and
bring him good luck. Really. Lots of cameramen do it. It's
an old tradition among news crews."

"Shut your face," said the Sergeant. "And that goes for
you men, too. There's no way a freak like this could have
qualified for the army news corp. Which means you two
are here illegally. Probably rebels as well as degenerates."

"Of course we're not rebels! Look, I'm Toby Shreck!
You must have seen my work!"

"I've seen it." The Sergeant looked at his men. "Shoot
them both."

Toby stood frozen in a moment that seemed to last forever. He had nothing to defend himself with, and there
was nowhere to run. Even if he could bring himself to
abandon Flynn. He watched helplessly as the marines
turned their guns on him, and all he could think was that
he hoped the camera was getting a good view of this. And
then his jaw dropped as the Sergeant and all his marines
simultaneously burst into flames. The marines dropped
their weapons and staggered back and froth, beating at
the flames with their bare hands and screaming shrilly
as the fires rose up to consume them. One by one they fell
to the ground as the flames stole the oxygen from their
lungs, and they lay kicking and twitching as their flesh
blackened and cooked, their hair burning with a bright
blue flame. And then two women with the same face
stepped out of the shadows, and Toby realized what had
happened. The Stevie Blues had come to the rescue again.

He grunted a quick thanks and bent over Flynn, who
was dazedly trying to sit up. The Blues hauled him up
onto his feet and hurried him down the street, with Toby
sticking close behind them. Even in the chaos of a town

on fire, people still had the sense to get out of the way of the Stevie Blues. They made good time, despite having to dodge roving companies of Imperial marines, hurrying down a series of narrow side streets that all looked the same to Toby, until finally they ended up before an anonymous door in a fairly untouched area. Stevie Three hammered on the door with her fist, and a sliding panel opened, revealing a pair of suspicious eyes. Stevie Three glared right back at them, and the panel slammed shut. There was the sound of locks turning and bolts being pulled back, and then the door opened, and the Stevies led Toby and Flynn inside. The door slammed shut behind them.

It wasn't much more than a bolt-hole, really—a single wide room with boarded-up windows and only the one exit. Guns and rifles lay stacked along one wall, along with open cases of ammunition. A dozen heavily armed men and women were staring out through cracks in the boarded-up windows. They barely spared Toby and Flynn a glance. The air was thick and close, and smelled of sweat and tension. Stevie One had a muttered conversation with one of the rebels, while Stevie Three found a gun she liked and started loading it. Toby found a chair and helped Flynn onto it. The cameraman was looking better, but was increasingly distressed at the state of his clothes.

"I mean, these were my best lacy set," he said bitterly. "I knew I shouldn't have risked wearing them down here."

"Damn right," said Toby. "They very nearly got both of us killed."

Flynn sniffed. "Marines have no fashion sense." The camera perched on his shoulder seemed to nod agreement.

Toby turned to Stevie Three. "What is this place?"

"What's left of a rebel cell, fairly low on the chain of command, which is probably why the troops haven't found it yet. We're using it as a check-in point, for rebels who got scattered when the invasion hit. We're waiting for orders, but I don't even know if there are any traces of the underground's organization left in this town. We've been hit hard. Communications have gone to hell, and there are hardly any espers here. You're lucky my sister and I were out looking for strays; we'd already decided it was the last run we were going to make. This town has fallen; it just doesn't know it yet."

"Have you got time for an interview?" said Toby. "Seeing as we've got nothing to do for the moment. There's always the chance someone's watching."

He gestured to Flynn, who nodded that his camera was still running. He settled it comfortably on his shoulder, and the camera turned its glowing, unblinking eye on Stevie Three.

"Not much to tell," the esper clone said quietly. "The invasion took us all by surprise. The chain of command among the rebels was shattered almost immediately. We have no idea how things are going in any of the main cities. Some of the rebels tried to surrender when they saw how bad things were going, but the Empire forces aren't interested in taking prisoners. My sister and I did what we could to help, taking out some of the smaller war machines with our fire, preying on troops that got separated from the main forces, but there were just so many of them . . . We're all tired. So many of us are dead. Our ammunition's getting low. Maybe all that's left to us is to die well. And take as many of the bastards with us as we can."

"They're here!" yelled Stevie One, glaring out one of the slits in the windows. Everyone pushed their guns through the cracks between the boards and opened fire on the advancing troops. The noise of so many projectile weapons firing in a confined space was deafening. Toby and Flynn clapped their hands to their ears. Smoke and the stench of cordite filled the air. And then an energy beam punched right through the solid wooden door, passing on through the body of the rebel standing guard behind it, before exiting through the far wall.

"War wagon!" yelled Stevie One. "It's got disrupter cannon!"

And then energy beams were hitting the room from all directions. They came slamming through the walls, catching most of the rebels before they could drop to the floor for cover. The beams filled the room with blinding light, crisscrossing like some glaring luminous spider's web. Most of the rebels were holed and blown apart in the first few seconds, their charred and scattered parts falling to lie twitching on the floor. One man's head was blown clean away, and his body managed half a dozen faltering steps before another beam took its legs out, and it fell.

Toby tried to burrow into the stone floor, his hands over his head. He'd grabbed Flynn and hit the deck the moment Stevie One yelled her first warning. He wasn't a fighter. The beams kept coming, riddling the walls with endless holes, filling the room with the stench of ionized air. A few people were crying out, in fear or shock or suffering, but that didn't last long. Finally the beams stopped, and all was quiet, save for quiet creaking noises from the weakened walls. Early-morning light streamed through the hundreds of holes in the walls, diffused by the drifting smoke. Toby slowly lifted his head and looked around him. The dead were everywhere. Torn apart and broken, like so many dolls deserted by angry children who didn't want to play anymore. Flynn was lying beside Toby, cradling his precious camera in his arms. He nodded to Toby to show he was okay, but made no move to get up. Stevie One and Stevie Three lay together, and only one of them was moving.

Stevie Three sat up slowly. Half her hair and half her face had been burned away from her head where an energy beam had touched her in passing, but otherwise she seemed unhurt. Stevie One had fared less well. She'd been hit several times, and her left arm had been shot away, the steaming wound roughly cauterized just above the elbow. Stevie Three cradled her in her arms. Stevie One groaned, and her eyes flickered open.

"Damn," she said thickly. "I think the odds just got worse."

"Shut up," said Stevie Three. "Rest. Save your strength."

"What for? It's over, love. The Empire's won."

"It's not over till we say it's over," said Stevie Three fiercely. "Don't you dare die and leave me alone. We lived together and we'll die together, and we'll do it on our feet. Get up, damn you. Come on, love. One last spit in the Empress's eye."

Stevie One smiled. "Right."

Stevie Three got them both on their feet, holding Stevie

One up till her legs firmed. They looked around for other
survivors, and saw Toby and Flynn looking up at them.
Stevie Three smiled.

"I might have known. Good men and women die, but
reporters go on forever. Stay down, boys. This isn't your
fight."

"What are you going to do?" said Toby.

Stevie Three looked at the door before her, and Toby
knew she was seeing the enemy massed outside. When
she spoke, her voice was almost calm, matter of fact.
"Once there were four of us. Clones, sisters, lovers; a
closer relationship than you can ever imagine. Two died,
fighting the Empire that created them, and now it's our
turn. We've always known we were born to burn. All
that's left is one last gesture of defiance."

"What are you going to do?" said Toby. "What can
you do?"

"Die well," said Stevie One, and Stevie Three nodded.

"Sometimes, that's all there is."

"No," said Toby, his voice roughened by unfamiliar
emotions. "There's got to be another way. There's always
another way."

"No," said Stevie Three, almost kindly. "Not always.
Every road comes to its end eventually. Get your camera
ready. We're going out."

She hauled her sister over to the door, carefully undid
the locks, and pulled back the bolts one by one. Flynn's
camera rose from his shoulder to get a better view. Stevie
Three yanked the door open and slammed it back against
the wall. The esper clones stood framed in the doorway a
moment, looking out at the men and machines arrayed
against them. From somewhere deep inside, Stevie One
found the strength to stand alone. Stevie Three glanced
back over her shoulder, and showed her teeth in a smile.

"See you in Hell, boys."

She turned back to stare out the doorway, and both the
Stevie Blues burst into flames. Bright blue fires burned
around them, strengthening and consuming them as they
focused all their last strength and rage into a final act of
defiance. They ran forward, yelling their war cry, fire
blazing from three outstretched hands to incinerate men
and machines alike. The Imperial marines opened fire.

Disrupter beams punched through the Stevie Blues again and again, shaking them like a dog shakes a rat. They fell together, and their flames went out, and there were no more Stevie Blues, anywhere at all.

Flynn got it all on film. Toby couldn't think of a damn thing to say.

A marine Sergeant came forward, and calmly stirred the dead espers with his boot, to make sure they were dead. He nodded, satisfied, and then walked unhurriedly forward to look through the door at Toby and Flynn. Toby waited to die. He had nowhere to go, and wouldn't have known what to do with a weapon if he'd had one. He felt strangely unconcerned, as though it felt wrong he should still be alive, when everyone else was dead. He glared up at the Sergeant unflinchingly, and hoped Flynn would keep filming to the last. The Sergeant stood over him and smiled.

"You're a lucky boy, Shreck. Turns out the Empress is something of a fan of yours. She's followed everything you've done recently. Think how surprised and delighted she was when the *Elegance* picked up your signal. So, you're coming with us. You and your cameraman are now official Imperial reporters, and the Empress wants you covering the fall of the Deathstalker Standing. And no, you don't get a choice. So hurry up, or you'll miss it."

He hauled Toby up onto his feet and slapped some of the dust off him. Flynn got up unaided. The Sergeant looked at him and winced.

"We'd better find you a cloak. Even reporters are supposed to have some standards. Come along, lads. The Empress wants the whole Empire to see what happens to people who dare rebel against her wise and just rule. Do a really good job, and maybe she won't have you executed afterward for fraternizing with the enemy. Now move it!"

Toby and Flynn walked unsteadily out of the room of death and into the waiting arms of the Empire.

In the ancient Standing of his Clan, David Deathstalker sat on the edge of his bed, watching his planet die on the viewscreen before him. He clicked through channel after channel, but the scene was always the same. His people, fighting and dying. Fighting ground troops or combat androids or war machines, but always dying. The villages and the towns and the cities burned, and the countryside was full of refugees being rounded up by Imperial troops. One in ten would be executed later, as an example. Lionstone was very keen on tradition.

David turned off the viewscreen, and the bedchamber was suddenly quiet. He hugged himself as tightly as he could stand, trying to hold himself together, despite the bloodsoaked bandages wrapped around his middle. The pain came and went now. He didn't know whether that was a good sign or not. When it was very bad all he could do was sit very still, gritting his teeth so he wouldn't call out, and wait for the pain to pass so he could think again. He felt hot and cold by turns, and sweat was dripping off his face. He tried desperately to think of something he could do to save the situation. His surrender had been turned down, and he couldn't get a signal offworld to call on the underground for help. Down below, the few staff still loyal to him or the rebellion were fighting to keep the Imperial forces out of the Standing. They wouldn't last long. Kit SummerIsle came through the open door, and David knew his news from his face.

"Captain Silence and the Investigator are leading a strike force against the main door. There's no way our people are going to be able to keep them out."

David nodded slowly. "They were never more than a holding action." He struggled to get up off the bed and onto his feet. Kit hurried over to help him. David hung on to him. His legs felt like they might go at any moment, but he wouldn't give in to them. He forced them straight and smiled at his friend.

"This is it, Kit. Once the Standing falls, the rebellion here is over. I think I finally understand what it means, to be a Deathstalker. To fight the good fight, to put it all on the line, even when you know you can't win." He gestured at the old holoportrait of the original Deathstalker, on the wall at the foot of his bed. "Look at him. Like some bad old barbarian mercenary, in his leathers and scalplock. Giles, my ancestor. I wonder what he would think of me. We never really had a chance to talk. And then there's Owen. I think I understand him a little better now. He tried to warn me, and I wouldn't listen. He said I'd never be able to hold Virimonde, and he was right. The Empress gives and the Empress takes away. God damn the Empress."

"You're feverish," said Kit. "Sit down again."

"No. If I sit down now, I'll never find the strength to get up again. Time we were leaving, I think."

Kit looked at him. "The Standing's surrounded, David. They have all the exits blocked."

"There's one they don't know about." David lurched over to the holoportrait and hit a hidden switch, and the portrait swung sideways, revealing a narrow passage. Lights came on, showing the passage stretching down into darkness. David smiled tiredly as he saw new hope rise in Kit's eyes. "Secret passage. Owen told me about it. Saved his ass when they came for him. Finishes up in the flyer bay, in the caves below the Standing. We'll grab a flyer, shove the throttle to max, and get the hell out of here before they know what's happening. I can't die yet, Kit. My people need me. If I can't save them, maybe I can arrange for them to be avenged. You know, Kit, it's taken a long time, but I think I've finally found my honor and my duty."

"You are feverish," said Kit. "Let's go."

They made their way slowly down the secret passage, David leaning heavily on Kit. Blood was running freely down his side now, and when he coughed, as he sometimes had to despite the pain, blood sprayed from his mouth along with the sound. But he kept going. He wouldn't give up. A Deathstalker never gives up. His head swam sickly, and sometimes he thought it was Owen there in the passage with him, and sometimes it was Giles. But when his head cleared, Kit was always there with him, the only real friend he'd ever had.

They reached the end of the passage, and came to a stop while Kit peered cautiously out into the flyer bay. He snapped his head back in immediately, and a disrupter beam hit the top of the tunnel mouth, blasting debris from the stone ceiling. David was caught off-balance and fell heavily to the floor, pulling Kit down with him. They lay together on the stone floor, breathing heavily. Kit fired his gun blindly out the passage mouth, to discourage anyone from coming in after them. He looked for David's gun, and found he didn't have one.

"David," he said urgently. "Where's your gun?"

"I gave it to Alice, just before we crashed. She's still got it." David spit blood onto the floor, and pulled a face. "Kit, I just tried to boost, and nothing happened. There's nothing left in me. No more fight. This is as far as I go."

"Shut up," said Kit. "Get your breath back, and we'll head back up the passage."

"No. I'm not going anywhere. I'm cold, Kit. So cold."

Kit sat up, put his back against the passage wall, and cradled David in his arms, holding him close, trying to share his warmth with the dying man.

"Had some good times here, didn't we, Kit?"

"The best."

"Pity about Alice. And Jenny."

"Yes."

"Leave me, Kit."

"What?"

"They want me, not you. Pointless, you dying here as well as me."

"I can't leave you, David. You're my friend."

"Then do as I ask. Don't die for nothing. Kill me, and then go out to them. My death will put you in good with Lionstone again. Show her my head, and she'll probably make you Lord of Virimonde. They'll think you're one of them, after all."

"David . . . please. I can't . . ."

"Yes you can. You have to. I don't want to die here, by inches, screaming when the pain gets really bad. Do it, Kit. Be my friend. One last time."

He coughed harshly, and couldn't stop. Blood spilled down his chin. He tried to speak again and couldn't. Kit hugged him tightly till the coughing stopped, then drew his knife and thrust it expertly between David's ribs. The breath went out of the Deathstalker in a long sigh, and then he was still. Kit sat there for a while, cradling the dead body in his arms. David had been quite right. The Empress would take him back, as David's executioner. She'd always had a soft spot for her smiling killer. And it wasn't as if he had anywhere else to go. The rebellion was over. Anyone could see that. So that just left Lionstone. He was a killer, and he had to go where the killing was. He carefully laid David's body down on the passage floor and arranged his arms and legs neatly. He drew his sword and leaned over David. The Deathstalker's face was very calm. Kit leaned down and kissed David on the bloody lips.

"My love."

He straightened up and raised his sword.

CHAPTER FOUR

EVERYONE GOES TO GOLGOTHA

And so the war finally began, almost by accident.

The live broadcast of Virimonde's destruction and the slaughter of its population by Imperial forces backfired badly. A roar of rage and condemnation spread across the whole Empire, planet after planet seeing its own possible future in the horrific images unfolding before them on their viewscreens. Insurrections arose spontaneously on world after world, sparks fanning into flames as the incoming images grew steadily worse. The lower classes took to the streets, protests quickly becoming riots, turning on anything that could be seen as representing Imperial authority. The moneyed classes were right out there with them, as often as not, driven from their complacency by shock and outrage, ready to fight and die rather than see their world mechanized like Virimonde.

The underground seized the opportunity before it, and sent its people out on every world they had access to, guiding and assisting the spontaneous uprisings. They supplied weapons, pointed crowds in the right directions, and put long-crafted plans into operation. Deep-planted sleeper agents committed sabotage, disrupted communications, and generally brought people together to do the most damage possible. The army responded by emptying its barracks and sending troops straight out onto the streets, with orders to shoot everything that moved. It might have worked, if so many people hadn't been shocked and sickened by what they'd seen happening on Virimonde. They were too angry now to be properly scared. Men and women spilled out onto the streets, armed with whatever weapons they could find or improvise, and fell upon the Imperial troops in such numbers that not even massed energy weapons could stop

them. All across the Empire, on world after world, there
was blood and slaughter in the towns and cities, and official buildings blazed like warning beacons of the battle
to come.

In the streets they cursed the name of the Widowmaker
Dram, and tore down the portraits and statues of the Iron
Bitch, and howled for revenge for the dead of Virimonde.

Increasingly isolated as well as outraged, the Lords
added their troops to the rebellion, sending their armed
forces out to fight the Imperial troops alongside the
rebels. The Families were nothing if not survivors, and
Lionstone had become a greater threat to them than any
momentary uprisings. They'd always known she was
crazy, but now she had become dangerously insane. If
Lionstone had consulted them first, about David or Virimonde or even the mechanization, things might have been
different. They'd have found some way to turn it to their
advantage. But the first they knew of any of it was when
their viewscreens showed them the rape of a Lord's
planet. It didn't take too much imagination for any of
them to see themselves as Lionstone's next object of
opportunity, outlawed so their planet could be next in line
for mechanization under Lionstone's direct rule. Faced
with a clear threat to their lives, their position, and their
wealth, it was inevitable that the Lords would tacitly
encourage the rebellion. The lower orders could always
be put back in their place later. And if many Lords saw in
the chaos an opportunity to place themselves on the Iron
Throne, they kept it to themselves, for the moment.

Suddenly, it seemed like everything was up for grabs.
Anything seemed possible. Every group and faction and
cause saw a chance to overthrow the way things were, and
went out into the streets to fight for it. People who
wouldn't normally have spoken to each other without
spitting became temporary allies, fighting side by side,
held together by the shared aim of throwing Lionstone off
the Iron Throne before she could destroy them all in her
madness. In city after city, on world after world, the
people went head-to-head with Imperial troops, and the
cry of rebellion was on everyone's lips.

The army and the Fleet could have coped with a few
planetwide rebellions, but not everything at once.

Stretched thinly across the Empire, attacked on every front and even from within by those sympathetic to the rebels and their cause, the Imperial forces were crippled by confusion. Starcruisers appeared over the worst trouble spots, but they'd never been intended to deal with planetside rebellions. Their only real threat was a scorching, and for the moment, at least, they were spread too thinly for that. Rebels in their crews sabotaged their communications, isolating them further. The underground had planned for this day, and the Empire, in its arrogance, had not.

On the planet Golgotha, homeworld of Empire, center of authority, outraged people filled the streets, rioting and looting and burning down the command centers. Because they'd had so much more to lose, they'd hesitated at first from open rebellion, but the underground had swiftly spread rumors that Lionstone was planning harsh new taxes, even more repressive laws, and was even planning to shut down their precious Arenas. After what they'd seen on Virimonde, the people were ready to believe anything of her, and these new threats hit them where they lived. Isolated protests were put down with such fury and bloodshed that even the hardened populace of Golgotha was shocked, and they rose up everywhere at once. The underground did its best to guide them in the right directions, while hiding its smiles. It had always known people need motivating, and what they won't do for the right reason, sometimes they will for the wrong reason.

The authorities sent out every armed trooper they had, with orders to stop the riots at all costs and not to bother with taking prisoners. This just made matters worse, infuriating an already defiant population, and as fast as troopers put the rebellion down in one place, it just popped up in another, regrouping and re-forming faster than it could be dispersed. The underground disrupted all levels of communication, while using espers to organize their own forces. The Clans took one look at the growing chaos, called back all their troops, and retreated into their pastel Towers, safe behind organized levels of security. Encouraging the fighting on other worlds was one thing, but this was too close to home. So they kept their heads well down, avoided attracting attention to themselves, and let the rebels concentrate their hatred on Lionstone's authority. And when the mess was over, and the rebels were tired and aimless once more, the Families would emerge and take control again, as they always had. Or so they thought. They didn't know about the underground—its plans and its powers. They didn't know about the people who'd been through the Madness Maze. They didn't realize that the great rebellion had finally begun.

Parliament convened and agreed to stand aside and support whoever came out on top. Which surprised no one.

Above the worlds of Empire, starships clashed in the night. The underground had put out a call to the Hadenmen, and their great golden ships were abroad in the night again. Huge and fast and awesome, they were more than a match for the scattered Imperial starcruisers. As far as numbers went, the Hadenman ships were greatly in the minority, but they ran rings around the slower Empire ships, outgunning and outperforming them on every level. The Empire crews panicked, faced with the legendary old Enemies of Humanity, and put out general distress calls, demanding that all Imperial ships forget about the rebellions to face the greater threat of the Hadenmen. Starcruisers all across the Empire ignored Lionstone's increasingly frantic orders and raced to meet the golden ships, only to fall one by one. Blazing wreckage cartwheeled slowly down through the atmospheres of unsuspecting planets. And the Hadenmen sailed on through the long night.

The Church of Christ the Warrior saw the second coming of the augmented men as a spiritual as well as a martial threat, and threw everything they had against the Hadenmen, ignoring the rebellion. They fared no better than the Fleet, once again distracting ships and troops that might have prevailed against the rebellion. The underground confused things even farther by spreading carefully placed rumors that Lionstone was planning to seize the Church's tithes to replace her missing taxes, thus alienating the Church even more. Every little bit helped.

If Lionstone had had more than just a few E class starcruisers to call on, with their new stardrives and superior weapons systems, things might have been different. But after the rebels destroyed the Wolfe stardrive factory on Technos III, there were only five E class ships in service, and they couldn't be everywhere at once. There were even open mutinies on some Imperial ships, as junior officers with rebel sympathies and underground connections led takeover bids on the control decks, backed by disgruntled lower ranks who hadn't been paid for months, because of Treasury shortfalls after the Tax systems crashed. A surprising number of these mutinies succeeded, and the new rebel ships withdrew themselves from combat. They wouldn't fight their own kind, but they would take no further part against the rebellion.

Meanwhile, Toby Shreck and his cameraman Flynn were right there in the thick of it all, getting everything on film, transmitting live as often as they could. Dragged from one bloody firefight to another by their Imperial minders, they did their best to cover everything as objectively as possible. The army officers supposed to be in charge of censoring their output were mostly too busy with their own problems.

On a battlefield pockmarked with craters on the planet Loki, the Imperial armies were overrun by wild-eyed rebel forces, and Toby and Flynn took the first opportunity to make a run for it. They didn't get far among the body-filled craters before they were stopped by the advancing rebel forces, who luckily recognized Toby. A few even asked for autographs. Toby pleaded eloquently to be sent to Golgotha, where the real story was, and after a certain amount of discussion the rebels were happy to send them on their way. They understood the need for good propaganda, and it seemed only fair to all concerned that the two men who had covered so much of the story should be there for the final act when it happened. Toby smiled and nodded and agreed modestly in all the right places, and prayed no one would ask awkward questions about who was going to pay all the bills. No one did, so Toby and Flynn set off on the first of half a dozen uncomfortable journeys that would take them eventually to Golgotha, Lionstone's Court, and the Hell that she had made there.

For it was on Golgotha that the real fighting, the clashes

that mattered, would take place. Who rules homeworld rules the Empire. Everyone knew that. And so Lionstone retreated into her Palace of gleaming steel and brass, set inside a massive steel bunker a mile and a half wide, sunk deep below the surface of the planet, and waited for her enemies to come to her.

They were burning the poets, hanging the troubadours, impaling the satirists. Blood and screams and horror. Just another day in Hell. The Court was a dark, dangerous place now, reflecting the mind of its ruler. The Empress Lionstone XIV, the worshiped and adored, sat on her Iron Throne as though she might leap down from it at any moment, to rend and savage some unfortunate enemy. She wore shimmering white battle armor, which together with her pale face and long blond hair made her look like some vengeful family ghost. Normally she wore her long mane of hair piled up on top of her head for Court appearances, but now it hung down in long uncared-for tresses, through which her icy blue eyes stared unwaveringly. And on her head the tall spiky crown, cut from a single huge diamond—the symbol of power and authority in the Empire.

At the base of her Throne, her maids-in-waiting crouched watchfully like the guard dogs they were. Naked and unashamed as animals, mindwiped and surgically altered to be loyal unto death, they watched the Court through cybernetic senses, ready for any threat to their beloved mistress. They would kill or die to protect her, and their ferocity was legendary. Their teeth were pointed and their fingers ended in implanted steel claws. Within their naked bodies they had other, nastier surprises, the best that money could buy. Once they had been as human as anyone else, with minds and lives of their own, but that was before Lionstone chose them, and took them away from their old lives to be a part of hers. They could be commoner or aristocrat; all were made equally vile under Lionstone's wishes. No one objected. No one dared. Besides, it was an honor to be a maid-in-waiting to the Empress.

Floating on the air before the Throne, dozens of view-screens showed scenes from all across the Empire. The

views changed rapidly, constantly updating themselves
on the growing path of the rebellion. Announcers with
sweating faces read the news almost apologetically. There
were charts showing rebel advances and Imperial losses.
Shaky cameras showed scenes of blood and chaos and
the roar of battle. They all looked much the same. Increasingly confused commentators chattered endlessly
about what it all meant. On some worlds the rebels had
seized control of communications, and triumphant smoke-
blackened faces called for the downtrodden to rise up and
overthrow the Iron Bitch. Screens blanked in and out as
the underground and their cyberat allies interfered with
the comm channels, but there were always more signals
coming in to replace them. The whole Empire was shouting at the top of its voice, desperate to be heard. The
Empress watched it all, her steady gaze cold as death
itself. For those who thought they knew her, her cold calm
was more worrying than her earlier shouted orders and
temper tantrums. It meant she was thinking. Planning.
Deliberating on her revenges, and the awful forms they
would take.

Standing quietly before the Iron Throne, at what they
hoped was a safe distance, were two of the few people
apart from guards and their victims still admitted to the
Imperial Court. General Shaw Beckett and the Warrior
Prime, the Lord High Dram. There were no courtiers present. No Lords and their Ladies, no representatives of the
great Families, no Members of Parliament, no one from
the one true Church, none of the usual celebrities and
characters and hangers-on. Lionstone didn't trust them
anymore. Any of them. And so Beckett and Dram stood
together, ignoring each other as best they could. They
were both men of war, but all they had in common was
their loyalty.

Tall and imposing, Dram wore his usual jet-black robes
over black battle armor, looking like some gore crow
fresh from the battlefield. He wore both gun and sword in
the presence of his Empress, one of the very few so
allowed. Beckett, on the other hand, looked a mess, as
always. His carefully tailored battle armor couldn't hide
the fact that he was seriously overweight, his robes were
decidedly scruffy, and he carried himself with immense

calm but little authority. He was smoking an evil-smelling cigar and not caring where the smoke went.

Around them, the Hell that Lionstone had fashioned for her Court. The light was bloodred, and the air was thick with the stench of brimstone. Great vents had opened up in the floor of the Court, through which sudden bursts of flame erupted, adding to the sweltering heat. And from far below came the faint screams of the damned and the suffering. Great pillars of stone rose up farther than the eye could follow, covered with carved tormented faces, screaming in silent agony, contorted by unimaginable pain.

And all around, the dead and the dying. Unfortunates who'd caught Lionstone's attention at just the wrong time. The hanged hung limply from their ropes or chains, the impaled had mostly stopped twitching on their bloody stakes, and only smoke rose from the charred and blackened figures burned in iron cages. There were others, denied an easy death. A ballerina with broken legs, a poet with his eyes gouged out, and a captured rebel leader with long ropes of purple guts hanging out of his torn-open stomach. And many more. They crawled around on their hands and knees, biting back their screams to prevent further punishment, begging quietly for just a little water. Beckett hoped that most of them were just holograms, computer-generated images called up by Lionstone to add to the atmosphere, but he couldn't make himself believe it. Particularly when they tugged at his boots with broken hands and pleaded quietly for just a word on their behalf. He didn't look down. He couldn't help them. He wasn't even sure he could help himself. To distract himself, he studied the armed guards standing in silent ranks behind the Throne. Lionstone had dressed them as devils, with curling horns on their helmets and blazing wings erupting from the back of their armor. Lionstone believed in every detail being perfect.

Finally she looked away from the viewscreens and turned her attention to Beckett and Dram. They both did their best to stand a little straighter. When she spoke her voice, like her gaze, was icy cold.

"General Beckett, we have called you here to place you

in sole charge of this planet's defenses. We put Golgotha into your hands. Guard it well and keep it safe."

Beckett stared at her blankly. "But . . . Your Majesty; I assumed I'd been brought here to take command of your fleet! I am the only one left with the experience and seniority to pull things back together. They'll listen to me! Who else is better qualified for this than I?"

"Don't presume to argue with us, General," said Lionstone, her voice dangerously calm. "You have your orders; carry them out."

Beckett bore down hard on his anger, to keep from saying something he might be made to regret later, turned on his heel, and strode out of the Court. He'd been loyal to the Iron Throne all his days, and couldn't change that now. No matter how much he was tempted. Lionstone watched him go, and then turned back to Dram.

"You will command my fleet, dear Dram. Beckett is too soft, for all his vaunted loyalty. He might hesitate to do the things that must be done. I admired your firmness, your thoroughness, on Virimonde, and I need someone at the helm that I can trust implicitly. So you're to be the man in charge, Dram. My man in charge. Don't fail me. Don't dare fail me. You'll give your orders from here, at my side. You'll be safe here, and I'll be able to consult with you, as necessary."

"Yes, Lionstone. But . . . will the Captains accept me as Commander in Chief? They know I don't have Beckett's experience."

"They'll serve the Warrior Prime. The man they think you are. That's all that matters. Take my fleet and crush my enemies, Dram. Break them and scatter them and show them no mercy. Just as you did on Virimonde. I am Empress, and I will be obeyed. And afterward . . . there will be a purging of all weak and disloyal elements such as no one has ever seen before."

She smiled an unpleasant smile, and Dram made himself nod in agreement. "As you will, Lionstone. Pardon me for asking, but . . . do you think you would do well to protect yourself further, even here? There's no telling what lengths the rebels or the elves might go to, for a chance to strike directly at you."

"Don't worry yourself about such things," Lionstone

said easily. "I have sent for the best of the best to come here to be my personal bodyguards. No one will get past Investigator Razor and Kid Death."

Up on the surface, the fighting went on, growing more bloody and more bitter all the time. Armies ran through the streets and crowded the open squares, fighting the Imperial troops for this cause or that, but all united against the monster Lionstone, the madwoman on the Iron Throne. The barracks had been emptied of troops to the very last man, and the two main forces slammed together wherever they met, each convinced that right and destiny were on their side. One fought for order, the other for justice, and there was no room for quarter or surrender in either camp. Both sides had to win overwhelmingly, or see themselves devastated by the victor. They fought with swords and axes, force shields and energy guns, and the disturbing, unfamiliar projectile weapons supplied by the underground. Blood sprayed on the air, and men and women fell to lie screaming on the gore-soaked streets, dying from their wounds, or simple shock, or just from the endless trampling feet of the close-packed fighters. No one had time to care for the wounded, and the dead were everywhere. They were kicked out of the way, or piled on street corners, forgotten by friends and enemies alike as the battles continued.

Some of Lionstone's troops were using the new stasis projectors. Within their narrowly focused fields, time came to a stop, and all those caught in the field were held there helpless, trapped in a moment taken out of time, like insects confined in amber. Advances were brought to crashing halts, and whole areas became impassable. But this was new technology, and the number of projectors was strictly limited. They were also unstable and unreliable. Sometimes just activating the machine was enough to blow the whole apparatus apart and kill everyone in a thirty-yard radius. Understandably, the troops were reluctant to use them. Sometimes officers had to stand there with them and put guns to their heads. But where the machines did work, the effects were dramatic. Within the projected field, time could be slowed to a crawl or sped up beyond counting. Those trapped in stasis could become living statues, removed from the conflict, or, more often, they could age horribly fast. Skin shrank, bodies warped with age, hearts failed and brains rotted in splitting skulls. Even on low power, the machines produced clinging tanglefields that could fill a street, slowing advancing forces and making them helpless targets for more traditional weapons.

But this success didn't last. As soon as the threat became clear, the cyberats infiltrated the machines' computer-aiming systems, and shut them down. Battle espers took out the projectors' operators from a safe distance, destroying their minds or setting them on fire. Where the troops were protected by esp-blockers, the espers used mind-bombs. Nasty high-tech devices built around dead esper brain tissues. When detonated, every non-esper in the mindbomb's range went horribly insane. The troops would turn on each other and tear each other apart with their bare hands, screaming and crying and howling wordlessly, soaked in their fellows' blood. The rebel forces pressed forward, overran the stasis projectors and their dead or insane crews, and moved on.

There would be time to think about the terrible things they'd had to do later.

The Empress gave orders to turn the Grendels, the merciless killing-machine aliens found in the Vaults of the Sleepers, loose in the streets. Vicious monsters in blood-red spiked silicon armor, they moved too swiftly for the human eye to follow, killing all they came across. Weapons were useless against them. Too strong to be fought, too fast to be faced, they moved inexorably through the crowded streets, leaving only blood and slaughter in their wake. Unfortunately, the Empress's control over these creatures was very limited. Once released from the enforced pacification of their cybernetic yokes, they killed every living thing they encountered, no matter which side they happened to be on. Beyond any control or guidance, they rampaged through the streets, scarlet devils from an alien hell, and the dead piled up behind them. If Lionstone had had more of them, they might have turned the tide. But their numbers were limited, and so was the damage they could cause in a city overrun with battling armies.

The underground sent battle espers against the aliens, but many of the espers died just from making contact with the Grendels' minds. They were too alien, too different, too awful to be faced. And so the underground called on the elves, the hard-line Esper Liberation Front, who sent in the polters and the firestarters. Soon roiling psistorms blazed through the streets, ripping the Grendels apart and incinerating the bloody fragments. The aliens fell one by one, fighting to the last against an enemy they could neither see nor reach, and as they were broken and consumed by raging fires, both sides cheered the espers as heroes. Never before had aliens been allowed to roam home-world's streets, killing humans, and many on both sides saw this as another sign of Lionstone's growing madness. Soldiers and civilians who had been forced to stand by helplessly as the Grendels butchered their comrades and loved ones now cursed the Empress and went to fight alongside the rebels.

The rebels didn't have it all their own way. The leg-endary Half A Man led his own army of troops through the Parade of the Endless, fighting from the front, putting down rebellion wherever he found it, by whatever means necessary. His successes and calm military demeanor inspired his soldiers, and almost through sheer force of personality he held the center of the city, and would not be moved, no matter what the odds against him. To the troops he was a hero as well as a legend, the protector of Humanity, and they stood their ground and fought to the death rather than fail him. So the rebels left them the center of the city, and went around them. For in the end he was only one man, and he couldn't be everywhere at once.

The cyberats hacked into Golgotha's main communica-tions systems and shut down every military comm channel they could reach. The troops were instantly shut off from each other and isolated in their own small pockets of fighting. Strategy became impossible and rein-forcements ran helplessly in circles. Imperial espers were no match for the organized underground telepaths, and the military and security organizations quickly fell apart. Orders never reached their destinations. Calls for help went unanswered. Chaos reigned. But the rioters wasted their energies on looting and trivial revenges, for all the underground could do to guide them. The rebels themselves remained outnumbered and outgunned, and the longer the fighting went on, the worse the odds against them grew. They had to strike quickly, while they still had the advantage of surprise, and take control of Golgotha, or the rebellion could still fall apart and fail, for all its successes. The military knew this, and played a waiting game, holding key areas and refusing to give way. And so blood spilled, and men and women died on both sides, the tides of battle went this way and that, and the leaders of the underground began to grow desperate. It was beginning to look as though all their hopes now depended on a small group of heroes and legends who hadn't even made an appearance yet, that the whole rebellion could stand or fall on the actions of Owen Deathstalker and his companions.

The Shandrakor Standing of Giles Deathstalker, the original home and sanctuary of the Deathstalker Clan, dropped out of hyperspace and fell into orbit over the planet Golgotha. A huge stone castle with its own stardrive and force shield, and many other hidden surprises, it hung silently over the homeworld of Empire like a specter from the past, from the great days of Empire, before the dream became a nightmare and good men fell as the bad came to power. The ancient stone gleamed whitely in the light of Golgotha's sun, pale as a ghost, the specter at the feast, the old retainer returned at last to kick the usurpers out. After 943 years, the Deathstalker Standing had finally come home.

Giles Deathstalker stood at parade rest in the great Hall of the Standing, his back to a blazing fire, studying the planet below as it turned slowly on the giant viewscreen at the end of the Hall. Clad in his usual battered armor, grubby furs, golden armlets, and mercenary's scalplock, he looked more like some barbarian warrior out of Humanity's distant past then the first Warrior Prime of the Empire, hero and legend to all the Empire for almost a millennium. His long sword hung in a scabbard down his back, the leather-wrapped hilt peering watchfully over his shoulder, as though only waiting to be called into action.

The original Deathstalker, namer and founder of his Clan, back from exile to a homeworld that knew him not.

His distant descendant, Owen Deathstalker, stood a little away, with his comrade in arms, Hazel d'Ark, at his side. There was a closeness between them that hadn't been so clear before, as though they had discovered something important about each other and themselves during the invasion of Mistworld. They stood tall and confident, and strength and power hung about them like an aura of greatness. They wore no armor, but while Owen bore only his sword and disrupter, Hazel was packing as many weapons as she could carry. Hazel believed in guns. They'd come a long way since they first met, in a field on Virimonde which no longer existed, and it was hard to see in Owen and Hazel the reclusive scholar and reluctant pirate they'd once been. They had come into their destiny, and it showed.

On the other side of the enormous fireplace stood Jack Random, the legendary professional rebel. The broken-down old man Owen had found hiding out in Mistport, such a short time ago, had disappeared now, replaced by a strong, muscular figure in the prime of his years. Jack Random had re-created himself, through his faith and his power and his courage, and the mysterious powers of the Madness Maze, to be a hero and a legend one more time. Just standing there, calm and relaxed, he looked ready to take on the whole damned Empire by himself. And if there were blood and savagery and slaughter of the foe along the way, that suited him just fine.

Close by his side, looking as though she belonged there and always had, Ruby Journey. She wore black leathers under white furs, and was as dauntingly attractive as the kind of flower whose pollen provides uneasy dreams. Just standing there, she looked dangerous as hell and damned pleased about it. Unlike the others who'd passed through the Madness Maze, Ruby Journey hadn't really changed much at all. It just ... refined her. As a bounty hunter, she'd mostly brought her victims in dead rather than alive, because it meant less paperwork. She sought out fights and battles and the most dangerous bounties, just to prove she was as nasty as everyone said she was. As a rebel, she'd just increased the size of her enemy. It was still all down to mayhem and looting, as far as she was concerned. She saw great opportunities for financial improvement in the chaos on Golgotha, and didn't intend to let herself be distracted by unimportant things like politics. Random could deal with things like that. He understood them.

Alexander Storm, that old and tired man, had been a part of the rebellion most of his life. As a young man he'd fought at Jack's side in battles beyond counting. Once a brilliant swordsman and a laughing adventurer, a hero almost as famous as Random, he was now weighed down with age and bitterness, and concentrated his remaining energies in helping to determine the underground's policies and strategies. And if he was jealous that his old friend Jack had somehow grown young and vital again, and he had not, he kept it to himself. Mostly.

And finally, there were Young Jack Random and Psycho Jenny. They stood together some distance away from the others, because no one else would stand next to them. And even they did their best to ignore each other. Young Jack had arrived on the scene out of nowhere, claiming to be the real professional rebel, and it had to be said he looked the part. Tall and powerful in his silver battle armor chased with gold, he positively radiated strength and wisdom, and his charisma almost outshone the overhead lights. Every inch the hero, people followed him almost instinctively, even into the most impossible of situations. Unbeatable with a sword in his hand, he charged barricades and mounted daring rescues with verve and courage and a constant dazzling smile. Already he was being hailed as the savior of Mistport during the invasion, as though he'd single-handedly turned back the Empire's invasion forces. Owen and Hazel could have told a different story, had they chosen, but they kept their peace. The rebellion needed its heroes to inspire the masses.

It still wasn't clear which of the two Randoms was the real one. They were both powerful fighters and cunning strategists. So the underground, expedient as ever, made use of both of them.

Jenny Psycho was a different matter. The Empire had broken something deep inside her, and it had healed crookedly. But then she was touched by the enigmatic uber-esper, Mater Mundi, and now Jenny Psycho was very powerful indeed. Her presence all but crackled on the air around her, like a thunderstorm waiting to happen. She lived only for revenge, relying on the rebellion to give her focus and purpose. She'd had another name once, and another life, but that seemed a long time ago, and most of the time she barely remembered the minor esper called Diana Vertue.

Owen Deathstalker looked about him unobtrusively, studying his companions thoughtfully. It seemed they'd all changed dramatically in the short time they'd been apart. Jack Random looked thirty years younger, and tough enough to chew up tin cans and spit nails. He looked a lot more like Young Jack, but there was still a clear difference. There was something almost inhuman about Young Jack's unwavering heroism, as though he was really a character from some holoaction drama, stepped out of the viewscreen and into reality with his charisma intact. Unlike his previously older self, Young Jack came across as though he'd never had a doubt or a failure in his life. Besides, he smiled too much. Owen didn't trust anyone who smiled a lot. It wasn't natural, not in this day and age. He still didn't have a clue who the hell Young Jack might really be, but he kept his suspicions to himself. If the man was an impostor, he was damned convincing, and the underground needed heroes to lead the masses into battle.

Even out-on-the-edge weirdos like Jenny Psycho. Owen worried about her. The espers would follow her blindly, just because she had once manifested the Mater Mundi, Our Mother of All Souls. They saw her as a saint now. A crazy saint, but none the less holy for that. And there was no denying she was powerful as hell. When Jenny really let loose, reality trembled. But with someone as maltreated and disturbed as Jenny Psycho, the balance of her mind was only a sometime thing now, and it was only a matter of time before she broke apart along the stress lines. Owen had already decided that when that happened, he wanted to be really far away.

Ruby Journey . . . looked as disturbing as ever. If she hadn't been Hazel's longtime friend, Owen thought he would probably have shot her on general principles by now. Having Ruby around was like sharing a very confined space with a paranoid attack dog that had slipped its leash. The best you could really hope for with Ruby Journey was to point her in the right direction and then follow the trail of bodies.

What Jack Random saw in her remained a mystery to Owen. Perhaps the man just liked living dangerously. There was no denying he'd been through some amazing changes. It was as though his body had turned back time, denying the passing years to become young and vital again. Owen wondered if aging was a thing of the past for all of them now, since they'd been altered by the Madness Maze. And if so, how long they might all live . . . Owen tried to visualize a future life stretching endlessly away before him, forever young, and then he smiled and shook his head. Much more likely they'd all be slaughtered down on Golgotha. Get through that first, and he'd worry about eternity later. He made himself concentrate on Random. The professional rebel looked sharp and deadly, eager to throw himself headlong into a battle he'd been looking forward to all his life. Despite himself, Owen worried about that, too. Such determination tended to be dangerously single-minded. Sometimes Owen thought Jack Random would walk right over the body of his best friend to reach the victory he craved.

Owen felt guilty thinking such things about his friends and comrades, but his discovery on Mistworld of how little he'd really understood about Hazel had started him thinking, and he couldn't seem to stop. It seemed they all had obsessions and private agendas, and the old togetherness that the Maze had gifted them with seemed to have vanished during their separation. He could still feel their presence around him, but he could no longer sense what they were thinking or feeling. The closeness that had them finishing each other's thoughts and sentences was gone. They were no longer linked, mind to mind, as though what they'd been through on their various missions had changed them so much they weren't the same people anymore.

He could still feel the Maze's power, burning brightly within them, and no more so than in his ancestor Giles.

Owen studied the man thoughtfully, his hand unconsciously dropping to the sword at his side. Giles was still
scowling at the view on the screen, lost in his own
thoughts, ignoring the others. Of them all, Giles had
seemed the most reluctant to investigate or use the powers
the Maze had bestowed on him. As though they were a
necessary evil, only to be used when there was no other
choice. On the one occasion Owen had raised the matter
with him, Giles had said curtly it was enough to be a
Deathstalker, and that was the end of that conversation.
Owen and Giles had always found it difficult to talk. They
came from very different times and backgrounds, for all
their shared name, and it seemed the only thing they had
in common was the rebellion. Giles had briefly tried to be
a father figure to Owen, after he had to kill his own es-
tranged son, the original Dram, but Owen had put a stop
to that. He'd had enough of his real father trying to run
his life. He was his own man, and if the life he'd made for
himself wasn't quite what he'd expected or intended, it
was still his, and he guarded it jealously.

And even beyond that, there were the quiet niggling
suspicions that murmured at the back of Owen's mind and
wouldn't be silenced. He couldn't help thinking that Giles
often seemed to be remarkably well informed on the current situation, for a man who had supposedly spent the
last 943 years in stasis . . . He pushed the thought aside,
for the moment, and moved over to join his ancestor
beside the viewscreen.

"How does it feel to be home again, after so long?" he
said quietly. "Is it what you expected?"

"No," said Giles, just as quietly, not looking away from
the screen. "Almost a thousand years have passed since I
last saw Golgotha, but it seems like only yesterday to me.
Everyone I ever knew or cared for down there is long
dead and gone to dust. Instead, the place is overrun with
clones and espers, the Families have grown soft or corrupt
or insane, and the Empire . . . the Empire I remember no
longer exists. I feel like a ghost, fighting a ghost's old
battles, not noticing that the world has moved on without
me. The Empire was falling apart even in my day, but I
never dreamed it would end up like this. I don't know
whether to save it or put it out of its misery. It's like a

sick distortion of everything I ever believed in. But I will put things right. I will wake the people from the nightmare of history and rebuild the Empire as it should be."

"With a little help from your friends," Owen said lightly.

Giles looked at him for the first time, his solid, lined face impassive. "Of course, kinsman. I couldn't have come this far alone. You and your friends have made all this possible. I'll never forget you. Now, time for a conference, I think, before the battle begins and we all go rushing off in different directions. It may be some time before we can talk again."

"What's there to talk about?" said Ruby, calmly manicuring her nails with the edge of an evil-looking dagger. "We go down, kill everything in a uniform, grab as much loot as we can carry, and then race to see who gets to kill Lionstone. My kind of party."

"There are things we need to discuss," Giles said stubbornly. "The Madness Maze changed us all, but apparently in different ways. According to the reports you filed since you returned, and Ruby, I'm still waiting for yours, it would seem our . . . abilities have been developing in different ways. I have learned to teleport. Owen has become a psychokinetic. Jack and Ruby have manifested pyrokinetic abilities. And Hazel can summon alternative versions of herself from different timelines. I don't even pretend to understand how that works. None of this is what I expected."

"Why shouldn't we have changed in different ways?" said Random. "We're different people. And what do we really know about the Maze? That it was probably an alien artifact, that no one knows how old it might have been, or what its original purpose was, and that the last people to go through it created the Hadenmen. Not much to go on, is it?"

"Unless you know more about it than you've been letting on," said Hazel. "How about it, Giles? You been holding out on us?"

"Of course not," said Giles. "I did study it briefly, before I was hounded away to Shandrakor, but I never did understand its purpose. I'm not sure if anything human could. Now that it's gone, I don't suppose we'll ever know. What matters is that we have all been bestowed marvelous gifts, and it's up to us to try and understand them. Contrary to Ruby's comments, the fighting down on Golgotha isn't going to be easy or straightforward. Lionstone's got a whole army of Security people down there, plus the various armed forces, plus whatever nasty surprises she has set in place for just such an occasion as this. Never underestimate a ruler's paranoia. Lionstone always knew a day like this might come, and you can bet she's got plans in place to frustrate us."

"Damn," said Hazel. "He makes even longer speeches than you do, Owen. Must run in the Family."

"Is there a point in all this?" said Random. "I would prefer to go down and get involved before it's all over."

"The point," said Giles, "is that we need to split up. Spread our talents as widely as possible, hit Lionstone on as many fronts as possible."

"Hold everything," said Owen. "We've always been strongest together. Remember the force shield we raised on the Wolfling World? That was strong enough to stand off massed disrupter cannon at point-blank range. And Hazel and I worked miracles together on Mistworld. Who knows what we might be capable of if we all stuck together?"

"We don't have the time to experiment," Giles said flatly. "The rebellion needs us now. I've put a lot of thought into this."

"Without consulting us," said Ruby.

"Right," said Random. "When was all this planning going on? The rest of us have been working our asses off on our missions."

"I don't sleep much," said Giles. "Now pay attention, please. We need to split into the following groups . . ."

"I'm not happy about this," said Hazel. "The last time we let the underground split us up, David and the SummerIsle went off on their own. Now David's dead, and Kid Death's joined the opposition."

"I miss David," Owen said suddenly. "I never really got to know him, and now I never will, but I miss him now he's gone. I'm the last of the direct line. The last of the Deathstalkers."

"That's not what's upsetting you," said Hazel. "You're

just angry because since Virimonde's been destroyed, you can't go home again. You can never have your old life back. That's all you ever really wanted out of this rebellion, isn't it?"

"I don't know," said Owen. "Maybe. I never wanted to be a warrior. I was happy, being a scholar and an historian, with no pressures and no responsibilities. But I wouldn't go back, even if I could. I've seen too much. And David . . . he was a pain in the ass, but he had potential. There was so much I could have taught him . . . and now he's gone. Murdered by Kit SummerIsle. The same smiling bastard who killed my father. Whatever happens down below, the SummerIsle is mine."

"Good," said Giles approvingly. "You're starting to sound like a Deathstalker. You've come a long way, historian."

"And if I don't always like what I've made of myself, whom do I blame?" said Owen. "Sometimes I think I've become everything I ever hated. A man of violence, driven by revenge. Just another pawn in my father's plots and schemes to bring down the Empress. Just another barbarian at the gates of Empire."

There was an awkward silence, broken by an urgent chiming from the viewscreen. Giles switched to the new incoming signal, and Golgotha disappeared, replaced by Finlay Campbell, Evangeline Shreck, and Julian Skye, their faces filling the screen. They looked harried.

"What's holding you people up?" said Finlay, not bothering with any amenities. "We need you down here now. Everything's gone to hell in a handcart in the Parade of the Endless, the one city above all we have to hold. We can't tell who's winning anymore, if anyone is. Our people are all out on the streets, doing what they can, but we need you to bring things together. Just your presence will help to inspire the fighters. You've become heroes, legends, not least through Toby Shreck's coverage, and people will follow you where they won't follow us."

"Tell me more about the situation," said Giles, refusing to be pressured. "Who's on top at the moment?"

"Depends on who you talk to," said Evangeline. "Things are falling apart in the governing bodies incredibly quickly, and we're doing all we can to take advantage of that, but then, it's all been precariously balanced for a long time. It only needed a spark to set the people off. If we'd known they were this close to the edge, we'd have provided a spark ourselves, even if we had to make one up. But there are still a hell of a lot of troops and Security people out in the streets, and they're a damned sight better armed than most of our people. So we need you. Your powers could be the turning point. God knows we need one. We're fighting on so many fronts it's hard to make any real breakthrough."

"What about the Hadenmen?" said Owen, cutting in. "I've been worried about them. I woke them from their Tomb because we needed them, but after all, they were the official Enemies of Humanity before Shub came along. Are they behaving themselves?"

"Surprisingly enough, yes," said Julian Skye. "Their ships are only taking out the targets we gave them, and their ground fighting has proved a blessing. They make great shock troops. Half the time, the army forces run away rather than face them. Not that I blame them in the slightest. But all in all, the augmented men have been behaving impeccably. We've even had reports they've been taking prisoners, rather than just killing everything that moves, which surprised everyone. Not least the prisoners. Maybe they found God, in their Tomb. So, one of your better ideas, Deathstalker."

"Right," said Evangeline. "Now if you're quite happy, perhaps we could return to more pressing matters, namely the unholy mess in the Parade of the Endless . . ."

"Get your collective asses down here," said Finlay sharply. "Right now. We have to hold this city."

"Understood," said Owen. "We'll be there. We haven't come this far to miss out on the ending."

Finlay nodded, and cut off the signal. The image of their serious faces barely had time to clear from the viewscreen before another signal came in. Everyone in the great Hall straightened up a little as a new face filled the screen, and a great many hands dropped instinctively to weapons. The broad, shaggy wolf's-head looking down on them was dominated by the long muzzle full of sharp teeth, and the darkly gleaming eyes above, large and intelligent and almost overpoweringly ferocious. It

was the Wolfling, the last of his kind, only survivor of the
Empire's first attempt to build a superior fighting man.
Last of a race butchered and slaughtered by a fearful
humankind. Once guardian of the Madness Maze, and
now protector of the sleeping Darkvoid Device. Giles
smiled broadly at him.

"Wulf! I've been waiting for you to contact me! When
will you be here?"

"I won't," said the Wolfling. His deep, dark voice was
as much a growl as anything else, but an underlying sad-
ness and tiredness took most of the threat out of it. "I told
you, Giles. I've had enough of fighting. I've seen too
much death and destruction to take pleasure in any more.
Lionstone has to fall. I know that. But she'll go whether
I'm there or not. You don't need me anymore, Giles.
You've moved beyond me."

"But . . . we spent so long arguing and scheming over
how we'd pull the Iron Bitch down! Don't do this to me,
Wulf. Don't leave me here alone. You're my oldest
friend, all I have left to remind me of the old days."

"That was always the difference between us, Giles. You
want to remember the past, and I just want to forget it. Let
your hatred go, Giles. I know all about hatred. Give it too
much hold over you, and it'll eat you alive till there's
nothing left in you but it. And that's no way to live. Do
what you have to because it's the right thing to do, not
because you enjoy it. I'm tired, Giles. I've lived too long,
seen the Empire change beyond recognition, watched my
race fall out of history and into legend. I think it's time
for me to let go and follow them."

"Isn't there anything I can do for you?" said Giles,
almost plaintively.

"Yes," said the Wolfling. "You can kill Lionstone for
me. Whatever happens, she mustn't be allowed to escape.
Kill her, Giles."

"Yes," said Giles. "I can do that for you."

The Wolfling nodded his great shaggy head, and the
viewscreen went blank. Giles stared at it for a long
moment, and then nodded slowly, as though listening to
some private, inner voice. He turned back to the others,
and his face was entirely calm and composed, as though
daring the others to comment on the emotions they'd seen

him display. When he spoke, his voice was brisk and formal.

"Aliens. We haven't discussed them yet. So far, there's been no sightings of any alien craft anywhere in the Empire since the attack on Golgotha, but we can't afford to forget them. They're out there somewhere, no doubt watching and planning. It's vital we get the rebellion over with as quickly as possible, and order restored. We can't afford to be caught helpless and divided by an invading alien force."

"And let's not forget Shub," said Owen. "There's always a chance the rogue AIs might try and take advantage of our divisions by launching an attack of their own."

"God, you're a cheerful lot," said Ruby. "Look, let's just get out of here and get this show on the road. We'll worry about aliens and AIs and plagues of frogs as and when they make an appearance."

"Right," said Hazel. "We're wasting time here."

"Good planning is never a waste," said Giles coldly. "Now pay attention. This is how we're going to do it. Owen's been doing some research on old records of the Imperial Palace, back when it was first being constructed. I suppose his being an historian had to come in useful someday. The only way into the Palace today is by the underground train system, run and monitored by the Palace's security systems. The train stations are well guarded, and the train compartments themselves are fitted with lethal gas jets, just in case. However, Owen has discovered records of a number of old maintenance tunnels, long abandoned and apparently forgotten. We can use those to bypass the Security guards entirely, and gain access to the trains safely. Owen, Hazel, and I will undertake this mission."

"Hold everything," said the AI Ozymandius in Owen's ear. "Sorry to interrupt, boss, but your ancestor's words have tripped a file hidden deep within my memory by your father. He knew about these trains and tunnels, and has given me all the necessary security codes to get you onto the trains and into the Palace."

"Are you sure about this?" said Owen, subvocalizing. "If you get just one of those codes wrong, we're all dead."

"Trust me," said the AI. "This is the real thing, Owen. Your father believed in planning ahead."

Owen passed on the AI's words, and there was an awkward pause. Owen had always maintained he'd used his Maze powers to completely destroy the treacherous AI Ozymandius when it turned out to be working for the Empire, and tried to use control words it had implanted in Owen and Hazel to make them kill the others. Only sometime later Oz, or something claiming to be Oz, turned up in Owen's head again. No one but Owen could hear its voice, but the information it occasionally volunteered was always reliable. For the rest of the time, Owen tried hard to ignore it.

"Your father would naturally have tried to gain access to those codes," Giles said slowly. "I suppose it's possible he could have hidden them in your AI for safekeeping. There's no way of testing them here. I suppose we'll find out whether they're the real thing when we get there. It would certainly simplify things a lot. Even with our powers, breaking out of the Palace station was always going to be a major undertaking. So, it would appear we'll just have to trust Oz. Whoever or whatever he really is."

"Thanks a whole bunch," Oz murmured in Owen's ear. Owen didn't pass that on.

Hazel shook her head. "Great. We're going to risk all our lives on a voice in Owen's head only he can hear. What do we do for an encore, make a sacrifice to the gods and read our fortune in its entrails?"

"Don't tempt me," said Giles. "Next, Jack Random and Ruby Journey will lead the gravity-sled attack on the Family Towers, as arranged with the underground. For the moment the Clans seem to have decided they're on no one's side but their own, but that won't last. The outlawing of David and the threatened mechanization of their planets hit them where they lived, but it won't take them long to realize that their financial and social well-being is irrevocably linked to the Empire as it is. A successful rebellion by the lower orders would be their worst nightmare come true. So, faced with the loss of their wealth and position, they'll finally have to commit their troops to defending the Empress, on the grounds that the crazy devil you know is still preferable to the devil with blood in his eyes and centuries of grudges to catch up on. At this stage, their troops might just be enough to turn things in the Empress's favor. It's therefore vital we keep them pinned down in their Towers, well away from the main action. We want them preoccupied with their own survival, rather than the Empress's.

"Random, we've been through the logistics of this with the underground. You know what to do. A flotilla of gravity sleds is waiting just outside the Parade of the Endless for you to lead them in. Apparently competition to man the sleds, and follow you into almost certain death for the majority, was very hard-fought. It would seem there are still a great many people who still believe in the professional rebel. But Random, while you're out there enjoying yourself raining death and destruction down on the heads of the Lords, remember we still need some of them left alive afterward to oversee the economy once the rebellion is over."

"I'll see what I can do," said Random calmly. "No promises."

Giles sighed, and shook his head. "Ruby Journey will, of course, accompany you. If only because no one else feels safe around her."

"You say the nicest things," said Ruby.

"If they're going, I'm going, too," said Alexander Storm firmly. "I haven't waited this long to miss out on the downfall of the Families. I've worked and fought all my life to see them go down in flames, and I'm damned if I'm being left behind. I might not be as young as some people, but I can still carry my weight."

"Oh, let him come," said Ruby. "He'll only sulk otherwise."

"Of course you're coming with us, Alex," Random said reassuringly. "I wouldn't dream of doing this without my old comrade at my side."

"You're using that word *old* again," said Storm ominously.

"All right, how about ancient?" said Ruby.

"Ruby . . ." said Random.

She sniffed, and went back to manicuring her nails with her dagger. She'd come to accept that Random had a blind spot where Storm was concerned. He still thought of his old friend as he used to be, when Storm was young and swift and daring and hell on wheels with a sword in his hand. He couldn't seem to accept that while he was young and strong again, Storm wasn't. Ruby decided to keep a watchful eye on Storm. She didn't care tuppence if he got himself killed, but she was damned if she'd let him drag Random down with them. In fact, it might be better all around if a stray bullet took Storm out right at the beginning. No one would notice where one stray shot came from, once the fighting started. Of course, she'd have to be careful. If Random ever found out . . . Ruby Journey frowned, thinking hard.

"Now that that's decided," said Giles loudly, bringing all eyes back to him, "we come to Young Jack Random. You will make your own landing dirtside, and team up with Finlay Campbell and Julian Skye. Your reputation will help to inspire their people, and throw a fright into the defending troops. Your mission is to take out and occupy the Security troops' main command center in the Parade of the Endless. They've still got comm channels open, so they're practically running the city's defenses single-handed. Once they're out of the loop, the Security forces will fall apart, and the Parade of the Endless will be ours for the taking. And once the city is ours, only the Empress herself stands between us and control of Golgotha. And from Golgotha, we will form the new Empire that rises from the ashes of the old."

"Rah rah rah," said Hazel. "Go, team, go. Save the inspirational pep talks, Giles. We all know why we're here. And can I just remind you that the rebellion is far from over. Right now, we're nothing more than a handful of terrorists with prices on our heads."

"Your point being?" Giles said icily.

"That we take things one step at a time. We can dream about the future once we've taken control of the present. I don't want any of us getting shot in the back because we were too busy dreaming of running the Empire instead of paying proper attention to what's going on around us."

"Don't worry, Hazel," said Young Jack calmly. "We will prevail. We are heroes. It is our destiny."

"And somebody shut him up before I puke," said Hazel. "I am not a hero, and never have been. Heroes tend to

come to glorious, painful, and rather sudden ends, and
have statues put up to them by the survivors. Personally, I
would much rather be a survivor than a statue."

"Right," said Ruby. "We haven't talked about the loot
yet, either. Can we talk about the loot?"

"Somebody sit on her," said Giles. "I'm getting a
headache. And finally . . ."

"About time you got around to me," said Jenny Psycho,
scowling fiercely. "I was beginning to think you'd forgotten all about me."

"If only that was possible," said Giles. "You will
orchestrate the use of espers on the planet's surface, and
liaise among the various rebel factions. Like the two Randoms, the espers should follow you unquestioningly, just
because of who you are. Try and keep your people under
control. Espers can do a lot of damage when they're all
pointed in the same direction, but the last thing we need
are esper loose cannon going off all over the place."

"You presume too much," said Jenny Psycho. "You're
not in charge here. In the end, the underground will win
this war, and the underground will decide what replaces
Lionstone's Empire. We've been preparing for this day
for centuries. Espers, clones, the committed, and the
faithful. We won't be brushed aside in the moment of our
triumph by a bunch of newcomers, even if they are heroes
and legends."

"We can argue about who gets the credit later," said
Random, cutting in firmly on what threatened to be a long
tirade. "First, we have to win this war. Let's make a
move, people. It's time to go to work."

"Right," said Hazel.

Owen grinned about him. "See you all in Hell."

In the huge Court of the Imperial Palace, the Hell that
Lionstone had made was growing worse. The surroundings continued to change from moment to moment,
reflecting the Empress's darkening mood, and the underworld grew steadily more disturbing. The light was more
scarlet than crimson now, absorbing all other colors, and
the stench of sulfur was almost overpowering. There
were other smells, too: piss and shit and blood, the smells
of fear. Batwinged shapes floated lazily overhead, dark

shadows too high up to be seen clearly, like cinders coughed up from the depths of the Pit. The maids-in-waiting clustered at the foot of the Iron Throne looked more like demons than ever. And the open Court itself was studded with row upon row of men and women impaled on stakes. There were so many of them Dram assumed they had to be holograms, but he didn't ask. He didn't want to know. Their screams had sounded real enough. He stood where he'd been told to stand, beside the Iron Throne, and did his best not to draw attention to himself.

Lionstone had grown too restless to stay sitting on the Throne, and now paced back and forth before it, shouting orders at people on the floating viewscreens. She was still in control of herself, but her rage grew with every reported rebel victory or Imperial setback. Lionstone had stopped seeing it as a political struggle for control of the Empire, and was now taking it as a series of personal attacks. Everyone was out to get her. No one could be trusted. Every Imperial failure was a betrayal of her. She gave orders in endless streams, sometimes contradicting herself. Dram didn't point this out to her. Lionstone's legendary self-control was finally fragmenting in the face of so many attacks on so many fronts.

Valentine Wolfe had been summoned to Court, and stood patiently before the Throne, poisoning the air just by being there and looking pleased as Punch about it. His long black curls had been freshly oiled, falling to his shoulders in artful disarray. His mascaraed eyes gleamed with fever-bright intensity from his bone-pale face, and his scarlet smile seemed wider than ever. He was calmly pulling the legs from some squealing black thing in his hands. Dram hoped it was an insect. Valentine Wolfe had come to Hell, and looked perfectly at home there.

Dram stood facing him, not because he chose to, but because Lionstone hadn't given him permission to move. He was still officially in charge of the Imperial Fleet, when Lionstone allowed him to be. He'd been doing his best, but his lack of real experience limited his insights and his options. Mostly, things were moving too fast for him to keep up. The Fleet was scattered all across the Empire, and the increasingly isolated ships were too busy fighting off Hadenmen and rebel mutineers to pay him much attention. Even if he'd had anything worthwhile to offer. Lionstone suddenly stopped her pacing and whirled on the two men.

"You! I should have you both executed! This is all your fault! I had things under control until you went mad on Virimonde! All you had to do was pacify one insignificant backwater planet, and you couldn't even do that for me. No, you were too busy running wild and killing anything that moved. Fools! Even a mechanized planet will need some people to work it! What use is there in being an Empress if you don't have peasants to rule?"

Both Dram and Valentine had been following Lionstone's specific instructions on Virimonde, but neither of them was stupid enough to remind her of that. Lionstone glared at them both, and the maids stirred menacingly, picking up on her mood. Dram could feel cold beads of sweat popping out on his forehead. He felt very much that he would have liked to turn and run, except that a maid would undoubtably have brought him down before he managed a dozen steps, and besides, there was nowhere he could run to. He had no friends anywhere after Virimonde. Not that he regretted one delightful moment of his time there. He'd never felt so alive. No, for better or worse, his destiny was tied to Lionstone's, the woman who had brought him into life from the cells of his dead original.

"I'm going to have to send you out to defend me, because you're all I've got," the Empress said finally, recovering some of her calm. "Valentine, you will take control of all the war machines currently on Golgotha. There aren't that many, but do what you can with them. Most of my beautiful engines of destruction are still stuck on Virimonde, and by the time I could get them back here the struggle would already be over. One way or the other. So don't waste any of them. Dram, I want you up on the surface, leading the troops in person. They'll follow the Warrior Prime. I'm giving control of the fleet over to Beckett. He was right, damn him. He has the experience. All I can do is hope the bastard stays loyal."

"I've done my best," Dram said cautiously. "But I'm sure you can trust Beckett to do his best, too."

"Very good," said Valentine. "Polite but supportive, without actually meaning anything. If we survive this, you may have a bright future as a courtier."

"I don't like leaving you here undefended," said Dram, ostentatiously ignoring the Wolfe.

"Investigator Razor and Lord SummerIsle are already waiting in my antechamber," said the Empress. "And there are . . . others on their way, too. Now get out of my sight, both of you. And don't fail me."

"I wouldn't dare," murmured Dram, and he and Valentine Wolfe bowed low and departed. They passed Razor and Kid Death coming in, but kept their eyes carefully averted. In her present state, Lionstone might well take a warning glance as evidence of treason. Dram and the Wolfe passed through the Court's great double doors, and out of Hell, walking as fast as they thought they could get away with.

Investigator Razor and Lord Kit SummerIsle approached the Iron Throne at a somewhat slower pace, stopped a safe distance from the maids-in-waiting, and bowed respectfully to the Empress. When they raised their heads, they were disturbed to find Lionstone smiling at them. It was truly said that the Empress was at her most dangerous when she was smiling. Her sense of humor was . . . not like other people's, and tended toward the vindictive. Razor and the SummerIsle stood their ground, faces carefully blank, and kept their hands well away from the weapons they'd been ordered to wear in her presence.

"Well, well," said Lionstone lightly. "My two favorite killers. How nice. Razor, I should be angry with you. I sent you to conquer Mistworld in my name, and you failed. But it wasn't really your fault. So many people failed me on that mission, but you stayed true. And Kid Death, my smiling assassin. You brought me the young Deathstalker's head, the only good thing to come out of that debacle. You always brought me the nicest presents, SummerIsle. I've got it here on a spike, somewhere.

"It is good to have you both back here with me. Good to have people around me I can depend on. Your duties here are simple, to protect me from any and all dangers. The odds against any of the rebels getting this far are vanishingly small, especially since I had the extra esp-blockers installed, but it seems I can no longer depend on all my people to do their duty. There are many layers of defense between my Palace and the surface, not all of them human, and I am not entirely helpless myself . . . but I'll feel better with you two watching over me. Any comments? Bearing in mind that they'd better be extremely constructive and to the point if you like your heads where they are."

"An honor to serve Your Majesty, as always," Razor said smoothly. "I take great pride in the confidence that you have invested in me. But I feel I should point out that with my sword to guard you, I really don't see the need for the SummerIsle's presence. I am a professional fighting man of long standing. The young Lord is, at best, a gifted amateur."

"An enthusiastic amateur with an exceptional track record has to be a better bet than a tired old man who's already been retired once," said Kit calmly. "Send this ancient obsolete away, Your Majesty. You don't need him while you've got me, and I don't want to be distracted trying to keep him alive as well as you, Your Highness."

"You don't have to like each other," said Lionstone. "Just do your job. And don't get too close to the maids. I haven't fed them recently." She smiled fondly at her two defenders. "Don't worry, my most loyal subjects. Once this nonsense is over, and order has been restored, as it will be, I promise you both all the killing you can handle. The executions will last all day and all night, and blood will flow in the streets like tides."

She turned away from them, ignoring their deep bows, and switched the floating viewscreens to the main news channels. The rebels were still shutting down military and Security comm channels as fast as new ones were set up, but they left the news channels alone. They wanted the people to see what was going on. All the floating screens showed a different news report, from all over Golgotha, but mainly from the Parade of the Endless, where the real fighting was. Urgent voices spilled out into the Court—loud, overlapping, almost hysterical. News of the rebellion was coming in from a hundred worlds at once, and the news stations were going crazy trying to keep up with it all. Lionstone fixed her attention on screen after screen, trying for an overview of the situation. She no longer trusted her own Security reports.

Scenes of bloodshed and fighting in the streets and buildings going up in flames filled the viewscreens, interrupted occasionally by news reporters and commentators. Their faces were flushed, and they talked too quickly. There'd never been a story like this, and with so much going on, most of it coming in live, there was little or no censorship anymore. Almost delirious with the truth, news editors threw caution to the winds and put everything on the air, irrespective of what it was or where it came from. Commentators were saying what they really meant for the first time in their lives, and couldn't seem to get enough of it. Neither could the audience, according to the latest viewing figures.

It seemed all those who weren't actually out in the streets fighting the revolution were glued to their viewscreens watching it. This is history in the making, said the news stations, and for once they weren't exaggerating. Lionstone came across a familiar face and stalked over to that screen to stand before it. Toby Shreck's fat sweating face stared back at her. There was chaos behind him, people running back and forth with weapons in their hands. Thick smoke drifted on the air from a gutted, fire-blackened building in the background. A troop of guards, their uniforms torn and bloody, ran past in full retreat, jostling the camera. Toby's face was smudged with smoke, and his clothes were a mess. He had to shout to be heard over the bedlam around him.

"This is Toby Shreck, for Imperial News, reporting from the center of the Parade of the Endless. Rebel forces are overrunning the whole city, driving demoralized and decimated Imperial forces before them. The slaughter is incredible. There are bodies everywhere. The wounded on both sides are being left to die in the streets because there's no more room in the hospitals. Civilians and noncombatants are running for their lives. There seems to be nowhere safe left for them to shelter. Imperial forces and the newly arrived war machines are treating everyone but themselves as the enemy. Security forces have been dragging civilians to the city squares and executing them, as a sign to others not to support the rebellion. If anything, this has had the opposite effect. Rebels are being seen as liberators. The Empress recently released a large number of the Grendel aliens onto the streets. No one knows how many civilians they killed. The body parts are too mixed up to make a count possible. Heroic espers from the underground took the aliens down eventually. This insane action on the part of the Empress would seem to indicate a growing desperation on her part, and a total disregard for the safety of her subjects."

"The fat traitor!" Lionstone cut the signal off, her eyes bulging with rage. "I'll have his head for this! How dare he!"

She ran from screen to screen, glaring at them as though she could force them to give her good news. But everywhere the story was the same. People fighting in anonymous streets, with smoke and fire in the background. Screams and shouts and incoherent orders. Flashing swords and axes, and blood flying on the air. The humming of force shields and the roar of discharging energy weapons. Quick shots of rubble that used to be buildings, and wild-eyed, traumatized children soaked in their own blood and others'. Women crying over still and broken bodies. Limp forms hanging from lampposts. Some wore uniforms. Some did not.

Swept along in the thrill of the unfolding story, the newscasters and commentators had given up trying to sound calm and objective. They grew steadily more excited and disheveled, gulping at glasses of water as their voices roughened from overuse. The first rebel victories were coming in. First it was cities, and then colonies, and finally whole planets, torn from Empire rule, starting at the Rim and working inward. Some channels still loyal to the Empress blanked out rather than show such news, while others were taken over by victorious rebel forces. Lionstone shut these channels down, but found it harder and harder to find broadcasts telling her what she wanted to hear. Eventually she shut them all down, and screamed into her comm implant for General Shaw Beckett. His face appeared on a screen floating before her. He looked tired. The top buttons of his uniform were undone.

"What do you want, Lionstone? I'm busy."

"Don't you dare talk to us that way, Beckett! This is your Empress! We have new orders for you, effective immediately. Identify all planets where rebel forces have taken control and scorch them, one after the other. You are not empowered to accept surrenders. We want those planets dead and lifeless."

Beckett stared impassively at her out of the screen. "And the billions of innocents who would die?"

"Expendable. They should have fought harder against the rebels. Confirm our order, General."

"I regret I am unable to do so, Your Majesty. Much as it pains me. What remains of the fleet is under constant Hadenman attack. Many of my ships have been destroyed or boarded. Those I have left are scattered too widely to be recalled. We don't have enough ships in any one place to attempt even a single scorching. We're having to fight with everything we've got just to survive, Empress. I would estimate more than 40 percent of your fleet has been destroyed, or is in enemy hands."

Lionstone lost it completely, and shouted and screamed abuse at Beckett's unmoved image. She threatened him with everything from demotion to immediate arrest and execution if he wouldn't carry out her orders, and still he wouldn't answer her. Lionstone finally regained some self-control and stood panting before the viewscreen, her hands clenched into fists. Beckett waited patiently while she got her breath back. Lionstone fixed him with a cold glare.

"Very well. Again, we are failed by those we are forced to trust. New orders, General. All starcruisers are to return immediately to protect the homeworld. No excuses, no exceptions. We require a shield of ships around Golgotha. No one is to pass. Whatever happens, the homeworld must not fall. Is that clear, General?"

Beckett sighed deeply. "Lionstone, it's over. We're too far away. Even if we were to abandon the people we're protecting from the Hadenmen, by the time we'd fought our way past their ships, it would all be over on Golgotha, bar the shouting. All I can offer you are my best wishes, and my hopes for your personal safety. There's nothing I can do for you anymore. Good-bye, Lionstone."

"Traitor!" screamed Lionstone, as his face disappeared

from the viewscreen. She breathed heavily, her eyes wide
and staring at some private inner image, and then she
moved quickly among the floating screens, calling up
Captains in her fleet personally. Many didn't answer, for
one reason or another, and those who did couldn't help
her. They had their own problems. She saved the E class
ships, her pride and joy, for last, but only one answered.
The *Endurance*.

The bridge was in flames. Emergency sirens and warnings were sounding everywhere, overlapping each other.
Crew members sat doggedly at their seats, manning the
surviving stations with desperate concentration. Shouted
orders and responses could barely be heard over the
bedlam, but the screams were clear enough. Dead bodies
scattered the bridge, some charred and blackened figures
still sitting at their exploded stations. Smoke was building
faster than the extractor fans could clear it. Wounded
were sobbing and crying out, but no one had the time to
tend them. Lionstone yelled for someone to report to her,
and finally a disheveled minor officer lurched to a halt
before the viewscreen. One of his sleeves was blackened
and crisped from flames only recently beaten out, and the
hair on one side of his head had been burned away. Half
his face was roasted an angry red. He pulled himself to
something like attention and saluted the screen. His eyes
were wild and staring, like some creature confronted by a
forest fire. Lionstone glared at him.

"Who are you? Where's the Captain? What's happening on the *Endurance*?"

"Navigation Officer Robert Campbell reporting, Your
Majesty. The Captain's dead. We're under attack by three
Hadenman ships. We're faster than they are, but they've
got better weapons and shields. Our shields are failing.
We've seriously disabled one of the Hadenman ships, but
doing so drained our reserves almost to zero. Power levels
all over the ship are dropping fast. But we won't give up,
Your Majesty. We'll fight till they tear this ship apart
around us. If nothing else, we'll buy you time."

A massive explosion rocked the bridge. The hull had
been breached. Air and smoke shrieked out the widening
hole. People not strapped into seats clung to their workstations to avoid being dragged away. The lights flickered

and went out, replaced by the dull red glow of emergency lighting. There was only one siren sounding now, loud and piercing, like a lost soul falling into eternal darkness. Robert Campbell clung to the edge of the screen and tried to shout something, but he couldn't get enough air into his lungs. He pulled himself away from the screen, heading across the devastated bridge toward the emergency exit. All around him, the workstations were exploding one by one, throwing their dead operators away or blowing them apart where they sat. And then the screen went suddenly blank, and the Court was quiet again. Lionstone stared at the screen for a long moment.

"Brave boy," she said finally. "Maybe I should have put him in charge. And the *Endurance* is gone. The finest of the E class ships. The ship that was supposed to be unbeatable."

"To be fair, I don't think the designers had Hademan ships in mind when they said that," said Razor, apparently unmoved. "And it did take three of the legendary golden ships to take down one E class ship."

"The ship didn't fail me," said Lionstone, her mood changing yet again. "It was the crew! Cowards and traitors and incompetents! Is there no one I can trust?"

Razor and Kid Death shared a glance, but said nothing.

Up on the surface of Golgotha, in the teeming streets of the Parade of the Endless, the fighting was getting dirty. The Imperial forces were being forced back on every front, and were not taking it at all well. They shot at everything that didn't wear a uniform, and pulled down buildings to cover their retreat. They had tried using women and children as human shields, but tended to shoot them themselves when they couldn't keep up. Most noncombatants had fled the city by now. Thick black smoke from the many burning buildings had gathered overhead, plunging the city into an early twilight. With most of the streetlights smashed, flickering crimson light from the hundreds of fires provided the only illumination. Dark figures moved through the bloody light with blood on their minds.

The Imperial forces hadn't given up yet. The Grendels might all be dead, but there were still other, secret, unpleasant weapons they hadn't used yet. Esp-blockers had been rushed to the front lines to hold back the elves, but the esper brains in their glass cases were limited in number and range. So they brought out the experimental living esp-blockers, captured espers brainwashed and conditioned into obedient shells. They weren't very bright, and had to be led everywhere in chains, but they were effective, and their range was staggering. The rebel espers had no choice but to fall back and make way for the standard fighters. The rebel advance slowed to a crawl in those areas, giving the Empire forces time to regroup.

So the clones went in, crowds of people with the same faces, armed to the teeth and wearing Born To Burn T-shirts in memory of the fallen Stevie Blues. Massed disrupter fire slammed through their ranks, cutting them down, but there were thousands of them, and they would not be stopped. They just kept running into the fire, jumping over the fallen, until the survivors stormed the barricades and fell on the troops. They always went for the esp-blockers first, giving them merciful deaths so that the elves could come swarming in behind them. A few hours after they'd been introduced, there were no living esp-blockers left anywhere in the city.

The underground brought forward its own awful weapons. Polters sent razor-edged psistorms barreling down the streets, ripping apart all they touched. Soldiers spontaneously combusted, burning with a fire no water could extinguish, as pyros went to work. And then there were the mindbombs, simple devices built around esper brain tissues. When activated, they spread madness and horror through all nonespers in the vicinity. Affected troops clawed their own eyes out, or turned on each other, and tore their companions limb from limb. The rebels pressed forward, overrunning Imperial positions again and again, and then Valentine's war machines appeared on the scene, and everything changed.

Huge hulking constructions stamped and rumbled down the wider streets, built-in disrupters cutting through the packed rebel ranks. Hundreds died in the first few minutes. People scrambled for cover, only to find there was nowhere the war machines couldn't reach. They smashed through walls and entire buildings to get at their prey, and projectile weapons were no use against them. Hand disrupters couldn't do enough damage to stop them. Espers came running from all directions to set their powers against the machines. Polters blasted them with chunks of fallen masonry, and barely dented the metal sides with their minds. Pyros swathed them with flames. But still the machines moved inexorably forward, street by street, block by block, retaking all the ground the Imperial forces had ceded. Troops pressed in after the machines, but were careful never to get in front of them. The war machines shot at everything that moved. Valentine could have distinguished between the two forces, but couldn't be bothered. He was having too much fun. His mind moved across the city, carried by the war machines, while his body lay safely cocooned in Tower Wolfe. He looked upon the death and destruction he was causing through a thousand sensors, and found it to be good.

The espers massed themselves before the oncoming machines, and prayed for a miracle. They got one. The Mater Mundi, Our Mother of All Souls, once again manifested through the entire esper force, burning brightly in every man and woman. For a moment they shone like gods, lighting the streets around them, and then their minds came together in a single expression of will, and an unstoppable psistorm raged through the streets, tearing the war machines apart and scattering the pieces. Metal shrapnel rained down on the retreating Imperial forces, until they, too, were swept away by the advancing psistorm. Every esper in the city roared with triumph, and the Parade of the Endless shook with the sound of it.

In his fortified retreat in Tower Wolfe, Valentine was thrown rudely from his war machines, and sat trembling and panting in his control center. One by one, the systems around him were shutting down, wrecked beyond repair. Valentine himself was dazed and disoriented, but lucky to be alive, and he knew it. The esper attack had followed him home and would have destroyed anything less than his chemically augmented and expanded mind. He could still feel the fringes of the esper contruct searching for him, as yet unable to get a grip on his slippery, evasive mind. He would have to leave Tower Wolfe and seek sanctuary elsewhere. But concentrate as he might, he couldn't think of anywhere else that would welcome him. Even Lionstone wouldn't want him after he'd failed to bring her victory with his war machines. Valentine Wolfe sat alone in the heart of his Family Tower and wondered what to do next.

The maintenance tunnels for the Palace's underground train systems had been sealed off and abandoned centuries ago, and the wait hadn't improved them. They had that particular darkness unique to the deep underground, an absolute blackness unreachable by any glint of surface light. They were cold as arctic ice, and the air was thick and musty. Even the smallest noise seemed to echo on forever, as though the tunnels were grateful for any sound after so many years of silence. And through the dark, claustrophobic passageways came Owen and Hazel and Giles, stumbling along the uneven floor and keeping their heads down to avoid banging them on the low ceiling. The cold barely touched them, thanks to the Maze, but even their incredible eyesight was useless in such utter darkness. Owen and Giles both carried lamps, their stark white light gleaming unpleasantly on the curving tunnel walls. Hazel had the map Owen had drawn out of computer records almost as old as the tunnels themselves. The passages interlinked with each other in an endless maze, and only one carefully traced route would get the rebels where they were going in time for it to do any good.

The pallid light on the pockmarked, cable-strewn walls looked increasingly disturbing, almost organic. Hazel muttered something about moving through the bowels of the earth, but no one laughed. They didn't feel much like speaking, lost in their own thoughts. After all the time and blood they'd given to the struggle, they were finally heading toward a confrontation that could mean the end of Lionstone's rule and the way things were. Owen tried to visualize the kind of Empire he might be responsible for creating and wasn't surprised to find he couldn't. As an historian he'd studied any number of ancient societies, including some that were officially banned from the records these days, based on all kinds of politics and beliefs, but all he'd ever known personally was the Empire of the Families and the Iron Throne. Random and Hazel had taken it in turns to explain their differing views of a democracy-based Empire, but much as he wanted to believe in them, they just sounded like chaos to him. And he was damned if he could see how he'd fit into either of their futures. But then, he'd never fitted in Lionstone's Empire, either. He smiled briefly, as it occurred to him that the chances of his living to see any of these futures were remote anyway, which made his worries somewhat irrelevant. Let him survive this mission, and he'd worry about such things then.

He still wasn't sure exactly what he was going to do when he finally forced his way into the Imperial Court and faced his Empress in the Iron Throne. All his life he'd been raised to revere and honor the Throne, irrespective of whoever occupied it, sworn to serve it all his life and to his death, if necessary. The Iron Throne was the source of all duty and honor and other things that could not easily be put into words. Overturning the Throne was like overturning God. Owen Deathstalker was an aristocrat, even if he had been outlawed, and he supposed in some ways he always would be. But he'd seen too much of the dark side of Empire, of the suffering and horrors on which his society of wealth and privilege was based, and he couldn't just look away and pretend he'd never seen it. Duty and honor and sheer humanity demanded he put a stop to it.

So he became a leader of the rebellion, a hero and an inspiration to others, and his life had been given over to avenging others whose lives had been broken and discarded on an Empress's whim. He was fighting now for all the poor and downtrodden, the espers and the clones and the other unpeople, for everyone whose lives had been ruined by an Empress who was supposed to protect them. And if sometimes he felt like an impostor, or unworthy to be part of the struggle, he comforted himself with the thought that no one else could do what he was doing. The Madness Maze had made him more than human, so he preserved his humanity by wielding his powers in the service of Humanity.

And all because Lionstone had outlawed him and taken

away his life of comforts and everything he ever cared for. He tried to tell himself it wasn't just revenge, that his fate gave him an insight into how so many other people had felt when the Empress ruined their lives, but he was basically too honest to lie well, even to himself. He wanted to make her suffer as he had, by taking away what she valued most.

But in the end none of that mattered. None of those reasons had brought him here, stumbling along in the darkness under the earth to topple an Empire. He was fighting for a child who'd lain crying helplessly in the blood-soaked snows of a Mistport back alley after he'd cut her down without thinking. She was a Blood addict, a street ganger, and she'd tried to kill him, but none of that mattered. He'd been forced into a position where he'd had no choice but to cripple and then kill her, and that didn't matter either. What mattered was that no one should have had to live like her, or die like her. Just a poor lost soul in the Hell Lionstone made. Her cries haunted him, and her blood would always be on his hands. He would overturn an Empire for her, throw down a whole way of life and everything he ever believed in, and he knew even then it wouldn't be enough to satisfy his guilt.

The tunnel they were following finally reached an end in a sealed hatchway. Owen and Giles put their shoulders and their Maze-given strength to it, and the heavy steel plate wrenched open on squealing hinges. Light spilled into the tunnel, so bright they all had to look away for a moment, till their eyes adjusted. Owen turned off his lamp, leaned out of the opening, and took a cautious look around, then signaled the others it was all clear. They took it in turns to jump lightly down from the tunnel opening to the station platform below.

The station was a massive, wide-open cavern, all gleaming tiles and overhead lights, with a single tube train standing at the spotlessly clean platform. The long vehicle was large enough to make them feel like children in its presence, all gleaming steel polished within an inch of its life. There were no windows, but a sliding door stood invitingly open. The platform was deserted, no guards anywhere, though security cameras watched openly from above. Hazel looked up at the high-arching ceiling, then at the richly decorated walls, and finally at the luxurious interior of the train, and tried hard not to seem impressed.

"Nice," she said, "in an overbearing sort of way."

"That's the aristocracy for you," said Owen. "They don't like to settle for anything less than perfection. Even if the surroundings aren't the first thing on your mind. Normally, if you're using one of these trains, you're too busy worrying about what nasty surprises Lionstone is going to hit you with once you get to Court. Sometimes the Court can be more dangerous than Lionstone is, which takes some doing. God knows what it looks like now, given her present mood. Still, no point in hanging about. Come, my lady Hazel, your carriage awaits."

"I am nobody's Lady," said Hazel, stepping warily through the open door into the train's carriage.

"That's for sure," Owen said gallantly.

Once inside, Giles sat down on the nearest seat and put his feet up. Hazel headed straight for the built-in bar, and Owen paid careful attention to the code panel set beside the door. The correct codes announced who you were, how many were in your party, and your level in Society. Without the right codes, the train wouldn't go anywhere. A really wrong code would activate the security systems, and the gas jets fitted in the carriage, and the only place you'd go after that would be the morgue. Oz claimed to have codes that would not only get them to the next station in perfect safety, but would also override the security systems, so that the gas jets couldn't be activated from the outside. Owen wasn't quite as convinced of that as he had been.

"Trust me," Oz said calmly in Owen's ear. "Your father's research was very thorough. The codes are correct. Just punch in the numbers as I give them to you."

Owen growled something indistinct under his breath, and did as he was told. The last number went in, and Owen braced himself for any hissing from the gas jets. He'd already decided that at the first whiff of anything suspicious, he was grabbing Hazel and leaving this carriage, even if he had to punch a hole through the solid steel wall to do it. But nothing happened, or at least, nothing unpleasant. The door slid shut, the engine fired up in its sealed compartment, and the train moved smoothly off. Owen looked around him, feeling there was something else he ought to be doing, and then shrugged and went to sit down beside Giles, who was leaning back in his luxuriously appointed seat, eyes closed, feet casually crossed before him, the epitome of relaxation. Owen sat on the edge of his seat and bit his lower lip. Trains gave him travel sickness.

Hazel had the bar open and was working her way through the decanters. She took a healthy swig from each till she found something she really liked, then came back to sit down opposite Owen and Giles, clutching the decanter to her. Owen gave her a hard look. Hazel wasn't in the least put out and offered him a sip. Owen politely declined. Giles opened an eye, looked at Hazel and the decanter, sniffed, and closed his eye again. Hazel made a rude gesture at him that Owen was glad Giles didn't see. He could feel his face getting warm. Giles had made it clear to Owen on more than one occasion that he didn't approve of Hazel. Entirely unsuitable as a match for the last of the Deathstalker line. He said it once in front of Hazel, and Owen had to restrain her from punching his ancestor out. Giles had got very sniffy, and said that just proved his point. Hazel had shrugged Owen off, said something very unkind about inbreeding in the aristocracy, and stalked off in a huff. Owen had been torn between a shouting match with his ancestor or hurrying after Hazel to calm her down, but in the end decided discretion was the better part of valor and left them both to their own devices. Some arguments you just knew you were never going to win.

"You know, this has almost been too easy," said Hazel, lowering the decanter and wiping her mouth with the back of her hand. "I mean, considering this is the only means of access to Lionstone's Court, I was expecting the station to be stuffed with security measures. Instead there's no armed guards, you punched in a few numbers, and off we went. That doesn't sound to me like the paranoid Iron Bitch we all know and loathe."

"Lionstone has always believed simple is best," said Owen. "It doesn't take much to make these trains secure.

Once they've started, there's no way of getting off, the carriage is sealed, and the gas jets in the ceiling can be activated by the Palace at the first sign of anything worrying. Hopefully the codes Oz and my father supplied are either blocking the carriage's sensors or preventing the Palace from flooding the carriage with gas. A slow and rather horrid death, or so I'm told."

Hazel glared at the nearest gas nozzle. "Hold everything. Are you telling me you don't know exactly what these codes do?"

"I'm afraid so. Oz doesn't have details like that. Apparently my father loaded the codes into the AI's memory some time back, but never got around to explaining their function. Which was typical of my father, who never explained anything unless he absolutely had to. So I'm afraid we'll just have to trust him."

"You want me to trust the word of an AI that's supposed to be dead, and only you can hear, programmed by a man who delighted in intrigue and treachery? All right; stop the train. Let me off. I'll walk the rest of the way."

"The trains are programmed not to stop anywhere except their destination," Owen said calmly. "I could break down the door and throw you out, but then you'd be facing a ten-mile walk. Alone. In the dark. Facing unknown security measures very definitely not covered by my codes."

Hazel scowled at him and took solace in her decanter. "I hate it when you're right. You go all smug and self-satisfied."

Owen hid a smile and looked round at Giles, who still had his eyes shut. "Everything all right, Giles?"

Giles opened his eyes and nodded to Owen, ignoring Hazel. "Couldn't be better, my boy. I've waited a long time for this. Dreamed for so long of finally coming home to put right the ancient wrongs done me. They threw me out, Owen. Outlawed me, after everything I'd done for them. I gave them my life and all my duty, fought their wars and killed their enemies, stained my honor with the Darkvoid Device, and even that wasn't enough for them. But now, after 943 years, I'm back to present them with the bill for what they did to me."

He stopped talking with an abruptness that suggested he

had nothing more to say on the subject, and stared straight ahead, eyes far away in a time of old hurts and betrayals. Owen stirred uncomfortably in his seat. The original Deathstalker had been a hero and a legend for so long it was hard to think of him as a real man, with real hurts and grievances. Owen couldn't help feeling that the great and glorious Deathstalker of old ought to be above such things. There wasn't room in what they had to do for such simple things as revenge anymore. Even he knew that. To be fair, Giles had never tried to hide the fact that he was in this for himself, and not for the underground or any of its causes. The rebellion was just a means to an end for him. On its own this would have been enough to cause Owen concern, but there was also the fact that for a man who'd spent the best part of a thousand years in stasis, Giles often seemed remarkably well informed and up-to-date. Owen sighed mentally. If you couldn't trust Giles Deathstalker, legendary hero and warrior, whom could you trust?

Assuming, of course, that this really was Giles Deathstalker.

The journey passed uneventfully, Hazel kept shooting suspicious glances at the gas jets in the ceiling, and significantly lowered the level of brandy in her decanter. Eventually this made Owen so nervous that he took the decanter away from her and put it back in the bar. It was a measure of their friendship that she let him do it, but she still didn't speak to him for the rest of the trip. The train finally slowed and slid to a halt. The door opened, and the engine shut itself down. It was suddenly very quiet. Owen got to his feet, his heart thudding uncomfortably in his chest. They'd finally come to Court. No more plans, no more arguments, no more quiet panics in the early hours of the morning when everyone else was fast asleep. And no turning back. Here, in the next few hours, his fate and that of the whole Empire would be decided, one way or another. He drew his sword and gun, took a deep breath, and stepped out onto the platform. He only managed a couple of steps, and then stopped dead. He heard Hazel and Giles leave the carriage behind him, but he only had eyes for the man waiting at the other end of the platform to meet them. As soon as

Owen saw him, he realized he should have expected him
to be there. That it was right that this man, above all
others, should be there to try and stop them going any farther. He was standing some distance down the brightly
illuminated platform, sword in hand, waiting patiently for
them to come to him. His energy half spit and crackled
loudly in the quiet.

Half A Man.

Hazel moved up beside Owen and swore quietly. "I
knew things had been going too smoothly. Why did it
have to be him, of all people? The one man in the Empire
who definitely can't be killed?"

"Because my loyalty is beyond question," said Half
A Man. "Because the sensors in the carriage told us
who was coming, and Lionstone knew someone of more
than usual valor would be needed to stop you. And
because I wanted to be here. Lionstone was quite annoyed
when the gas jets wouldn't function, but I wasn't. That
would have been such a . . . petty way to win. This way
is better. It's only fitting that the truest man in the Empire should face such infamous traitors to the Crown.
I suppose it's too late even now to talk you out of this
madness?"

"Far too late," said Giles.

"And it's not madness," said Owen. "It's necessary.
The Empire has become corrupt, sick, evil. It has to be put
down, so that something better can take its place."

"I've heard all that before," said Half A Man. His half
face was unreadable, but his voice was firm. "It doesn't
mean anything compared to the evil waiting outside the
Empire. The aliens that destroyed my ship and my crew
and did this to me are still out there, somewhere, waiting
for us to grow weak and divided so they can move in and
destroy us. And the petty evils that so concern you are
nothing to what the aliens would do to Humanity. I saw
and experienced horrors beyond your worst nightmares in
their ship. We're nothing compared to them. Only the
combined strength of the Empire has a chance of stopping
them. By this rebellion, you put the survival of our very
species at risk."

"Stuff that shit," said Hazel. "I've been hearing that all
my life, and there's still no sign of your aliens. If they

were coming, they'd have been here long ago. These days, it's just an excuse to keep people like you in power. That lets people like you do whatever you want to people like me. Let the aliens come. They couldn't be worse than the life you people wanted to condemn me to. You're the real aliens. You have nothing in common with the people whose lives you control."

"Hazel's right," said Owen. "You've held the threat of the aliens' coming over everyone's heads for so long, you've come to the point where you can use it to justify any damn thing you want. If you really want to ensure the Empire's survival, stand aside. Let us overthrow Lionstone, and put things right in the Empire."

"You wouldn't know what to do with an Empire," said Half A Man. "You people would loot and pillage and destroy the traditions of centuries, just to satisfy your own needs and pleasures. I can understand what drives a mercenary like the d'Ark woman, but what the hell are Deathstalkers doing here? You took an oath, upon your name and your blood and your honor, to be true to the Empress and serve her all your days."

"No," said Giles. "Our oath was to the Throne, not to the madwoman who currently sits on it."

"A distinction without meaning." Half A Man moved unhurriedly toward them, the sound of his one human foot slapping on the platform sounding loud and distinct in the hush. It felt to Owen as though the whole Empire was listening and holding its breath to see what would happen next. "We have nothing to talk about, outlaws," said Half A Man. "We don't even speak the same language anymore."

"I don't think we ever did," said Owen, just a little sadly. "Throw down your sword. You don't stand a chance against the three of us."

"You can't kill me," said Half A Man. "No one can."

"You never met us before," said Giles. "We're different."

"So we've heard," said Half A Man. He stopped a few yards short of them, and his half mouth moved in something that might have been a smile. "Know what this is?"

And he held up in his human hand a small metal box with a red button on it. Owen, Hazel, and Giles just had time to recognize it as a mindbomb, and then Half A Man pressed the button. The tech in the box stimulated the esper brain tissues, and a psionic signal leaped out, falling across the three rebels like a thunderstorm in their heads. Owen and Hazel and Giles rocked on their feet, hands pressed to their heads, trying to force the hideous howl out of their thoughts. Owen staggered back a step, his eyes bulging, his thoughts slow and churning and not entirely his own. Bright lights flared around him, and there were mad voices in his ears. There was something walking up and down in his head and it wasn't he. Pain and weakness chewed through his body, but even through all that was happening to him, Owen could still hear Half A Man talking.

"Interesting. We weren't sure what effect the mindbomb would have on you, since we were fairly sure that whatever you are, you aren't actually espers, but the odds seemed good that it would mess you up nicely. My own unique nature makes me immune, of course. There's really no point in struggling. This particular mindbomb has been augmented far beyond its usual strength and range, just for you. If you were normal mortals, your brains would be leaking out your ears by now. But don't worry. Just hold still for a moment, and I'll put you out of your misery."

Owen had dropped his gun. His hands felt like they belonged to someone else. He only knew he still had hold of his sword because when he looked down he could see it in his white-knuckled grip. Giles was on his knees beside him, twitching and trembling as his nerves fired at random, his eyes wide and unseeing. Hazel lay on her back on the platform, her mouth stretched in a feral grimace of helpless pain and rage, her empty hands clenching and unclenching. They were fighting the mindbomb's influence and getting nowhere, so Owen decided to stop fighting. He withdrew deep inside himself, and shut down all his Maze-given gifts. They were no use to him now. They had become the means whereby the mindbomb was able to torment him.

It was hard, deliberately blinding and deafening himself as Half A Man advanced on him with deadly intent, but somehow he knew his only real defense lay inside him, not outside. The mindbomb was designed to work on humans, but though he wasn't an esper, he wasn't human anymore either. And if his thoughts were still human, it was only because he chose so. There were other ways of thinking, and even as that idea came to him, he seemed to see another direction he could move in, another form of thought, above and beyond human limitations. So he went that way, in a direction that was more than a direction, and suddenly his mind was clear again. He opened his eyes to find Half A Man looming over him, sword in hand, mindbomb hanging from his belt. And it was the easiest thing in the world for Owen to lash out with his sword and cut through the cord holding the mindbomb to the belt. The small steel box fell clattering to the platform, and Owen crushed it with one blow of his golden fist.

In a moment the mindbomb's influence was gone, and Owen was himself again. Half A Man retreated quickly to a safe distance, surprise and shock clear in his half face. Hazel and Giles came back to themselves and scrambled to their feet, shaking their heads confusedly. And that part of Owen's mind that had come briefly alive when he needed it shut itself down again, now that it was no longer needed. On some deep basic level Owen knew he couldn't continue to think that way and still be himself, so he deliberately turned away from a direction that was already fading from his memory. He was Owen again, and only Owen, and that was enough. He smiled at the warily watching Half A Man, and the humor in that smile was very dark. Half A Man lifted his sword slightly.

"I'm impressed, Deathstalker," he said evenly. "But not really surprised. They told me their new and improved mindbomb would fry your minds, but I was never convinced. Not after all the things you've done. You're becoming a legend, just like me. You won't like it. People will make up stories and songs about you, and worship your image on the viewscreen, but they'll never get near the real truth of who you are. They'll make a giant out of you, and then be ever so upset when you let them down by being only human. Still, not to worry. I'll see your story ends here, then you'll never have to hear the lies they'll tell in your name."

"You died a long time ago," said Owen, moving calmly forward. "Time for you to lie down and admit it."

"I can't die," said Half A Man. "My alien half won't let me. Come to me, Deathstalker, and I'll make it quick."

"Shut up and fight," said Owen.

They came together, and their swords clashed and flew apart in a shower of sparks. Half A Man moved and struck with several lifetimes' speed and experience, never still, endlessly circling around his opponent, pressing Owen's skills to the limit. Owen moved with him, limiting himself to purely defensive moves as he studied his opponent's style, moving round and round in slow, cautious circles, searching out Half A Man's weaknesses and vulnerabilities. It didn't take Owen long to realize that Half A Man didn't have any. The energy half supplied him with endless strength and speed, so he never grew tired, and he knew more about swordsmanship than Owen ever would. Owen boosted, becoming immediately faster and stronger, and launched his own attack. Half A Man sped right up with him, and calmly stood off everything Owen could throw at him. Strength burned in Owen's arms, and he sped up again, pushing his boost to the limits. His sword moved so fast it was only a blur. And for the first time, Half A Man fell back a step.

Owen pressed the attack, cutting at Half A Man's defending sword like a woodsman attacking a stubborn tree. In that moment, Half A Man represented to him everything he hated about the Empire, and he laughed aloud as he threw himself at his enemy. Half A Man had stopped smiling, but held his ground and would not retreat another step. And it occurred to Owen that whereas Half A Man's great strength and speed came from the endless store of his energy half, Owen's boost was of strictly limited duration. Which meant, if he didn't find a way to finish this fight soon, the odds were he wouldn't be finishing it at all. So he put all his strength and speed into one attack, a hammering blow with all his Maze-given talents behind it that slammed right past Half A Man's defense, and crashed down on his human skull.

For a long moment Owen's sword seemed to hesitate, as though frustrated by some unseen energy barrier, and then all the Maze's gifts and strengths concentrated themselves in Owen's blow, a more-than-human impetus that would not be denied, and the sword crashed on. The great and heavy blade cut down through Half A Man's human face, right next to the energy's dividing line, and then carried on down, cutting the human half away from the energy until the crimson blade erupted from the groin in a rush of blood and guts. Owen staggered backwards as his sword came free, all his strength and speed disappearing as he dropped out of boost. Hazel and Giles caught him and kept him from falling. And together they watched as Half A Man's human half fell to lie thrashing and bleeding to death on the platform. The energy half still stood where it was, motionless.

"How the hell did you do that?" said Hazel.

"Damned if I know," said Owen.

They moved forward to stand over the twitching human half, giving the energy half a wide berth. The human half was dying by inches, but it was dying. Guts and organs had fallen out of the huge wound down its side, and blood streamed across the platform, welled over the edge, and dripped onto the tracks below. Owen watched the half man die with divided feelings. Half A Man had been his enemy, opposed to everything Owen now believed in, but it was hard not to see in him a man shaped by implacable outside forces into a legend he had never chosen for himself. Owen could understand that. It was the story of his life, too. He knelt down beside the half body, and took the trembling hand in his. The eye in the half head had sunk right back in the socket, but it rolled slowly over to look up at Owen. Half A Man tried desperately to say something, but couldn't make his mouth work. Owen leaned over him, but his enemy was already dead. Owen gently pulled his hand free from the dead grip and got to his feet.

"What do you suppose he would have said?" murmured Hazel.

"Damn you to hell, probably," said Owen. "He always was single-minded, for a man with only half a brain."

Giles clapped Owen on the shoulder, making him jump.

"Well done, kinsman. You fought a good fight, for an historian."

"I could have used some help," said Owen. "Why didn't you two join in?"

"Oh, I couldn't allow that," said Giles. "It wouldn't have been sporting."

"Stuff sport," said Owen. "This is war."

"And war is the greatest sport of all," said Giles. "You're an historian. You should know that."

"It's only sport to the victors," said Owen. "Not to the victims and the orphaned and all the poor bastards dragged into it against their will."

"Uh, guys," said Hazel. "I think we have a problem . . ."

They both looked round to follow her pointing hand. The sundered energy half was still standing where they'd left it, but its shape was slowly changing. The coruscating energy pulsed and flowed, pushing at the boundaries of its form. It was becoming something else, something different, no longer bound or dictated by its human half. The slowly changing shape grew more disturbing as it became more distinct, until Owen had to fight not to look away. It was becoming alien, and more than alien. It had width and breadth and depth, and other dimensions, too. Owen couldn't see so much as sense them, and they made his head hurt. Hazel fired her disrupter at it, and the energy beam bounced harmlessly away. The energy shape burned horribly brightly, like a hole cut in reality through which some malign god's light was shining. And then it was gone, and the memory of it faded thankfully from Owen's mind like a nightmare best not remembered. Owen let his breath out in a long shuddering sigh, and only then discovered that Hazel was gripping his arm so hard it hurt. She let go as soon as he saw it and pulled her composure briskly about herself again.

"Well, that was different," she said, just a little breathlessly. "Anyone here have any ideas as to what the hell that was? Or what it was becoming?"

"A problem for the future," said Owen. "As I have a horrible feeling it'll be back someday, along with the aliens that created it. We may only have traded one threat for another."

"Let them come," said Giles. "Let them all come. They'll

be no match for the Empire we shall create. Now let's go. We don't want to keep the Empress waiting."

He strode off down the platform, and Owen and Hazel fell in after him. Hazel looked at Owen.

"I hate it when he gets all confident like that. It's just asking for trouble."

"I couldn't agree more," said Owen. "But at least as long as he's in front of us, I don't have to worry about what he might be doing."

"And when the shooting starts, we can hide behind him," said Hazel. "He's wide enough."

"I can hear every word you're saying," said Giles calmly. "And I don't find it in the least amusing."

"Tough," said Hazel. "Serves you right for eavesdropping. And get a move on, or I'll kick your ankles."

"I wonder if it's too late to go back to the rebel leaders, and ask for some new companions," Owen said wistfully.

They came flying out of the scarlet sun on the early-morning skies, a vast armada of fast-flying gravity sleds. There were thousands of them, blackening the sky, one-man sleds with souped-up engines for more speed, armed to the teeth with bolted-down energy guns and heavy projectile weapons, with long ribbons of bullets. They came in low, well below the usual sensor levels, and were over the Parade of the Endless and heading for the pastel Towers of the Families before any of the Clans even knew they were coming. They whipped between the tall buildings of the city, rising and falling on the thermals, flashing by too fast for the automated weapons systems to draw a bead on them. Thousands of sleds shot across the city, manned by rebels, espers, clones, anyone with a raging need for justice in their hearts, and a willingness to fly into Hell itself for a chance at bringing down the Families.

They swept over the struggling crowds in the streets below, ignoring the fighting. That wasn't their mission. An occasional weapon fired up at them from the heaving masses below, but the sleds were small, evasive targets, hard to hit. The Empire's huge gravity barges tried to block their way, hovering in place like floating battle stations, but there were only a few of them, and the sleds just soared over and around them, come and gone in seconds, too unpredictable for the barges' computerized firing systems. No one had ever thought to use one-man sleds like this before. Until Jack Random did. They filled the skies, thundering along, with the sun at their back, heading for the Towers, an army of retribution flying on wings of fury.

Jack Random, Ruby Journey, and Alexander Storm led the way, flying side by side. They'd lowered the sleds' force shields for more speed, and the wind of their passing whipped at their faces, driving tears from their eyes. The early-morning chill cut right through them, despite the heating units in their outfits, but they ignored it, intent on what was to come. Storm felt it the worst in his old bones, but he just clenched his teeth to keep them from chattering, and concentrated on keeping up with the others. He wasn't going to be left behind.

Random looked down at the Parade of the Endless flashing by below him, and found it hard to believe that after all the many years and all the many battles, he'd finally brought his crusade home to Golgotha. To the Families who ran and ruined everything in the name of profit and privilege. They outlawed him and banished him, did their best to break and kill him, but now here he was, back to present them with the bill. And payback was going to be a real bitch.

He laughed aloud, the wind whipping the sound away almost before he heard it. The Empire was going to fall today, and he was going to help bring it down. And when he had it on its knees and begging for mercy, he'd spit in its eye and kick it in the teeth. He worked the sled's throttle mercilessly, trying to force out even more speed, but the sled was already exceeding its safety limits. Random could see the first of the Towers in the distance, and he couldn't wait to get to them. The Clans had to know he was coming by now. They'd have set up their defenses, adjusted their computer aiming systems to compensate for the sleds' speed and maneuverability. They'd be waiting for him. And he didn't give a damn. This was judgment day, and he was bringing down the hammer. It was almost enough to make a man believe in religion. He grinned harshly, the wind forcing his lips back into a wolf's snarl. It was a good day for someone else to die.

He looked across at Ruby Journey. In her black leathers and white furs, standing rock-steady on her bucking sled, face grim and implacable, she looked like some dark Valkyrie out of legend, come to take the dead heroes to Valhalla, whether they wanted to go or not. Her sled was loaded down with weapons of all kinds, right up to the last ounce of weight that wouldn't interfere with her speed. Everything from energy guns to grenades to throwing knives. Ruby liked to be prepared. She looked around, caught his eye on her, and grinned at him. She was on her way to a lifetime best in looting and mayhem, or quite possibly her own death, and she'd never looked happier.

Random smiled back at her, then turned to look at Storm, flying on his other side. The canny old warrior had strapped himself securely onto his sled, but even so he still seemed to shake and shudder with every sudden movement of his craft. His long mane of white hair flew out behind him as he stared unflinchingly into the rushing wind. He was too old for this kind of mission, and everyone knew it, including him, but he'd insisted on coming along, and Random hadn't had the heart to say no. He understood Storm's need to be in at the kill after giving so much of his life to the struggle against the Empire. So he'd put the old man right next to him, where he could keep an eye on him, and just hoped Storm could keep up. Hopefully the old warrior's reflexes would keep him alive long enough to reach the Towers. A lot of people weren't going to make it. There were bound to be heavy losses once the armada hit the Towers' main defenses. Everyone in the armada knew that. But they'd all volunteered anyway. They knew the one-man sleds were the only force fast enough, mobile enough, and versatile enough to get past the defenses and into the Towers. Where the Families thought they were so safe.

Ground forces would have had to struggle for days against the heavily manned and armed Towers, fighting their way up floor by floor to reach the Families barricaded in their heavily defended top floor. Losses on both sides would have been enormous, with no guarantee that the Families wouldn't just abandon their Towers and flee elsewhere before they could be captured. Gravity barges had guns strong enough to blast a way in, but they were too slow, too unwieldy. The Towers' superior firepower would have blown them out of the sky before they could get close enough to do any real damage. Espers were helpless in the face of so many known esp-blockers. Which was why the Clans had retired to the Towers—the one place where they felt really safe—at the first sign of real trouble.

Random was here to teach them different. He'd thought about this plan for years, in the trenches and foxholes of endless battles on endless worlds, dreaming of what he'd do when he finally brought the war home to homeworld. He'd thought of every problem, refined every detail, and now here he was, living his dream. Do or die. Death or glory. And he couldn't have been happier either.

Gravity barges lifted off from the Towers' private landing fields and launched themselves into the sky to meet the armada. They were great lumbering ships, with heavy armor and superior firepower, but the sleds were upon them in seconds, and ran rings around them. They snapped back and forth, whipping around the slow-moving barges, too small and too fast for the larger ships' tracking computers. They'd been programmed for vessels their own size, or stationary targets. The sleds shot past them, more and more all the time, so the barges opened fire anyway, disrupter cannon blazing from the huge vessels' sides, aimed at what seemed like the greatest concentrations of sleds.

The sleds scattered immediately, but there were so many of them the barges couldn't miss all the time. With no force shields to protect them, they exploded into flames and fell from the sky like so many burning leaves. Dozens were blown apart in the first few seconds, screams sounding briefly in the wind, and then the survivors of the first rank of sleds threw themselves in close to the barges, so they couldn't keep firing without hitting each other. Ducking and dodging the barges' few smaller weapons, the sleds opened up with their own

disrupters. At first they were too few to hurt the barges'
force shields, but soon there were hundreds of them, and
hundreds more, buzzing around the barges like bees
around a bear, hitting the shields again and again until
they overloaded and burned out, unable to cope with
being hit so often in so many places at once. The sleds
fell on the barges, their weapons tearing ragged holes
through the heavy armor by sheer persistence. As the
sleds' fire continued, inner explosions rocked the barges,
and smoke billowed out the holes, thick and black and
shot with flames. One by one the great heavy ships
lurched or tilted helplessly in the air, drifting in the wind,
already beginning their slow but inevitable descent to the
ground. The armada of one-man sleds, only slightly
depleted, left them behind and headed for the first of the
pastel Towers, standing tall and proud against the early-
morning sky.

The sleds filled the sky now, thousands of them descending inexorably on the last redoubts of the Clans. The
Towers waited till they were safely in range, then opened
up with their own disrupter cannon, blowing great holes
in the armada. Sleds plummeted from the sky, twisted
metal wrecks leaving long shaky trails of smoke and
fire behind them. The majority pressed on. There would
be time for grieving later. The Towers' guns punched
through the massed sleds again and again, filling the sky
with blood and screams, explosions and shrapnel, but still
the armada pressed on. There was no point in turning back
now. The Towers would only shoot them in the back. And
this close to their target, there was no longer any point in
evasive tactics, so they just opened their throttles all the
way and bore in on the Towers like so many guided mis-
siles, driven by rage and determination and a lifetime's
grievances. Random was still right there at the front, with
Ruby and Storm at his sides. He was howling and roaring
now, shouting old battle cries and slogans, and hundreds
of responses rose up behind him. For many, Jack
Random's name was battle cry enough. The rebels fell
howling on the Towers, and the sound of their blood rage
filled the morning sky.

The Towers' disrupters fired again and again, blasting
sleds out of the sky, their blackened husks falling on all

sides. Hundreds of good men and women died, blown apart with their craft, consumed in fire, or thrown from their sleds by the impact of nearby explosions. They screamed in fear and pain and rage as they fell to the earth far below. Random and Ruby and Storm still led the advance, fire and explosions and people dying all around them, whipping their sleds through daring, dangerous maneuvers as the thermals around the Towers rose up to meet them. Behind them, the oncoming sleds darkened the sky, casting a dark, looming shadow over the Towers. For all the hundreds that had fallen, and continued to fall, there were still thousands of them, and they would not be denied. And the leading sleds were close now, so close the Towers' disrupter cannon could no longer train on them. They shot inside the defensive perimeter, heading for the great steelglass windows on the top floors. Random thought he could see faces staring out, eyes wide with fear and shock, and his heart warmed at the sight.

He was still grinning when a disrupter beam from Tower Chojiro hit his sled. He grabbed the controls and hung on grimly as the sled bucked beneath him, and then the whole control panel exploded. Blinded by smoke and flames, Random hung on to the dead throttle as the sled dropped out beneath him. The sled fell like a brick, leaving the smoke behind, and Random could see the armada falling away above him, leaving him behind. Random cursed and struggled with what was left of the controls. He wasn't afraid of dying. He was too angry. He hadn't come this far, been through this much, to fail now.

The sled's engine coughed briefly, and the sled lurched beneath him, almost throwing him off. Random snarled something indistinct, and concentrated on the controls, trying to coax a miracle out of the burning remnants of the crippled sled. And one of the gods he was praying to must have been listening, because the sled's engine fired back into life. It sounded ragged and uncertain, and the sled lurched and tilted this way and that, but gradually its headlong plummet slowed to a halt, and then, as Random whooped and howled and shook his fist in triumph, the sled slowly began to rise again, heading up the side of the Tower Chojiro toward the Family on the top floor.

The sled's engine wanted to cut out at any moment, but Random wouldn't let it, nursing the controls along with scowling concentration. The armada was still flooding by above him, dark shapes racing unstoppably toward the many Towers. The guns still sounded, and great ragged gaps were appearing in the dark tide, but still the sleds pressed on. Some had already made contact, blowing holes in the steelglass windows and crashing into the top floors of the Towers. There were troops waiting for them with sword and gun, but the first wave of rebels fought well, with a fierce desperation, refusing to die until they had established a beachhead for those coming after them. Many of them died anyway, cut down by overwhelming odds, but more rebels were appearing all the time, and slowly, foot by foot, they forced their way into the Towers.

It was a fight the Families had never expected to have to fight. After the Wolfes' sled attack on Tower Campbell, most Families had added extra disrupter cannon on the roofs, and invested in a few gravity barges, but they'd never anticipated such a near-suicidal charge.

More and more gravity sleds made it past the Towers' defenses and crashed their way into the top floors. Random cursed regretfully as his sled slowly rose nearer the top floor of Tower Chojiro. He'd always meant to be one of the first in, fighting to provide a landing ground for those coming behind him. Jack Random had always believed in leading from the front. He couldn't see what had happened to Ruby Journey and Alexander Storm, but he couldn't think about them now. The sled lurched up past the last few floors, and came to a halt facing the top floor of Tower Chojiro. And Random's stomach lurched as he found himself facing a dozen leveled hand disrupters. Someone had smashed a hole through the steelglass window but obviously hadn't survived it. Random's adrenaline kicked in, and everything seemed to move very slowly. He seemed to have all the time in the world to study the situation and think about what to do. He didn't trust his control over the sled enough to risk dropping below the guns' range, and he was moving too slowly to

rise above it. And if he used up his last few moments
trying to raise the sled's force shield, only to find it didn't
work, the disrupters wouldn't leave enough of him to
bury. So Random did the only thing he could, as time
crashed up to speed again. He gave the sled all the speed
it had, and slammed the craft right into the waiting
guards.

Their shots went wild as he was suddenly among them,
but some hit anyway. The sled exploded, throwing
Random forward over the controls in a cloud of flames.
He flew blindly through the air, smarting from the heat of
the flames, trying to get his feet under him. The guards
scattered as what was left of the sled crash-landed among
them and exploded again. Random hit the carpeted floor
hard, driving the breath from his lungs. He curled into a
ball, hoping the smoke from the explosions would hide
him, desperately trying to draw his sword and gun. He
could hear shouting and the crackle of flames and general
chaos. And then what was left of the fiercely burning sled
crashed down on top of him, pinning him to the floor, and
there was only blazing heat and the roar of the fire all
around him.

The surviving guards called for reinforcements as they
fought the fires breaking out all over the top floor. The
Clan Chojiro had already retreated to the floor below
sometime back. More men arrived, and some fought the
fires while others took up positions at the broken windows, keeping up a steady fire on the advancing sleds.
Tower Chojiro had more disrupter cannon on the roof
than most, and for the moment most of the one-man sleds
were concentrating their efforts on the less well defended
Towers. A handful of guards cautiously approached the
blazing wreckage of the downed sled. There was no way
anyone could have survived such a crash and its after-
math, but the guards were taking no chances. They'd been
hearing disturbing things about some of the rebels. One of
the braver guards leaned over the wreckage and poked it
gingerly with the tip of his sword. The heat from the fire
kept him from getting any closer, but he thought he could
see a single blackened leg protruding from under the rear
of the wreckage. He poked that with his sword too, and
then leaped back as the leg twitched. He scrambled back-

wards to rejoin his fellows, and the whole wreckage
lurched to one side as something underneath it rose up
from certain death, determined to be free. The burning
sled overbalanced and fell away, revealing a dark human
figure. Its clothes were charred and smoldering, and the
bare face and hands were blackened and red raw from
burns. But its back was straight and its head erect, and the
blistered hands held gun and sword securely. The eyes
were pale slits in the dark face, but white teeth flashed
suddenly in a disturbing smile.

"I don't die that easily," said Jack Random.

The guards stood where they were for a long moment,
paralyzed at the sight of something that should have been
dead and still, but instead had risen up to challenge them
again. But they were trained Tower guards, conditioned to
serve their Family unto death, and the moment passed.
They threw the fear off with a cold shrug and started forward, swords raised to carve the burnt specter into a hundred pieces and see if it rose again. Random aimed his
disrupter carefully and took out three of the guards with a
single shot. They fell silently, and the rest came on.
Random put his gun back in its charred holster, took a
firm grip on his sword, and wondered how many he might
take with him before they finally pulled him down. Even
he had his limitations, and he could feel how close they
were. Surviving the crash had taken a lot out of him, and
he wasn't going to be given enough time to recover. He
would have shrugged if it hadn't hurt so much. He'd
always known he's die alone, overrun at last by too many
enemies. And that was when Ruby Journey's voice suddenly grated in his ears.

"Hit the floor, Random!"

He threw himself down without questioning, and the
room was immediately full of the roar of gunfire as Ruby
opened up with the heavy projectile weapon mounted
on her gravity sled, hovering outside the shattered windows. The guards jerked and convulsed as the bullets
tore through them, falling helpless before a weapon they
had never been prepared for. The few shots they got off
went wild, and soon they were all dead, lying in tangled
bloody heaps on the expensive carpeting. The gun finally
shut off, and the sudden quiet in the room was almost

deafening. Thick trails of smoke curled lazily on the air.
Ruby ripped the heavy gun from its moorings, jumped
easily through the shattered window, and hurried over
to Random, who raised a tired hand in greeting. Ruby
stared at the charred and blistered hand, then at his red
raw face.

"Jack . . . you look awful."

"Thanks a whole bunch. I think it probably looks worse
than it feels, though it feels pretty bad. But I'm healing. I
can feel it. I'm still in the game." He looked down at the
projectile weapon she had cradled in her arms. "Guess
you were right to bring that thing along after all. Is it as
much fun as it looked?"

Ruby chuckled. "Bet your ass. Hold it for a while." She
dropped it into his arms, and moved purposefully toward
the dead guards. She knelt beside them and began going
through their pockets with professional speed and skill.
Random frowned.

"Ruby, what are you doing?"

"Just looking for valuables. Credits, jewelry, anything
going."

"We don't have time for looting!"

"There's always time for looting. When I joined up
with this rebellion, I was promised all the loot I could
carry, and this is the first down payment. Though I have
to say we're talking lean pickings here. Cheap bunch.
Still, by this time tomorrow, I fully intend to have
stripped this entire Tower bare. If it's small and valuable
and can be carried somewhere on my person, I'm having it."

Random shook his head sadly and moved over to
the stairs. No point in trying the elevator; it was bound
to be booby-trapped. It was what he would have done.
The Family would be on the next floor down, no doubt
barricaded in, and surrounded by a small army of protec-
tors. Not that it would do them any good. Random
grinned like a wolf, and felt the skin of his face crackle.
He reached up automatically and rubbed at his mouth.
Black flecks of dead skin fell away. He peered at a small
mirror set on the wall by the stairs. Fresh new skin
showed where the dead had peeled away. He was healing.
He still felt like shit, but he didn't have time to bother

with that. He pushed open the stairway door and peered down the brightly lit metal stairs. Quite deserted and utterly quiet.

Random smiled again. He had no doubt Clan Chojiro had all kinds of unpleasant surprises lying in wait for him. But they wouldn't stop him. Nothing was going to stop him now, not all the armed forces in Golgotha or all the loot in the world. He'd chosen Tower Chojiro for his target quite deliberately. He had long acquaintance with the treacheries of the Chojiros, and now he was finally here, he was going to send all their souls shrieking down to Hell, whatever it took and whatever it cost him. He called sharply to Ruby, and she paused just to pull a few more rings from a few more fingers, then hurried over to join him, her pockets bulging with all sorts of expensive items. She took the projectile weapon back from him, cradling it tenderly in her arms. She'd have a few sharp words with him later, for having dared snap at her as much as for interrupting her looting, but for the moment she was content to follow wherever Random led, secure in the thought that the journey would no doubt involve satisfactory amounts of blood, savagery, and general mayhem. She took the lead when Random indicated, and started down the stairs, Random right behind her.

They hadn't got far when a determined band of elite troops came hammering up the metal stairs to meet them. Ruby opened up with her gun at once, the sound horribly loud in the confined space, but the guards had already turned on their personal force shields, those at the rear holding them over their heads. Bullets ricochetted harmlessly from the shields, and Ruby had to stop firing as her own bullets came flying back at her from the walls of the stairwell. She dropped her gun and drew her sword, expecting the guards to lower their force shields and charge with drawn swords. But instead, the shielded guards moved slowly forward, filling the stairs, forcing Ruby and Random to back away before them. There was nowhere else they could go. It was a simple tactic, its only function to keep the rebels from getting to the Clan. With anyone else it might have worked, but Ruby and Random had been touched by the Madness Maze. They reached out to each other mentally, linked their thoughts, and pyrokinetic fire roared away from them, filling the stairwell with a heat so extreme the metal steps and walls began to twist and bubble. The brilliant white flames swept around and over the guards' force shields, blasting them out of the way, and incinerated them all in a few moments. Some had time to scream, and a few turned to run, but the fire was everywhere, and when it finally disappeared, the stairwell was full of charred and blackened bodies and the thick heavy smell of burnt meat. Ruby and Random broke their mental link and looked dispassionately upon what they'd done. There was no room in them for quarter or mercy anymore. Ruby winced back from the heated air, and scowled at the twisted bodies blocking the stairway.

"I suppose we're going to have to shift them out of the way before we can go any farther. Maybe we should have let them run after all."

"No," said Random. "A foe you let run away is a foe who might come back to fight you another day. Let's get to work. All these obstacles are making me impatient."

Ruby pulled on a pair of gloves to protect her hands, and they set about lifting and pushing the charred bodies to one side. Ruby wrinkled her nose at the smell, but Random didn't seem to notice. He'd smelled worse in his time. Thick black specks fell away from his face and hands as he worked, revealing pink new skin underneath. And though he started out looking much like the bodies he was shifting, by the time they'd finished he looked much like his old self again. His clothes were still a mess, but there wasn't a lot he could do about that.

He and Ruby were just manhandling the last of the bodies out of the way when they heard a single set of footsteps coming hurriedly down the stairs from above. Ruby quickly grabbed up her projectile weapon, and Random drew his disrupter. They stood back-to-back, looking up and down the stairs, just in case the footsteps were a feint to draw their attention away from the real attack. The footsteps seemed to take a long time to arrive, and then Alexander Storm rounded the corner of the stairwell, stopped, and blinked mildly at the gun Ruby was training on him.

"If you were a man, I could make a very damaging psychological remark about the need to carry such a large gun," he said calmly. "But as it's you, Ruby, I don't think I'll bother."

Ruby looked back at Random. "Is he saying what I think he's saying?"

"We'll discuss it later," Random said diplomatically. He lowered his gun and grinned up at Storm. "About time you got here, Alex. I was wondering what was keeping you."

"Traffic was murder," said Storm. He sniffed the air and pulled a face. "I see you two have been raising hell again."

"Just doing what we have to," said Random. "Fall in behind us, Alex, but don't start dragging your feet, or we'll leave you behind. We're right on the Chojiros' heels now. I can feel it."

"Yeah," said Ruby. "Time for all fate's revenges to come home."

"You've been reading those Gothic romances again," said Random.

Storm sniffed. "It's a revelation to me that she can read."

"Keep talking, Storm," said Ruby. "There's still room for another spare rib on the barbecue."

"God, I swear it's like being in charge of children," said Random. "Shut it, both of you, and follow me. I don't want to keep the Chojiros waiting."

He set off down the stairs, Ruby right behind him. Storm wrapped himself in his great cloak to protect himself from the worst of the heat only slowly dissipating in the stairwell, and went after them.

They went cautiously but met no resistance. No more troops, no booby traps, no guns hidden in the walls. Just the metal steps, falling away before them. Random grew increasingly wary and gripped his gun and sword so tightly his fingers ached. This wasn't the Clan Chojiro he remembered, with a trap for every choice of action, a trip for every footstep, and layer upon layer of treachery and deceit. Such easy going could only mean the Chojiros wanted him to reach them. Which in turn could only mean they had something really unpleasant and devastating in store for him. Random grinned his wolfish smile. It didn't matter what they had, or thought they had; nothing was going to stop him now.

They reached the foot of the stairs and carefully approached the blank metal door that led off to the next floor. Everything was still and quiet. Ruby peered over the railings and down the stairwell, in case there were troops waiting below, but the stairwell was empty for as far as she could see. Random studied the door and the walls around it carefully, but couldn't detect any booby traps. He was pretty sure he would have been able to sense anything wrong or out of place, but he still felt a small but definite sense of relief when he turned the door handle and eased the door open, and nothing nasty happened. He gestured for Ruby to join him, and she moved in beside him without making a sound, her gun at the ready. Random counted to three silently, then they both hit the door together and stormed into the next floor, Storm right behind them. A quick glance around assured Random there were no troops waiting, and no obvious traps; just a man and a woman standing together, waiting to greet their visitors with ostentatiously empty hands.

BB Chojiro and Gregor Shreck.

BB was a petite doll of a woman, with long dark hair and sharp oriental features. She wore a kimono of bright scarlet, wrapped tightly in all the right places. It was easy to see why Julian Skye had once fallen in love with her. The Shreck, on the other hand, was a short fat butterball of a man, with a bulging fleshy face and deep-set eyes. A tricky, dangerous, vindictive man, by all accounts.

Random moved slowly forward, stopping carefully out of reach of the Chojiro or the Shreck. Ruby and Storm moved in on either side of him, guns trained. BB Chojiro bowed deeply to them. Gregor managed a stiff nod.

"Who the hell are these people?" said Ruby, not bothering to lower her voice.

"I do wish you'd keep up on the briefings," said Random, not taking his eyes off the two before him. "The woman speaks for the Chojiros in negotiations, and the like. She's also Blue Block, though we're not supposed to know that."

"Perhaps she wants to negotiate the Clan's surrender," said Storm.

Ruby frowned. "Would you accept it, Jack?"

"Not a chance in hell," said Jack Random, his voice flat and cold as death. "They've got nothing I want more than their destruction. You ought to recognize Gregor Shreck at least, Ruby. Chief slimeball in a totally disreputable Clan. Rebel when it suits him, but always a member of the Families."

"Toby's uncle?"

"That's the one."

"Oh yeah, I've heard of him. I'll toss you for who gets first hack at him."

"Oh no you won't," said Random. "I've seen that double-headed coin of yours."

"If we do end up negotiating something, please leave the talking to me," said Storm. "You two could talk your way out of a lottery win. I have experience in this sort of thing."

"There isn't going to be any negotiating," said Random. "I've waited a long time to bring down Clan Chojiro. The Shreck is just a bonus."

"Let them speak," said Storm. "What harm can it do?"

"If nothing else," said Ruby, "they might tell us where the rest of the Chojiros are hiding out. Or where they've hidden the valuables."

Random nodded curtly. BB Chojiro smiled charmingly at her three visitors. It had no obvious effect, but she kept smiling anyway.

"Welcome, honored guests. Please excuse the earlier armed responses; at that time the Families had yet to reach agreement on the best course of action to take, and they felt the need to defend themselves while the talks continued. I am happy to be able to inform you that all discussions have now ended, and I am empowered to speak for all the Clans. The Shreck is here to confirm my words. Basically, we wish to surrender."

Random's jaw dropped just a little. Of all the situations he'd expected to face this day, that wasn't one of them. "What? All the Families?"

"I speak for every Clan in the Empire," said BB. "We see no point in continuing in an armed struggle."

"Don't let her throw you," said Ruby. "Remember why you came here. She's just trying to distract you."

"If she is, it's working," said Storm. "There's got to be a catch."

"Our surrender is of course dependent on our agreeing to certain conditions," said BB.

"That sounds more like it," said Storm.

"The Families are prepared to give up their Lordships and associated privileges," said BB calmly, "in return for their survival. Essentially, the aristocracy will disappear, to be replaced by family-owned business operations. The Clans will continue to run their particular financial concerns, but will take no further part in the governing of the Empire. It's really quite a simple deal. You call off your dogs, guarantee our safety, and we give up politics. We're not so blind that we can't see the old order is finished and a new way is beginning. And isn't that what you really wanted, Jack? An end to established, inherited wielding of power in the Empire?"

"How can we be sure you speak for all the Families?" said Random. "You've never agreed over anything before."

"Because I'm Blue Block," said BB, still smiling. "No one Family is greater than Blue Block."

"Jesus," said Ruby. "I always thought they were just a myth. Young Family members conditioned to be utterly loyal to death and beyond, right? Infiltrated everywhere, hidden in deep cover, the Families' last weapon against Lionstone. You're that Blue Block?"

"Oh yes," said BB Chojiro. "Only down the many years we slowly evolved into something more than was originally intended. Our loyalty now is to the protection and survival of all the Families, not just the Clans that birthed us. This came as something of a surprise to the heads of the various Clans, but they were quick to grasp the possibilities. Particularly when we proposed this plan to ensure the Families' survival. There were those who took some convincing. Who were so sure they were impregnable in their ancient Towers. Your unexpected form of attack changed all that, Jack. As soon as your people started crashing through their defenses and smashing their way into the top floors of their precious Towers, it was amazing how fast the recalcitrant Families changed their tune, and told us to go ahead and make the deal. Isn't that right, Gregor?"

"Get on with it," growled the Shreck. "Just because a thing's necessary, it doesn't mean I like having to bow down to rebel scum. You haven't won, Random, and we haven't lost. It's a stalemate. You could stick to your original plan and try to take us down, but I swear we'd fight to the last survivor of each Clan, and see most of your people dead in the process. You could still win; but you'd lose thousands of your people doing it. Well, Random? Is your need for revenge worth the deaths of so many of your followers? When you can save them and win the day, with just a word?"

"I don't know," said Random. "It might be. As long as people like you live and go unpunished, the rebellion will have been for nothing. All those who died to help us get this far will have died for nothing The system has to fall, and you're part of the system."

"If we go down, it won't be just the system that falls," said Gregor, grinning nastily. "You've had the carrot; now here's the stick. You reject the deal, and we'll use our financial power to destroy the Empire's economic base. We can do it. We can use our computers to crash the banking system so thoroughly it would take centuries to recover. It's already precarious after what your friend Deathstalker did to the Tax computers. We could push it over the edge with just a nudge here and there. Money would become worthless. Credit would disappear. Trade would become impossible. Planets would be cut off from each other. Millions would starve, and millions more would fight over the crumbs that remained. What of your glorious rebellion then, Random? Destroy us, and we'll destroy the people you've been fighting to save."

"Could they do that?" said Ruby to Random. "Could they really do that?"

"Oh yeah," said Random. "That's just the kind of thing the Families would do."

"The order of things changes, but we go on," said BB. "We have so much to offer a new regime."

"The rebellion isn't actually over yet," said Storm thoughtfully. "The Empress could still make a comeback."

"The Empress is mad," said Gregor. "We can read the writing on the wall, especially when it's written in blood. Now are we going to agree to the deal or not? As long as we're standing here talking, people on both sides are dying needlessly. Not that I give a damn, but you're supposed to care about such things. Decide, Random. We know the underground will abide by your decision."

"Don't listen to him, Jack," said Ruby urgently. "We haven't come this far to give up now. We can tear the Families down, just like you always wanted!"

"You heard the price," said Random. "I always fought for the good of the people, not my own needs and wishes. What good is there in burning down an Empire, if all we have left to live in is ashes? The needs of the people come first. That's why I became a rebel in the first place. If I put their future at risk for the sake of my own revenge, then everything I've ever fought for becomes a lie. Who knows; with the Families removed from political power, maybe we can . . . civilize them."

"And what about the Chojiros?" said Ruby hotly. "All the vows you made to kill them all and piss on their graves? Do they mean nothing anymore?"

"I have more reason to hate the Chojiros than you'll ever know," Random said coldly. "I want them dead so badly I'd give up my life to destroy them all, root and branch. But I won't, I can't, give up innocent lives to my old hurts. And after all—maybe there'll still be room for a little private revenge, after the rebellion is over."

"Yes," said BB, still smiling. "Clan Chojiro has always appreciated the honorable art of vendetta."

"So we have a deal?" said Gregor.

"Yes, damn you," said Jack Random. "We have a deal. Stand down your people, and I'll halt the attack. Stay in your Towers till the rebellion's over, and we'll hammer out the details afterward. And no, I'm not going to shake your hands. I have to keep some self-respect."

"I don't believe this!" said Ruby, stepping back a pace

so that her projectile weapon covered them all. "And I haven't agreed to anything! You're selling out the rebellion, Jack, selling out every promise you ever made. All the things you said to me, all the things you wanted me to believe, and now the day of judgment's come, and you're making deals!"

"It's called politics, love," said Random. "Sometimes the price of ideals can be too high. And if I can live with this, you can."

"You were born an aristo," said Ruby. "And you're still one at heart after all. Make your deal, Jack. But I'll never believe anything you tell me, ever again."

And in the end, it was as simple as that. The word went out, the armada broke off its assault on the Towers, and both sides stood down. Many of the rebels still cried out for revenge, for those who had fallen this day as well as for all the many the Families had trampled underfoot down the centuries, but in the end the carrot and the stick convinced them. And as Random said, no one had ruled out the possibilities of some private revenges, afterward.

Some unexpected good came from the deal. Valentine Wolfe didn't trust it to guarantee his safety, after all he'd done, and so he fled Tower Wolfe to take sanctuary in Lionstone's Court. By leaving his Tower he broke the deal, and made himself a legitimate target for anyone who wanted to go after him. Ordinary people began to stream back into the city, sensing that the worst of the fighting was over. They cheered the rebels and called for the downfall of the Empress. They tore down her statues and spit on them, torched public buildings, and generally ran riot in the streets, drunk on the promise of freedom. The underground had to direct people away from the fighting to control the growing jubilation and prevent widespread looting, which put something of a dent in their general popularity. The underground had no choice but to ignore that. They had more important things to think about. They knew the war wasn't over while Lionstone was still safe and secure in her steel bunker, deep below the surface, far away from the fighting.

Back in Tower Chojiro, Gregor Shreck and BB Chojiro

had left to carry the good word back to their respective people, leaving Jack Random, Ruby Journey, and Alexander Storm alone. Random had already contacted the underground and apprised them of the deal, and was now thinking hard, trying to work out all the angles, desperate to be sure he hadn't, after all, made a terrible mistake. Ruby was stomping up and down, fuming quietly, kicking the furniture and helping herself to any bright and shiny thing that took her fancy. Storm watched them both and for a time said nothing. Random finally looked around and caught the expression on Storm's face.

"What is it, Alex? The rebellion's all over now, bar the shouting."

"No," said Storm. "It isn't over as long as the Empress still sits on the Iron Throne. She has access to all kinds of support. Weapons, people, secrets that the underground knows nothing about. She could still turn it all around, and the people in the streets would cheer her victory just as loudly as they're now calling for her head. Lionstone always knew a day like this might come. Do you think the Families are the only ones who could made doomsday threats?"

"If she had any last nasty surprises, she'd have used them by now," said Ruby.

"Is that what's upsetting you?" said Random. "Forget it. Ruby's right. Come on, cheer up. I haven't seen you smile once since we got here."

"They came to you to make the deal," said Storm. "Not to me. Even though I represent the underground. They trusted your word, not mine. A small thing, perhaps, but the last of many." He looked at Random almost helplessly. "But it's still going to be harder than I thought."

"What is?" said Random. "Look, if you've got something to say, spit it out. I haven't got time to worry over your hurt feelings."

"Time," said Storm. "This has all been about time, really. Time steals our life away, day by day, and we don't notice how much we've lost till it's too late. We fought for years, you and I, and all for nothing. Gave up our youth, and all our chances for love and marriage and children and happiness, all for a dream that never came true. When we started, you promised me power and suc-

cess, victory over our foes and justice for all, and I never
saw any of it. Just hard fighting and harder living, cold
food and bad liquor, and one lost battle after another.
Running from world to world with nothing to show for it
but more dead friends and a few new scars to nurse. And
that was my life with Jack Random."

"But that was then," said Random. "We've moved on.
Things have changed. We've changed . . ."

"Yes," said Storm. "We got old. But you got young
again. That was the last straw, really. I could have stood it
if Time had cheated us both equally, but you got a new
life again, and I didn't. You were right, Jack; there's
always time for a little personal revenge. Thanks for
helping me think this through. You've made this so much
easier. Jack, Code Zero Zero Red Two."

Jack Random convulsed, his back arching as though
he'd been hit from behind. He sank to his knees, trying to
force words out of a contorted mouth. Ruby was quickly
at his side, kneeling down and holding his shaking hands
in hers. "What is it, Jack? What?"

"He can't hear you," said Storm, almost regretfully.
"You see, when the med techs had him in their nasty little
hands, not all that long ago, they took the precaution
of implanting certain control words in his head, just
in case he ever got away from them. And they gave
those words to me, when I agreed to become an Imperial
spy, their agent in the heart of the underground. They
always thought there was a chance we might meet
again, eventually. And how right they were. Ever since
then, it's just been a question of waiting for the right
moment. I kept putting it off and putting it off, hoping for
a return of the old camaraderie we used to share. Hoping
for a chance to be a hero again. But he wouldn't even
allow me that. So in the end, I am the Empress's man.
And now, so is he."

"But you were a hero!" said Ruby. "Everybody
said so!"

"And now I'm a traitor. Only if the Empress wins, then
I'll be the hero, and he'll be the traitor. It's all a matter of
how you look at things. And who are you to judge me?
You always said you were only in this for the loot. Well,
now so am I."

"You bastard!" said Ruby. Letting Random go and scrambling to her feet, she reached for her sword.

"I never liked you," said Storm. "Jack, shut this bitch up."

Random rose to his feet. Ruby turned on him, sword in hand, her face desperate. Random slapped her sword aside and hit her once on the jaw, snapping back her head. She fell to the floor, and lay still. Storm moved over and kicked her in the ribs. Her head lolled helplessly. Storm nodded, satisfied. "Very good, Jack. Now pick her up and follow me. Lionstone is waiting for us to join her."

And so they left the Tower and made their way through the confusion of the streets, then down beneath the surface, descending to the Imperial Palace by secret, hidden ways. And so they went down into darkness, heading for Hell.

Elsewhere in the chaotic streets of the Parade of the Endless, Finlay Campbell and Evangeline Shreck and Julian Skye followed Young Jack Random as he led a small army of rebels and underground supporters toward the Imperial ground troops' main command center in the city. The center was supposed to contain the main decision makers and strategists of the planetside military. And despite everything the underground had done to try to cut them off from their forces, they were still very much in charge. So all that was left was to shut them down the hard way, by brute force. Unfortunately, since the command center was set inside a massive steel-and-stone bunker and guarded with practically every weapon known to man, it promised to be a very hard job. Which was why the underground leaders had volunteered Young Jack Random and the others to go and do the job. That was what happened when you got a reputation for achieving the impossible.

So Finlay slogged his way through the streets, shooting at everything wearing a uniform, and wondering what the hell he was going to do if and when he finally reached the bunker. He had no doubt he'd think of something annoying to do to it, probably involving high explosives. He was on a roll, after all. He could feel it. But somehow he had a strong feeling that breaking into the bunker was going to be a real bastard. He didn't even have any of the incredible Maze people with him this time. Just one possibly rejuvenated esper, Julian Skye. Still, they were being led by the legendary Young Jack Random, hero and savior, who apparently could do no wrong. According to all reports he'd practically turned back the Imperial invasion on Mistworld single-handed. Maybe he'd think of something.

Finlay wasn't sure how he felt about Young Jack. The man was brave and daring and a great fighter, to be sure, and heroic as all hell, and he always seemed to know just the right thing to say to motivate his followers, but . . . Perhaps it was just that the man was too perfect. Even the greatest of heroes was supposed to have some flaws. Young Jack didn't even belch after a good dinner. Finlay smiled despite himself. It had been a long time since he'd felt jealous of anyone. As the Masked Gladiator, he'd been unbeatable in the Arena, and adored by all. And now here he was, following Young Jack Random like all the others, forgotten and ignored in the great hero's shadow. Finlay shrugged. He could live with that, for now. There was work to be done.

Evangeline was also lost in her own thoughts. She was back on Golgotha again, back in the Parade of the Endless, not far from her father. Her hated, despised father, who loved her as a woman, not a daughter. Evangeline had fled to Shannon's World, but now she was back. And it wouldn't be long before Gregor Shreck found out, and then the threats of torture or death to her friend Penny would begin again. Evangeline scowled, barely seeing the crowd around her. Maybe she could get the underground leaders to promise Gregor's safety, in return for Penny's release, unharmed. They owed her a favor, after all she'd done for them. If Penny was still alive . . . she wouldn't put it past her father to have killed Penny in her absence, out of spite. He was quite capable of such a thing. In which case she would find him and kill him, and to hell with the consequences. Finlay would understand. He knew all about revenge.

Julian Skye was thinking about revenge, too. About Blue Block in general, and BB Chojiro in particular. He had loved her with all his heart, and she betrayed him to the torturers and the mind techs. And sometimes it seemed all he lived for now was a chance to make her pay. Now, at last, they were in the same city again. When the rebellion was over, he'd find her, no matter where she hid, and then he'd make her suffer as he had. (Or maybe he'd fall on his knees and promise her anything, if only she'd love him again. He still dreamed that, sometimes. In his worst nightmares.) Julian Sky gripped his sword tightly, and the smile that stretched his mouth had little of humor in it. First the rebellion, and the cause he'd given his life to. There'd be time for personal revenge afterward.

All three had volunteered to be part of the gravity-sled armada, for their various reasons, but the underground leaders had been unwaveringly firm that they were needed here more. So they fought their way through the packed streets, following Young Jack Random, and did their best to keep their inner turmoil at arm's length until they had time to pay attention to it.

And so they fought their way through the madness in the streets, taking on troops, Security men, and anything else the Empire could throw at them. At every turn there were more armed men, as the increasingly desperate Imperials struggled to stop the rebel forces advancing on the command center. Energy guns flared, explosives tore holes in the packed forces on both sides, and swords and axes swung in bloody arcs. Dead and wounded alike fell to be trampled underfoot. No one had the time to see to them. There was only the endless, almost hysterical push forward by the rebels, and the slow, panicking retreat of the Imperials. Steel blades swung in short, brutal arcs, punching into yielding flesh and out again, and blood ran like rivers in the street, choking the overflowing gutters. Men fell and the push went on, and the command center drew slowly nearer.

And right there, at the front of it all, Young Jack Random stood tall and proud, swinging his great sword with both hands, and no man could stand against him. Their swords could not touch him or defend them from his wrath, and the men behind him roared his name as a battle cry. Finlay and Evangeline stuck close behind him, and were too busy to be jealous. Finlay was fighting at the peak of his powers, a dazzling display of swordsmanship that would have drawn cheers from his old Arena fans. Men actually tried to turn and run rather than face him. Finlay smiled his wolfish smile and killed them all anyway. He was doing what he was born to do and savoring every minute.

Evangeline guarded his back and his blind spots with dogged efficiency. Finlay had taught her how to use a sword, though she never felt any of his dark joy for slaughter. She fought as a means to an end and nothing more, and only sometimes suspected that for Finlay the means was the end. Julian Skye's esper powers crackled on the air around them, deflecting disrupter beams and the occasional grenade. Now and again he'd gather his strength and let rip with a psistorm that sent armed troops flying helplessly in the grip of sudden storm winds, but mostly the fighters of both sides were packed too closely together for him to achieve much. He carried a sword and a gun, and used them with brisk efficiency. The fighting went on, time lengthening beyond counting, till both sides were ready to drop from exhaustion. And still Young Jack called his people on, to death or glory, and the destruction of Empire.

The rebels pressed forward, inch by inch, paying for every step with blood and death, until finally the command center's steel-and-stone bunker appeared at the end of the street before them. The sight gave new heart to the rebels, and they roared their triumph as they surged forward behind Young Jack, driving the demoralized defenders back and back. Only the narrowness of the street and the fact that there was nowhere for the troops to run prevented a complete rout. And so the troops fought viciously, like the cornered rats they were, and through sheer desperation again slowed the rebel advance to a crawl.

The struggle went on, tides in the fighting moving this way and that, and Toby Shreck and his cameraman Flynn were there to cover it all, broadcasting live to the watching Empire. They hovered precariously above the crowd on a commandeered gravity sled, just high enough to keep out of range of the fighting while still close enough to get all the gory details in close-up. Flynn sent his camera swooping back and forth over the surging crowd, searching out the best footage, while Toby hung over the edge of the sled, narrating a breathless commentary with a voice grown rough through smoke inhalation and overuse. Both men were using every upper in Toby's collection to keep them sharp and alert after so long on the air, and they had long since abandoned impartiality and distance for an almost hysterical need to capture history in the making. They both knew they'd never cover so important a story again. They spied the familiar faces of Finlay, Evangeline, and Julian, waved cheerfully, and called for them to smile for the camera. Finlay gave a short but very emphatic answer indicating that he was rather busy just at the moment, and Toby made a mental note to edit that bit out of any future repeat broadcasts. Flynn kept his camera rocketing back and forth, getting as much coverage of the bloodletting as he could. The viewers knew what they liked, and had to be coaxed to keep watching, even if this was history in the making.

Young Jack hacked and cut his way through an army of defenders, blood spilling onto the ground and streaming around his feet. His muscular arm rose and fell tirelessly, and none of the enemy could even touch him. His broad grin never wavered, and his calm eyes never blinked, no matter how close a sword blow came. He went for body shots, mostly. Short, vicious arcs that slammed his long sword into stomach and rib cage, and out again in a flurry of blood and guts. Traumatic wounds that stopped enemies immediately, but still left them staggering around to get in the way of their fellows. Their cries of pain and horror had great psychological effect on the enemy troops, while heartening the rebel side. And perhaps only Finlay and Evangeline and Julian found time to consider that such unpleasant methods weren't really what might be expected from a renowned hero like Jack Random. Young Jack fought on, calling his followers on to victory. His enemies fell before him, and he trampled them underfoot, still smiling. His clothes were soaked with blood, none of it his. Near the end of the street, with the command center only yards away, he paused just long enough to throw a smile and a wink at Flynn's hovering camera.

"You know; there has to be an easier way to overthrow an Empire . . ."

And then he got back to work, and the killing continued. Up on the sled, Toby gave Flynn a high five. A hero, a bladesman, and charming with it. Young Jack was a godsend. The audience would eat this up with spoons. The networks would be repeating that particular moment on news anthologies for years to come, no matter who won the rebellion. Toby had to admit he much preferred the Young Jack Random to the older counterpart he'd met on Technos III. Young Jack understood the importance of a good sound bite. Toby was glad someone here did. Most of the rebels were too busy to talk to him, and those who would were usually too earthy in their comments. You could only bleep so much.

Toby steered the sled as close to Young Jack as he could. When in doubt, follow the story. And so he and Flynn were perfectly placed to see the grenade come arcing out of the defenders and tumble almost unhurriedly through the air toward Young Jack. It passed right in front of Flynn's camera, hung on the air for a long moment at the top of its loop, and then dropped directly toward Young Jack. Many of the rebels saw it coming, and screamed warnings, but in the tightly packed crowd of fighters, there was nowhere for Young Jack to go. The grenade exploded right in front of him, and his body took the full force of the explosion. The blast threw him to one side, crashing through friend and foe alike, and slammed him into the high stone wall that overlooked that side of the street. The wall swayed and then fell forward, collapsing on top of the people below. Dozens of other people, rebels and troops, had been hit by shrapnel from the grenade and they lay screaming in the street.

Finlay and Evangeline and Julian had been protected behind Julian's hastily thrown-up force shield. As it dropped, Finlay quickly yelled for rebels to come forward and hold back the troops while he dug through the rubble of the fallen wall. Men and women rushed forward into the gap, yelling for Finlay to save Young Jack. Finlay was pretty sure the man had to be dead, but if there was even a chance ... He bent over the rubble and started pulling away bricks, and soon Evangeline and Julian were there to help him. More people pushed forward, wanting to help but only getting in the way. Julian put up a force shield to hold them back, until they got the message. Finlay and Evangéline kept digging. It didn't take them long to find the first body parts. People had been torn literally limb from limb by the force of the explosion. They kept digging, forcing their way down through the bloody remains. Flynn's camera hovered overhead, getting it all. Some of the body parts were still twitching. Finlay and Evangeline dug down through the pitiful scraps and remnants, arms bloody to the elbow, and finally they came to what was left of Young Jack Random. For a second they just stood there, stunned, and then Finlay turned and glared back at Toby and Flynn.

"Cut off the live feed! Do it now!"

Toby leaned off the edge of the sled to argue, looked past Finlay and saw what he saw, and made a sharp chopping gesture to Flynn. The cameraman nodded, and cut off the live broadcast, but kept the camera in place, still recording. Toby moved the gravity sled in over Finlay and Evangeline as they bent over the revealed body of the thing called Young Jack Random. The force of the grenade's explosion had torn away much of his skin, revealing the gleaming blue steel beneath. His face was gone, leaving only a metal skull. The eye sockets were empty, but the white teeth remained, giving the metal skull a disturbingly human smile. Young Jack Random was a Fury, a spy from Shub, a machine in the shape of a man, hiding under a human appearance. And it was still alive. The lower part of the body was seriously crushed by the fallen wall, and one arm was missing, but the torso and head were pretty much intact. The Fury raised its metal head slightly and nodded to Finlay and Evangeline. When it spoke, the slightly echoing voice was calm, almost friendly.

"All right, I'm a machine. But that doesn't mean we can't still be friends. You need me. Or who I'm pretending to be. I can be repaired. Cover my face, and no one will know the difference. Some of the truth is bound to leak out, but we can just tell everyone that I'm a cyborg. An augmented man. They'll buy that, after all Jack Random's supposed to have been through. You need me, Campbell. The rebels will follow a hero like me where they won't follow someone like you. So get a cloak to wrap me in, stick me on the Shreck's gravity sled, and I'll lead your people right into the command center."

"Do you really think that any member of Humanity would follow a thing from Shub?" said Finlay, his voice cold and tight. "Do you think we would? You represent the Enemies of Humanity. Sworn to wipe us out to the last man, woman, and child. No wonder you enjoyed the slaughter here so much. And what would you do, after the rebellion is over? Be a party to our plans and hopes, just when we're at our most vulnerable? Do you really think we'd let a metal wolf like you into our fold?"

"You don't really have much of a choice," said the machine calmly. "My systems are already repairing themselves, and you don't have any weapons here strong enough to destroy me. The grenade took me by surprise. It was unexpectedly powerful for its size. But soon I will be operating at acceptable efficiency levels again, and if you will not help me to pass as Jack Random, then I will fulfill my secondary programming, and kill every human here. What will that do to your push on the command center? Like it or not, you're stuck with me."

"Like hell," said Finlay. "Julian, stamp this tin soldier flat."

"Gladly," said Julian. he called up his psistorm, compressed and focused it into a hammer of pure force, and brought it slamming down on the crippled Fury. The human-shaped machine flattened out like a starship had fallen on it, the metal cracking and shattering in a thousand places. Julian smiled coldly as the metal shape crumpled under the pressure of his mind. The esper concentrated, and the flattened metal rolled itself into a ball, shrinking and further compacting until all that remained was a solid sphere of metal, with no trace of life left in it. Julian smiled again.

"Repair that, you bastard."

Finlay and Evangeline buried the sphere under a pile of body parts. Julian looked up at Flynn's camera, still hovering overhead, and scowled thoughtfully.

"Oh no, not the camera, please!" said Toby. "We don't have another!"

"We can't let this piece of news get out," said Julian. "No one must ever know."

"We know how to keep our mouths shut," said Toby. "This wouldn't be the first piece of film I've had to bury. Ask the Campbell; he'll vouch for me."

"I don't know if I'd go that far," said Finlay. "But I think we can trust him to understand that if this piece of film ever surfaces again, there will be a queue of people waiting to kill him in slow and interesting ways. Right, Shreck?"

"Couldn't have put it better myself," said Toby. "I've seen you people in action. I don't want you coming after me. It doesn't really matter. I've already got enough great footage to make me immortal."

"What about me?" said Flynn. "Don't I get to be immortal, too?"

"I said immortal, not immoral. You just point the camera and leave the thinking to me."

Flynn glared at him coldly. "I am an artist. It's in my contract."

"I know what you are," said Toby. "Now shut up and point the camera."

"Bully," said Flynn. "You wait till your next direct to camera. I'll make you look really podgy."

"You'd swear they were married, wouldn't you?" said Julian. "Finlay, we have to get our people moving again, before they have time to think about what's happened here. If they panic, the whole push will fall apart."

"Got it," said Finlay. He stepped up onto the rubble so all the rebels could see him. "Jack Random is dead! The Empire killed him. Are you going to let his death be for nothing? Or will you fight on, as he would have wanted? Then follow me, to death or glory!"

It was as basic as that, but it worked. The rebels roared their defiance to the Empire and surged forward again, howling for revenge. Finlay led the way, with Evangeline and Julian at his sides. He'd never doubted that the rebels would follow him, in Random's name. Sometimes a rebel leader can be a greater inspiration dead than alive. The defending troops had held their ground while they thought

Random's death would demoralize the rebels, but the new, even more determined attack was just too much for them. Outnumbered and outfought, they cracked and turned and ran, some throwing away their weapons to show they were no longer a part of the war, and as quickly as that the battle was over. The troops ran in all directions, desperate to escape the killing grounds, and the rebels cut down those who didn't run fast enough.

Finlay stormed forward, heading for the huge steel doors that were the only entrance to the command-center bunker. Disrupters built into the bunker walls opened up, but Julian deflected the beams with his esp until rebel sharpshooters had blown the guns out of their emplacements. And then they were all at the door, and Evangeline punched in the entry codes that the underground leaders had provided. Nothing happened. Evangeline tried again, hitting each number carefully, but the door remained stubbornly closed. Finlay could hear the crowd growing restive behind them.

"Typical," he said briskly. "Have to do everything ourselves. Julian, get this door open."

"I'm on it," said Julian. He concentrated, ignoring the familiar headache growing behind his temples, and hit the door with a psychokinetic hammer blow that punched the door right out of its supports and back into the bunker. The rebels cheered, and Finlay led the way through the opening. He hadn't got far before he came to a sudden halt. Evangeline and Julian, close behind, almost crashed into him. Before them, guarding the entry corridor with a drawn sword, stood a single figure in an anonymous tunic, with a featureless black-steel helm covering his head. A familiar sight to anyone who'd ever watched the fights in the Arenas. It was the undefeated champion himself, the Masked Gladiator.

"No," said Finlay. "No. Not you . . ."

"Of course it's me," said the calm voice behind the helm. "I've always been loyal to the Iron Throne, come what may. Which means you have to get past me to get any farther. And one man in the right place can stop an army if he's good enough. And the Masked Gladiator has never been defeated."

476 Simon R. Green

"Don't do this," said Finlay. "I don't want to have to fight you."

"They shall not pass," said the Masked Gladiator. "No exceptions. Not even you, Finlay."

"The hell you say," said Julian. He stepped forward, and his face contorted with an anger so overwhelming he was almost unrecognizable. "I've waited a long time for this, you bastard. You killed my brother, Auric Skye!"

"I've killed a lot of people," said the voice behind the featureless helm. "I don't remember names anymore."

"I remember," said Julian Skye, and he lashed out with his mind. An irresistible force hit the Masked Gladiator like a hammer, smashing him off his feet. He hung in midair, feet kicking helplessly above the ground, and blood flew from every joint in his armor, as the body within was crushed by a cold, vengeful force. He didn't cry out, but eventually he stopped convulsing, and Julian dropped him. He hit the floor hard and lay still. Blood pooled around him. Julian leaned over him, breathing heavily. Blood was running thickly from one of his nostrils. He spit on the featureless helmet.

"That was for you, Auric."

He started forward into the command center, and the rebels poured after him, cheering the man who'd beaten the undefeated Masked Gladiator. Toby and Flynn hurried after them on foot. None of them even noticed Finlay and Evangeline kneel beside the fallen man. Finlay waited till the last of the rebels had passed by, and then gently removed the dying man's helmet, revealing the blood-smeared face of Georg McCrackin, the original Masked Gladiator. The man who'd taught Finlay everything he knew, and then allowed him to replace him in the Arena. Georg tried to smile up at Finlay and Evangeline, but his teeth were red with his own blood.

"Now we'll never know . . . whether you could have beaten me, Finlay. Should never have expected a fair chance from an esper."

"I killed his brother," said Finlay. "I'm so sorry, Georg. I never meant . . . Why did you go back to the Arena? I thought you retired."

"Someone had to be the Masked Gladiator after you left, and there wasn't anyone ready to take your place."

Georg swallowed hard, and his voice cleared a little. "Besides, I wanted to see if I still had what it took. To be the best again. I was doing well, too, until this nonsense started, and the Empress herself called me here, to defend the command center." He coughed harshly, and blood welled from his mouth and ran down his chin. "Damn. I'm hurt bad, Finlay. That esper bastard really screwed me up." He tried to smile at Finlay again, and blood leaked out the corners of his mouth. "So you're a rebel now, Finlay. I was surprised when I heard. I never understood politics. Not for me, though. The Empire's been good to me. Can't say I'm sorry it's all over. Shouldn't think there'd be anyplace for the likes of me in what's to come. Better to go out with some dignity."

He stopped, as though considering what to say next. Finlay waited, and only after a moment realized that Georg McCrackin was dead. Finlay closed the man's eyes and got to his feet. Evangeline stood up with him and put a comforting hand on his arm. He didn't notice. He was still looking down at the dead man.

"Julian doesn't need to know," he said finally. "Let him think he killed his brother's killer. It's simpler, that way."

"For the moment," said Evangeline. "But what happens if he ever finds out the truth? That you were his brother's killer, and he killed an innocent man?"

"No one's innocent anymore," said Finlay. "And what's one more secret, to the likes of us?"

He strode off into the depths of the command center, following the distant sounds of combat and the screams of the dying, not looking to see whether Evangeline was following him.

All across the planet of Golgotha, in towns and cities and starports, the rebels moved unstoppably forward, driving back the Imperial forces on all fronts. Their one trump card, the huge war machines, now stood dead and lifeless, empty metal shells with nothing to guide them. The Imperial troops looked defeat in the face, and reacted in the only way they knew how. They broke out the biggest weapons they had, and opened fire on everyone who wasn't them. They cut down rebels and civilians alike, and flooded the streets with blood. They took crowds of women and children hostage, used them as human shields, and threatened to execute them in batches of ten if the rebels didn't back off. They blew up important installations and power plants and hospitals rather than let the rebels take them. They destroyed whole towns and their populations in order to save them. Such widespread savagery and slaughter had been expected, and theoretically allowed for, but in practice the sheer coldbloodedness of it shocked the rebels to their souls, even after all they'd seen on Virimonde. All over the world the rebel advances slowed and stopped, confronted by an evil too great for their simple tactics. The rebels were willing to give their own lives for victory, but faced with the responsibility for mass slaughter of civilians, they hesitated, and were lost. The rebellion faltered, and suddenly everything seemed in the balance again.

And that was when the Mater Mundi manifested again, all across the planet. Our Mother of All Souls, the uberesper, slammed into every esper's mind simultaneously, hundreds of thousands of espers suddenly transformed and transfigured into a whole new order of being. Linked into one great massmind, they acted as one, the psistorms flashed through towns and cities all over Golgotha, sweeping away the Imperial troops while not touching the rebels or civilians. Polters and pyros destroyed Imperial buildings and refuges, torched barracks and tore down barricades, unstoppable avatars of destruction. Telepathic storms swept through the troops, jumping from mind to mind, washing away sanity and memories and leaving nothing behind. In other places, esper-driven nightmares ran riot through helpless minds, and hardened soldiers tore out their own eyes rather than see what they were being shown. Other troops gunned down their fellows, then turned their guns on themselves.

And as quickly as that the tide turned again, and resistance to the rebel forces was swept away. Mater Mundi looked upon her work and saw it to be good, and withdrew herself from the thousands of esper minds. The rebel forces mopped up the mess she'd left behind and took control of the towns and cities, whose populations praised them as saviors. The war on the surface was over.

But the Mater Mundi wasn't finished yet. Manifesting through an old friend, Jenny Psycho, the Mater Mundi reached out and snagged two more useful souls, and teleported all three of them to where they could do the most good. They disappeared silently, air rushing in to fill the space where they'd been, and in the general chaos no one even noticed they'd gone. Satisfied that she'd done all that was necessary, the Mater Mundi shut herself down until she might be needed again.

In Lionstone's Court, Hell had taken root and bloomed like a dark and poisonous flower. There were flames everywhere, their golden and scarlet light sometimes all the illumination there was against the lowering dark. The air was thick with the stench of sulfur, spilled blood, and cooked human flesh. Captured rebels had been impaled on rough wooden stakes or hung on traceries of metal thorns that slowly pulled them apart. Corpses of dead advisors hung from chains. Ravens ate their eyes and tore at their faces, and spoke shrilly in human voices. It had become dangerous to fail the Empress in anything now. Bloodred angels with burning wings stood in ranks behind the Iron Throne, bearing monofilament swords. Dishonorable weapons, but Lionstone was past caring about such niceties.

Captain Silence, Investigator Frost, and Security Officer Stelmach made their way cautiously through the crimson-tinged mists of Hell, carefully skirting the yellow sulfur fogs that belched up out of the glowing ash pits. They stuck close together, tried not to look around too much, and headed for Lionstone's spotlit Throne by the most direct route. Small bones crunched under their boots from time to time. They looked like they came from birds or animals. Or possibly small children. Some of them still had tatters of flesh and skin attached. Sometimes the people hanging from chains or transfixed on steel-bladed trees cried out to them as they passed, begging for help or death or just a little water. Silence and Frost stared straight ahead, and did not answer. They knew there was nothing they could do. Nothing they'd be allowed to do. Stelmach was crying quietly, sniffing back tears.

They'd been called back to Golgotha, and then down to the Imperial Palace, on direct orders from the Empress herself, using top emergency codes only ever to be used when the Throne itself was endangered. So of course they came, ignoring the rebels and their battles, ignoring cries for help from beleagured Imperial forces, driven by the urgency of their summons. They didn't know yet that the war on the surface had been lost, but it wouldn't have surprised them. They'd seen the live broadcasts from Virimonde, and even the Investigator had been shocked. Silence had said only a madwoman could have given such orders, and neither Frost nor Stelmach had reproached him. They discussed the rebellion on their way back to Golgotha, but their loyalty was never in doubt, despite all that had happened. They were sworn to the Iron Throne, and their Empress, and you didn't betray your honor just because things were going badly. Sometimes, when things were going really badly, all you had left was your honor.

And so they walked through Hell, through the heat and the mists and the suffering of the damned. There were no guards to accompany them, this time. Silence wondered if this was meant as a mark of trust, or if Lionstone was just short of guards. It didn't matter. They were here now, called back from disgrace, their ship and crew's honor restored. Silence had been hoping to use this opportunity to talk a little cautious sense into Lionstone. But having seen the Court's current incarnation, he wasn't sure that was possible anymore. The Court was an extension of the Empress's mind, and it seemed both had gone to Hell.

Finally they came to the Iron Throne. Jets of flame shot high up into the air, like fountains of fire, eerily silent, casting a crimson satanic aspect over Lionstone and her Throne. The maids clustered together at her feet, alert and snarling, metal claws flexing from under their fingernails, staring hungrily with their artificial eyes at the newcomers before the Throne. The burning angels stood silently, swords at the ready. Lionstone should have looked utterly safe and secure, but she didn't. She sat forward, right on the edge of her seat, staring grimly at the viewscreen floating before her, studying reports from the few Imperial-controlled channels still on the air, watching helplessly as her Empire fell apart around her. Silence and Frost and Stelmach came to a halt before the Iron Throne, and bowed deeply to her, and she acknowledged them with a mere flap of her hand. When she finally deigned to turn and look at them, her eyes were wide and staring, and her smile was strangely fixed, as though she'd forgotten just how one did such a thing.

"So, you're finally here. My Captain, my Investigator, my Security Officer. Sworn to me, to death and beyond. Traitors!"

"No, Your Majesty," Silence said quickly. "We are loyal to you. We always have been."

"Then why did you keep secrets from me? Why did you try and hide what you've become? Why didn't you tell me about the powers you gained on the Wolfling World?"

Silence and Frost looked at each other, and then at Stelmach, who shook his head. He hadn't told. Silence looked back at Lionstone, and kept his voice even and calm. "For a long time we didn't understand what was happening to us. It seems our time in the Madness Maze, brief though it was, was enough to change us on levels we still don't fully comprehend. We have done our best to serve you faithfully while we struggled for some kind of control over our new . . . abilities."

"And what about you, Security Officer?" said Lionstone. "I gave you specific orders to watch these two and report on them!"

"I have tried to do my duty as I saw best," said Stelmach. His face was deathly pale, and his hands were shaking, but his gaze and his voice were unflinching. "It was not a simple matter. There were . . . ambiguities to the situation."

"Words," said Lionstone, leaning back on her Throne. Her cold eyes moved back and forth across the three of them. "Nothing but empty words. It's too late for such evasiveness now. I won't have it. The barbarians are pounding on the gates of Empire. I need weapons to hold them back while I plan how to undo my reverses. You're going to be those weapons. Tell me about your powers. Tell me everything. Or die here at my feet."

Just for a moment, Silence considered defying her. She

had no real power over them anymore. All the armed guards in her Court couldn't compel him or Frost to do a single damn thing they didn't want to. Not after everything they'd become. But the moment passed, as he'd known it would. She was his Empress. He and Frost had kept their powers to themselves out of a very real fear of ending up as lab rats. Possibly even vivisected lab rats. But the time for such weakness was past. He could recognize fate when it came knocking on his window. So he told the Empress, as clearly as he could, of the strange strengths and abilities and intuitions that he and Frost had manifested since their time on lost Haden, also known as the Wolfling World.

It took a while, not least because Lionstone kept interrupting, pressing him for details and explanations he didn't always have. As he spoke, two new figures appeared in the Court, breasting the sulfurous mists on their way to the Throne. First came Valentine Wolfe, the dandy in black with the long white face. He stopped a respectful distance away, quite happy to watch and listen while Silence spoke. His crimson mouth was stretched in its usual constant smile, and his heavily mascaraed eyes were fever-bright from the impact of the dozen drugs roaring through his veins. Valentine wasn't used to losing, and his recent reverses had stunned him. His response had been to amplify his whirling thoughts with stimulant after stimulant, trying to force his mind to come up with answers to his problems. The end result had been something of a chemical stalemate, where his thoughts crashed emptily together, canceling each other out. And so he'd come to Court; not just for his own safety, but because that was in the end where all the real decisions of Empire were made. Whatever happened here, he was confident he'd find some way to turn it to is advantage. He always did.

He had hoped to call on favors from his previous dalliance with the underground, but it hadn't taken him long to discover that the esper leaders had promised his head to Finlay Campbell, in return for the Campbell's services. You couldn't trust anyone these days. Still, it wasn't a complete loss. Finlay might yet die during the rebellion, with a little help, and afterward Valentine was confident he'd find some way to bargain himself back into the underground's good graces. Or, if things somehow went the other way, and Lionstone yet pulled off some miraculous victory, or more likely some form of compromise with the rebels, she would need someone to speak for her to the underground. Someone with good connections. And who better than the widely experienced Valentine Wolfe?

He laughed quietly, quite at home in Hell, and stood patiently before the Iron Throne, winking at the snarling maids. His body twitched and seethed with possibilities, his thoughts running a mile a second in all directions at once. So he stood still and said nothing. Let others speak. He would listen. He'd find a way to profit. He always did. And then let his enemies beware.

The second figure to appear was, of course, the Lord High Dram, Consort and Widowmaker. He looked rather battered around the edges. There were tears and scorch marks on his clothes, and blood, too, some of it his. He'd been driven from the surface fighting by one rebel victory after another. When the war machines stalled and the Mater Mundi manifested, Dram knew a lost cause when he saw one. He deserted his men, disguised himself, and made his way back to Court. He felt angry rather than guilty. Lionstone kept expecting him to do things that only the original Dram, with all his experience, could have pulled off. While he was only a clone, barely finished, trying to learn on the run and stay alive while men died all around him. It wasn't his fault he didn't know how to cope with overwhelming odds and strange new weapons and espers with the powers of gods. Even the original Dram had never had to face a ubiquitous Mater Mundi. And so he ran away and came home to Lionstone, like a child beaten by bullies at school, hoping not to be beaten again for losing.

A viewscreen chimed, and Lionstone quieted Silence with a sharp wave of her hand. She activated the screen, and General Shaw Beckett appeared. He looked tired, beaten down. There was chaos on his ship's bridge behind him, with people shouting and cursing and running back and forth. Alarm sirens were sounding. Beckett looked steadily out of the screen at Lionstone, and raised his voice to be sure his words could be heard clearly over the bedlam.

"Your Majesty, I have done my best to defend your Empire and yourself with all the powers at my command, but I regret to inform you that I have failed. The war in space is over. My fleet is scattered and destroyed, my ground forces have been overrun on all the worlds I can still get reports from, and I have nothing left to fight with. I can see no scheme or strategy that might enable me to overcome these reverses. Therefore, in order to save as many of my people as possible, in space and on the ground, I have contacted the rebel leaders and offered them my surrender.

"My advice to Your Majesty is to do the same, for the best possible concessions, while you still can. I will hand over control of the fleet to whatever authority replaces Your Majesty. I'm sorry, Lionstone, but I have my men to think of. There's been enough death and suffering. Who knows; perhaps this was all for the best anyway. Good luck, Your Majesty. If we both survive, perhaps we'll meet again in happier times."

He signed off, and the viewscreen went blank while Lionstone was still drawing breath to scream abuse at him. She stared unseeingly about her for a long moment, beating on the arms of her Throne with her fists. The maids stirred uneasily below her, picking up on her mood. Finally her gaze fell on Silence and Frost, and she nodded slowly.

"I am surrounded by incompetents and traitors. But I still have you. My secret weapons. I place command of all my forces in your hands, Captain and Investigator. Defend the Empire. Slaughter the scum rioting in my streets. Don't dare fail me." And the rage boiled up in her again, and her voice rose in a frustrated scream. "Is there no one else to defend me from the rabble?"

"Well, there's always me," said Alexander Storm.

Everyone looked round, startled, as the old rebel came strolling unhurriedly through the horrors of Hell. Jack Random walked behind him, pulling along a heavily chained and restrained Ruby Journey by a leash around her neck. When she tried to slow down or pull back, Random just tightened the leash till she couldn't breathe,

and had no choice but to hurry and catch up. Alexander
Storm came to a halt a respectful distance away from the
maids, signaled Random to halt, and then bowed courteously to Lionstone and the others present.

"Your Majesty, honored guests; may I present my two
prisoners, those most damnable rebels and traitors, Jack
Random and Ruby Journey. Yours to do with as you
wish."

There was a long silence, and then the Empress Lionstone laughed and clapped her hands together girlishly.
"You see, my friends? It's not over till I say it's over."

Owen Deathstalker, his ancestor Giles, and Hazel
d'Ark had arrived in the great antechamber that was the
only access to Lionstone's Court. A huge open chamber
of gleaming steel and brass, with huge intricately carved
pillars of gold and silver, it stretched away in all directions, vast and empty and echoing. Normally it would
have been full of the movers and shakers of Empire, all
waiting impatiently for the great steel doors to open, and
their chance to gain the ear of the Empress. But now the
great antechamber stood deserted and abandoned. Owen
and Giles and Hazel stood before the closed double doors,
and looked at them thoughtfully.

"Bound to be locked," said Owen.

"Oh, bound to be," said Hazel. "I take it you don't
have any codes for this?"

"Afraid not," said Owen. "Don't suppose you brought
any explosives with you, by any chance?"

"Afraid not," said Hazel. "Guess we'll just have to
smash our way through by brute force and ignorance."

"Get on with it," said Giles. "I've come a long way to
be here, and I have much to do."

Owen and Hazel exchanged a glance, but before they
could say anything, there was a bright flash of light and
Jenny Psycho, Toby Shreck, and Flynn appeared suddenly
out of nowhere. Jenny surrounded herself with a psionic
force shield, then dropped it a moment later as she realized
no one was attacking her. Toby and Flynn checked to see
that their camera was still with them and looked around
with open mouths. Toby realized who was standing before

him, and where he was, and gestured urgently for Flynn to start filming.

"What the hell are you doing here?" said Hazel, not all that welcomingly.

"The Mater Mundi wanted us here," said Jenny Psycho. "Any problems, take it up with her. Apparently she wants the downfall of the Empress shown live throughout the Empire. Why she wants me here as well . . . isn't yet clear to me. No doubt I'll find out shortly. So, bring me up to date. What lies between us and the Court?"

"Well, basically, these doors," said Owen. "Personally, I thought there'd be more security than this."

He broke off and they all looked round as they heard the sound of approaching running feet. There seemed to be a hell of a lot of them. Those who had them drew swords and guns. Jenny gathered her power around her till it crackled on the air. Flynn sent his camera up to the ceiling, made sure it was pointing in the right direction, and then moved quickly to join Toby in hiding behind the others. He'd barely made it when a small army of Lionstone's personal guards came charging into the antechamber, armed with drawn swords and personal force shields. Owen took a firm grip on his sword. There had to be at least two hundred of them. Hazel glared at him.

"You had to open your big mouth."

"Surrender!" yelled the officer in charge of the guards. "You're massively outnumbered. You don't stand a chance."

Owen grinned at Giles. "He doesn't know us very well, does he?"

"Finish them quickly," said Giles. "Lionstone could be trying to distract us while she makes her escape."

"Can I just point out, in an extremely nonthreatening way, that Flynn and I are very definitely noncombatants," said Toby, from the rear.

"Kill them all," snapped the guard officer, and led the way forward.

Jenny Psycho levitated into the air, spread her arms wide, and lightning blazed from her hands, striking down the first dozen guards. Hazel d'Ark shimmered, and suddenly there were a dozen of her. Hazels that might have been from other timestreams, all of them grinning nastily at the prospect of battle. Giles teleported back and forth among the guards, striking men down and disappearing again before he could be attacked. Owen smiled and shook his head. Show-offs. He hefted his sword, boosted, and went to meet the guards with death in his eyes. Two men and two women went to war against an army, and the numbers were no problem to them, no problem at all.

At first. The rebels cut their way through the guards with grim efficiency, and soon dead bodies lay everywhere, getting underfoot. The rebels killed and killed, but still the guards kept coming. Owen fought on, swinging his sword with both hands, and no one could stand against him. He was boosting, and strength and speed sang in his arms, but for every guard that fell, it seemed there were two more pressing forward to take his place. They swarmed around him, coming at him from all directions, and soon there wasn't enough room to swing his sword anymore, and all he could do was cut and stab. Backed by his boosted strength and speed, such blows were still devastating and deadly, but with enemies at his back as well as his front he couldn't relax for a moment. He fought on, spinning this way and that, holding his enemies at bay, knowing that if slowed down or hesitated even for a moment, he was a dead man.

Quick glances around suggested his friends weren't doing any better. The Hazels had become separated, scattered the length of the antechamber, but still fighting furiously. Owen had to smile. It seemed that whatever reality the various Hazels came from, she was always a hell of a scrapper. One of the Hazels was forced back in his direction, and Owen was glad to see it was the original. They moved quickly to fight back-to-back, and Owen was happy to have her there. They'd always made an excellent team.

He could see Giles fighting some distance away, roaring his ancient battle cries and bringing his huge long sword down like a hammer, guards surrounding him like attack dogs struggling to bring down a bear. He'd had to stop teleporting. There wasn't enough space left among the fighters for him to teleport into. It seemed to Owen that there were even more guards now than when they'd started, for all the dead bodies cluttering up the floor. They must be bringing in reinforcements. The cheats. Jenny Psycho was still hanging in the air, wreathed in lightning, but didn't seem to be lashing out with it anymore. This puzzled Owen till he saw the guards bringing in esp-blocker after esp-blocker, piling up the brains in their glass cases, trying to shut down Jenny's amplified powers by sheer attrition.

And for the first time it occurred to Owen that just maybe this was as far as he was going to get. He'd come so far, fought his way through so many obstacles, but even he had his limitations. Even a boosted man couldn't stand off a whole army. He remembered how it had all started, so long ago now, with him standing alone against a crowd of his own turncoat guards on Virimonde, outnumbered and about to die. Maybe he'd come full circle; only this time Hazel wasn't going to be able to save him. She was as deep in trouble as he was. It seemed crazy to Owen that after all he'd been through, he was finally going to fall to a bunch of armed guards, just because there were so many of them. He reached inside himself, trying to find the power he'd used on Mistworld to bring a whole building down, but there was nothing there. Nothing came to answer his call, no matter how desperately he tried. And he had no idea why.

He was soaked in sweat now, and he had to keep blinking it out of his eyes as it ran down his face. He was breathing hard, and it seemed to him that he wasn't quite as fast as he had been. Some of the guards' blows were beginning to get through. Just a minor cut here and there, barely felt in his boosted condition, but a wound was a wound and blood was blood. Enough blood loss would slow him down, despite the boost. And the boost wouldn't last forever. Beyond a certain point, the flame that burned so brightly would start to consume him. Just as it had on Mistworld. He cut and hacked and blocked blows from every direction. He was a Deathstalker, and guards fell dead and dying all around him. He could hear Hazel grunting and bumping against his back as she fought, so he knew she was still with him. But over on the other side of the antechamber, he saw another Hazel with dark skin and dreadlocks go down suddenly under a dozen hacking swords, and though he watched as long as he could, she didn't rise again. Giles was backed up against a wall, cut in a dozen places, blood streaming down his face from a long cut on his temple. There was no sign of Jenny Psycho anywhere.

And then he heard Hazel cry out in shock and pain behind him, and her back slammed against his for a moment before she fell to her knees. Owen spun around, swinging his sword with all his strength, forcing the guards back. Hazel sat slumped at his feet, bent over a gut wound. She'd dropped her sword. She was trying to hold the great ragged wound together by wrapping her arms tightly around her, but blood was pouring out of her. There was already a great pool of it forming around her. Owen knew a death wound when he saw it. He tried to say her name, but couldn't seem to get his breath. He dropped out of boost, and his sword arm fell. The guards rushed in. And all the rage and horror rose up in Owen, igniting his power once again, filling him with a blazing energy that would not be denied. He gave himself up to it, and it roared out of him like an unstoppable tide. The guards nearest him were consumed in a moment, like moths in a flame, and then more died screaming as the energy rushed on. The guards tried to turn and run, but it was upon them in seconds, destroying them all without quarter or mercy. In the space of a few seconds, every guard in the antechamber was dead, and only Giles and Jenny, Toby and Flynn and a handful of Hazels were left standing. Owen shut the power down, looked at all the dead, and didn't give a damn.

He sank down beside Hazel, and took her gently in his arms. She laid her head against his chest, and he cradled her to him. She felt very light in his arms, as though she was already drifting away from him. He was quickly soaked in the blood leaking out of her, but he didn't notice. He tried reaching for the power again, but there was no response. Whatever the Madness Maze had given him, it was a thing of death and destruction, and not healing. He could slay an army, but he couldn't save the one person who mattered to him most. His chest was tight, and he couldn't get his breath. Hazel lifted her head slowly, and tried to smile up at him. Her teeth were red with blood. Owen started to cry, great rasping sobs that shook his whole body. Hazel tried to say something to him, and then her breath went out of her in a series of shudders, and she lay dead in his arms. Owen held her close and rocked her like a sleeping child.

"I did it for you," he tried to say past his tears. "I did it all for you, Hazel."

He heard footsteps approaching, but he didn't look up. He had nothing to say to anyone. And then someone with Hazel's voice said his name. He stopped crying, a wild hope jumping in his heart, but it was only when the dead Hazel disappeared from his arms that he finally believed it. He made himself look up, and there was Hazel d'Ark standing over him. The real original, this time. He scrambled to his feet, and then just stood there and stared at her, afraid to touch her in case she disappeared, too. Finally she reached out and took him in her arms, and he hugged her fiercely to him, like a drowning man clinging to the only thing that could save him. They stood that way for a long time, both of them breathing hard.

"I thought I'd lost you," Owen said finally. "I really thought I'd lost you."

"It's all right, Owen," said Hazel. "I'm here. I'll always be here for you."

After a while they let go and stepped back to look at each other. Owen wiped the last of the tears from his eyes with the back of his hand. Hazel smiled at him awkwardly. She looked around at the dead bodies heaped on the antechamber floor, and nodded, impressed.

"Way to go, aristo. Remind me never to get you angry at me."

"Never happen," said Owen, his voice still just a little unsteady. "Hazel, I . . ."

"I know. But we can talk about that later. Right now, we still have an Empire to overthrow."

Owen shook his head. "It's always business first with you, isn't it, Hazel?"

Jenny and Giles came forward to join them. Jenny had been busy smashing the esp-blockers, and Giles had tied a handkerchief round his head to stop the bleeding. It wasn't the cleanest of handkerchiefs, but Owen didn't think he'd say anything. With the blood still drying on his face, the old warrior looked not unlike a pirate of old.

"Nice show, Deathstalker," said Jenny briskly. "I'm impressed. Are you sure you're not the Mater Mundi in disguise?"

"Positive," said Owen. "Whatever I'm becoming, it's not an esper. It's . . . more than that."

"Still, you did well, kinsman," said Giles. "You were wasted as a scholar, boy."

Toby and Flynn emerged from the alcove where they'd been hiding, and hurried over to join the others, Flynn's camera tagging along behind them.

"We're fine, too, just in case anybody cares," said Toby, just a little hurt.

"Oh, we never worried about you," said Hazel. "Everyone knows journalists are harder to kill than cockroaches."

And then, by some unspoken agreement, they all turned and looked at the great steel double doors that led into Lionstone's Court. It was very quiet in the antechamber, as though even the dead were waiting to see what would happen next.

"Do we knock?" said Hazel. "Or do we blast our way in?"

"I don't think we need to knock," said Giles. "Lionstone knows we're here. She also knows she can't keep us out."

As if on cue, the doors swung slowly open, silent for all their massive size and weight. Bloodred light spilled out into the antechamber, along with the stench of blood and brimstone. Owen and Hazel started forward, sword and gun in hand, and they all walked forward into Hell.

In Court, before the Iron Throne, Alexander Storm gave in to his need to strut a bit. His existence as an Imperial agent deep within the rebel structure had of necessity involved hiding who and what he really was, so now he took the opportunity to show off a little. The Empress was smiling down at him approvingly, and Dram and Valentine looked quite jealous. Razor and the SummerIsle stared coldly at him from their positions just behind the Throne, but Storm didn't care about their opinions. Razor was an Investigator, the Kid was a psychopath. Silence and Frost and Stelmach didn't matter either. They were renowned for failing the Empress, whereas he had succeeded brilliantly.

"I've been an Imperial agent ever since the rebels got their heads handed to them on Cold Rock," he said proudly to his audience. "I saw Jack fall and be taken, and knew that was the end of any real hopes for the rebellion. And I'd fought for so very long, with nothing to show for it. So I surrendered and struck a deal. It wasn't difficult. They were glad to have me. They recognized my worth. And all these years I've wormed my way deeper and deeper into the heart of the underground, trusted by one damn fool after another, sabotaging and undermining their operations pretty much at will. No one every suspected me. I was Alexander Storm, the great rebel hero, friend and companion to the legendary Jack Random.

"I was a bit worried when Jack turned up again, but the mind techs had done a good job on him. They saw to it he never remembered much of his time on Cold Rock, let alone my desertion and turning. He never even remembered how I helped the mind techs torture and condition him, to prove my loyalty to my new masters. So when he reappeared, and I finally had to meet him because putting it off any longer might have seemed suspicious. Well, it was all old friends together again, and he never saw past my smile to see the contempt in my eyes. After that, it was just a case of waiting for the best time to use the control words the mind techs had planted in Jack's subconscious. And here he is now, standing before Your Majesty, harmless as a newborn kitten."

"What about the bounty hunter?" said Razor. "There have been reports of her developing psi powers . . ."

"Don't worry about her," said Storm. "She's drugged to the eyeballs and loaded down with so many chains and restraints it's a wonder she can still stand." He wandered over to her and kicked her behind the knee. She fell heavily to her knees, her chains clanking loudly. Storm laughed, and moved back before the Throne.

"I thought Jack Random was your friend," said Captain Silence.

Storm shrugged. "He was. And then he let me down, by

being only human. Legends shouldn't get old and tired
and slow, and lose more often than they win. I was tired
of being a loser. I wanted to be on the winning side, to
have wealth and luxuries and an easy life, to make up for
all my years of nothing. No one was ever grateful to me
for all the times I risked my life on their behalf, the bastards. No one ever said thanks, you've done enough, let
someone else take over now. No, they just wanted more.
Even Jack. Into battle one more time, on some godfor-
saken rock I'd never even heard of, leading dumb peasants against trained Imperial troops, and all of it for
nothing. All the blood and the fear and the death of
friends. I just got tired of it all. So when Jack fell and was
taken, I had a moment of very clear insight, and saw the
futility of rebellion. Even if we were to win, and overthrow the Empress, she'd only be replaced by someone
just like her. It's the nature of the job, and the way things
are. So I gave up poverty and hopelessness for wealth
and security. And a chance to strike back at the rebels and
make them pay for all the years of my life they had
wasted."

"He was still your friend," said Silence.

Storm glared at him. "Is he? I don't know who this is
anymore. He should be my age, but he's young, and I'm
not. He's a man of power and destiny again, and I'm not.
All my life has been unfair, and he's always been the
most unfair thing in it."

"Kill you," said Ruby Journey thickly. They all turned
to look at her, kneeling and weighed down with chains,
fighting to hold her head up. She glared at Storm. "He
trusted you. Loved you like a brother. Fought beside you.
I'll kill you slowly, you treacherous bastard. Rip your
heart out and make you eat it before you die. Chains
won't hold me. Drugs wear off. I'll see you dead before
I am."

"Oh shut up," said Storm. He swaggered over to her,
and punched her in the mouth. She fell backwards. "I
never liked you, bitch." He started kicking her.

"That's quite enough of that," said Owen Deathstalker.

His voice rang across the Court, sharp and commanding, and Storm fell back in spite of himself. Everyone
turned to see Owen leading his companions through the

inferno, toward the Iron Throne. Two Deathstalkers, both legends and men of destiny. Hazel d'Ark, the pirate turned hero. Psycho Jenny, the sacred madwoman of the esper underground. And, like two crows with great experience of battlefields, Toby and Flynn brought up the rear, there for the end of the story, whatever it might be.

Investigator Razor and Kit SummerIsle moved quickly to stand between the Throne and the newcomers. Storm hurried back to join Dram and Valentine Wolfe. Silence and Frost drew their swords. Stelmach drew his gun. The maids-in-waiting stirred angrily, and hissed at the new arrivals as Owen led them toward the Throne. They stopped beside Ruby Journey, who looked up at them and spit out a mouthful of blood.

"Took you long enough to get here."

"Sorry," said Owen. "We got distracted. Need a hand?"

"In your dreams, aristo." Ruby stood up and flexed her arms, and the enveloping chains shattered and fell away from her. Ruby smiled nastily at the stunned Storm. "You didn't really think drugs and chains would hold someone like me, did you?"

Owen looked around him, taking in the smoldering ash pits, the burning angels, the great vents in the floor from which arose the screams of the damned. The crimson light, the rows of the impaled dead, and the tortured sinners hanging on their barbed chains. When he finally looked back at Lionstone, his voice was as flat and cold as his gaze. "Nice place you've got here, Lionstone. It's you. Your taste always tended to the extreme, but I think you've really outdone yourself this time. You've progressed from the disturbed to the actually psychotic. You've become a sick person, Lionstone, a mad dog, a rabid animal; and it's our job to shut you down."

Lionstone leaned back in her Throne, apparently unmoved. "Welcome to our Court, outlaw. We've been expecting you. We even have a few guests here to greet you, specially invited with you in mind. For instance . . ."

She snapped her fingers, and a masking holoillusion dropped away, revealing the huge wooden cross set up behind the Iron Throne. And nailed to that cross, Mother Superior Beatrice Christiana, the saint of Technos III.

Her nun's robes were torn and bloodied, and her wimple was gone, replaced by a crown of thorns. Dried blood encrusted thickly around her pierced wrists and ankles, and more had run down her face from where the crown had been jammed forcefully onto her head. She was still alive and still conscious enough to feel the awful pain that wracked her. Her face was twisted away from its usual serenity, dragged beyond humanity into pure animal suffering.

"She seemed so eager to be a martyr that I thought I'd oblige her," said Lionstone. "If she's really sincere in her religion, she should take it as a compliment. A martyr's death is supposed to be the highest honor they can hope to obtain in this life. Isn't that right?"

"You bitch! You stinking bitch!" Surprisingly, it was Toby Shreck who broke first. He lunged forward, enraged beyond reason, as though he planned to free Beatrice by brute force. Flynn had to grab him and hold him back. "Let me go!" said Toby, struggling to break free. "I won't stand for this! Not her! She's the only decent person I ever met!"

"You'd be dead before you could get anywhere near her, boss," said Flynn, almost shouting at Toby as he held him firmly. "She wants someone to try something, so she can set her maids on them, as an example."

"He's right, Shreck," said Giles. "Listen to your friend. We'll deal with this. It's what we're here for."

"Right," said Hazel. "Make sure your camera's working. You're about to witness the death of an Empress. Convenient of you to build your own Hell, Lionstone. It means you won't have too far to go when we drag you down off your Throne, and cut your damned head off."

"The show isn't over yet," said Lionstone. "Beatrice, this is your moment. Come on down, and kill these vermin for me."

And as the rebels watched incredulously, Beatrice raised her head on the cross and smiled down at them. With one convulsive movement, she ripped her arms and legs free from the blocky nails holding her to the wood, and dropped lightly to the ground. She started toward the rebels, still smiling, and everyone by the Throne hurried to get out of her way. Lionstone was laughing. Toby stared stupidly for a moment, then gestured urgently to make sure Flynn was getting it all.

"She's not the real thing," said Hazel. "She can't be. Nothing human could have freed itself that easily."

"Right," said Owen. "It's some kind of Fury, a machine. Lionstone just had it nailed up there to upset us."

"And it worked," said Toby. "I can't believe I was fooled again. Is nobody what they appear to be anymore?"

"You'd be surprised," said Owen. "Now stand back and give us some room, journalist. This could get a little messy."

"I knew you'd like her," said Lionstone. "Dear Valentine donated her. He had her constructed as a sex toy originally, when he couldn't get his hands on the real thing, but he quite rightly thought I'd get more use out of her. I've even had some special augmentations added, just for you. Aren't I good to you? Beatrice, dear, kill them all and bring me their heads."

The thing that looked like Beatrice Christiana surged forward incredibly quickly. Disrupter muzzles emerged from the holes in her hands. Dazzlingly bright energy beams blazed through the crimson air, narrowly missing Owen and Hazel as they threw themselves to one side, and striking Giles square in the chest. The impact threw him to the ground. Hazel brought up her projectile weapon and opened fire, but the bullets rebounded harmlessly from the steel chassis under the flesh covering. Owen fired his disrupter, but the machine just ducked under the energy beam and kept coming. She was on Hazel before she could drop the gun and draw her disrupter, grabbed her by the throat with one hand, and lifted her up into the air. Hazel dangled helplessly, choking as the metal fingers cut off her air. She clawed at the metal arm with both hands, feet kicking a good yard above the floor.

Owen threw himself at the machine from behind, but she wheeled inhumanly quickly, and slapped him away with her free hand like a bothersome child. Hazel's eyes bulged as she fought for air. Owen was quickly back on his feet, boosted, and came at the Fury again. He ducked under the sweeping arm this time, and drove his sword at not-Beatrice's unprotected throat. Steel slammed against steel, and the impact jarred the sword out of Owen's hand. He didn't hesitate and slammed his fist into its metallic side with all his boosted strength behind it. Amazingly, the steel ribs dented under the blow, and she staggered to one side, still holding on to Hazel. Owen hit it again and again, ignoring the pain of his skinned knuckles, doing damage, but not enough to make her drop her prey.

And then Jenny Psycho stepped forward, a sword blade of shimmering psi energy emerging from her hand. She chopped down, and the energy blade sheared clean through the machine's arm. Hazel crashed to the ground, the steel hand still crushing her throat. She thrashed back and forth, tearing at it with both hands. Owen was quickly there beside her, and between them they broke the metal fingers one by one and pulled the hand away. Owen threw it to one side, and it lay twitching on the ground like a giant malformed spider.

The thing that looked like Beatrice stood facing Jenny Psycho, who grinned at it nastily. The energy sword disappeared from her hand, and she made a beckoning gesture. Beatrice looked at the esper for a moment, a quizzical expression on her artificial face, then suddenly she convulsed, her back arching. Strange noises came from her mouth, and her chest and sides bellowed in and out. And then her mouth stretched impossibly as all her artificial guts came fountaining up and out, pushing the teeth aside as they came. More and more flew from her mouth, torn out by Jenny's esp, and she staggered back and forth as the high-tech contents fell to the ground at her feet. Finally there was nothing left of it but an artificial shell, tottering on its feet. Her workings lay steaming and twitching on the ground, spread over a wide area. Jenny smiled again, made a pushing gesture with one finger, and the lifeless shell crashed to the ground and lay still. Owen and Hazel got to their feet, and looked at it.

"The girl had guts," said Hazel, her voice just a little rough.

Owen winced, and moved over to Giles, who was sitting up and shaking his head muzzily. Owen helped him up. "You took a disrupter blast point-blank in the chest," he said, almost accusingly. "Why aren't you dead?"

"Force shield," said Giles briskly. "I've been working on it since Haceldama. Takes a lot out of me, but I think I'm getting the hang of it. You could do it, too, if you practiced."

"Never seem to have the time," said Owen. "You know how it is; when you're running a rebellion, it's one damned thing after another."

The rebels dusted themselves off, and turned back to face the Throne. Lionstone stared back at them unflinchingly. "You always break my favorite toys. Very well, let's try something else. Owen Deathstalker, Hazel d'Ark, Code Blue Two Two."

She smiled triumphantly as she spoke the control words implanted in Owen's and Hazel's minds by the treacherous AI Ozymandius, but then her smile faltered as they just stood there, unmoved. Lionstone tried the control words again. Owen smiled at her.

"That won't work anymore. We've moved beyond that."

Lionstone spun on Jack Random. "You are still my creature. Obey me. Kill your friends!"

Random smiled, and shook his head. "Sorry, Lionstone. I'm not under your control. Never was. Control words won't work on what we've become. I only went along to be sure of ending up here, right in front of you, just in case Owen and the others didn't make it. Ruby went along with it, once she realized what I was up to."

Ruby sniffed. "If I'd known it entailed being chained up like an escape artist and kicked around like a rag doll, I'd have thought twice about it."

"I had to be convincing," said Random. "Besides, you're always telling me how tough you are. I knew you could take it."

"Well next time, I'll be the one in charge, and you can get chained up, and see how you like it."

"Kinky," said Random. "Remember, Ruby, it's all for the cause."

"Stuff the cause. I'm in this for the money, and don't you forget it."

Random sighed, shook his head, and turned to look at

Alexander Storm. The two men who used to be friends stared at each other.

"I'd been having my suspicions about you for quite a while, Alex," Random said finally. "Little things I was beginning to remember about Cold Rock. Things about you that didn't add up, compared to the man I used to know. I put it down to age at first. We all change as we get older. But I didn't want to believe how much you'd changed, till you used the control words on me. So I went along, to find out who you really were these days. Damn it, Alex; did I really let you down so badly? I never meant for you to be hurt."

"Oh, you always meant well, Jack," said Storm. "You promised me all kinds of things, but you never delivered. So I went to people who would keep their promises. People I could trust. They looked after me, treated me well. More than you ever did."

Storm was trembling with anger by the time he finished, almost spitting the words at Random, trying to hurt him, even now. Random sighed, and met Storm's gaze unflinchingly. "You poor bastard. You could have come to me anytime. Told me. We could have worked something out. I would have understood. You were my friend, Alex."

"You were always so bloody understanding! Saint Jack, the hero and savior of the downtrodden, who had time for everyone but his friends! I got sick of your endless nobility, of having to be the selfless hero again and again, and to hell with the lives we might have made for ourselves. This is all your fault, Jack. You made me what I am. You're responsible for everything I've done. And now I'm going to die here, because of you. I know that. But I'll hurt you one last time, before I go."

He surged forward, a hidden knife suddenly in his hand, heading not for Jack Random, but Ruby Journey. His knife flashed for her throat before Random could even begin to react. But Ruby's hand came up impossibly quickly, slapped the knife aside, and then she punched Storm over the heart with all her strength behind it. Her fist sank in as far as the wrist, right under the sternum. Storm stopped in his charge, as though he'd run into a brick wall. All the color went out of his face, and he crumpled to the floor, just an old man who'd been hurt so badly he couldn't even breathe. The knife fell from his hand as the feeling went out of his fingers. Random was quickly there at his side, but by the time he'd taken Storm gently by the shoulders, the old man was already dead, his heart crushed to a pulp by a single blow. Random stood up and looked at Ruby.

"He was my friend, for a long time."

"I know," said Ruby. "That's why I killed him. So you wouldn't have to."

Random nodded. He couldn't bring himself to thank her, not now. Maybe later.

"This is all very interesting, not to say sentimental and downright sickening," said Lionstone. "But the game isn't over yet. I still have a few cards left to play. Let's try an obvious one, this time. Guards! A Lordship to whoever brings me the Deathstalker's head!"

The guards standing in ranks behind the Throne rushed forward as one, their holographic disguises as burning angels falling away to reveal the armored men beneath. The monofilament swords in their hands were real enough, though, power-driven swords with an edge a single molecule thick, capable of cutting through anything. That many men, with that kind of weapon, could have stopped an army in its tracks. So the rebels didn't let the guards reach them. Jenny Psycho gestured, the power units that maintained the monofilament edge suddenly shorted out, and the swords were suddenly just swords again. While the guards were coming to terms with that, Random and Ruby hit them with a rolling wave of pyrokinetic fire. The guards burst into flames, some dying immediately, others turning and running, as though they could leave the deadly flames behind. As they ran they lit the Court like so many blazing candles, until one by one they fell, and guttered out.

Lionstone stared blankly at the charred and steaming carnage around her Throne, and then turned to her maids-in-waiting. "Kill them! Kill them all!"

The maids surged forward like attack dogs unleashed. Pointed teeth showed in their snarling mouths, and steel claws snapped out from under their fingernails. They were trained and deadly beasts of prey, conditioned to die rather than fail, packed with cybernetic augmentations. And Jenny Psycho stepped forward to meet them alone.

"This has gone on for far too long. It's time to end it now."

Her mind leaped out and dropped upon the maids, sinking deep into their minds and battling the conditioning at its roots. The maids fell to the ground, screaming and crying out, rolling and clawing at the floor like animals as an invisible war was waged in their minds. Jenny ripped away the conditioning with her esp, undid the neural connections and reconstituted the damaged brain tissues, returning the maids to who they had been before Lionstone took them to be her slaves. It was all over in a few moments, and then Jenny withdrew from their minds. The maids stopped their animal behavior and sat up, suddenly human again for the first time in years. At first they were stunned, and then slowly they came to themselves—their old selves. Some screamed, and tried to hide their nakedness. Some screamed, remembering what they had done, had been commanded to do, by Lionstone. They shook and shuddered, unable to cry with their artificial eyes. And some just looked around them in utter confusion. Toby Shreck stared intently at one of the maids, and then stepped forward.

"Clarissa? Clarissa, is that you?"

She looked at him blankly for a moment, and then recognition flooded her altered face. "Toby! Cousin Toby!"

She ran forward into his arms. He held her tightly for a moment, and then took off his bantered jacket and wrapped her up in it. Clarissa looked around her, at the Hell Lionstone had made.

"Are we dead, Toby?"

"No, love. You're alive again. The rebellion is here, and all the prisoners are being set free." He looked back at the others. "She's Family. Gregor's niece. Lionstone took her as a maid and made a monster out of her, and there was nothing any of us could do. Thank you, Jenny. Strikes me there are a lot of people who are going to want to thank you, too."

"No big deal," said Jenny Psycho. "I think there's been enough fighting and killing. That's Lionstone's way.

We're supposed to be different. You and Flynn look after the maids. We still have work to do."

And as Toby and Flynn gathered up the maids and ushered them away out of the line of fire, Jenny moved back to confront Lionstone again. And then she stopped, and looked around sharply as Captain Silence moved uncertainly forward, staring at her searchingly. She looked at him flatly, not making it any easier for him, but eventually recognition flooded into Silence's face.

"Diana?"

"Not anymore," said Jenny. "That was somebody else."

"I hardly recognized you. You look so . . . different."

"It's called growing up, Captain. Happens to everyone eventually."

"You know this person?" said Lionstone, frowning.

"Of course he does," said Frost. "This is his daughter, Diana Vertue. Ship's esper on his last command."

Silence looked at Frost. "You knew? How long have you known?"

"I recognized her face on a Security posting some months back."

"Then why didn't you tell me!"

"You weren't ready to handle something like this. I'm not sure you're ready now. And I didn't want you distracted from your other responsibilities."

Silence turned back to Jenny. "I'd heard you joined the underground. But what happened to you? To your voice? You look . . ."

"Like I've been through Hell? That's because I have. This place doesn't frighten me. I've seen the real thing. I'm not Diana Vertue anymore. She died screaming in the esper interrogation cells in Silo Nine. Also known as Wormboy Hell. I'm Jenny Psycho now. For now and always. But then, we're both different people than we used to be, aren't we, Father? You've changed, too. This close, I can feel the Maze's energies working within you. How does it feel, Father, to know you've become the same kind of person you used to track down and kill?"

"Diana . . ."

"Jenny. I'm Jenny now."

"All right, Jenny. I never knew they'd put you into Silo Nine. If I'd known, I'd have . . ."

"You'd have what? Smashed your way into one of the Empire's most strongly guarded prisons to save me?"

"Yes," said Silence simply. "If I'd known, I would have come for you."

Jenny nodded slowly. "Yes. Maybe you would have at that. But you didn't. On the planet Unseeli, you promised me you'd never let me be hurt again. You lied, Daddy."

"I'm sorry, baby. I'm so sorry."

"And now here we are, on different sides of the war, and all because of the Iron Bitch. How can you still defend her, after all she's done? After all she had done to me?"

"She's my Empress," said Silence.

Lionstone jumped down from her Throne, stalked over to Silence, and slapped him hard on the face. His head rocked under the blow, but he held his ground. Lionstone stuck her face right in front of his, so close that when she spoke, her spittle sprayed his cheeks. "Traitor! Damned traitor! You hid your powers from me, you failed in every mission I gave you, and now I find your own daughter is one of my greatest enemies!"

"That's all true," Silence said steadily. "But you are still my Empress."

Lionstone laughed in his face, and drew back her hand for another blow. And then she gasped, her eyes widening as an unseen force gripped her hand firmly and jerked it back. She tried to break free, and couldn't. She looked across at Jenny Psycho, who was scowling at her.

"That's enough of that, bitch. That's my dad you're messing with."

"I appreciate the gesture," said Silence. "But let her go, Jenny. Please."

Jenny sniffed, released her hold, and gave the Empress a mental shove that sent her stumbling back toward her Throne. Lionstone quickly regained her balance and seated herself on her Throne again with defiant dignity. She was still the Empress, and she still had weapons she could use. She glared around her, and her gaze fell on Valentine Wolfe.

"Don't look at me," said Valentine. "I know a lost cause when I see one. I could fight for you, I suppose. I have drugs for that. But I really don't see the point. The rebellion's time has come. It would seem I jumped ship from the underground a little too early. So. I will withdraw to the sidelines and offer my services to whoever comes out on top. People like me are always useful."

"You're not fighting because you're afraid your makeup would get smudged," said Hazel.

Valentine smiled. "That too."

"Do you really think you can be forgiven for what your war machines did on Virimonde?" said Owen. "For the slaughter and suffering and horror you brought to a helpless farming people?"

The Wolfe shrugged. "I was only obeying orders. Not an original excuse, I'll admit, but then the old jokes are always the best. And I can be very loyal, for the right rewards. And I'm sure the underground leaders will recognize my worth. I know things, you see. Things the underground will need to know, if it's to take control of the Empire without unnecessary suffering and destruction. Which is more important to you, Deathstalker, seeing me punished or rebuilding the Empire with the minimum of bloodshed? No, they'll pardon me, no matter how much the rabble scream for my head. I'm just too valuable to waste. Not to worry, Deathstalker. You've still got Lionstone to kill. Enjoy yourself. Knock yourself out. It's not every day you get to murder an Empress."

"Execute," said Owen.

Valentine smiled. "Don't you just love euphemisms?"

Lionstone turned desperately on her Throne to her two bodyguards. "Razor! SummerIsle! Defend me!"

"No," said Kit calmly. "I don't think so. Because of you, David died on Virimonde. I only came back here for a chance to watch you die at close quarters. And do the job myself, if necessary. My David is dead. I'll enjoy watching you die, Lionstone."

Razor drew his sword and spun it around in a vicious sideways arc aimed at Kit's neck. But for all his Investigator's swiftness, he couldn't catch the SummerIsle off guard. Kit's sword was in just the right place to block the blow, as though he'd known all along what Razor was going to do. And maybe he had. He was Kid Death, after all. The two men sprang apart, and then circled each other warily, two practiced killers come together at last in a match that would finally decide which of them was better. Their swords slammed together, withdrew, and then spun through a dazzling series of cuts and parries. Razor was an Investigator, trained since childhood to be the perfect killing machine in the Empire's interests. Kit SummerIsle, Kid Death, was a natural-born psychopath, with a genius for swordplay and slaughter, who had killed his whole Family just for the fun of it. Two men who had taken Death as their mistress, and knew nothing of quarter or mercy. And in the end talent won out over training, as Kit dared Razor into a corps a corps, smiled at him over the crossed swords, then stuck a dagger in Razor's ribs with his other hand. Razor looked startled for a moment, as though he couldn't believe it was happening, then he fell to his knees as the strength suddenly went out of his legs. Kit knelt down with him and pushed the dagger in a little deeper. Razor dropped his sword. He met Kid Death's eyes unflinchingly and even managed a sneer.

"You only beat me because I'm old and slow, boy."

"No," said Kit. "I beat you because you still cared whether you lived or died. And I never have. Now shut up and die. I have business to be about."

He pushed the dagger in one more inch, and the light went out of Razor's eyes. He fell backwards and lay still. Kit waited a moment, to hear the last dying breath go out of his enemy, and then he smiled briefly, took back his dagger, and got to his feet. He nodded to Owen.

"The Empire killed David. Not me. He was the only friend I ever had. Guess I'm back in the rebellion again."

"What makes you think we want a lunatic like you?" said Jenny.

Kit raised an eyebrow. "Hark who's talking. No, they'll take me back. You'll always need someone like me. Someone to do the dirty jobs no one else wants to do. I don't care. I'm a killer. I go where the killing is."

One of Lionstone's hands rose slowly to tangle its fingers in her hair, pulling loose long curls of pale blond strands. Her eyes were wild and staring, her mouth a flat thin line. "Will no one defend the Empress in her hour of need? Is there not one loyal subject left to me?"

"Hell," said Dram. "I suppose there's always me." He

strode forward and set himself between the Throne and
the rebels. "I've always been yours, Lionstone, till death
do us part. You gave me life. Gave me everything. And if
my life's been a little shorter than most, it sure as hell
hasn't been boring." He grinned at Owen. "I had a great
time on Virimonde, Deathstalker. Watching your peasants
run before me, striking them down and trampling them
underfoot. Stamping the spilt blood into the furrowed
earth, and watching the towns burn in the early-morning
light. I ate your world up and spit it out, Deathstalker, and
loved every minute of it. I am Dram, the Widowmaker,
the undefeated. And after I've killed you and your friends,
I'll lead the forces that will drive your rebellion back into
the gutter, where it belongs. You never really stood a
chance. You're scum, the lowest of the low, the dirt under
our boots. Step forward, Deathstalker, and I'll cut your
stupid head off and stick it on a pike."

"Damn," said Hazel. "He makes even longer speeches
than you do, Owen."

"Not to worry," said Owen. "I'll soon put a stop to
that."

"No," said Giles Deathstalker, putting a staying hand
on Owen's arm as he started forward. "This one belongs
to me." He stepped forward, and Dram fell into a warrior's crouch, sword at the ready. Giles shook his head.
"Amateur. You're not Dram, whoever you are. Dram was
my son, and I trained him to be a far better swordsman
than you'll ever be. I killed him, on Haden. It was necessary. When I walked in here, and saw you standing by the
Throne, I knew I'd have to do it again. Killing my son
almost destroyed me, but I don't think I'll have any
problem killing a clone."

Dram looked at him strangely. "You're my *father*? I
never knew. Lionstone never told me. I never knew I had
a Family. You mean I'm a Deathstalker, too?"

"No," said Giles. "You're just a clone."

"Wait," said Dram. "We have to talk about this."

"No we don't," said Giles. "You're not my son. You're
not even human. How dare you wear my son's face?"

He aimed his disrupter and shot Dram right in the face.
The energy blast tore the clone's head off his body, which
crumpled slowly to the floor. Lionstone looked at Giles,

shocked. He smiled coldly at her. "What did you expect? Another duel? Another matter of honor, settled sword to sword? I've done that. This wasn't anything as clean as a killing. Just exterminating some garbage that should never have existed in the first place."

He turned away, put up a hand to stop Owen when he moved forward to comfort him, and walked a little away, to be by himself. Lionstone sat speechlessly on her Throne, looking at the headless corpse lying at her feet. Captain Silence and Investigator Frost looked at each other.

"Looks like it's down to us, Investigator."

"Not for the first time, Captain."

Silence nodded to Lionstone. "We've been through a lot of changes, Your Majesty, whether we wanted them or not, but our loyalty has never been in question. And if we kept our powers to ourselves, it was only so we could serve you better. Come on, Frost, time to snatch victory from the jaws of defeat one more time." He smiled at Owen and Hazel. "And we do have some unfinished business, you and I, don't we?"

"Damn right," said Hazel, sweeping her sword back and forth before her like a cat twitching its tail.

"Daddy . . ." said Jenny.

"I'm sorry," said Silence. "But this is a matter of duty. And I've always known my duty."

"Damn it, we don't have time for all this posing," said Ruby Journey. "If I wanted to watch fencing displays and grudge matches, I'd go to the Arena, so I could do it in a comfortable seat with a cold drink and a big bag of peanuts. We're supposed to be fighting a rebellion here. This is just keeping us from the more important things. Like looting. Head up, Lionstone. Giles had the right idea."

And she raised her disrupter and opened fire on the Empress. But even as Ruby was taking aim, Stelmach shouted something incoherent and threw himself between Ruby and the Empress. He took the energy blast high on the chest. It tore away his right arm and vaporized much of the upper right side of his chest, leaving him lying twitching and moaning at the foot of the Throne. Silence and Frost were quickly there at his side, but it was clear the Security Officer was dying. He put out his remaining hand to Silence, who took it firmly in his.

"All I ever wanted . . . was to serve," said Valiant Stelmach. "To be loyal. To give my life for the Empress."

"No one ever doubted your loyalty," said Silence, but he was saying it to a dead man. He gently placed Stelmach's hand on his chest and patted it twice, saying good-bye.

"Pity," said Frost. "He was a good man, in his way."

"I'm surprised you cared," said Silence.

"I liked him," said Frost. "He was a coward, a weakling, and probably harbored rebel sympathies, but he did his best to be brave and do the right thing anyway. It's easy for us to be brave, with our training and abilities. All he had was guts. And a willingness to die for his Empress."

"And now it's our turn," said Silence. He got to his feet, Frost beside him, and together they took up their places before the Throne. Silence smiled once at Jenny, then nodded to Owen. "Let's do it, Deathstalker."

Owen stepped up to face Silence, and Hazel moved forward to face Frost. Owen hefted his sword casually. "From what I've been hearing, Captain, you and the Investigator gained abilities similar to ours from the Madness Maze. Which means we could raise our powers, go head-to-head, reduce the Court to rubble, and kill everyone in it, and still end up in a stalemate. So what say we do this the honorable way. Just sword to sword. How does that sound to you?"

"Honorable," said Silence. "And what I'd expect from a Deathstalker. Besides, we've always wanted to know which of us is better with a blade, haven't we?"

"Damn right," said Frost.

"Then let's do it," said Hazel. "One last fight, as humans. Before we forget how."

And so they went forward to meet each other, the last great champions of Empire and rebellion, four good people whose differing beliefs could not be reconciled, only decided at the point of a sword. Owen and Silence circled each other slowly, their swords clashing lightly, tip to tip, as they studied each other's style for openings and vulnerabilities. Hazel and Frost went straight at each other, hacking and cutting, slamming their blades together, fueled by a rivalry that was stronger than hate or rage.

Owen and Silence stamped and lunged and recovered, both of them cold and calculating, testing their strength and skills to the limits, both trained in harsh and unforgiving schools. Their blades crashed together, sparks flying on the air, neither man prepared to give an inch or retreat a step. Their swords flew so fast the eye could barely keep up, driven by skills and reflexes almost too quick for human thought. Owen didn't boost. It never occurred to him. He wanted to win this one fairly. He was fighting for a set of ideals, his own as well as the rebellion's, and either he won fairly, or his whole life had no meaning. Silence put all his strength into every blow, all his speed into every cut and parry, and still had to struggle to match the Deathstalker's attacks. The young rebel fought as though his life no longer mattered, only the winning. Silence tried to feel that way, too. The whole Empire depended on him now. Everything he'd ever believed in and fought for. Everything that had given his life shape and meaning. But in the end, his surety wasn't as certain as Owen's, and perhaps that was why his sword was finally just that fraction slower, and Owen beat his blade aside, stepped forward, and set the point of his sword at Silence's throat. For a long moment the two men just stood there, face-to-face, breathing hard from their exertions. They looked into each other's eyes, and recognized what they saw there.

"I can't kill you," Owen said finally. "It would be like killing myself. Surrender, Captain. Put down your sword, and I guarantee your safety. The rebellion's going to need someone like you to help us rebuild."

"My loyalty . . ."

"Is to the people of the Empire. Help us preserve the best, so we don't throw it out along with the bad."

Captain John Silence looked back at his Empress, then around at the Hell she'd made of her Court, and slowly opened his hand and let his sword drop to the floor. It made hardly any sound. Owen lowered his blade. They nodded respectfully to each other, then turned to look at Hazel d'Ark and Investigator Frost. They'd dueled each other to a standstill, standing face-to-face, breathing hard and harsh, swords shaking in their exhausted hands. Their eyes were as fierce as ever, but they had driven themselves beyond strength or stamina, and they were both too proud to draw on their unnatural strength and skills.

"Give it up, Hazel," said Owen. "You're never going to win, either of you. And neither of you is ever going to yield. You're too alike. Call it a day, and let's get on with what we came here for."

Hazel considered it, frowning thoughtfully as sweat dripped off her face. "What the hell," she said finally. "We can always try this again later, when we've got more time. What do you say, Investigator? I'll step back if you will."

"Never," said Frost. "I'm an Investigator. The Empire made me what I am. I'll never give up, never give in. Kill me if you can, rebel."

"It doesn't have to be this way," said Owen.

"Yes it does," said Frost. "This is my life. My meaning. My purpose. I'll never back down. It's not in me. Kill me if you can."

Hazel lowered her sword. "I can't. Not like this."

"I can," said Kit SummerIsle. And in a movement so fast no one recognized it till it was too late, he drew a hidden dagger and threw it at Frost with all his strength behind it. She turned slightly as he spoke, and the knife took her in the throat. Blood spurted thickly, running down her chest in streams. She dropped her sword and clutched at her throat with both hands. Blood welled between her fingers. She started to pull the knife free, and then sat down suddenly as the strength went out of her. Silence was quickly there at her side, holding her in his arms. She shuddered uncontrollably, and he held her tighter. She looked shocked, confused, as though she couldn't believe this was happening to her.

"Stupid way to die," she said, her voice thick and labored. Blood sprayed from her mouth in a fine red mist. "I feel cold. So cold."

"I've got you, Frost," said Silence. "I'm right here."

"Never thought . . . it would end like this."

"Hush," said Silence. "Save your strength till we can get a medic in here."

"No," said Frost. "We never lied to each other, Captain. Don't start now."

"Then heal yourself! I did!"

"Too late, Captain. Too late."

"You were a good soldier," said Silence, his voice breaking. "The best, right to the end."

"Of course. I'm an Investigator. John . . ."

"Yes?" said Silence, but the breath just went out of her in a long bloody sigh, and she was gone. Silence hugged her to him. "Good soldier. Good soldier." Eventually he let her go and got to his feet. His uniform was soaked with her blood. He looked at the SummerIsle, who smiled back at him.

"Why?" said Silence. "Why her, and not me?"

"You killed my David," said Kit. "Now you know what I felt. Want to try and kill me now, old man?"

"Not right now," said Silence. "There's been enough killing here. And she never would have surrendered. Just stay out of my sight, killer."

He turned away to face Owen and Hazel, as though he didn't know what to do next. Stelmach and Frost were dead, and he had repudiated his Empress. It didn't seem possible that his whole life could have been destroyed in such a short time.

"I'm sorry about the Investigator," said Owen. "Sometimes, it just isn't possible for everyone to win."

"You loved her, didn't you?" said Hazel. "Did you ever tell her?"

"She wouldn't have known how to answer me," said Silence. "She was an Investigator."

There was nothing more to say, so they all turned to look at Lionstone, alone on her Throne. She glared back at them defiantly. All her champions were dead or defeated, but she still hadn't given up. It was an almost perfect moment of opposition, and it hung endlessly on the air, as though neither side wanted to break it. Hell had grown very quiet. The angel guards were dead, the maids-in-waiting were human again, and even the hologram illusions were still, as though waiting to see what would happen next. Owen moved slowly forward to stand alone at the foot of the Iron Throne. He'd come a long way to reach this place, this moment. To stand before the woman who'd destroyed his life and taken away everything he'd ever had or cared for. Because of her he'd been sent wandering through the Empire, always running from the hounds on his trail, never to feel safe or secure again. Because of her he'd been forced to become someone he still wasn't sure he approved of, the kind of man his Family had always wanted him to be—a warrior. Fighting for a cause he wasn't always sure he really believed in. But every time he wavered, all he had to do was remember a young girl lying bloodied on the Mistport snows, crippled by his sword, crying helplessly till he killed her out of mercy. Time to end it all, now. He nodded almost familiarly to the Empress.

"It's over, Lionstone. Time to go. Step down."

"No," said Giles. "Not yet. It isn't over till I say it's over. Step away from the Throne, Owen. This isn't your moment; it's mine."

Everyone turned to look at him. The old warrior in his barbarian's furs, the legendary hero of centuries past, stood calmly a little distance away from the others, his sword in his hand. He smiled at them, and something in that smile made them all shiver. He lifted his blade and set the edge against his mercenary's scalplock. He sawed through the thick hair with ease, and then held it thoughtfully in his hand for a moment, before throwing it away.

"That's it," he said calmly. "No more a mercenary. No more fighting for other men's causes. I am my own man again, the Deathstalker, and I will take the crown now, as it was always meant I should. I will be Emperor, and put things right again. I'm the only one who understands what needs to be done to restore the Empire. To make it strong again, before the aliens or the Hadenmen or Shub rise up to destroy Humanity. The people will follow me. They've always had a soft spot for heroes and legends. I will remake the old Empire, as it was a thousand years ago, before the rot set in. No more clones or espers or other genetic abominations. It was always meant that the Empire should be a human Empire."

He smiled at Owen in a fatherly fashion. "It was always

meant to be me, Owen. I knew when I went into stasis, 943 years ago, that I would have to plan for the long term. Step outside of time, so I could wait to return till the odds were in my favor again. All during that time, the computers in my Standing monitored events and maintained contact with my Clan. They planned and plotted, shaping events, preparing for my eventual return. Your father was the last contact, Owen. A very adroit agent. He set the final plans in motion—funded the rebels on Mistworld, created the Abraxus Information Center, and was finally planning a trip to Shandrakor to wake me when he made a misstep, drew attention to himself at just the wrong moment, and the Empress sent Kid Death to put an end to his intrigues.

"It was a major blow. Your father had always been meant to be the leader of the coming rebellion, a warrior-politician with the legendary Deathstalker name. The people would have followed him, as he prepared them for my return. But then he was gone, and I had no choice but to replace him with you, a feeble historian who never even wanted to be the warrior his inheritance demanded.

"To temper the steel that will become a sword blade, you beat the hell out of it and test it almost to the point of destruction. So I tempered you. It wasn't difficult for some of my agents to convince Lionstone to outlaw you, and thus set you on the path that would eventually bring you to me. The Maze . . . confused things. It was only ever intended that I should pass through the Maze and gain the powers it promised but under the pressure of events I had no choice but to allow you and your companions to pass through, too. You were never meant to become superhuman, like me. Still, you haven't turned out too badly, Owen. I've made you a warrior in spite of yourself. A credit to your Family name. But now it's time for you to step aside.

"It was never meant to be you, boy. This is my moment, my destiny. I will be Emperor, as it was always meant I should."

Owen stared at Giles for a long moment, and then shook his head. "To hell with that. I didn't come this far, spill this much blood, just to replace one tyrant with another. Even if he is Family. Put down your sword, Giles. You left it too late. Your time is over; we do things differently now. The rebellion grew from the clone and esper undergrounds, not your meddling. We've had enough of Families and Emperors. It's time for . . . something new."

Giles slowly advanced on Owen, who raised his sword warningly. Giles stopped. "Don't do this, boy. Don't make me kill you."

"You wouldn't really kill me," said Owen. "Not your own Family. The last of your descendants. The last Deathstalker."

"I can always start a new line," said Giles calmly. "I never promised you wealth or fame or an easy death, Owen. Just a chance to be a legend. Whether that's a living legend is up to you. I am . . . fond of you, in my way. The last of my original line. My child, in every way that matters. Don't get in my way, boy. I've done . . . awful things, terrible things. I created the Darkvoid Device and put out a thousand suns. This is my chance to atone, to put things right. To make things the way they should be. Don't take that away from me. You've come a long way, fought well, tried hard to do the right thing, uphold the Family name. I love you, Owen."

"*I don't care!*" said Owen, and swung his sword double-handed at Giles's neck. Giles's sword swept up to meet Owen's, and sparks flew as the blades crashed together. In a moment they were circling each other, eyes narrowed, searching for a weakness to exploit. Everyone else stayed back. They understood this was personal. Still, Hazel held her disrupter down by her side. She knew Owen would never forgive her if she interfered in the fight, but she'd already decided that if Giles won and Owen died, she was going to shoot Giles in the back of the head, and to hell with the consequences.

Owen and Giles could have used their Maze-given powers, but they didn't. This was a Family matter. They stamped and lunged and parried, swords flashing in and out, surprisingly evenly matched. Giles was the first Warrior Prime, a legendary swordsman, but as he said, Owen had come a long way. The once insular historian and scholar had been plunged into battle after battle, refining and expanding his skills all the time, until he was every bit the legendary swordsman, too. It was, after all, his inheritance. The two men fought to their limits, pushing their strength and speed into the inhuman levels of boost and beyond without even noticing.

And so they went on, hacking and cutting at each other, drawing blood after blood, neither able to slam home a blow serious enough to cause a mortal hurt. They both grew tired and measurably slower as even their immense strength began to run out. And for the first time it occurred to Giles that just possibly he might not win this battle. No one had tested him like this since the days of his prime. He could lose. But that was an intolerable thought, and not to be allowed. He hadn't waited 943 years to be denied his destiny by an upstart descendant. He scowled, and reached inwardly for his Maze-given powers. All he had to do was teleport behind Owen and run him through, and the fight would be over. Honor had become irrelevant, in the scheme of things. But reach as hard as he might, he couldn't find his power. It was blocked, canceled out by Owen's powers. On some basic level, Giles slowly realized that neither of them could use his powers against another altered by the Maze. It was a safety guard, installed by the Maze, the knowledge only to be revealed when necessary.

Giles was shaken. He'd grown used to depending on his powers, to having an unbeatable ace up his sleeve. He quickly brought himself back under control. If he couldn't win that way, there were other ways. Giles hadn't become a legendary warrior without learning a few dirty tricks along the way. The SummerIsle had had the right idea. Like Kit, Giles had a hidden dagger. He'd never told Owen about it. Never saw the need. All he had to do was lure Owen in close and stick the dagger in while the boy was distracted. Simple. Owen would never expect him to use a dirty trick like Kid Death's. Giles smiled.

And so he carefully maneuvered Owen into a corps a corps, making him think it was his idea, and the two men came face-to-face, glaring at each other over the crossed swords, so close their panting breaths moved in and out of each other's mouths. They were both pushing with all their strength, legs braced, holding them where they were.

Giles locked eyes with Owen, holding his attention, while his free hand surreptitiously drew his hidden dagger. He smiled at Owen, and thrust it up into Owen's ribs. Only to meet Owen's golden Hadenman hand coming down to block it. The steel blade shattered on the golden hand. And Giles realized Owen had been waiting for just such a trick. He lurched forward, off-balance, and Owen slammed his head forward and head-butted Giles in the face. There was a loud crack as Giles's nose broke, and he staggered backwards, blood spilling down over his mouth. And in that moment of confusion and indecision, it was the easiest thing in the world for Owen to step forward and run Giles through.

For a moment they stared at each other over Owen's extended sword. Giles's sword dropped to the floor as his fingers grew numb. He looked down at the sword protruding from his chest, but he did not fall. Owen wondered crazily if he'd have to cut off the man's head to finish him. And then Giles's legs buckled, and he fell to his knees. Owen pulled his sword out, and Giles fell forward onto his face and lay still. Owen stood over his dead ancestor, breathing hard. Hazel came forward and put a comforting hand on his shoulder.

"I'm the last one now," said Owen. "There were only ever Giles and David and me, and now I'm the only one left. The last of the Deathstalkers."

"How very touching," said Lionstone from her Throne. Her voice was brittle, but still controlled. "Well, much as I enjoy watching my enemies slaughter each other in front of me, I think it's time I brought this nonsense to an end. Didn't it ever occur to you that I might have foreseen such a situation as this, and planned accordingly? I have insurance, you see, a little something I put aside for a rainy day. To be exact—a planet-buster bomb, buried deep in the planet's core, right next to the geothermal tap that powers my Palace. Yes, I know, such things have been banned for centuries, but I never let a little thing like that bother me. All it takes is a simple activation code from me, and Golgotha will blow apart into so much glowing rubble. So either all of you surrender to me unconditionally, right now, or I'll take you and this world and your precious rebellion down into Hell with me. Your choice. Which is more important, your victory, or the billions of people who will die with us?"

Silence looked at her, shocked. "You wouldn't destroy the homeworld of Humanity!"

Lionstone smiled. "Try me."

Ruby looked at Random. "What do you think? Is she bluffing?"

"I doubt it," said Random. "After all, one of her ancestors gave the order to use the Darkvoid Device. And she's just desperate and crazy enough to see death as a victory. If she can't play with the toys, at least she can make sure no one else will have them."

"She's bluffing," said Kid Death. "I'll kill her, if you're not up to it."

"Hold it!" said Owen. "Odds are the bomb's boobytrapped to go off if she dies."

"How well you know me," said Lionstone.

"We can't surrender," said Hazel. "Not after all we've been through. Not after we've got so close!"

"What else can we do?" said Owen. "We can't get to the bomb, and we can't let billions of innocent people die!"

"God, you guys go to pieces easily," said Jenny Psycho. She reached out with her mind and suddenly they were all linked, their Maze-given powers merging with hers into a white-hot flame that burned in all their minds. Their collective mind dropped through the floor of Hell, and plummeted down into the earth, Jenny leading the way as though born to it. Thousands of miles flashed by in a moment as they descended through the many layers of the planet, heading for the bomb at the heart of the world. It was well protected, but nothing could defy them now. They deactivated it with a thought, checked around to be sure there weren't any other nasty surprises, and then turned their back on the harmless device and surged up through the earth and back into Lionstone's Court.

"Wow," said Ruby. "Some trip."

"Sorry to disappoint you," Random said cheerfully to Lionstone, "but we just defused your bomb. All part of the service."

"You *cheats*!" Lionstone screamed, after she sent the

activation codes and nothing happened. She rose up to
stand on her Throne, and threw aside her battle armor,
revealing her bare arms. Hidden disrupter implants suddenly rose up through the skin of her arms, and opened
fire on the rebels. They threw themselves in all directions
as energy beams flashed through the space where they'd
been standing. More energy weapons emerged from Lionstone's body, poking their metal snouts out of her shoulders and rib cage. Long steel blades with serrated edges
slid out of the backs of her hands. *Of course she'd have
implants,* Owen thought as he hit the floor rolling. *A
paranoid like her would want to be prepared for anything. And she could afford the best.*

He reached out with his mind to the others, and together
they raised a force shield between them and the Throne.
They'd done it once before, on the Wolfling World, and
that shield had stood off the combined firepower of an
Imperial pinnace at point-blank range. And so they stood
their ground, unharmed, as Lionstone's weapons exhausted themselves against the force shield, and she had
nothing left to throw at them. She screamed with rage and
jumped down from her Throne. Owen reached out with
the group's mind and psychokinetically seized all of
Lionstone's implants and ripped them out of her body.
She screamed again as her flesh tore open, and her implants burrowed up out through her skin and fell bloodily
to the floor. Lionstone fell to the floor as well, eyes wild
and staring, and clung desperately to the side of her
Throne. She was panting heavily, only shock shielding
her from what had been done to her. Owen dropped the
force shield, and the group mind fell apart. He walked
slowly forward to stand over Lionstone. She snarled up at
him, mortally hurt and cornered, but still refusing to be
beaten.

"You can't kill me, Deathstalker. I'm your Empress."

"I want to kill you, Lionstone," Owen said slowly.
"You don't know how much I want to. For all the things
you did to me, and to your people. For all the dead of
Virimonde, and for all who lived in fear and pain because
of you. But I won't kill you. That's your way. You're
going to stand trial, Lionstone. Let the people judge you.
It's their right, as your victims."

"Well done, Owen," said Hazel, as she came up beside him. "You finally got it right."

And then the floating viewscreens suddenly reappeared on the air around them, and turned themselves on. Young Jack Random's face appeared on every screen, smiling easily. Being dead didn't seem to have bothered him at all. "Hello, everyone," he said calmly. "We're using this face as you're familiar with it. For those of you who haven't been keeping up, I speak for the AIs of Shub. It's time for you to hear some of the truths we've been hiding from you. Shub owns the computer Matrix of Golgotha. We infiltrated it long ago, making contact with the AIs that were spontaneously generating in the Matrix, and used them to take control of the larger business entities as they evolved. All part of our plan to control Humanity through its own tech.

"Not only did we thus have access to all of Humanity's business information, which we manipulated to our own ends and for our own amusement, but we have also been destroying human minds as they entered the Matrix, occupying their empty bodies and sending them forth as spies. Even better and more undetectable than Furies. How does it feel, knowing we walk among you, unsuspected? People you'd know, too. We're everywhere. You can't trust anyone, these days. Still, I'm not here to chat. Dear Lionstone, you've looked better. But we can still save you from your enemies. You have a home with us on Shub, if you wish. You'll have to leave your body behind, but it's such a limited thing anyway. Open your mind to us, through your comm implants, and we'll do the rest. Come to Shub and live forever. You'll have to give up your Humanity, but you'll live forever."

"Anything for revenge," said Lionstone, and opened her comm implants. Something from outside seized her mind and tore it out of her body. Her consciousness surged up and out, leaving Golgotha and human cares and limitations behind. Her face replaced Young Jack's on all the viewscreens, laughing triumphantly, and then she was gone, and the screens shut down again. It was very quiet in the Court. The rebels moved slowly forward and looked down at Lionstone's body, lying bloodied and broken before the Iron Throne. It was still breathing. They all looked at each other, and then Kit SummerIsle leaned over and cut off her head.

"For you, David," he said softly, and he straightened up holding the head up by the hair for the others to see. "Just in case. And we'll want something to show the people. Let them think her dead and gone. It's for the best."

, "Er, sorry," said Toby Shreck from the back, where everyone had forgotten about him. "But this has all being going out live through Flynn's camera, remember? The whole Empire's been watching this."

"Right," said Flynn. "Got some great close-ups, too."

"Ah well," said Random. "At least now they know what kind of creature they had for an Empress."

Owen shook his head. "Great. More problems. You realize we're going to have to send the cyberats into the Matrix to clean it out before we can use it? Assuming they're as good as they claim they are."

"What about the AIs in human form?" said Ruby. "Now that is one hell of a spooky thought. They said we'd know some of them."

"They probably just said that to mess with our heads," said Hazel.

"Are you ready to put money on that?" said Ruby.

"Either way," said Random. "The struggle isn't over, just because Lionstone's no longer on the Iron Throne. Right, Owen? Owen?"

They all looked round, to where Owen was standing at the foot of the Throne. Lionstone's diamond crown had fallen off when Kit decapitated the empty body, and it was lying right at his feet. It filled his sight. The crown that ruled the Empire. He stood there, in the abandoned Court, blood dripping from the sword in his hand, at the end of his quest, and what did he have to show for it all? He could pick up the crown, place it on his head, and declare himself Emperor. He could. He was the last Deathstalker, almost as big a legend as the original. Hero of the rebellion, Redeemer of the lost Hadenmen, Savior of Mistworld. There were any number of people and causes he could count on to support him, for their various reasons. He could be Emperor. He might have to kill or imprison a few old friends, abandon a few beliefs, but he could rule the Empire. Put things right. Make it over in his image. He reached down and picked up the crown.

"Well?" said Hazel quietly, at his side. "Do you want it?"

Owen weighed the crown in his hands, and then let it drop to the floor. "No. It's too heavy for me."

"You have a legitimate claim," Random said carefully.

"No," said Owen. "I was tempted, but only for a moment. I never wanted to be a ruler, any more than I wanted to be a warrior. Maybe now this is all over, I'll be allowed to go back to being an historian and scholar again, of no importance to anyone but myself. It's all I ever really wanted." He looked at the Iron Throne. "No more crowns. No more Thrones. They corrupt people, bringing out the worst in them. Even good people, like Giles." He clenched his fists and glared at the Throne. It cracked apart from top to bottom, and collapsed into dark broken pieces. "No more Thrones. No more rulers. It's time we ruled ourselves."

"Well said, Owen," said Jack Random, moving forward to clap him on the shoulder. "But it's not over yet, for you or me. The aliens are still out there. And Shub. Someone's got to rebuild the Empire and make Humanity strong again. We're going to be needed more than ever."

"You know, we never did decide just what kind of system we're going to replace the Empire with," said Hazel. "There are a lot of people in the rebellion who had nothing in common but a desire to bring Lionstone down. I foresee a lot of arguments and raised voices in the near future."

"Good," said Random. "Healthy debate is the cornerstone of democracy."

"And if we don't like what they're saying, we can always kick their asses," said Ruby. Random looked at her. Ruby raised an eyebrow. "What?"

"That is a problem for tomorrow," said Owen. "Savor today's victory. We paid enough for it, in blood and the loss of friends and loved ones."

"Some of us are still here," said Hazel.

"Quite right," said Owen. And he took her in his arms and kissed her. Hazel pulled back.

"Don't take too much for granted, stud." And then she kissed him.

"Zoom in for a close-up," Toby whispered to Flynn. "Don't you just love a happy ending?"

EPILOGUE

The story isn't over yet.

After the rebellion the real struggle begins, as the various factions fight it out over which political system will replace the Empire. Old friends become enemies, and old enemies become reluctant allies. Old debts are paid in blood, hidden movers behind the scenes are revealed, and long-established plans and conspiracies come to a head. The war over the Iron Throne is ended, but the struggle for the soul of Humanity goes on.

There's something alive in the Darkvoid. The Hadenmen reveal their own, inhuman, agenda. The true nature of the Mater Mundi is revealed. The Madness Maze returns to lost Haden. And the aliens are coming back.

And in the end, it will all come down to one man, Owen Deathstalker, to face his final destiny in the back streets of Mistport, and save or damn the future of Humanity.

The Bestselling
DEATHSTALKER Saga
by Simon R. Green

Owen Deathstalker, a reluctant hero destined for greatness, guards the secret of his identity from the corrupt powers that run the Empire—an Empire he hopes to protect by leading a rebellion against it!

Praise for the DEATHSTALKER Saga:

"[Simon R.] Green invokes some powerful mythologies."
—*Publishers Weekly*

"A huge novel of sweeping scope, told with a strong sense of legend." —*Locus*

THE ULTIMATE IN
SCIENCE FICTION AND FANTASY!

From magical tales of distant worlds to stories of
technological advances beyond the grasp of man, Penguin has
everything you need to stretch your imagination to its limits.

penguin.com

ACE
Get the latest information on favorites like
William Gibson, T.A. Barron, Brian Jacques,
Ursula K. Le Guin, Sharon Shinn, Charlaine Harris,
Patricia Briggs, and Marjorie M. Liu,
as well as updates on the best new authors.

ROC
Escape with Jim Butcher, Harry Turtledove, Anne Bishop,
S.M. Stirling, Simon R. Green, E.E. Knight, Kat Richardson,
Rachel Caine, and many others—plus news on the
latest and hottest in science fiction and fantasy.

DAW
Patrick Rothfuss, Mercedes Lackey, Kristen Britain,
Tanya Huff, Tad Williams, C.J. Cherryh, and many more—
DAW has something to satisfy the cravings of any
science fiction and fantasy lover.
Also visit dawbooks.com.

*Get the best of science fiction and fantasy
at your fingertips!*